The
BEST
AMERICAN
ESSAYS
of the Century

The
BEST
AMERICAN
ESSAYS
of the Century

Joyce Carol Oates EDITOR

Robert Atwan COEDITOR

WITH AN INTRODUCTION
BY JOYCE CAROL OATES

HOUGHTON MIFFLIN COMPANY
BOSTON · NEW YORK 2000

ISSN 0888-3742   ISBN 0-618-04370-5

Book design by Robert Overholtzer

Printed in the United States of America

QUM 10 9 8 7 6 5 4 3 2 1

Ernest Hemingway, "Pamplona in July." First published as "World's Series of Bull Fighting a Mad, Whirling Carnival"
in the *Toronto Star Weekly*, 1923; collected in *By-Line: Ernest Hemingway*, edited by William White, 1967. Reprinted with
permission of Scribner, a Division of Simon & Schuster, from *By-Line: Ernest Hemingway*, edited by William White.
Copyright © 1967 by Mary Hemingway. • H. L. Mencken, "The Hills of Zion." From *Prejudices, 5th Series* by H. L.
Mencken. First published as a dispatch in the *Baltimore Evening Sun* in July 1925. Collected in *Prejudices, 5th Series*, 1926.
Copyright 1926 by Alfred A. Knopf, Inc., and renewed 1954 by H. L. Mencken. Reprinted by permission of Alfred
A. Knopf, a division of Random House, Inc. • Zora Neale Hurston, "How It Feels to Be Colored Me." From *World To-
morrow* (May 1928). Used with the permission of the Estate of Zora Neale Hurston. • Edmund Wilson, "The Old Stone
House." First published in *Scribner's*, 1933; collected in *Travels in Two Democracies*, 1936, and in *The American Earthquake*,
1958, by Edmund Wilson. Copyright © 1958 by Edmund Wilson. Copyright renewed © 1986 by Helen Miranda Wilson.
Reprinted by permission of Farrar, Straus & Giroux, LLC. • Gertrude Stein, "What Are Master-pieces and Why Are
There So Few of Them." Used by permission. • F. Scott Fitzgerald, "The Crack-Up." From *The Crack-Up*, edited by
Edmund Wilson. Copyright 1945 by New Directions Publishing Corp. First published in *Esquire*, February–April 1936;
collected in Fitzgerald, *The Crack-Up*, edited by Edmund Wilson, 1945. Reprinted by permission of New Directions
Publishing Corp. • James Thurber, "Sex Ex Machina." From *Let Your Mind Alone! And Other More or Less Inspirational Pieces* by James Thurber (New York: Harper & Bros., 1937). First published in *The New Yorker*, 1937. Used by permission. • Richard Wright, "The Ethics of Living Jim Crow: An Autobiographical Sketch." From *Uncle Tom's Children* by
Richard Wright. Copyright 1937 by Richard Wright. Copyright renewed © 1965 by Ellen Wright. First published in *American Stuff: WPA Writers' Anthology*, 1937; reprinted as the introduction to the second printing of *Uncle Tom's Children*,
1940. Reprinted by permission of HarperCollins Publishers, Inc. • James Agee, "Knoxville: Summer of 1915." First published in *Partisan Review*, 1938; reprinted as the prologue to Agee's posthumously published novel *A Death in the Family*.
Copyright © 1957 by The James Agee Trust, renewed 1985 by Mia Agee. Used by permission of Grosset & Dunlap, Inc., a
division of Penguin Putnam Inc. • Robert Frost, "The Figure a Poem Makes." From *The Selected Prose of Robert Frost*, edited by Hyde Cox and Edward Connery Lathem. Copyright 1946, © 1956, 1959 by Robert Frost. Copyright 1949, 1954,
© 1966 by Henry Holt & Co., LLC. Reprinted by permission of Henry Holt & Co., LLC. • E. B. White, "Once More to the
Lake." From *One Man's Meat* by E. B. White. Text copyright 1941 by E. B. White. Reprinted by permission of Tilbury
House, Publishers, Gardiner, Maine. • S. J. Perelman, "Insert Flap 'A' and Throw Away." From *The Most of S. J. Perelman*
by S. J. Perelman (New York: Simon & Schuster, 1958). First published in *The New Yorker*, 1944. Copyright 1944 by S. J.
Perelman. Reprinted by permission of Harold Ober Associates Inc. • Langston Hughes, "Bop." First published in *The
Chicago Defender*, 1949; revised and collected in *Simple Takes a Wife*, 1953, and in *The Best of Simple*, 1961. Copyright
© 1961 by Langston Hughes. Copyright renewed © 1989 by George Houston Bass. Reprinted by permission of Hill and
Wang, a division of Farrar, Straus & Giroux, LLC, and by permission of Harold Ober Associates Inc. • Katherine Anne
Porter, "The Future Is Now." From *The Collected Essays and Occasional Writings of Katherine Anne Porter* (New York:
Delacorte Press/Seymour Lawrence, 1970). Originally published in *Mademoiselle* (November 1950). Reprinted with the
permission of Barbara Thompson Davis, Literary Trustee for the Estate of Katherine Anne Porter, c/o The Permissions
Company, High Bridge, New Jersey, USA. • Mary McCarthy, "Artists in Uniform." First published in *Harper's Magazine*,
1953; collected in *On the Contrary* by Mary McCarthy, 1961. Copyright © by The Mary McCarthy Literary Trust. Reprinted
by permission of The Mary McCarthy Literary Trust. • Rachel Carson, "The Marginal World." From *The Edge of the
Sea* by Rachel Carson (Boston: Houghton Mifflin, 1955). Used by permission. • James Baldwin, "Notes of a Native
Son." From *Notes of a Native Son* by James Baldwin. Copyright © 1955, renewed 1983, by James Baldwin. First published in *Harper's Magazine*, 1955; collected in *Notes of a Native Son*, 1955. Reprinted by permission of Beacon Press,
Boston. • Loren Eiseley, "The Brown Wasps." First published in *Gentry*, 1956–57; collected in *The Night Country*, 1971. Re-
printed with permission of Scribner, a Division of Simon & Schuster, from *The Night Country* by Loren Eiseley. Copy-

Contents

Foreword

The Essay in the Twentieth Century

When I was very young, my father purchased a small, uniform set of cheap literary classics. Why, I never knew. He was not a reader. Perhaps he had been duped by a door-to-door salesman. Perhaps he had aspirations for his children. The books crowded the only bookshelf in a cramped two-family house hedged in by humming factories on a narrow street that dead-ended into the mysterious and spectacular sumac-lined banks of the Passaic River in Paterson, New Jersey. As a result of his once-in-a-lifetime purchase I grew up with the privilege of knowing that Emerson was not merely the name of a television set.

I found Emerson's message bracing and liberating. I can see it now as self-help elevated to the highest literary standard, but reading "Self-Reliance" as an adolescent I simply took heart from his exhortations to resist conformity, trust in oneself, and not feel pressured by conventions, parties, and authority: "I am ashamed to think how easily we capitulate to badges and names, to large societies and dead institutions," he said. "If I know your sect, I anticipate your argument," he said. "Insist on yourself; never imitate," he said. He warned about the physical pain of forced smiles and acknowledged the advantages of being misunderstood. If the writings of the medieval Jewish philosopher Maimonides comprised a *Guide for the Perplexed*, Emerson's essays provided a *Guide for the Intimidated*. His independent, freethinking, inquisitive mind shaped American thought and writing, and his spiritual heirs invented the twentieth-century essay.

Although Emerson may be said to hover over the volume, his presence can be detected more directly in one of his most prominent descendants, William James. Although this selection of great American essays begins in 1901, one could argue that the symbolic origins of the twentieth-century essay go back to the day in 1842 when Emerson was invited by the James family to visit their New York apartment and "bless" young William in his cradle. As a teacher, lecturer, physician, scientist, and one of the founders of modern psychology, William James would exert a powerful influence over the new century. Two of his students, W.E.B. Du Bois and Gertrude Stein, would permanently alter the course of the American essay by initiating two new modes of literary introspection: Du Bois's "double-consciousness" grounded in racial identity and Stein's experiments with "stream of consciousness." Both originated in the critical first decade of the century, and their literary legacies can be felt throughout this collection.

The twentieth-century essay also emerged from a resistance to the "familiar" or "polite" essay that had been a literary staple of the preceding era. Proper, congenial, Anglophilic, the genteel essay survived, even against the skepticism and irascibility of the Mark Twains, Randolph Bournes, and H. L. Menckens, who did their best to bury it. By the 1930s, however, some writers were lamenting its demise, and in the most curious metaphors. "The familiar essay, that lavender-scented little old lady of literature, has passed away," one wrote, regretting that magazines now filled their pages with "crisp articles, blatant exposés, or statistic-laden surveys," and concluding that one day "her pale ghost will not appear at all, and the hard young sociologists can have her pages all to themselves." But the "pale ghost" did not vanish all at once. It lived on in college courses and gave the essay a bad name for decades. The goal of English teachers, the novelist Kurt Vonnegut recalls, was to get you "to write like cultivated Englishmen of a century or more ago."

This collection features none of those "lavender-scented" essays, not even for historical reasons. Our object was not to construct a Museum of the American Essay. Although some vestiges of "gentility" or essayistic "leisure" may have seeped in here and there, the ruling idea behind the volume was that the essays should speak to the present, not merely represent the past. So you will find more "hard young sociologists" here than "cultivated" literati. After all, some of those young social scientists were Jane Addams, Zora Neale Hurston, and a youthful Saul Bellow, who happened to be studying sociology and anthropology at Northwestern at precisely the same time the genteel essayists were lamenting their own demise. The sociologists, accompanied by such self-taught social critics as Edmund Wilson, Richard Wright, and James Agee, brought the essay out of the library and into the American factories, city streets, courthouses, and tenant farms. For many of them, ardent pacifists and reformers, writing essays would amount to what James called "the moral equivalent of war."

Unlike their predecessors, twentieth-century essayists were eager to confront inner as well as outer strife. To be sure, the genteel essay was personal, but no matter how "familiar," it always politely stopped short of full disclosure. Here, too, William James made his presence felt. The brilliant chapters "The Divided Self" and "The Sick Soul" in his monumental *The Varieties of Religious Experience* (1902) would become a valuable resource for essayists seeking ways to articulate despair, breakdowns, aberrant states of consciousness, psychic confusion, the ineffable in general. F. Scott Fitzgerald's famous observation in "The Crack-Up" — "The test of a first-rate intelligence is the ability to hold two opposed ideas in the mind at the same time, and still retain the ability to function" — laid out a course for future essayists and expanded the possibilities of self-disclosure. As writers began amplifying the personal essay into what is now known singularly as "the memoir," the processes of confession would know no limits.

What next? Will this new century reject our "best" essays as dramatically as the twentieth discarded those of James Russell Lowell and Oliver Wendell Holmes? The 1890s, too, saw astonishing changes in technology, rapid changes that frightened Henry Adams as he wondered what the "Law of Acceleration" would finally lead to. We have reached his speculative end point — visionary though he was, he never imagined a world transformed by electronics. The Internet is already generating new sources of essays. Will it somehow channel the usual processes of prose into new literary forms the way some thought the typewriter had once done? Will young essayists discover audiences without having to sweat through the hundreds of rejection slips James Thurber received before he could break into print? And will they do what few from any century have ever done: make a living writing essays? These remain to be seen, but what I think we can say for certain is that whatever new forms the essay takes, if they are wonderful, they will have the blessing of William James and his legitimate heirs.

About This Collection

This volume is not a "best of the best." I founded *The Best American Essays* series in 1986, and therefore Joyce Carol Oates and I had only a small slice of the century to provide us with essays that had already achieved an annual "best" status. Only seven of the essays in this volume come from the series. We wish we could have included many more of the superb contemporary writers who have contributed to the yearly books, but it was of course not possible. Our consolation is that their work is still accessible to readers and that the annual books are for the most part available in libraries and bookstores. It was important that we include writers from previous generations who may not be well known to today's readers and who in our opinion still very much deserve an audience.

I proceeded with this book in much the same way that I have with the annual volumes. I screened a good number of essays — though far, far more than usual — and turned them over to Joyce Carol Oates for a final decision. There were hundreds of essays to consider and so little space. But we winnowed and winnowed and arrived at these fifty-five. We tried to include the best of as many different kinds of essay as possible — personal, critical, philosophical, humorous, pastoral, autobiographical, scientific, documentary, political. Obviously we had to pull back in many cases. A comparable volume could be assembled to showcase each one of these categories. I also exercised one final choice: I insisted that Oates's essay from *The Best American Essays 1996*, "They All Just Went Away," be included.

"Essays end up in books," Susan Sontag writes, "but they start their lives in magazines." That fact may not interest many readers, but it played a large role in the research for this book, since between an essay's debut in a periodical and its inclusion in a collection, a good deal of revision often occurs. Vladimir Nabokov's memoir of his father, for example, went through three very distinct publishing stages. It began life as "The Perfect Past" in *The New Yorker* in 1950, but Nabokov, dissatisfied with some of the editing, returned to his original typescript when he included (and expanded) it as the opening chapter of his 1951 autobiography, *Conclusive Evidence*. When he revised that book as *Speak, Memory: An Autobiography Revisited* in 1966, he expanded the essay yet again. Of the three published versions, we chose — as we did with many of the selections — to reprint the final version, as it would reflect and respect the author's final decisions. But in some instances (consistency "is the hobgoblin of little minds," Emerson said), we selected the first or a different published version.

Some essays start out looking like essays only to reemerge in unexpected contexts. James Agee's lovely childhood reminiscence, "Knoxville: Summer of 1915," started out in *Partisan Review* in 1938 but was given a new twist when an editor cleverly borrowed and italicized it in 1957 to serve as the introduction to Agee's posthumously published novel, *A Death in the Family*. Other essays in this book were also put to service by their authors to introduce works of fiction: Richard Wright's "The Ethics of Living Jim Crow" became the preface to his collection of stories *Uncle Tom's Children*, and N. Scott Momaday's "The Way to Rainy Mountain" now serves as the prologue to his popular novel of the same title.

I discovered that there is rarely only one version of an essay. Susan Sontag's useful observation sometimes gets reversed: an essay starts out in book form and ends up in a magazine. Several essays in this volume were skillfully carved out of books and re-created either by their authors or a magazine's editors as independent essays. Usually, what's required is the removal of the interstitial glue that connects a book's separate chapters. For example, the opening sections of Maya Angelou's 1970 memoir, *I Know Why the Caged Bird Sings*, were transformed into a memorable childhood reminiscence of the same title in *Harper's Magazine*.

Because essays may go through so many publishing variations, settling on a precise date for each selection was no easy matter. I proceeded largely case by case. Nabokov's 1966 essay on his father was so transformed from its 1950 origins that it seemed only reasonable to use the later date. So, too, I decided to use the final publication date for John Muir's Alaskan adventures with his unforgettable companion Stickeen; it was that version, and not the earlier and now forgotten essay, that became his most popular work. But occasionally I thought it would be misleading to use the final date of publication. Langston Hughes's "Bop," for example, clearly comes out of the forties; though it was revised considerably for subsequent book publication, to place it in a later decade would distort its contemporary flavor. An essay like Mark Twain's "Corn-pone Opinions," never published in the author's lifetime, is listed by date of composition.

For the reader's convenience, I have attached brief notes to each essay outlining its publishing history and supplying relevant contextual information. I have placed an asterisk before the source used for this collection. I have also translated foreign words and phrases within brackets when it seemed necessary. Additional information is contained in the Biographical Notes in the back of the book, where I included pertinent information on the writer's career, relevant details to establish a context for the selected essay, and titles of books and collections (with the emphasis on nonfiction) that will direct interested readers to more books by that writer.

Writers and magazine editors interested in submitting published essays for the annual volumes should send complimentary issues, subscriptions, or appropriate material to Robert Atwan, Series Editor, The Best American Essays, Box 220, Readville, Massachusetts 02137-9998. Criteria and guidelines can be found in the annual book.

Acknowledgments

As I researched books and periodicals for this unprecedented volume, I often felt like Henry Adams, poised at the crossroads of two time periods: the rapidly accelerating age of cyberspace that instantly furnishes vast amounts of information and the old-fashioned era of dim library stacks and dusty, out-of-print books. The experience was both high-tech and low-tech. If it was satisfying to sit at my desk and click a few keys for immediate access to material that only a few years ago would have required frequent library visits, it was even more satisfying to hold in my hand hardcover first editions of books like Martin Luther King's *Why We Can't Wait* or H. L. Mencken's *Prejudices*. Even obtaining these books involved travel in both worlds: through the Internet I could enter my local library's regional network, discover books it didn't own, and conveniently order them online. A day or two later — and sometimes within hours — I would be experiencing the tactile and intellectual pleasures of handling some of the treasured pieces of our literary heritage. For their invaluable assistance, then, I want to thank especially the staff of the Milton Public Library as well as all the other institutions connected with the Old Colony Library Network in Massachusetts.

What I was unable to find, my researcher could. Much of the knottier research — establishing the original source or date of an essay, or tracking down an elusive periodical — was performed by Donna Ashley, who relied on the superb resources of the libraries at the Massachusetts Institute of Technology, Boston University, Boston College, and the Boston Public Library. Nearly all of the source notes attached to each essay derive from her dogged research; without her assistance this project might have taken another year to complete. I want to thank, too, Arthur Johnson for his generous help in providing permissions data for all of the essays. I borrowed a good deal of biographical information about the essayists from some of my previous anthologies and would like to thank a few coeditors for their contributions: Martha Banta, Bruce Forer, Justin Kaplan, Donald McQuade, David Minter, Jon Roberts, Robert Stepto, and William Vesterman. I'm enormously grateful to Charles H. Christensen for his advice and encouragement over the years. The Houghton Mifflin staff has been helpful and supportive as always, and I'd like to thank Janet Silver, Sean Lawler, Larry Cooper, Bridget Marmion, Dean Johnson, and Bruce Cantley for all their efforts. My wife, Hélène Atwan, kindly read over portions of the manuscript and offered many valuable suggestions for which I am very grateful. Finally, it was a great pleasure to work once again with Joyce Carol Oates. Her broad knowledge of American writing and her literary judgment transformed what seemed like a paralyzing critical task — reducing several hundred great essays to a mere fifty-five — into a spirited, illuminating assessment of the modern American essayist's struggle to encompass the creative energies and social emergencies of a century that had no shortage of either.

ROBERT ATWAN

Introduction

The Art of the (American) Essay

HERE IS a history of America told in many voices.

It's an elliptical tale, or a compendium of tales, of the American twentieth century by way of individual essays that, fitting together into a kind of mobile mosaic, suggest where we've come from, and who we are, and where we are going. In his probing, provocative "The Creation Myth of Cooperstown," Stephen Jay Gould asks: "Why do we prefer creation myths to evolutionary stories?" The more we know of history, of both the natural and the civilized worlds, the more we understand that our tangled lives are ever evolving, and that our culture, far from being timeless, is a living expression of Time.

The essay, in its directness and intimacy, in its first-person authority, is the ideal literary form to convey such a vision. By tradition essays have been categorized as formal or informal; yet it can be argued that all essays are an expression of the human voice addressing an imagined audience, seeking to shift opinion, to influence judgment, to appeal to another in his or her common humanity. Even the most artfully composed essay suggests a naturalness of discourse. As our precursor Montaigne advised, "We must remove the mask."

The essays in this volume have all been written by writers who have published at least one collection of essays or nonfiction. Not only did this principle allow the editors a reasonable means of limiting selections, it is an acknowledgment that writing is a vocation, not merely an avocation. In a historical overview of a century virtually teeming with talent, I wanted to honor those writers who have made writing their life's work. I didn't see my role as one to reward the lucky amateur who writes a single good essay, then disappears forever. Better to search for little-known but excellent essays by, for instance, writers of historical significance like John Jay Chapman, Jane Addams, Edmund Wilson. Most of the essays are "informal"; but this isn't to suggest that they are innocent, unmediated utterances lacking the stratagems of art. Even Mark Twain's "Corn-pone Opinions," delivered in the author's characteristic forthright voice, is driven by a passionate intellectual conviction regarding the gullibility of mankind and the tragic consequences of this gullibility.

My general theme in the assemblage of this volume has been a search for the expression of personal experience within the historical, the individual talent within the tradition (to paraphrase T. S. Eliot). My preference was always to essays that, springing from intense personal experience, are nonetheless significantly linked to larger issues, even if, as in the case of James Thurber and S. J. Perelman, these issues are viewed playfully. The emotion I felt when beginning to read most of the essays gathered here was one of great excitement and anticipation; even, at times, a distinct visceral thrill. As an editor, I am primarily a reader. I could not countenance including essays out of duty's sake that, in fact, I found deadly dull. For the many essays considered for this volume, the majority of which ultimately had to be excluded, I was the ideal reader: I wanted to like what I read, and I was committed to reading the entire essay with sympathy. If you will substitute "literature" for "poetry" in this famous remark in a letter of Emily Dickinson's, you have my basic criterion for the work included in *The Best American Essays of the Century:* "If I read a book [and] it makes my whole body so cold no fire can ever warm me I know that is poetry. If I feel physically as if the top of my head were taken off, I know *that* is poetry."

And what powerful openings in certain of these exemplary essays:

> We are met to commemorate the anniversary of one of the most terrible crimes in history — not for the purpose of condemning it, but to repent of our share in it.
>
> — John Jay Chapman, "Coatesville" (1912)

> The knowledge of the existence of Devil Baby burst upon the residents of Hull House one day when three Italian women, with an excited rush through the door, demanded that he be shown to them.
>
> — Jane Addams, "The Devil Baby at Hull-House" (1916)

> Of course all life is a process of breaking down, but the blows that do the dramatic side of the work — the big sudden blows that come, or seem to

come, from outside — the ones you remember and blame things on and, in
moments of weakness, tell your friends about, don't show their effect all at
once. There is another sort of blow that comes from within — that you don't
feel until it's too late to do anything about it, until you realize with finality
that in some regard you will never be as good a man again.

— F. Scott Fitzgerald, "The Crack-Up" (1936)

The cradle rocks above an abyss, and common sense tells us that our existence is but a brief crack of light between two eternities of darkness.

— Vladimir Nabokov, "Perfect Past" (1950)

On the twenty-ninth of July, in 1943, my father died. On the same day, a few
hours later, his last child was born. Over a month before this, while all our
energies were concentrated in waiting for these events, there had been, in
Detroit, one of the bloodiest race riots of the century.

— James Baldwin, "Notes of a Native Son" (1955)

The decaying, downtown shopping section of Memphis — still another
Main Street — lay, the weekend before Martin Luther King's funeral, under a
siege.

— Elizabeth Hardwick, "The Apotheosis of Martin Luther King" (1968)

We were all strapped into the seats of the Chinook, fifty of us, and something, someone was hitting it from the outside with an enormous hammer.
How do they do that? I thought, we're a thousand feet in the air!

— Michael Herr, "Illumination Rounds" (1977)

We tell ourselves stories in order to live.

— Joan Didion, "The White Album" (1978)

Of course there are crucial distinctions between the art of the essay
and the art of prose fiction, yet to the reader the immediate experience
in reading is an engagement with that mysterious presence we call *voice*.
Reading, we "hear" another's speech replicated in our heads as if by
magic. Where in life we sometimes (allegedly infrequently) fall in love
at first sight, in reading we may fall in love with the special, singular
qualities of another's voice; we may become mesmerized, haunted; we
may be provoked, shocked, illuminated; we may be galvanized into action; we may be enraged, revulsed, and yet! — drawn irresistibly to experience this *voice* again, and again. It's a writer's unique employment
of language to which we, as readers, are drawn, though we assume
we admire the writer primarily for what he or she "has to say." For consider: how many intelligent, earnest, right-minded commentators published essays on such important subjects as racial conflict in twentieth-

century America, social and personal disintegration in the thirties, morality, democracy, nostalgia-for-a-vanishing-America; class struggle, civil rights, Martin Luther King, Jr., the Vietnam War, the mystical experience of nature, ethnic diversity, various American "myths" — and how few of these are worth rereading, let alone enshrining, in this new century. To be an editor in so massive an undertaking, committed to reading with sympathy countless essays of high worth and distinction published in the most prestigious journals of their era, beginning in about 1900 and sweeping through the decades, is to experience firsthand that quickening of dread, which Nabokov calls mere "common sense," in the realization of human mortality. So many meritorious voices, so much evidence of American good will and wisdom, and so many fallen by the wayside! There were times when I felt as if I were indeed standing at the edge of an abyss, entrusted with rescuing pages of impeccable prose being blown past me into oblivion, preserving what I could, surrendering all the rest. (Those excellent essayists of a bygone time John Muir, Randolph Bourne, and John Jay Chapman are preserved here; surrendered to the exigencies of space limitations are John Burroughs, George Santayana, Joseph Wood Krutch, Ellen Glasgow, and others listed in the Appendix.)

My belief is that art should not be comforting; for comfort, we have mass entertainment, and one another. Art should provoke, disturb, arouse our emotions, expand our sympathies in directions we may not anticipate and may not even wish. Art should certainly aspire to beauty, but there are myriad sorts of beauty: the presentation of a subject in the most economical way, for instance; a precise choice of language, of detail. There is beauty in the calibrated ugliness of the opening of William Gass's meditation on suicide and art, "The Doomed in Their Sinking," because it is so finely calibrated; there is beauty in the eloquent, elegiac expression of hurt, rage, and despair in James Baldwin's "Notes of a Native Son," because it is eloquent and elegiac, in the service of art. That staple of traditional essay collections, the unhurried musings of a disembodied (Caucasian, male, privileged) consciousness, is missing here, except for its highest, most lyric expression in E. B. White's classic "Once More to the Lake" and its total transmogrification in Edward Hoagland's powerful "Heaven and Nature" — which is about neither heaven nor nature. (Hoagland, one of the few American writers who has forged a brilliant career out of essays, is our Chopin of the genre. Though best known for such nature essays as "The Courage of Turtles," "Red Wolves and Black Bears," and "Earth's Eye," in the tradition of

Thoreau, Hoagland is equally memorable as a recorder of startling, confessional utterances of a kind the very private Thoreau would not have dared.) Though there are deeply moving essays in the nostalgic/ musing mode by such fine writers as White, James Agee, Eudora Welty, and John Updike, I have given more space to what might be called a radical expansion of this familiar genre, essays that have the power of personal nostalgia yet are not sentimental, and in which private contemplation touches on crucial public issues, as Zora Neale Hurston's "How It Feels to Be Colored Me," Richard Wright's "The Ethics of Living Jim Crow," Baldwin's "Notes of a Native Son," Loren Eiseley's "The Brown Wasps," N. Scott Momaday's "The Way to Rainy Mountain," Maya Angelou's "I Know Why the Caged Bird Sings," Richard Rodriguez's "Aria: A Memoir of a Bilingual Childhood," and others. If you begin Edmund Wilson's "The Old Stone House" presuming it to be another nostalgic lament for a vanishing America, you will be shocked by the author's conclusion:

> And what about me? As I come back in the train, I find that — other causes contributing — my depression of Talcottville deepens. I did not find the river and the forest of my dream — I did not find the magic of the past . . . I would not go back to that old life if I could: the civilization of northern New York — why should I idealize it? — was too lonely, too poor, too provincial.

Similarly, Donald Hall's "A Hundred Thousand Straightened Nails" is both a sympathetic portrait of an older relative of the writer's and a devastating critique of the romance of American rural eccentricity, the stock material of how many homespun reminiscences in the Norman Rockwell mode:

> [Washington Woodward] worked hard all his life at being himself, but there were no principles to examine when his life was over . . . The life that he could recall totally was not worth recalling; it was a box of string too short to be saved.

Apart from being first-rate reportage, Joan Didion's "The White Album" can be seen as a radical variant of the genre of nostalgia as well, in which the essayist positions her intimate, interior life ("an attack of vertigo and nausea does not seem to me an inappropriate response to the summer of 1968") within the larger, wayward, and "poorly comprehended" life of our culture circa 1966–1978, with the defiant conclusion "writing [this] has not yet helped me to see what it means": the antithesis of the traditional essay, which was organized around a principle, or epiphany, toward which it confidently moved. So too Michael Herr's "Illumination Rounds," from *Dispatches*, is appropriately ironically titled, for little is finally illuminated in this account of a young American journalist's visit to Vietnam in the mid-seventies, at the height of that protracted and tragic war; the techniques of vividly cinematic fiction writing are here employed in the service of the author's vision, but there is, conspicuously, no "moral" — no "moralizing." This is the art of the contemporary essay, or memoir: a heightened, *trompe l'oeil* attention to detail that allows the reader to see, hear, witness, as if at first hand, what the essayist has witnessed. Though this is "informal" writing, there is no lack of form. Postmodernist strategies of fragmentation and collage have replaced that of exposition, summary, and argument.

For all their diversity, essays tend to fall into three general types: those that present opinions primarily, and have been written to "instruct"; those that impart information and knowledge; and those that record personal impressionistic experiences, especially memories. These categories often overlap, of course, as in the outstanding essays named above, and in recent years, judging from the annual series *The Best American Essays*, from which essays in this volume published since 1985 have been taken, the genre has evolved into a form closely akin to prose fiction and prose poetry, employing dialogue, dramatic scenes, withheld information, suspense.

The essay of opinion, of which Montaigne (1533–1592) was an early, highly influential master, was for centuries the quintessential essay. Here, you find no dialogue or dramatic scenes, only a rational, reasoning voice. Such an essay is an argument, often couched in conversational terms; its intention is to instruct, to illuminate, to influence. Except for editorial and op-ed pages of newspapers, in which they appear in miniature form, and in a very few general-interest magazines like *Harper's* and the *Atlantic*, such essays are not much favored today. In our egalitarian culture we tend to feel, rightly or wrongly, that an essayist's opinion is only as good as his or her expertise, and in such uncharted areas as ethics, morals, and general wisdom, whose opinion should be taken more seriously than anyone else's? In the past, however, the gentlemanly art of opinion-offering was commonplace; Ralph Waldo Emerson is the North American master of this form. With the publication of "Nature" in 1836, Emerson's prestige and influence through the whole of the nineteenth century was incalculable. Here was a brilliant aphoristic-philosophical mind expressed in an elegantly idiosyncratic language. Henry David Thoreau, Emerson's younger contemporary, combines strong opinions with a wealth of observed information and firsthand experience in a crystalline, poetic prose, and for this reason seems to us more modern, and far more accessible, than Emerson. There is a rich subcategory of American essays, the confrontation of nature by a refined, fastidiously observing consciousness, that has descended to us from Thoreau; I would have dearly liked to include more practitioners of this sort but had room for only John Muir, Rachel Carson, Loren Eiseley, Annie Dillard, and Gretel Ehrlich. (But all these essays are gems.) In general, our patience tends to wear thin when we're confronted with sermonizing in its many forms; I most often encountered such essays among those published in the first four or five decades of the century, when magazines seemed to have unlimited space for rambling, genial prose by men with nothing especially urgent on their minds apart from platitudes of nature and morality. Who were the readers of these essays, I wondered. The more elusive the subject, the more verbose the style, as in two fascinating masterpieces of ellipsis, indirection, and irresolution by Henry James at his most baroque, "Is There a Life after Death?" (1910) and "Within the Rim" (1915). ("Is There a Life after Death?" was initially included in this volume, and then reluctantly excluded; then included again, and finally excluded. A longtime admirer of Henry James, I wanted badly for him to be represented, but the essay is, one might say, "Jamesian," and long, and could hardly be justified as among the best of the century. And "Within the Rim," on the apparent theme of war, is even more abstruse.)

Yet for all their unfashionableness, the opinion essays included here are, I think, excellent, and will repay the sort of close, sympathetic reading required for prose that isn't immediately gripping and specific. Henry Adams's "A Law of Acceleration," from the classic *The Education of Henry Adams*, is a bravura work of astonishing intellectual abstraction; written nearly one hundred years ago, it strikes a disturbingly contemporary note in its somber contemplation of a mechanistic universe reduced to a series of "relations" and mankind itself reduced to "Motion in a universe of Motions, with an acceleration . . . of vertiginous violence." With the authority of science, Adams says, history has no right to meddle, since science "now lay in a plane where scarcely one or two hundred minds in the world could follow its mathematical processes." Fittingly, William James's famous "The Moral Equivalent of War" was written in the same year, 1910, as Henry James's "Is There a Life after Death?" Though William James is a far more lucid prose stylist than his younger brother, both brothers are concerned with profound questions of life and death; William James broods upon the future of civilization itself in a prophetic work that looks ahead to Freud's late, melancholic *Civilization and Its Discontents* (1930). What is history but a bloodbath? "The horrors make the fascination. War is the *strong* life; it is life *in extremis;* war-taxes are the only ones men never hesitate to pay, as the budgets of all nations show us." John Jay Chapman, once considered an essayist of nearly Emerson's stature, is not much read today, yet his passionate meditation upon a notorious lynching that took place in Coatesville, Pennsylvania, in 1911 transcends its time and tragic circumstances.

The two most influential literary essays of the twentieth century are perhaps T. S. Eliot's "Tradition and the Individual Talent" ("The emotion of art is impersonal") and Robert Frost's "The Figure a Poem Makes" ("No tears in the writer, no tears in the reader"); each gains from being read in conjunction with the other. *Sui generis* is Gertrude Stein's "What Are Master-pieces and Why Are There So Few of Them," itself a masterpiece of polemics, an argument that convinces by sheer repetition:

> . . . One has not identity [when] one is in the act of doing anything. Identity is recognition, you know who you are because you and others remember anything about yourself but essentially you are not that when you are doing anything. I am I because my little dog knows me but, creatively speaking the little dog knowing that you are you and your recognizing that he knows, is what destroys creation.

H. L. Mencken's "The Hills of Zion" is, like many of Mencken's essays and columns, a passionate repudiation of evangelical Christianity and anti-intellectualism. This is sermonizing disguised as social satire, zestful in its accumulation of damning details; one can see why the young Negro Richard Wright was so impressed by Mencken's example, seeing the older white man as "fighting, fighting with words . . . using words as a weapon . . . as one would use a club." Katherine Anne Porter's "The Future Is Now" is an almost purely cerebral opinion piece, less compelling perhaps than Porter's elegantly composed short stories, but gracefully argued nonetheless, while "Artists in Uniform," one of Mary McCarthy's most anthologized essays, smoothly combines her satirical gifts with her passion for intellectual discourse. Susan Sontag's "Notes on Camp" is both opinion essay and cultural criticism of a high order; Adrienne Rich's dramatically fragmented "Women and Honor: Some

Notes on Lying" might be defined as an essay of opinion in a unique, poetic form. Essays by Alice Walker, Richard Rodriguez, N. Scott Momaday, and Cynthia Ozick advance arguments by means of an accumulation of memoirist detail, and each presents us with the wonder of how, in Ozick's words, "a writer is dreamed and transfigured into being." And essays that seem to be primarily concerned with the imparting of information and description, like Loren Eiseley's "The Brown Wasps," Tom Wolfe's "Putting Daddy On," Elizabeth Hardwick's "The Apotheosis of Martin Luther King," Lewis Thomas's "The Lives of a Cell," Annie Dillard's "Total Eclipse," among others, contain arguments of subtlety and insight. Saul Bellow's "Graven Images" is a meditation in the author's characteristic ironic mode on photography as a violation of personal dignity and privacy and the "revolutionary transformation" of a world that no longer honors such values. John McPhee's wonderfully original "The Search for Marvin Gardens" makes of the popular American board game an allegory of capitalist adventure, and rewards us with the unexpected discovery of the secluded middle-class bastion Marvin Gardens, the security-patrolled "suburb within a suburb" that is one's reward for winning the game.

The earliest essay in the anthology, Mark Twain's "Corn-pone Opinions," is a superbly modulated argument that begins with an engaging portrait of a young black slave (this is the Missouri of Twain's childhood, in the 1850s) and proceeds to a ringing denunciation of cultural chauvinism that is as relevant to our time as it was to Twain's:

> Broadly speaking, there are none but corn-pone opinions. And broadly speaking, corn-pone stands for self-approval. Self-approval is acquired mainly from the approval of other people. The result is conformity.

By which Twain means that deathly conformity that leads to an acceptance of slavery, lynchings, white bigotry, and injustice in a nation constituted as a democracy.

Twain's essay strikes a chord that resounds through the anthology: the ever-shifting, ever-evolving issue of race in America. It can't be an accident that the essays in this volume by men and women of ethnic minority backgrounds are outstanding; to paraphrase Melville, to write a "mighty" work of prose you must have a "mighty" theme. And what mightier, what more challenging and passionate theme for both writer and reader than how it feels to be of minority status in America, from the time of W.E.B. Du Bois in the first decade of the century to our contemporaries Maya Angelou, N. Scott Momaday, Maxine Hong Kingston, Alice Walker, Richard Rodriguez, and Gerald Early? For historical reasons obviously having to do with slavery, the experience of blacks in America has been significantly different from that of other minorities, and this fact is reflected in the essays included here.

W.E.B. Du Bois's "Of the Coming of John," from *The Souls of Black Folk* (1903), is a chillingly prophetic work that traces the intellectual and spiritual evolution of a seemingly ordinary black boy from southeastern Georgia who is sent north to be educated in a Negro school, returns after seven years to his hometown so thoroughly changed that he seems more foreign to his former relatives and neighbors than a Georgian white man would be, and is given advice by the kindly white Judge:

> "... You and I both know, John, that in this country the Negro must remain subordinate, and can never expect to be the equal of white men. In their place, you people can be honest and respectful; and God knows, I'll do what I can to help them. But when they want to reverse nature ... by God! we'll hold them under if we have to lynch every Nigger in the land."

Zora Neale Hurston in "How It Feels to Be Colored Me" (1928) defines herself very differently from Du Bois's tragic protagonist, partly because she has been raised in a "colored town" in Florida, Eatonville. Her defiance strikes us as courageous, and touching:

> At certain times I have no race, I am *me* ... Sometimes, I feel discriminated against, but it does not make me angry. It merely astonishes me. How *can* any deny themselves the pleasure of my company! It's beyond me.

Richard Wright's "The Ethics of Living Jim Crow: An Autobiographical Sketch," the preface to Wright's 1938 collection of novellas, *Uncle Tom's Children*, would become a section of his heralded *Black Boy* (1945). Wright's education in Jim Crow "wisdom" begins ironically with a beating his mother gives him for having dared to fight with white boys, and carries him into a prematurely cynical adolescence; it's a vision of the American South contiguous with that of New York City in the 1940s experienced by Langston Hughes.

Perhaps the preeminent essayist of the American twentieth century is James Baldwin, and it seems fitting that Baldwin wrote his most powerful and influential nonfiction works, *Notes of a Native Son, Nobody Knows My Name,* and *The Fire Next Time,* at about midcentury. Baldwin was a natural master of a kind of nonfiction narration we associate with the most engaging fiction, in which personal, familial experience is linked with a larger social and political context that enhances it as myth. Like his mentor Richard Wright, James Baldwin was a poet of irony; his bitterness and rage at social injustice was so finely distilled, his use of language so impassioned and fluent, he made of the most tragically debased materials a world of startling beauty. Baldwin's is a secular mystical vision that seems to us quintessentially American:

> All of my [newly deceased] father's texts and songs, which I had decided were meaningless, were arranged before me at his death like empty bottles, waiting to hold the meaning which life would give them for me. This was his legacy: nothing is ever escaped . . . The dead man mattered, the new life mattered; blackness and whiteness did not matter; to believe they did was to acquiesce in one's own destruction. Hatred, which could destroy so much, never failed to destroy the man who hated and this man was an immutable law.

This is the vision of Martin Luther King, Jr., expressed in his historic 1963 "Letter from Birmingham Jail": "One who breaks an unjust law must do it *openly, lovingly* . . . and with a willingness to accept the penalty."

Robert Atwan, who has been an invaluable series editor for the highly regarded *The Best American Essays* since its inception in 1986, assisted me tirelessly and with inspiration in our months-long effort of sifting through any and all essays that were possibilities for this anthology. We have been limited, or, one might say, assisted, in our selections only since 1986, being obliged to choose essays from the series anthology after that date; before 1986, we had no restrictions. Our decision to reprint essays only by writers who have published nonfiction books helped to limit our search, as did our exclusion of journalism, excepting unique reportage like Hemingway's "Pamplona in July" and Michael Herr's "Illumination Rounds." We hoped to avoid prose fiction in essay form, though such prose pieces as W.E.B. Du Bois's "Of the Coming of John" and Langston Hughes's "Bop" certainly employ fictional techniques; we excluded literary criticism — though some of our finest writers, like Randall Jarrell, Jacques Barzun, and Lionel Trilling, have excelled in it — and footnote-laden academic essays for a limited readership, even by Hannah Arendt. Much as I wanted to include Henry James, as I've noted above, I could not justify reprinting a long, convoluted skein of words that few readers would read. Nor could I include another major twentieth-century writer, Willa Cather, whose available essays were simply inappropriate, and lengthy. Of Norman Mailer's nonfiction work, "The Fight" would have been my choice for this volume, but it's book length (and has already appeared in *The Best American Sports Writing of the Century*); other essays of Mailer's, like "The White Negro," controversial in their time, are badly dated today. Gay Talese, a brilliant practitioner of what has come to be known as New Journalism, has written no "essays" per se. William Carlos Williams, Ralph Ellison, John Hersey, Wallace Stegner, Barbara Tuchman, Gore Vidal, most painfully William Faulkner: these important writers had no single appropriate essay. Faulkner in particular seems to have had little aptitude, or perhaps inspiration, for the essay form.

Of contemporary essayists there are so many — so very many! — who might well be included here, it isn't possible to list their names except in the Appendix. Quite apart from the numerous memoirs of high quality being written today, and published to much acclaim, this is a remarkably fruitful era for the personal essay. The triumph, one might say, of the mysterious pronoun "I."

It was the aim of the editors to tell a more or less chronological story of America as the century unfolded, with representative essays from each decade, as we have done; yet, the reader will note, the traumatic experiences of World War II, vividly described by William Manchester in "Okinawa: The Bloodiest Battle of All," does not appear in the forties but decades later, in 1987; and numerous other essays, stimulated by memory and meditation, have been written years after the occasion of their subjects. The ideal essay, in any case, is as timeless as any work of art, transcending the circumstances of its inception. It moves, as Robert Frost says of the ideal poem, from delight to wisdom, and "rides on its own melting," like ice on a hot stove.

Joyce Carol Oates

Mark Twain

....

Corn-pone Opinions

FIFTY YEARS AGO, when I was a boy of fifteen and helping to inhabit a Missourian village on the banks of the Mississippi, I had a friend whose society was very dear to me because I was forbidden by my mother to partake of it. He was a gay and impudent and satirical and delightful young black man — a slave — who daily preached sermons from the top of his master's woodpile, with me for sole audience. He imitated the pulpit style of the several clergymen of the village, and did it well, and with fine passion and energy. To me he was a wonder. I believed he was the greatest orator in the United States and would some day be heard from. But it did not happen; in the distribution of rewards he was overlooked. It is the way, in this world.

He interrupted his preaching, now and then, to saw a stick of wood; but the sawing was a pretense — he did it with his mouth; exactly imitating the sound the bucksaw makes in shrieking its way through the wood. But it served its purpose; it kept his master from coming out to see how the work was getting along. I listened to the sermons from the open window of a lumber room at the back of the house. One of his texts was this:

"You tell me whar a man gits his corn pone, en I'll tell you what his 'pinions is."

I can never forget it. It was deeply impressed upon me. By my mother. Not upon my memory, but elsewhere. She had slipped in upon

Unpublished in Twain's lifetime. His notebooks and the opening sentence suggest the essay was written early in 1901. It was first published in *Europe and Elsewhere*, edited by Albert Bigelow Paine, 1923.

Throughout, the asterisk indicates the source used for this collection.

me while I was absorbed and not watching. The black philosopher's idea was that a man is not independent, and cannot afford views which might interfere with his bread and butter. If he would prosper, he must train with the majority; in matters of large moment, like politics and religion, he must think and feel with the bulk of his neighbors, or suffer damage in his social standing and in his business prosperities. He must restrict himself to corn-pone opinions — at least on the surface. He must get his opinions from other people; he must reason out none for himself; he must have no first-hand views.

I think Jerry was right, in the main, but I think he did not go far enough.

1. It was his idea that a man conforms to the majority view of his locality by calculation and intention.

This happens, but I think it is not the rule.

2. It was his idea that there is such a thing as a first-hand opinion; an original opinion; an opinion which is coldly reasoned out in a man's head, by a searching analysis of the facts involved, with the heart unconsulted, and the jury room closed against outside influences. It may be that such an opinion has been born somewhere, at some time or other, but I suppose it got away before they could catch it and stuff it and put it in the museum.

I am persuaded that a coldly-thought-out and independent verdict upon a fashion in clothes, or manners, or literature, or politics, or religion, or any other matter that is projected into the field of our notice and interest, is a most rare thing — if it has indeed ever existed.

A new thing in costume appears — the flaring hoopskirt, for example — and the passers-by are shocked, and the irreverent laugh. Six months later everybody is reconciled; the fashion has established itself; it is admired, now, and no one laughs. Public opinion resented it before, public opinion accepts it now, and is happy in it. Why? Was the resentment reasoned out? Was the acceptance reasoned out? No. The instinct that moves to conformity did the work. It is our nature to conform; it is a force which not many can successfully resist. What is its seat? The inborn requirement of self-approval. We all have to bow to that; there are no exceptions. Even the woman who refuses from first to last to wear the hoopskirt comes under that law and is its slave; she could not wear the skirt and have her own approval; and that she *must* have, she cannot help herself. But as a rule our self-approval has its source in but one place and not elsewhere — the approval of other people. A person of vast consequences can introduce any kind of novelty in dress and the general world will presently adopt it — moved to do it, in the first place, by the natural instinct to passively yield to that vague something recognized as authority, and in the second place by the human instinct to train with the multitude and have its approval. An empress introduced the hoopskirt, and we know the result. A nobody introduced the bloomer, and we know the result. If Eve should come again, in her ripe renown, and reintroduce her quaint styles — well, we know what would happen. And we should be cruelly embarrassed, along at first.

The hoopskirt runs its course and disappears. Nobody reasons about it. One woman abandons the fashion; her neighbor notices this and follows her lead; this influences the next woman; and so on and so on, and presently the skirt has vanished out of the world, no one knows how nor why, nor cares, for that matter. It will come again, by and by and in due course will go again.

Twenty-five years ago, in England, six or eight wine glasses stood grouped by each person's plate at a dinner party, and they were used, not left idle and empty; to-day there are but three or four in the group, and the average guest sparingly uses about two of them. We have not adopted this new fashion yet, but we shall do it presently. We shall not think it out; we shall merely conform, and let it go at that. We get our notions and habits and opinions from outside influences; we do not have to study them out.

Our table manners, and company manners, and street manners change from time to time, but the changes are not reasoned out; we merely notice and conform. We are creatures of outside influences; as a rule we do not think, we only imitate. We cannot invent standards that will stick; what we mistake for standards are only fashions, and perishable. We may continue to admire them, but we drop the use of them. We notice this in literature. Shakespeare is a standard, and fifty years ago we used to write tragedies which we couldn't tell from — from somebody else's; but we don't do it any more, now. Our prose standard, three quarters of a century ago, was ornate and diffuse; some authority or other changed it in the direction of compactness and simplicity, and conformity followed, without argument. The historical novel starts up suddenly, and sweeps the land. Everybody writes one, and the nation is glad. We had historical novels before; but nobody read them, and the rest of us conformed — without reasoning it out. We are conforming in the other way, now, because it is another case of everybody.

The outside influences are always pouring in upon us, and we are always obeying their orders and accepting their verdicts. The Smiths like the new play; the Joneses go to see it, and they copy the Smith verdict. Morals, religions, politics, get their following from surrounding influences and atmospheres, almost entirely; not from study, not from thinking. A man must and will have his own approval first of all, in each and every moment and circumstance of his life — even if he must repent of a self-approved act the moment after its commission, in order to get his self-approval *again:* but, speaking in general terms, a man's self-approval in the large concerns of life has its source in the approval of the peoples about him, and not in a searching personal examination of the matter. Mohammedans are Mohammedans because they are born and reared among that sect, not because they have thought it out and can furnish sound reasons for being Mohammedans; we know why Catholics are Catholics; why Presbyterians are Presbyterians; why Baptists are Baptists; why Mormons are Mormons; why thieves are thieves; why monarchists are monarchists; why Republicans are Republicans and Democrats, Democrats. We know it is a matter of association and sympathy, not reasoning and examination; that hardly a man in the world has an opinion upon morals, politics, or religion which he got otherwise than through his associations and sympathies. Broadly speaking, there are none but corn-pone opinions. And broadly speaking, corn-pone stands for self-approval. Self-approval is acquired mainly from the approval of other people. The result is conformity. Sometimes conformity has a sordid business interest — the bread-and-butter interest — but not in most cases, I think. I think that in the majority of cases it is unconscious and not calculated; that it is born of the human being's natural yearning to stand well with his fellows and have their inspiring approval and praise — a yearning which is commonly so strong and so insistent that it cannot be effectually resisted, and must have its way.

A political emergency brings out the corn-pone opinion in fine force in its two chief varieties — the pocketbook variety, which has its origin in self-interest, and the bigger variety, the sentimental variety — the one which can't bear to be outside the pale; can't bear to be in disfavor; can't endure the averted face and the cold shoulder; wants to stand well with his friends, wants to be smiled upon, wants to be welcome, wants to hear the precious words, "*He's* on the right track!" Uttered, perhaps by an ass, but still an ass of high degree, an ass whose approval is gold and diamonds to a smaller ass, and confers glory and honor and happiness, and membership in the herd. For these gauds many a man will dump his life-long principles into the street, and his conscience along with them. We have seen it happen. In some millions of instances.

Men think they think upon great political questions, and they do; but they think with their party, not independently; they read its literature, but not that of the other side; they arrive at convictions, but they are drawn from a partial view of the matter in hand and are of no particular value. They swarm with their party, they feel with their party, they are happy in their party's approval; and where the party leads they will follow, whether for right and honor, or through blood and dirt and a mush of mutilated morals.

In our late canvass half of the nation passionately believed that in silver lay salvation, the other half as passionately believed that that way lay destruction. Do you believe that a tenth part of the people, on either side, had any rational excuse for having an opinion about the matter at all? I studied that mighty question to the bottom — came out empty. Half of our people passionately believe in high tariff, the other half believe otherwise. Does this mean study and examination, or only feeling? The latter, I think. I have deeply studied that question, too — and didn't arrive. We all do no end of feeling, and we mistake it for thinking. And out of it we get an aggregation which we consider a boon. Its name is Public Opinion. It is held in reverence. It settles everything. Some think it the Voice of God.

W.E.B. Du Bois

Of the Coming of John

What bring they 'neath the midnight,
    Beside the River-sea?
They bring the human heart wherein
    No nightly calm can be;
That droppeth never with the wind,
    Nor drieth with the dew;
O calm it, God; thy calm is broad
    To cover spirits too.
    The river floweth on.
                Mrs. Browning

CARLISLE STREET runs westward from the centre of Johnstown, across a great black bridge, down a hill and up again, by little shops and meat-markets, past single-storied homes, until suddenly it stops against a wide green lawn. It is a broad, restful place, with two large buildings outlined against the west. When at evening the winds come swelling from the east, and the great pall of the city's smoke hangs wearily above

First published in *The Souls of Black Folk, 1903. Each of the first thirteen essays in Souls is prefaced with a poetic epigraph followed by a bar from a Negro spiritual, which Du Bois called a "sorrow song." This one is from "You May Bury Me in the East." Although "Of the Coming of John" reads like a short story, Du Bois clearly considered it an essay. See biographical note for additional information.

the valley, then the red west glows like a dreamland down Carlisle Street, and, at the tolling of the supper-bell, throws the passing forms of students in dark silhouette against the sky. Tall and black, they move slowly by, and seem in the sinister light to flit before the city like dim warning ghosts. Perhaps they are; for this is Wells Institute, and these black students have few dealings with the white city below.

And if you will notice, night after night, there is one dark form that ever hurries last and late toward the twinkling lights of Swain Hall, — for Jones is never on time. A long, straggling fellow he is, brown and hard-haired, who seems to be growing straight out of his clothes, and walks with a half-apologetic roll. He used perpetually to set the quiet dining-room into waves of merriment, as he stole to his place after the bell had tapped for prayers; he seemed so perfectly awkward. And yet one glance at his face made one forgive him much, — that broad, good-natured smile in which lay no bit of art or artifice, but seemed just bubbling good-nature and genuine satisfaction with the world.

He came to us from Altamaha, away down there beneath the gnarled oaks of Southeastern Georgia, where the sea croons to the sands and the sands listen till they sink half drowned beneath the waters, rising only here and there in long, low islands. The white folk of Altamaha voted John a good boy, — fine plough-hand, good in the rice-fields, handy everywhere, and always good-natured and respectful. But they shook their heads when his mother wanted to send him off to school. "It'll spoil him, — ruin him," they said; and they talked as though they knew. But full half the black folk followed him proudly to the station, and carried his queer little trunk and many bundles. And there they shook and shook hands, and the girls kissed him shyly and the boys clapped him on the back. So the train came, and he pinched his little sister lovingly, and put his great arms about his mother's neck, and then was away with a puff and a roar into the great yellow world that flamed and flared about the doubtful pilgrim. Up the coast they hurried, past the squares and palmettos of Savannah, through the cotton-fields and through the weary night, to Millville, and came with the morning to the noise and bustle of Johnstown.

And they that stood behind, that morning in Altamaha, and watched the train as it noisily bore playmate and brother and son away to the world, had thereafter one ever-recurring word, — "When John comes." Then what parties were to be, and what speakings in the churches; what new furniture in the front room, — perhaps even a new front room; and there would be a new schoolhouse, with John as teacher; and then perhaps a big wedding; all this and more — when John comes. But the white people shook their heads.

At first he was coming at Christmas-time, — but the vacation proved too short; and then, the next summer, — but times were hard and schooling costly, and so, instead, he worked in Johnstown. And so it drifted to the next summer, and the next, — till playmates scattered, and mother grew gray, and sister went up to the Judge's kitchen to work. And still the legend lingered, — "When John comes."

Up at the Judge's they rather liked this refrain; for they too had a John — a fair-haired, smooth-faced boy, who had played many a long summer's day to its close with his darker namesake. "Yes, sir! John is at Princeton, sir," said the broad-shouldered gray-haired Judge every morning as he marched down to the post-office. "Showing the Yankees what a Southern gentleman can do," he added; and strode home again with his letters and papers. Up at the great pillared house they lingered long over the Princeton letter, — the Judge and his frail wife, his sister and growing daughters. "It'll make a man of him," said the Judge, "college is the place." And then he asked the shy little waitress, "Well, Jennie, how's your John?" and added reflectively, "Too bad, too bad your mother sent him off, — it will spoil him." And the waitress wondered.

Thus in the far-away Southern village the world lay waiting, half consciously, the coming of two young men, and dreamed in an inarticulate way of new things that would be done and new thoughts that all would think. And yet it was singular that few thought of two Johns, — for the black folk thought of one John, and he was black; and the white folk thought of another John, and he was white. And neither world thought the other world's thought, save with a vague unrest.

Up in Johnstown, at the Institute, we were long puzzled at the case of John Jones. For a long time the clay seemed unfit for any sort of moulding. He was loud and boisterous, always laughing and singing, and never able to work consecutively at anything. He did not know how to study; he had no idea of thoroughness; and with his tardiness, carelessness, and appalling good-humor, we were sore perplexed. One night we sat in faculty-meeting, worried and serious; for Jones was in trouble again. This last escapade was too much, and so we solemnly voted "that Jones, on account of repeated disorder and inattention to work, be suspended for the rest of the term."

It seemed to us that the first time life ever struck Jones as a really serious thing was when the Dean told him he must leave school. He stared at the gray-haired man blankly, with great eyes. "Why, — why," he faltered, "but — I haven't graduated!" Then the Dean slowly and clearly explained, reminding him of the tardiness and the carelessness, of the poor lessons and neglected work, of the noise and disorder, until the fellow hung his head in confusion. Then he said quickly, "But you won't tell mammy and sister, — you won't write mammy, now will you? For if you won't I'll go out into the city and work, and come back next term and show you something." So the Dean promised faithfully, and John shouldered his little trunk, giving neither word nor look to the giggling boys, and walked down Carlisle Street to the great city, with sober eyes and a set and serious face.

Perhaps we imagined it, but someway it seemed to us that the serious look that crept over his boyish face that afternoon never left it again. When he came back to us he went to work with all his rugged strength. It was a hard struggle, for things did not come easily to him, — few crowding memories of early life and teaching came to help him on his new way; but all the world toward which he strove was of his own building, and he builded slow and hard. As the light dawned lingeringly on his new creations, he sat rapt and silent before the vision, or wandered alone over the green campus peering through and beyond the world of men into a world of thought. And the thoughts at times puzzled him sorely; he could not see just why the circle was not square, and carried it out fifty-six decimal places one midnight, — would have gone further, indeed, had not the matron rapped for lights out. He caught terrible colds lying on his back in the meadows of nights, trying to think out the solar system; he had grave doubts as to the ethics of the Fall of Rome, and strongly suspected the Germans of being thieves and rascals, despite his text-books; he pondered long over every new Greek word, and wondered why this meant that and why it couldn't mean something else, and how it must have felt to think all things in Greek. So he thought and puzzled along for himself, — pausing perplexed where others skipped merrily, and walking steadily through the difficulties where the rest stopped and surrendered.

Thus he grew in body and soul, and with him his clothes seemed to grow and arrange themselves; coat sleeves got longer, cuffs appeared, and collars got less soiled. Now and then his boots shone, and a new dignity crept into his walk. And we who saw daily a new thoughtfulness growing in his eyes began to expect something of this plodding boy. Thus he passed out of the preparatory school into college, and we who watched him felt four more years of change, which almost transformed the tall, grave man who bowed to us commencement morning. He had left his queer thought-world and come back to a world of motion and of men. He looked now for the first time sharply about him, and wondered he had seen so little before. He grew slowly to feel almost for the first time the Veil that lay between him and the white world; he first noticed now the oppression that had not seemed oppression before, differences that erstwhile seemed natural, restraints and slights that in his boyhood days had gone unnoticed or been greeted with a laugh. He felt angry now when men did not call him "Mister," he clenched his hands at the "Jim Crow" cars, and chafed at the color-line that hemmed in him and his. A tinge of sarcasm crept into his speech, and a vague bitterness into his life; and he sat long hours wondering and planning a way around these crooked things. Daily he found himself shrinking from the choked and narrow life of his native town. And yet he always planned to go back to Altamaha, — always planned to work there. Still, more and more as the day approached he hesitated with a nameless dread; and even the day after graduation he seized with eagerness the offer of the Dean to send him North with the quartette during the summer vacation, to sing for the Institute. A breath of air before the plunge, he said to himself in half apology.

It was a bright September afternoon, and the streets of New York were brilliant with moving men. They reminded John of the sea, as he sat in the square and watched them, so changelessly changing, so bright and dark, so grave and gay. He scanned their rich and faultless clothes, the way they carried their hands, the shape of their hats; he peered into the hurrying carriages. Then, leaning back with a sigh, he said, "This is the World." The notion suddenly seized him to see where the world was going; since many of the richer and brighter seemed hurrying all one way. So when a tall, light-haired young man and a little talkative lady came by, he rose half hesitatingly and followed them. Up the street they went, past stores and gay shops, across a broad square, until with a hundred others they entered the high portal of a great building.

He was pushed toward the ticket-office with the others, and felt in his pocket for the new five-dollar bill he had hoarded. There seemed really no time for hesitation, so he drew it bravely out, passed it to the busy clerk, and received simply a ticket but no change. When at last he realized that he had paid five dollars to enter he knew not what, he stood stock-still amazed. "Be careful," said a low voice behind him; "you must not lynch the colored gentleman simply because he's in your way," and a girl looked up roguishly into the eyes of her fair-haired escort. A shade of annoyance passed over the escort's face. "You *will* not understand us at the South," he said half impatiently, as if continuing an argument. "With all your professions, one never sees in the North so cordial and intimate relations between white and black as are everyday occurrences with us. Why, I remember my closest playfellow in boyhood was a little Negro named after me, and surely no two, — *well!*" The man stopped short and flushed to the roots of his hair, for there directly beside his reserved orchestra chairs sat the Negro he had stumbled over in the hallway. He hesitated and grew pale with anger, called the usher and gave him his card, with a few peremptory words, and slowly sat down. The lady deftly changed the subject.

All this John did not see, for he sat in a half-maze minding the scene about him; the delicate beauty of the hall, the faint perfume, the moving myriad of men, the rich clothing and low hum of talking seemed all a part of a world so different from his, so strangely more beautiful than anything he had known, that he sat in dreamland, and started when, after a hush, rose high and clear the music of Lohengrin's swan. The infinite beauty of the wail lingered and swept through every muscle of his frame, and put it all a-tune. He closed his eyes and grasped the elbows of the chair, touching unwittingly the lady's arm. And the lady drew away. A deep longing swelled in all his heart to rise with that clear music out of the dirt and dust of that low life that held him prisoned and befouled. If he could only live up in the free air where birds sang and setting suns had no touch of blood! Who had called him to be the slave and butt of all? And if he had called, what right had he to call when a world like this lay open before men?

Then the movement changed, and fuller, mightier harmony swelled away. He looked thoughtfully across the hall, and wondered why the beautiful gray-haired woman looked so listless, and what the little man could be whispering about. He would not like to be listless and idle, he thought, for he felt with the music the movement of power within him. If he but had some master-work, some life-service, hard, — aye, bitter hard, but without the cringing and sickening servility, without the cruel hurt that hardened his heart and soul. When at last a soft sorrow crept across the violins, there came to him the vision of a far-off home, — the great eyes of his sister, and the dark drawn face of his mother. And his heart sank below the waters, even as the sea-sand sinks by the shores of Altamaha, only to be lifted aloft again with that last ethereal wail of the swan that quivered and faded away into the sky.

It left John sitting so silent and rapt that he did not for some time notice the usher tapping him lightly on the shoulder and saying politely, "Will you step this way, please, sir?" A little surprised, he arose quickly at the last tap, and, turning to leave his seat, looked full into the face of the fair-haired young man. For the first time the young man recognized his dark boyhood playmate, and John knew that it was the Judge's son. The white John started, lifted his hand, and then froze into his chair; the black John smiled lightly, then grimly, and followed the usher down the aisle. The manager was sorry, very, very sorry, — but he explained that some mistake had been made in selling the gentleman a seat already disposed of; he would refund the money, of course, — and indeed felt the matter keenly, and so forth, and — before he had finished John was gone, walking hurriedly across the square and down the broad streets, and as he passed the park he buttoned his coat and said, "John Jones, you're a natural-born fool." Then he went to his lodgings and wrote a letter, and tore it up; he wrote another, and threw it in the fire. Then he seized a scrap of paper and wrote: "Dear Mother and Sister — I am coming — John."

"Perhaps," said John, as he settled himself on the train, "perhaps I am to blame myself in struggling against my manifest destiny simply because it looks hard and unpleasant. Here is my duty to Altamaha plain before me; perhaps they'll let me help settle the Negro problems there, — perhaps they won't. 'I will go in to the King, which is not according to the law; and if I perish, I perish.'" And then he mused and dreamed, and planned a life-work; and the train flew south.

Down in Altamaha, after seven long years, all the world knew John was coming. The homes were scrubbed and scoured, — above all, one; the gardens and yards had an unwonted trimness, and Jennie bought a new gingham. With some finesse and negotiation, all the dark Methodists and Presbyterians were induced to join in a monster welcome at the Baptist Church; and as the day drew near, warm discussions arose on every corner as to the exact extent and nature of John's accomplishments. It was noontide on a gray and cloudy day when he came. The black town flocked to the depot, with a little of the white at the edges, — a happy throng, with "Good-mawnings" and "Howdys" and laughing and joking and jostling. Mother sat yonder in the window watching; but sister Jennie stood on the platform, nervously fingering her dress, — tall and lithe, with soft brown skin and loving eyes peering from out a tangled wilderness of hair. John rose gloomily as the train stopped, for he was thinking of the "Jim Crow" car; he stepped to the platform, and paused: a little dingy station, a black crowd gaudy and dirty, a half-mile of dilapidated shanties along a straggling ditch of mud. An over-whelming sense of the sordidness and narrowness of it all seized him; he looked in vain for his mother, kissed coldly the tall, strange girl who called him brother, spoke a short, dry word here and there; then, lingering neither for hand-shaking nor gossip, started silently up the street, raising his hat merely to the last eager old aunty, to her open-mouthed astonishment. The people were distinctly bewildered. This si-lent, cold man, — was this John? Where was his smile and hearty hand-grasp? "'Peared kind o' down in the mouf," said the Methodist preacher thoughtfully. "Seemed monstus stuck up," complained a Baptist sister. But the white postmaster from the edge of the crowd expressed the opinion of his folks plainly. "That damn Nigger," said he, as he shoul-dered the mail and arranged his tobacco, "has gone North and got plum full o' fool notions; but they won't work in Altamaha." And the crowd melted away.

The meeting of welcome at the Baptist Church was a failure. Rain spoiled the barbecue, and thunder turned the milk in the ice-cream. When the speaking came at night, the house was crowded to overflow-ing. The three preachers had especially prepared themselves, but some-how John's manner seemed to throw a blanket over everything, — he seemed so cold and preoccupied, and had so strange an air of restraint that the Methodist brother could not warm up to his theme and elicited not a single "Amen"; the Presbyterian prayer was but feebly responded to, and even the Baptist preacher, though he wakened faint enthusiasm, got so mixed up in his favorite sentence that he had to close it by stop-ping fully fifteen minutes sooner than he meant. The people moved un-easily in their seats as John rose to reply. He spoke slowly and methodi-cally. The age, he said, demanded new ideas; we were far different from those men of the seventeenth and eighteenth centuries, — with broader ideas of human brotherhood and destiny. Then he spoke of the rise of charity and popular education, and particularly of the spread of wealth and work. The question was, then, he added reflectively, looking at the low discolored ceiling, what part the Negroes of this land would take in the striving of the new century. He sketched in vague outline the new Industrial School that might rise among these pines, he spoke in detail of the charitable and philanthropic work that might be organized, of money that might be saved for banks and business. Finally he urged unity, and deprecated especially religious and denominational bicker-ing. "To-day," he said, with a smile, "the world cares little whether a man be Baptist or Methodist, or indeed a churchman at all, so long as he is good and true. What difference does it make whether a man be baptized in river or wash-bowl, or not at all? Let's leave all that little- ness, and look higher." Then, thinking of nothing else, he slowly sat down. A painful hush seized that crowded mass. Little had they under- stood of what he said, for he spoke an unknown tongue, save the last word about baptism; that they knew, and they sat very still while the clock ticked. Then at last a low suppressed snarl came from the Amen corner, and an old bent man arose, walked over the seats, and climbed straight up into the pulpit. He was wrinkled and black, with scant gray and tufted hair; his voice and hands shook as with palsy; but on his face lay the intense rapt look of the religious fanatic. He seized the Bible with his rough, huge hands; twice he raised it inarticulate, and then fairly burst into the words, with rude and awful eloquence. He quivered, swayed, and bent; then rose aloft in perfect majesty, till the people moaned and wept, wailed and shouted, and a wild shrieking arose from the corners where all the pent-up feeling of the hour gathered itself and rushed into the air. John never knew clearly what the old man said; he only felt himself held up to scorn and scathing denunciation for tram- pling on the true Religion, and he realized with amazement that all un- knowingly he had put rough, rude hands on something this little world held sacred. He arose silently, and passed out into the night. Down to- ward the sea he went, in the fitful starlight, half conscious of the girl who followed timidly after him. When at last he stood upon the bluff, he turned to his little sister and looked upon her sorrowfully, re- membering with sudden pain how little thought he had given her. He put his arm about her and let her passion of tears spend itself on his shoulder.

Long they stood together, peering over the gray unresting water.

"John," she said, "does it make every one — unhappy when they study and learn lots of things?"

He paused and smiled. "I am afraid it does," he said.

"And, John, are you glad you studied?"

"Yes," came the answer, slowly but positively.

She watched the flickering lights upon the sea, and said thoughtfully, "I wish I was unhappy, — and — and," putting both arms about his neck, "I think I am, a little, John."

It was several days later that John walked up to the Judge's house to ask for the privilege of teaching the Negro school. The Judge him- self met him at the front door, stared a little hard at him, and said brusquely, "Go 'round to the kitchen door, John, and wait." Sitting on the kitchen steps, John stared at the corn, thoroughly perplexed. What on earth had come over him? Every step he made offended some one. He had come to save his people, and before he left the depot he had hurt them. He sought to teach them at the church, and had outraged their deepest feelings. He had schooled himself to be respectful to the Judge, and then blundered into his front door. And all the time he had meant right, — and yet, and yet, somehow he found it so hard and strange to fit his old surroundings again, to find his place in the world about him. He could not remember that he used to have any difficulty in the past, when life was glad and gay. The world seemed smooth and easy then. Perhaps, — but his sister came to the kitchen door just then and said the Judge awaited him.

The Judge sat in the dining-room amid his morning's mail, and he did not ask John to sit down. He plunged squarely into the business. "You've come for the school, I suppose. Well, John, I want to speak to you plainly. You know I'm a friend to your people. I've helped you and your family, and would have done more if you hadn't got the notion of going off. Now I like the colored people, and sympathize with all their reasonable aspirations; but you and I both know, John, that in this country the Negro must remain subordinate, and can never expect to be the equal of white men. In their place, your people can be honest and respectful; and God knows, I'll do what I can to help them. But when they want to reverse nature, and rule white men, and marry white women, and sit in my parlor, then, by God! we'll hold them under if we have to lynch every Nigger in the land. Now, John, the question is, are you, with your education and Northern notions, going to accept the situation and teach the darkies to be faithful servants and laborers as your fathers were, — I knew your father, John, he belonged to my brother, and he was a good Nigger. Well — well, are you going to be like him, or are you going to try to put fool ideas of rising and equality into these folks' heads, and make them discontented and unhappy?"

"I am going to accept the situation, Judge Henderson," answered John, with a brevity that did not escape the keen old man. He hesitated a moment, and then said shortly, "Very well, — we'll try you awhile. Good-morning."

It was a full month after the opening of the Negro school that the other John came home, tall, gay, and headstrong. The mother wept, the sisters sang. The whole white town was glad. A proud man was the Judge, and it was a goodly sight to see the two swinging down Main Street together. And yet all did not go smoothly between them, for the younger man could not and did not veil his contempt for the little town, and plainly had his heart set on New York. Now the one cherished ambition of the Judge was to see his son mayor of Altamaha, representative to the legislature, and — who could say? — governor of Georgia. So the argument often waxed hot between them. "Good heavens, father," the younger man would say after dinner, as he lighted a cigar and stood by the fireplace, "you surely don't expect a young fellow like me to settle down permanently in this — this God-forgotten town with nothing but mud and Negroes?" "*I* did," the Judge would answer laconically; and on this particular day it seemed from the gathering scowl that he was about to add something more emphatic, but neighbors had already begun to drop in to admire his son, and the conversation drifted.

"Heah that John is livenin' things up at the darky school," volunteered the postmaster, after a pause.

"What now?" asked the Judge, sharply.

"Oh, nothin' in particulah, — just his almighty air and uppish ways. B'lieve I did heah somethin' about his givin' talks on the French Revolution, equality, and such like. He's what I call a dangerous Nigger."

"Have you heard him say anything out of the way?"

"Why, no, — but Sally, our girl, told my wife a lot of rot. Then, too, I don't need to heah: a Nigger what won't say 'sir' to a white man, or —"

"Who is this John?" interrupted the son.

"Why, it's little black John, Peggy's son, — your old playfellow."

The young man's face flushed angrily, and then he laughed.

"Oh," said he, "it's the darky that tried to force himself into a seat beside the lady I was escorting —"

But Judge Henderson waited to hear no more. He had been nettled all day, and now at this he rose with a half-smothered oath, took his hat and cane, and walked straight to the schoolhouse.

For John, it had been a long, hard pull to get things started in the rickety old shanty that sheltered his school. The Negroes were rent into factions for and against him, the parents were careless, the children irregular and dirty, and books, pencils, and slates largely missing. Nevertheless, he struggled hopefully on, and seemed to see at last some glimmering of dawn. The attendance was larger and the children were a shade cleaner this week. Even the booby class in reading showed a little comforting progress. So John settled himself with renewed patience this afternoon.

"Now, Mandy," he said cheerfully, "that's better; but you mustn't chop your words up so: 'If — the — man — goes.' Why, your little brother even wouldn't tell a story that way, now would he?"

"Naw, suh, he cain't talk."

"All right; now let's try again: 'If the man —'"

"John!"

The whole school started in surprise, and the teacher half arose, as the red, angry face of the Judge appeared in the open doorway.

"John, this school is closed. You children can go home and get to work. The white people of Altamaha are not spending their money on black folks to have their heads crammed with impudence and lies. Clear out! I'll lock the door myself."

Up at the great pillared house the tall young son wandered aimlessly about after his father's abrupt departure. In the house there was little to interest him; the books were old and stale, the local newspaper flat, and the women had retired with headaches and sewing. He tried a nap, but it was too warm. So he sauntered out into the fields, complaining disconsolately, "Good Lord! how long will this imprisonment last!" He was not a bad fellow, — just a little spoiled and self-indulgent, and as headstrong as his proud father. He seemed a young man pleasant to look upon, as he sat on the great black stump at the edge of the pines idly swinging his legs and smoking. "Why, there isn't even a girl worth getting up a respectable flirtation with," he growled. Just then his eye caught a tall, willowy figure hurrying toward him on the narrow path. He looked with interest at first, and then burst into a laugh as he said, "Well, I declare, if it isn't Jennie, the little brown kitchen-maid! Why, I never noticed before what a trim little body she is. Hello, Jennie! Why, you haven't kissed me since I came home," he said gaily. The young girl stared at him in surprise and confusion, — faltered something inarticulate, and attempted to pass. But a wilful mood had seized the young idler, and he caught at her arm. Frightened, she slipped by; and half mischievously he turned and ran after her through the tall pines.

Yonder, toward the sea, at the end of the path, came John slowly, with his head down. He had turned wearily homeward from the schoolhouse; then, thinking to shield his mother from the blow, started to meet his sister as she came from work and break the news of his dismissal to her. "I'll go away," he said slowly; "I'll go away and find work, and send for them. I cannot live here longer." And then the fierce, buried anger surged up into his throat. He waved his arms and hurried wildly up the path.

The great brown sea lay silent. The air scarce breathed. The dying day bathed the twisted oaks and mighty pines in black and gold. There came from the wind no warning, not a whisper from the cloudless sky. There was only a black man hurrying on with an ache in his heart, seeing neither sun nor sea, but starting as from a dream at the frightened cry that woke the pines, to see his dark sister struggling in the arms of a tall and fair-haired man.

He said not a word, but, seizing a fallen limb, struck him with all the pent-up hatred of his great black arm; and the body lay white and still beneath the pines, all bathed in sunshine and in blood. John looked at it dreamily, then walked back to the house briskly, and said in a soft voice, "Mammy, I'm going away, — I'm going to be free."

She gazed at him dimly and faltered, "No'th, honey, is yo' gwine No'th agin?"

He looked out where the North Star glistened pale above the waters, and said, "Yes, mammy, I'm going — North."

Then, without another word, he went out into the narrow lane, up by the straight pines, to the same winding path, and seated himself on the great black stump, looking at the blood where the body had lain. Yonder in the gray past he had played with that dead boy, romping together under the solemn trees. The night deepened; he thought of the boys at Johnstown. He wondered how Brown had turned out, and Carey? And Jones, — Jones? Why, *he* was Jones, and he wondered what they would all say when they knew, when they knew, in that great long dining-room with its hundreds of merry eyes. Then as the sheen of the starlight stole over him, he thought of the gilded ceiling of that vast concert hall, and heard stealing toward him the faint sweet music of the swan. Hark! was it music, or the hurry and shouting of men? Yes, surely! Clear and high the faint sweet melody rose and fluttered like a living thing, so that the very earth trembled as with the tramp of horses and murmur of angry men.

He leaned back and smiled toward the sea, whence rose the strange melody, away from the dark shadows where lay the noise of horses galloping, galloping on. With an effort he roused himself, bent forward, and looked steadily down the pathway, softly humming the "Song of the Bride," —

"Freudig geführt, ziehet dahin."
["Joyfully led, drawn onward."]

Amid the trees in the dim morning twilight he watched their shadows dancing and heard their horses thundering toward him, until at last they came sweeping like a storm, and he saw in front that haggard white-haired man, whose eyes flashed red with fury. Oh, how he pitied him, — pitied him, — and wondered if he had the coiling twisted rope. Then, as the storm burst round him, he rose slowly to his feet and turned his closed eyes toward the Sea.

And the world whistled in his ears.

Henry Adams

A Law of Acceleration

IMAGES are not arguments, rarely even lead to proof, but the mind craves them, and, of late more than ever, the keenest experimenters find twenty images better than one, especially if contradictory; since the human mind has already learned to deal in contradictions.

The image needed here is that of a new center, or preponderating mass, artificially introduced on earth in the midst of a system of attractive forces that previously made their own equilibrium, and constantly induced to accelerate its motion till it shall establish a new equilibrium. A dynamic theory would begin by assuming that all history, terrestrial or cosmic, mechanical or intellectual, would be reduceable to this formula if we knew the facts.

For convenience, the most familiar image should come first; and this is probably that of the comet, or meteoric streams, like the Leonids and Perseids; a complex of minute mechanical agencies, reacting within and without, and guided by the sum of forces attracting or deflecting it. Nothing forbids one to assume that the man-meteorite might grow, as an acorn does, absorbing light, heat, electricity, — or thought; for, in recent times, such transference of energy has become a familiar idea; but the simplest figure, at first, is that of a perfect comet, — say that of 1843, — which drops from space, in a straight line, at the regular acceleration of speed, directly into the sun, and after wheeling sharply about it, in heat that ought to dissipate any known substance, turns back un-

Written in 1905, the essay was published as chapter 34 of *The Education of Henry Adams*, which was *privately printed in 1906 and brought out posthumously in a trade edition in 1918. The book was awarded one of the earliest Pulitzer Prizes in 1919.

harmed, in defiance of law, by the path on which it came. The mind, by analogy, may figure as such a comet, the better because it also defies law.

Motion is the ultimate object of science, and measures of motion are many; but with thought as with matter, the true measure is mass in its astronomic sense — the sum or difference of attractive forces. Science has quite enough trouble in measuring its material motions without volunteering help to the historian, but the historian needs not much help to measure some kinds of social movement; and especially in the nineteenth century, society by common accord agreed in measuring its progress by the coal-output. The ratio of increase in the volume of coal-power may serve as dynamometer.

The coal-output of the world, speaking roughly, doubled every ten years between 1800 and 1900, in the form of utilized power, for the ton of coal yielded three or four times as much power in 1900 as in 1840. Rapid as this rate of acceleration in volume seems, it may be tested in a thousand ways without greatly reducing it. Perhaps the ocean steamer is nearest unity and easiest to measure, for anyone might hire, in 1905, for a small sum of money, the use of 30,000 steam-horse-power to cross the ocean, and by halving this figure every ten years, he got back to 234 horse power for 1835, which was accuracy enough for his purposes. In truth, his chief trouble came not from the ratio in volume of heat, but from the intensity, since he could get no basis for a ratio there. All ages of history have known high intensities, like the iron-furnace, the burning-glass, the blow-pipe; but no society has ever used high-intensities on any large scale till now, nor can a mere bystander decide what range of temperature is now in common use. Loosely guessing that science controls habitually the whole range from absolute zero to 3000° Centigrade, one might assume, for convenience, that the ten-year ratio for volume could be used temporarily for intensity; and still there remained a ratio to be guessed for other forces than heat. Since 1800 scores of new forces had been discovered; old forces had been raised to higher powers, as could be measured in the navy-gun; great regions of chemistry had been opened up, and connected with other regions of physics. Within ten years a new universe of force had been revealed in radiation. Complexity had extended itself on immense horizons, and arithmetical ratios were useless for any attempt at accuracy. The force evolved seemed more like explosion than gravitation, and followed closely the curve of steam; but, at all events, the ten-year ratio seemed carefully conservative. Unless the calculator was prepared to be instantly overwhelmed by physical force and mental complexity, he must stop there.

Thus, taking the year 1900 as the starting point for carrying back the series, nothing was easier than to assume a ten-year period of retardation as far back as 1820, but beyond that point the statistician failed, and only the mathematician could help. La Place would have found it child's-play to fix a ratio of progression in mathematical science between Descartes, Leibnitz, Newton and himself. Watt could have given in pounds the increase of power between Newcomen's engines and his own. Volta and Benjamin Franklin would have stated their progress as absolute creation of power. Dalton could have measured minutely his advance on Boerhave. Napoleon I must have had a distinct notion of his own numerical relation to Louis XIV. No one in 1789 doubted the progress of force, least of all those who were to lose their heads by it.

Pending agreement between these authorities, theory may assume what it likes — say a fifty, or even a five-and-twenty-year period of reduplication for the eighteenth century, for the period matters little until the acceleration itself is admitted. The subject is even more amusing in the seventeenth than in the eighteenth century, because Galileo and Kepler, Descartes, Huyghens and Isaac Newton took vast pains to fix the laws of acceleration for moving bodies, while Lord Bacon and William Harvey were content with showing experimentally the fact of acceleration in knowledge; but from their combined results a historian might be tempted to maintain a similar rate of movement back to 1600, subject to correction from the historians of mathematics.

The mathematicians might carry their calculations back as far as the fourteenth century when algebra seems to have become for the first time, the standard measure of mechanical progress in western Europe; for not only Copernicus and Tycho Brahe, but even artists like Leonardo, Michael Angelo and Albert Dürer worked by mathematical processes, and their testimony would probably give results more exact than that of Montaigne or Shakespeare; but, to save trouble, one might tentatively carry back the same ratio of acceleration, or retardation, to the year 1400, with the help of Columbus and Gutenberg, so taking a uniform rate during the whole four centuries (1400–1800), and leaving to statisticians the task of correcting it.

Or better, one might, for convenience, use the formula of squares to serve for a law of mind. Any other formula would do as well, either of chemical explosion, or electrolysis, or vegetable growth, or of expansion or contraction in innumerable forms; but this happens to be simple and convenient. Its force increases in the direct ratio of its squares. As the human meteoroid approached the sun or centre of attractive force, the attraction of one century squared itself to give the measure of attraction in the next.

Behind the year 1400, the process certainly went on, but the progress became so slight as to be hardly measureable. What was gained in the east or elsewhere, cannot be known; but forces, called loosely Greek fire and gunpowder, came into use in the west in the thirteenth century, as well as instruments like the compass, the blow-pipe, clocks and spectacles, and materials like paper; Arabic notation and algebra were introduced, while metaphysics and theology acted as violent stimulants to mind. An architect might detect a sequence between the Church of St. Peter's at Rome, the Amiens Cathedral, the Duomo at Pisa, San Marco at Venice, Sancta Sofia at Constantinople and the churches at Ravenna. All the historian dares affirm is that a sequence is manifestly there, and he has a right to carry back his ratio, to represent the fact, without assuming its numerical correctness. On the human mind as a moving body, the break in acceleration in the middle-ages is only apparent; the attraction worked through shifting forms of force, as the sun works by light or heat, electricity, gravitation, or what not, on different organs with different sensibilities, but with invariable law.

The science of prehistoric man has no value except to prove that the law went back into indefinite antiquity. A stone arrowhead is as convincing as a steam-engine. The values were as clear a hundred thousand years ago as now, and extended equally over the whole world. The motion at last became infinitely slight, but cannot be proved to have stopped. The motion of Newton's comet at aphelion may be equally slight. To evolutionists may be left the processes of evolution; to historians the single interest is the law of reaction between force and force, — between mind and nature, — the law of progress.

The great division of history into phases by Turgot and Comte first affirmed this law in its outlines by asserting the unity of progress, for a mere phase interrupts no growth, and nature shows innumerable such phases. The development of coal-power in the nineteenth century furnished the first means of assigning closer values to the elements; and the appearance of supersensual forces towards 1900 made this calculation a pressing necessity; since the next step became infinitely serious.

A law of acceleration, definite and constant as any law of mechanics, cannot be supposed to relax its energy to suit the convenience of man. No one is likely to suggest a theory that man's convenience has been consulted by nature at any time, or that nature has consulted the convenience of any of her creations, except perhaps the *Terebratula*. In every age man has bitterly and justly complained that nature hurried and hustled him, for inertia almost invariably has ended in tragedy. Resistance is its law, and resistance to superior mass is futile and fatal.

Fifty years ago, science took for granted that the rate of acceleration could not last. The world forgets quickly, but even to-day the habit remains of founding statistics on the faith that consumption will continue nearly stationary. Two generations, with John Stuart Mill, talked of this stationary period, which was to follow the explosion of new power. All the men who were elderly in the forties died in this faith, and other men grew old, nursing the same conviction, and happy in it; while science, for fifty years, permitted, or encouraged, society to think that force would prove to be limited in supply. This mental inertia of science lasted through the eighties before showing signs of breaking up; and nothing short of radium fairly wakened men to the fact, long since evident, that force was inexhaustible. Even then the scientific authorities vehemently resisted.

Nothing so revolutionary had happened since the year 300. Thought had more than once been upset, but never caught and whirled about in the vortex of infinite forces. Power leaped from every atom, and enough of it to supply the stellar universe showed itself running to waste at every pore of matter. Man could no longer hold it off. Forces grasped his wrists and flung him about as though he had hold of a live wire or a runaway automobile; which was very nearly the exact truth for the purposes of an elderly and timid single gentleman in Paris, who never drove down the Champs Elysées without expecting an accident, and commonly witnessing one; or found himself in the neighborhood of an official without calculating the chances of a bomb. So long as the rates of progress held good, these bombs would double in force and number every ten years.

Impossibilities no longer stood in the way. One's life had fattened on impossibilities. Before the boy was six years old, he had seen four impossibilities made actual, — the ocean-steamer, the railway, the electric telegraph, and the Daguerreotype; nor could he ever learn which of the four had most hurried others to come. He had seen the coal-output of the United States grow from nothing to three hundred million tons or more. What was far more serious, he had seen the number of minds, engaged in pursuing force — the truest measure of its attraction — increase from a few scores or hundreds, in 1838, to many thousands in

1905, trained to sharpness never before reached, and armed with instruments amounting to new senses of indefinite power and accuracy, while they chased force into hiding-places where nature herself had never known it to be, making analyses that contradicted being, and syntheses that endangered the elements. No one could say that the social mind now failed to respond to new force, even when the new force annoyed it horribly. Every day nature violently revolted, causing so-called accidents with enormous destruction of property and life, while plainly laughing at man, who helplessly groaned and shrieked and shuddered, but never for a single instant could stop. The railways alone approached the carnage of war; automobiles and fire-arms ravaged society, until an earthquake became almost a nervous relaxation. An immense volume of force had detached itself from the unknown universe of energy, while still vaster reservoirs, supposed to be infinite, steadily revealed themselves, attracting mankind with more compulsive course than all the Pontic Seas or Gods or Gold that ever existed, and feeling still less of retiring ebb.

In 1850, science would have smiled at such a romance as this, but, in 1900, as far as history could learn, few men of science thought it a laughing matter. If a perplexed but laborious follower could venture to guess their drift, it seemed in their minds a toss-up between anarchy and order. Unless they should be more honest with themselves in the future than ever they were in the past, they would be more astonished than their followers when they reached the end. If Karl Pearson's notions of the universe were sound, men like Galileo, Descartes, Leibnitz and Newton should have stopped the progress of science before 1700, supposing them to have been honest in the religious convictions they expressed. In 1900 they were plainly forced back on faith in a unity unproved and an order they had themselves disproved. They had reduced their universe to a series of relations to themselves. They had reduced themselves to Motion in a universe of Motions, with an acceleration, in their own case, of vertiginous violence. With the correctness of their science, history had no right to meddle, since their science now lay in a plane where scarcely one or two hundred minds in the world could follow its mathematical processes; but bombs educate vigorously, and even wireless telegraphy or air-ships might require the reconstruction of society. If any analogy whatever existed between the human mind, on one side, and the laws of motion, on the other, the mind had already entered a field of attraction so violent that it must immediately pass beyond, into new equilibrium, like the Comet of Newton, or suffer dissipation altogether, like meteoroids in the earth's atmosphere. If it behaved like an explosive, it must rapidly recover equilibrium; if it behaved like a vegetable, it must reach its limits of growth; and even if it acted like the earlier creations of energy, — the Saurians and Sharks, — it must have nearly reached the limits of its expansion. If science were to go on doubling or quadrupling its complexities every ten years, even mathematics would soon succumb. An average mind had succumbed already in 1850; it could no longer understand the problem in 1900.

Fortunately, a student of history had no responsibility for the problem; he took it as science gave it, and waited only to be taught. With science or with society, he had no quarrel and claimed no share of authority. He had never been able to acquire knowledge, still less to impart it; and if he had, at times, felt serious differences with the American of the nineteenth century, he felt none with the American of the twentieth. For this new creation, born since 1900, a historian asked no longer to be teacher or even friend; he asked only to be a pupil, and promised to be docile, for once, even though trodden under foot; for he could see that the new American, — the child of incalculable coal-power, chemical power, electric power, and radiating energy, as well as of new forces yet undetermined, — must be a sort of God compared with any former creation of nature. At the rate of progress since 1800, every American who lived into the year 2000 would know how to control unlimited power. He would think in complexities unimaginable to an earlier mind. He would deal with problems altogether beyond the range of earlier society. To him the nineteenth century would stand on the same plane with the fourth, — equally childlike, — and he would only wonder how both of them, knowing so little, and so weak in force, should have done so much. Perhaps even he might go back, in 1964, to sit with Gibbon on the steps of Ara Coeli.

Meanwhile he was getting education. With that, a teacher who had failed to educate even the generation of 1870, dared not interfere. The new forces would educate. History saw few lessons in the past that would be useful in the future; but one, at least, it did see. The attempt of the American of 1800 to educate the American of 1900 had not often been surpassed for folly; and since 1800 the forces and their complications had increased a thousand times or more. The attempt of the American of 1900 to educate the American of 2000, must be even blinder than that of the Congressman of 1800, except so far as he had learned his ignorance. During a million or two of years, every generation in turn had toiled with endless agony to attain and apply power, all the while betraying the deepest alarm and horror at the power they created. The teacher of 1900, if foolhardy, might stimulate; if foolish, might resist; if intelligent, might balance, as wise and foolish have often tried to do from the beginning; but the forces would continue to educate, and the mind would continue to react. All the teacher could hope was to teach it reaction.

Even there his difficulty was extreme. The most elementary books of science betrayed the inadequacy of old implements of thought. Chapter after chapter closed with phrases such as one never met in older literature: — "The cause of this phenomenon is not understood"; "science no longer ventures to explain causes"; "the first step towards a causal explanation still remains to be taken"; "opinions are very much divided"; "in spite of the contradictions involved"; "science gets on only by adopting different theories, sometimes contradictory." Evidently the new American would need to think in contradictions, and instead of Kant's famous four antinomies, the new universe would know no law that could not be proved by its anti-law.

To educate — oneself to begin with — had been the effort of one's life for sixty years; and the difficulties of education had gone on doubling with the coal output, until the prospect of waiting another ten years, in order to face a seventh doubling of complexities, allured one's imagination but slightly. The law of acceleration was definite, and did not require ten years more study except to show whether it held good. No scheme could be suggested to the new American, and no fault needed to be found, or complaint made; but the next great influx of new forces seemed near at hand, and its style of education promised to be violently coercive. The movement from unity into multiplicity, between 1200 and 1900, was unbroken in sequence, and rapid in acceleration. Prolonged one generation longer, it would require a new social mind. As though thought were common salt in indefinite solution it must enter a new phase subject to new laws. Thus far, since five or ten thousand years, the mind had successfully reacted, and nothing yet proved that it would fail to react, — but it would need to jump.

1909

John Muir

....

Stickeen

IN THE SUMMER of 1880 I set out from Fort Wrangel in a canoe to continue the exploration of the icy region of southeastern Alaska, begun in
the fall of 1879. After the necessary provisions, blankets, etc., had been
collected and stowed away, and my Indian crew were in their places
ready to start, while a crowd of their relatives and friends on the wharf
were bidding them good-by and good-luck, my companion, the Rev.
S. H. Young, for whom we were waiting, at last came aboard, followed
by a little black dog, that immediately made himself at home by curling
up in a hollow among the baggage. I like dogs, but this one seemed so
small and worthless that I objected to his going, and asked the missionary why he was taking him.

"Such a little helpless creature will only be in the way," I said; "you
had better pass him up to the Indian boys on the wharf, to be taken
home to play with the children. This trip is not likely to be good for toy-
dogs. The poor silly thing will be in rain and snow for weeks or months,
and will require care like a baby."

But his master assured me that he would be no trouble at all; that he
was a perfect wonder of a dog, could endure cold and hunger like a
bear, swim like a seal, and was wondrous wise and cunning, etc., making out a list of virtues to show he might be the most interesting member of the party.

Nobody could hope to unravel the lines of his ancestry. In all the

---

The essay grew out of Muir's fascination with "a little black dog" while on an expedition
in Taylor Bay, Alaska, in 1880. It was first published in a different version and under a
different title in *The Century* in 1897, but Muir continued to work on the essay, and the
final version was published in book form as *Stickeen in 1909.

wonderfully mixed and varied dog-tribe I never saw any creature very much like him, though in some of his sly, soft, gliding motions and gestures he brought the fox to mind. He was short-legged and bunchy-bodied, and his hair, though smooth, was long and silky and slightly waved, so that when the wind was at his back it ruffled, making him look shaggy. At first sight his only noticeable feature was his fine tail, which was about as airy and shady as a squirrel's, and was carried curling forward almost to his nose. On closer inspection you might notice his thin sensitive ears, and sharp eyes with cunning tan-spots above them. Mr. Young told me that when the little fellow was a pup about the size of a woodrat he was presented to his wife by an Irish prospector at Sitka, and that on his arrival at Fort Wrangel he was adopted with enthusiasm by the Stickeen Indians as a sort of new good-luck totem, was named "Stickeen" for the tribe, and became a universal favorite; petted, protected, and admired wherever he went, and regarded as a mysterious fountain of wisdom.

On our trip he soon proved himself a queer character — odd, concealed, independent, keeping invincibly quiet, and doing many little puzzling things that piqued my curiosity. As we sailed week after week through the long intricate channels and inlets among the innumerable islands and mountains of the coast, he spent most of the dull days in sluggish ease, motionless, and apparently as unobserving as if in deep sleep. But I discovered that somehow he always knew what was going on. When the Indians were about to shoot at ducks or seals, or when anything along the shore was exciting our attention, he would rest his chin on the edge of the canoe and calmly look out like a dreamy-eyed tourist. And when he heard us talking about making a landing, he immediately roused himself to see what sort of a place we were coming to, and made ready to jump overboard and swim ashore as soon as the canoe neared the beach. Then, with a vigorous shake to get rid of the brine in his hair, he ran into the woods to hunt small game. But though always the first out of the canoe, he was always the last to get into it. When we were ready to start he could never be found, and refused to come to our call. We soon found out, however, that though we could not see him at such times, he saw us, and from the cover of the briers and huckleberry bushes in the fringe of the woods was watching the canoe with wary eye. For as soon as we were fairly off he came trotting down the beach, plunged into the surf, and swam after us, knowing well that we would cease rowing and take him in. When the contrary little vagabond came alongside, he was lifted by the neck, held at arm's length a moment to drip, and dropped aboard. We tried to cure him of this trick by compelling him to swim a long way, as if we had a mind to abandon him; but this did no good: the longer the swim the better he seemed to like it.

Though capable of great idleness, he never failed to be ready for all sorts of adventures and excursions. One pitch-dark rainy night we landed about ten o'clock at the mouth of a salmon stream when the water was phosphorescent. The salmon were running, and the myriad fins of the onrushing multitude were churning all the stream into a silvery glow, wonderfully beautiful and impressive in the ebon darkness. To get a good view of the show I set out with one of the Indians and sailed up through the midst of it to the foot of a rapid about half a mile from camp, where the swift current dashing over rocks made the luminous glow most glorious. Happening to look back down the stream, while the Indian was catching a few of the struggling fish, I saw a long spreading fan of light like the tail of a comet, which we thought must be made by some big strange animal that was pursuing us. On it came with its magnificent train, until we imagined we could see the monster's head and eyes; but it was only Stickeen, who, finding I had left the camp, came swimming after me to see what was up.

When we camped early, the best hunter of the crew usually went to the woods for a deer, and Stickeen was sure to be at his heels, provided I had not gone out. For, strange to say, though I never carried a gun, he always followed me, forsaking the hunter and even his master to share my wanderings. The days that were too stormy for sailing I spent in the woods, or on the adjacent mountains, wherever my studies called me; and Stickeen always insisted on going with me, however wild the weather, gliding like a fox through dripping huckleberry bushes and thorny tangles of panax and rubus, scarce stirring their rain-laden leaves; wading and wallowing through snow, swimming icy streams, skipping over logs and rocks and the crevasses of glaciers with the patience and endurance of a determined mountaineer, never tiring or getting discouraged. Once he followed me over a glacier the surface of which was so crusty and rough that it cut his feet until every step was marked with blood; but he trotted on with Indian fortitude until I noticed his red track, and, taking pity on him, made him a set of moccasins out of a handkerchief. However great his troubles he never asked help or made any complaint, as if, like a philosopher, he had learned that without hard work and suffering there could be no pleasure worth having.

Yet none of us was able to make out what Stickeen was really good for. He seemed to meet danger and hardships without anything like reason, insisted on having his own way, never obeyed an order, and the hunter could never set him on anything, or make him fetch the birds he shot. His equanimity was so steady it seemed due to want of feeling; ordinary storms were pleasures to him, and as for mere rain, he flourished in it like a vegetable. No matter what advances you might make, scarce a glance or a tail-wag would you get for your pains. But though he was apparently as cold as a glacier and about as impervious to fun, I tried hard to make his acquaintance, guessing there must be something worth while hidden beneath so much courage, endurance, and love of wild-weathery adventure. No superannuated mastiff or bulldog grown old in office surpassed this fluffy midget in stoic dignity. He sometimes reminded me of a small, squat, unshakable desert cactus. For he never displayed a single trace of the merry, tricksy, elfish fun of the terriers and collies that we all know, nor of their touching affection and devotion. Like children, most small dogs beg to be loved and allowed to love; but Stickeen seemed a very Diogenes, asking only to be let alone: a true child of the wilderness, holding the even tenor of his hidden life with the silence and serenity of nature. His strength of character lay in his eyes. They looked as old as the hills, and as young, and as wild. I never tired of looking into them: it was like looking into a landscape; but they were small and rather deep-set, and had no explaining lines around them to give out particulars. I was accustomed to look into the faces of plants and animals, and I watched the little sphinx more and more keenly as an interesting study. But there is no estimating the wit and wisdom concealed and latent in our lower fellow mortals until made manifest by profound experiences; for it is through suffering that dogs as well as saints are developed and made perfect.

After we had explored the Sundum and Tahkoo fiords and their glaciers, we sailed through Stephen's Passage into Lynn Canal and thence through Icy Strait into Cross Sound, searching for unexplored inlets leading toward the great fountain ice-fields of the Fairweather Range. Here, while the tide was in our favor, we were accompanied by a fleet of icebergs drifting out to the ocean from Glacier Bay. Slowly we paddled around Vancouver's Point, Wimbleton, our frail canoe tossed like a feather on the massive heaving swells coming in past Cape Spenser. For miles the sound is bounded by precipitous mural cliffs, which, lashed with wave-spray and their heads hidden in clouds, looked terribly threatening and stern. Had our canoe been crushed or upset we

could have made no landing here, for the cliffs, as high as those of Yosemite, sink sheer into deep water. Eagerly we scanned the wall on the
north side for the first sign of an opening fiord or harbor, all of us anxious except Stickeen, who dozed in peace or gazed dreamily at the tremendous precipices when he heard us talking about them. At length we
made the joyful discovery of the mouth of the inlet now called "Taylor
Bay," and about five o'clock reached the head of it and encamped in a
spruce grove near the front of a large glacier.

While camp was being made, Joe the hunter climbed the mountain
wall on the east side of the fiord in pursuit of wild goats, while Mr.
Young and I went to the glacier. We found that it is separated from the
waters of the inlet by a tide-washed moraine, and extends, an abrupt
barrier, all the way across from wall to wall of the inlet, a distance of
about three miles. But our most interesting discovery was that it had recently advanced, though again slightly receding. A portion of the terminal moraine had been plowed up and shoved forward, uprooting and
overwhelming the woods on the east side. Many of the trees were down
and buried, or nearly so, others were leaning away from the ice-cliffs,
ready to fall, and some stood erect, with the bottom of the ice-plow still
beneath their roots and its lofty crystal spires towering high above their
tops. The spectacle presented by these century-old trees standing close
beside a spiry wall of ice, with their branches almost touching it, was
most novel and striking. And when I climbed around the front, and a
little way up the west side of the glacier, I found that it had swelled and
increased in height and width in accordance with its advance, and carried away the outer ranks of trees on its bank.

On our way back to camp after these first observations I planned a
far-and-wide excursion for the morrow. I awoke early, called not only
by the glacier, which had been on my mind all night, but by a grand
flood-storm. The wind was blowing a gale from the north and the rain
was flying with the clouds in a wide passionate horizontal flood, as if it
were all passing over the country instead of falling on it. The main pe-
rennial streams were booming high above their banks, and hundreds of
new ones, roaring like the sea, almost covered the lofty gray walls of the
inlet with white cascades and falls. I had intended making a cup of coffee and getting something like a breakfast before starting, but when I
heard the storm and looked out I made haste to join it; for many of Nature's finest lessons are to be found in her storms, and if careful to keep
in right relations with them, we may go safely abroad with them, rejoic-
ing in the grandeur and beauty of their works and ways, and chanting

with the old Norsemen, "The blast of the tempest aids our oars, the hurricane is our servant and drives us whither we wish to go." So, omitting breakfast, I put a piece of bread in my pocket and hurried away.

Mr. Young and the Indians were asleep, and so, I hoped, was Stickeen; but I had not gone a dozen rods before he left his bed in the tent and came boring through the blast after me. That a man should welcome storms for their exhilarating music and motion, and go forth to see God making landscapes, is reasonable enough; but what fascination could there be in such tremendous weather for a dog? Surely nothing akin to human enthusiasm for scenery or geology. Anyhow, on he came, breakfastless, through the choking blast. I stopped and did my best to turn him back. "Now don't," I said, shouting to make myself heard in the storm, "now don't, Stickeen. What has got into your queer noddle now? You must be daft. This wild day has nothing for you. There is no game abroad, nothing but weather. Go back to camp and keep warm, get a good breakfast with your master, and be sensible for once. I can't carry you all day or feed you, and this storm will kill you."

But Nature, it seems, was at the bottom of the affair, and she gains her ends with dogs as well as with men, making us do as she likes, shoving and pulling us along her ways, however rough, all but killing us at times in getting her lessons driven hard home. After I had stopped again and again, shouting good warning advice, I saw that he was not to be shaken off; as well might the earth try to shake off the moon. I had once led his master into trouble, when he fell on one of the topmost jags of a mountain and dislocated his arm; now the turn of his humble companion was coming. The pitiful little wanderer just stood there in the wind, drenched and blinking, saying doggedly, "Where thou goest I will go." So at last I told him to come on if he must, and gave him a piece of the bread I had in my pocket; then we struggled on together, and thus began the most memorable of all my wild days.

The level flood, driving hard in our faces, thrashed and washed us wildly until we got into the shelter of a grove on the east side of the glacier near the front, where we stopped awhile for breath and to listen and look out. The exploration of the glacier was my main object, but the wind was too high to allow excursions over its open surface, where one might be dangerously shoved while balancing for a jump on the brink of a crevasse. In the mean time the storm was a fine study. Here the end of the glacier, descending an abrupt swell of resisting rock about five hundred feet high, leans forward and falls in ice cascades. And as the storm came down the glacier from the North, Stickeen and I were beneath the main current of the blast, while favorably located to see and hear it. What a psalm the storm was singing, and how fresh the smell of the washed earth and leaves, and how sweet the still small voices of the storm! Detached wafts and swirls were coming through the woods, with music from the leaves and branches and furrowed boles, and even from the splintered rocks and ice-crags overhead, many of the tones soft and low and flute-like, as if each leaf and tree, crag and spire were a tuned reed. A broad torrent, draining the side of the glacier, now swollen by scores of new streams from the mountains, was rolling boulders along its rocky channel, with thudding, bumping, muffled sounds, rushing towards the bay with tremendous energy, as if in haste to get out of the mountains; the waters above and beneath calling to each other, and all to the ocean, their home.

Looking southward from our shelter, we had this great torrent and the forested mountain wall above it on our left, the spiry ice-crags on our right, and smooth gray gloom ahead. I tried to draw the marvelous scene in my note-book, but the rain blurred the page in spite of all my pains to shelter it, and the sketch was almost worthless. When the wind began to abate, I traced the east side of the glacier. All the trees standing on the edge of the woods were barked and bruised, showing high-ice mark in a very telling way, while tens of thousands of those that had stood for centuries on the bank of the glacier farther out lay crushed and being crushed. In many places I could see down fifty feet or so beneath the margin of the glacier-mill, where trunks from one to two feet in diameter were being ground to pulp against outstanding rock-ribs and bosses of the bank.

About three miles above the front of the glacier I climbed to the surface of it by means of axe-steps made easy for Stickeen. As far as the eye could reach, the level, or nearly level, glacier stretched away indefinitely beneath the gray sky, a seemingly boundless prairie of ice. The rain continued, and grew colder, which I did not mind, but a dim snowy look in the drooping clouds made me hesitate about venturing far from land. No trace of the west shore was visible, and in case the clouds should settle and give snow, or the wind again become violent, I feared getting caught in a tangle of crevasses. Snow-crystals, the flowers of the mountain clouds, are frail, beautiful things, but terrible when flying on storm-winds in darkening, benumbing swarms, or, when welded together into glaciers full of deadly crevasses. Watching the weather, I sauntered about on the crystal sea. For a mile or two out I found the ice remarkably safe. The marginal crevasses were mostly narrow, while the few wider ones were easily avoided by passing around them, and the clouds began to open here and there.

Thus encouraged, I at last pushed out for the other side; for Nature can make us do anything she likes. At first we made rapid progress, and the sky was not very threatening, while I took bearings occasionally with a pocket compass to enable me to find my way back more surely in case the storm should become blinding; but the structure lines of the glacier were my main guide. Toward the west side we came to a closely crevassed section in which we had to make long, narrow tacks and doublings, tracing the edges of tremendous transverse and longitudinal crevasses, many of which were from twenty to thirty feet wide, and perhaps a thousand feet deep — beautiful and awful. In working a way through them I was severely cautious, but Stickeen came on as unhesitating as the flying clouds. The widest crevasse that I could jump he would leap without so much as halting to take a look at it. The weather was now making quick changes, scattering bits of dazzling brightness through the wintry gloom; at rare intervals, when the sun broke forth wholly free, the glacier was seen from shore to shore with a bright array of encompassing mountains partly revealed, wearing the clouds as garments, while the prairie bloomed and sparkled with irised light from myriads of washed crystals. Then suddenly all the glorious show would be darkened and blotted out.

Stickeen seemed to care for none of these things, bright or dark, nor for the crevasses, wells, moulins, or swift flashing streams into which he might fall. The little adventurer was only about two years old, yet nothing seemed novel to him, nothing daunted him. He showed neither caution nor curiosity, wonder nor fear, but bravely trotted on as if glaciers were playgrounds. His stout, muffled body seemed all one skipping muscle, and it was truly wonderful to see how swiftly and to all appearance heedlessly he flashed across nerve-trying chasms six or eight feet wide. His courage was so unwavering that it seemed to be due to dullness of perception, as if he were only blindly bold; and I kept warning him to be careful. For we had been close companions on so many wilderness trips that I had formed the habit of talking to him as if he were a boy and understood every word.

We gained the west shore in about three hours; the width of the glacier here being about seven miles. Then I pushed northward in order to see as far back as possible into the fountains of the Fairweather Mountains, in case the clouds should rise. The walking was easy along the margin of the forest, which, of course, like that on the other side, had been invaded and crushed by the swollen, overflowing glacier. In an hour or so, after passing a massive headland, we came suddenly on a branch of the glacier, which, in the form of a magnificent ice-cascade two miles wide, was pouring over the rim of the main basin in a westerly direction, its surface broken into wave-shaped blades and shattered blocks, suggesting the wildest updashing, heaving, plunging motion of a great river cataract. Tracing it down three or four miles, I found that it discharged into a lake, filling it with icebergs.

I would gladly have followed the lake outlet to tide-water, but the day was already far spent, and the threatening sky called for haste on the return trip to get off the ice before dark. I decided therefore to go no farther, and, after taking a general view of the wonderful region, turned back, hoping to see it again under more favorable auspices. We made good speed up the cañon of the great ice-torrent, and out on the main glacier until we had left the west shore about two miles behind us. Here we got into a difficult network of crevasses, the gathering clouds began to drop misty fringes, and soon the dreaded snow came flying thick and fast. I now began to feel anxious about finding a way in the blurring storm. Stickeen showed no trace of fear. He was still the same silent, able little hero. I noticed, however, that after the storm-darkness came on he kept close up behind me. The snow urged us to make still greater haste, but at the same time hid our way. I pushed on as best I could, jumping innumerable crevasses, and for every hundred rods or so of direct advance traveling a mile in doubling up and down in the turmoil of chasms and dislocated ice-blocks. After an hour or two of this work we came to a series of longitudinal crevasses of appalling width, and almost straight and regular in trend, like immense furrows. These I traced with firm nerve, excited and strengthened by the danger, making wide jumps, poising cautiously on their dizzy edges after cutting hollows for my feet before making the spring, to avoid possible slipping or any uncertainty on the farther sides, where only one trial is granted — exercise at once frightful and inspiring. Stickeen followed seemingly without effort.

Many a mile we thus traveled, mostly up and down, making but little real headway in crossing, running instead of walking most of the time as the danger of being compelled to spend the night on the glacier became threatening. Stickeen seemed able for anything. Doubtless we could have weathered the storm for one night, dancing on a flat spot to keep from freezing, and I faced the threat without feeling anything like despair; but we were hungry and wet, and the wind from the mountains was still thick with snow and bitterly cold, so of course that night would have seemed a very long one. I could not see far enough through the blurring snow to judge in which general direction the least dangerous route lay, while the few dim, momentary glimpses I caught of mountains through rifts in the flying clouds were far from encouraging either as weather signs or as guides. I had simply to grope my way from crevasse to crevasse, holding a general direction by the ice-structure, which was not to be seen everywhere, and partly by the wind. Again and again I was put to my mettle, but Stickeen followed easily, his nerve apparently growing more unflinching as the danger increased. So it always is with mountaineers when hard beset. Running hard and jumping, holding every minute of the remaining daylight, poor as it was, precious, we doggedly persevered and tried to hope that every difficult crevasse we overcame would prove to be the last of its kind. But on the contrary, as we advanced they became more deadly trying.

At length our way was barred by a very wide and straight crevasse, which I traced rapidly northward a mile or so without finding a crossing or hope of one; then down the glacier about as far, to where it united with another uncrossable crevasse. In all this distance of perhaps two miles there was only one place where I could possibly jump it, but the width of this jump was the utmost I dared attempt, while the danger of slipping on the farther side was so great that I was loath to try it. Furthermore, the side I was on was about a foot higher than the other, and even with this advantage the crevasse seemed dangerously wide. One is liable to underestimate the width of crevasses where the magnitudes in general are great. I therefore stared at this one mighty keenly, estimating its width and the shape of the edge on the farther side, until I thought that I could jump it if necessary, but that in case I should be compelled to jump back from the lower side I might fail. Now, a cautious mountaineer seldom takes a step on unknown ground which seems at all dangerous that he cannot retrace in case he should be stopped by unseen obstacles ahead. This is the rule of mountaineers who live long, and, though in haste, I compelled myself to sit down and calmly deliberate before I broke it.

Retracing my devious path in imagination as if it were drawn on a chart, I saw that I was recrossing the glacier a mile or two farther upstream than the course pursued in the morning, and that I was now entangled in a section I had not before seen. Should I risk this dangerous jump, or try to regain the woods on the west shore, make a fire, and have only hunger to endure while waiting for a new day? I had already crossed so broad a stretch of dangerous ice that I saw it would be difficult to get back to the woods through the storm, before dark, and the attempt would most likely result in a dismal night-dance on the glacier; while just beyond the present barrier the surface seemed more promising, and the east shore was now perhaps about as near as the west. I was therefore eager to go on. But this wide jump was a dreadful obstacle.

At length, because of the dangers already behind me, I determined to venture against those that might be ahead, jumped and landed well, but with so little to spare that I more than ever dreaded being compelled to take that jump back from the lower side. Stickeen followed, making nothing of it, and we ran eagerly forward, hoping we were leaving all our troubles behind. But within the distance of a few hundred yards we were stopped by the widest crevasse yet encountered. Of course I made haste to explore it, hoping all might yet be remedied by finding a bridge or a way around either end. About three-fourths of a mile upstream I found that it united with the one we had just crossed, as I feared it would. Then, tracing it down, I found it joined the same crevasse at the lower end also, maintaining throughout its whole course a width of forty to fifty feet. Thus to my dismay I discovered that we were on a narrow island about two miles long, with two barely possible ways of escape: one back by the way we came, the other ahead by an almost inaccessible sliver-bridge that crossed the great crevasse from near the middle of it!

After this nerve-trying discovery I ran back to the sliver-bridge and cautiously examined it. Crevasses, caused by strains from variations in the rate of motion of different parts of the glacier and convexities in the channel, are mere cracks when they first open, so narrow as hardly to admit the blade of a pocket-knife, and gradually widen according to the extent of the strain and the depth of the glacier. Now some of these cracks are interrupted, like the cracks in wood, and in opening, the strip of ice between overlapping ends is dragged out, and may maintain a continuous connection between the sides, just as the two sides of a slivered crack in wood that is being split are connected. Some crevasses remain open for months or even years, and by the melting of their sides continue to increase in width long after the opening strain has ceased; while the sliver-bridges, level on top at first and perfectly safe, are at length melted to thin, vertical, knife-edged blades, the upper portion being most exposed to the weather; and since the exposure is greatest in the middle, they at length curve downward like the cables of suspension bridges. This one was evidently very old, for it had been weathered and wasted until it was the most dangerous and inaccessible that ever lay in my way. The width of the crevasse was here about fifty feet, and the sliver crossing diagonally was about seventy feet long; its thin knife-edge near the middle was depressed twenty-five or thirty feet below the level of the glacier, and the upcurving ends were attached to the sides eight or ten feet below the brink. Getting down the nearly vertical wall to the end of the sliver and up the other side were the main difficulties, and they seemed all but insurmountable. Of the many perils encountered in my years of wandering on mountains and glaciers none seemed so plain and stern and merciless as this. And it was presented when we were wet to the skin and hungry, the sky dark with quick driving snow, and the night near. But we were forced to face it. It was a tremendous necessity.

Beginning, not immediately above the sunken end of the bridge, but a little to one side, I cut a deep hollow on the brink for my knees to rest in. Then, leaning over, with my short-handled axe I cut a step sixteen or eighteen inches below, which on account of the sheerness of the wall was necessarily shallow. That step, however, was well made; its floor sloped slightly inward and formed a good hold for my heels. Then, slipping cautiously upon it, and crouching as low as possible, with my left side toward the wall, I steadied myself against the wind with my left hand in a slight notch, while with the right I cut other similar steps and notches in succession, guarding against losing balance by glinting of the axe, or by wind-gusts, for life and death were in every stroke and in the niceness of finish of every foothold.

After the end of the bridge was reached I chipped it down until I had made a level platform six or eight inches wide, and it was a trying thing to poise on this little slippery platform while bending over to get safely astride of the sliver. Crossing was then comparatively easy by chipping off the sharp edge with short, careful strokes, and hitching forward an inch or two at a time, keeping my balance with my knees pressed against the sides. The tremendous abyss on either hand I studiously ignored. To me the edge of that blue sliver was then all the world. But the most trying part of the adventure, after working my way across inch by inch and chipping another small platform, was to rise from the safe position astride and to cut a step-ladder in the nearly vertical face of the wall, — chipping, climbing, holding on with feet and fingers in mere notches. At such times one's whole body is eye, and common skill and fortitude are replaced by power beyond our call or knowledge. Never before had I been so long under deadly strain. How I got up that cliff I never could tell. The thing seemed to have been done by somebody else. I never have held death in contempt, though in the course of my explorations I have oftentimes felt that to meet one's fate on a noble mountain, or in the heart of a glacier, would be blessed as compared with death from disease, or from some shabby lowland accident. But the best death, quick and crystal-pure, set so glaringly open before us, is hard enough to face, even though we feel gratefully sure that we have already had happiness enough for a dozen lives.

But poor Stickeen, the wee, hairy, sleekit beastie, think of him! When I had decided to dare the bridge, and while I was on my knees chipping a hollow on the rounded brow above it, he came behind me, pushed his head past my shoulder, looked down and across, scanned the sliver and its approaches with his mysterious eyes, then looked me in the face with a startled air of surprise and concern, and began to mutter and whine; saying as plainly as if speaking with words, "Surely, you are not going into that awful place." This was the first time I had seen him gaze deliberately into a crevasse, or into my face with an eager, speaking, troubled look. That he should have recognized and appreciated the danger at the first glance showed wonderful sagacity. Never before had the daring midget seemed to know that ice was slippery or that there was any such thing as danger anywhere. His looks and tones of voice when he began to complain and speak his fears were so human that I unconsciously talked to him in sympathy as I would to a frightened boy, and in trying to calm his fears perhaps in some measure moderated my own. "Hush your fears, my boy," I said, "we will get across safe, though it is not going to be easy. No right way is easy in this rough world. We must risk our lives to save them. At the worst we can only slip, and then how grand a grave we will have, and by and by our nice bones will do good in the terminal moraine."

But my sermon was far from reassuring him: he began to cry, and after taking another piercing look at the tremendous gulf, ran away in desperate excitement, seeking some other crossing. By the time he got back, baffled of course, I had made a step or two. I dared not look back, but he made himself heard; and when he saw that I was certainly bent on crossing he cried aloud in despair. The danger was enough to daunt anybody, but it seems wonderful that he should have been able to weigh and appreciate it so justly. No mountaineer could have seen it more quickly or judged it more wisely, discriminating between real and apparent peril.

When I gained the other side, he screamed louder than ever, and after running back and forth in vain search for a way of escape, he would return to the brink of the crevasse above the bridge, moaning and wailing as if in the bitterness of death. Could this be the silent, philosophic Stickeen? I shouted encouragement, telling him the bridge was not so bad as it looked, that I had left it flat and safe for his feet, and he could walk it easily. But he was afraid to try. Strange so small an animal should be capable of such big, wise fears. I called again and again in a reassuring tone to come on and fear nothing; that he could come if he would only try. He would hush for a moment, look down again at the bridge, and shout his unshakable conviction that he could never, never come that way; then lie back in despair, as if howling, "O-o-oh! what a place! No-o-o, I can never go-o-o down there!" His natural composure and courage had vanished utterly in a tumultuous storm of fear. Had the danger been less, his distress would have seemed ridiculous. But in this dismal, merciless abyss lay the shadow of death, and his heartrending cries might well have called Heaven to his help. Perhaps they did. So hidden before, he was now transparent, and one could see the workings of his heart and mind like the movements of a clock out of its case. His voice and gestures, hopes and fears, were so perfectly human that none could mistake them; while he seemed to understand every word of mine. I was troubled at the thought of having to leave him out all night, and of the danger of not finding him in the morning. It seemed impossible to get him to venture. To compel him to try through fear of being abandoned, I started off as if leaving him to his fate, and disappeared back of a hummock; but this did no good; he only lay down and moaned in utter hopeless misery. So, after hiding a few minutes, I went back to the brink of the crevasse and in a severe tone of voice shouted across to him that now I must certainly leave him, I could wait no longer, and that, if he would not come, all I could promise was that I would return to seek him next day. I warned him that if he went back to the woods the wolves would kill him, and finished by urging him once more by words and gestures to come on, come on.

He knew very well what I meant, and at last, with the courage of despair, hushed and breathless, he crouched down on the brink in the hollow I had made for my knees, pressed his body against the ice as if trying to get the advantage of the friction of every hair, gazed into the first step, put his little feet together and slid them slowly, slowly over the edge and down into it, bunching all four in it and almost standing on his head. Then, without lifting his feet, as well as I could see through the snow, he slowly worked them over the edge of the step and down into the next and the next in succession in the same way, and gained the end of the bridge. Then, lifting his feet with the regularity and slowness of the vibrations of a seconds pendulum, as if counting and measuring *one-two-three*, holding himself steady against the gusty wind, and giving separate attention to each little step, he gained the foot of the cliff, while I was on my knees leaning over to give him a lift should he succeed in getting within reach of my arm. Here he halted in dead silence, and it was here I feared he might fail, for dogs are poor climbers. I had no cord. If I had had one, I would have dropped a noose over his head and hauled him up. But while I was thinking whether an available cord might be made out of clothing, he was looking keenly into the series of notched steps and finger-holds I had made, as if counting them, and fixing the position of each one of them in his mind. Then suddenly up he came in a springy rush, hooking his paws into the steps and notches so quickly that I could not see how it was done, and whizzed past my head, safe at last!

And now came a scene! "Well done, well done, little boy! Brave boy!" I cried, trying to catch and caress him; but he would not be caught. Never before or since have I seen anything like so passionate a revulsion from the depths of despair to exultant, triumphant, uncontrollable joy. He flashed and darted hither and thither as if fairly demented, screaming and shouting, swirling round and round in giddy loops and circles like a leaf in a whirlwind, lying down, and rolling over and over, sidewise and heels over head, and pouring forth a tumultuous flood of hysterical cries and sobs and gasping mutterings. When I ran up to him to shake him, fearing he might die of joy, he flashed off two or three hundred yards, his feet in a mist of motion; then, turning suddenly, came back in a wild rush and launched himself at my face, almost knocking me down, all the time screeching and screaming and shouting as if saying, "Saved! saved! saved!" Then away again, dropping suddenly at times with his feet in the air, trembling and fairly sobbing. Such passionate emotion was enough to kill him. Moses' stately song of triumph after escaping the Egyptians and the Red Sea was nothing to it. Who could have guessed the capacity of the dull, enduring little fellow for all that most stirs this mortal frame? Nobody could have helped crying with him!

But there is nothing like work for toning down excessive fear or joy. So I ran ahead, calling him in as gruff a voice as I could command to come on and stop his nonsense, for we had far to go and it would soon be dark. Neither of us feared another trial like this. Heaven would surely count one enough for a lifetime. The ice ahead was gashed by thousands of crevasses, but they were common ones. The joy of deliverance burned in us like fire, and we ran without fatigue, every muscle with immense rebound glorying in its strength. Stickeen flew across everything in his way, and not till dark did he settle into his normal fox-like trot. At last the cloudy mountains came in sight, and we soon felt the solid rock beneath our feet, and were safe. Then came weakness. Danger had vanished, and so had our strength. We tottered down the lateral moraine in the dark, over boulders and tree trunks, through the bushes and devil-club thickets of the grove where we had sheltered ourselves in the morning, and across the level mud-slope of the terminal moraine. We reached camp about ten o'clock, and found a big fire and a big supper. A party of Hoona Indians had visited Mr. Young, bringing a gift of porpoise meat and wild strawberries, and Hunter Joe had brought in a wild goat. But we lay down, too tired to eat much, and soon fell into a troubled sleep. The man who said, "The harder the toil, the sweeter the rest," never was profoundly tired. Stickeen kept springing up and muttering in his sleep, no doubt dreaming that he was still on the brink of the crevasse; and so did I, that night and many others long afterward, when I was overtired.

Thereafter Stickeen was a changed dog. During the rest of the trip, instead of holding aloof, he always lay by my side, tried to keep me constantly in sight, and would hardly accept a morsel of food, however tempting, from any hand but mine. At night, when all was quiet about the camp-fire, he would come to me and rest his head on my knee with a look of devotion as if I were his god. And often as he caught my eye he seemed to be trying to say, "Wasn't that an awful time we had together on the glacier?"

Nothing in after years has dimmed that Alaska storm-day. As I write it all comes rushing and roaring to mind as if I were again in the heart of it. Again I see the gray flying clouds with their rain-floods and snow, the ice-cliffs towering above the shrinking forest, the majestic ice-cascade, the vast glacier outspread before its white mountain fountains, and in the heart of it the tremendous crevasse, — emblem of the valley of the shadow of death, — low clouds trailing over it, the snow falling into it; and on its brink I see little Stickeen, and I hear his cries for help and his shouts of joy. I have known many dogs, and many a story I could tell of their wisdom and devotion; but to none do I owe so much as to Stickeen. At first the least promising and least known of my dog-friends, he suddenly became the best known of them all. Our storm-battle for life brought him to light, and through him as through a window I have ever since been looking with deeper sympathy into all my fellow mortals.

None of Stickeen's friends knows what finally became of him. After my work for the season was done I departed for California, and I never saw the dear little fellow again. In reply to anxious inquiries his master wrote me that in the summer of 1883 he was stolen by a tourist at Fort Wrangel and taken away on a steamer. His fate is wrapped in mystery. Doubtless he has left this world — crossed the last crevasse — and gone to another. But he will not be forgotten. To me Stickeen is immortal.

1910

William James

The Moral Equivalent of War

THE WAR against war is going to be no holiday excursion or camping party. The military feelings are too deeply grounded to abdicate their place among our ideals until better substitutes are offered than the glory and shame that come to nations as well as to individuals from the ups and downs of politics and the vicissitudes of trade. There is something highly paradoxical in the modern man's relation to war. Ask all our millions, north and south, whether they would vote now (were such a thing possible) to have our war for the Union expunged from history, and the record of a peaceful transition to the present time substituted for that of its marches and battles, and probably hardly a handful of eccentrics would say yes. Those ancestors, those efforts, those memories and legends, are the most ideal part of what we now own together, a sacred spiritual possession worth more than all the blood poured out. Yet ask those same people whether they would be willing in cold blood to start another civil war now to gain another similar possession, and not one man or woman would vote for the proposition. In modern eyes, precious though wars may be, they must not be waged solely for the sake of the ideal harvest. Only when forced upon one, only when an enemy's injustice leaves us no alternative, is a war now thought permissible.

It was not thus in ancient times. The earlier men were hunting men, and to hunt a neighboring tribe, kill the males, loot the village and possess the females, was the most profitable, as well as the most exciting,

First published as a *pamphlet by the Association for International Conciliation in 1910 and also in *McClure's*, 1910. The essay was a revision of a talk first given at Stanford in 1906.

way of living. Thus were the more martial tribes selected, and in chiefs and peoples a pure pugnacity and love of glory came to mingle with the more fundamental appetite for plunder.

Modern war is so expensive that we feel trade to be a better avenue to plunder; but modern man inherits all the innate pugnacity and all the love of glory of his ancestors. Showing war's irrationality and horror is of no effect upon him. The horrors make the fascination. War is the *strong* life; it is life *in extremis;* war-taxes are the only ones men never hesitate to pay, as the budgets of all nations show us.

History is a bath of blood. The Iliad is one long recital of how Diomedes and Ajax, Sarpedon and Hector *killed.* No detail of the wounds they made is spared us, and the Greek mind fed upon the story. Greek history is a panorama of jingoism and imperialism — war for war's sake, all the citizens being warriors. It is horrible reading, because of the irrationality of it all — save for the purpose of making "history" — and the history is that of the utter ruin of a civilization in intellectual respects perhaps the highest the earth has ever seen.

Those wars were purely piratical. Pride, gold, women, slaves, excitement, were their only motives. In the Peloponnesian war, for example, the Athenians ask the inhabitants of Melos (the island where the "Venus of Milo" was found), hitherto neutral, to own their lordship. The envoys meet, and hold a debate which Thucydides gives in full, and which, for sweet reasonableness of form, would have satisfied Matthew Arnold. "The powerful exact what they can," said the Athenians, "and the weak grant what they must." When the Meleans say that sooner than be slaves they will appeal to the gods, the Athenians reply: "Of the gods we believe and of men we know that, by a law of their nature, wherever they can rule they will. This law was not made by us, and we are not the first to have acted upon it; we did but inherit it, and we know that you and all mankind, if you were as strong as we are, would do as we do. So much for the gods; we have told you why we expect to stand as high in their good opinion as you." Well, the Meleans still refused, and their town was taken. "The Athenians," Thucydides quietly says, "thereupon put to death all who were of military age and made slaves of the women and children. They then colonized the island, sending thither five hundred settlers of their own."

Alexander's career was piracy pure and simple, nothing but an orgy of power and plunder, made romantic by the character of the hero. There was no rational principle in it, and the moment he died his generals and governors attacked one another. The cruelty of those times is incredible. When Rome finally conquered Greece, Paulus Aemilius was told by the Roman Senate to reward his soldiers for their toil by "giving" them the old kingdom of Epirus. They sacked seventy cities and carried off a hundred and fifty thousand inhabitants as slaves. How many they killed I know not; but in Etolia they killed all the senators, five hundred and fifty in number. Brutus was "the noblest Roman of them all," but to reanimate his soldiers on the eve of Philippi he similarly promises to give them the cities of Sparta and Thessalonica to ravage, if they win the fight.

Such was the gory nurse that trained societies to cohesiveness. We inherit the warlike type; and for most of the capacities of heroism that the human race is full of we have to thank this cruel history. Dead men tell no tales, and if there were any tribes of other type than this they have left no survivors. Our ancestors have bred pugnacity into our bone and marrow, and thousands of years of peace won't breed it out of us. The popular imagination fairly fattens on the thought of wars. Let public opinion once reach a certain fighting pitch, and no ruler can withstand it. In the Boer war both governments began with bluff, but couldn't stay there, the military tension was too much for them. In 1898 our people had read the word WAR in letters three inches high for three months in every newspaper. The pliant politician McKinley was swept away by their eagerness, and our squalid war with Spain became a necessity.

At the present day, civilized opinion is a curious mental mixture. The military instincts and ideals are as strong as ever, but are confronted by reflective criticisms which sorely curb their ancient freedom. Innumerable writers are showing up the bestial side of military service. Pure loot and mastery seem no longer morally avowable motives, and pretexts must be found for attributing them solely to the enemy. England and we, our army and navy authorities repeat without ceasing, arm solely for "peace," Germany and Japan it is who are bent on loot and glory. "Peace" in military mouths to-day is a synonym for "war expected." The word has become a pure provocative, and no government wishing peace sincerely should allow it ever to be printed in a newspaper. Every up-to-date Dictionary should say that "peace" and "war" mean the same thing, now *in posse*, now *in actu*. It may even reasonably be said that the intensely sharp competitive *preparation* for war by the nations *is the real war*, permanent, unceasing; and that the battles are only a sort of public verification of the mastery gained during the "peace"-interval.

It is plain that on this subject civilized man has developed a sort of double personality. If we take European nations, no legitimate interest of any one of them would seem to justify the tremendous destructions which a war to compass it would necessarily entail. It would seem as though common sense and reason ought to find a way to reach agreement in every conflict of honest interests. I myself think it our bounden duty to believe in such international rationality as possible. But, as things stand, I see how desperately hard it is to bring the peace-party and the war-party together, and I believe that the difficulty is due to certain deficiencies in the program of pacificism which set the militarist imagination strongly, and to a certain extent justifiably, against it. In the whole discussion both sides are on imaginative and sentimental ground. It is but one utopia against another, and everything one says must be abstract and hypothetical. Subject to this criticism and caution, I will try to characterize in abstract strokes the opposite imaginative forces, and point out what to my own very fallible mind seems the best utopian hypothesis, the most promising line of conciliation.

In my remarks, pacificist tho' I am, I will refuse to speak of the bestial side of the war-regime (already done justice to by many writers) and consider only the higher aspects of militaristic sentiment. Patriotism no one thinks discreditable; nor does any one deny that war is the romance of history. But inordinate ambitions are the soul of every patriotism, and the possibility of violent death the soul of all romance. The militarily patriotic and romantic-minded everywhere, and especially the professional military class, refuse to admit for a moment that war may be a transitory phenomenon in social evolution. The notion of a sheep's paradise like that revolts, they say, our higher imagination. Where then would be the steeps of life? If war had ever stopped, we should have to reinvent it, on this view, to redeem life from flat degeneration.

Reflective apologists for war at the present day all take it religiously. It is a sort of sacrament. Its profits are to the vanquished as well as to the victor; and quite apart from any question of profit, it is an absolute good, we are told, for it is human nature at its highest dynamic. Its "horrors" are a cheap price to pay for rescue from the only alternative supposed, of a world of clerks and teachers, of co-education and zoophily, of "consumer's leagues" and "associated charities," of industrialism unlimited, and feminism unabashed. No scorn, no hardness, no valor any more! Fie upon such a cattleyard of a planet!

So far as the central essence of this feeling goes, no healthy minded person, it seems to me, can help to some degree partaking of it. Militarism is the great preserver of our ideals of hardihood, and human life with no use for hardihood would be contemptible. Without risks or prizes for the darer, history would be insipid indeed; and there is a type of military character which every one feels that the race should never cease to breed, for every one is sensitive to its superiority. The duty is incumbent on mankind, of keeping military characters in stock — of keeping them, if not for use, then as ends in themselves and as pure pieces of perfection, — so that Roosevelt's weaklings and mollycoddles may not end by making everything else disappear from the face of nature.

This natural sort of feeling forms, I think, the innermost soul of army-writings. Without any exception known to me, militarist authors take a highly mystical view of their subject, and regard war as a biological or sociological necessity, uncontrolled by ordinary psychological checks and motives. When the time of development is ripe the war must come, reason or no reason, for the justifications pleaded are invariably fictitious. War is, in short, a permanent human *obligation*. General Homer Lea, in his recent book "the Valor of Ignorance," plants himself squarely on this ground. Readiness for war is for him the essence of nationality, and ability in it the supreme measure of the health of nations.

Nations, General Lea says, are never stationary — they must necessarily expand or shrink, according to their vitality or decrepitude. Japan now is culminating; and by the fatal law in question it is impossible that her statesmen should not long since have entered, with extraordinary foresight, upon a vast policy of conquest — the game in which the first moves were her wars with China and Russia and her treaty with England, and of which the final objective is the capture of the Philippines, the Hawaiian Islands, Alaska, and the whole of our Coast west of the Sierra Passes. This will give Japan what her ineluctable vocation as a state absolutely forces her to claim, the possession of the entire Pacific Ocean; and to oppose these deep designs we Americans have, according to our author, nothing but our conceit, our ignorance, our commercialism, our corruption, and our feminism. General Lea makes a minute technical comparison of the military strength which we at present could oppose to the strength of Japan, and concludes that the islands, Alaska, Oregon, and Southern California, would fall almost without resistance, that San Francisco must surrender in a fortnight to a Japanese investment, that in three or four months the war would be over, and our republic, unable to regain what it had heedlessly neglected to protect sufficiently, would then "disintegrate," until perhaps some Caesar should arise to weld us again into a nation.

A dismal forecast indeed! Yet not unplausible, if the mentality of Japan's statesmen be of the Caesarian type of which history shows so many examples, and which is all that General Lea seems able to imagine. But there is no reason to think that women can no longer be the mothers of Napoleonic or Alexandrian characters; and if these come in Japan and find their opportunity, just such surprises as "the Valor of Ignorance" paints may lurk in ambush for us. Ignorant as we still are of the innermost recesses of Japanese mentality, we may be foolhardy to disregard such possibilities.

Other militarists are more complex and more moral in their considerations. The "Philosophie des Krieges," by S. R. Steinmetz is a good example. War, according to this author, is an ordeal instituted by God, who weighs the nations in its balance. It is the essential form of the State, and the only function in which peoples can employ all their powers at once and convergently. No victory is possible save as the resultant of a totality of virtues, no defeat for which some vice or weakness is not responsible. Fidelity, cohesiveness, tenacity, heroism, conscience, education, inventiveness, economy, wealth, physical health and vigor — there isn't a moral or intellectual point of superiority that doesn't tell, when God holds his assizes and hurls the peoples upon one another. Die Weltgeschichte ist das Weltgericht ["The unfolding of history is the unfolding of right."]; and Dr. Steinmetz does not believe that in the long run chance and luck play any part in apportioning the issues.

The virtues that prevail, it must be noted, are virtues anyhow, superiorities that count in peaceful as well as in military competition; but the strain on them, being infinitely intenser in the latter case, makes war infinitely more searching as a trial. No ordeal is comparable to its winnowings. Its dread hammer is the welder of men into cohesive states, and nowhere but in such states can human nature adequately develop its capacity. The only alternative is "degeneration."

Dr. Steinmetz is a conscientious thinker, and his book, short as it is, takes much into account. Its upshot can, it seems to me, be summed up in Simon Patten's word, that mankind was nursed in pain and fear, and that the transition to a "pleasure-economy" may be fatal to a being wielding no powers of defense against its disintegrative influences. If we speak of the fear of emancipation from the fear-regime, we put the whole situation into a single phrase; fear regarding ourselves now taking the place of the ancient fear of the enemy.

Turn the fear over as I will in my mind, it all seems to lead back to two unwillingnesses of the imagination, one esthetic, and the other moral: unwillingness, first to envisage a future in which army-life, with its many elements of charm, shall be forever impossible, and in which the destinies of peoples shall nevermore be decided quickly, thrillingly, and tragically, by force, but only gradually and insipidly by "evolution"; and, secondly, unwillingness to see the supreme theatre of human strenuousness closed, and the splendid military aptitudes of men doomed to keep always in a state of latency and never show themselves in action. These insistent unwillingnesses, no less than other esthetic and ethical insistencies have, it seems to me, to be listened to and respected. One cannot meet them effectively by mere counter-insistency on war's expensiveness and horror. The horror makes the thrill; and when the question is of getting the extremest and supremest out of human nature, talk of expense sounds ignominious. The weakness of so much merely negative criticism is evident — pacificism makes no converts from the military party. The military party denies neither the bestiality nor the horror, nor the expense; it only says that these things tell but half the story. It only says that war is *worth* them; that, taking human nature as a whole, its wars are its best protection against its weaker and more cowardly self, and that mankind cannot *afford* to adopt a peace-economy.

Pacificists ought to enter more deeply into the esthetical and ethical point of view of their opponents. Do that first in any controversy, says J. J. Chapman, *then move the point*, and your opponent will follow. So long as anti-militarists propose no substitute for war's disciplinary function, no *moral equivalent* of war, analogous, as one might say, to the mechanical equivalent of heat, so long they fail to realize the full inwardness of the situation. And as a rule they do fail. The duties, penalties, and sanctions pictured in the utopias they paint are all too weak and tame to touch the military-minded. Tolstoy's pacificism is the only exception to this rule, for it is profoundly pessimistic as regards all this world's values, and makes the fear of the Lord furnish the moral spur provided elsewhere by the fear of the enemy. But our socialistic peace-advocates all believe absolutely in this world's values; and instead of the fear of the Lord and the fear of the enemy, the only fear they reckon with is the fear of poverty if one be lazy. This weakness pervades all the socialistic literature with which I am acquainted. Even in Lowes Dickinson's exquisite dialogue,* high wages and short hours are the

* *Justice and Liberty*, N.Y., 1909.

only forces invoked for overcoming man's distaste for repulsive kinds of labor. Meanwhile men at large still live as they always have lived, under a pain-and-fear economy — for those of us who live in an ease-economy are but an island in the stormy ocean — and the whole atmosphere of present-day utopian literature tastes mawkish and dishwatery to people who still keep a sense for life's more bitter flavors. It suggests, in truth, ubiquitous inferiority.

Inferiority is always with us, and merciless scorn of it is the keynote of the military temper. "Dogs, would you live forever?" shouted Frederick the Great. "Yes," say our utopians, "let us live forever, and raise our level gradually." The best thing about our "inferiors" to-day is that they are as tough as nails, and physically and morally almost as insensitive. Utopianism would see them soft and squeamish, while militarism would keep their callousness, but transfigure it into a meritorious characteristic, needed by "the service," and redeemed by that from the suspicion of inferiority. All the qualities of a man acquire dignity when he knows that the service of the collectivity that owns him needs them. If proud of the collectivity, his own pride rises in proportion. No collectivity is like an army for nourishing such pride; but it has to be confessed that the only sentiment which the image of pacific cosmopolitan industrialism is capable of arousing in countless worthy breasts is shame at the idea of belonging to *such* a collectivity. It is obvious that the United States of America as they exist to-day impress a mind like General Lea's as so much human blubber. Where is the sharpness and precipitousness, the contempt for life, whether one's own, or another's? Where is the savage "yes" and "no," the unconditional duty? Where is the conscription? Where is the blood-tax? Where is anything that one feels honored by belonging to?

Having said thus much in preparation, I will now confess my own utopia. I devoutly believe in the reign of peace and in the gradual advent of some sort of a socialistic equilibrium. The fatalistic view of the war-function is to me nonsense, for I know that war-making is due to definite motives and subject to prudential checks and reasonable criticisms, just like any other form of enterprise. And when whole nations are the armies, and the science of destruction vies in intellectual refinement with the sciences of production, I see that war becomes absurd and impossible from its own monstrosity. Extravagant ambitions will have to be replaced by reasonable claims, and nations must make common cause against them. I see no reason why all this should not apply to yellow as well as to white countries, and I look forward to a future when acts of war shall be formally outlawed as between civilized peoples.

All these beliefs of mine put me squarely into the anti-militarist party. But I do not believe that peace either ought to be or will be permanent on this globe, unless the states pacifically organized preserve some of the old elements of army-discipline. A permanently successful peace-economy cannot be a simple pleasure-economy. In the more or less socialistic future towards which mankind seems drifting we must still subject ourselves collectively to those severities which answer to our real position upon this only partly hospitable globe. We must make new energies and hardihoods continue the manliness to which the military mind so faithfully clings. Martial virtues must be the enduring cement; intrepidity, contempt of softness, surrender of private interest, obedience to command, must still remain the rock upon which states are built — unless, indeed, we wish for dangerous reactions against commonwealths fit only for contempt, and liable to invite attack whenever a centre of crystallization for military-minded enterprise gets formed anywhere in their neighborhood.

The war-party is assuredly right in affirming and reaffirming that the martial virtues, although originally gained by the race through war, are absolute and permanent human goods. Patriotic pride and ambition in their military form are, after all, only specifications of a more general competitive passion. They are its first form, but that is no reason for supposing them to be its last form. Men now are proud of belonging to a conquering nation, and without a murmur they lay down their persons and their wealth, if by so doing they may fend off subjection. But who can be sure that *other aspects of one's country* may not, with time and education and suggestion enough, come to be regarded with similarly effective feelings of pride and shame? Why should men not some day feel that it is worth a blood-tax to belong to a collectivity superior in *any* ideal respect? Why should they not blush with indignant shame if the community that owns them is vile in any way whatsoever? Individuals, daily more numerous, now feel this civic passion. It is only a question of blowing on the spark till the whole population gets incandescent, and on the ruins of the old morals of military honour, a stable system of morals of civic honour builds itself up. What the whole community comes to believe in grasps the individual as in a vise. The war-function has graspt us so far; but constructive interests may some day seem no less imperative, and impose on the individual a hardly lighter burden.

Let me illustrate my idea more concretely. There is nothing to make one indignant in the mere fact that life is hard, that men should toil and suffer pain. The planetary conditions once for all are such, and we can stand it. But that so many men, by mere accidents of birth and opportunity, should have a life of *nothing else* but toil and pain and hardness and inferiority imposed upon them, should have *no* vacation, while others natively no more deserving never get any taste of this campaigning life at all, — *this* is capable of arousing indignation in reflective minds. It may end by seeming shameful to all of us that some of us have nothing but campaigning, and others nothing but unmanly ease. If now — and this is my idea — there were, instead of military conscription a conscription of the whole youthful population to form for a certain number of years a part of the army enlisted against *Nature,* the injustice would tend to be evened out, and numerous other goods to the commonwealth would follow. The military ideals of hardihood and discipline would be wrought into the growing fibre of the people; no one would remain blind as the luxurious classes now are blind, to man's real relations to the globe he lives on, and to the permanently sour and hard foundations of his higher life. To coal and iron mines, to freight trains, to fishing fleets in December, to dish-washing, clothes-washing, and window-washing, to road-building and tunnel-making, to foundries and stoke-holes, and to the frames of skyscrapers, would our gilded youths be drafted off, according to their choice, to get the childishness knocked out of them, and to come back into society with healthier sympathies and soberer ideas. They would have paid their blood-tax, done their own part in the immemorial human warfare against nature, they would tread the earth more proudly, the women would value them more highly, they would be better fathers and teachers of the following generation.

Such a conscription, with the state of public opinion that would have required it, and the many moral fruits it would bear, would preserve in the midst of a pacific civilization the manly virtues which the military party is so afraid of seeing disappear in peace. We should get toughness without callousness, authority with as little criminal cruelty as possible, and painful work done cheerily because the duty is temporary, and threatens not, as now, to degrade the whole remainder of one's life. I spoke of the "moral equivalent" of war. So far, war has been the only force that can discipline a whole community, and until an equivalent discipline is organized, I believe that war must have its way. But I have no serious doubt that the ordinary prides and shames of social man, once developed to a certain intensity, are capable of organizing such a moral equivalent as I have sketched, or some other just as effective for preserving manliness of type. It is but a question of time, of skillful propagandism, and of opinion-making men seizing historic opportunities.

The martial type of character can be bred without war. Strenuous honour and disinterestedness abound elsewhere. Priests and medical men are in a fashion educated to it, and we should all feel some degree of it imperative if we were conscious of our work as an obligatory service to the state. We should be *owned*, as soldiers are by the army, and our pride would rise accordingly. We could be poor, then, without humiliation, as army officers now are. The only thing needed henceforward is to inflame the civic temper as past history has inflamed the military temper. H. G. Wells, as usual, sees the centre of the situation. "In many ways," he says, "military organization is the most peaceful of activities. When the contemporary man steps from the street, of clamorous insincere advertisement, push, adulteration, underselling and intermittent employment, into the barrack-yard, he steps on to a higher social plane, into an atmosphere of service and co-operation and of infinitely more honourable emulations. Here at least men are not flung out of employment to degenerate because there is no immediate work for them to do. They are fed and drilled and trained for better services. Here at least a man is supposed to win promotion by self forgetfulness and not by self-seeking. And beside the feeble and irregular endowment of research by commercialism, its little short-sighted snatches at profit by innovation and scientific economy, see how remarkable is the steady and rapid development of method and appliances in naval and military affairs! Nothing is more striking than to compare the progress of civil conveniences which has been left almost entirely to the trader, to the progress in military apparatus during the last few decades. The house-appliances of to-day for example, are little better than they were fifty years ago. A house of to-day is still almost as ill-ventilated, badly heated by wasteful fires, clumsily arranged and furnished as the house of 1858. Houses a couple of hundred years old are still satisfactory places of residence, so little have our standards risen. But the rifle or battleship of fifty years ago was beyond all comparison inferior to those we possess;

in power, in speed, in convenience alike. No one has a use now for such superannuated things."*

Wells adds† that he thinks that the conceptions of order and discipline, the tradition of service and devotion, of physical fitness, unstinted exertion, and universal responsibility, which universal military duty is now teaching European nations, will remain a permanent acquisition, when the last ammunition has been used in the fireworks that celebrate the final peace. I believe as he does. It would be simply preposterous if the only force that could work ideals of honour and standards of efficiency into English or American natures should be the fear of being killed by the Germans or the Japanese. Great indeed is Fear; but it is not, as our military enthusiasts believe and try to make us believe, the only stimulus known for awakening the higher ranges of men's spiritual energy. The amount of alteration in public opinion which my utopia postulates is vastly less than the difference between the mentality of those black warriors who pursued Stanley's party on the Congo with their cannibal war-cry of "Meat! Meat" and that of the "general-staff" of any civilized nation. History has seen the latter interval bridged over: the former one can be bridged over much more easily.

* *First and Last Things*, 1908, p. 215.
† Ibid., p. 226.

Randolph Bourne

....

The Handicapped

IT WOULD NOT perhaps be thought, ordinarily, that the man whom physical disabilities have made so helpless that he is unable to move around among his fellows can bear his lot more happily, even though he suffer pain, and face life with a more cheerful and contented spirit, than can the man whose deformities are merely enough to mark him out from the rest of his fellows without preventing him from entering with them into most of their common affairs and experiences. But the fact is that the former's very helplessness makes him content to rest and not to strive. I know a young man so helplessly deformed that he has to be carried about, who is happy in reading a little, playing chess, taking a course or two in college, and all with the sunniest goodwill in the world, and a happiness that seems strange and unaccountable to my restlessness. He does not cry for the moon.

When one, however, is in full possession of his faculties, and can move about freely, bearing simply a crooked back and an unsightly face, he is perforce drawn into all the currents of life. Particularly if he has his own way in the world to make, his road is apt to be hard and rugged, and he will penetrate to an unusual depth in his interpretation both of the world's attitude toward such misfortunes, and of the attitude toward the world which such misfortunes tend to cultivate in men like him. For he has all the battles of a stronger man to fight, and he is at a double disadvantage in fighting them. He has constantly with him the sense of being obliged to make extra efforts to overcome the bad impression of his physical defects, and he is haunted with a constant feel-

First published anonymously as "The Handicapped — By One of Them" in *The Atlantic Monthly*, 1911; revised and collected in *Youth and Life*, 1913.

ing of weakness and low vitality which makes effort more difficult and renders him easily fainthearted and discouraged by failure. He is never confident of himself, because he has grown up in an atmosphere where nobody has been very confident of him; and yet his environment and circumstances call out all sorts of ambitions and energies in him which, from the nature of his case, are bound to be immediately thwarted. This attitude is likely to keep him at a generally low level of accomplishment unless he have an unusually strong will, and a strong will is perhaps the last thing to develop under such circumstances.

That vague sense of physical uncomfortableness which is with him nearly every minute of his waking day serves, too, to make steady application for hours to any particular kind of work much more irksome than it is even to the lazy man. No one but the deformed man can realize just what the mere fact of sitting a foot lower than the normal means in discomfort and annoyance. For one cannot carry one's special chair everywhere, to theatre and library and train and schoolroom. This sounds trivial, I know, but I mention it because it furnishes a real, even though usually dim, "background of consciousness" which one had to reckon with during all one's solid work or enjoyment. The things that the world deems hardest for the deformed man to bear are perhaps really the easiest of all. I can truthfully say, for instance, that I have never suffered so much as a pang from the interested comments on my personal appearance made by urchins in the street, nor from the curious looks of people in the street and public places. To ignore this vulgar curiosity is the simplest and easiest thing in the world. It does not worry me in the least to appear on a platform if I have anything to say and there is anybody to listen. What one does get sensitive to is rather the inevitable way that people, acquaintances and strangers alike, have of discounting in advance what one does or says.

The deformed man is always conscious that the world does not expect very much from him. And it takes him a long time to see in this a challenge instead of a firm pressing down to a low level of accomplishment. As a result, he does not expect very much of himself; he is timid in approaching people, and distrustful of his ability to persuade and convince. He becomes extraordinarily sensitive to other people's first impressions of him. Those who are to be his friends he knows instantly, and further acquaintance adds little to the intimacy and warm friendship that he at once feels for them. On the other hand, those who do not respond to him immediately cannot by any effort either on his part or theirs overcome that first alienation.

This sensitiveness has both its good and bad sides. It makes friendship that most precious thing in the world to him, and he finds that he arrives at a much richer and wider intimacy with his friends than do ordinary men with their light, surface friendships, based on good fellowship or the convenience of the moment. But on the other hand this sensitiveness absolutely unfits him for business and the practice of a profession, where one must be "all things to all men," and the professional manner is indispensable to success. For here, where he has to meet a constant stream of men of all sorts and conditions, his sensitiveness to these first impressions will make his case hopeless. Except with those few who by some secret sympathy will seem to respond, his deformity will stand like a huge barrier between his personality and other men's. The magical good fortune of attractive personal appearance makes its way almost without effort in the world, breaking down all sorts of walls of disapproval and lack of interest. Even the homely person can attract by personal charm. But deformity cannot even be charming.

The doors of the deformed man are always locked, and the key is on the outside. He may have treasures of charm inside, but they will never be revealed unless the person outside cooperates with him in unlocking the door. A friend becomes, to a much greater degree than with the ordinary man, the indispensable means of discovering one's own personality. One only exists, so to speak, with friends. It is easy to see how hopelessly such a sensitiveness incapacitates a man for business, professional, or social life, where the hasty and superficial impression is everything, and disaster is the fate of the man who has not all the treasures of his personality in the front window, where they can be readily inspected and appraised.

It thus takes the deformed man a long time to get adjusted to his world. Childhood is perhaps the hardest time of all. As a child he is a strange creature in a strange land. It was my own fate to be just strong enough to play about with the other boys, and attempt all their games and "stunts," without being strong enough actually to succeed in any of them. It never used to occur to me that my failures and lack of skill were due to circumstances beyond my control, but I would always impute them, in consequence of my rigid Calvinistic bringing-up, I suppose, to some moral weakness of my own. I suffered tortures in trying to learn to skate, to climb trees, to play ball, to conform in general to the ways of the world. I never resigned myself to the inevitable, but overexerted myself constantly in a grim determination to succeed. I was good at my lessons, and through timidity rather than priggishness, I hope, a very well-behaved boy at school; I was devoted, too, to music, and learned to play the piano pretty well. But I despised my reputation for excellence in these things, and instead of adapting myself philosophically to the situation, I strove (and have been striving ever since) to do the things I could not.

As I look back now it seems perfectly natural that I should have followed the standards of the crowd, and loathed my high marks in lessons and deportment, and the concerts to which I was sent by my aunt, and the exhibitions of my musical skill that I had to give before admiring ladies. Whether or not such an experience is typical of handicapped children, there is tragedy there for those situated as I was. For had I been a little weaker physically, I should have been thrown back on reading omnivorously and cultivating my music, with some possible results; while if I had been a little stronger, I could have participated in the play on an equal footing with the rest. As it was, I simply tantalized myself, and grew up with a deepening sense of failure, and a lack of pride in what I really excelled at.

When the world become one of dances and parties and social evenings and boy-and-girl attachments — the world of youth — I was to find myself still less adapted to it. And this was the harder to bear because I was naturally sociable, and all these things appealed tremendously to me. This world of admiration and gayety and smiles and favors and quick interest and companionship, however, is only for the well-begotten and the debonair. It was not through any cruelty or dislike, I think, that I was refused admittance; indeed they were always very kind about inviting me. But it was more as if a ragged urchin had been asked to come and look through the window at the light and warmth of a glittering party; I was truly in the world, but not of the world. Indeed there were times when one would almost prefer conscious cruelty to this silent, unconscious, gentle oblivion. And this is the tragedy, I suppose, not only of the deformed, but of all the ill-favored and unattractive to a greater or less degree. The world of youth is a world of so many conventions, and the abnormal in any direction is so glaringly and hideously abnormal.

Although it took me a long time to understand this, and I continue to attribute my failure mostly to my own character, trying hard to compensate for my physical deficiencies by skill and cleverness, I suffered comparatively few pangs, and got much better adjusted to this world than to the other, For I was older, and I had acquired a lively interest in all the social politics; I would get so interested in watching how people behaved, and in sizing them up, that only at rare intervals would I remember that I was really having no hand in the game. This interest just in the ways people are human has become more and more a positive advantage in my life, and has kept sweet many a situation that might easily have cost me a pang. Not that a person with my disabilities should be a sort of detective, evil-mindedly using his social opportunities for spying out and analyzing his friends' foibles, but that, if he does acquire an interest in people quite apart from their relation to him, he may go into society with an easy conscience and a certainty that he will be entertained and possibly entertaining, even though he cuts a poor enough social figure. He must simply not expect too much.

Perhaps the bitterest struggles of the handicapped man come when he tackles the business world. If he has to go out for himself to look for work, without fortune, training, or influence, as I personally did, his way will indeed be rugged. His disability will work against him for any position where he must be much in the eyes of men, and his general insignificance has a subtle influence in convincing those to whom he applies that he is unfitted for any kind of work. As I have suggested, his keen sensitiveness to other people's impressions of him makes him more than unusually timid and unable to counteract that fatal first impression by any display of personal force and will. He cannot get his personality over across that barrier. The cards seem stacked against him from the start. With training and influence something might be done, but alone and unaided his case is almost hopeless. At least, this was my own experience. We were poor relations, and our prosperous relatives thought they had done quite enough for us without sending me through college, and I did not seem strong enough to work my way through (although I have since done it). I started out auspiciously enough, becoming a sort of apprentice to a musician who had invented a machine for turning out music-rolls. Here, with steady work, good pay, and the comfortable consciousness that I was "helping support the family," I got the first pleasurable sensation of self-respect, I think, that I ever had. But with the failure of this business I was precipitated against the real world.

It would be futile to recount the story of my struggles: how I besieged for nearly two years firm after firm, in search of a permanent position, trying everything in New York in which I thought I had the slightest chance of success, meanwhile making a precarious living by a few music lessons. The attitude toward me ranged from "You can't expect us to create a place for you," to, "How could it enter your head that we should find any use for a man like you?" My situation was doubtless unusual. Few men handicapped as I was would be likely to go so long without arousing some interest and support in relative or friend. But my experience serves to illustrate the peculiar difficulties that a handicapped man meets if he has his own way to make in the world. He is discounted at the start: it is not business to make allowances for anybody; and while people were not cruel or unkind, it was the hopeless finality of the thing that filled one's heart with despair.

The environment of a big city is perhaps the worst possible that a man in such a situation could have. For the thousands of seeming opportunities lead one restlessly on and on, and keep one's mind perpetually unsettled and depressed. There is a poignant mental torture that comes with such an experience — the urgent need, the repeated failure, or rather the repeated failure even to obtain a chance to fail, the realization that those at home can ill afford to have you idle, the growing dread of encountering people — all this is something that those who have never been through it can never realize. Personally I know of no particular way of escape. One can expect to do little by one's own unaided efforts. I solved my difficulties only by evading them, by throwing overboard some of my responsibility, and taking the desperate step of entering college on a scholarship. Desultory work is not nearly so humiliating when one is using one's time to some advantage, and college furnishes an ideal environment where the things at which a man handicapped like myself can succeed really count. One's self-respect can begin to grow like a weed.

For at the bottom of all the difficulties of a man like me is really the fact that his self-respect is so slow in growing up. Accustomed from childhood to being discounted, his self-respect is not naturally very strong, and it would require pretty constant success in a congenial line of work really to confirm it. If he could only more easily separate the factors that are due to his physical disability from those that are due to his weak will and character, he might more quickly attain self-respect, for he would realize what he is responsible for, and what he is not. But at the beginning he rarely makes allowances for himself; he is his own severest judge. He longs for a "strong will," and yet the experience of having his efforts promptly nipped off at the beginning is the last thing on earth to produce that will.

Life, particularly if he is brought into harsh and direct touch with the real world, is a much more complex thing to him than to the ordinary man. Many of his inherited platitudes vanish at the first touch. Life appears to him as a grim struggle, where ability does not necessarily mean opportunity and success, nor piety sympathy, and where helplessness cannot count on assistance and kindly interest. Human affairs seem to be running on a wholly irrational plan, and success to be founded on chance as much as on anything. But if he can stand the first shock of disillusionment, he may find himself enormously interested in discovering how they actually do run, and he will want to burrow into the motives of men, and find the reasons for the crass inequalities and injustices of the world he sees around him. He has practically to construct anew a world of his own, and explain a great many things to himself that the ordinary person never dreams of finding unintelligible at all. He will be filled with a profound sympathy for all who are despised and ignored in the world. When he has been through the neglect and struggles of a handicapped and ill-favored man himself, he will begin to understand the feelings of all the horde of the unpresentable and the unemployable, the incompetent and the ugly, the queer and crotchety people who make up so large a proportion of human folk.

We are perhaps too prone to get our ideas and standards of worth from the successful, without reflecting that the interpretations of life which patriotic legend, copybook philosophy, and the sayings of the wealthy give us are pitifully inadequate for those who fall behind in the race. Surely there are enough people to whom the task of making a decent living and maintaining themselves and their families in their social class, or of winning and keeping the respect of their fellows, is a hard and bitter task, to make a philosophy gained through personal disability and failure as just and true a method of appraising the life around us as the cheap optimism of the ordinary professional man. And certainly a kindlier, for it has no shade of contempt or disparagement about it.

It irritates me as if I had been spoken of contemptuously myself, to hear people called "common" or "ordinary," or to see that deadly and delicate feeling for social gradations crop out, which so many of our upper-middle-class women seem to have. It makes me wince to hear a man spoken of as a failure, or to have it said of one that he "doesn't amount to much." Instantly I want to know why he has not succeeded, and what have been the forces that have been working against him. He is the truly interesting person, and yet how little our eager-pressing, on-rushing world cares about such aspects of life, and how hideously though unconsciously cruel and heartless it usually is.

Often I had tried in arguments to show my friends how much of circumstance and chance go to the making of success; and when I reached the age of sober reading, a long series of the works of radical social philosophers, beginning with Henry George, provided me with the materials for a philosophy which explained why men were miserable and overworked, and why there was on the whole so little joy and gladness among us — and which fixed the blame. Here was suggested a goal, and a definite glorious future, toward which all good men might work. My own working hours became filled with visions of how men could be brought to see all that this meant, and how I in particular might work some great and wonderful thing for human betterment. In more recent years, the study of history and social psychology and ethics has made those crude outlines sounder and more normal, and brought them into a saner relation to other aspects of life and thought, but I have not lost the first glow of enthusiasm, nor my belief in social progress as the first right and permanent interest for every thinking and truehearted man or woman.

I am ashamed that my experience has given me so little chance to count in any way toward either the spreading of such a philosophy or toward direct influence and action. Nor do I yet see clearly how I shall be able to count effectually toward this ideal. Of one thing I am sure, however: that life will have little meaning for me except as I am able to contribute toward some such ideal of social betterment, if not in deed, then in word. For this is the faith that I believe we need today, all of us — a truly religious belief in human progress, a thorough social consciousness, an eager delight in every sign and promise of social improvement, and best of all, a new spirit of courage that will dare. I want to give to the young men whom I see — who, with fine intellect and high principles, lack just that light of the future on their faces that would give them a purpose and meaning in life — to them I want to give some touch of this philosophy — that will energize their lives, and save them from the disheartening effects of that poisonous counsel of timidity and distrust of human ideals which pours out in steady stream from reactionary press and pulpit.

It is hard to tell just how much of this philosophy has been due to my handicaps. If it is solely to my physical misfortunes that I owe its existence, the price has not been a heavy one to pay. For it has given me something that I should not know how to be without. For, however gained, this radical philosophy has not only made the world intelligible and dynamic to me, but has furnished me with the strongest spiritual support. I know that many people, handicapped by physical weakness and failure, find consolation and satisfaction in a very different sort of faith — in an evangelical religion, and a feeling of close dependence on God and close communion with him. But my experience has made my ideal of character militant rather than long-suffering.

I very early experienced a revulsion against the rigid Presbyterianism in which I had been brought up — a purely intellectual revulsion, I believe, because my mind was occupied for a long time afterward with theological questions, and the only feeling that entered into it was a sort of disgust at the arrogance of damning so great a proportion of the human race. I read T. W. Higginson's *The Sympathy of Religions* with the greatest satisfaction, and attended the Unitarian Church whenever I could slip away. This faith, while it still appeals to me, seems at times a little too static and refined to satisfy me with completeness. For some time there was a considerable bitterness in my heart at the narrowness of the people who could still find comfort in the old faith. Reading Buckle and Oliver Wendell Holmes gave me a new contempt for "conventionality," and my social philosophy still further tortured me by throwing the burden for the misery of the world on these same good neighbors. And all this, although I think I did not make a nuisance of myself, made me feel a spiritual and intellectual isolation in addition to my more or less effective physical isolation.

Happily these days are over. The world has righted itself, and I have been able to appreciate and realize how people count in a social and group capacity as well as in an individual and personal one, and to separate the two in my thinking. Really to believe in human nature while striving to know the thousand forces that warp it from its ideal development — to call for and expect much from men and women, and not to be disappointed and embittered if they fall short — to try to do good with people rather than to them — this is my religion on its human side. And if God exists, I think that He must be in the warm sun, in the kindly actions of the people we know and read of, in the beautiful things of art and nature, and in the closeness of friendships. He may also be in heaven, in life, in suffering, but it is only in these simple moments of happiness that I feel Him and know that He is there.

Death I do not understand at all. I have seen it in its cruelest, most irrational forms, where there has seemed no excuse, no palliation. I have only known that if we were more careful, and more relentless in fighting evil, if we knew more of medical science, such things would not be. I know that a sound body, intelligent care and training, prolong life, and that the death of a very old person is neither sad nor shocking, but sweet and fitting. I see in death a perpetual warning of how much there is to be known and done in the way of human progress and betterment. And equally, it seems to me, is this true of disease. So all the crises and deeper implications of life seem inevitably to lead back to that question of social improvement, and militant learning and doing.

This, then, is the goal of my religion — the bringing of fuller, richer life to more people on this earth. All institutions and all works that do not have this for their object are useless and pernicious. And this is not to be a mere philosophic precept which may well be buried under a host of more immediate matters, but a living faith, to permeate one's thought, and transfuse one's life. Prevention must be the method against evil. To remove temptation from men, and to apply the stimulus which shall call forth their highest endeavors — these seem to me the only right principles of ethical endeavor. Not to keep waging the age-long battle with sin and poverty, but to make the air around men so pure that foul lungs cannot breathe it — this should be our noblest religious aim.

Education — knowledge and training — I have felt so keenly my lack of these things that I count them as the greatest of means toward making life noble and happy. The lack of stimulus has tended with me to dissipate the power which might otherwise have been concentrated in some one productive direction. Or perhaps it was the many weak stimuli that constantly incited me and thus kept me from following one particular bent. I look back on what seems a long waste of intellectual power, time frittered away in groping and moping, which might easily have been spent constructively. A defect in one of the physical senses often means a keener sensitiveness in the others, but it seems that unless the sphere of action that the handicapped man has is very much narrowed, his intellectual ability will not grow in compensation for his physical defects. He will always feel that, had he been strong or even successful, he would have been further advanced intellectually, and would have attained greater command over his powers. For his mind tends to be cultivated extensively, rather than intensively. He has so many problems to meet, so many things to explain to himself, that he acquires a wide rather than a profound knowledge. Perhaps eventually, by eliminating most of these interests as practicable fields, he may tie himself down to one line of work; but at first he is pretty apt to find his mind rebellious. If he is eager and active, he will get a smattering of too many things, and his imperfect, badly trained organism will make intense application very difficult.

Now that I have talked a little of my philosophy of life, particularly about what I want to put into it, there is something to be said also of its enjoyment, and what I may hope to get out of it. I have said that my ideal of character was militant rather than long-suffering. It is true that my world has been one of failure and deficit — I have accomplished practically nothing alone, and can count only two or three instances where I have received kindly counsel and suggestion; moreover it still seems a miracle to me that money can be spent for anything beyond the necessities without being first carefully weighed and pondered over — but it has not been a world of suffering and sacrifice, my health has been almost criminally perfect in the light of my actual achievement, and life has appeared to me, at least since my more pressing responsibilities were removed, as a challenge and an arena, rather than a vale of tears. I do not like the idea of helplessly suffering one's misfortunes, of passively bearing one's lot. The Stoics depress me. I do not want to look on my life as an eternal making the best of a bad bargain. Granting all the circumstances, admitting all my disabilities, I want too to "warm both hands before the fire of life." What satisfactions I have, and they are many and precious, I do not want to look on as compensations, but as positive goods.

The difference between what the strongest of the strong and the most winning of the attractive can get out of life, and what I can, is after all so slight. Our experiences and enjoyments, both his and mine, are so infinitesimal compared with the great mass of possibilities; and there must be a division of labor. If he takes the world of physical satisfactions and of material success, I at least can occupy the far richer kingdom of mental effort and artistic appreciation. And on the side of what we are to put into life, although I admit that achievement on my part will be harder relatively to encompass than on his, at least I may have the field of artistic creation and intellectual achievement for my own. Indeed, as one gets older, the fact of one's disabilities fades dimmer and dimmer away from consciousness. One's enemy is now one's own weak will, and the struggle is to attain the artistic ideal one has set.

But one must have grown up, to get this attitude. And that is the best thing the handicapped man can do. Growing up will have given him one of the greatest, and certainly the most durable satisfaction of his life. It will mean at least that he is out of the woods. Childhood has nothing to offer him; youth little more. They are things to be gotten through with as soon as possible. For he will not understand, and he will not be understood. He finds himself simply a bundle of chaotic impulses and emotions and ambitions, very few of which, from the nature of the case, can possibly be realized or satisfied. He is bound to be at cross-grains with the world, and he has to look sharp that he does not grow up with a bad temper and a hateful disposition, and become cynical and bitter against those who turn him away. But grown up, his horizon will broaden; he will get a better perspective, and will not take the world so seriously as he used to, nor will failure frighten him so much. He can look back and see how inevitable it all was, and understand how precarious and problematic even the best regulated of human affairs may be. And if he feels that there were times when he should have been able to count upon the help and kindly counsel of relatives and acquaintances who remained dumb and uninterested, he will not put their behavior down as proof of the depravity of human nature, but as due to an unfortunate blindness which it will be his work to avoid in himself by looking out for others when he has the power.

When he has grown up, he will find that people of his own age and experience are willing to make those large allowances for what is out of the ordinary which were impossible to his younger friends, and that grown-up people touch each other on planes other than the purely superficial. With a broadening of his own interests, he will find himself overlapping other people's personalities at new points, and will discover with rare delight that he is beginning to be understood and appreciated — at least to a greater degree than when he had to keep his real interests hid as something unusual. For he will begin to see in his friends, his music and books, and his interest in people and social betterment, his true life; many of his restless ambitions will fade gradually away, and he will come to recognize all the more clearly some true ambition of his life that is within the range of his capabilities. He will have built up his world, and have sifted out the things that are not going to concern him, and participation in which will only serve to vex and harass him. He may well come to count his deformity even as a blessing, for it has made impossible to him at last many things in the pursuit of which he would only fritter away his time and dissipate his interest. He must not think of "resigning himself to his fate"; above all he must insist on his own personality. For once really grown up, he will find that he has acquired self-respect and personality. Grown-upness, I think, is not a mere question of age, but of being able to look back and understand and find satisfaction in one's experience, no matter how bitter it may have been.

So to all who are situated as I am, I would say — Grow up as fast as you can. Cultivate the widest interests you can, and cherish all your

friends. Cultivate some artistic talent, for you will find it the most durable of satisfactions, and perhaps one of the surest means of livelihood as
well. Achievement is, of course, on the knees of the gods; but you will at
least have the thrill of trial, and, after all, not to try is to fail. Taking your
disabilities for granted, and assuming constantly that they are being
taken for granted, make your social intercourse as broad and as constant as possible. Do not take the world too seriously, nor let too many
social conventions oppress you. Keep sweet your sense of humor, and
above all do not let any morbid feelings of inferiority creep into your
soul. You will find yourself sensitive enough to the sympathy of others,
and if you do not find people who like you and are willing to meet you
more than halfway, it will be because you have let your disability narrow your vision and shrink up your soul. It will be really your own
fault, and not that of your circumstances. In a word, keep looking outward; look out eagerly for those things that interest you, for people who
will interest you and be friends with you, for new interests and for opportunities to express yourself. You will find that your disability will
come to have little meaning for you, that it will begin to fade quite completely out of your sight; you will wake up some fine morning and find
yourself, after all the struggles that seemed so bitter to you, really and
truly adjusted to the world.

I am perhaps not yet sufficiently out of the wilderness to utter all
these brave words. For, I must confess, I find myself hopelessly dependent on my friends, and my environment. My friends have come to mean
more to me than almost anything else in the world. If it is far harder
work for a man in my situation to make friendships quickly, at least
friendships once made have a depth and intimacy quite beyond ordinary attachments. For a man such as I am has little prestige; people do
not want to impress him. They are genuine and sincere, talk to him
freely about themselves, and are generally far less reticent about revealing their real personality and history and aspirations. And particularly
is this so in friendships with young women. I have found their friendships the most delightful and satisfying of all. For all that social convention that insists that every friendship between a young man and woman
must be on a romantic basis is necessarily absent in our case. There is
no fringe around us to make our acquaintance anything but a charming
companionship. With all my friends, the same thing is true. The first
barrier of strangeness broken down, our interest is really in each other,
and not in what each is going to think of the other, how he is to be impressed, or whether we are going to fall in love with each other. When

one of my friends moves away, I feel as if a great hole had been left in my life. There is a whole side of my personality that I cannot express without him. I shudder to think of any change that will deprive me of their constant companionship. Without friends I feel as if even my music and books and interests would turn stale on my hands. I confess that I am not grown up enough to get along without them.

But if I am not yet out of the wilderness, at least I think I see the way to happiness. With health and a modicum of achievement, I shall not see my lot as unenviable. And if misfortune comes, it will only be something flowing from the common lot of men, not from my own particular disability. Most of the difficulties that flow from that I flatter myself I have met by this time of my twenty-fifth year, have looked full in the face, have grappled with, and find in nowise so formidable as the world usually deems them; no bar to my real ambitions and ideals.

1912

John Jay Chapman

....

Coatesville

WE ARE MET to commemorate the anniversary of one of the most dreadful crimes in history — not for the purpose of condemning it, but to repent of our share in it. We do not start any agitation with regard to that particular crime. I understand that an attempt to prosecute the chief criminals has been made, and has entirely failed; because the whole community, and in a sense our whole people, are really involved in the guilt. The failure of the prosecution in this case, in all such cases, is only a proof of the magnitude of the guilt, and of the awful fact that everyone shares in it.

I will tell you why I am here; I will tell you what happened to me. When I read in the newspapers of August 14, a year ago, about the burning alive of a human being, and of how a few desperate, fiend-minded men had been permitted to torture a man chained to an iron bedstead, burning alive, thrust back by pitchforks when he struggled out of it, while around about stood hundreds of well-dressed American citizens, both from the vicinity and from afar, coming on foot and in wagons, assembling on telephone call, as if by magic, silent, whether from terror or indifference, fascinated and impotent, hundreds of persons watching this awful sight and making no attempt to stay the wickedness, and no one man among them all who was inspired to risk his life in an attempt to stop it, no one man to name the name of Christ, of humanity, of government! As I read the newspaper accounts of the scene enacted here in

Bitterly distressed by the lynching of a black man in Coatesville, Pennsylvania, in August 1911, Chapman decided to go there himself a year later and deliver an address at a prayer meeting commemorating the event. Two people attended. The address was first published in *Harper's Weekly* in 1912 and collected in *Memories and Milestones*, 1915.

Coatesville a year ago, I seemed to get a glimpse into the unconscious soul of this country. I saw a seldom revealed picture of the American heart and of the American nature. I seemed to be looking into the heart of the criminal — a cold thing, an awful thing.

I said to myself, "I shall forget this, we shall all forget it; but it will be there. What I have seen is not an illusion. It is the truth. I have seen death in the heart of this people." For to look at the agony of a fellow-being and remain aloof means death in the heart of the onlooker. Religious fanaticism has sometimes lifted men to the frenzy of such cruelty, political passion has sometimes done it, personal hatred might do it, the excitement of the amphitheater in the degenerate days of Roman luxury could do it. But here an audience chosen by chance in America has stood spellbound through an improvised *auto-da-fé*, irregular, illegal, having no religious significance, not sanctioned by custom, having no immediate provocation, the audience standing by merely in cold dislike.

I saw during one moment something beyond all argument in the depth of its significance. You might call it the paralysis of the nerves about the heart in a people habitually and unconsciously given over to selfish aims, an ignorant people who knew not what spectacle they were providing, or what part they were playing in a judgment-play which history was exhibiting on that day.

No theories about the race problem, no statistics, legislation, or mere educational endeavor, can quite meet the lack which that day revealed in the American people. For what we saw was death. The people stood like blighted things, like ghosts about Acheron, waiting for someone or something to determine their destiny for them.

Whatever life itself is, that thing must be replenished in us. The opposite of hate is love, the opposite of cold is heat; what we need is the love of God and reverence for human nature. For one moment I knew that I had seen our true need; and I was afraid that I should forget it and that I should go about framing arguments and agitations and starting schemes of education, when the need was deeper than education. And I became filled with one idea, that I must not forget what I had seen, and that I must do something to remember it. And I am here today chiefly that I may remember that vision. It seems fitting to come to this town where the crime occurred and hold a prayer-meeting, so that our hearts may be turned to God through whom mercy may flow into us.

Let me say one thing more about the whole matter. The subject we are dealing with is not local. The act, to be sure, took place at Coatesville and everyone looked to Coatesville to follow it up. Some months ago I asked a friend who lives not far from here something about this case, and about the expected prosecutions, and he replied to me: "It wasn't in my county," and that made me wonder whose county it was in. And it seemed to be in my county. I live on the Hudson River; but I knew that this great wickedness that happened in Coatesville is not the wickedness of Coatesville nor of to-day. It is the wickedness of all America and of three hundred years — the wickedness of the slave trade. All of us are tinctured by it. No special place, no special persons, are to blame. A nation cannot practice a course of inhuman crime for three hundred years and then suddenly throw off the effects of it. Less than fifty years ago domestic slavery was abolished among us; and in one way and another the marks of that vice are in our faces. There is no country in Europe where the Coatesville tragedy or anything remotely like it could have been enacted, probably no country in the world.

On the day of the calamity, those people in the automobiles came by the hundred and watched the torture, and passers-by came in a great multitude and watched it — and did nothing. On the next morning the newspapers spread the news and spread the paralysis until the whole country seemed to be helplessly watching this awful murder, as awful as anything ever done on the earth; and the whole of our people seemed to be looking on helplessly, not able to respond, not knowing what to do next. That spectacle has been in my mind.

The trouble has come down to us out of the past. The only reason that slavery is wrong is that it is cruel and makes men cruel and leaves them cruel. Someone may say that you and I cannot repent because we did not do the act. But we are involved in it. We are still looking on. Do you not see that this whole event is merely the last parable, the most vivid, the most terrible illustration that ever was given by man or imagined by a Jewish prophet, of the relation between good and evil in this world, and of the relation of men to one another?

This whole matter has been an historic episode; but it is a part, not only of our national history, but of the personal history of each one of us. With the great disease (slavery) came the climax (the war), and after the climax gradually began the cure, and in the process of cure comes now the knowledge of what the evil was. I say that our need is new life, and that books and resolutions will not save us, but only such disposition in our hearts and souls as will enable the new life, love, force, hope, virtue, which surround us always, to enter into us.

This is the discovery that each man must make for himself — the discovery that what he really stands in need of he cannot get for himself, but must wait till God gives it to him. I have felt the impulse to come here to-day to testify to this truth.

The occasion is not small; the occasion looks back on three centuries and embraces a hemisphere. Yet the occasion is small compared with the truth it leads us to. For this truth touches all ages and affects every soul in the world.

1916

Jane Addams

....

The Devil Baby at Hull-House

I

The knowledge of the existence of the Devil Baby burst upon the residents of Hull-House one day when three Italian women, with an excited rush through the door, demanded that he be shown to them. No amount of denial convinced them that he was not there, for they knew exactly what he was like, with his cloven hoofs, his pointed ears and diminutive tail; moreover, the Devil Baby had been able to speak as soon as he was born and was most shockingly profane.

The three women were but the forerunners of a veritable multitude; for six weeks the streams of visitors from every part of the city and suburbs to this mythical baby poured in all day long, and so far into the night that the regular activities of the settlement were almost swamped.

The Italian version, with a hundred variations, dealt with a pious Italian girl married to an atheist. Her husband vehemently tore a holy picture from the bedroom wall, saying that he would quite as soon have a devil in the house as that; whereupon the devil incarnated himself in her coming child. As soon as the Devil Baby was born, he ran about the table shaking his finger in deep reproach at his father, who finally caught him and in fear and trembling brought him to Hull-House. When the residents there, in spite of the baby's shocking appearance, wishing to save his soul, took him to church for baptism, they found that the shawl was empty and the Devil Baby, fleeing from the holy water, ran lightly over the backs of the pews.

First published in *The Atlantic Monthly,* 1916; collected in *The Long Road of Woman's Memory,* 1916; and incorporated into *The Second Twenty Years at Hull-House,* 1930.

The Jewish version, again with variations, was to the effect that the father of six daughters had said before the birth of a seventh child that he would rather have a devil in the house than another girl, whereupon the Devil Baby promptly appeared.

Save for a red automobile which occasionally figured in the story, and a stray cigar which, in some versions, the newborn child snatched from his father's lips, the tale might have been fashioned a thousand years ago.

Although the visitors to the Devil Baby included people of every degree of prosperity and education, even physicians and trained nurses who assured us of their scientific interest, the story constantly demonstrated the power of an old wives' tale among thousands of people in modern society who are living in a corner of their own, their vision fixed, their intelligence held by some iron chain of silent habit. To such primitive people the metaphor apparently is still the very 'stuff of life'; or, rather, no other form of statement reaches them, and the tremendous tonnage of current writing for them has no existence. It was in keeping with their simple habits that the reputed presence of the Devil Baby at Hull-House did not reach the newspapers until the fifth week of his sojourn — after thousands of people had already been informed of his whereabouts by the old method of passing news from mouth to mouth.

During the weeks of excitement it was the old women who really seemed to have come into their own, and perhaps the most significant result of the incident was the reaction of the story upon them. It stirred their minds and memories as with a magic touch; it loosened their tongues and revealed the inner life and thoughts of those who are so often inarticulate. These old women enjoyed a moment of triumph, as if they had made good at last and had come into a region of sanctions and punishments which they understood.

Throughout six weeks, as I went about Hull-House, I would hear a voice at the telephone repeating for the hundredth time that day, 'No, there is no such baby'; 'No, we never had it here'; 'No, he couldn't have seen it for fifty cents'; 'We didn't send it anywhere because we never had it'; 'I don't mean to say that your sister-in-law lied, but there must be some mistake'; 'There is no use getting up an excursion from Milwaukee, for there isn't any Devil Baby at Hull-House'; 'We can't give reduced rates because we are not exhibiting anything'; and so on and on. As I came near the front door, I would catch snatches of arguments that were often acrimonious: 'Why do you let so many people believe it, if it isn't here?' 'We have taken three lines of cars to come, and we have as much right to see it as anybody else'; 'This is a pretty big place, of course you could hide it easy enough'; 'What you saying that for — are you going to raise the price of admission?' We had doubtless struck a case of what the psychologists call the 'contagion of emotion,' added to that 'aesthetic sociability' which impels any one of us to drag the entire household to the window when a procession comes into the street or a rainbow appears in the sky.

But the Devil Baby of course was worth many processions and rainbows, and I will confess that, as the empty show went on day after day, I quite revolted against such a vapid manifestation of an admirable human trait. There was always one exception, however: whenever I heard the high eager voices of old women, I was irresistibly interested and left anything I might be doing in order to listen to them.

II

Perhaps my many talks with these aged visitors crystallized thoughts and impressions that I had been receiving through years; or the tale itself may have ignited a fire, as it were, whose light illumined some of my darkest memories of neglected and uncomfortable old age, of old peasant women who had ruthlessly probed into the ugly depths of human nature in themselves and others. Many of them who came to see the Devil Baby had been forced to face tragic human experiences; the powers of brutality and horror had had full scope in their lives, and for years they had had acquaintance with disaster and death. Such old women do not shirk life's misery by feeble idealism, for they are long past the stage of make-believe. They relate without flinching the most hideous experiences. 'My face has had this queer twist now for nearly sixty years; I was ten when it got that way, the night after I saw my father do my mother to death with his knife.' 'Yes, I had fourteen children; only two grew to be men and both of them were killed in the same explosion. I was never sure they brought home the right bodies.' But even the most hideous sorrows which the old women related had apparently subsided into the paler emotion of ineffectual regret, after Memory had long done her work upon them; the old people seemed, in some unaccountable way, to lose all bitterness and resentment against life, or rather they were so completely without it that they must have lost it long since.

Perhaps those women, because they had come to expect nothing more from life and had perforce ceased from grasping and striving, had obtained, if not renunciation, at least that quiet endurance which allows the wounds of the spirit to heal. Through their stored-up habit of acquiescence, they vouchsafed a fleeting glimpse of that translucent wisdom so often embodied in old women but so difficult to portray. I recall a conversation with one of them, a woman whose fine mind and indomitable spirit I had long admired; I had known her for years, and yet the recital of her sufferings, added to those the Devil Baby had already induced other women to tell me, pierced me afresh.

'I had eleven children, some born in Bohemia and some born here; nine of them boys; all of the children died when they were little, but my dear Liboucha, you know all about her. She died last winter in the insane asylum. She was only twelve years old when her father, in a fit of delirium tremens, killed himself after he had chased us around the room trying to kill us first. She saw it all; the blood splashed on the wall stayed in her mind the worst; she shivered and shook all that night through, and the next morning she had lost her voice, couldn't speak out loud for terror. After a while her voice came back, although it was never very natural, and she went to school again. She seemed to do as well as ever and was awful pleased when she got into High School. All the money we had, I earned scrubbing in a public dispensary, although sometimes I got a little more by interpreting for the patients, for I know three languages, one as well as the other. But I was determined that, whatever happened to me, Liboucha was to be educated. My husband's father was a doctor in the old country, and Liboucha was always a clever child. I wouldn't have her live the kind of life I had, with no use for my mind except to make me restless and bitter. I was pretty old and worn out for such hard work, but when I used to see Liboucha on a Sunday morning, ready for church in her white dress with her long yellow hair braided round her beautiful pale face, lying there in bed as I was, — being brought up a freethinker and needing to rest my aching bones for the next week's work, — I'd feel almost happy, in spite of everything.

'But of course no such peace could last in my life; the second year at High School, Liboucha began to seem different and to do strange things. You know the time she wandered away for three days and we were all wild with fright, although a kind woman had taken her in and no harm came to her. I could never be easy after that; she was always gentle, but she was awful sly about running away, and at last I had to send her to the asylum. She stayed there off and on for five years, but I saw her every week of my life and she was always company for me, what with sewing for her, washing and ironing her clothes, cooking little things to take out to her and saving a bit of money to buy fruit for her. At any rate, I had stopped feeling so bitter, and got some comfort out of seeing the one thing that belonged to me on this side of the water, when all of a sudden she died of heart failure, and they never took the trouble to send for me until the next day.'

She stopped as if wondering afresh that the Fates could have been so casual, but with a sudden illumination, as if she had been awakened out of the burden and intensity of her restricted personal interests into a consciousness of those larger relations that are, for the most part, so strangely invisible. It was as if the young mother of the grotesque Devil Baby, that victim of wrong-doing on the part of others, had revealed to this tragic woman, much more clearly than soft words had ever done, that the return of a deed of violence upon the head of the innocent is inevitable; as if she had realized that, although she was destined to walk all the days of her life with that piteous multitude who bear the undeserved wrongs of the world, she would walk henceforth with a sense of companionship.

Among the visitors were pitiful old women who, although they had already reconciled themselves to much misery, were still enduring more. 'You might say it's a disgrace to have your son beat you up for the sake of a bit of money you've earned by scrubbing — your own man is different — but I haven't the heart to blame the boy for doing what he's seen all his life; his father forever went wild when the drink was in him and struck me to the very day of his death. The ugliness was born in the boy as the marks of the devil was born in the poor child upstairs.'

This more primitive type embodies the eternal patience of those humble toiling women who through the generations have been held of little value, save as their drudgery ministered to their men. One of them related her habit of going through the pockets of her drunken son every pay-day, and complained that she had never got so little as the night before, only twenty-five cents out of fifteen dollars he had promised for the rent long overdue. 'I had to get that as he lay in the alley before the door; I couldn't pull him in, and the copper who helped him home left as soon as he heard me coming and pretended he didn't see me. I have no food in the house nor coffee to sober him up with. I know perfectly well that you will ask me to eat something here, but if I can't carry it home, I won't take a bite nor a sup. I have never told you so much before. Since one of the nurses said he could be arrested for my non-support, I have been awfully close-mouthed. It's the foolish way all the women in our street are talking about the Devil Baby that's loosened my tongue — more shame to me.'

There are those, if possible more piteous still, who have become absolutely helpless and can therefore no longer perform the household services exacted from them. One last wish has been denied them. 'I hoped to go before I became a burden, but it was not to be'; and the long days of unwonted idleness are darkened by the haunting fear that 'they' will come to think the burden too heavy and decide that the poorhouse is 'the best.' Even then there is no word of blame for undutiful children or heedless grandchildren, for apparently all that is petty and transitory falls away from austere old age; the fires are burnt out, resentments, hatreds, and even cherished sorrows have become actually unintelligible. It is as if the horrors through which these old people had passed had never existed for them, and, facing death as they are, they seem anxious to speak only such words of groping wisdom as they are able.

This aspect of memory has never been more clearly stated than by Gilbert Murray in his *Life of Euripides*. He tells us that the aged poet, when he was officially declared to be one of 'the old men of Athens,' said, 'Even yet the age-worn minstrel can turn Memory into song'; and the memory of which he spoke was that of history and tradition, rather than his own. The aged poet turned into song even the hideous story of Medea, transmuting it into 'a beautiful remote song about far-off children who have been slain in legend, children who are now at peace and whose ancient pain has become part mystery and part music. Memory — that Memory who is the mother of the Muses — having done her work upon them.'

The vivid interest of so many old women in the story of the Devil Baby may have been an unconscious, although powerful testimony that tragic experiences gradually become dressed in such trappings in order that their spent agony may prove of some use to a world which learns at the hardest; and that the strivings and sufferings of men and women long since dead, their emotions no longer connected with flesh and blood, are thus transmuted into legendary wisdom. The young are forced to heed the warning in such a tale, although for the most part it is so easy for them to disregard the words of the aged. That the old women who came to visit the Devil Baby believed that the story would secure them a hearing at home, was evident, and as they prepared themselves with every detail of it, their old faces shone with a timid satisfaction. Their features, worn and scarred by harsh living, even as effigies built into the floor of an old church become dim and defaced by rough-shod feet, grew poignant and solemn. In the midst of their double bewilderment, both that the younger generation were walking in such strange paths and that no one would listen to them, for one moment there flickered up that last hope of a disappointed life, that it may at least serve as a warning while affording material for exciting narrations.

Sometimes in talking to one of them, who was 'but a hair's breadth this side of the darkness,' one realized that old age has its own expression for the mystic renunciation of the world. The impatience with all non-essentials, the craving to be free from hampering bonds and soft conditions, was perhaps typified in our own generation by Tolstoï's last impetuous journey, the light of his genius for a moment making comprehensible to us that unintelligible impulse of the aged.

Often, in the midst of a conversation, one of these touching old women would quietly express a longing for death, as if it were a natural fulfillment of an inmost desire. Her sincerity and anticipation were so genuine that I would feel abashed in her presence, ashamed to 'cling to this strange thing that shines in the sunlight, and to be sick with love for it.' Such impressions were in their essence transitory, but one result from the hypothetical visit of the Devil Baby to Hull-House will, I think, remain: a realization of the sifting and reconciling power inherent in Memory itself. The old women, with much to aggravate and little to soften the habitual bodily discomforts of old age, exhibited an emotional serenity so vast and reassuring that I found myself perpetually speculating as to how soon the fleeting and petty emotions which seem so unduly important to us now might be thus transmuted; at what moment we might expect the perplexities of life to be brought under this appeasing Memory, with its ultimate power to increase the elements of Beauty and Significance and to reduce, if not to eliminate, stupidity and resentment.

III

As our visitors to the Devil Baby came day by day, it was gradually evident that the simpler women were moved not wholly by curiosity, but that many of them prized the story as a valuable instrument in the business of living.

The legend exhibited all the persistence of one of those tales which have doubtless been preserved through the centuries because of their taming effects upon recalcitrant husbands and fathers. Shamefaced men brought by their women-folk to see the baby but ill-concealed their triumph when there proved to be no such visible sign of retribution for domestic derelictions. On the other hand, numbers of men came by themselves. One group from a neighboring factory, on their 'own time,' offered to pay twenty-five cents, a half dollar, two dollars apiece to see the child, insisting that it must be at Hull-House because 'the women folks had seen it.' To my query as to whether they supposed we would exhibit for money a poor little deformed baby, if one had been born in the neighborhood, they replied, 'Sure, why not?' and 'It teaches a good lesson, too,' they added as an afterthought, or perhaps as a concession to the strange moral standards of a place like Hull-House. All the members in this group of hard-working men, in spite of a certain swagger toward one another and a tendency to bully the derelict showman, wore that hang-dog look betraying the sense of unfair treatment which a man is so apt to feel when his womankind makes an appeal to the supernatural. In their determination to see the child, the men recklessly divulged much more concerning their motives than they had meant to do, and their talk confirmed my impression that such a story may still act as a restraining influence in that sphere of marital conduct which, next to primitive religion itself, we are told, has always afforded the most fertile field for irrational tabus and savage punishments.

What story more than this could be calculated to secure sympathy for the mother of too many daughters, and contumely for the irritated father? The touch of mysticism, the supernatural sphere in which it was placed, would render a man perfectly helpless.

The story of the Devil Baby, evolved to-day as it might have been centuries before in response to the imperative needs of anxious wives and mothers, recalled the theory that woman first fashioned the fairy-story, that combination of wisdom and romance, in an effort to tame her mate and to make him a better father to her children, until such stories finally became a rude creed for domestic conduct, softening the treatment that men accorded to women.

These first pitiful efforts of women, so widespread and powerful that we have not yet escaped their influence, still cast vague shadows upon the vast spaces of life, shadows that are dim and distorted because of their distant origin. They remind us that for thousands of years women had nothing to oppose against unthinkable brutality save 'the charm of words,' no other implement with which to subdue the fiercenesses of the world about them.

During the weeks that the Devil Baby drew multitudes of visitors to Hull-House, my mind was opened to the fact that new knowledge derived from concrete experience is continually being made available for the guidance of human life; that humble women are still establishing rules of conduct as best they may, to counteract the base temptations of a man's world. Thousands of women, for instance, make it a standard of domestic virtue that a man must not touch his pay envelope, but bring it home unopened to his wife. High praise is contained in the phrase, 'We have been married twenty years and he never once opened his own envelope'; or covert blame in the statement, 'Of course he got to gambling; what can you expect from a man who always opens his own pay?'

The women are so fatalistically certain of this relation of punishment to domestic sin, of reward to domestic virtue, that when they talk about it, as they so constantly did in connection with the Devil Baby, it often sounds as if they were using the words of a widely known ritual. Even the young girls seized upon it as a palpable punishment, to be held over the heads of reckless friends. That the tale was useful was evidenced by many letters similar to the anonymous epistle here given.

'me and my friends we work in talor shop and when we are going home on the roby street car where we get off that car at blue island ave. we will meet some fellows sitting at that street where they drink some beer from pail. they keep look in cars all time and they will wait and see if we will come sometimes we will have to work, but they will wait so long they are tired and they don't care they get rest so long but a girl what works in twine mill saw them talk with us we know her good and she say what youse talk with old drunk man for we shall come to thier dance when it will be they will tell us and we should know all about where to see them that girl she say oh if you will go with them you will get devils baby like some other girls did who we knows. she say Jane Addams she will show one like that in Hull House if you will go down there we shall come sometime and we will see if that is trouth we do not believe her for she is friendly with them old men herself when she go out from her work they will wink to her and say something else to. We will go down and see you and make a lie from what she say.'

IV

The story evidently held some special comfort for hundreds of forlorn women, representatives of that vast horde of the denied and proscribed, who had long found themselves confronted by those mysterious and impersonal wrongs which are apparently nobody's fault but seem to be inherent in the very nature of things.

Because the Devil Baby embodied an undeserved wrong to a poor mother, whose tender child had been claimed by the forces of evil, his merely reputed presence had power to attract to Hull-House hundreds of women who had been humbled and disgraced by their children; mothers of the feeble-minded, of the vicious, of the criminal, of the prostitute. In their talk it was as if their long rôle of maternal apology and protective reticence had at last broken down; as if they could speak out freely because for once a man responsible for an ill-begotten child had been 'met up with' and had received his deserts. Their sinister version of the story was that the father of the Devil Baby had married without confessing a hideous crime committed years before, thus basely deceiving both his innocent young bride and the good priest who performed the solemn ceremony; that the sin had become incarnate in his child which, to the horror of the young and trusting mother, had been born with all the outward aspects of the devil himself.

As if drawn by a magnet, week after week, a procession of forlorn women in search of the Devil Baby came to Hull-House from every part of the city, issuing forth from the many homes in which dwelt 'the two unprofitable goddesses, Poverty and Impossibility.' With an understanding quickened perhaps through my own acquaintance with the mysterious child, I listened to many tragic tales from the visiting women: of premature births, 'because he kicked me in the side'; of children maimed and burned because 'I had no one to leave them with when I went to work.' These women had seen the tender flesh of growing little bodies given over to death because 'he wouldn't let me send for the doctor,' or because 'there was no money to pay for the medicine.' But even these mothers, rendered childless through insensate brutality, were less pitiful than some of the others, who might well have cried aloud of their children as did a distracted mother of her child centuries ago, —

> That God should send this one thing more
> Of hunger and of dread, a door
> Set wide to every wind of pain!

Such was the mother of a feeble-minded boy who said, 'I didn't have a devil baby myself, but I bore a poor "innocent," who made me fight devils for twenty-three years.' She told of her son's experiences from the time the other little boys had put him up to stealing that they might hide in safety and leave him to be found with 'the goods' on him, until, grown into a huge man, he fell into the hands of professional burglars; he was evidently the dupe and stool-pigeon of the vicious and criminal until the very day he was locked into the State Penitentiary. 'If people played with him a little, he went right off and did anything they told him to, and now he's been sent up for life. We call such innocents "God's Fools" in the old country, but over here the Devil himself gets them. I've fought off bad men and boys from the poor lamb with my very fists; nobody ever came near the house except such like and the police officers who were always arresting him.'

There were a goodly number of visitors, of the type of those to be found in every large city, who are on the verge of nervous collapse or who exhibit many symptoms of mental aberration and yet are sufficiently normal to be at large most of the time and to support themselves by drudgery which requires little mental effort, although the exhaustion resulting from the work they are able to do is the one thing from which they should be most carefully protected. One such woman, evidently obtaining inscrutable comfort from the story of the Devil Baby even after she had become convinced that we harbored no such creature, came many times to tell of her longing for her son who had joined the army some eighteen months before and was stationed in Alaska. She always began with the same words. 'When spring comes and the snow melts so that I know he could get out, I can hardly stand it. You know I was once in the Insane Asylum for three years at a stretch, and since then I haven't had much use of my mind except to worry with. Of course I know that it is dangerous for me, but what can I do? I think something like this: "The snow is melting, now he could get out, but his officers won't let him off, and if he runs away he'll be shot for a deserter — either way I'll never see him again; I'll die without seeing him" — and then I begin all over again with the snow.' After a pause, she said, 'The recruiting officer ought not to have taken him; he's my only son and I'm a widow; it's against the rules, but he was so crazy to go that I guess he lied a little. At any rate, the government has him now and I can't get him back. Without this worry about him, my mind would be all right; if he was here he would be earning money and keeping me and we would be happy all day long.'

Recalling the vagabondish lad who had never earned much money and had certainly never 'kept' his hard-working mother, I ventured to suggest that, even if he were at home, he might not have work these

hard times, that he might get into trouble and be arrested, — I did not
need to remind her that he had already been arrested twice, — that he
was now fed and sheltered and under discipline, and I added hopefully
something about seeing the world. She looked at me out of her withdrawn harried eyes, as if I were speaking a foreign tongue. 'That
wouldn't make any real difference to me — the work, the money, his be-
having well and all that, if I could cook and wash for him; I don't need
all the money I earn scrubbing that factory; I only take bread and tea
for supper, and I choke over that, thinking of him.'

v

A sorrowful woman clad in heavy black, who came one day, exhibited
such a capacity for prolonged weeping that it was evidence in itself of
the truth of at least half her statement, that she had cried herself to
sleep every night of her life for fourteen years in fulfillment of a 'curse'
laid upon her by an angry man that 'her pillow would be wet with tears
as long as she lived.' Her respectable husband had kept a shop in the
Red Light district, because he found it profitable to sell to the men and
women who lived there. She had kept house in the rooms 'over the
store,' from the time she was a bride newly come from Russia, and her
five daughters had been born there, but never a son to gladden her husband's heart.

She took such a feverish interest in the Devil Baby that when I was
obliged to disillusion her, I found it hard to take away her comfort in
the belief that the Powers that Be are on the side of the woman, when
her husband resents too many daughters. But, after all, the birth of
daughters was but an incident in her tale of unmitigated woe, for the
scoldings of a disappointed husband were as nothing to the curse of a
strange enemy, although she doubtless had a confused impression that
if there was retribution for one in the general scheme of things, there
might be for the other.

When the weeping woman finally put the events of her disordered
life in some sort of sequence, it was clear that about fifteen years ago she
had reported to the police a vicious house whose back door opened
into her own yard. Her husband had forbidden her to do anything
about it and had said that it would only get them into trouble, but she
had been made desperate one day when she saw her little girl, then
twelve years old, come out of the door, gleefully showing her younger
sister a present of money. Because the poor woman had tried for ten

years, without success, to induce her husband to move from the vicinity of such houses, she was certain that she could save her child only by forcing out 'the bad people' from her own door-yard. She therefore made her one frantic effort, found her way to the city hall, and there reported the house to the chief himself. Of course, 'the bad people' 'stood in with the police,' and nothing happened to them except, perhaps, a fresh levy of blackmail; but the keeper of the house, beside himself with rage, made the dire threat and laid the curse upon her. In less than a year from that time he had enticed her daughter into a disreputable house in another part of the district. The poor woman, ringing one doorbell after another, had never been able to find her, but the girl's sisters, who in time came to know where she was, had been dazzled by her mode of life. The weeping mother was quite sure that two of her daughters, while still outwardly respectable and 'working downtown,' earned money in the devious ways which they had learned all about when they were little children, although for the past five years the now prosperous husband had allowed the family to live in a suburb where the two younger daughters were 'growing up respectable.'

At moments it seemed possible that these simple women, representing an earlier development, eagerly seized upon the story simply because it was primitive in form and substance. Certainly one evening a long-forgotten ballad made an unceasing effort to come to the surface of my mind, as I talked to a feeble woman who, in the last stages of an incurable disease from which she soon afterwards died, had been helped off the street-car in front of Hull-House.

The ballad tells that the lover of a proud and jealous mistress, who demanded as a final test of devotion that he bring her the heart of his mother, had quickly cut the heart from his mother's breast and impetuously returned to his lady bearing it upon a salver; but that, when stumbling in his gallant haste, he stooped to replace upon the silver plate his mother's heart which had rolled upon the ground, the heart, still beating with tender solicitude, whispered the hope that her child was not hurt.

The ballad itself was scarcely more exaggerated than the story of our visitor that evening, who had made the desperate effort of a journey from home in order to see the Devil Baby. I was familiar with her vicissitudes: the shiftless drinking husband and the large family of children, all of whom had brought her sorrow and disgrace; and I knew that her heart's desire was to see again before she died her youngest son, who was a life prisoner in the penitentiary. She was confident that the last piteous stage of her disease would secure him a week's parole, founding this forlorn hope upon the fact that 'they sometimes let them out to attend a mother's funeral, and perhaps they'd let Joe come a few days ahead; he could pay his fare afterwards from the insurance money. It wouldn't take much to bury me.'

Again we went over the hideous story. Joe had violently quarreled with a woman, the proprietor of the house in which his disreputable wife lived, because she withheld from him a part of his wife's 'earnings,' and in the altercation had killed her — a situation, one would say, which it would be difficult for even a mother to condone. But not at all: her thin gray face worked with emotion, her trembling hands restlessly pulled at her shabby skirt as the hands of the dying pluck at the sheets, but she put all the vitality she could muster into his defense. She told us he had legally married the girl who supported him, 'although Lily had been so long in that life that few men would have done it. Of course such a girl must have a protector or everybody would fleece her; poor Lily said to the day of her death that he was the kindest man she ever knew, and treated her the whitest; that she herself was to blame for the murder because she told on the old miser, and Joe was so hot-headed she might have known that he would draw a gun for her.' The gasping mother concluded, 'He was always that handsome and had such a way. One winter when I was scrubbing in an office-building, I'd never get home much before twelve o'clock; but Joe would open the door for me just as pleasant as if he had n't been waked out of a sound sleep.'

She was so triumphantly unconscious of the incongruity of a sturdy son in bed while his mother earned his food, that her auditors said never a word, and in silence we saw a hero evolved before our eyes: a defender of the oppressed, the best beloved of his mother, who was losing his high spirits and eating his heart out behind prison bars. He could well defy the world even there, surrounded as he was by that invincible affection which assures both the fortunate and unfortunate alike that we are loved, not according to our deserts, but in response to some profounder law.

This imposing revelation of maternal solicitude was an instance of what continually happened in connection with the Devil Baby. In the midst of the most tragic recitals there remained that something in the souls of these mothers which has been called the great revelation of tragedy, or sometimes the great illusion of tragedy — that which has power in its own right to make life acceptable and at rare moments even beautiful.

At least, during the weeks when the Devil Baby seemed to occupy every room in Hull-House, one was conscious that all human vicissitudes are in the end melted down into reminiscence, and that a metaphorical statement of those profound experiences which are implicit in human nature itself, however crude in form the story may be, has a singular power of healing the distracted spirit.

If it has always been the mission of literature to translate the particular act into something of the universal, to reduce the element of crude pain in the isolated experience by bringing to the sufferer a realization that his is but the common lot, this mission may have been performed through such stories as this for simple hard-working women, who, after all, at any given moment compose the bulk of the women in the world.

1919

T. S. Eliot

··

Tradition and the Individual Talent

IN ENGLISH WRITING we seldom speak of tradition, though we occasionally apply its name in deploring its absence. We cannot refer to "the tradition" or to "a tradition"; at most, we employ the adjective in saying that the poetry of So-and-so is "traditional" or even "too traditional." Seldom, perhaps, does the word appear except in a phrase of censure. If otherwise, it is vaguely approbative, with the implication, as to the work approved, of some pleasing archaeological reconstruction. You can hardly make the word agreeable to English ears without this comfortable reference to the reassuring science of archaeology.

Certainly the word is not likely to appear in our appreciations of living or dead writers. Every nation, every race, has not only its own creative, but its own critical turn of mind; and is even more oblivious of the shortcomings and limitations of its critical habits than of those of its creative genius. We know, or think we know, from the enormous mass of critical writing that has appeared in the French language the critical method or habit of the French; we only conclude (we are such unconscious people) that the French are "more critical" than we, and sometimes even plume ourselves a little with the fact, as if the French were the less spontaneous. Perhaps they are; but we might remind ourselves that criticism is as inevitable as breathing, and that we should be none the worse for articulating what passes in our minds when we read a book and feel an emotion about it, for criticizing our own minds in their work of criticism. One of the facts that might come to light in this process is our tendency to insist, when we praise a poet, upon those aspects of his work in which he least resembles any one else. In these as-

First published in *The Egoist*, 1919, and collected in *The Sacred Wood*, 1920.

pects or parts of his work we pretend to find what is individual, what is the peculiar essence of the man. We dwell with satisfaction upon the poet's difference from his predecessors, especially his immediate predecessors; we endeavour to find something that can be isolated in order to be enjoyed. Whereas if we approach a poet without this prejudice we shall often find that not only the best, but the most individual parts of his work may be those in which the dead poets, his ancestors, assert their immortality most vigorously. And I do not mean the impressionable period of adolescence, but the period of full maturity.

Yet if the only form of tradition, of handing down, consisted in following the ways of the immediate generation before us in a blind or timid adherence to its successes, "tradition" should positively be discouraged. We have seen many such simple currents soon lost in the sand; and novelty is better than repetition. Tradition is a matter of much wider significance. It cannot be inherited, and if you want it you must obtain it by great labour. It involves, in the first place, the historical sense, which we may call nearly indispensable to any one who would continue to be a poet beyond his twenty-fifth year; and the historical sense involves a perception, not only of the pastness of the past, but of its presence; the historical sense compels a man to write not merely with his own generation in his bones, but with a feeling that the whole of the literature of Europe from Homer and within it the whole of the literature of his own country has a simultaneous existence and composes a simultaneous order. This historical sense, which is a sense of the timeless as well as of the temporal and of the timeless and of the temporal together, is what makes a writer traditional. And it is at the same time what makes a writer most acutely conscious of his place in time, of his own contemporaneity.

No poet, no artist of any art, has his complete meaning alone. His significance, his appreciation is the appreciation of his relation to the dead poets and artists. You cannot value him alone; you must set him, for contrast and comparison, among the dead. I mean this as a principle of aesthetic, not merely historical, criticism. The necessity that he shall conform, that he shall cohere, is not onesided; what happens when a new work of art is created is something that happens simultaneously to all the works of art which preceded it. The existing monuments form an ideal order among themselves, which is modified by the introduction of the new (the really new) work of art among them. The existing order is complete before the new work arrives; for order to persist after the supervention of novelty, the *whole* existing order must be, if ever so slightly, altered; and so the relations, proportions, values of each work of art toward the whole are readjusted; and this is conformity between the old and the new. Whoever has approved this idea of order, of the form of European, of English literature will not find it preposterous that the past should be altered by the present as much as the present is directed by the past. And the poet who is aware of this will be aware of great difficulties and responsibilities.

In a peculiar sense he will be aware also that he must inevitably be judged by the standards of the past. I say judged, not amputated, by them; not judged to be as good as, or worse or better than, the dead; and certainly not judged by the canons of dead critics. It is a judgment, a comparison, in which two things are measured by each other. To conform merely would be for the new work not really to conform at all; it would not be new, and would therefore not be a work of art. And we do not quite say that the new is more valuable because it fits in; but its fitting in is a test of its value — a test, it is true, which can only be slowly and cautiously applied, for we are none of us infallible judges of conformity. We say: it appears to conform, and is perhaps individual, or it appears individual, and may conform; but we are hardly likely to find that it is one and not the other.

To proceed to a more intelligible exposition of the relation of the poet to the past: he can neither take the past as a lump, an indiscriminate bolus, nor can he form himself wholly on one or two private admirations, nor can he form himself wholly upon one preferred period. The first course is inadmissible, the second is an important experience of youth, and the third is a pleasant and highly desirable supplement. The poet must be very conscious of the main current, which does not at all flow invariably through the most distinguished reputations. He must be quite aware of the obvious fact that art never improves, but that the material of art is never quite the same. He must be aware that the mind of Europe — the mind of his own country — a mind which he learns in time to be much more important than his own private mind — is a mind which changes, and that this change is a development which abandons nothing en route, which does not superannuate either Shakespeare, or Homer, or the rock drawing of the Magdalenian draughtsmen. That this development, refinement perhaps, complication certainly, is not, from the point of view of the artist, any improvement. Perhaps not even an improvement from the point of view of the psychologist or not to the extent which we imagine; perhaps only in the end based upon a complication in economics and machinery. But the difference between the present and the past is that the conscious present is an awareness of the past in a way and to an extent which the past's awareness of itself cannot show.

Some one said: "The dead writers are remote from us because we *know* so much more than they did." Precisely, and they are that which we know.

I am alive to a usual objection to what is clearly part of my programme for the *métier* of poetry. The objection is that the doctrine requires a ridiculous amount of erudition (pedantry), a claim which can be rejected by appeal to the lives of poets in any pantheon. It will even be affirmed that much learning deadens or perverts poetic sensibility. While, however, we persist in believing that a poet ought to know as much as will not encroach upon his necessary receptivity and necessary laziness, it is not desirable to confine knowledge to whatever can be put into a useful shape for examinations, drawing-rooms, or the still more pretentious modes of publicity. Some can absorb knowledge, the more tardy must sweat for it. Shakespeare acquired more essential history from Plutarch than most men could from the whole British Museum. What is to be insisted upon is that the poet must develop or procure the consciousness of the past and that he should continue to develop this consciousness throughout his career.

What happens is a continual surrender of himself as he is at the moment to something which is more valuable. The progress of an artist is a continual self-sacrifice, a continual extinction of personality.

There remains to define this process of depersonalization and its relation to the sense of tradition. It is in this depersonalization that art may be said to approach the condition of science. I, therefore, invite you to consider, as a suggestive analogy, the action which takes place when a bit of finely filiated platinum is introduced into a chamber containing oxygen and sulphur dioxide.

II

Honest criticism and sensitive appreciation are directed not upon the poet but upon the poetry. If we attend to the confused cries of the newspaper critics and the *susurrus* of popular repetition that follows, we shall hear the names of poets in great numbers; if we seek not Blue-book knowledge but the enjoyment of poetry, and ask for a poem, we shall seldom find it. I have tried to point out the importance of the relation of the poem to other poems by other authors, and suggested the conception of poetry as a living whole of all the poetry that has ever been written. The other aspect of this Impersonal theory of poetry is the relation of the poem to its author. And I hinted, by an analogy, that the mind of the mature poet differs from that of the immature one not precisely in any valuation of "personality," not being necessarily more interesting, or having "more to say," but rather by being a more finely perfected medium in which special, or very varied, feelings are at liberty to enter into new combinations.

The analogy was that of the catalyst. When the two gases previously mentioned are mixed in the presence of a filament of platinum, they form sulphurous acid. This combination takes place only if the platinum is present; nevertheless the newly formed acid contains no trace of platinum, and the platinum itself is apparently unaffected; has remained inert, neutral, and unchanged. The mind of the poet is the shred of platinum. It may partly or exclusively operate upon the experience of the man himself; but, the more perfect the artist, the more completely separate in him will be the man who suffers and the mind which creates; the more perfectly will the mind digest and transmute the passions which are its material.

The experience, you will notice, the elements which enter the presence of the transforming catalyst, are of two kinds: emotions and feelings. The effect of a work of art upon the person who enjoys it is an experience different in kind from any experience not of art. It may be formed out of one emotion, or may be a combination of several; and various feelings, inhering for the writer in particular words or phrases or images, may be added to compose the final result. Or great poetry may be made without the direct use of any emotion whatever: composed out of feelings solely. Canto XV of the *Inferno* (Brunetto Latini) is a working up of the emotion evident in the situation; but the effect, though single as that of any work of art, is obtained by considerable complexity of detail. The last quatrain gives an image, a feeling attaching to an image, which "came," which did not develop simply out of what precedes, but which was probably in suspension in the poet's mind until the proper combination arrived for it to add itself to. The poet's mind is in fact a receptacle for seizing and storing up numberless feelings, phrases, images, which remain there until all the particles which can unite to form a new compound are present together.

If you compare several representative passages of the greatest poetry you see how great is the variety of types of combination, and also how completely any semi-ethical criterion of "sublimity" misses the mark.

For it is not the "greatness," the intensity, of the emotions, the components, but the intensity of the artistic process, the pressure, so to speak, under which the fusion takes place, that counts. The episode of Paolo and Francesca employs a definite emotion, but the intensity of the poetry is something quite different from whatever intensity in the supposed experience it may give the impression of. It is no more intense, furthermore, than Canto XXVI, the voyage of Ulysses, which has not the direct dependence upon an emotion. Great variety is possible in the process of transmutation of emotion: the murder of Agamemnon, or the agony of Othello, gives an artistic effect apparently closer to a possible original than the scenes from Dante.

In the *Agamemnon*, the artistic emotion approximates to the emotion of an actual spectator; in *Othello* to the emotion of the protagonist himself. But the difference between art and the event is always absolute; the combination which is the murder of Agamemnon is probably as complex as that which is the voyage of Ulysses. In either case there has been a fusion of elements. The ode of Keats contains a number of feelings which have nothing particular to do with the nightingale, but which the nightingale, partly, perhaps, because of its attractive name, and partly because of its reputation, served to bring together.

The point of view which I am struggling to attack is perhaps related to the metaphysical theory of the substantial unity of the soul: for my meaning is, that the poet has, not a "personality" to express, but a particular medium, which is only a medium and not a personality, in which impressions and experiences combine in peculiar and unexpected ways. Impressions and experiences which are important for the man may take no place in the poetry, and those which become important in the poetry may play quite a negligible part in the man, the personality.

I will quote a passage which is unfamiliar enough to be regarded with fresh attention in the light — or darkness — of these observations:

> And now methinks I could e'en chide myself
> For doating on her beauty, though her death
> Shall be revenged after no common action.
> Does the silkworm expend her yellow labours
> For thee? For thee does she undo herself?
> Are lordships sold to maintain ladyships
> For the poor benefit of a bewildering minute?
> Why does yon fellow falsify highways,
> And put his life between the judge's lips,

To refine such a thing — keeps horse and men
To beat their valours for her? . . .
[Cyril Tourneur, *The Revenger's Tragedy*]

In this passage (as is evident if it is taken in its context) there is a combination of positive and negative emotions: an intensely strong attraction
toward beauty and an equally intense fascination by the ugliness which
is contrasted with it and which destroys it. This balance of contrasted
emotion is in the dramatic situation to which the speech is pertinent,
but that situation alone is inadequate to it. This is, so to speak, the
structural emotion, provided by the drama. But the whole effect, the
dominant tone, is due to the fact that a number of floating feelings,
having an affinity to this emotion by no means superficially evident,
have combined with it to give us a new art emotion.

It is not in his personal emotions, the emotions provoked by particular events in his life, that the poet is in any way remarkable or interesting. His particular emotions may be simple, or crude, or flat. The
emotion in his poetry will be a very complex thing, but not with the
complexity of the emotions of people who have very complex or unusual emotions in life. One error, in fact, of eccentricity in poetry is to
seek for new human emotions to express; and in this search for novelty
in the wrong place it discovers the perverse. The business of the poet is
not to find new emotions, but to use the ordinary ones and, in working
them up into poetry, to express feelings which are not in actual emotions at all. And emotions which he has never experienced will serve his
turn as well as those familiar to him. Consequently, we must believe
that "emotion recollected," in tranquillity" is an inexact formula. For it
is neither emotion, nor recollection, nor, without distortion of meaning, tranquillity. It is a concentration, and a new thing resulting from
the concentration, of a very great number of experiences which to the
practical and active person would not seem to be experiences at all; it is
a concentration which does not happen consciously or of deliberation.
These experiences are not "recollected," and they finally unite in an atmosphere which is "tranquil" only in that it is a passive attending upon
the event. Of course this is not quite the whole story. There is a great
deal, in the writing of poetry, which must be conscious and deliberate.
In fact, the bad poet is usually unconscious where he ought to be conscious, and conscious where he ought to be unconscious. Both errors
tend to make him "personal." Poetry is not a turning loose of emotion,
but an escape from emotion; it is not the expression of personality, but

an escape from personality. But, of course, only those who have personality and emotions know what it means to want to escape from these things.

III

ὁ δέ νοῦς ἴσως θειότερόν τι καὶ ἀπαθές ἐστιν.

["The mind is, no doubt, something more divine and therefore unaffected." — Aristotle]

This essay proposes to halt at the frontier of metaphysics or mysticism, and confine itself to such practical conclusions as can be applied by the responsible person interested in poetry. To divert interest from the poet to the poetry is a laudable aim: for it would conduce to a juster estimation of actual poetry, good and bad. There are many people who appreciate the expression of sincere emotion in verse, and there is a smaller number of people who can appreciate technical excellence. But very few know when there is an expression of *significant* emotion, emotion which has its life in the poem and not in the history of the poet. The emotion of art is impersonal. And the poet cannot reach this impersonality without surrendering himself wholly to the work to be done. And he is not likely to know what is to be done unless he lives in what is not merely the present, but the present moment of the past, unless he is conscious, not of what is dead, but of what is already living.

1923

Ernest Hemingway

Pamplona in July

IN PAMPLONA, a white-walled, sun-baked town high up in the hills of Navarre, is held in the first two weeks of July each year the World's Series of bull fighting.

Bull fight fans from all Spain jam into the little town. Hotels double their prices and fill every room. The cafes under the wide arcades that run around the Plaza de la Constitucion have every table crowded, the tall Pilgrim Father sombreros of Andalusia sitting over the same table with straw hats from Madrid and the flat blue Basque caps of Navarre and the Basque country.

Really beautiful girls, gorgeous, bright shawls over their shoulders, dark, dark-eyed, black-lace mantillas over their hair, walk with their escorts in the crowds that pass from morning until night along the narrow walk that runs between inner and outer belts of cafe tables under the shade of the arcade out of the white glare of the Plaza de la Constitucion. All day and all night there is dancing in the streets. Bands of blue-shirted peasants whirl and lift and swing behind a drum, fife and reed instruments in the ancient Basque Riau-Riau dances. And at night there is the throb of the big drums and the military band as the whole town dances in the great open square of the Plaza.

We landed at Pamplona at night. The streets were solid with people dancing. Music was pounding and throbbing. Fireworks were being set off from the big public square. All the carnivals I had ever seen paled down in comparison. A rocket exploded over our heads with a blinding

First published as "World's Series of Bull Fighting a Mad, Whirling Carnival" in the *Toronto Star Weekly,* 1923; collected in *By-Line: Ernest Hemingway,* edited by William White, 1967.

burst and the stick came swirling and whishing down. Dancers, snapping their fingers and whirling in perfect time through the crowd, bumped into us before we could get our bags down from the top of the station bus. Finally I got the bags through the crowd to the hotel.

We had wired and written for rooms two weeks ahead. Nothing had been saved. We were offered a single room with a single bed opening on to the kitchen ventilator shaft for seven dollars a day apiece. There was a big row with the landlady, who stood in front of her desk with her hands on her hips, and her broad Indian face perfectly placid, and told us in a few words of French and much Basque Spanish that she had to make all her money for the whole year in the next ten days. That people would come and that people would have to pay what she asked. She could show us a better room for ten dollars apiece. We said it would be preferable to sleep in the streets with the pigs. The landlady agreed that might be possible. We said we preferred it to such a hotel. All perfectly amicable. The landlady considered. We stood our ground. Mrs. Hemingway sat down on our rucksacks.

"I can get you a room in a house in the town. You can eat here," said the landlady.

"How much?"

"Five dollars."

We started off through the dark, narrow, carnival-mad streets with a boy carrying our rucksacks. It was a lovely big room in an old Spanish house with walls thick as a fortress. A cool, pleasant room, with a red tile floor and two big, comfortable beds set back in an alcove. A window opened on to an iron grilled porch out over the street. We were very comfortable.

All night long the wild music kept up in the street below. Several times in the night there was a wild roll of drumming, and I got out of bed and across the tiled floor to the balcony. But it was always the same. Men, blue-shirted, bareheaded, whirling and floating in a wild fantastic dance down the street behind the rolling drums and shrill fifes.

Just at daylight there was a crash of music in the street below. Real military music. Herself was up, dressed, at the window.

"Come on," she said. "They're all going somewhere." Down below the street was full of people. It was five o'clock in the morning. They were all going in one direction. I dressed in a hurry and we started after them.

The crowd was all going toward the great public square. People were pouring into it from every street and moving out of it toward the open country we could see through the narrow gaps in the high walls.

"Let's get some coffee," said Herself.

"Do you think we've got time? Hey, what's going to happen?" I asked a newsboy.

"Encierro," he said scornfully. "The encierro commences at six o'clock."

"What's the encierro?" I asked him.

"Oh, ask me to-morrow," he said, and started to run. The entire crowd was running now.

"I've got to have my coffee. No matter what it is," Herself said.

The waiter poured two streams of coffee and milk into the glass out of his big kettles. The crowd was still running, coming from all the streets that fed into the Plaza.

"What is this encierro anyway?" Herself asked, gulping the coffee.

"All I know is that they let the bulls out into the streets."

We started out after the crowd. Out of a narrow gate into a great yellow open space of country with the new concrete bull ring standing high and white and black with people. The yellow and red Spanish flag blowing in the early morning breeze. Across the open and once inside the bull ring, we mounted to the top looking toward the town. It cost a peseta to go up to the top. All the other levels were free. There were easily twenty thousand people there. Everyone jammed on the outside of the big concrete amphitheatre, looking toward the yellow town with the bright red roofs, where a long wooden pen ran from the entrance of the city gate across the open, bare ground to the bull ring.

It was really a double wooden fence, making a long entryway from the main street of the town into the bull ring itself. It made a runway about two hundred and fifty yards long. People were jammed solid on each side of it. Looking up it toward the main street.

Then far away there was a dull report.

"They're off," everybody shouted.

"What is it?" I asked a man next to me who was leaning far out over the concrete rail.

"The bulls! They have released them from the corrals on the far side of the city. They are racing through the city."

"Whew," said Herself. "What do they do that for?"

Then down the narrow fenced-in runway came a crowd of men and boys running. Running as hard as they could go. The gate feeding into the bull ring was opened and they all ran pell-mell under the entrance levels into the ring. Then there came another crowd. Running even harder. Straight up the long pen from the town.

"Where are the bulls?" asked Herself.

Then they came in sight. Eight bulls galloping along, full tilt, heavy set, black, glistening, sinister, their horns bare, tossing their heads. And running with them three steers with bells on their necks. They ran in a solid mass, and ahead of them sprinted, tore, ran and bolted the rear guard of the men and boys of Pamplona who had allowed themselves to be chased through the streets for a morning's pleasure.

A boy in his blue shirt, red sash, white canvas shoes with the inevitable leather wine bottle hung from his shoulders, stumbled as he sprinted down the straightaway. The first bull lowered his head and made a jerky, sideways toss. The boy crashed up against the fence and lay there limp, the herd running solidly together passed him up. The crowd roared.

Everybody made a dash for the inside of the ring, and we got into a box just in time to see the bulls come into the ring filled with men. The men ran in a panic to each side. The bulls, still bunched solidly together, ran straight with the trained steers across the ring and into the entrance that led to the pens.

That was the entry. Every morning during the bull fighting festival of San Fermin at Pamplona the bulls that are to fight in the afternoon are released from their corrals at six o'clock in the morning and race through the main street of the town for a mile and a half to the pen. The men who run ahead of them do it for the fun of the thing. It has been going on each year since a couple of hundred years before Columbus had his historic interview with Queen Isabella in the camp outside of Granada.

There are two things in favor of there being no accidents. First, that fighting bulls are not aroused and vicious when they are together. Second, that the steers are relied upon to keep them moving.

Sometimes things go wrong, a bull will be detached from the herd as they pile through into the pen and with his crest up, a ton of speed and viciousness, his needle-sharp horns lowered, will charge again and again into the packed mass of men and boys in the bull ring. There is no place for the men to get out of the ring. It is too jammed for them to climb over the barrera or red fence that rims the field. They have to stay in and take it. Eventually the steers get the bull out of the ring and into the pen. He may wound or kill thirty men before they can get him out. No armed men are allowed to oppose him. That is the chance the Pamplona bull fight fans take every morning during the Feria. It is the Pamplona tradition of giving the bulls a final shot at everyone in town before they enter the pens. They will not leave until they come out into the glare of the arena to die in the afternoon.

Consequently Pamplona is the toughest bull fight town in the world. The amateur fight that comes immediately after the bulls have entered the pens proves that. Every seat in the great amphitheatre is packed. About three hundred men, with capes, odd pieces of cloth, old shirts, anything that will imitate a bull fighter's cape, are singing and dancing in the arena. There is a shout, and the bull pen opens. Out comes a young bull just as fast as he can come. On his horns are leather knobs to prevent his goring anyone. He charges and hits a man. Tosses him high in the air, and the crowd roars. The man comes down on the ground, and the bull goes for him, bumping him with his head. Worrying him with his horns. Several amateur bull fighters are flopping their capes in his face to make the bull charge and leave the man on the ground. Then the bull charges and bags another man. The crowd roars with delight.

Then the bull will turn like a cat and get somebody who has been acting very brave about ten feet behind him. Then he will toss a man over the fence. Then he picks out one man and follows him in a wild twisting charge through the entire crowd until he bags him. The barrera is packed with men and boys sitting along the top, and the bull decides to clear them all off. He goes along, hooking carefully with his horn and dropping them off with a toss of his horns like a man pitching hay.

Each time the bull bags someone the crowd roars with joy. Most of it is home talent stuff. The braver the man has been or the more elegant pass he has attempted with his cape before the bull gets him the more the crowd roars. No one is armed. No one hurts or plagues the bull in any way. A man who grabbed the bull by the tail and tried to hang on was hissed and booed by the crowd and the next time he tried it was knocked down by another man in the bull ring. No one enjoys it all more than the bull.

As soon as he shows signs of tiring from his charges, the two old steers, one brown and the other looking like a big Holstein, come trotting in and alongside the young bull who falls in behind them like a dog and follows them meekly on a tour of the arena and then out.

*

Another comes right in, and the charging and tossing, the ineffectual cape waving, and wonderful music are repeated right over again. But always different. Some of the animals in this morning amateur fight are steers. Fighting bulls from the best strain who had some imperfection or other in build so they could never command the high prices paid for combat animals, $2,000 to $3,000 apiece. But there is nothing lacking in their fighting spirit.

The show comes off every morning. Everybody in town turns out at five-thirty when the military bands go through the streets. Many of them stay up all night for it. We didn't miss one, and it is quelque sporting event that will get us both up at five-thirty o'clock in the morning for six days running.

As far as I know we were the only English-speaking people in Pamplona during the Feria of last year.

There were three minor earthquakes while we were there. Terrific cloud bursts in the mountains and the Ebro River flooded out Zaragossa. For two days the bull ring was under water and the Corrida had to be suspended for the first time in over a hundred years. That was during the middle of the fair. Everyone was desperate. On the third day it looked gloomier than ever, poured rain all morning, and then at noon the clouds rolled away up across the valley, the sun came out bright and hot and baking and that afternoon there was the greatest bull fight I will perhaps ever see.

There were rockets going up into the air and the arena was nearly full when we got into our regular seats. The sun was hot and baking. Over on the other side we could see the bull fighters standing ready to come in. All wearing their oldest clothes because of the heavy, muddy going in the arena. We picked out the three matadors of the afternoon with our glasses. Only one of them was new. Olmos, a chubby faced, jolly looking man, something like Tris Speaker. The others we had seen often before. Maera, dark, spare and deadly looking, one of the very greatest toreros of all time. The third, young Algabeno, the son of a famous bull fighter, a slim young Andalusian with a charming Indian looking face. All were wearing the suits they had probably started bull fighting with, too tight, old fashioned, outmoded.

There was the procession of entrance, the wild bull fight music played, the preliminaries were quickly over, the picadors retired along the red fence with their horses, the heralds sounded their trumpets and the door of the bull pen swung open. The bull came out in a rush, saw a man standing near the barrera and charged him. The man vaulted over the fence and the bull charged the barrera. He crashed into the fence in full charge and ripped a two by eight plank solidly out in a splintering smash. He broke his horn doing it and the crowd called for a new bull. The trained steers trotted in, the bull fell in meekly behind them, and the three of them trotted out of the arena.

The next bull came in with the same rush. He was Maera's bull and after perfect cape play Maera planted the banderillos. Maera is Herself's favorite bull fighter. And if you want to keep any conception of yourself as a brave, hard, perfectly balanced, thoroughly competent man in your wife's mind never take her to a real bull fight. I used to go into the amateur fights in the morning to try and win back a small amount of her esteem but the more I discovered that bull fighting required a very great quantity of a certain type of courage of which I had an almost complete lack the more it became apparent that any admiration she might ever redevelop for me would have to be simply an antidote to the real admiration for Maera and Villalta. You cannot compete with bull fighters on their own ground. If anywhere. The only way most husbands are able to keep any drag with their wives at all is that, first there are only a limited number of bull fighters, second there are only a limited number of wives who have ever seen bull fights.

Maera planted his first pair of banderillos sitting down on the edge of the little step-up that runs around the barrera. He snarled at the bull and as the animal charged leaned back tight against the fence and as the horns struck on either side of him, swung forward over the brute's head and planted the two darts in his hump. He planted the next pair the same way, so near to us we could have leaned over and touched him. Then he went out to kill the bull and after he had made absolutely unbelievable passes with the little red cloth of the muleta drew up his sword and as the bull charged Maera thrust. The sword shot out of his hand and the bull caught him. He went up in the air on the horns of the bull and then came down. Young Algabeno flopped his cape in the bull's face. The bull charged him and Maera staggered to his feet. But his wrist was sprained.

With his wrist sprained, so that every time he raised it to sight for a thrust it brought beads of sweat out on his face, Maera tried again and again to make his death thrust. He lost his sword again and again, picked it up with his left hand from the mud floor of the arena and transferred it to the right for the thrust. Finally he made it and the bull went over. The bull nearly got him twenty times. As he came in to stand up under us at the barrera side his wrist was swollen to twice normal size. I thought of prize fighters I had seen quit because they had hurt their hands.

There was almost no pause while the mules galloped in and hitched on to the first bull and dragged him out and the second came in with a rush. The picadors took the first shock of him with their bull lances. There was the snort and charge, the shock and the mass against the sky, the wonderful defense by the picador with his lance that held off the bull, and then Rosario Olmos stepped out with his cape.

Once he flopped the cape at the bull and floated it around in an easy graceful swing. Then he tried the same swing, the classic "Veronica," and the bull caught him at the end of it. Instead of stopping at the finish the bull charged on in. He caught Olmos squarely with his horn, hoisted him high in the air. He fell heavily and the bull was on top of him, driving his horns again and again into him. Olmos lay on the sand, his head on his arms. One of his teammates was flopping his cape madly in the bull's face. The bull lifted his head for an instant and charged and got his man. Just one terrific toss. Then he whirled and chased a man just in back of him toward the barrera. The man was running full tilt and as he put his hand on the fence to vault it the bull had him and caught him with his horn, shooting him way up into the crowd. He rushed toward the fallen man he had tossed who was getting to his feet and all alone — Algabeno grabbed him by the tail. He hung on until I thought he or the bull would break. The wounded man got to his feet and started away.

The bull turned like a cat and charged Algabeno and Algabeno met him with the cape. Once, twice, three times he made the perfect, floating, slow swing with the cape, perfectly, graceful, debonair, back on his heels, baffling the bull. And he had command of the situation. There never was such a scene at any world's series game.

There are no substitute matadors allowed. Maera was finished. His wrist could not lift a sword for weeks. Olmos had been gored badly through the body. It was Algabeno's bull. This one and the next five.

He handled them all. Did it all. Cape play easy, graceful, confident. Beautiful work with the muleta. And serious, deadly killing. Five bulls he killed, one after the other, and each one was a separate problem to be worked out with death. At the end there was nothing debonair about him. It was only a question if he would last through or if the bulls would get him. They were all very wonderful bulls.

"He is a very great kid," said Herself. "He is only twenty."

"I wish we knew him," I said.

"Maybe we will some day," she said. Then considered a moment. "He will probably be spoiled by then."

They make twenty thousand a year.

That was just three months ago. It seems in a different century now, working in an office. It is a very long way from the sun baked town of Pamplona, where the men race through the streets in the mornings ahead of the bulls to the morning ride to work on a Bay-Caledonia car. But it is only fourteen days by water to Spain and there is no need for a castle. There is always that room at 5 Calle de Eslava, and a son, if he is to redeem the family reputation as a bull fighter, must start very early.

1925

H. L. Mencken

The Hills of Zion

IT WAS HOT WEATHER when they tried the infidel Scopes at Dayton, Tenn., but I went down there very willingly, for I was eager to see something of evangelical Christianity as a going concern. In the big cities of the Republic, despite the endless efforts of consecrated men, it is laid up with a wasting disease. The very Sunday-school superintendents, taking jazz from the stealthy radio, shake their fire-proof legs; their pupils, moving into adolescence, no longer respond to the proliferating hormones by enlisting for missionary service in Africa, but resort to necking instead. Even in Dayton, I found, though the mob was up to do execution upon Scopes, there was a strong smell of antinomianism. The nine churches of the village were all half empty on Sunday, and weeds choked their yards. Only two or three of the resident pastors managed to sustain themselves by their ghostly science; the rest had to take orders for mail-order pantaloons or work in the adjacent strawberry fields; one, I heard, was a barber. On the courthouse green a score of sweating theologians debated the darker passages of Holy Writ day and night, but I soon found that they were all volunteers, and that the local faithful, while interested in their exegesis as an intellectual exercise, did not permit it to impede the indigenous debaucheries. Exactly twelve minutes after I reached the village I was taken in tow by a Christian man and introduced to the favorite tipple of the Cumberland Range: half corn liquor and half Coca-Cola. It seemed a dreadful dose to me, but I

First published as a dispatch to the *Baltimore Evening Sun* in July 1925. Mencken noted he "wrote it on a roaring hot Sunday afternoon in a Chattanooga hotel room, naked above the waist and with only a pair of BVDs below." Collected in *Prejudices: Fifth Series*, 1926.

found that the Dayton illuminati got it down with gusto, rubbing their
tummies and rolling their eyes. I include among them the chief local
proponents of the Mosaic cosmogony. They were all hot for Genesis,
but their faces were far too florid to belong to teetotalers, and when a
pretty girl came tripping down the main street, which was very often,
they reached for the places where their neckties should have been with
all the amorous enterprise of movie actors. It seemed somehow strange.

An amiable newspaper woman of Chattanooga, familiar with those
uplands, presently enlightened me. Dayton, she explained, was simply a
great capital like any other. That is to say, it was to Rhea county what
Atlanta was to Georgia or Paris to France. That is to say, it was predomi-
nantly epicurean and sinful. A country girl from some remote valley of
the county, coming into town for her semi-annual bottle of Lydia
Pinkham's Vegetable Compound, shivered on approaching Robinson's
drug-store quite as a country girl from up-State New York might shiver
on approaching the Metropolitan Opera House. In every village lout
she saw a potential white-slaver. The hard sidewalks hurt her feet.
Temptations of the flesh bristled to all sides of her, luring her to Hell.
This newspaper woman told me of a session with just such a visitor,
holden a few days before. The latter waited outside one of the town hot-
dog and Coca-Cola shops while her husband negotiated with a hardware merchant across the street. The newspaper woman, idling along
and observing that the stranger was badly used by the heat, invited her
to step into the shop for a glass of Coca-Cola. The invitation brought
forth only a gurgle of terror. Coca-Cola, it quickly appeared, was prohibited by the country lady's pastor, as a levantine and Hell-sent narcotic. He also prohibited coffee and tea — and pies! He had his doubts
about white bread and boughten meat. The newspaper woman, interested, inquired about ice-cream. It was, she found, not specifically prohibited, but going into a Coca-Cola shop to get it would be clearly sinful. So she offered to get a saucer of it, and bring it out to the sidewalk.
The visitor vacillated — and came near being lost. But God saved her in
the nick of time. When the newspaper woman emerged from the place
she was in full flight up the street. Later on her husband, mounted on a
mule, overtook her four miles out the mountain pike.

This newspaper woman, whose kindness covered city infidels as well
as Alpine Christians, offered to take me back in the hills to a place
where the old-time religion was genuinely on tap. The Scopes jury, she
explained, was composed mainly of its customers, with a few Dayton
sophisticates added to leaven the mass. It would thus be instructive to

climb the heights and observe the former at their ceremonies. The trip, fortunately, might be made by automobile. There was a road running out of Dayton to Morgantown, in the mountains to the westward, and thence beyond. But foreigners, it appeared, would have to approach the sacred grove cautiously, for the upland worshipers were very shy, and at the first sight of a strange face they would adjourn their orgy and slink into the forest. They were not to be feared, for God had long since forbidden them to practise assassination, or even assault, but if they were alarmed a rough trip would go for naught. So, after dreadful bumpings up a long and narrow road, we parked our car in a little woodpath a mile or two beyond the tiny village of Morgantown, and made the rest of the approach on foot, deployed like skirmishers. Far off in a dark, romantic glade a flickering light was visible, and out of the silence came the rumble of exhortation. We could distinguish the figure of the preacher only as a moving mote in the light: it was like looking down the tube of a dark-field microscope. Slowly and cautiously we crossed what seemed to be a pasture, and then we stealthily edged further and further. The light now grew larger and we could begin to make out what was going on. We went ahead on all fours, like snakes in the grass.

From the great limb of a mighty oak hung a couple of crude torches of the sort that car inspectors thrust under Pullman cars when a train pulls in at night. In the guttering glare was the preacher, and for a while we could see no one else. He was an immensely tall and thin mountaineer in blue jeans, his collarless shirt open at the neck and his hair a tousled mop. As he preached he paced up and down under the smoking flambeaux, and at each turn he thrust his arms into the air and yelled "Glory to God!" We crept nearer in the shadow of the cornfield, and began to hear more of his discourse. He was preaching on the Day of Judgment. The high kings of the earth, he roared, would all fall down and die; only the sanctified would stand up to receive the Lord God of Hosts. One of these kings he mentioned by name, the king of what he called Greece-y. The king of Greece-y, he said, was doomed to Hell. We crawled forward a few more yards and began to see the audience. It was seated on benches ranged round the preacher in a circle. Behind him sat a row of elders, men and women. In front were the younger folk. We crept on cautiously, and individuals rose out of the ghostly gloom. A young mother sat suckling her baby, rocking as the preacher paced up and down. Two scared little girls hugged each other, their pigtails down their backs. An immensely huge mountain woman, in a gingham dress, cut in one piece, rolled on her heels at every "Glory to God!" To one

side, and but half visible, was what appeared to be a bed. We found afterward that half a dozen babies were asleep upon it.

The preacher stopped at last, and there arose out of the darkness a
woman with her hair pulled back into a little tight knot. She began so
quietly that we couldn't hear what she said, but soon her voice rose res-
onantly and we could follow her. She was denouncing the reading of
books. Some wandering book agent, it appeared, had come to her cabin
and tried to sell her a specimen of his wares. She refused to touch it.
Why, indeed, read a book? If what was in it was true, then everything
in it was already in the Bible. If it was false, then reading it would im-
peril the soul. This syllogism from the Caliph Omar complete, she sat
down. There followed a hymn, led by a somewhat fat brother wearing
silver-rimmed country spectacles. It droned on for half a dozen stan-
zas, and then the first speaker resumed the floor. He argued that the gift
of tongues was real and that education was a snare. Once his children could read the Bible, he said, they had enough. Beyond lay only
infidelity and damnation. Sin stalked the cities. Dayton itself was a
Sodom. Even Morgantown had begun to forget God. He sat down, and
a female aurochs in gingham got up. She began quietly, but was soon
leaping and roaring, and it was hard to follow her. Under cover of the
turmoil we sneaked a bit closer.

A couple of other discourses followed, and there were two or three
hymns. Suddenly a change of mood began to make itself felt. The last
hymn ran longer than the others, and dropped gradually into a monot-
onous, unintelligible chant. The leader beat time with his book. The
faithful broke out with exultations. When the singing ended there was a
brief palaver that we could not hear, and two of the men moved a bench
into the circle of light directly under the flambeaux. Then a half-grown
girl emerged from the darkness and threw herself upon it. We noticed
with astonishment that she had bobbed hair. "This sister," said the
leader, "has asked for prayers." We moved a bit closer. We could now see
faces plainly, and hear every word. At a signal all the faithful crowded
up to the bench and began to pray — not in unison, but each for himself. At another they all fell on their knees, their arms over the penitent.
The leader kneeled facing us, his head alternately thrown back dramatically or buried in his hands. Words spouted from his lips like bullets
from a machine-gun — appeals to God to pull the penitent back out of
Hell, defiances of the demons of the air, a vast impassioned jargon of
apocalyptic texts. Suddenly he rose to his feet, threw back his head and

began to speak in the tongues — blub-blub-blub, gurgle-gurgle-gurgle. His voice rose to a higher register. The climax was a shrill, inarticulate squawk, like that of a man throttled. He fell headlong across the pyramid of supplicants.

From the squirming and jabbering mass a young woman gradually detached herself — a woman not uncomely, with a pathetic homemade cap on her head. Her head jerked back, the veins of her neck swelled, and her fists went to her throat as if she were fighting for breath. She bent backward until she was like half a hoop. Then she suddenly snapped forward. We caught a flash of the whites of her eyes. Presently her whole body began to be convulsed — great throes that began at the shoulders and ended at the hips. She would leap to her feet, thrust her arms in air, and then hurl herself upon the heap. Her praying flattened out into a mere delirious caterwauling. I describe the thing discreetly, and as a strict behaviorist. The lady's subjective sensations I leave to infidel pathologists, privy to the works of Ellis, Freud and Moll. Whatever they were, they were obviously not painful, for they were accompanied by vast heavings and gurglings of a joyful and even ecstatic nature. And they seemed to be contagious, too, for soon a second penitent, also female, joined the first, and then came a third, and a fourth, and a fifth. The last one had an extraordinary violent attack. She began with mild enough jerks of the head, but in a moment she was bounding all over the place, like a chicken with its head cut off. Every time her head came up a stream of hosannas would issue out of it. Once she collided with a dark, undersized brother, hitherto silent and stolid. Contact with her set him off as if he had been kicked by a mule. He leaped into the air, threw back his head, and began to gargle as if with a mouthful of BB shot. Then he loosed one tremendous, stentorian sentence in the tongues, and collapsed.

By this time the performers were quite oblivious to the profane universe and so it was safe to go still closer. We left our hiding and came up to the little circle of light. We slipped into the vacant seats on one of the rickety benches. The heap of mourners was directly before us. They bounced into us as they cavorted. The smell that they radiated, sweating there in that obscene heap, half suffocated us. Not all of them, of course, did the thing in the grand manner. Some merely moaned and rolled their eyes. The female ox in gingham flung her great bulk on the ground and jabbered an unintelligible prayer. One of the men, in the intervals between fits, put on his spectacles and read his Bible. Beside me on the bench sat the young mother and her baby. She suckled it through the whole orgy, obviously fascinated by what was going on, but never venturing to take any hand in it. On the bed just outside the light the half a dozen other babies slept peacefully. In the shadows, suddenly appearing and as suddenly going away, were vague figures, whether of believers or of scoffers I do not know. They seemed to come and go in couples. Now and then a couple at the ringside would step out and vanish into the black night. After a while some came back, the males looking somewhat sheepish. There was whispering outside the circle of vision. A couple of Model T Fords lurched up the road, cutting holes in the darkness with their lights. Once someone out of sight loosed a bray of laughter.

All this went on for an hour or so. The original penitent, by this time, was buried three deep beneath the heap. One caught a glimpse, now and then, of her yellow bobbed hair, but then she would vanish again. How she breathed down there I don't know; it was hard enough six feet away, with a strong five-cent cigar to help. When the praying brothers would rise up for a bout with the tongues their faces were streaming with perspiration. The fat harridan in gingham sweated like a longshoreman. Her hair got loose and fell down over her face. She fanned herself with her skirt. A powerful old gal she was, plainly equal in her day to a bout with obstetrics and a week's washing on the same morning, but this was worse than a week's washing. Finally, she fell into a heap, breathing in great, convulsive gasps.

Finally, we got tired of the show and returned to Dayton. It was nearly eleven o'clock — an immensely late hour for those latitudes — but the whole town was still gathered in the courthouse yard, listening to the disputes of theologians. The Scopes trial had brought them in from all directions. There was a friar wearing a sandwich sign announcing that he was the Bible champion of the world. There was a Seventh Day Adventist arguing that Clarence Darrow was the beast with seven heads and ten horns described in Revelation xiii, and that the end of the world was at hand. There was an evangelist made up like Andy Gump, with the news that atheists in Cincinnati were preparing to descend upon Dayton, hang the eminent Judge Raulston, and burn the town. There was an ancient who maintained that no Catholic could be a Christian. There was the eloquent Dr. T. T. Martin, of Blue Mountain, Miss., come to town with a truck-load of torches and hymn-books to put Darwin in his place. There was a singing brother bellowing apocalyptic hymns. There was William Jennings Bryan, followed everywhere by a gaping crowd. Dayton was having a roaring time. It was better than the circus. But the note of devotion was simply not there; the Daytonians, after listening a while, would slip away to Robinson's drug-store to regale themselves with Coca-Cola, or to the lobby of the Aqua Hotel, where the learned Raulston sat in state, judicially picking his teeth. The real religion was not present. It began at the bridge over the town creek, where the road makes off for the hills.

1928

Zora Neale Hurston

How It Feels to Be Colored Me

I AM COLORED but I offer nothing in the way of extenuating circumstances except the fact that I am the only Negro in the United States whose grandfather on the mother's side was *not* an Indian chief.

I remember the very day that I became colored. Up to my thirteenth year I lived in the little Negro town of Eatonville, Florida. It is exclusively a colored town. The only white people I knew passed through the town going to or coming from Orlando. The native whites rode dusty horses, the Northern tourists chugged down the sandy village road in automobiles. The town knew the Southerners and never stopped cane chewing when they passed. But the Northerners were something else again. They were peered at cautiously from behind curtains by the timid. The more venturesome would come out on the porch to watch them go past and got just as much pleasure out of the tourists as the tourists got out of the village.

The front porch might seem a daring place for the rest of the town, but it was a gallery seat to me. My favorite place was atop the gate-post. Proscenium box for a born first-nighter. Not only did I enjoy the show, but I didn't mind the actors knowing that I liked it. I actually spoke to them in passing. I'd wave at them and when they returned my salute, I would say something like this: "Howdy-do-well-I-thank-you-where-you-goin'?" Usually automobile or the horse paused at this, and after a queer exchange of compliments, I would probably "go a piece of the way" with them, as we say in farthest Florida. If one of my family hap-

First published in *The World Tomorrow, May 1928. The essay was never collected by Hurston or reprinted during her lifetime.

MAIN STREET BOOKS

25% discount on one paperback after purchase of ten paperbacks

25% discount on one hardcover after purchase of five hardcovers

Does not include sale books or other discounts

HARDCOVER

BOOK CLUB

PERBACK

MAIN STREET BOOKS

46 Main Street   Orleans, MA 02653
508•255•3343

www.mainstreetbookstore.com

	1
	2
	3
	4
	5
25%	25%

1	2
3	4
5	6
7	8
9	10

pened to come to the front in time to see me, of course negotiations would be rudely broken off. But even so, it is clear that I was the first "welcome-to-our-state" Floridian, and I hope the Miami Chamber of Commerce will please take notice.

During this period, white people differed from colored to me only in that they rode through town and never lived there. They liked to hear me "speak pieces" and sing and wanted to see me dance the parse-me-la, and gave me generously of their small silver for doing these things, which seemed strange to me for I wanted to do them so much that I needed bribing to stop. Only they didn't know it. The colored people gave no dimes. They deplored any joyful tendencies in me, but I was their Zora nevertheless. I belonged to them, to the nearby hotels, to the county — everybody's Zora.

But changes came in the family when I was thirteen, and I was sent to school in Jacksonville. I left Eatonville, the town of the oleanders, as Zora. When I disembarked from the riverboat at Jacksonville, she was no more. It seemed that I had suffered a sea change. I was not Zora of Orange County any more, I was now a little colored girl. I found it out in certain ways. In my heart as well as in the mirror, I became a fast brown — warranted not to rub nor run.

But I am not tragically colored. There is no great sorrow dammed up in my soul, nor lurking behind my eyes. I do not mind at all. I do not belong to the sobbing school of Negrohood who hold that nature somehow has given them a low-down dirty deal and whose feelings are all hurt about it. Even in the helter-skelter skirmish that is my life, I have seen that the world is to the strong regardless of a little pigmentation more or less. No, I do not weep at the world — I am too busy sharpening my oyster knife.

Someone is always at my elbow reminding me that I am the grand-daughter of slaves. It fails to register depression with me. Slavery is sixty years in the past. The operation was successful and the patient is doing well, thank you. The terrible struggle that made me an American out of a potential slave said "On the line!" The Reconstruction said "Get set!"; and the generation before said "Go!" I am off to a flying start and I must not halt in the stretch to look behind and weep. Slavery is the price I paid for civilization, and the choice was not with me. It is a bully adventure and worth all that I have paid through my ancestors for it. No one on earth ever had a greater chance for glory. The world to be won and nothing to be lost. It is thrilling to think — to know that for any act of mine, I shall get twice as much praise or twice as much

blame. It is quite exciting to hold the center of the nation...
the spectators not knowing whether to laugh or to weep.

The position of my white neighbor is much more difficul...
specter pulls up a chair beside me when I sit down to eat. N...
thrusts its leg against mine in bed. The game of keeping wh...
never so exciting as the game of getting.

I do not always feel colored. Even now I often achieve...
scious Zora of Eatonville before the Hegira. I feel most co...
am thrown against a sharp white background.

For instance at Barnard. "Beside the waters of the Huds...
race. Among the thousand white persons, I am a dark...
upon, overswept by a creamy sea. I am surged upon and o...
through it all, I remain myself. When covered by the wate...
the ebb but reveals me again.

Sometimes it is the other way around. A white person i...
our midst, but the contrast is just as sharp for me. For inst...
sit in the drafty basement that is The New World Cabaret...
person, my color comes. We enter chatting about any little...
we have in common and are seated by the jazz waiters. I...
way that jazz orchestras have, this one plunges into a nu...
no time in circumlocutions, but gets right down to busi...
stricts the thorax and splits the heart with its tempo and...
monies. This orchestra grows rambunctious, rears on its l...
attacks the tonal veil with primitive fury, rending it, claw...
breaks through to the jungle beyond. I follow those heat...
them exultingly. I dance wildly inside myself; I yell withi...
shake my assegai above my head, I hurl it true to the mark...
am in the jungle and living in the jungle way. My face is pa...
yellow, and my body is painted blue. My pulse is throbbi...
drum. I want to slaughter something — give pain, give de...
do not know. But the piece ends. The men of the orchest...
lips and rest their fingers. I creep back slowly to the veneer...
zation with the last tone and find the white friend sitting...
his seat, smoking calmly.

"Good music they have here," he remarks, drumming t...
his fingertips.

Music! The great blobs of purple and red emotion have...
him. He has only heard what I felt. He is far away and...
dimly across the ocean and the continent that have falle...
He is so pale with his whiteness then and I am so colored.

At certain times I have no race, I am *me*. When I set my hat at a certain angle and saunter down Seventh Avenue, Harlem City, feeling as snooty as the lions in front of the Forty-Second Street Library, for instance. So far as my feelings are concerned, Peggy Hopkins Joyce on the Boule Mich with her gorgeous raiment, stately carriage, knees knocking together in a most aristocratic manner, has nothing on me. The cosmic Zora emerges. I belong to no race nor time, I am the eternal feminine with its string of beads.

I have no separate feeling about being an American citizen and colored. I am merely a fragment of the Great Soul that surges within the boundaries. My country, right or wrong.

Sometimes, I feel discriminated against, but it does not make me angry. It merely astonishes me. How *can* any deny themselves the pleasure of my company! It's beyond me.

But in the main, I feel like a brown bag of miscellany propped against a wall. Against a wall in company with other bags, white, red and yellow. Pour out the contents, and there is discovered a jumble of small things priceless and worthless. A first-water diamond, an empty spool, bits of broken glass, lengths of string, a key to a door long since crumbled away, a rusty knife-blade, old shoes saved for a road that never was and never will be, a nail bent under the weight of things too heavy for any nail, a dried flower or two, still a little fragrant. In your hand is the brown bag. On the ground before you is the jumble it held — so much like the jumble in the bags, could they be emptied, that all might be dumped in a single heap and the bags refilled without altering the content of any greatly. A bit of colored glass more or less would not matter. Perhaps that is how the Great Stuffer of Bags filled them in the first place — who knows?

1933

Edmund Wilson

The Old Stone House

As I GO NORTH for the first time in years, in the slow, the constantly stopping, milk train — which carries passengers only in the back part of the hind car and has an old stove to heat it in winter — I look out through the dirt-yellowed double pane and remember how once, as a child, I used to feel thwarted in summer till I had got the windows open and there was nothing between me and the widening pastures, the great boulders, the black and white cattle, the rivers, stony and thin, the lone elms like feather-dusters, the high air which sharpens all outlines, makes all colors so breathtakingly vivid, in the clear light of late afternoon.

The little stations again: Barnevald, Stittville, Steuben — a tribute to the Prussian general who helped drill our troops for the Revolution. The woman behind me in the train talks to the conductor with a German accent. They came over here for land and freedom.

Boonville: that pale boxlike building, smooth gray, with three floors of slots that look in on darkness and a roof like a flat overlapping lid — cold dark clear air, fresh water. Like nothing else but upstate New York. Rivers that run quick among stones, or, deeper, stained dark with dead leaves. I used to love to follow them — should still. A fresh breath of water off the Black River, where the blue closed gentians grow. Those forests, those boulder-strewn pastures, those fabulous distant falls!

There was never any train to Talcottville. Our house was the center of the town. It is strange to get back to this now: it seems not quite like

---

First published in *Scribner's*, 1933; collected in *Travels in Two Democracies*, 1936, and *The American Earthquake*, 1958.

anything else that I have ever known. But is this merely the apparent uniqueness of places associated with childhood?

The settlers of this part of New York were a first westward migration from New England. At the end of the eighteenth century, they drove ox-teams from Connecticut and Massachusetts over into the wild northern country below Lake Ontario and the St. Lawrence River, and they established here an extension of New England.

Yet an extension that was already something new. I happened last week to be in Ipswich, Mass., the town from which one branch of my family came; and, for all the New England pride of white houses and green blinds, I was oppressed by the ancient crampedness. Even the House of the Seven Gables, which stimulated the imagination of Haw-thorne, though it is grim perhaps, is not romantic. It, too, has the tight-ness and the self-sufficiency of that little provincial merchant society, which at its best produced an intense little culture, quite English in its concreteness and practicality — as the block letters of the signs along the docks make Boston look like Liverpool. But life must have hit its head on those close and low-ceilinged coops. That narrowness, that meagerness, that stinginess, still grips New England today: the drab summer cottages along the shore seem almost as slit-windowed and pinched as the gray twin-houses of a mill town like Lawrence or Fall River. I can feel the relief myself of coming away from Boston to these first uplands of the Adirondacks, where, discarding the New England religion but still speaking the language of New England, the settlers found limitless space. They were a part of the new America, now forever for a century on the move; and they were to move on themselves before they would be able to build here anything comparable to the New England civilization. The country, magnificent and vast, has never really been humanized as New England has: the landscape still overwhelms the people. But this house, one of the few of its kind among later wooden houses and towns, was an attempt to found a civilization. It blends in a peculiar fashion the amenities of the eastern seaboard with the rudeness and toughness of the new frontier.

It was built at the end of the eighteenth century: the first event recorded in connection with it is a memorial service for General Washington. It took four or five years in the building. The stone had to be quarried and brought out of the river. The walls are a foot and a half thick, and the plaster was applied to the stone without any intervening lattice. The beams were secured by enormous nails, made by hand and some of them eighteen inches long. Solid and simple as a fortress, the place has also the charm of something which has been made to order. There is a front porch with white wooden columns which support a white wooden balcony that runs along the second floor. The roof comes down close over the balcony, and the balcony and the porch are draped with vines. Large ferns grow along the porch, and there are stone hitching-posts and curious stone ornaments, cut out of the quarry like the house: on one side, a round-bottomed bowl in which red geraniums bloom, and on the other, an unnamable object, crudely sculptured and vaguely pagoda-like. The front door is especially handsome: the door itself is dark green and equipped with a brass knocker, and the woodwork which frames it is white; it is crowned with a wide fanlight and flanked by two narrow panes of glass, in which a white filigree of ironwork makes a webbing like ice over winter ponds. On one of the broad sides of the building, where the mortar has come off the stone, there is a dappling of dark gray under pale gray like the dappling of light in shallow water, and the feathers of the elms make dapplings of sun among their shadows of large lace on the grass.

The lawn is ungraded and uneven like the pastures, and it merges eventually with the fields. Behind, there are great clotted masses of myrtle-beds, lilac-bushes, clumps of pink phlox and other things I cannot identify; pink and white hollyhocks, some of them leaning, fine blue and purple dye of larkspur; a considerable vegetable garden, with long rows of ripe gooseberries and currants, a patch of yellow pumpkin flowers, and bushes of raspberries, both white and red — among which are sprinkled like confetti the little flimsy California poppies, pink, orange, white and red. In an old dark red barn behind, where the hayloft is almost collapsing, I find spinning-wheels, a carder, candle-molds, a patent bootjack, obsolete implements of carpentry, little clusters of baskets for berry-picking and a gigantic pair of scales such as is nowadays only seen in the hands of allegorical figures.

The house was built by the Talcotts, after whom the town was named. They owned the large farm in front of the house, which stretches down to the river and beyond. They also had a profitable grist mill, but — I learn from the county history — were thought to have "adopted a policy adverse to the building up of the village at the point where natural advantages greatly favored," since they "refused to sell village lots to mechanics, and retained the water power on Sugar River, although parties offered to invest liberally in manufactures." In time, there were only two Talcotts left, an old maid and her widowed sister. My great-grandfather

Thomas Baker, who lived across the street and had been left by the death of his wife with a son and eight daughters, paid court to Miss Talcott and married her. She was kind to the children, and they remembered her with affection. My great-grandfather acquired in this way the house, the farm and the quarry.

All but two of my great-grandfather's daughters, of whom my grandmother was one — "six of them beauties," I understand — got married and went away. Only one of them was left in the house at the time when I first remember Talcottville: my great-aunt Rosalind, a more or less professional invalid and a figure of romantic melancholy, whose fiancé had been lost at sea. When I knew her, she was very old. It was impressive and rather frightening to call on her — you did it only by special arrangement, since she had to prepare herself to be seen. She would be beautifully dressed in a lace cap, a lavender dress and a white crocheted shawl, but she had become so bloodless and shrunken as dreadfully to resemble a mummy and reminded one uncomfortably of Miss Havisham in Dickens's *Great Expectations*. She had a certain high and formal coquetry and was the only person I ever knew who really talked like the characters in old novels. When she had been able to get about, she had habitually treated the townspeople with a condescension almost baronial. According to the family legend, the great-grandmother of great-grandmother Baker had been a daughter of one of the Earls of Essex, who had eloped with a gardener to America.

Another of my Baker great-aunts, who was one of my favorite relatives, had married and lived in the town and had suffered tragic disappointments. Only her strong intellectual interests and a mind capable of philosophic pessimism had maintained her through the wreck of her domestic life. She used to tell me how, a young married woman, she had taught herself French by the dictionary and grammar, sitting up at night alone by the stove through one of their cold and dark winters. She had read a great deal of French, subscribed to French magazines, without ever having learned to pronounce it. She had rejected revealed religion and did not believe in immortality; and when she felt that she had been relieved of the last of her family obligations — though her hair was now turning gray — she came on to New York City and lived there alone for years, occupying herself with the theater, reading, visits to her nephews and nieces — with whom she was extremely popular — and all the spectacle and news of the larger world which she had always loved so much but from which she had spent most of her life removed.

When she died, only the youngest of the family was left, the sole brother, my great-uncle Tom. His mother must have been worn out with childbearing — she died after the birth of this ninth child — and he had not turned out so well as the others. He had been born with no roof to his mouth and was obliged to wear a false gold palate, and it was difficult to understand him. He was not really simple-minded — he had held a small political job under Cleveland, and he usually beat me at checkers — but he was childlike and ill-equipped to deal with life in any very effective way. He sold the farm to a German and the quarry to the town. Then he died, and the house was empty, except when my mother and father would come here to open it up for two or three months in the summer.

I have not been back here in years, and I have never before examined the place carefully. It has become for me something like a remembered dream — unearthly with the powerful impressions of childhood. Even now that I am here again, I find I have to shake off the dream. I keep walking from room to room, inside and outside, upstairs and down, with uneasy sensations of complacency that are always falling through to depression.

These rooms are very well proportioned; the white mantelpieces are elegant and chaste, and the carving on each one is different. The larger of the two living rooms now seems a little bare because the various members of the family have claimed and taken away so many things; and there are some disagreeable curtains and carpets, for which the wife of my great-uncle Tom is to blame. But here are all the things, I take note, that are nowadays sold in antique stores: red Bohemian-glass decanters; a rusty silver snuff-box; a mirror with the American eagle painted at the top of the glass. Little mahogany tables with slim legs; a set of curly-maple furniture, deep seasoned yellow like satin; a yellow comb-backed rocker, with a design of green conch-shells that look like snails. A small bust of Dante with the nose chipped, left behind as defective by one of my cousins when its companion piece, Beethoven, was taken away; a little mahogany melodeon on which my Aunt "Lin" once played. Large engravings of the family of Washington and of the "Reformers Presenting Their Famous Protest before the Diet of Spires"; a later engraving of Dickens. Old tongs and poker, impossibly heavy. A brown mahogany desk inlaid with yellow birdwood, which contains a pair of steel-rimmed spectacles and a thing for shaking sand on wet ink. Daguerreotypes in fancy cases: they seem to last much better than photographs — my grandmother looks fresh and cunning — I remember that I used to hear that the first time my grandfather saw her, she was riding on a load of hay — he came back up here to marry her as soon as he had got out of medical school. An old wooden flute — originally brought over from New England, I remember my great-uncle's telling me, at the time when they traveled by ox-team — he used to get a lonely piping out of it — I try it but cannot make a sound. Two big oval paintings, in tarnished gilt frames, of landscapes romantic and mountainous: they came from the Utica house of my great-grandfather Baker's brother — he married a rich wife and invented excelsior — made out of the northern lumber — and was presented with a solid-silver table service by the grateful city of Utica.

Wallpaper molded by the damp from the stone; uninviting old black haircloth furniture. A bowl of those enormous up-country sweet peas, incredibly fragrant and bright — they used to awe and trouble me — why?

In the dining room, a mahogany china closet, which originally — in the days when letters were few and great-grandfather Baker was postmaster — was the whole of the village post office. My grandmother's pewter tea-service, with its design of oak-leaves and acorns, which I remember from her house in New Jersey. Black iron cranes, pipkins and kettles for cooking in the fireplace; a kind of flat iron pitchfork for lifting the bread in and out, when they baked at the back of the hearth. On the sideboard, a glass decanter with a gilt black-letter label: "J. Rum." If there were only some rum in the decanter! — if the life of the house were not now all past! — the kitchens that trail out behind are almost too old-smelling, too long deserted, to make them agreeable to visit — in spite of the delightful brown crocks with long-tailed blue birds painted on them, a different kind of bird on each crock.

In the ample hall with its staircase, two large colored pictures of trout, one rising to bait, one leaping. Upstairs, a wooden pestle and mortar; a perforated tin box for hot coals to keep the feet warm in church or on sleigh-rides; a stuffed heron; a horrible bust of my cousin Dorothy Read in her girlhood, which her mother had done of her in Germany. The hair-ribbon and the ruffles are faithfully reproduced in marble, and the eyes have engraved pupils. It stands on a high pedestal, and it used to be possible, by pressing a button, to make it turn around. My Cousin Grace, Dorothy's mother, used to show it off and invite comparison with the original, especially calling attention to the nose; but what her mother had never known was that Dorothy had injured her nose in some rather disgraceful row with her sister. One day when the family were making an excursion, Dorothy pleaded indisposition and bribed a man with a truck to take the bust away and drop it into a pond. But Uncle Tom got this out of the man, dredged the statue up and replaced it on its pedestal. An ugly chair with a round rag back; an ugly bed with the head of Columbus sticking out above the pillows like a figurehead. Charming old bedquilts, with patterns of rhomboids in softened browns, greens and pinks, or of blue polka-dotted hearts that ray out on stiff phallic stalks. A footstool covered in white, which, however, when you step on a tab at the side, opens up into a cuspidor — some relic, no doubt, of the times when the house was used for local meetings. (There used to be a musical chair, also brought back from Germany, but it seems to have disappeared.) A jar of hardly odorous dried rose-leaves, and a jar of little pebbles and shells that keep their bright colors in alcohol.

The original old panes up here have wavy lines in the glass. There are cobweb-filthy books, which I try to examine: many religious works, the annals of the state legislature, a book called *The Young Wife, or Duties of Women in the Marriage Relation,* published in Boston in 1838 and containing a warning against tea and coffee, which "loosen the tongue, fire the eye, produce mirth and wit, excite the animal passions, and lead to remarks about ourselves and others, that we should not have made in other circumstances, and which it were better for us and the world, never to have made." But there is also, I noticed downstairs, Grant Allan's *The Woman Who Did* from 1893.

I come upon the *History of Lewis County* and read it with a certain pride. I am glad to say to myself that it is a creditable piece of work — admirably full in its information on geology, flora and fauna, on history and local politics; diversified with anecdotes and biographies never overflattering and often pungent; and written in a sound English style. Could anyone in the county today, I wonder, command such a sound English style? I note with gratification that the bone of a prehistoric cuttlefish, discovered in one of the limestone caves, is the largest of its kind on record, and that a flock of wild swans was seen here in 1821. In the eighties, there were still wolves and panthers. There are still bears and deer today.

I also look into the proceedings of the New York State Assembly. My great-grandfather Thomas Baker was primarily a politician and at that time a member of the Assembly. I have heard that he was a Jacksonian Democrat, and that he made a furious scene when my grandmother came back from New Jersey and announced that she had become a Republican: it "spoiled her whole visit." There is a photograph of great-grandfather Baker in an oval gilt frame, with his hair sticking out in three spikes and a wide and declamatory mouth. I look through the Assembly record to see what sort of role he played. It is the forties; the Democrats are still angry over the Bank of United States. But when I look up Thomas Baker in the index, it turns out that he figures solely as either not being present or as requesting leave of absence. They tell me he used to go West to buy cattle.

That sealed-up space on the second floor which my father had knocked out — who did they tell me was hidden in it? I have just learned from one of the new road-signs which explain historical associations that there are caves somewhere here in which slaves were hidden. Could this have been a part of the underground route for smuggling Negroes over the border into Canada? Is the attic, the "kitchen chamber," which is always so suffocating in summer, still full of those carpet-bags and crinolines and bonnets and beaver-hats that we used to get out of the old cowhide trunks and use to dress up for charades?

It was the custom for the married Baker daughters to bring their children back in the summer; and their children in time brought their children. In those days, how I loved coming up here! It was a reunion with cousins from Boston and New York, Ohio and Wisconsin, as well as with the Talcottville and Utica ones: we fished and swam in the rivers, had all sorts of excursions and games. Later on, I got to dislike it: the older generation died, the younger did not much come. I wanted to be elsewhere, too. The very fullness with life of the past, the memory of those many families of cousins and uncles and aunts, made the emptiness of the present more oppressive. Isn't it still? — didn't my gloom come from that, the night of my first arrival? Wasn't it the dread of that that kept me away? I am aware, as I walk through the rooms, of the amplitude and completeness of the place — the home of a big old-fashioned family that had to be a city in itself. And not merely did it house a clan: the whole life of the community passed through it. And now for five sixths of the year it is nothing but an unheated shell, a storehouse of unused antiques, with no intimate relation to the county.

The community itself today is somewhat smaller than the community of those days, and its condition has very much changed. It must seem to the summer traveler merely one of the clusters of houses that he shoots through along the state highway; and there may presently be little left save our house confronting, across the road, the hot-dog stand and the gasoline station.

For years I have had a recurrent dream. I take a road that runs toward the west. It is summer; I pass by a strange summer forest, in which there are mysterious beings, though I know that, on the whole, they are shy and benign. If I am fortunate and find the way, I arrive at a wonderful river, which runs among boulders, with rapids, between alders and high weedy trees, through a countryside fresh, green and wide. We go in swimming; it is miles away from anywhere. We plunge in the smooth flowing pools. We make our way to the middle of the stream and climb up on the pale round gray stones and sit naked in the sun and the air, while the river glides away below us. And I know that it is the place for which I have always longed, the place of wildness and freedom, to find which is the height of what one may hope for — the place of unalloyed delight.

As I walk about Talcottville now, I discover that the being-haunted forest is a big grove which even in daytime used to be lonely and dark and where great white Canadian violets used to grow out of the deep black leaf-mold. Today it is no longer dark, because half the trees have been cut down. The river of my dream, I see, is simply an idealized version of the farther and less frequented and more adventurous bank of Sugar River, which had to be reached by wading. Both river and forest are west of the road that runs through the village, which accounts for my always taking that direction in my dream. I remember how Sugar River — out of the stone of which our house is built — used, in my boyhood, so to fascinate me that I had an enlargement made of one of the photographs I had taken of it — a view of "the Big Falls" — and kept it in my room all winter. Today the nearer bank has been largely blasted away to get stone for the new state highway, and what we used to call "the Little Falls" is gone.

I visit the house of my favorite great-aunt, and my gloom returns and overwhelms me. The huge root of an elm has split the thick slabs of the pavement so that you have to walk over a hump; and one of the big square stone fence-posts is toppling. Her flowers, with no one to tend them, go on raggedly blooming in their seasons. There has been nobody in her house since she died. It is all too appropriate to her pessimism — that dead end she always foresaw. As I walk around the house, I remember how, once on the back porch there, she sang me old English ballads, including that gruesome one, "Oh, where have you been, Randall, my son?" — about the man who had gone to Pretty Peggy's house and been given snakes to eat:

"What had you for supper, Randall, my son?"
"Fresh fish fried in butter. Oh, make my bed soon!
For I'm sick at my heart and I fain would lie down!"

She was old then — round-shouldered and dumpy — after the years when she had looked so handsome, straight-backed and with the fashionable aigrette in her hair. And the song she sang seemed to have been drawn out of such barbarous reaches of the past, out of something so surprisingly different from the college-women's hotels in New York in which I had always known her as living: that England to which, far though she had come from it, she was yet so much nearer than I — that queer troubling world of legend which I knew from Percy's *Reliques* but with which she had maintained a real contact through centuries of women's voices — for she sang it without a smile, completely possessed by its spirit — that it made my flesh creep, disconcerted me.

My great-aunt is dead, and all her generation are dead — and the new generations of the family have long ago left Talcottville behind and have turned into something quite different. They were already headed for the cities by the middle of the last century, as can be seen by the rapid dispersal of great-grandfather Baker's daughters. Yet there were still, in my childhood, a few who stayed on in this country as farmers. They were very impressive people, the survivors of a sovereign race who had owned their own pastures and fields and governed their own community. Today the descendants of these are performing mainly minor functions in a machine which they do not control. They have most of them become thoroughly urbanized, and they are farther from great-grandfather Baker than my grandmother, his daughter, was when she came back from New Jersey a Republican. One of her children, a retired importer in New York, was complaining to me the other day that the outrageous demands of the farmers were making business recovery impossible, and protesting that if the advocates of the income tax had their way, the best people would no longer be able to live up to their social positions. A cousin, who bears the name of one of his Ipswich ancestors, a mining engineer on the Coast and a classmate and admirer of Hoover, invested and has lost heavily in Mexican real estate and the industrial speculations of the boom. Another, with another of the old local names, is now at the head of an organization whose frankly avowed

purpose is to rescue the New York manufacturers from taxation and social legislation. He has seen his native city of Utica decline as a textile
center through the removal of its mills to the South, where taxes are
lighter and labor is cheaper; and he is honestly convinced that his efforts are directed toward civic betterment.

Thus the family has come imperceptibly to identify its interests with
those of what my great-grandfather Baker would have called the
"money power." They work for it and acquiesce in it — they are no
longer the sovereign race of the first settlers of Lewis County, and in the
cities they have achieved no sovereignty. They are much too scrupulous
and decent, and their tastes are too comparatively simple for them ever
to have rolled up great fortunes during the years of expansion and
plunder. They have still the frank accent and the friendly eye of the
older American world, and they seem rather taken aback by the turn
that things have been taking.

And what about me? As I come back in the train, I find that — other
causes contributing — my depression of Talcottville deepens. I did not
find the river and the forest of my dream — I did not find the magic of
the past. I have been too close to the past: there in that house, in that remote little town which has never known industrial progress since the
Talcotts first obstructed the development of the water power of Sugar
River, you can see exactly how rural Americans were living a century
and a half ago. And who would go back to it? Not I. Let people who
have never known country life complain that the farmer has been
spoiled by his radio and his Ford. Along with the memory of exaltation
at the immensity and freedom of that countryside, I have memories
of horror at its loneliness: houses burning down at night, sometimes
with people in them, where there was no fire department to save them,
and husbands or wives left alone by death — the dark nights and the
prisoning winters. I do not grudge the sacrifice of the Sugar River falls
for the building of the new state highway, and I do not resent the hot-
dog stand. I am at first a little shocked at the sight of a transformer on
the road between Talcottville and Boonville, but when I get to the Talcottville house, I am obliged to be thankful for it — no more oil-lamps
in the evenings! And I would not go back to that old life if I could: that
civilization of northern New York — why should I idealize it? — was too
lonely, too poor, too provincial.

I look out across the Hudson and see Newburgh: with the neat-win-
dowed cubes of its dwellings and docks, distinct as if cut by a burin,

built so densely up the slope of the bank and pierced by an occasional steeple, undwarfed by tall modern buildings and with only the little old-fashioned ferry to connect it with the opposite bank, it might still be an eighteenth-century city. My father's mother came from there. She was the granddaughter of a carpet-importer from Rotterdam. From him came the thick Spanish coins which the children of my father's family were supposed to cut their teeth on. The business, which had been a considerable one, declined as the sea trade of the Hudson became concentrated in New York. My father and mother went once — a good many years ago — to visit the old store by the docks, and were amazed to find a solitary old clerk still scratching up orders and sales on a slate that hung behind the counter.

And the slate and the Spanish coins, though they symbolize a kind of life somewhat different from that evoked by Talcottville, associate themselves in my mind with such things as the old post office turned china closet. And as I happen to be reading Herndon's *Life of Lincoln*, that, too, goes to flood out the vision with its extension still further west, still further from the civilized seaboard, of the life of the early frontier. Through Herndon's extraordinary memoir, one of the few really great American books of its kind, which America has never accepted, preferring to it the sentimentalities of Sandburg and the ladies who write Christmas stories — the past confronts me even more plainly than through the bootjacks and daguerreotypes of Talcottville, and makes me even more uneasy. Here you are back again amid the crudeness and the poverty of the American frontier, and here is a man of genius coming out of it and perfecting himself. The story is not merely moving, it becomes almost agonizing. The ungainly boorish boy from the settler's clearing, with nobody and nothing behind him, hoping that his grandfather had been a planter as my great-aunt Rosalind hoped that she was a descendant of the Earls of Essex, the morbid young man looking passionately toward the refinement and the training of the East but unable to bring himself to marry the women who represented it for him — rejoining across days in country stores, nights in godforsaken hotels, rejoining by heroic self-discipline the creative intelligence of the race, to find himself the conscious focus of its terrible unconscious parturition — his miseries burden his grandeur. At least they do for me at this moment.

> Old Abe Lincoln came out of the wilderness,
> Out of the wilderness, out of the wilderness —

The echo of the song in my mind inspires me with a kind of awe — I can hardly bear the thought of Lincoln.

Great-grandfather Baker's politics and the Talcottville general store, in which people sat around and talked before the new chain store took its place — Lincoln's school was not so very much different. And I would not go back to that.

Yet as I walk up the steps of my house in New York, I am forced to recognize, with a sinking, that I have never been able to leave it. This old wooden booth I have taken between First and Second Avenues — what is it but the same old provincial America? And as I open the door with its loose knob and breathe in the musty smell of the stair-carpet, it seems to me that I have not merely stuck in the world where my fathers lived but have actually, in some ways, lost ground in it. This gray paintless clapboarded front, these lumpy and rubbed yellow walls — they were probably once respectable, but they must always have been commonplace. They have never had even the dignity of the house in Lewis County. But I have rented them because, in my youth, I had been used to living in houses and have grown to loathe city apartments.

So here, it seems, is where I must live: in an old cramped and sour frame-house — having failed even worse than my relatives at getting out of the American big-business era the luxuries and the prestige that I unquestionably should very much have enjoyed. Here is where I end by living — among the worst instead of the best of this city that took the trade away from Newburgh — the sordid and unhealthy children of my sordid and unhealthy neighbors, who howl outside my windows night and day. It is this, in the last analysis — there is no doubt about it now! — which has been rankling and causing my gloom: to have left that early world behind yet never to have really succeeded in what was till yesterday the new.

1935

Gertrude Stein

....

What Are Master-pieces and
Why Are There So Few of Them

I WAS ALMOST going to talk this lecture and not write and read it because all the lectures that I have written and read in America have been
printed and although possibly for you they might even being read be as
if they had not been printed still there is something about what has
been written having been printed which makes it no longer the property of the one who wrote it and therefore there is no more reason why
the writer should say it out loud than anybody else and therefore one
does not.

Therefore I was going to talk to you but actually it is impossible to
talk about master-pieces and what they are because talking essentially
has nothing to do with creation. I talk a lot I like to talk and I talk even
more than that I may say I talk most of the time and I listen a fair
amount too and as I have said the essence of being a genius is to be able
to talk and listen to listen while talking and talk while listening but and
this is very important very important indeed talking has nothing to do
with creation. What are master-pieces and why after all are there so few
of them. You may say after all there are a good many of them but in any
kind of proportion with everything that anybody who does anything is
doing there are really very few of them. All this summer I meditated
and wrote about this subject and it finally came to be a discussion of the
relation of human nature and the human mind and identity. The thing
one gradually comes to find out is that one has no identity that is when

---

Written in 1935 and delivered as a lecture at Oxford and Cambridge in 1936; first published in the book *What Are Master-pieces, 1940.

one is in the act of doing anything. Identity is recognition, you know who you are because you and others remember anything about yourself but essentially you are not that when you are doing anything. I am I because my little dog knows me but, creatively speaking the little dog knowing that you are you and your recognising that he knows, that is what destroys creation. That is what makes school. Picasso once remarked I do not care who it is that has or does influence me as long as it is not myself.

It is very difficult so difficult that it always has been difficult but even more difficult now to know what is the relation of human nature to the human mind because one has to know what is the relation of the act of creation to the subject the creator uses to create that thing. There is a great deal of nonsense talked about the subject of anything. After all there is always the same subject there are the things you see and there are human beings and animal beings and everybody you might say since the beginning of time knows practically commencing at the beginning and going to the end everything about these things. After all any woman in any village or men either if you like or even children know as much of human psychology as any writer that ever lived. After all there are things you do know each one in his or her way knows all of them and it is not this knowledge that makes master-pieces. Not at all not at all at all. Those who recognise master-pieces say that is the reason but it is not. It is not the way Hamlet reacts to his father's ghost that makes the master-piece, he might have reacted according to Shakespeare in a dozen other ways and everybody would have been as much impressed by the psychology of it. But there is no psychology in it, that is not probably the way any young man would react to the ghost of his father and there is no particular reason why they should. If it were the way a young man could react to the ghost of his father then that would be something anybody in any village would know they could talk about it talk about it endlessly but that would not make a master-piece and that brings us once more back to the subject of identity. At any moment when you are you you are you without the memory of yourself because if you remember yourself while you are you you are not for purposes of creating you. This is so important because it has so much to do with the question of a writer to his audience. One of the things that I discovered in lecturing was that gradually one ceased to hear what one said one heard what the audience hears one say, that is the reason that oratory is practically never a master-piece very rarely and very rarely history, because history deals with people who are orators who hear not what they are not what they say but what their audience hears them say. It is very interesting that letter writing has the same difficulty, the letter writes what the other person is to hear and so entity does not exist there are two present instead of one and so once again creation breaks down. I once wrote in writing *The Making of Americans* I write for myself and strangers but that was merely a literary formalism for if I did write for myself and strangers if I did I would not really be writing because already then identity would take the place of entity. It is awfully difficult, action is direct and effective but after all action is necessary and anything that is necessary has to do with human nature and not with the human mind. Therefore a master-piece has essentially not to be necessary, it has to be that is it has to exist but it does not have to be necessary it is not in response to necessity as action is because the minute it is necessary it has in it no possibility of going on.

To come back to what a master-piece has as its subject. In writing about painting I said that a picture exists for and in itself and the painter has to use objects landscapes and people as a way the only way that he is able to get the picture to exist. That is every one's trouble and particularly the trouble just now when every one who writes or paints has gotten to be abnormally conscious of the things he uses that is the events the people the objects and the landscapes and fundamentally the minute one is conscious deeply conscious of these things as a subject the interest in them does not exist.

You can tell that so well in the difficulty of writing novels or poetry these days. The tradition has always been that you may more or less describe the things that happen you imagine them of course but you more or less describe the things that happen but nowadays everybody all day long knows what is happening and so what is happening is not really interesting, one knows it by radios cinemas newspapers biographies autobiographies until what is happening does not really thrill any one, it excites them a little but it does not really thrill them. The painter can no longer say that what he does is as the world looks to him because he cannot look at the world any more, it has been photographed too much and he has to say that he does something else. In former times a painter said he painted what he saw of course he didn't but anyway he could say it, now he does not want to say it because seeing it is not interesting. This has something to do with master-pieces and why there are so few of them but not everything.

So you see why talking has nothing to do with creation, talking is really human nature as it is and human nature has nothing to do with master-pieces. It is very curious but the detective story which is you might say the only really modern novel form that has come into existence gets rid of human nature by having the man dead to begin with the hero is dead to begin with and so you have so to speak got rid of the event before the book begins. There is another very curious thing about detective stories. In real life people are interested in the crime more than they are in detection, it is the crime that is the thing the shock the thrill the horror but in the story it is the detection that holds the interest and that is natural enough because the necessity as far as action is concerned is the dead man, it is another function that has very little to do with human nature that makes the detection interesting. And so always it is true that the master-piece has nothing to do with human nature or with identity, it has to do with the human mind and the entity that is with a thing in itself and not in relation. The moment it is in relation it is common knowledge and anybody can feel and know it and it is not a master-piece. At the same time every one in a curious way sooner or later does feel the reality of a master-piece. The thing in itself of which the human nature is only its clothing does hold the attention. I have meditated a great deal about that. Another curious thing about master-pieces is, nobody when it is created there is in the thing that we call the human mind something that makes it hold itself just the same. The manner and habits of Bible times or Greek or Chinese have nothing to do with ours today but the master-pieces exist just the same and they do not exist because of their identity, that is what any one remembering then remembered then, they do not exist by human nature because everybody always knows everything there is to know about human nature, they exist because they came to be as something that is an end in itself and in that respect it is opposed to the business of living which is relation and necessity. That is what a master-piece is not although it may easily be what a master-piece talks about. It is another one of the curious difficulties a master-piece has that is to begin and end, because actually a master-piece does not do that it does not begin and end if it did it would be of necessity and in relation and that is just what a master-piece is not. Everybody worries about that just now everybody that is what makes them talk about abstract and worry about punctuation and capitals and small letters and what a history is. Everybody worries about that not because everybody knows what a masterpiece is but because a certain number have found out what a masterpiece is not. Even the very master-pieces have always been very bothered about beginning and ending because essentially that is what a master-piece is not. And yet after all like the subject of human nature master-pieces have to use beginning and ending to become existing. Well anyway anybody who is trying to do anything today is desperately not having a beginning and an ending but nevertheless in some way one does have to stop. I stop.

I do not know whether I have made any of this very clear, it is clear, but unfortunately I have written it all down all summer and in spite of everything I am now remembering and when you remember it is never clear. This is what makes secondary writing, it is remembering, it is very curious you begin to write something and suddenly you remember something and if you continue to remember your writing gets very confused. If you do not remember while you are writing, it may seem confused to others but actually it is clear and eventually that clarity will be clear, that is what a master-piece is, but if you remember while you are writing it will seem clear at the time to any one but the clarity will go out of it that is what a master-piece is not.

All this sounds awfully complicated but it is not complicated at all, it is just what happens. Any of you when you write you try to remember what you are about to write and you will see immediately how lifeless the writing becomes that is why expository writing is so dull because it is all remembered, that is why illustration is so dull because you remember what somebody looked like and you make your illustration look like it. The minute your memory functions while you are doing anything it may be very popular but actually it is dull. And that is what a master-piece is not, it may be unwelcome but it is never dull.

And so then why are there so few of them. There are so few of them because mostly people live in identity and memory that is when they think. They know they are they because their little dog knows them, and so they are not an entity but an identity. And being so memory is necessary to make them exist and so they cannot create master-pieces. It has been said of geniuses that they are eternally young. I once said what is the use of being a boy if you are going to grow up to be a man, the boy and the man have nothing to do with each other, except in respect to memory and identity, and if they have anything to do with each other in respect to memory and identity then they will never produce a master-piece. Do you do you understand well it really does not make much difference because after all master-pieces are what they are and the reason why is that there are very few of them. The reason why is any of you try it just not to be you are you because your little dog knows you. The second you are you because your little dog knows you you cannot make a master-piece and that is all of that.

It is not extremely difficult not to have identity but it is extremely difficult the knowing not having identity. One might say it is impossible but that it is not impossible is proved by the existence of master-pieces which are just that. They are knowing that there is no identity and producing while identity is not.

That is what a master-piece is.

And so we do know what a master-piece is and we also know why there are so few of them. Everything is against them. Everything that makes life go on makes identity and everything that makes identity is of necessity a necessity. And the pleasures of life as well as the necessities help the necessity of identity. The pleasures that are soothing all have to do with identity and the pleasures that are exciting all have to do with identity and moreover there is all the pride and vanity which play about master-pieces as well as about every one and these too all have to do with identity, and so naturally it is natural that there is more identity that one knows about than anything else one knows about and the worst of all is that the only thing that any one thinks about is identity and thinking is something that does so nearly need to be memory and if it is then of course it has nothing to do with a master-piece.

But what can a master-piece be about mostly it is about identity and all it does and in being so it must not have any. I was just thinking about anything and in thinking about anything I saw something. In seeing that thing shall we see it without it turning into identity, the moment is not a moment and the sight is not the thing seen and yet it is. Moments are not important because of course master-pieces have no more time than they have identity although time like identity is what they concern themselves about of course that is what they do concern themselves about.

Once when one has said what one says it is not true or too true. That is what is the trouble with time. That is what makes what women say truer than what men say. That is undoubtedly what is the trouble with time and always in its relation to master-pieces. I once said that nothing could bother me more than the way a thing goes dead once it has been said. And if it does it it is because of there being this trouble about time.

Time is very important in connection with master-pieces, of course it makes identity time does make identity and identity does stop the creation of master-pieces. But time does something by itself to interfere with the creation of master-pieces as well as being part of what makes identity. If you do not keep remembering yourself you have no identity and if you have no time you do not keep remembering yourself and as you remember yourself you do not create anybody can and does know that.

Think about how you create if you do create you do not remember yourself as you do create. And yet time and identity is what you tell about as you create only while you create they do not exist. That is really what it is.

And do you create yes if you exist but time and identity do not exist. We live in time and identity but as we are we do not know time and identity everybody knows that quite simply. It is so simple that anybody does know that. But to know what one knows is frightening to live what one lives is soothing and though everybody likes to be frightened what they really have to have is soothing and so the master-pieces are so few not that the master-pieces themselves are frightening no of course not because if the creator of the master-piece is frightened then he does not exist without the memory of time and identity, and insofar as he is that then he is frightened and insofar as he is frightened the master-piece does not exist, it looks like it and it feels like it, but the memory of the fright destroys it as a master-piece. Robinson Crusoe and the footstep of the man Friday is one of the most perfect examples of the non-existence of time and identity which makes a master-piece. I hope you do see what I mean but any way everybody who knows about Robinson Crusoe and the footstep of Friday knows that that is true. There is no time and identity in the way it happened and that is why there is no fright.

And so there are very few master-pieces of course there are very few master-pieces because to be able to know that is not to have identity and time but not to mind talking as if there was because it does not interfere with anything and to go on being not as if there were no time and identity but as if there were and at the same time existing without time and identity is so very simple that it is difficult to have many who are that. And of course that is what a master-piece is and that is why there are so few of them and anybody really anybody can know that.

What is the use of being a boy if you are going to grow up to be a man. And what is the use there is no use from the standpoint of master-pieces there is no use. Anybody can really know that.

There is really no use in being a boy if you are going to grow up to be a man because then man and boy you can be certain that that is continuing and a master-piece does not continue it is as it is but it does not continue. It is very interesting that no one is content with being a man and boy but he must also be a son and a father and the fact that they all die has something to do with time but it has nothing to do with a master-piece. The word timely as used in our speech is very interesting but you can any one can see that it has nothing to do with master-pieces we all readily know that. The word timely tells that master-pieces have nothing to do with time.

It is very interesting to have it be inside one that never as you know yourself you know yourself without looking and feeling and looking and feeling make it be that you are some one you have seen. If you have seen any one you know them as you see them whether it is yourself or any other one and so the identity consists in recognition and in recognising you lose identity because after all nobody looks as they look like, they do not look like that we all know that of ourselves and of any one. And therefore in every way it is a trouble and so you write anybody does write to confirm what any one is and the more one does the more one looks like what one was and in being so identity is made more so and that identity is not what any one can have as a thing to be but as a thing to see. And it being a thing to see no master-piece can see what it can see if it does then it is timely and as it is timely it is not a master-piece.

There are so many things to say. If there was no identity no one could be governed, but everybody is governed by everybody and that is why they make no master-pieces, and also why governing has nothing to do with master-pieces it has completely to do with identity but it has nothing to do with master-pieces. And that is why governing is occupying but not interesting, governments are occupying but not interesting because master-pieces are exactly what they are not.

There is another thing to say. When you are writing before there is an audience anything written is as important as any other thing and you cherish anything and everything that you have written. After the audience begins, naturally they create something that is they create you, and so not everything is so important, something is more important than another thing, which was not true when you were you that is when you were not you as your little dog knows you.

And so there we are and there is so much to say but anyway I do not say that there is no doubt that master-pieces are master-pieces in that way and there are very few of them.

1936

F. Scott Fitzgerald

....

The Crack-Up

OF COURSE all life is a process of breaking down, but the blows that do the dramatic side of the work — the big sudden blows that come, or seem to come, from outside — the ones you remember and blame things on and, in moments of weakness, tell your friends about, don't show their effect all at once. There is another sort of blow that comes from within — that you don't feel until it's too late to do anything about it, until you realize with finality that in some regard you will never be as good a man again. The first sort of breakage seems to happen quick — the second kind happens almost without your knowing it but is realized suddenly indeed.

Before I go on with this short history, let me make a general observation — the test of a first-rate intelligence is the ability to hold two opposed ideas in the mind at the same time, and still retain the ability to function. One should, for example, be able to see that things are hopeless and yet be determined to make them otherwise. This philosophy fitted on to my early adult life, when I saw the improbable, the implausible, often the "impossible," come true. Life was something you dominated if you were any good. Life yielded easily to intelligence and effort, or to what proportion could be mustered of both. It seemed a romantic business to be a successful literary man — you were not ever going to be as famous as a movie star but what note you had was probably longer-lived — you were never going to have the power of a man of strong political or religious convictions but you were certainly more independ-

First published in *Esquire*, February–April 1936; collected in *The Crack-Up*, edited by Edmund Wilson, 1945.

ent. Of course within the practice of your trade you were forever unsatisfied — but I, for one, would not have chosen any other.

As the twenties passed, with my own twenties marching a little ahead of them, my two juvenile regrets — at not being big enough (or good enough) to play football in college, and at not getting overseas during the war — resolved themselves into childish waking dreams of imaginary heroism that were good enough to go to sleep on in restless nights. The big problems of life seemed to solve themselves, and if the business of fixing them was difficult, it made one too tired to think of more general problems.

Life, ten years ago, was largely a personal matter. I must hold in balance the sense of the futility of effort and the sense of the necessity to struggle; the conviction of the inevitability of failure and still the determination to "succeed" — and, more than these, the contradiction between the dead hand of the past and the high intentions of the future. If I could do this through the common ills — domestic, professional and personal — then the ego would continue as an arrow shot from nothingness to nothingness with such force that only gravity would bring it to earth at last.

For seventeen years, with a year of deliberate loafing and resting out in the center — things went on like that, with a new chore only a nice prospect for the next day. I was living hard, too, but: "Up to forty-nine it'll be all right," I said. "I can count on that. For a man who's lived as I have, that's all you could ask."

— And then, ten years this side of forty-nine, I suddenly realized that I had prematurely cracked.

II

Now a man can crack in many ways — can crack in the head — in which case the power of decision is taken from you by others! or in the body, when one can but submit to the white hospital world; or in the nerves. William Seabrook in an unsympathetic book tells, with some pride and a movie ending, of how he became a public charge. What led to his alcoholism or was bound up with it, was a collapse of his nervous system. Though the present writer was not so entangled — having at the time not tasted so much as a glass of beer for six months — it was his nervous reflexes that were giving way — too much anger and too many tears.

Moreover, to go back to my thesis that life has a varying offensive, the realization of having cracked was not simultaneous with a blow, but with a reprieve.

Not long before, I had sat in the office of a great doctor and listened to a grave sentence. With what, in retrospect, seems some equanimity, I had gone on about my affairs in the city where I was then living, not caring much, not thinking how much had been left undone, or what would become of this and that responsibility, like people do in books; I was well insured and anyhow I had been only a mediocre caretaker of most of the things left in my hands, even of my talent.

But I had a strong sudden instinct that I must be alone. I didn't want to see any people at all. I had seen so many people all my life — I was an average mixer, but more than average in a tendency to identify myself, my ideas, my destiny, with those of all classes that I came in contact with. I was always saving or being saved — in a single morning I would go through the emotions ascribable to Wellington at Waterloo. I lived in a world of inscrutable hostiles and inalienable friends and supporters.

But now I wanted to be absolutely alone and so arranged a certain insulation from ordinary cares.

It was not an unhappy time. I went away and there were fewer people. I found I was good-and-tired. I could lie around and was glad to, sleeping or dozing sometimes twenty hours a day and in the intervals trying resolutely not to think — instead I made lists — made lists and tore them up, hundreds of lists: of cavalry leaders and football players and cities, and popular tunes and pitchers, and happy times, and hobbies and houses lived in and how many suits since I left the army and how many pairs of shoes (I didn't count the suit I bought in Sorrento that shrunk, nor the pumps and dress shirt and collar that I carried around for years and never wore, because the pumps got damp and grainy and the shirt and collar got yellow and starch-rotted). And lists of women I'd liked, and of the times I had let myself be snubbed by people who had not been my betters in character or ability.

— And then suddenly, surprisingly, I got better.

— And cracked like an old plate as soon as I heard the news.

That is the real end of this story. What was to be done about it will have to rest in what used to be called the "womb of time." Suffice it to say that after about an hour of solitary pillow-hugging, I began to realize that for two years my life had been a drawing on resources that I did not possess, that I had been mortgaging myself physically and spiritually up to the hilt. What was the small gift of life given back in comparison to that? — when there had once been a pride of direction and a confidence in enduring independence.

I realized that in those two years, in order to preserve something — an inner hush maybe, maybe not — I had weaned myself from all the things I used to love — that every act of life from the morning toothbrush to the friend at dinner had become an effort. I saw that for a long time I had not liked people and things, but only followed the rickety old pretense of liking. I saw that even my love for those closest to me was become only an attempt to love, that my casual relations — with an editor, a tobacco seller, the child of a friend, were only what I remembered I *should* do, from other days. All in the same month I became bitter about such things as the sound of the radio, the advertisements in the magazines, the screech of tracks, the dead silence of the country — contemptuous at human softness, immediately (if secretively) quarrelsome toward hardness — hating the night when I couldn't sleep and hating the day because it went toward night. I slept on the heart side now because I knew that the sooner I could tire that out, even a little, the sooner would come that blessed hour of nightmare which, like a catharsis, would enable me to better meet the new day.

There were certain spots, certain faces I could look at. Like most Middle Westerners, I have never had any but the vaguest race prejudices — I always had a secret yen for the lovely Scandinavian blondes who sat on porches in St. Paul but hadn't emerged enough economically to be part of what was then society. They were too nice to be "chickens" and too quickly off the farmlands to seize a place in the sun, but I remember going round blocks to catch a single glimpse of shining hair — the bright shock of a girl I'd never know. This is urban, unpopular talk. It strays afield from the fact that in these latter days I couldn't stand the sight of Celts, English, Politicians, Strangers, Virginians, Negroes (light or dark), Hunting People, or retail clerks, and middlemen in general, all writers (I avoided writers very carefully because they can perpetuate trouble as no one else can) — and all the classes as classes and most of them as members of their class . . .

Trying to cling to something, I liked doctors and girl children up to the age of about thirteen and well-brought-up boy children from about eight years old on. I could have peace and happiness with these few categories of people. I forgot to add that I liked old men — men over seventy, sometimes over sixty if their faces looked seasoned. I liked Katharine Hepburn's face on the screen, no matter what was said about her pretentiousness, and Miriam Hopkins' face, and old friends if I only saw them once a year and could remember their ghosts.

All rather inhuman and undernourished, isn't it? Well, that, children, is the true sign of cracking up.

It is not a pretty picture. Inevitably it was carted here and there within its frame and exposed to various critics. One of them can only be described as a person whose life makes other people's lives seem like death — even this time when she was cast in the usually unappealing role of Job's comforter. In spite of the fact that this story is over, let me append our conversation as a sort of postscript:

"Instead of being so sorry for yourself, listen —" she said. (She always says "Listen," because she thinks while she talks — *really* thinks.) So she said: "Listen. Suppose this wasn't a crack in you — suppose it was a crack in the Grand Canyon."

"The crack's in me," I said heroically.

"Listen! The world only exists in your eyes — your conception of it. You can make it as big or as small as you want to. And you're trying to be a little puny individual. By God, if I ever cracked, I'd try to make the world crack with me. Listen! The world only exists through your apprehension of it, and so it's much better to say that it's not you that's cracked — it's the Grand Canyon."

"Baby et up all her Spinoza?"

"I don't know anything about Spinoza. I know —" She spoke, then, of old woes of her own, that seemed, in the telling, to have been more dolorous than mine, and how she had met them, over-ridden them, beaten them.

I felt a certain reaction to what she said, but I am a slow-thinking man, and it occurred to me simultaneously that of all natural forces, vitality is the incommunicable one. In days when juice came into one as an article without duty, one tried to distribute it — but always without success; to further mix metaphors, vitality never "takes." You have it or you haven't it, like health or brown eyes or honor or a baritone voice. I might have asked some of it from her, neatly wrapped and ready for home cooking and digestion, but I could never have got it — not if I'd waited around for a thousand hours with the tin cup of self-pity. I could walk from her door, holding myself very carefully like cracked crockery, and go away into the world of bitterness, where I was making

a home with such materials as are found there — and quote to myself
after I left her door:
"*Ye are the salt of the earth. But if the salt hath lost its savour, where-
with shall it be salted?*"
Matthew 5:13.

Pasting It Together

In a previous article this writer told about his realization that what he
had before him was not the dish that he had ordered for his forties. In
fact — since he and the dish were one, he described himself as a cracked
plate, the kind that one wonders whether it is worth preserving. Your
editor thought that the article suggested too many aspects without regarding them closely, and probably many readers felt the same way —
and there are always those to whom all self-revelation is contemptible,
unless it ends with a noble thanks to the gods for the Unconquerable
Soul.

But I had been thanking the gods too long, and thanking them for
nothing. I wanted to put a lament into my record, without even the
background of the Euganean Hills to give it color. There weren't any
Euganean hills that I could see.

Sometimes, though, the cracked plate has to be retained in the pan-
try, has to be kept in service as a household necessity. It can never again
be warmed on the stove nor shuffled with the other plates in the
dishpan; it will not be brought out for company, but it will do to hold
crackers late at night or to go into the ice box under left-overs . . .

Hence this sequel — a cracked plate's further history.

Now the standard cure for one who is sunk is to consider those in actual destitution or physical suffering — this is an all-weather beatitude
for gloom in general and fairly salutory day-time advice for everyone.
But at three o'clock in the morning, a forgotten package has the same
tragic importance as a death sentence, and the cure doesn't work — and
in a real dark night of the soul it is always three o'clock in the morning,
day after day. At that hour the tendency is to refuse to face things as
long as possible by retiring into an infantile dream — but one is continually startled out of this by various contacts with the world. One meets
these occasions as quickly and carelessly as possible and retires once
more back into the dream, hoping that things will adjust themselves by
some great material or spiritual bonanza. But as the withdrawal persists
there is less and less chance of the bonanza — one is not waiting for the

fade-out of a single sorrow, but rather being an unwilling witness of an execution, the disintegration of one's own personality . . .

Unless madness or drugs or drink come into it, this phase comes to a dead-end, eventually, and is succeeded by a vacuous quiet. In this you can try to estimate what has been sheared away and what is left. Only when this quiet came to me, did I realize that I had gone through two parallel experiences.

The first time was twenty years ago, when I left Princeton in junior year with a complaint diagnosed as malaria. It transpired, through an X-ray taken a dozen years later, that it had been tuberculosis — a mild case, and after a few months of rest I went back to college. But I had lost certain offices, the chief one was the presidency of the Triangle Club, a musical comedy idea, and also I dropped back a class. To me college would never be the same. There were to be no badges of pride, no medals, after all. It seemed on one March afternoon that I had lost every single thing I wanted — and that night was the first time that I hunted down the spectre of womanhood that, for a little while, makes everything else seem unimportant.

Years later I realized that my failure as a big shot in college was all right — instead of serving on committees, I took a beating on English poetry; when I got the idea of what it was all about, I set about learning how to write. On Shaw's principle that "If you don't get what you like, you better like what you get," it was a lucky break — at the moment it was a harsh and bitter business to know that my career as a leader of men was over.

Since that day I have not been able to fire a bad servant, and I am astonished and impressed by people who can. Some old desire for personal dominance was broken and gone. Life around me was a solemn dream, and I lived on the letters I wrote to a girl in another city. A man does not recover from such jolts — he becomes a different person and, eventually, the new person finds new things to care about.

The other episode parallel to my current situation took place after the war, when I had again over-extended my flank. It was one of those tragic loves doomed for lack of money, and one day the girl closed it out on the basis of common sense. During a long summer of despair I wrote a novel instead of letters, so it came out all right, but it came out all right for a different person. The man with the jingle of money in his pocket who married the girl a year later would always cherish an abiding distrust, an animosity, toward the leisure class — not the conviction of a revolutionist but the smouldering hatred of a peasant. In the years since then I have never been able to stop wondering where my friends' money came from, nor to stop thinking that at one time a sort of *droit de seigneur* might have been exercised to give one of them my girl.

For sixteen years I lived pretty much as this latter person, distrusting the rich, yet working for money with which to share their mobility and the grace that some of them brought into their lives. During this time I had plenty of the usual horses shot from under me — I remember some of their names — *Punctured Pride, Thwarted Expectation, Faithless, Show-off, Hard Hit, Never Again*. And after awhile I wasn't twenty-five, then not even thirty-five, and nothing was quite as good. But in all these years I don't remember a moment of discouragement. I saw honest men through moods of suicidal gloom — some of them gave up and died; others adjusted themselves and went on to a larger success than mine; but my morale never sank below the level of self-disgust when I had put on some unsightly personal show. Trouble has no necessary connection with discouragement — discouragement has a germ of its own, as different from trouble as arthritis is different from a stiff joint.

When a new sky cut off the sun last spring, I didn't at first relate it to what had happened fifteen or twenty years ago. Only gradually did a certain family resemblance come through — an over-extension of the flank, a burning of the candle at both ends; a call upon physical resources that I did not command, like a man over-drawing at his bank. In its impact this blow was more violent than the other two but it was the same in kind — a feeling that I was standing at twilight on a deserted range, with an empty rifle in my hands and the targets down. No problem set — simply a silence with only the sound of my own breathing.

In this silence there was a vast irresponsibility toward every obligation, a deflation of all my values. A passionate belief in order, a disregard of motives or consequences in favor of guess work and prophecy, a feeling that craft and industry would have a place in any world — one by one, these and other convictions were swept away. I saw that the novel, which at my maturity was the strongest and supplest medium for conveying thought and emotion from one human being to another, was becoming subordinated to a mechanical and communal art that, whether in the hands of Hollywood merchants or Russian idealists, was capable of reflecting only the tritest thought, the most obvious emotion. It was an art in which words were subordinate to images, where personality was worn down to the inevitable low gear of collaboration. As long past as 1930, I had a hunch that the talkies would make even the best selling novelist as archaic as silent pictures. People still read, if only Professor Canby's book of the month — curious children nosed at the slime of Mr. Tiffany Thayer in the drug-store libraries — but there was a rankling indignity, that to me had become almost an obsession, in seeing the power of the written word subordinated to another power, a more glittering, a grosser power . . .

I set that down as an example of what haunted me during the long night — this was something I could neither accept nor struggle against, something which tended to make my efforts obsolescent, as the chain stores have crippled the small merchant, an exterior force, unbeatable —

(I have the sense of lecturing now, looking at a watch on the desk before me and seeing how many more minutes —).

Well, when I had reached this period of silence, I was forced into a measure that no one ever adopts voluntarily: I was impelled to think. God, was it difficult! The moving about of great secret trunks. In the first exhausted halt, I wondered whether I had ever thought. After a long time I came to these conclusions, just as I write them here:

(1) That I had done very little thinking, save within the problems of my craft. For twenty years a certain man had been my intellectual conscience. That was Edmund Wilson.

(2) That another man represented my sense of the "good life," though I saw him once in a decade, and since then he might have been hung. He is in the fur business in the Northwest and wouldn't like his name set down here. But in difficult situations I had tried to think what *he* would have thought, how *he* would have acted.

(3) That a third contemporary had been an artistic conscience to me — I had not imitated his infectious style, because my own style, such as it is, was formed before he published anything, but there was an awful pull toward him when I was on a spot.

(4) That a fourth man had come to dictate my relations with other people when these relations were successful: how to do, what to say. How to make people at least momentarily happy (in opposition to Mrs. Post's theories of how to make everyone thoroughly uncomfortable with a sort of systematized vulgarity). This always confused me and made me want to go out and get drunk, but this man had seen the game, analyzed it and beaten it, and his word was good enough for me.

(5) That my political conscience had scarcely existed for ten years save as an element of irony in my stuff. When I became again concerned with the system I should function under, it was a man much younger

than myself who brought it to me, with a mixture of passion and fresh air.

So there was not an "I" any more — not a basis on which I could organize my self-respect — save my limitless capacity for toil that it seemed I possessed no more. It was strange to have no self — to be like a little boy left alone in a big house, who knew that now he could do anything he wanted to do, but found that there was nothing that he wanted to do —

(The watch is past the hour and I have barely reached my thesis. I have some doubts as to whether this is of general interest, but if anyone wants more, there is plenty left, and your editor will tell me. If you've had enough, say so — but not too loud, because I have the feeling that someone, I'm not sure who, is sound asleep — someone who could have helped me to keep my shop open. It wasn't Lenin, and it wasn't God.)

Handle with Care

I have spoken in these pages of how an exceptionally optimistic young man experienced a crack-up of all values, a crack-up that he scarcely knew of until long after it occurred. I told of the succeeding period of desolation and of the necessity of going on, but without benefit of Henley's familiar heroics, "my head is bloody but unbowed." For a check-up of my spiritual liabilities indicated that I had no particular head to be bowed or unbowed. Once I had had a heart but that was about all I was sure of.

This was at least a starting place out of the morass in which I floundered: "I felt — therefore I was." At one time or another there had been many people who had leaned on me, come to me in difficulties or written me from afar, believed implicitly in my advice and my attitude toward life. The dullest platitude monger or the most unscrupulous Rasputin who can influence the destinies of many people must have some individuality, so the question became one of finding why and where I had changed, where was the leak through which, unknown to myself, my enthusiasm and my vitality had been steadily and prematurely trickling away.

One harassed and despairing night I packed a brief case and went off a thousand miles to think it over. I took a dollar room in a drab little town where I knew no one and sunk all the money I had with me in a stock of potted meat, crackers and apples. But don't let me suggest that the change from a rather overstuffed world to a comparative asceticism was any Research Magnificent — I only wanted absolute quiet to think out why I had developed a sad attitude toward sadness, a melancholy attitude toward melancholy and a tragic attitude toward tragedy — *why I had become identified with the objects of my horror or compassion.*

Does this seem a fine distinction? It isn't: identification such as this spells the death of accomplishment. It is something like this that keeps insane people from working. Lenin did not willingly endure the sufferings of his proletariat, nor Washington of his troops, nor Dickens of his London poor. And when Tolstoy tried some such merging of himself with the objects of his attention, it was a fake and a failure. I mention these because they are the men best known to us all.

It was dangerous mist. When Wordsworth decided that "there had passed away a glory from the earth," he felt no compulsion to pass away with it, and the Fiery Particle Keats never ceased his struggle against t.b. nor in his last moments relinquished his hope of being among the English poets.

My self-immolation was something sodden-dark. It was very distinctly not modern — yet I saw it in others, saw it in a dozen men of honor and industry since the war. (I heard you, but that's too easy — there were Marxians among these men.) I had stood by while one famous contemporary of mine played with the idea of the Big Out for half a year; I had watched when another, equally eminent, spent months in an asylum unable to endure any contact with his fellow men. And of those who had given up and passed on I could list a score.

This led me to the idea that the ones who had survived had made some sort of clean break. This is a big word and is no parallel to a jailbreak when one is probably headed for a new jail or will be forced back to the old one. The famous "Escape" or "run away from it all" is an excursion in a trap even if the trap includes the south seas, which are only for those who want to paint them or sail them. A clean break is something you cannot come back from; that is irretrievable because it makes the past cease to exist. So, since I could no longer fulfill the obligations that life had set for me or that I had set for myself, why not slay the empty shell who had been posturing at it for four years? I must continue to be a writer because that was my only way of life, but I would cease any attempts to be a person — to be kind, just or generous. There were plenty of counterfeit coins around that would pass instead of these and I knew where I could get them at a nickel on the dollar. In thirty-nine years an observant eye has learned to detect where the milk is watered and the sugar is sanded, the rhinestone passed for diamond and the stucco for stone. There was to be no more giving of myself — all giving was to be outlawed henceforth under a new name, and that name was Waste.

The decision made me rather exuberant, like anything that is both real and new. As a sort of beginning there was a whole shaft of letters to be tipped into the waste basket when I went home, letters that wanted something for nothing — to read this man's manuscript, market this man's poem, speak free on the radio, indite notes of introduction, give this interview, help with the plot of this play, with this domestic situation, perform this act of thoughtfulness or charity.

The conjuror's hat was empty. To draw things out of it had long been a sort of sleight of hand, and now, to change the metaphor, I was off the dispensing end of the relief roll forever.

The heady villainous feeling continued.

I felt like the beady-eyed men I used to see on the commuting train from Great Neck fifteen years back — men who didn't care whether the world tumbled into chaos tomorrow if it spared their houses. I was one with them now, one with the smooth articles who said:

"I'm sorry but business is business." Or:

"You ought to have thought of that before you got into this trouble." Or:

"I'm not the person to see about that."

And a smile — ah, I would get me a smile. I'm still working on that smile. It is to combine the best qualities of a hotel manager, an experienced old social weasel, a headmaster on visitors' day, a colored elevator man, a pansy pulling a profile, a producer getting stuff at half its market value, a trained nurse coming on a new job, a body-vender in her first rotogravure, a hopeful extra swept near the camera, a ballet dancer with an infected toe, and of course the great beam of loving kindness common to all those from Washington to Beverly Hills who must exist by virtue of the contorted pan.

The voice too — I am working with a teacher on the voice. When I have perfected it the larynx will show no ring of conviction except the conviction of the person I am talking to. Since it will be largely called upon for the elicitation of the word "Yes," my teacher (a lawyer) and I are concentrating on that, but in extra hours. I am learning to bring into it that polite acerbity that makes people feel that far from being welcome they are not even tolerated and are under continual and scathing analysis at every moment. These times will of course not coincide with the smile. This will be reserved exclusively for those from whom I have nothing to gain, old worn-out people or young struggling people. They won't mind — what the hell, they get it most of the time anyhow.

But enough. It is not a matter of levity. If you are young and you should write asking to see me and learn how to be a sombre literary man writing pieces upon the state of emotional exhaustion that often overtakes writers in their prime — if you should be so young and so fatuous as to do this, I would not do so much as acknowledge your letter, unless you were related to someone very rich and important indeed. And if you were dying of starvation outside my window, I would go out quickly and give you the smile and the voice (if no longer the hand) and stick around till somebody raised a nickel to phone for the ambulance, that is if I thought there would be any copy in it for me.

I have now at last become a writer only. The man I had persistently tried to be became such a burden that I have "cut him loose" with as little compunction as a Negro lady cuts loose a rival on Saturday night. Let the good people function as such — let the overworked doctors die in harness, with one week's "vacation" a year that they can devote to straightening out their family affairs, and let the underworked doctors scramble for cases at one dollar a throw; let the soldiers be killed and enter immediately into the Valhalla of their profession. That is their contract with the gods. A writer need have no such ideals unless he makes them for himself, and this one has quit. The old dream of being an entire man in the Goethe-Byron-Shaw tradition, with an opulent American touch, a sort of combination of J. P. Morgan, Topham Beauclerk and St. Francis of Assisi, has been relegated to the junk heap of the shoulder pads worn for one day on the Princeton freshman football field and the overseas cap never worn overseas.

So what? This is what I think now: that the natural state of the sentient adult is a qualified unhappiness. I think also that in an adult the desire to be finer in grain than you are, "a constant striving" (as those people say who gain their bread by saying it) only adds to this unhappiness in the end — that end that comes to our youth and hope. My own happiness in the past often approached such an ecstasy that I could not share it even with the person dearest to me but had to walk it away in quiet streets and lanes with only fragments of it to distil into little lines in books — and I think that my happiness, or talent for self-delusion or what you will, was an exception. It was not the natural thing but the unnatural — unnatural as the Boom; and my recent experience parallels the wave of despair that swept the nation when the Boom was over.

I shall manage to live with the new dispensation, though it has taken some months to be certain of the fact. And just as the laughing stoicism which has enabled the American Negro to endure the intolerable conditions of his existence has cost him his sense of the truth — so in my case there is a price to pay. I do not any longer like the postman, nor the grocer, nor the editor, nor the cousin's husband, and he in turn will come to dislike me, so that life will never be very pleasant again, and the sign *Cave Canem* is hung permanently just above my door. I will try to be a correct animal though, and if you throw me a bone with enough meat on it I may even lick your hand.

1937

James Thurber

Sex Ex Machina

WITH THE DISAPPEARANCE of the gas mantle and the advent of the short circuit, man's tranquility began to be threatened by everything he put his hand on. Many people believe that it was a sad day indeed when Benjamin Franklin tied that key to a kite string and flew the kite in a thunderstorm; other people believed that if it hadn't been Franklin, it would have been someone else. As, of course, it was in the case of the harnessing of steam and the invention of the gas engine. At any rate, it has come about that so-called civilized man finds himself today surrounded by the myriad mechanical devices of a technological world. Writers of books on how to control your nerves, how to conquer fear, how to cultivate calm, how to be happy in spite of everything, are of several minds as regards the relation of man and the machine. Some of them are prone to believe that the mind and body, if properly disciplined, can get the upper hand of this mechanized existence. Others merely ignore the situation and go on to the profitable writing of more facile chapters of inspiration. Still others attribute the whole menace of the machine to sex, and so confuse the average reader that he cannot always be certain whether he has been knocked down by an automobile or is merely in love.

Dr. Bisch, the Be-Glad-You're-Neurotic man, has a remarkable chapter which deals, in part, with man, sex, and the machine. He examines the case of three hypothetical men who start across a street on a red light and get in the way of an oncoming automobile. A dodges successfully; B stands still, "accepting the situation with calm and resignation,"

First published in *The New Yorker*, 1937; collected in *Let Your Mind Alone! And Other More or Less Inspirational Pieces*, 1937.

thus becoming one of my favorite heroes in modern belles-lettres; and C hesitates, wavers, jumps backward and forward, and finally runs head on into the car. To lead you through Dr. Bisch's complete analysis of what was wrong with B and C would occupy your whole day. He mentions what the McDougallians would say ("Instinct!"), what the Freudians would retort ("Complexes!"), and what the behaviorists would shout ("Conditioned reflexes!"). He also brings in what the physiologists would say — deficient thyroid, hypoadrenal functioning, and so on. The average sedentary man of our time who is at all suggestible must emerge from this chapter believing that his chances of surviving a combination of instinct, complexes, reflexes, glands, sex, and present-day traffic conditions are about equal to those of a one-legged blind man trying to get out of a labyrinth.

Let us single out what Dr. Bisch thinks the Freudians would say about poor Mr. C, who ran right into the car. He writes, "'Sex hunger,' the Freudians would declare. 'Always keyed up and irritable because of it. Undoubtedly suffers from insomnia and when he does sleep his dream life must be productive, distorted, and possibly frightening. Automobile unquestionably has sex significance for him . . . to C the car is both enticing and menacing at one and the same time. . . . A thorough analysis is indicated. . . . It might take months. But then, the man needs an analysis as much as food. He is heading for a complete nervous collapse.'" It is my studied opinion, not to put too fine a point on it, that Mr. C is heading for a good mangling, and that if he gets away with only a nervous collapse, it will be a miracle.

I have not always, I am sorry to say, been able to go the whole way with the Freudians, or even a very considerable distance. Even though, as Dr. Bisch says, "One must admit that the Freudians have had the best of it thus far. At least they have received the most publicity." It is in matters like their analysis of men and machines, of Mr. C and the automobile, that the Freudians and I part company. Of course, the analysis above is simply Dr. Bisch's idea of what the Freudians would say, but I think he has got it down pretty well. Dr. Bisch himself leans toward the Freudian analysis of Mr. C, for he says in this same chapter, "An automobile bearing down upon you may be a sex symbol at that, you know, especially if you dream it." It is my contention, of course, that even if you dream it, it is probably not a sex symbol, but merely an automobile bearing down upon you. And if it bears down upon you in real life, I am sure it is an automobile. I have seen the same behavior that characterized Mr. C displayed by a squirrel (Mr. S) that lives in the grounds of my house in the country. He is a fairly tame squirrel, happily mated and not sex-hungry, if I am any judge, but nevertheless he frequently runs out toward my automobile when I start down the driveway, and then hesitates, wavers, jumps forward and backward, and occasionally would run right into the car except that he is awfully fast on his feet and that I always hurriedly put on the brakes of the 1935 V-8 Sex Symbol that I drive.

I have seen this same behavior in the case of rabbits (notoriously uninfluenced by any sex symbols save those of other rabbits), dogs, pigeons, a doe, a young hawk (which flew at my car), a blue heron that I encountered on a country road in Vermont, and once, near Paul Smith's in the Adirondacks, a fox. They all acted exactly like Mr. C. The hawk, unhappily, was killed. All the others escaped with nothing worse, I suppose, than a complete nervous collapse. Although I cannot claim to have been conversant with the private life and the secret compulsions, the psychoneuroses and the glandular activities of all these animals, it is nevertheless my confident and unswervable belief that there was nothing at all the matter with any one of them. Like Mr. C, they suddenly saw a car swiftly bearing down upon them, got excited, and lost their heads. I do not believe, you see, there was anything the matter with Mr. C, either. But I do believe that, after a thorough analysis lasting months, with a lot of harping on the incident of the automobile, something might very well come to be the matter with him. He might even actually get to suffering from the delusion that he believes automobiles are sex symbols.

It seems to me worthy of note that Dr. Bisch, in reciting the reactions of three persons in the face of an oncoming car, selected three men. What would have happened had they been Mrs. A, Mrs. B, and Mrs. C? You know as well as I do: all three of them would have hesitated, wavered, jumped forward and backward, and finally run head on into the car if some man hadn't grabbed them. (I used to know a motorist who, every time he approached a woman standing on a curb preparing to cross the street, shouted, "Hold it, stupid!") It is not too much to say that, with a car bearing down upon them, ninety-five women out of a hundred would act like Mr. C — or Mr. S, the squirrel, or Mr. F, the fox. But it is certainly too much to say that ninety-five out of every hundred women look upon an automobile as a sex symbol. For one thing, Dr. Bisch points out that the automobile serves as a sex symbol because of the "mechanical principle involved." But only one woman in a thousand really knows anything about the mechanical principle involved in an automobile. And yet, as I have said, ninety-five out of a hundred would hesitate, waver, and jump, just as Mr. C did. I think we have the Freudians here. If we haven't proved our case with rabbits and a blue heron, we have certainly proved it with women.

To my notion, the effect of the automobile and of other mechanical contrivances on the state of our nerves, minds, and spirits is a problem which the popular psychologists whom I have dealt with know very little about. The sexual explanation of the relationship of man and the machine is not good enough. To arrive at the real explanation, we have to begin very far back, as far back as Franklin and the kite, or at least as far back as a certain man and woman who appear in a book of stories written more than sixty years ago by Max Adeler. One story in this book tells about a housewife who bought a combination ironing board and card table, which some New England genius had thought up in his spare time. The husband, coming home to find the devilish contraption in the parlor, was appalled. "What is that thing?" he demanded. His wife explained that it was a card table, but that if you pressed a button underneath, it would become an ironing board. Whereupon she pushed the button and the table leaped a foot into the air, extended itself, and became an ironing board. The story goes on to tell how the thing finally became so finely sensitized that it would change back and forth if you merely touched it — you didn't have to push the button. The husband stuck it in the attic (after it had leaped up and struck him a couple of times while he was playing euchre), and on windy nights it could be heard flopping and banging around, changing from a card table to an ironing board and back. The story serves as one example of our dread heritage of annoyance, shock, and terror arising out of the nature of mechanical contrivances *per se.* The mechanical principle involved in this damnable invention had, I believe, no relationship to sex whatsoever. There are certain analysts who see sex in anything, even a leaping ironing board, but I think we can ignore these scientists.

No man (to go on) who has wrestled with a self-adjusting card table can ever be quite the man he once was. If he arrives at the state where he hesitates, wavers, and jumps at every mechanical device he encounters, it is not, I submit, because he recognizes the enticements of sex in the device, but only because he recognizes the menace of the machine as such. There might very well be, in every descendant of the man we have been discussing, an inherited desire to jump at, and conquer, mechanical devices before they have a chance to turn into something twice as big and twice as menacing. It is not reasonable to expect that his children and their children will have entirely escaped the stigma of such traumata. I myself will never be the man I once was, nor will my descendants probably ever amount to much, because of a certain experience I had with an automobile.

I had gone out to the barn of my country place, a barn which was used both as a garage and a kennel, to quiet some large black poodles. It was 1 A.M. of a pitch-dark night in winter and the poodles had apparently been terrified by some kind of a prowler, a tramp, a turtle, or perhaps a fiend of some sort. Both my poodles and I myself believed, at the time, in fiends, and still do. Fiends who materialize out of nothing and nowhere, like winged pigweed or Russian thistle. I had quite a time quieting the dogs, because their panic spread to me and mine spread back to them again, in a kind of vicious circle. Finally, a hush as ominous as their uproar fell upon them, but they kept looking over their shoulders, in a kind of apprehensive way. "There's nothing to be afraid of," I told them as firmly as I could, and just at that moment the klaxon of my car, which was just behind me, began to shriek. Everybody has heard a klaxon on a car suddenly begin to sound; I understand it is a short circuit that causes it. But very few people have heard one scream behind them while they were quieting six or eight alarmed poodles in the middle of the night in an old barn. I jump now whenever I hear a klaxon, even the klaxon on my own car when I push the button intentionally. The experience has left its mark. Everybody, from the day of the jumping card table to the day of the screaming klaxon, has had similar shocks. You can see the result, entirely unsuperinduced by sex, in the strained faces and muttering lips of people who pass you on the streets of great, highly mechanized cities. There goes a man who picked up one of those trick matchboxes that whir in your hands; there goes a woman who tried to change a fuse without turning off the current; and yonder toddles an ancient who cranked an old Reo with the spark advanced. Every person carries in his consciousness the old scar, or the fresh wound, of some harrowing misadventure with a contraption of some sort. I know people who would not deposit a nickel and a dime in a cigarette-vending machine and push the lever even if a diamond necklace came out. I know dozens who would not climb into an airplane even if it didn't move off the ground. In none of these people have I discerned what I would call a neurosis, an "exaggerated" fear; I have discerned only a natural caution in a world made up of gadgets that whir and whine and whiz and shriek and sometimes explode.

I should like to end with the case history of a friend of mine in Ohio named Harvey Lake. When he was only nineteen, the steering bar of an old electric runabout broke off in his hand, causing the machine to carry him through a fence and into the grounds of the Columbus School for Girls. He developed a fear of automobiles, trains, and every other kind of vehicle that was not pulled by a horse. Now, the psychologists would call this a complex and represent the fear as abnormal, but I see it as a purely reasonable apprehension. If Harvey Lake had, because he was catapulted into the grounds of the Columbus School for Girls, developed a fear of girls, I would call that a complex; but I don't call his normal fear of machines a complex. Harvey Lake never in his life got into a plane (he died in a fall from a porch), but I do not regard that as neurotic, either, but only sensible.

I have, to be sure, encountered men with complexes. There was, for example, Marvin Belt. He had a complex about airplanes that was quite interesting. He was not afraid of machinery, or of high places, or of crashes. He was simply afraid that the pilot of any plane he got into might lose his mind. "I imagine myself high over Montana," he once said to me, "in a huge, perfectly safe tri-motored plane. Several of the passengers are dozing, others are reading, but I am keeping my eyes glued on the door to the cockpit. Suddenly the pilot steps out of it, a wild light in his eyes, and in a falsetto like that of a little girl he says to me, 'Conductor, will you please let me off at One-Hundred-and-Twenty-fifth Street?'" "But," I said to Belt, "even if the pilot does go crazy, there is still the co-pilot." "No, there isn't," said Belt. "The pilot has hit the co-pilot over the head with something and killed him." Yes, the psychoanalysts can have Marvin Belt. But they can't have Harvey Lake, or Mr. C, or Mr. S, or Mr. F, or, while I have my strength, me.

1937

Richard Wright

....

The Ethics of Living Jim Crow:
An Autobiographical Sketch

I

MY FIRST LESSON in how to live as a Negro came when I was quite small. We were living in Arkansas. Our house stood behind the railroad tracks. Its skimpy yard was paved with black cinders. Nothing green ever grew in that yard. The only touch of green we could see was far away, beyond the tracks, over where the white folks lived. But cinders were good enough for me and I never missed the green growing things. And anyhow cinders were fine weapons. You could always have a nice hot war with huge black cinders. All you had to do was crouch behind the brick pillars of a house with your hands full of gritty ammunition. And the first woolly black head you saw pop out from behind another row of pillars was your target. You tried your very best to knock it off. It was great fun.

I never fully realized the appalling disadvantages of a cinder environment till one day the gang to which I belonged found itself engaged in a war with the white boys who lived beyond the tracks. As usual we laid down our cinder barrage, thinking that this would wipe the white boys out. But they replied with a steady bombardment of broken bottles. We doubled our cinder barrage, but they hid behind trees, hedges, and the sloping embankments of their lawns. Having no such fortifications, we retreated to the brick pillars of our homes. During the retreat a broken

First published in *American Stuff: WPA Writers' Anthology*, 1937; included as the introduction to the second printing of * *Uncle Tom's Children*, 1940.

milk bottle caught me behind the ear, opening a deep gash which bled profusely. The sight of blood pouring over my face completely demoralized our ranks. My fellow-combatants left me standing paralyzed in the center of the yard, and scurried for their homes. A kind neighbor saw me and rushed me to a doctor, who took three stitches in my neck.

I sat brooding on my front steps, nursing my wound and waiting for my mother to come from work. I felt that a grave injustice had been done me. It was all right to throw cinders. The greatest harm a cinder could do was leave a bruise. But broken bottles were dangerous; they left you cut, bleeding, and helpless.

When night fell, my mother came from the white folks' kitchen. I raced down the street to meet her. I could just feel in my bones that she would understand. I knew she would tell me exactly what to do next time. I grabbed her hand and babbled out the whole story. She examined my wound, then slapped me.

"How come yuh didn't hide?" she asked me. "How come yuh awways fightin'?"

I was outraged, and bawled. Between sobs I told her that I didn't have any trees or hedges to hide behind. There wasn't a thing I could have used as a trench. And you couldn't throw very far when you were hiding behind the brick pillars of a house. She grabbed a barrel stave, dragged me home, stripped me naked, and beat me till I had a fever of one hundred and two. She would smack my rump with the stave, and, while the skin was still smarting, impart to me gems of Jim Crow wisdom. I was never to throw cinders any more. I was never to fight any more wars. I was never, never, under any conditions, to fight *white* folks again. And they were absolutely right in clouting me with the broken milk bottle. Didn't I know she was working hard every day in the hot kitchens of the white folks to make money to take care of me? When was I ever going to learn to be a good boy? She couldn't be bothered with my fights. She finished by telling me that I ought to be thankful to God as long as I lived that they didn't kill me.

All that night I was delirious and could not sleep. Each time I closed my eyes I saw monstrous white faces suspended from the ceiling, leering at me.

From that time on, the charm of my cinder yard was gone. The green trees, the trimmed hedges, the cropped lawns grew very meaningful, became a symbol. Even today when I think of white folks, the hard, sharp outlines of white houses surrounded by trees, lawns, and hedges are present somewhere in the background of my mind. Through the years they grew into an overreaching symbol of fear.

It was a long time before I came in close contact with white folks again. We moved from Arkansas to Mississippi. Here we had the good fortune not to live behind the railroad tracks, or close to white neighborhoods. We lived in the very heart of the local Black Belt. There were black churches and black preachers, there were black schools and black teachers; black groceries and black clerks. In fact, everything was so solidly black that for a long time I did not even think of white folks, save in remote and vague terms. But this could not last forever. As one grows older one eats more. One's clothing costs more. When I finished grammar school I had to go to work. My mother could no longer feed and clothe me on her cooking job.

There is but one place where a black boy who knows no trade can get a job, and that's where the houses and faces are white, where the trees, lawns, and hedges are green. My first job was with an optical company in Jackson, Mississippi. The morning I applied I stood straight and neat before the boss, answering all his questions with sharp yessirs and nosirs. I was very careful to pronounce my *sirs* distinctly, in order that he might know that I was polite, that I knew where I was, and that I knew he was a *white* man. I wanted that job badly.

He looked me over as though he were examining a prize poodle. He questioned me closely about my schooling, being particularly insistent about how much mathematics I had had. He seemed very pleased when I told him I had had two years of algebra.

"Boy, how would you like to try to learn something around here?" he asked me.

"I'd like it fine, sir," I said, happy. I had visions of "working my way up." Even Negroes have those visions.

"All right," he said. "Come on."

I followed him to the small factory.

"Pease," he said to a white man of about thirty-five, "this is Richard. He's going to work for us."

Pease looked at me and nodded.

I was then taken to a white boy of about seventeen.

"Morrie, this is Richard, who's going to work for us."

"Whut yuh sayin' there, boy!" Morrie boomed at me.

"Fine!" I answered.

The boss instructed these two to help me, teach me, give me jobs to do, and let me learn what I could in my spare time.

My wages were five dollars a week.

I worked hard, trying to please. For the first month I got along O.K. Both Pease and Morrie seemed to like me. But one thing was missing. And I kept thinking about it. I was not learning anything and nobody was volunteering to help me. Thinking they had forgotten that I was to learn something about the mechanics of grinding lenses, I asked Morrie one day to tell me about the work. He grew red.

"Whut yuh tryin' t' do, nigger, get smart?" he asked.

"Naw; I ain' tryin' t' git smart," I said.

"Well, don't, if yuh know whut's good for yuh!"

I was puzzled. Maybe he just doesn't want to help me, I thought. I went to Pease.

"Say, are yuh crazy, you black bastard?" Pease asked me, his gray eyes growing hard.

I spoke out, reminding him that the boss had said I was to be given a chance to learn something.

"Nigger, you think you're *white*, don't you?"

"Naw, sir!"

"Well, you're acting mighty like it!"

"But, Mr. Pease, the boss said . . ."

Pease shook his fist in my face.

"This is a *white* man's work around here, and you better watch your-self!"

From then on they changed toward me. They said good-morning no more. When I was just a bit slow in performing some duty, I was called a lazy black son-of-a-bitch.

Once I thought of reporting all this to the boss. But the mere idea of what would happen to me if Pease and Morrie should learn that I had "snitched" stopped me. And after all the boss was a white man, too. What was the use?

The climax came at noon one summer day. Pease called me to his work-bench. To get to him I had to go between two narrow benches and stand with my back against a wall.

"Yes, sir," I said.

"Richard, I want to ask you something," Pease began pleasantly, not looking up from his work.

"Yes, sir," I said again.

Morrie came over, blocking the narrow passage between the benches. He folded his arms, staring at me solemnly.

I looked from one to the other, sensing that something was coming.

"Yes, sir," I said for the third time.

Pease looked up and spoke very slowly.

"Richard, *Mr.* Morrie here tells me you called me *Pease.*"

I stiffened. A void seemed to open up in me. I knew this was the show-down.

He meant that I had failed to call him Mr. Pease. I looked at Morrie. He was gripping a steel bar in his hands. I opened my mouth to speak, to protest, to assure Pease that I had never called him simply *Pease,* and that I had never had any intentions of doing so, when Morrie grabbed me by the collar, ramming my head against the wall.

"Now, be careful, nigger!" snarled Morrie, baring his teeth. "*I* heard yuh call 'im *Pease!* 'N' if yuh say yuh didn't, yuh're callin' me a *lie,* see?" He waved the steel bar threateningly.

If I had said: No, sir, Mr. Pease, I never called you *Pease,* I would have been automatically calling Morrie a liar. And if I had said: Yes, sir, Mr. Pease, I called you *Pease,* I would have been pleading guilty to having uttered the worst insult that a Negro can utter to a southern white man. I stood hesitating, trying to frame a neutral reply.

"Richard, I asked you a question!" said Pease. Anger was creeping into his voice.

"I don't remember calling you *Pease,* Mr. Pease," I said cautiously. "And if I did, I sure didn't mean . . ."

"You black son-of-a-bitch! You called me *Pease,* then!" he spat, slapping me till I bent sideways over a bench. Morrie was on top of me, demanding:

"Didn't yuh call 'im *Pease?* If yuh say yuh didn't, I'll rip yo' gut string loose with this bar, yuh black granny dodger! Yuh can't call a white man a lie 'n' git erway with it, you black son-of-a-bitch!"

I wilted. I begged them not to bother me. I knew what they wanted. They wanted me to leave.

"I'll leave," I promised. "I'll leave right *now.*"

They gave me a minute to get out of the factory. I was warned not to show up again, or tell the boss.

I went.

When I told the folks at home what had happened, they called me a fool. They told me that I must never again attempt to exceed my boundaries. When you are working for white folks, they said, you got to "stay in your place" if you want to keep working.

II

My Jim Crow education continued on my next job, which was portering in a clothing store. One morning, while polishing brass out front, the boss and his twenty-year-old son got out of their car and half dragged and half kicked a Negro woman into the store. A policeman standing at the corner looked on, twirling his night-stick. I watched out of the corner of my eye, never slackening the strokes of my chamois upon the brass. After a few minutes, I heard shrill screams coming from the rear of the store. Later the woman stumbled out, bleeding, crying, and holding her stomach. When she reached the end of the block, the policeman grabbed her and accused her of being drunk. Silently, I watched him throw her into a patrol wagon.

When I went to the rear of the store, the boss and his son were washing their hands at the sink. They were chuckling. The floor was bloody and strewn with wisps of hair and clothing. No doubt I must have appeared pretty shocked, for the boss slapped me reassuringly on the back.

"Boy, that's what we do to niggers when they don't want to pay their bills," he said, laughing.

His son looked at me and grinned.

"Here, hava cigarette," he said.

Not knowing what to do, I took it. He lit his and held the match for me. This was a gesture of kindness, indicating that even if they had beaten the poor old woman, they would not beat me if I knew enough to keep my mouth shut.

"Yes, sir," I said, and asked no questions.

After they had gone, I sat on the edge of a packing box and stared at the bloody floor till the cigarette went out.

That day at noon, while eating in a hamburger joint, I told my fellow Negro porters what had happened. No one seemed surprised. One fellow, after swallowing a huge bite, turned to me and asked:

"Huh! Is tha' all they did t' her?"

"Yeah. Wasn't tha' enough?" I asked.

"Shucks! Man, she's a lucky bitch!" he said, burying his lips deep into a juicy hamburger. "Hell, it's a wonder they didn't lay her when they got through."

III

I was learning fast, but not quite fast enough. One day, while I was delivering packages in the suburbs, my bicycle tire was punctured. I walked along the hot, dusty road, sweating and leading my bicycle by the handle-bars.

A car slowed at my side.

"What's the matter, boy?" a white man called.

I told him my bicycle was broken and I was walking back to town.

"That's too bad," he said. "Hop on the running board."

He stopped the car. I clutched hard at my bicycle with one hand and clung to the side of the car with the other.

"All set?"

"Yes, sir," I answered. The car started.

It was full of young white men. They were drinking. I watched the flask pass from mouth to mouth.

"Wanna drink, boy?" one asked.

I laughed as the wind whipped my face. Instinctively obeying the freshly planted precepts of my mother, I said:

"Oh, no!"

The words were hardly out of my mouth before I felt something hard and cold smash me between the eyes. It was an empty whisky bottle. I saw stars, and fell backwards from the speeding car into the dust of the road, my feet becoming entangled in the steel spokes of my bicycle. The white men piled out and stood over me.

"Nigger, ain' yuh learned no better sense'n tha' yet?" asked the man who hit me. "Ain' yuh learned t' say *sir* t' a white man yet?"

Dazed, I pulled to my feet. My elbows and legs were bleeding. Fists doubled, the white man advanced, kicking my bicycle out of the way.

"Aw, leave the bastard alone. He's got enough," said one.

They stood looking at me. I rubbed my shins, trying to stop the flow of blood. No doubt they felt a sort of contemptuous pity, for one asked:

"Yuh wanna ride t' town now, nigger? Yuh reckon yuh know enough t' ride now?"

"I wanna walk," I said, simply.

Maybe it sounded funny. They laughed.

"Well, walk, yuh black son-of-a-bitch!"

When they left they comforted me with:

"Nigger, yuh sho better be damn glad it wuz us yuh talked t' tha' way.

Yuh're a lucky bastard, 'cause if yuh'd said tha' t' somebody else, yuh might've been a dead nigger now."

IV

Negroes who have lived South know the dread of being caught alone upon the streets in white neighborhoods after the sun has set. In such a simple situation as this the plight of the Negro in America is graphically symbolized. While white strangers may be in these neighborhoods trying to get home, they can pass unmolested. But the color of a Negro's skin makes him easily recognizable, makes him suspect, converts him into a defenseless target.

Late one Saturday night I made some deliveries in a white neighborhood. I was pedaling my bicycle back to the store as fast as I could, when a police car, swerving toward me, jammed me into the curbing.

"Get down and put up your hands!" the policemen ordered.

I did. They climbed out of the car, guns drawn, faces set, and advanced slowly.

"Keep still!" they ordered.

I reached my hands higher. They searched my pockets and packages. They seemed dissatisfied when they could find nothing incriminating. Finally, one of them said:

"Boy, tell your boss not to send you out in white neighborhoods after sundown."

As usual, I said:

"Yes, sir."

V

My next job was as hall-boy in a hotel. Here my Jim Crow education broadened and deepened. When the bell-boys were busy, I was often called to assist them. As many of the rooms in the hotel were occupied by prostitutes, I was constantly called to carry them liquor and cigarettes. These women were nude most of the time. They did not bother about clothing, even for bell-boys. When you went into their rooms, you were supposed to take their nakedness for granted, as though it startled you no more than a blue vase or a red rug. Your presence awoke in them no sense of shame, for you were not regarded as human. If they were alone, you could steal sidelong glimpses at them. But if they were receiving men, not a flicker of your eyelids could show. I remember one incident vividly. A new woman, a huge, snowy-skinned blonde, took a room on my floor. I was sent to wait upon her. She was in bed with a thick-set man; both were nude and uncovered. She said she wanted some liquor and slid out of bed and waddled across the floor to get her money from a dresser drawer. I watched her.

"Nigger, what in hell you looking at?" the white man asked me, raising himself upon his elbows.

"Nothing," I answered, looking miles deep into the blank wall of the room.

"Keep your eyes where they belong, if you want to be healthy!" he said.

"Yes, sir."

VI

One of the bell-boys I knew in this hotel was keeping steady company with one of the Negro maids. Out of a clear sky the police descended upon his home and arrested him, accusing him of bastardy. The poor boy swore he had had no intimate relations with the girl. Nevertheless, they forced him to marry her. When the child arrived, it was found to be much lighter in complexion than either of the two supposedly legal parents. The white men around the hotel made a great joke of it. They spread the rumor that some white cow must have scared the poor girl while she was carrying the baby. If you were in their presence when this explanation was offered, you were supposed to laugh.

VII

One of the bell-boys was caught in bed with a white prostitute. He was castrated and run out of town. Immediately after this all the bell-boys and hall-boys were called together and warned. We were given to understand that the boy who had been castrated was a "mighty, mighty lucky bastard." We were impressed with the fact that next time the management of the hotel would not be responsible for the lives of "troublemakin' niggers." We were silent.

VIII

One night, just as I was about to go home, I met one of the Negro maids. She lived in my direction, and we fell in to walk part of the way

home together. As we passed the white night-watchman, he slapped the
maid on her buttock. I turned around, amazed. The watchman looked
at me with a long, hard, fixed-under stare. Suddenly he pulled his gun
and asked:

"Nigger, don't yuh like it?"

I hesitated.

"I asked yuh don't yuh like it?" he asked again, stepping forward.

"Yes, sir," I mumbled.

"Talk like it, then!"

"Oh, yes, sir!" I said with as much heartiness as I could muster.

Outside, I walked ahead of the girl, ashamed to face her. She caught
up with me and said:

"Don't be a fool! Yuh couldn't help it!"

This watchman boasted of having killed two Negroes in self-defense.

Yet, in spite of all this, the life of the hotel ran with an amazing
smoothness. It would have been impossible for a stranger to detect anything. The maids, the hall-boys, and the bell-boys were all smiles. They
had to be.

IX

I had learned my Jim Crow lessons so thoroughly that I kept the hotel
job till I left Jackson for Memphis. It so happened that while in Memphis I applied for a job at a branch of the optical company. I was hired.
And for some reason, as long as I worked there, they never brought my
past against me.

Here my Jim Crow education assumed quite a different form. It was
no longer brutally cruel, but subtly cruel. Here I learned to lie, to steal,
to dissemble. I learned to play that dual role which every Negro must
play if he wants to eat and live.

For example, it was almost impossible to get a book to read. It was assumed that after a Negro had imbibed what scanty schooling the state
furnished he had no further need for books. I was always borrowing
books from men on the job. One day I mustered enough courage to ask
one of the men to let me get books from the library in his name. Surprisingly, he consented. I cannot help but think that he consented because he was a Roman Catholic and felt a vague sympathy for Negroes,
being himself an object of hatred. Armed with a library card, I obtained
books in the following manner: I would write a note to the librarian,

saying: "Please let this nigger boy have the following books." I would then sign it with the white man's name.

When I went to the library, I would stand at the desk, hat in hand, looking as unbookish as possible. When I received the books desired I would take them home. If the books listed in the note happened to be out, I would sneak into the lobby and forge a new one. I never took any chances guessing with the white librarian about what the fictitious white man would want to read. No doubt if any of the white patrons had suspected that some of the volumes they enjoyed had been in the home of a Negro, they would not have tolerated it for an instant.

The factory force of the optical company in Memphis was much larger than that in Jackson, and more urbanized. At least they liked to talk, and would engage the Negro help in conversation whenever possible. By this means I found that many subjects were taboo from the white man's point of view. Among the topics they did not like to discuss with Negroes were the following: American white women; the Ku Klux Klan; France, and how Negro soldiers fared while there; French women; Jack Johnson; the entire northern part of the United States; the Civil War; Abraham Lincoln; U. S. Grant; General Sherman; Catholics; the Pope; Jews; the Republican Party; slavery; social equality; Communism; Socialism; the 13th and 14th Amendments to the Constitution; or any topic calling for positive knowledge or manly self-assertion on the part of the Negro. The most accepted topics were sex and religion.

There were many times when I had to exercise a great deal of ingenuity to keep out of trouble. It is a southern custom that all men must take off their hats when they enter an elevator. And especially did this apply to us blacks with rigid force. One day I stepped into an elevator with my arms full of packages. I was forced to ride with my hat on. Two white men stared at me coldly. Then one of them very kindly lifted my hat and placed it upon my armful of packages. Now the most accepted response for a Negro to make under such circumstances is to look at the white man out of the corner of his eye and grin. To have said: "Thank you!" would have made the white man *think* that you *thought* you were receiving from him a personal service. For such an act I have seen Negroes take a blow in the mouth. Finding the first alternative distasteful, and the second dangerous, I hit upon an acceptable course of action which fell safely between these two poles. I immediately — no sooner than my hat was lifted — pretended that my packages were about to spill, and appeared deeply distressed with keeping them in my arms. In this fashion I evaded having to acknowledge his service, and, in spite of adverse circumstances, salvaged a slender shred of personal pride.

How do Negroes feel about the way they have to live? How do they discuss it when alone among themselves? I think this question can be answered in a single sentence. A friend of mine who ran an elevator once told me:

"Lawd, man! Ef it wuzn't fer them polices 'n' them ol' lynch-mobs, there wouldn't be nothin' but uproar down here!"

1938

James Agee

Knoxville: Summer of 1915

WE ARE TALKING NOW of summer evenings in Knoxville, Tennessee, in the time that I lived there so successfully disguised to myself as a child. It was a little bit mixed sort of block, fairly solidly lower middle class, with one or two juts apiece on either side of that. The houses corresponded: middle-sized gracefully fretted wood houses built in the late nineties and early nineteen hundreds, with small front and side and more spacious back yards, and trees in the yard, and porches. These were softwooded trees, poplars, tulip trees, cottonwoods. There were fences around one or two of the houses, but mainly the yards ran into each other with only now and then a low hedge that wasn't doing very well. There were few good friends among the grown people, and they were not poor enough for the other sort of intimate acquaintance, but everyone nodded and spoke, and even might talk short times, trivially, and at the two extremes of the general or the particular, and ordinarily nextdoor neighbors talked quite a bit when they happened to run into each other, and never paid calls. The men were mostly small businessmen, one or two very modestly executives, one or two worked with their hands, most of them clerical, and most of them between thirty and forty-five.

But it is of these evenings, I speak.

Supper was at six and was over by half past. There was still daylight, shining softly and with a tarnish, like the lining of a shell; and the carbon lamps lifted at the corners were on in the light, and the locusts were

First published in *Partisan Review*, 1938, and reprinted as the prologue to *A Death in the Family*, 1957.

started, and the fire flies were out, and a few frogs were flopping in the dewy grass, by the time the fathers and the children came out. The children ran out first hell bent and yelling those names by which they were known; then the fathers sank out leisurely in crossed suspenders, their collars removed and their necks looking tall and shy. The mothers stayed back in the kitchen washing and drying, putting things away, recrossing their traceless footsteps like the lifetime journeys of bees, measuring out the dry cocoa for breakfast. When they came out they had taken off their aprons and their skirts were dampened and they sat in rockers on their porches quietly.

It is not of the games children play in the evening that I want to speak now, it is of a contemporaneous atmosphere that has little to do with them: that of the fathers of families, each in his space of lawn, his shirt fishlike pale in the unnatural light and his face nearly anonymous, hosing their lawns. The hoses were attached at spiggots that stood out of the brick foundations of the houses. The nozzles were variously set but usually so there was a long sweet stream of spray, the nozzle wet in the hand, the water trickling the right forearm and the peeled-back cuff, and the water whishing out a long loose and low-curved cone, and so gentle a sound. First an insane noise of violence in the nozzle, then the still irregular sound of adjustment, then the smoothing into steadiness and a pitch as accurately tuned to the size and style of stream as any violin. So many qualities of sound out of one hose: so many choral differences out of those several hoses that were in earshot. Out of any one hose, the almost dead silence of the release, and the short still arch of the separate big drops, silent as a held breath, and the only noise the flattering noise on leaves and the slapped grass at the fall of each big drop. That, and the intense hiss with the intense stream; that, and that same intensity not growing less but growing more quiet and delicate with the turn of the nozzle, up to that extreme tender whisper when the water was just a wide bell of film. Chiefly, though, the hoses were set much alike, in a compromise between distance and tenderness of spray (and quite surely a sense of art behind this compromise, and a quiet deep joy, too real to recognize itself), and the sounds therefore were pitched much alike; pointed by the snorting start of a new hose; decorated by some man playful with the nozzle; left empty, like God by the sparrow's fall, when any single one of them desists: and all, though near alike, of various pitch; and in this unison. These sweet pale streamings in the light lift out their pallors and their voices all together, mothers hushing their children, the hushing unnaturally prolonged, the men gentle and silent and each snail-like withdrawn into the quietude of what he singly is doing, the urination of huge children stood loosely military against an invisible wall, and gentle happy and peaceful, tasting the mean goodness of their living like the last of their suppers in their mouths; while the locusts carry on this noise of hoses on their much higher and sharper key. The noise of the locust is dry, and it seems not to be rasped or vibrated but urged from him as if through a small orifice by a breath that can never give out. Also there is never one locust but an illusion of at least a thousand. The noise of each locust is pitched in some classic locust range out of which none of them varies more than two full tones: and yet you seem to hear each locust discrete from all the rest, and there is a long, slow, pulse in their noise, like the scarcely defined arch of a long and high set bridge. They are all around in every tree, so that the noise seems to come from nowhere and everywhere at once, from the whole shell heaven, shivering in your flesh and teasing your eardrums, the boldest of all the sounds of night. And yet it is habitual to summer nights, and is of the great order of noises, like the noises of the sea and of the blood her precocious grandchild, which you realize you are hearing only when you catch yourself listening. Meantime from low in the dark, just outside the swaying horizons of the hoses, conveying always grass in the damp of dew and its strong green-black smear of smell, the regular yet spaced noises of the crickets, each a sweet cold silver noise three-noted, like the slipping each time of three matched links of a small chain.

But the men by now, one by one, have silenced their hoses and drained and coiled them. Now only two, and now only one, is left, and you see only ghostlike shirt with the sleeve garters, and sober mystery of his mild face like the lifted face of large cattle enquiring of your presence in a pitchdark pool of meadow; and now he too is gone; and it has become that time of evening when people sit on their porches, rocking gently and talking gently and watching the street and the standing up into their sphere of possession of the trees, of birds hung havens, hangars. People go by; things go by. A horse, drawing a buggy, breaking his hollow iron music on the asphalt; a loud auto; a quiet auto; people in pairs, not in a hurry, scuffling, switching their weight of aestival body, talking casually, the taste hovering over them of vanilla, strawberry, pasteboard and starched milk, the image upon them of lovers and horsemen, squared with clowns in hueless amber. A street car raising its

iron moan; stopping, belling and starting; stertorous; rousing and raising again its iron increasing moan and swimming its gold windows and
straw seats on past and past and past, the bleak spark crackling and
cursing above it like a small malignant spirit set to dog its tracks; the
iron whine rises on rising speed; still risen, faints; halts; the faint stinging bell; rises again, still fainter, fainting, lifting, lifts, faints forgone: forgotten. Now is the night one blue dew.

> Now is the night one blue dew, my father has drained, he has coiled the
> hose.
> Low on the length of lawns, a frailing of fire who breathes.
> Content, silver, like peeps of light, each cricket makes his comment over
> and over in the drowned grass.
> A cold toad thumpily flounders.
> Within the edges of damp shadows of side yards are hovering children
> nearly sick with joy of fear, who watch the unguarding of a telephone
> pole.
> Around white carbon corner lamps bugs of all sizes are lifted elliptic, so-
> lar systems. Big hardshells bruise themselves, assailant: he is fallen on
> his back, legs squiggling.
> Parents on porches: rock and rock: From damp strings morning glories:
> hang their ancient faces.
> The dry and exalted noise of the locusts from all the air at once en-
> chants my eardrums.

On the rough wet grass of the back yard my father and mother have
spread quilts. We all lie there, my mother, my father, my uncle, my aunt,
and I too am lying there. First we were sitting up, then one of us lay
down, and then we all lay down, on our stomachs, or on our sides, or on
our backs, and they have kept on talking. They are not talking much,
and the talk is quiet, of nothing in particular, of nothing at all in particular, of nothing at all. The stars are wide and alive, they seem each like a
smile of great sweetness, and they seem very near. All my people are
larger bodies than mine, quiet, with voices gentle and meaningless like
the voices of sleeping birds. One is an artist, he is living at home. One is
a musician, she is living at home. One is my mother who is good to me.
One is my father who is good to me. By some chance, here they are, all
on this earth; and who shall ever tell the sorrow of being on this earth,
lying, on quilts, on the grass, in a summer evening, among the sounds
of night. May God bless my people, my uncle, my aunt, my mother, my

good father, oh, remember them kindly in their time of trouble; and in the hour of their taking away.

After a little I am taken in and put to bed. Sleep, soft smiling, draws me unto her: and those receive me, who quietly treat me, as one familiar and well-beloved in that home: but will not, oh, will not, not now, not ever; but will not ever tell me who I am.

1939

Robert Frost

··

The Figure a Poem Makes

ABSTRACTION is an old story with the philosophers, but it has been like a new toy in the hands of the artists of our day. Why can't we have any one quality of poetry we choose by itself? We can have in thought. Then it will go hard if we can't in practice. Our lives for it.

Granted no one but a humanist much cares how sound a poem is if it is only *a* sound. The sound is the gold in the ore. Then we will have the sound out alone and dispense with the inessential. We do till we make the discovery that the object in writing poetry is to make all poems sound as different as possible from each other, and the resources for that of vowels, consonants, punctuation, syntax, words, sentences, meter are not enough. We need the help of context — meaning — subject matter. That is the greatest help towards variety. All that can be done with words is soon told. So also with meters — particularly in our language where there are virtually but two, strict iambic and loose iambic. The ancients with many were still poor if they depended on meters for all tune. It is painful to watch our sprung-rhythmists straining at the point of omitting one short from a foot for relief from monotony. The possibilities for tune from the dramatic tones of meaning struck across the rigidity of a limited meter are endless. And we are back in poetry as merely one more art of having something to say, sound or unsound. Probably better if sound, because deeper and from wider experience.

Then there is this wildness whereof it is spoken. Granted again that it has an equal claim with sound to being a poem's better half. If it is a wild tune, it is a poem. Our problem then is, as modern abstractionists, to have the wildness pure; to be wild with nothing to be wild about. We

Preface to *Collected Poems, 1939.

bring up as aberrationists, giving way to undirected associations and kicking ourselves from one chance suggestion to another in all directions as of a hot afternoon in the life of a grasshopper. Theme alone can steady us down. Just as the first mystery was how a poem could have a tune in such a straightness as meter, so the second mystery is how a poem can have wildness and at the same time a subject that shall be fulfilled.

It should be of the pleasure of a poem itself to tell how it can. The figure a poem makes. It begins in delight and ends in wisdom. The figure is the same as for love. No one can really hold that the ecstasy should be static and stand still in one place. It begins in delight, it inclines to the impulse, it assumes direction with the first line laid down, it runs a course of lucky events, and ends in a clarification of life — not necessarily a great clarification, such as sects and cults are founded on, but in a momentary stay against confusion. It has denouement. It has an outcome that though unforeseen was predestined from the first image of the original mood — and indeed from the very mood. It is but a trick poem and no poem at all if the best of it was thought of first and saved for the last. It finds its own name as it goes and discovers the best waiting for it in some final phrase at once wise and sad — the happy-sad blend of the drinking song.

No tears in the writer, no tears in the reader. No surprise for the writer, no surprise for the reader. For me the initial delight is in the surprise of remembering something I didn't know I knew. I am in a place, in a situation, as if I had materialized from cloud or risen out of the ground. There is a glad recognition of the long lost and the rest follows. Step by step the wonder of unexpected supply keeps growing. The impressions most useful to my purpose seem always those I was unaware of and so made no note of at the time when taken, and the conclusion is come to that like giants we are always hurling experience ahead of us to pave the future with against the day when we may want to strike a line of purpose across it for somewhere. The line will have the more charm for not being mechanically straight. We enjoy the straight crookedness of a good walking stick. Modern instruments of precision are being used to make things crooked as if by eye and hand in the old days.

I tell how there may be a better wildness of logic than of inconsequence. But the logic is backward, in retrospect, after the act. It must be more felt than seen ahead like prophecy. It must be a revelation, or a series of revelations, as much for the poet as for the reader. For it to be that there must have been the greatest freedom of the material to move about in it and to establish relations in it regardless of time and space, previous relation, and everything but affinity. We prate of freedom. We call our schools free because we are not free to stay away from them till we are sixteen years of age. I have given up my democratic prejudices and now willingly set the lower classes free to be completely taken care of by the upper classes. Political freedom is nothing to me. I bestow it right and left. All I would keep for myself is the freedom of my material — the condition of body and mind now and then to summons aptly from the vast chaos of all I have lived through.

Scholars and artists thrown together are often annoyed at the puzzle of where they differ. Both work from knowledge; but I suspect they differ most importantly in the way their knowledge is come by. Scholars get theirs with conscientious thoroughness along projected lines of logic; poets theirs cavalierly and as it happens in and out of books. They stick to nothing deliberately, but let what will stick to them like burrs where they walk in the fields. No acquirement is on assignment, or even self-assignment. Knowledge of the second kind is much more available in the wild free ways of wit and art. A school boy may be defined as one who can tell you what he knows in the order in which he learned it. The artist must value himself as he snatches a thing from some previous order in time and space into a new order with not so much as a ligature clinging to it of the old place where it was organic.

More than once I should have lost my soul to radicalism if it had been the originality it was mistaken for by its young converts. Originality and initiative are what I ask for my country. For myself the originality need be no more than the freshness of a poem run in the way I have described: from delight to wisdom. The figure is the same as for love. Like a piece of ice on a hot stove the poem must ride on its own melting. A poem may be worked over once it is in being, but may not be worried into being. Its most precious quality will remain its having run itself and carried away the poet with it. Read it a hundred times: it will forever keep its freshness as a metal keeps its fragrance. It can never lose its sense of a meaning that once unfolded by surprise as it went.

E. B. White

....

Once More to the Lake

ONE SUMMER, along about 1904, my father rented a camp on a lake in Maine and took us all there for the month of August. We all got ring-worm from some kittens and had to rub Pond's Extract on our arms and legs night and morning, and my father rolled over in a canoe with all his clothes on; but outside of that the vacation was a success and from then on none of us ever thought there was any place in the world like that lake in Maine. We returned summer after summer — always on August 1 for one month. I have since become a salt-water man, but sometimes in summer there are days when the restlessness of the tides and the fearful cold of the sea water and the incessant wind that blows across the afternoon and into the evening make me wish for the placid-ity of a lake in the woods. A few weeks ago this feeling got so strong I bought myself a couple of bass hooks and a spinner and returned to the lake where we used to go, for a week's fishing and to revisit old haunts.

I took along my son, who had never had any fresh water up his nose and who had seen lily pads only from train windows. On the journey over to the lake I began to wonder what it would be like. I wondered how time would have marred this unique, this holy spot — the coves and streams, the hills that the sun set behind, the camps and the paths behind the camps. I was sure that the tarred road would have found it out, and I wondered in what other ways it would be desolated. It is strange how much you can remember about places like that once you

First published in *Harper's Magazine*, 1941; collected in *One Man's Meat*, 1942, and with slight revisions in *The Essays of E. B. White*, 1977.

allow your mind to return into the grooves that lead back. You remember one thing, and that suddenly reminds you of another thing. I guess I remembered clearest of all the early mornings, when the lake was cool and motionless, remembered how the bedroom smelled of the lumber it was made of and of the wet woods whose scent entered through the screen. The partitions in the camp were thin and did not extend clear to the top of the rooms, and as I was always the first up I would dress softly so as not to wake the others, and sneak out into the sweet outdoors and start out in the canoe, keeping close along the shore in the long shadows of the pines. I remembered being very careful never to rub my paddle against the gunwale for fear of disturbing the stillness of the cathedral.

The lake had never been what you would call a wild lake. There were cottages sprinkled around the shores, and it was in farming country although the shores of the lake were quite heavily wooded. Some of the cottages were owned by nearby farmers, and you would live at the shore and eat your meals at the farmhouse. That's what our family did. But although it wasn't wild, it was a fairly large and undisturbed lake and there were places in it that, to a child at least, seemed infinitely remote and primeval.

I was right about the tar: it led to within half a mile of the shore. But when I got back there, with my boy, and we settled into a camp near a farmhouse and into the kind of summertime I had known, I could tell that it was going to be pretty much the same as it had been before — I knew it, lying in bed the first morning, smelling the bedroom and hearing the boy sneak quietly out and go off along the shore in a boat. I began to sustain the illusion that he was I, and therefore, by simple transposition, that I was my father. This sensation persisted, kept cropping up all the time we were there. It was not an entirely new feeling, but in this setting it grew much stronger. I seemed to be living a dual existence. I would be in the middle of some simple act, I would be picking up a bait box or laying down a table fork, or I would be saying something, and suddenly it would be not I but my father who was saying the words or making the gesture. It gave me a creepy sensation.

We went fishing the first morning. I felt the same damp moss covering the worms in the bait can, and saw the dragonfly alight on the tip of my rod as it hovered a few inches from the surface of the water. It was the arrival of this fly that convinced me beyond any doubt that everything was as it always had been, that the years were a mirage and that there had been no years. The small waves were the same, chucking the rowboat under the chin as we fished at anchor, and the boat was the same boat, the same color green and the ribs broken in the same places, and under the floorboards the same fresh-water leavings and débris — the dead helgramite, the wisps of moss, the rusty discarded fishhook, and dried blood from yesterday's catch. We stared silently at the tips of our rods, at the dragonflies that came and went. I lowered the tip of mine into the water, tentatively, pensively dislodging the fly, which darted two feet away, poised, darted two feet back, and came to rest again a little farther up the rod. There had been no years between the ducking of this dragonfly and the other one — the one that was part of memory. I looked at the boy, who was silently watching his fly, and it was my hands that held his rod, my eyes watching. I felt dizzy and didn't know which rod I was at the end of.

We caught two bass, hauling them in briskly as though they were mackerel, pulling them over the side of the boat in a businesslike manner without any landing net, and stunning them with a blow on the back of the head. When we got back for a swim before lunch, the lake was exactly where we had left it, the same number of inches from the dock, and there was only the merest suggestion of a breeze. This seemed an utterly enchanted sea, this lake you could leave to its own devices for a few hours and come back to, and find that it had not stirred, this constant and trustworthy body of water. In the shallows, the dark, water-soaked sticks and twigs, smooth and old, were undulating in clusters on the bottom against the clean ribbed sand, and the track of the mussel was plain. A school of minnows swam by, each minnow with its small individual shadow, doubling the attendance, so clear and sharp in the sunlight. Some of the other campers were in swimming, along the shore, one of them with a cake of soap, and the water felt thin and clear and unsubstantial. Over the years there had been this person with the cake of soap, this cultist, and here he was. There had been no years.

Up to the farmhouse to dinner through the teeming, dusty field, the road under our sneakers was only a two-track road. The middle track was missing, the one with the marks of the hooves and the splotches of dried, flaky manure. There had always been three tracks to choose from in choosing which track to walk in; now the choice was narrowed down to two. For a moment I missed terribly the middle alternative. But the way led past the tennis court, and something about the way it lay there in the sun reassured me; the tape had loosened along the backline, the alleys were green with plantains and other weeds, and the net (installed in June and removed in September) sagged in the dry noon, and the whole place steamed with midday heat and hunger and emptiness. There was a choice of pie for dessert, and one was blueberry and one was apple, and the waitresses were the same country girls, there having been no passage of time, only the illusion of it as in a dropped curtain — the waitresses were still fifteen; their hair had been washed, that was the only difference — they had been to the movies and seen the pretty girls with the clean hair.

Summertime, oh, summertime, pattern of life indelible, the fade-proof lake, the woods unshatterable, the pasture with the sweetfern and the juniper forever and ever, summer without end; this was the background, and the life along the shore was the design, the cottagers with their innocent and tranquil design, their tiny docks with the flagpole and the American flag floating against the white clouds in the blue sky, the little paths over the roots of the trees leading from camp to camp and the paths leading back to the outhouses and the can of lime for sprinkling, and at the souvenir counters at the store the miniature birch-bark canoes and the postcards that showed things looking a little better than they looked. This was the American family at play, escaping the city heat, wondering whether the newcomers in the camp at the head of the cove were "common" or "nice," wondering whether it was true that the people who drove up for Sunday dinner at the farmhouse were turned away because there wasn't enough chicken.

It seemed to me, as I kept remembering all this, that those times and those summers had been infinitely precious and worth saving. There had been jollity and peace and goodness. The arriving (at the beginning of August) had been so big a business in itself, at the railway station the farm wagon drawn up, the first smell of the pine-laden air, the first glimpse of the smiling farmer, and the great importance of the trunks and your father's enormous authority in such matters, and the feel of the wagon under you for the long ten-mile haul, and at the top of the last long hill catching the first view of the lake after eleven months of not seeing this cherished body of water. The shouts and cries of the other campers when they saw you, and the trunks to be unpacked, to give up their rich burden. (Arriving was less exciting nowadays, when you sneaked up in your car and parked it under a tree near the camp and took out the bags and in five minutes it was all over, no fuss, no loud wonderful fuss about trunks.)

Peace and goodness and jollity. The only thing that was wrong now, really, was the sound of the place, an unfamiliar nervous sound of the outboard motors. This was the note that jarred, the one thing that would sometimes break the illusion and set the years moving. In those other summertimes all motors were inboard; and when they were at a little distance, the noise they made was a sedative, an ingredient of summer sleep. They were one-cylinder and two-cylinder engines, and some were make-and-break and some were jump-spark, but they all made a sleepy sound across the lake. The one-lungers throbbed and fluttered, and the twin-cylinder ones purred and purred, and that was a quiet sound, too. But now the campers all had outboards. In the daytime, in the hot mornings, these motors made a petulant, irritable sound; at night, in the still evening when the afterglow lit the water, they whined about one's ears like mosquitoes. My boy loved our rented outboard, and his great desire was to achieve single-handed mastery over it, and authority, and he soon learned the trick of choking it a little (but not too much), and the adjustment of the needle valve. Watching him I would remember the things you could do with the old one-cylinder engine with the heavy flywheel, how you could have it eating out of your hand if you got really close to it spiritually. Motorboats in those days didn't have clutches, and you would make a landing by shutting off the motor at the proper time and coasting in with a dead rudder. But there was a way of reversing them, if you learned the trick, by cutting the switch and putting it on again exactly on the final dying revolution of the flywheel, so that it would kick back against compression and begin reversing. Approaching a dock in a strong following breeze, it was difficult to slow up sufficiently by the ordinary coasting method, and if a boy felt he had complete mastery over his motor, he was tempted to keep it running beyond its time and then reverse it a few feet from the dock. It took a cool nerve, because if you threw the switch a twentieth of a second too soon you would catch the flywheel when it still had speed enough to go up past center, and the boat would leap ahead, charging bull-fashion at the dock.

We had a good week at the camp. The bass were biting well and the sun shone endlessly, day after day. We would be tired at night and lie down in the accumulated heat of the little bedrooms after the long hot day and the breeze would stir almost imperceptibly outside and the smell of the swamp drift in through the rusty screens. Sleep would come easily and in the morning the red squirrel would be on the roof, tapping out his gay routine. I kept remembering everything, lying in bed in the mornings — the small steamboat that had a long rounded stern like the lip of a Ubangi, and how quietly she ran on the moonlight sails, when the older boys played their mandolins and the girls sang and we ate doughnuts dipped in sugar, and how sweet the music was on the water in the shining night, and what it had felt like to think about girls then. After breakfast we would go up to the store and the things were in the same place — the minnows in a bottle, the plugs and spinners disarranged and pawed over by the youngsters from the boys' camp, the Fig Newtons and the Beeman's gum. Outside, the road was tarred and cars stood in front of the store. Inside, all was just as it had always been, except there was more Coca-Cola and not so much Moxie and root beer and birch beer and sarsaparilla. We would walk out with the bottle of pop apiece and sometimes the pop would backfire up our noses and hurt. We explored the streams, quietly, where the turtles slid off the sunny logs and dug their way into the soft bottom; and we lay on the town wharf and fed worms to the tame bass. Everywhere we went I had trouble making out which was I, the one walking at my side, the one walking in my pants.

One afternoon while we were there at that lake a thunderstorm came up. It was like the revival of an old melodrama that I had seen long ago with childish awe. The second-act climax of the drama of the electrical disturbance over a lake in America had not changed in any important respect. This was the big scene, still the big scene. The whole thing was so familiar, the first feeling of oppression and heat and a general air around camp of not wanting to go very far away. In mid-afternoon (it was all the same) a curious darkening of the sky, and a lull in everything that had made life tick; and then the way the boats suddenly swung the other way at their moorings with the coming of a breeze out of the new quarter, and the premonitory rumble. Then the kettle drum, then the snare, then the bass drum and cymbals, then crackling light against the dark, and the gods grinning and licking their chops in the hills. Afterward the calm, the rain steadily rustling in the calm lake, the return of light and hope and spirits, and the campers running out in joy and relief to go swimming in the rain, their bright cries perpetuating the deathless joke about how they were getting simply drenched, and the children screaming with delight at the new sensation of bathing in the rain, and the joke about getting drenched linking the generations in a strong indestructible chain. And the comedian who waded in carrying an umbrella.

When the others went swimming, my son said he was going in, too. He pulled his dripping trunks from the line where they had hung all through the shower and wrung them out. Languidly, and with no thought of going in, I watched him, his hard little body, skinny and bare, saw him wince slightly as he pulled up around his vitals the small, soggy, icy garment. As he buckled the swollen belt, suddenly my groin felt the chill of death.

1944

S. J. Perelman

Insert Flap "A" and Throw Away

ONE STIFLING summer afternoon last August, in the attic of a tiny stone house in Pennsylvania, I made a most interesting discovery: the shortest, cheapest method of inducing a nervous breakdown ever perfected. In this technique (eventually adopted by the psychology department of Duke University, which will adopt anything), the subject is placed in a sharply sloping attic heated to 340° F. and given a mothproof closet known as the Jiffy-Cloz to assemble. The Jiffy-Cloz, procurable at any department store or neighborhood insane asylum, consists of half a dozen gigantic sheets of red cardboard, two plywood doors, a clothes rack, and a packet of staples. With these is included a set of instructions mimeographed in pale-violet ink, fruity with phrases like "Pass Section F through Slot AA, taking care not to fold tabs behind washers (see Fig. 9)." The cardboard is so processed that as the subject struggles convulsively to force the staple through, it suddenly buckles, plunging the staple deep into his thumb. He thereupon springs up with a dolorous cry and smites his knob (Section K) on the rafters (RR). As a final demonic touch, the Jiffy-Cloz people cunningly omit four of the staples necessary to finish the job, so that after indescribable purgatory, the best the subject can possibly achieve is a sleazy, capricious structure which would reduce any self-respecting moth to helpless laughter. The cumulative frustration, the tropical heat, and the soft, ghostly chuckling of the moths are calculated to unseat the strongest mentality.

In a period of rapid technological change, however, it was inevitable that a method as cumbersome as the Jiffy-Cloz would be super-

First published in *The New Yorker*, 1944; collected in *Acres and Pains*, 1947, and **The Most of S. J. Perelman*, 1958.

seded. It was superseded at exactly nine-thirty Christmas morning by a device called the Self-Running 10-Inch Scale-Model Delivery-Truck Kit Powered by Magic Motor, costing twenty-nine cents. About nine on that particular morning, I was spread-eagled on my bed, indulging in my favorite sport of mouth-breathing, when a cork fired from a child's air gun mysteriously lodged in my throat. The pellet proved awkward for a while, but I finally ejected it by flailing the little marksman (and his sister, for good measure) until their welkins rang, and sauntered in to breakfast. Before I could choke down a healing fruit juice, my consort, a tall, regal creature indistinguishable from Cornelia, the Mother of the Gracchi, except that her foot was entangled in a roller skate, swept in. She extended a large, unmistakable box covered with diagrams.

"Now don't start making excuses," she whined. "It's just a simple cardboard toy. The directions are on the back —"

"Look, dear," I interrupted, rising hurriedly and pulling on my overcoat, "it clean slipped my mind. I'm supposed to take a lesson in crosshatching at Zim's School of Cartooning today."

"On Christmas?" she asked suspiciously.

"Yes, it's the only time they could fit me in," I countered glibly. "This is the big week for crosshatching, you know, between Christmas and New Year's."

"Do you think you ought to go in your pajamas?" she asked.

"Oh, that's O. K.," I smiled. "We often work in our pajamas up at Zim's. Well, goodbye now. If I'm not home by Thursday, you'll find a cold snack in the safe-deposit box." My subterfuge, unluckily, went for naught, and in a trice I was sprawled on the nursery floor, surrounded by two lambkins and ninety-eight segments of the Self-Running 10-Inch Scale-Model Delivery-Truck Construction Kit.

The theory of the kit was simplicity itself, easily intelligible to Kettering of General Motors, Professor Millikan, or any first-rate physicist. Taking as my starting point the only sentence I could comprehend, "Fold down on all lines marked 'fold down'; fold up on all lines marked 'fold up,'" I set the children to work and myself folded up with an album of views of Chili Williams. In a few moments, my skin was suffused with a delightful tingling sensation and I was ready for the second phase, lightly referred to in the directions as "Preparing the Spring Motor Unit." As nearly as I could determine after twenty minutes of mumbling, the Magic Motor ("No Electricity — No Batteries — Nothing to Wind — Motor Never Wears Out") was an accordion-pleated affair operating by torsion, attached to the axles. "It is necessary," said the text, "to cut a slight notch in each of the axles with a knife (see Fig. C). To find the exact place to cut this notch, lay one of the axles over diagram at bottom of page."

"Well, *now* we're getting someplace!" I boomed, with a false gusto that deceived nobody. "Here, Buster, run in and get Daddy a knife."

"I dowanna," quavered the boy, backing away. "You always cut yourself at this stage." I gave the wee fellow an indulgent pat on the head that flattened it slightly, to teach him civility, and commandeered a long, serrated bread knife from the kitchen. "Now watch me closely, children," I ordered. "We place the axle on the diagram as in Fig. C, applying a strong downward pressure on the knife handle at all times." The axle must have been a factory second, because an instant later I was in the bathroom grinding my teeth in agony and attempting to stanch the flow of blood. Ultimately, I succeeded in contriving a rough bandage and slipped back into the nursery without awakening the children's suspicions. An agreeable surprise awaited me. Displaying a mechanical aptitude clearly inherited from their sire, the rascals had put together the chassis of the delivery truck.

"Very good indeed," I complimented (naturally, one has to exaggerate praise to develop a child's self-confidence). "Let's see — what's the next step? Ah, yes. 'Lock into box shape by inserting tabs C, D, E, F, G, H, J, K, and L into slots C, D, E, F, G, H, J, K, and L. Ends of front axles should be pushed through holes A and B.'" While marshaling the indicated parts in their proper order, I emphasized to my rapt listeners the necessity of patience and perseverance. "Haste makes waste, you know," I reminded them. "Rome wasn't built in a day. Remember, your daddy isn't always going to be here to show you."

"Where *are* you going to be?" they demanded.

"In the movies, if I can arrange it," I snarled. Poising tabs C, D, E, F, G, H, J, K, and L in one hand and the corresponding slots in the other, I essayed a union of the two, but in vain. The moment I made one set fast and tackled another, tab and slot would part company, thumbing their noses at me. Although the children were too immature to understand, I saw in a flash where the trouble lay. Some idiotic employee at the factory had punched out the wrong design, probably out of sheer spite. So that was his game, eh? I set my lips in a grim line and, throwing one hundred and fifty-seven pounds of fighting fat into the effort, pounded the component parts into a homogeneous mass.

"There," I said with a gasp, "that's close enough. Now then, who wants candy? One, two, three — everybody off to the candy store!" "We wanna finish the delivery truck!" they wailed. "Mummy, he won't let us finish the delivery truck!" Threats, cajolery, bribes were of no avail. In their jungle code, a twenty-nine-cent gewgaw bulked larger than a parent's love. Realizing that I was dealing with a pair of mono-maniacs, I determined to show them who was master and wildly began locking the cardboard units helter-skelter, without any regard for the directions. When sections refused to fit, I gouged them with my nails and forced them together, cackling shrilly. The side panels collapsed; with a bestial oath, I drove a safety pin through them and lashed them to the roof. I used paper clips, bobby pins, anything I could lay my hands on. My fingers fairly flew and my breath whistled in my throat. "You want a delivery truck, do you?" I panted. "All right, I'll show you!" As merciful blackness closed in, I was on my hands and knees, bunting the infernal thing along with my nose and whinnying, "Roll, confound you, roll!"

"Absolute quiet," a carefully modulated voice was saying, "and fifteen of the white tablets every four hours." I opened my eyes carefully in the darkened room. Dimly I picked out a knifelike character actor in pince-nez lenses and a morning coat folding a stethoscope into his bag. "Yes," he added thoughtfully, "if we play our cards right, this ought to be a long, expensive recovery." From far away, I could hear my wife's voice bravely trying to control her anxiety.

"What if he becomes restless, Doctor?"

"Get him a detective story," returned the leech. "Or better still, a nice, soothing picture puzzle — something he can do with his hands."

1949

Langston Hughes

Bop

SOMEBODY upstairs in Simple's house had the combination turned up loud with an old Dizzy Gillespie record spinning like mad filling the Sabbath with Bop as I passed.

"Set down here on the stoop with me and listen to the music," said Simple.

"I've heard your landlady doesn't like tenants sitting on her stoop," I said.

"Pay it no mind," said Simple. "Ool-ya-koo," he sang. "Hey Ba-Ba-Re-Bop! Be-Bop! Mop!"

"All that nonsense singing reminds me of Cab Calloway back in the old *scat* days," I said, "around 1930 when he was chanting, 'Hi-de-*hie*-de-ho! Hee-de-*hee*-de-hee!'"

"Not at all," said Simple, "absolutely not at all."

"Re-Bop certainly sounds like scat to me," I insisted.

"No," said Simple, "Daddy-o, you are wrong. Besides, it was not *Re*-Bop. It is *Be*-Bop."

"What's the difference," I asked, "between *Re* and *Be?*"

"A lot," said Simple. "Re-Bop was an imitation like most of the white boys play. Be-Bop is the real thing like the colored boys play."

"You bring race into everything," I said, "even music."

"It is in everything," said Simple.

"Anyway, Be-Bop is passé, gone, finished."

"It may be gone, but its riffs remain behind," said Simple. "Be-Bop

---

First published in *The Chicago Defender*, 1949; revised and collected in *Simple Takes a Wife*, 1953, and in *The Best of Simple*, 1961.

music was certainly colored folks' music — which is why white folks found it so hard to imitate. But there are some few white boys that latched onto it right well. And no wonder, because they sat and listened to Dizzy, Thelonius, Tad Dameron, Charlie Parker, also Mary Lou, all night long every time they got a chance, and bought their records by the dozens to copy their riffs. The ones that sing tried to make up new Be-Bop words, but them white folks don't know what they are singing about, even yet."

"It all sounds like pure nonsense syllables to me."

"Nonsense, nothing!" cried Simple. "Bop makes plenty of sense."

"What kind of sense?"

"You must not know where Bop comes from," said Simple, astonished at my ignorance.

"I do not know," I said. "Where?"

"From the police," said Simple.

"What do you mean, from the police?"

"From the police beating Negroes' heads," said Simple. "Every time a cop hits a Negro with his billy club, that old club says, 'BOP! BOP! . . . BE-BOP! . . . MOP! . . . BOP!'

"That Negro hollers, 'Ooool-ya-koo! Ou-o-o!'

"Old Cop just keeps on, 'MOP! MOP! . . . BE-BOP! . . . MOP!' That's where Be-Bop came from, beaten right out of some Negro's head into them horns and saxophones and piano keys that plays it. Do you call that nonsense?"

"If it's true, I do not," I said.

"That's why so many white folks don't dig Bop," said Simple. "White folks do not get their heads beat *just for being white*. But me — a cop is liable to grab me almost any time and beat my head — *just* for being colored.

"In some parts of this American country as soon as the polices see me, they say, 'Boy, what are you doing in this neighborhood?'

"I say, 'Coming from work, sir.'

"They say, 'Where do you work?'

"Then I have to go into my whole pedigree because I am a black man in a white neighborhood. And if my answers do not satisfy them, BOP! MOP! . . . BE-BOP! . . . MOP! If they do not hit me, they have already hurt my soul. *A dark man shall see dark days.* Bop comes out of them dark days. That's why real Bop is mad, wild, frantic, crazy — and not to be dug unless you've seen dark days, too. Folks who ain't suffered much cannot play Bop, neither appreciate it. They think Bop is nonsense —

like you. They think it's just *crazy* crazy. They do not know Bop is also MAD CRAZY, SAD CRAZY, FRANTIC WILD CRAZY — beat out of somebody's head! That's what Bop is. Them young colored kids who started it, they know what Bop is."

"Your explanation depresses me," I said.

"Your nonsense depresses me," said Simple.

1950

Katherine Anne Porter

....

The Future Is Now

NOT SO LONG AGO I was reading in a magazine with an enormous circulation some instructions as to how to behave if and when we see that
flash brighter than the sun which means that the atom bomb has arrived. I read of course with the intense interest of one who has everything to learn on this subject; but at the end, the advice dwindled to
this: the only real safety seems to lie in simply being somewhere else at
the time, the farther away the better; the next best, failing access to deep
shelters, bombproof cellars and all, is to get under a stout table — that
is, just what you might do if someone were throwing bricks through
your window and you were too nervous to throw them back.

This comic anticlimax to what I had been taking as a serious educational piece surprised me into real laughter, hearty and carefree. It is
such a relief to be told the truth, or even just the facts, so pleasant not to
be coddled with unreasonable hopes. That very evening I was drawn
away from my work table to my fifth-story window by one of those
shrill terror-screaming sirens which our excitement-loving city government used then to affect for so many occasions: A fire? Police chasing
a gangster? Somebody being got to the hospital in a hurry? Some
distinguished public guest being transferred from one point to another? Strange aircraft coming over, maybe? Under the lights of the corner crossing of the great avenue, a huge closed vehicle whizzed past,
screaming. I never knew what it was, had not in fact expected to know;
no one I could possibly ask would know. Now that we have bells clamoring away instead for such events, we all have one doubt less, if per-

First published in *Mademoiselle*, 1950; collected in *The Days Before*, 1952, and ** The Collected Essays*, 1970.

haps one expectancy more. The single siren's voice means to tell us only one thing.

But at that doubtful moment, framed in a lighted window level with mine in the apartment house across the street, I saw a young man in a white T-shirt and white shorts at work polishing a long, beautiful dark table top. It was obviously his own table in his own flat, and he was enjoying his occupation. He was bent over in perfect concentration, rubbing, sandpapering, running the flat of his palm over the surface, standing back now and then to get the sheen of light on the fine wood. I am sure he had not even raised his head at the noise of the siren, much less had he come to the window. I stood there admiring his workmanlike devotion to a good job worth doing, and there flashed through me one of those pure fallacies of feeling which suddenly overleap reason: surely all that effort and energy so irreproachably employed were not going to be wasted on a table that was to be used merely for crawling under at some unspecified date. Then why take all those pains to make it beautiful? Any sort of old board would do.

I was so shocked at this treachery of the lurking Foul Fiend (despair *is* a foul fiend, and this was despair) I stood a moment longer, looking out and around, trying to collect my feelings, trying to think a little. Two windows away and a floor down in the house across the street, a young woman was lolling in a deep chair, reading and eating fruit from a little basket. On the sidewalk, a boy and a girl dressed alike in checkerboard cotton shirts and skin-tight blue denims, a costume which displayed acutely the structural differences of their shapes, strolled along with their arms around each other. I believe this custom of lovers walking enwreathed in public was imported by our soldiers of the First World War from France, from Paris indeed. "You didn't see that sort of thing here before," certain members of the older generation were heard to remark quite often, in a tone of voice. Well, one sees quite a lot of it now, and it is a very pretty, reassuring sight. Other citizens of all sizes and kinds and ages were crossing back and forth; lights flashed red and green, punctually. Motors zoomed by, and over the great city — but where am I going? I never read other peoples' descriptions of great cities, more particularly if it is a great city I know. It doesn't belong here anyway, except that I had again that quieting sense of the continuity of human experience on this earth, its perpetual aspirations, set-backs, failures and re-beginnings in eternal hope; and that, with some appreciable differences of dress, customs and means of conveyance, so people have lived and moved in the cities they have built for more millennia than we are yet able to account for, and will no doubt build and live for as many more.

Why did this console me? I cannot say; my mind is of the sort that can often be soothed with large generalities of that nature. The silence of the spaces between the stars does not affright me, as it did Pascal, because I am unable to imagine it except poetically; and my awe is not for the silence and space of the endless universe but for the inspired imagination of man, who can think and feel so, and turn a phrase like that to communicate it to us. Then too, I like the kind of honesty and directness of the young soldier who lately answered someone who asked him if he knew what he was fighting for. "I sure do," he said, "I am fighting to live." And as for the future, I was once reading the first writings of a young girl, an apprentice author, who was quite impatient to get on with the business and find her way into print. There is very little one can say of use in such matters, but I advised her against haste — she could so easily regret it. "Give yourself time," I said, "the future will take care of itself." This opinionated young person looked down her little nose at me and said, "The future is now." She may have heard the phrase somewhere and liked it, or she may just have naturally belonged to that school of metaphysics; I am sure she was too young to have investigated the thought deeply. But maybe she was right and the future does arrive every day and it is all we have, from one second to the next.

So I glanced again at the young man at work, a proper-looking candidate for the armed services, and realized the plain, homely fact: he was not preparing a possible shelter, something to cower under trembling; he was restoring a beautiful surface to put his books and papers on, to serve his plates from, to hold his cocktail tray and his lamp. He was full of the deep, right, instinctive, human belief that he and the table were going to be around together for a long time. Even if he is off to the army next week, it will be there when he gets back. At the very least, he is doing something he feels is worth doing now, and that is no small thing.

At once the difficulty, and the hope, of our special time in this world of Western Europe and America is that we have been brought up for many generations in the belief, however tacit, that all humanity was almost unanimously engaged in going forward, naturally to better things and to higher reaches. Since the eighteenth century at least when the Encyclopedists seized upon the Platonic theory that the highest pleasure of mankind was pursuit of the good, the true, and the beautiful, progress, in precisely the sense of perpetual, gradual amelioration of the hard human lot, has been taught popularly not just as theory of possibility but as an article of faith and the groundwork of a whole political doctrine. Mr. Toynbee has even simplified this view for us with picture diagrams of various sections of humanity, each in its own cycle rising to its own height, struggling beautifully on from craggy level to level, but always upward. Whole peoples are arrested at certain points, and perish there, but others go on. There is also the school of thought, Oriental and very ancient, which gives to life the spiral shape, and the spiral moves by nature upward. Even adherents of the circular or recurring-cycle school, also ancient and honorable, somehow do finally allow that the circle is a thread that spins itself out one layer above another, so that even though it is perpetually at every moment passing over a place it has been before, yet by its own width it will have risen just so much higher.

These are admirable attempts to get a little meaning and order into our view of our destiny, in that same spirit which moves the artist to labor with his little handful of chaos, bringing it to coherency within a frame; but on the visible evidence we must admit that in human nature the spirit of contradiction more than holds its own. Mankind has always built a little more than he has hitherto been able or willing to destroy; got more children than he has been able to kill; invented more laws and customs than he had any intention of observing; founded more religions than he was able to practice or even to believe in; made in general many more promises than he could keep; and has been known more than once to commit suicide through mere fear of death. Now in our time, in his pride to explore his universe to its unimaginable limits and to exceed his possible powers, he has at last produced an embarrassing series of engines too powerful for their containers and too tricky for their mechanicians; millions of labor-saving gadgets which can be rendered totally useless by the mere failure of the public power plants, and has reduced himself to such helplessness that a dozen or less of the enemy could disable a whole city by throwing a few switches. This paradoxical creature has committed all these extravagances and created all these dangers and sufferings in a quest — we are told — for peace and security.

How much of this are we to believe, when with the pride of Lucifer, the recklessness of Icarus, the boldness of Prometheus and the intellectual curiosity of Adam and Eve (yes, intellectual; the serpent promised them wisdom if . . .) man has obviously outreached himself, to the point where he cannot understand his own science or control his own inventions. Indeed he has become as the gods, who have over and over again suffered defeat and downfall at the hands of their creatures. Having devised the most exquisite and instantaneous means of communication to all corners of the earth, for years upon years friends were unable even to get a postcard message to each other across national frontiers.* The newspapers assure us that from the kitchen tap there flows a chemical, cheap and available, to make a bomb more disturbing to the imagination even than the one we so appallingly have; yet no machine has been invented to purify that water so that it will not spoil even the best tea or coffee. Or at any rate, it is not in use. We are the proud possessors of rocket bombs that go higher and farther and faster than any ever before, and there is some talk of a rocket ship shortly to take off for the moon. (My plan is to stow away.) We may indeed reach the moon some day, and I dare predict that will happen before we have devised a decent system of city garbage disposal.

This lunatic atom bomb has succeeded in rousing the people of all nations to the highest point of unanimous moral dudgeon; great numbers of persons are frightened who never really had much cause to be frightened before. This world has always been a desperately dangerous place to live for the greater part of the earth's inhabitants; it was, however reluctantly, endured as the natural state of affairs. Yet the invention of every new weapon of war has always been greeted with horror and righteous indignation, especially by those who failed to invent it, or who were threatened with it first . . . bows and arrows, stone cannon balls, gunpowder, flintlocks, pistols, the dumdum bullet, the Maxim silencer, the machine gun, poison gas, armored tanks, and on and on to the grand climax — if it should prove to be — of the experiment on Hiroshima. Nagasaki was bombed too, remember? Or were we already growing accustomed to the idea? And as for Hiroshima, surely it could not have been the notion of sudden death of others that shocked us? How could it be, when in two great wars within one generation we have become familiar with millions of shocking deaths, by sudden violence of most cruel devices, and by agonies prolonged for years in prisons and hospitals and concentration camps. We take with apparent calmness the news of the deaths of millions by flood, famine, plague — no, all the frontiers of danger are down now, no one is safe, no one, and that, alas, really means all of us. It is our own deaths we fear, and so let's

---

* Fall, 1952. The hydrogen bomb has just been exploded, very successfully, to the satisfaction of the criminals who caused it to be made.

out with it and give up our fine debauch of moralistic frenzy over Hiroshima. I fail entirely to see why it is more criminal to kill a few thousand persons in one instant than it is to kill the same number slowly over a given stretch of time. If I have a choice, I'd as lief be killed by an atom bomb as by a hand grenade or a flame thrower. If dropping the atom bomb is an immoral act, then the making of it was too; and writing of the formula was a crime, since those who wrote it must have known what such a contrivance was good for. So, morally speaking, the bomb is only a magnified hand grenade, and the crime, if crime it is, is still murder. It was never anything else. Our protocriminal then was the man who first struck fire from flint, for from that moment we have been coming steadily to this day and this weapon and this use of it. What would you have advised instead? That the human race should have gone on sitting in caves gnawing raw meat and beating each other over the head with the bones?

And yet it may be that what we have is a world not on the verge of flying apart, but an uncreated one — still in shapeless fragments waiting to be put together properly. I imagine that when we want something better, we may have it: at perhaps no greater price than we have already paid for the worse.

1953

Mary McCarthy

....

Artists in Uniform

The Colonel went out sailing,
He spoke with Turk and Jew . . .

"POUR IT ON, COLONEL," cried the young man in the Dacron suit excitedly, making his first sortie into the club-car conversation. His face
was white as Roquefort and of a glistening, cheeselike texture; he had a
shock of tow-colored hair, badly cut and greasy, and a snub nose with
large gray pores. Under his darting eyes were two black craters. He appeared to be under some intense nervous strain and had sat the night
before in the club car drinking bourbon with beer chasers and leafing
through magazines which he frowningly tossed aside, like cards into a
discard heap. This morning he had come in late, with a hangdog, hang-
over look, and had been sitting tensely forward on a settee, smoking
cigarettes and following the conversation with little twitches of the nose
and quivers of the body, as a dog follows a human conversation, veering
its mistrustful eyeballs from one speaker to another and raising its head
eagerly at its master's voice. The colonel's voice, rich and light and plausible, had in fact abruptly risen and swollen, as he pronounced his last
sentence. "I can tell you one thing," he had said harshly. "They weren't
named Ryan or Murphy!"

A sort of sigh, as of consummation, ran through the club car. "Pour it
on, Colonel, give it to them, Colonel, that's right, Colonel," urged the
young man in a transport of admiration. The colonel fingered his collar
and modestly smiled. He was a thin, hawklike, black-haired handsome
man with a bright blue bloodshot eye and a well-pressed, well-tailored

First published in *Harper's Magazine*, 1953; collected in *On the Contrary, 1961.

uniform that did not show the effects of the heat — the train, west-
bound for St. Louis, was passing through Indiana, and, as usual in a
heat wave, the air-conditioning had not met the test. He wore the Air
Force insignia, and there was something in his light-boned, spruce figure and keen, knifelike profile that suggested a classic image of the avia-
tor, ready to cut, piercing, into space. In base fact, however, the colonel
was in procurement, as we heard him tell the mining engineer who had
just bought him a drink. From several silken hints that parachuted into
the talk, it was patent to us that the colonel was a man who knew how
to enjoy this earth and its pleasures: he led, he gave us to think, a bache-
lor's life of abstemious dissipation and well-rounded sensuality. He had
accepted the engineer's drink with a mere nod of the glass in acknowledgment, like a genial Mars quaffing a libation; there was clearly no
prospect of his buying a second in return, not if the train were to travel
from here to the Mojave Desert. In the same way, an understanding had
arisen that I, the only woman in the club car, had become the colonel's
perquisite; it was taken for granted, without an invitation's being issued,
that I was to lunch with him in St. Louis, where we each had a wait between trains — my plans for seeing the city in a taxicab were dished.

From the beginning, as we eyed each other over my volume of Dickens (*"The Christmas Carol?"* suggested the colonel, opening relations), I
had guessed that the colonel was of Irish stock, and this, I felt, gave me
an advantage, for he did not suspect the same of me; strangely so, for I
am supposed to have the map of Ireland written on my features. In fact,
he had just wagered, with a jaunty, sidelong grin at the mining engineer,
that my people "came from Boston from way back," and that I — narrowed glance, running, like steel measuring-tape, up and down my
form — was a professional sculptress. I might have laughed this off, as a
crudely bad guess like his *Christmas Carol,* if I had not seen the engineer nodding gravely, like an idol, and the peculiar young man bobbing
his head up and down in mute applause and agreement. I was wearing a
bright apple-green raw silk blouse and a dark-green rather full raw silk
skirt, plus a pair of pink glass earrings; my hair was done up in a bun. It
came to me, for the first time, with a sort of dawning horror, that I had
begun, in the course of years, without ever guessing it, to look irrevocably Bohemian. Refracted from the three men's eyes was a strange vision
of myself as an artist, through and through, stained with my occupation like the dyer's hand. All I lacked, apparently, was a pair of sandals.
My sick heart sank to my Ferragamo shoes; I had always particularly
preened myself on being an artist in disguise. And it was not only a

question of personal vanity — it seemed to me that the writer or intellectual had a certain missionary usefulness in just such accidental gatherings as this, if he spoke not as an intellectual but as a normal member of the public. Now, thanks to the colonel, I slowly became aware that my contributions to the club-car conversation were being watched and assessed as coming from *a certain quarter.* My costume, it seemed, carefully assembled as it had been at an expensive shop, was to these observers simply a uniform that blazoned a caste and allegiance just as plainly as the colonel's khaki and eagles. *"Gardez,"* I said to myself. But, as the conversation grew tenser and I endeavored to keep cool, I began to writhe within myself, and every time I looked down, my contrasting greens seemed to be growing more and more lurid and taking on an almost menacing light, like leaves just before a storm that lift their bright undersides as the air becomes darker. We had been speaking, of course, of Russia, and I had mentioned a study that had been made at Harvard of political attitudes among Iron Curtain refugees. Suddenly, the colonel had smiled. "They're pretty Red at Harvard, I'm given to understand," he observed in a comfortable tone, while the young man twitched and quivered urgently. The eyes of all the men settled on me and waited. I flushed as I saw myself reflected. The woodland greens of my dress were turning to their complementary red, like a color-experiment in psychology or a traffic light changing. Down at the other end of the club car, a man looked up from his paper. I pulled myself together. "Set your mind at rest, Colonel," I remarked dryly. "I know Harvard very well and they're conservative to the point of dullness. The only thing crimson is the football team." This disparagement had its effect. "So . . . ?" queried the colonel. "I thought there was some professor. . . ." I shook my head. "Absolutely not. There used to be a few fellow-travelers, but they're very quiet these days, when they haven't absolutely recanted. The general atmosphere is more anti-Communist than the Vatican." The colonel and the mining engineer exchanged a thoughtful stare and seemed to agree that the Delphic oracle that had just pronounced knew whereof it spoke. "Glad to hear it," said the colonel. The engineer frowned and shook his fat wattles; he was a stately, gray-haired, plump man with small hands and feet and the pampered, finical tidiness of a small-town widow. "There's so much hearsay these days," he exclaimed vexedly. "You don't know *what* to believe."

I reopened my book with an air of having closed the subject and read a paragraph three times over. I exulted to think that I had made a modest contribution to sanity in our times, and I imagined my words pyramiding like a chain letter — the colonel telling a fellow-officer on the veranda of a club in Texas, the engineer halting a works-superintendent in a Colorado mine shaft: "I met a woman on the train who claims . . . Yes, absolutely. . . ." Of course, I did not know Harvard as thoroughly as I pretended, but I forgave myself by thinking it was the convention of such club-car symposia in our positivistic country to speak from the horse's mouth.

Meanwhile, across the aisle, the engineer and the colonel continued their talk in slightly lowered voices. From time to time, the colonel's polished index-fingernail scratched his burnished black head and his knowing blue eye forayed occasionally toward me. I saw that still I was a doubtful quantity to them, a movement in the bushes, a noise, a flicker, that was figuring in their crenelated thought as "she." The subject of Reds in our colleges had not, alas, been finished; they were speaking now of another university and a woman faculty-member who had been issuing Communist statements. This story somehow, I thought angrily, had managed to appear in the newspapers without my knowledge, while these men were conversant with it; I recognized a big chink in the armor of my authority. Looking up from my book, I began to question them sharply, as though they were reporting some unheard-of natural phenomenon. "When?" I demanded. "Where did you see it? What was her name?" This request for the professor's name was a headlong attempt on my part to buttress my position, the implication being that the identities of all university professors were known to me and that if I were but given the name I could promptly clarify the matter. To admit that there was a single Communist in our academic system whose activities were hidden from me imperiled, I instinctively felt, all the small good I had done here. Moreover, in the back of my mind, I had a supreme confidence that these men were wrong: the story, I supposed, was some tattered piece of misinformation they had picked up from a gossip column. Pride, as usual, preceded my fall. To the colonel, the demand for the name was not specific but generic: what *kind* of name was the question he presumed me to be asking. "Oh," he said slowly with a luxurious yawn, "Finkelstein or Fishbein or Feinstein." He lolled back in his seat with a side glance at the engineer, who deeply nodded. There was a voluptuary pause, as the implication sank in. I bit my lip, regarding this as a mere diversionary tactic. "Please!" I said impatiently. "Can't you remember exactly?" The colonel shook his head and then his spare cheekbones suddenly reddened and he looked directly at me. "I can tell you one thing," he exclaimed irefully. "They weren't named Ryan or Murphy."

The colonel went no further; it was quite unnecessary. In an instant, the young man was at his side, yapping excitedly and actually picking at the military sleeve. The poor thing was transformed, like some creature in a fairy tale whom a magic word releases from silence. "That's right, Colonel," he happily repeated. "I know them. *I* was at Harvard in the business school, studying accountancy. I left. I couldn't take it." He threw a poisonous glance at me, and the colonel, who had been regarding him somewhat doubtfully, now put on an alert expression and inclined an ear for his confidences. The man at the other end of the car folded his newspaper solemnly and took a seat by the young man's side. "They're all Reds, Colonel," said the young man. "They teach it in the classroom. I came back here to Missouri. It made me sick to listen to the stuff they handed out. If you didn't hand it back, they flunked you. Don't let anybody tell you different." "You are wrong," I said coldly and closed my book and rose. The young man was still talking eagerly, and the three men were leaning forward to catch his every gasping word, like three astute detectives over a dying informer, when I reached the door and cast a last look over my shoulder at them. For an instant, the colonel's eye met mine and I felt his scrutiny processing my green back as I tugged open the door and met a blast of hot air, blowing my full skirt wide. Behind me, in my fancy, I saw four sets of shrugging brows.

In my own car, I sat down, opposite two fat nuns, and tried to assemble my thoughts. I ought to have spoken, I felt, and yet what could I have said? It occurred to me that the four men had perhaps not realized why I had left the club car with such abruptness: was it possible that they thought I was a Communist, who feared to be unmasked? I spurned this possibility, and yet it made me uneasy. For some reason, it troubled my *amour-propre* to think of my anti-Communist self living on, so to speak, green in their collective memory as a Communist or fellow-traveler. In fact, though I did not give a fig for the men, I hated the idea, while a few years ago I should have counted it a great joke. This, it seemed to me, was a measure of the change in the social climate. I had always scoffed at the notion of liberals "living in fear" of political demagoguery in America, but now I had to admit that if I was not fearful, I was at least uncomfortable in the supposition that anybody, anybody whatever, could think of me, precious me, as a Communist. A remoter possibility was, of course, that back there my departure was being ascribed to Jewishness, and this too annoyed me. I am in fact a quarter Jewish, and though I did not "hate" the idea of being taken for a Jew, I did not precisely like it, particularly under these circumstances. I wished it to be clear that I had left the club car for intellectual and principled reasons; I wanted those men to know that it was not I, but my principles, that had been offended. To let them conjecture that I had left because I was Jewish would imply that only a Jew could be affronted by an anti-Semitic outburst; a terrible idea. Aside from anything else, it voided the whole concept of transcendence, which was very close to my heart, the concept that man is more than his circumstances, more even than himself.

However you looked at the episode, I said to myself nervously, I had not acquitted myself well. I ought to have done or said something concrete and unmistakable. From this, I slid glassily to the thought that those men ought to be punished, the colonel, in particular, who occupied a responsible position. In a minute, I was framing a businesslike letter to the Chief of Staff, deploring the colonel's conduct as unbecoming to an officer and identifying him by rank and post, since unfortunately I did not know his name. Earlier in the conversation, he had passed some comments on "Harry" that bordered positively on treason, I said to myself triumphantly. A vivid image of the proceedings against him presented itself to my imagination: the long military tribunal with a row of stern soldierly faces glaring down at the colonel. I myself occupied only an inconspicuous corner of this tableau, for, to tell the truth, I did not relish the role of the witness. Perhaps it would be wiser to let the matter drop . . . ? We were nearing St. Louis now; the colonel had come back into my car, and the young accountant had followed him, still talking feverishly. I pretended not to see them and turned to the two nuns, as if for sanctuary from this world and its hatred and revenges. Out of the corner of my eye, I watched the colonel, who now looked wry and restless; he shrank against the window as the young man made a place for himself amid the colonel's smart luggage and continued to express his views in a pale breathless voice. I smiled to think that the colonel was paying the piper. For the colonel, anti-Semitism was simply an aspect of urbanity, like a knowledge of hotels or women. This frantic psychopath of an accountant was serving him as a nemesis, just as the German people had been served by their psychopath, Hitler. Colonel, I adjured him, you have chosen, between him and me; measure the depth of your error and make the best of it! No intervention on my part was now necessary; justice had been meted out. Nevertheless, my heart was still throbbing violently, as if I were on the verge of some dangerous action. What was I to do, I kept asking myself, as I chatted with the nuns, if the colonel were to hold me to that lunch? And I slowly and apprehensively revolved this question, just as though it were a matter of the most serious import. It seemed to me that if I did not lunch with him — and I had no intention of doing so — I had the dreadful obligation of telling him why.

He was waiting for me as I descended the car steps. "Aren't you coming to lunch with me?" he called out and moved up to take my elbow. I began to tremble with audacity. "No," I said firmly, picking up my suitcase and draping an olive-green linen duster over my arm. "I can't lunch with you." He quirked a wiry black eyebrow. "Why not?" he said. "I understood it was all arranged." He reached for my suitcase. "No," I said, holding on to the suitcase. "I can't." I took a deep breath. "I have to tell you. I think you should be *ashamed* of yourself, Colonel, for what you said in the club car." The colonel stared: I mechanically waved for a redcap, who took my bag and coat and went off. The colonel and I stood facing each other on the emptying platform. "What do you mean?" he inquired in a low, almost clandestine tone. "Those anti-Semitic remarks," I muttered, resolutely. "You ought to be *ashamed*." The colonel gave a quick, relieved laugh. "Oh, come now," he protested. "I'm sorry," I said. "I can't have lunch with anybody who feels that way about the Jews." The colonel put down his attaché case and scratched the back of his lean neck. "Oh, come now," he repeated, with a look of amusement. "You're not Jewish, are you?" "No," I said quickly. "Well, then . . ." said the colonel, spreading his hands in a gesture of bafflement. I saw that he was truly surprised and slightly hurt by my criticism, and this made me feel wretchedly embarrassed and even apologetic, on my side, as though I had called attention to some physical defect in him, of which he himself was unconscious. "But I might have been," I stammered. "You had no way of knowing. You oughtn't to talk like that." I recognized, too late, that I was strangely reducing the whole matter to a question of etiquette: "Don't start anti-Semitic talk before making sure there are no Jews present." "Oh, hell," said the colonel, easily. "I can tell a Jew." "No, you can't," I retorted, thinking of my Jewish grandmother, for by Nazi criteria I was Jewish. "Of course I can," he insisted. "So can you." We had begun to walk down the platform side by side, disputing with a restrained passion that isolated us like a pair of lovers. All at once, the colonel halted, as though struck with a thought. "What *are* you, anyway?" he said meditatively, regarding my dark hair, green blouse, and pink earrings. Inside myself, I began to laugh. "Oh," I said gaily, playing out the trump I had been saving. "I'm Irish, like you, Colonel." "How did you know?" he said amazedly. I laughed aloud. "I can tell an Irishman," I taunted. The colonel frowned. "What's your family name?" he said brusquely. "McCarthy." He lifted an eyebrow, in defeat, and then quickly took note of my wedding ring. "That your maiden name?" I nodded. Under this peremptory questioning, I had the peculiar sensation that I get when I am lying; I began to feel that "McCarthy" was a nom de plume, a coinage of my artistic personality. But the colonel appeared to be satisfied. "Hell," he said, "come on to lunch, then. With a fine name like that, you and I should be friends." I still shook my head, though by this time we were pacing outside the station restaurant; my baggage had been checked in a locker; sweat was running down my face and I felt exhausted and hungry. I knew that I was weakening and I wanted only an excuse to yield and go inside with him. The colonel seemed to sense this. "Hell," he conceded. "You've got me wrong. I've nothing against the Jews. Back there in the club car, I was just stating a simple fact: you won't find an Irishman sounding off for the Commies. You can't deny that, can you?"

His voice rose persuasively; he took my arm. In the heat, I wilted and we went into the air-conditioned cocktail lounge. The colonel ordered two old-fashioneds. The room was dark as a cave and produced, in the midst of the hot midday, a hallucinated feeling, as though time had ceased, with the weather, and we were in eternity together. As the colonel prepared to relax, I made a tremendous effort to guide the conversation along rational, purposive lines; my only justification for being here would be to convert the colonel. "There *have* been Irishmen associated with the Communist party," I said suddenly, when the drinks came. "I can think of two." "Oh, hell," said the colonel, "every race and nation has its traitors. What I mean is, you won't find them in numbers. You've got to admit the Communists in this country are ninety per cent Jewish." "But the Jews in this country aren't ninety per cent Communist," I retorted.

As he stirred his drink, restively, I began to try to show him the reasons why the Communist movement in America had attracted such a large number, relatively, of Jews: how the Communists had been anti-Nazi when nobody else seemed to care what happened to the Jews in Germany; how the Communists still capitalized on a Jewish fear of fascism; how many Jews had become, after Buchenwald, traumatized by this fear. . . .

But the colonel was scarcely listening. An impatient frown rested on his jaunty features. "I don't get it," he said slowly. "Why should you be for them, with a name like yours?" "I'm *not* for the Communists," I cried. "I'm just trying to explain to you —" "For the Jews," the colonel interrupted, irritable now himself. "I've heard of such people but I never met one before." "I'm not 'for' them," I protested. "You don't understand. I'm not for *any* race or nation. I'm against those who are against them." This word, *them*, with a sort of slurring circle drawn round it, was beginning to sound ugly to me. Automatically, in arguing with him, I seemed to have slipped into the colonel's style of thought. It occurred to me that defense of the Jews could be a subtle and safe form of anti-Semitism, an exercise of patronage: as a rational Gentile, one could feel superior both to the Jews and the anti-Semites. There could be no doubt that the Jewish question evoked a curious stealthy lust or concupiscence. I could feel it now vibrating between us over the dark table. If I had been a good person, I should unquestionably have got up and left.

"I don't get it," repeated the colonel. "How were you brought up? Were your people this way too?" It was manifest that an odd reversal had taken place; each of us regarded the other as "abnormal" and was attempting to understand the etiology of a disease. "Many of my people think just as you do," I said, smiling coldly. "It seems to be a sickness to which the Irish are prone. Perhaps it's due to the potato diet," I said sweetly, having divined that the colonel came from a social stratum somewhat lower than my own.

But the colonel's hide was tough. "You've got me wrong," he reiterated, with an almost plaintive laugh. "I don't dislike the Jews. I've got a lot of Jewish friends. Among themselves, they think just as I do, mark my words. I tell you what it is," he added ruminatively, with a thoughtful prod of his muddler, "I draw a distinction between a kike and a Jew." I groaned. "Colonel, I've never heard an anti-Semite who didn't draw that distinction. You know what Otto Kahn said? 'A kike is a Jewish gentleman who has just left the room.'" The colonel did not laugh. "I don't hold it against some of them," he persisted, in a tone of pensive justice. "It's not their fault if they were born that way. That's what I tell them, and they respect me for my honesty. I've had a lot of discussions; in procurement, you have to do business with them, and the Jews are the first to admit that you'll find more chiselers among their race than among the rest of mankind." "It's not a race," I interjected wearily, but the colonel pressed on. "If I deal with a Jewish manufacturer, I can't bank on his word. I've seen it again and again, every damned time. When I deal with a Gentile, I can trust him to make delivery as promised. That's the difference between the two races. They're just a different breed. They don't have standards of honesty, even among each other." I sighed, feeling unequal to arguing the colonel's personal experience.

"Look," I said, "you may be dealing with an industry where the Jewish manufacturers are the most recent comers and feel they have to cut corners to compete with the established firms. I've heard that said about Jewish cattle-dealers, who are supposed to be extra sharp. But what I think, really, is that you notice it when a Jewish firm fails to meet an agreement and don't notice it when it's a Yankee." "Hah," said the colonel. "They'll tell you what I'm telling you themselves, if you get to know them and go into their homes. You won't believe it, but some of my best friends are Jews," he said, simply and thoughtfully, with an air of originality. "They may be *your* best friends, Colonel," I retorted, "but you are not theirs. I defy you to tell me that you talk to them as you're talking now." "Sure," said the colonel, easily. "More or less." "They must be very queer Jews you know," I observed tartly, and I began to wonder whether there indeed existed a peculiar class of Jews whose function in life was to be "friends" with such people as the colonel. It was difficult to think that all the anti-Semites who made the colonel's assertion were the victims of a cruel self-deception.

A dispirited silence followed. I was not one of those liberals who believed that the Jews, alone among peoples, possessed no characteristics whatever of a distinguishing nature — this would mean they had no history and no culture, a charge which should be leveled against them only by an anti-Semite. Certainly, types of Jews could be noted and patterns of Jewish thought and feeling: Jewish humor, Jewish rationality, and so on, not that every Jew reflected every attribute of Jewish life or history. But somehow, with the colonel, I dared not concede that there was such a thing as a Jew: I saw the sad meaning of the assertion that a Jew was a person whom other people thought was Jewish.

Hopeless, however, to convey this to the colonel. The desolate truth was that the colonel was extremely stupid, and it came to me, as we sat there, glumly ordering lunch, that for extremely stupid people anti-Semitism was a form of intellectuality, the sole form of intellectuality of which they were capable. It represented, in a rudimentary way, the ability to make categories, to generalize. Hence a thing I had noted before but never understood: the fact that anti-Semitic statements were generally delivered in an atmosphere of profundity. Furrowed brows attended these speculative distinctions between a kike and a Jew, these little empirical laws that you can't know one without knowing them all. To arrive, indeed, at the idea of a Jew was, for these grouping minds, an exercise in Platonic thought, a discovery of essence, and to be able to add the great corollary, "Some of my best friends are Jews," was to find the philosopher's cleft between essence and existence. From this, it would seem, followed the querulous obstinacy with which the anti-Semite clung to his concept; to be deprived of this intellectual tool by missionaries of tolerance would be, for persons like the colonel, the equivalent of Western man's losing the syllogism: a lapse into animal darkness. In the club car, we had just witnessed an example: the colonel with his anti-Semitic observation had come to the mute young man like the paraclete, bearing the gift of tongues.

Here in the bar, it grew plainer and plainer that the colonel did not regard himself as an anti-Semite but merely as a heavy thinker. The idea that I considered him anti-Semitic sincerely outraged his feelings. "Prejudice" was the last trait he could have imputed to himself. He looked on me, almost respectfully, as a "Jew-lover," a kind of being he had heard of but never actually encountered, like a centaur or a Siamese twin, and the interest of relating this prodigy to the natural state of mankind overrode any personal distaste. There I sat, the exception which was "proving" or testing the rule, and he kept pressing me for details of my history that might explain my deviation in terms of the norm. On my side, of course, I had become fiercely resolved that he would learn nothing from me that would make it possible for him to dismiss my anti-anti-Semitism as the product of special circumstances: I was stubbornly sitting on the fact of my Jewish grandmother like a hen on a golden egg. I was bent on making *him* see himself as a monster, a deviation, a heretic from Church and State. Unfortunately, the colonel, owing perhaps to his military training, had not the glimmering of an idea of what democracy meant; to him, it was simply a slogan that was sometimes useful in war. The notion of an ordained inequality was to him "scientific."

"Honestly," he was saying in lowered tones, as our drinks were taken away and the waitress set down my sandwich and his corned-beef hash, "don't you, brought up the way you were, feel about them the way I do? Just between ourselves, isn't there a sort of inborn feeling of horror that the very word, Jew, suggests?" I shook my head, roundly. The idea of an *innate* anti-Semitism was in keeping with the rest of the colonel's thought, yet it shocked me more than anything he had yet said. "No," I sharply replied. "It doesn't evoke any feeling one way or the other." "Honest Injun?" said the colonel. "Think back; when you were a kid, didn't the word, Jew, make you feel sick?" There was a dreadful sincerity about this that made me answer in an almost kindly tone. "No, truthfully, I assure you. When we were children, we learned to call the old-clothes man a sheeny, but that was just a dirty word to us, like 'Hun' that we used to call after workmen we thought were Germans."

"I don't get it," pondered the colonel, eating a pickle. "There must be something wrong with you. Everybody is born with that feeling. It's natural; it's part of nature." "On the contrary," I said. "It's something very unnatural that you must have been taught as a child." "It's not something you're *taught*," he protested. "You must have been," I said. "You simply don't remember it. In any case, you're a man now; you must rid yourself of that feeling. It's psychopathic, like that horrible young man on the train." "You thought he was crazy?" mused the colonel, in an idle, dreamy tone. I shrugged my shoulders. "Of course. Think of his color. He was probably just out of a mental institution. People don't get that tattletale gray except in prison or mental hospitals." The colonel suddenly grinned. "You might be right," he said. "He was quite a case." He chuckled.

I leaned forward. "You know, Colonel," I said quickly, "anti-Semitism is contrary to the Church's teaching. God will make you do penance for hating the Jews. Ask your priest; he'll tell you I'm right. You'll have a long spell in Purgatory, if you don't rid yourself of this sin. It's a deliberate violation of Christ's commandment, 'Love thy neighbor.' The Church holds that the Jews have a sacred place in God's design. Mary was a Jew and Christ was a Jew. The Jews are under God's special protection. The Church teaches that the millennium can't come until the conversion of the Jews; therefore, the Jews must be preserved that the Divine Will may be accomplished. Woe to them that harm them, for they controvert God's Will!" In the course of speaking, I had swept myself away with the solemnity of the doctrine. The Great Reconciliation between God and His chosen people, as envisioned by the Evangelist, had for me at that moment a piercing, majestic beauty, like some awesome Tintoretto. I saw a noble spectacle of blue sky, thronged with gray clouds, and a vast white desert, across which God and Israel advanced to meet each other, while below in hell the demons of disunion shrieked and gnashed their teeth.

"Hell," said the colonel, jovially, "I don't believe in all that. I lost my faith when I was a kid. I saw that all this God stuff was a lot of bushwa." I gazed at him in stupefaction. His confidence had completely returned. The blue eyes glittered debonairly, the eagles glittered; the narrow polished head cocked and listened to itself like a trilling bird. I was up against an airman with a bird's-eye view, a man who believed in nothing but the law of kind: the epitome of godless materialism. "You still don't hold with that bunk?" the colonel inquired in an undertone, with an expression of stealthy curiosity. "No," I confessed, sad to admit to a meeting of minds. "You know what got me?" exclaimed the colonel. "That birth-control stuff. Didn't it kill you?" I made a neutral sound. "I was beginning to play around," said the colonel, with a significant beam of the eye, "and I just couldn't take that guff. When I saw through the birth-control talk, I saw through the whole thing. They claimed it was against nature, but I claim, if that's so, an operation's against nature. I told my old man that when he was having his kidney stones out. You ought to have heard him yell!" A rich, reminiscent satisfaction dwelt in the colonel's face.

This period of his life, in which he had thrown off the claims of the spiritual and adopted a practical approach, was evidently one of those "turning points" to which a man looks back with pride. He lingered over the story of his break with church and parents with a curious sort of heat, as though the flames of old sexual conquests stirred within his body at the memory of those old quarrels. The looks he rested on me, as a sharer of that experience, grew more and more lickerish and assaying. "What got *you* down?" he finally inquired, settling back in his chair and pushing his coffee cup aside. "Oh," I said wearily, "it's a long story. You can read it when it's published." "You're an author?" cried the colonel, who was really very slow-witted. I nodded, and the colonel regarded me afresh. "What do you write? Love stories?" He gave a half-wink. "No," I said. "Various things. Articles. Books. Highbrowish stories." A suspicion darkened in the colonel's sharp face. "That McCarthy," he said. "Is that your pen name?" "Yes," I said, "but it's my real name too. It's the name I write under *and* my maiden name." The colonel digested this thought. "Oh," he concluded.

A new idea seemed to visit him. Quite cruelly, I watched it take possession. He was thinking of the power of the press and the indiscretions of other military figures, who had been rewarded with demotion. The consciousness of the uniform he wore appeared to seep uneasily into his body. He straightened his shoulders and called thoughtfully for the check. We paid in silence, the colonel making no effort to forestall my dive into my pocketbook. I should not have let him pay in any case, but it startled me that he did not try to do so, if only for reasons of vanity. The whole business of paying, apparently, was painful to him; I watched his facial muscles contract as he pocketed the change and slipped two dimes for the waitress onto the table, not daring quite to hide them under the coffee cup — he had short-changed me on the bill and the tip, and we both knew it. We walked out into the steaming station and I took my baggage out of the checking locker. The colonel carried my suitcase and we strolled along without speaking. Again, I felt horribly embarrassed for him. He was meditative, and I supposed that he too was mortified by his meanness about the tip.

"Don't get me wrong," he said suddenly, setting the suitcase down and turning squarely to face me, as though he had taken a big decision. "I may have said a few things back there about the Jews getting what they deserved in Germany." I looked at him in surprise; actually, he had not said that to me. Perhaps he had let it drop in the club car after I had left. "But that doesn't mean I approve of Hitler." "I should hope not," I said. "What I mean is," said the colonel, "that they probably gave the Germans a lot of provocation, but that doesn't excuse what Hitler did." "No," I said, somewhat ironically, but the colonel was unaware of anything satiric in the air. His face was grave and determined; he was sorting out his philosophy for the record. "I mean, I don't approve of his methods," he finally stated. "No," I agreed. "You mean, you don't approve of the gas chamber." The colonel shook his head very severely. "Absolutely not! That was terrible." He shuddered and drew out a handkerchief and slowly wiped his brow. "For God's sake," he said, "don't get me wrong. I think they're human beings." "Yes," I assented, and we walked along to my track. The colonel's spirits lifted, as though, having stated his credo, he had both got himself in line with public policy and achieved an autonomous thought. "I mean," he resumed, "you may not care for them, but that's not the same as killing them, in cold blood, like that." "No, Colonel," I said.

He swung my bag onto the car's platform and I climbed up behind it. He stood below, smiling, with upturned face. "I'll look for your article," he cried, as the train whistle blew. I nodded, and the colonel waved, and I could not stop myself from waving back at him and even giving him the corner of a smile. After all, I said to myself, looking down at him, the colonel was "a human being." There followed one of those inane intervals in which one prays for the train to leave. We both glanced at our watches. "See you some time," he called. "What's your married name?" "Broadwater," I called back. The whistle blew again. "Brodwater?" shouted the colonel, with a dazed look of unbelief and growing enlightenment; he was not the first person to hear it as a Jewish name, on the model of Goldwater. "B-r-o-a-d," I began, automatically, but then I stopped. I disdained to spell it out for him; the victory was his. "One of the chosen, eh?" his brief grimace seemed to commiserate. For the last time, and in the final fullness of understanding, the hawk eye patrolled the green dress, the duster, and the earrings; the narrow flue of his nostril contracted as he curtly turned away. The train commenced to move.

1955

Rachel Carson

The Marginal World

THE EDGE of the sea is a strange and beautiful place. All through the long history of Earth it has been an area of unrest where waves have broken heavily against the land, where the tides have pressed forward over the continents, receded, and then returned. For no two successive days is the shore line precisely the same. Not only do the tides advance and retreat in their eternal rhythms, but the level of the sea itself is never at rest. It rises or falls as the glaciers melt or grow, as the floor of the deep ocean basins shifts under its increasing load of sediments, or as the earth's crust along the continental margins warps up or down in adjustment to strain and tension. Today a little more land may belong to the sea, tomorrow a little less. Always the edge of the sea remains an elusive and indefinable boundary.

The shore has a dual nature, changing with the swing of the tides, belonging now to the land, now to the sea. On the ebb tide it knows the harsh extremes of the land world, being exposed to heat and cold, to wind, to rain and drying sun. On the flood tide it is a water world, returning briefly to the relative stability of the open sea.

Only the most hardy and adaptable can survive in a region so mutable, yet the area between the tide lines is crowded with plants and animals. In this difficult world of the shore, life displays its enormous toughness and vitality by occupying almost every conceivable niche. Visibly, it carpets the intertidal rocks; or half hidden, it descends into fissures and crevices, or hides under boulders, or lurks in the wet gloom of sea caves. Invisibly, where the casual observer would say there is no

First published in *The Edge of the Sea, 1955; a condensed version appeared the same year in The New Yorker.

life, it lies deep in the sand, in burrows and tubes and passageways. It tunnels into solid rock and bores into peat and clay. It encrusts weeds or drifting spars or the hard, chitinous shell of a lobster. It exists minutely, as the film of bacteria that spreads over a rock surface or a wharf piling; as spheres of protozoa, small as pinpricks, sparkling at the surface of the sea; and as Lilliputian beings swimming through dark pools that lie between the grains of sand.

The shore is an ancient world, for as long as there has been an earth and sea there has been this place of the meeting of land and water. Yet it is a world that keeps alive the sense of continuing creation and of the relentless drive of life. Each time that I enter it, I gain some new awareness of its beauty and its deeper meanings, sensing that intricate fabric of life by which one creature is linked with another, and each with its surroundings.

In my thoughts of the shore, one place stands apart for its revelation of exquisite beauty. It is a pool hidden within a cave that one can visit only rarely and briefly when the lowest of the year's low tides fall below it, and perhaps from that very fact it acquires some of its special beauty. Choosing such a tide, I hoped for a glimpse of the pool. The ebb was to fall early in the morning. I knew that if the wind held from the northwest and no interfering swell ran in from a distant storm the level of the sea should drop below the entrance to the pool. There had been sudden ominous showers in the night, with rain like handfuls of gravel flung on the roof. When I looked out into the early morning the sky was full of a gray dawn light but the sun had not yet risen. Water and air were pallid. Across the bay the moon was a luminous disc in the western sky, suspended above the dim line of distant shore — the full August moon, drawing the tide to the low, low levels of the threshold of the alien sea world. As I watched, a gull flew by, above the spruces. Its breast was rosy with the light of the unrisen sun. The day was, after all, to be fair.

Later, as I stood above the tide near the entrance to the pool, the promise of that rosy light was sustained. From the base of the steep wall of rock on which I stood, a moss-covered ledge jutted seaward into deep water. In the surge at the rim of the ledge the dark fronds of oarweeds swayed, smooth and gleaming as leather. The projecting ledge was the path to the small hidden cave and its pool. Occasionally a swell, stronger than the rest, rolled smoothly over the rim and broke in foam against the cliff. But the intervals between such swells were long enough to admit me to the ledge and long enough for a glimpse of that fairy pool, so seldom and so briefly exposed.

And so I knelt on the wet carpet of sea moss and looked back into the dark cavern that held the pool in a shallow basin. The floor of the cave was only a few inches below the roof, and a mirror had been created in which all that grew on the ceiling was reflected in the still water below.

Under water that was clear as glass the pool was carpeted with green sponge. Gray patches of sea squirts glistened on the ceiling and colonies of soft coral were a pale apricot color. In the moment when I looked into the cave a little elfin starfish hung down, suspended by the merest thread, perhaps by only a single tube foot. It reached down to touch its own reflection, so perfectly delineated that there might have been, not one starfish, but two. The beauty of the reflected images and of the limpid pool itself was the poignant beauty of things that are ephemeral, existing only until the sea should return to fill the little cave.

Whenever I go down into this magical zone of the low water of the spring tides, I look for the most delicately beautiful of all the shore's inhabitants — flowers that are not plant but animal, blooming on the threshold of the deeper sea. In that fairy cave I was not disappointed. Hanging from its roof were the pendent flowers of the hydroid Tubularia, pale pink, fringed and delicate as the wind flower. Here were creatures so exquisitely fashioned that they seemed unreal, their beauty too fragile to exist in a world of crushing force. Yet every detail was functionally useful, every stalk and hydranth and petal-like tentacle fashioned for dealing with the realities of existence. I knew that they were merely waiting, in that moment of the tide's ebbing, for the return of the sea. Then in the rush of water, in the surge of surf and the pressure of the incoming tide, the delicate flower heads would stir with life. They would sway on their slender stalks, and their long tentacles would sweep the returning water, finding in it all that they needed for life.

And so in that enchanted place on the threshold of the sea the realities that possessed my mind were far from those of the land world I had left an hour before. In a different way the same sense of remoteness and of a world apart came to me in a twilight hour on a great beach on the coast of Georgia. I had come down after sunset and walked far out over sands that lay wet and gleaming, to the very edge of the retreating sea. Looking back across that immense flat, crossed by winding, water-filled gullies and here and there holding shallow pools left by the tide, I was filled with awareness that this intertidal area, although abandoned briefly and rhythmically by the sea, is always reclaimed by the rising tide. There at the edge of low water the beach with its reminders of the land seemed far away. The only sounds were those of the wind and the sea and the birds. There was one sound of wind moving over water, and another of water sliding over the sand and tumbling down the faces of its own wave forms. The flats were astir with birds, and the voice of the willet rang insistently. One of them stood at the edge of the water and gave its loud, urgent cry; an answer came from far up the beach and the two birds flew to join each other.

The flats took on a mysterious quality as dusk approached and the last evening light was reflected from the scattered pools and creeks. Then birds became only dark shadows, with no color discernible. Sanderlings scurried across the beach like little ghosts, and here and there the darker forms of the willets stood out. Often I could come very close to them before they would start up in alarm — the sanderlings running, the willets flying up, crying. Black skimmers flew along the ocean's edge silhouetted against the dull, metallic gleam, or they went flitting above the sand like large, dimly seen moths. Sometimes they "skimmed" the winding creeks of tidal water, where little spreading surface ripples marked the presence of small fish.

The shore at night is a different world, in which the very darkness that hides the distractions of daylight brings into sharper focus the elemental realities. Once, exploring the night beach, I surprised a small ghost crab in the searching beam of my torch. He was lying in a pit he had dug just above the surf, as though watching the sea and waiting. The blackness of the night possessed water, air, and beach. It was the darkness of an older world, before Man. There was no sound but the all-enveloping, primeval sounds of wind blowing over water and sand, and of waves crashing on the beach. There was no other visible life — just one small crab near the sea. I have seen hundreds of ghost crabs in other settings, but suddenly I was filled with the odd sensation that for the first time I knew the creature in its own world — that I understood, as never before, the essence of its being. In that moment time was suspended; the world to which I belonged did not exist and I might have been an onlooker from outer space. The little crab alone with the sea became a symbol that stood for life itself — for the delicate, destructible, yet incredibly vital force that somehow holds its place amid the harsh realities of the inorganic world.

The sense of creation comes with memories of a southern coast, where the sea and the mangroves, working together, are building a wilderness of thousands of small islands off the southwestern coast of Florida, separated from each other by a tortuous pattern of bays, lagoons, and narrow waterways. I remember a winter day when the sky was blue and drenched with sunlight; though there was no wind one was conscious of flowing air like cold clear crystal. I had landed on the surf-washed tip of one of those islands, and then worked my way around to the sheltered bay side. There I found the tide far out, exposing the broad mud flat of a cove bordered by the mangroves with their twisted branches, their glossy leaves, and their long prop roots reaching down, grasping and holding the mud, building the land out a little more, then again a little more.

The mud flats were strewn with the shells of that small, exquisitely colored mollusk, the rose tellin, looking like scattered petals of pink roses. There must have been a colony nearby, living buried just under the surface of the mud. At first the only creature visible was a small heron in gray and rusty plumage — a reddish egret that waded across the flat with the stealthy, hesitant movements of its kind. But other land creatures had been there, for a line of fresh tracks wound in and out among the mangrove roots, marking the path of a raccoon feeding on the oysters that gripped the supporting roots with projections from their shells. Soon I found the tracks of a shore bird, probably a sanderling, and followed them a little; then they turned toward the water and were lost, for the tide had erased them and made them as though they had never been.

Looking out over the cove I felt a strong sense of the interchangeability of land and sea in this marginal world of the shore, and of the links between the life of the two. There was also an awareness of the past and of the continuing flow of time, obliterating much that had gone before, as the sea had that morning washed away the tracks of the bird.

The sequence and meaning of the drift of time were quietly summarized in the existence of hundreds of small snails — the mangrove periwinkles — browsing on the branches and roots of the trees. Once their ancestors had been sea dwellers, bound to the salt waters by every tie of their life processes. Little by little over the thousands and millions of years the ties had been broken, the snails had adjusted themselves to life out of water, and now today they were living many feet above the tide to which they only occasionally returned. And perhaps, who could say how many ages hence, there would be in their descendants not even this gesture of remembrance for the sea.

The spiral shells of other snails — these quite minute — left winding tracks on the mud as they moved about in search of food. They were horn shells, and when I saw them I had a nostalgic moment when I wished I might see what Audubon saw, a century and more ago. For such little horn shells were the food of the flamingo, once so numerous on this coast, and when I half closed my eyes I could almost imagine a flock of these magnificent flame birds feeding in that cove, filling it with their color. It was a mere yesterday in the life of the earth that they were there; in nature, time and space are relative matters, perhaps most truly perceived subjectively in occasional flashes of insight, sparked by such a magical hour and place.

There is a common thread that links these scenes and memories — the spectacle of life in all its varied manifestations as it has appeared, evolved, and sometimes died out. Underlying the beauty of the spectacle there is meaning and significance. It is the elusiveness of that meaning that haunts us, that sends us again and again into the natural world where the key to the riddle is hidden. It sends us back to the edge of the sea, where the drama of life played its first scene on earth and perhaps even its prelude; where the forces of evolution are at work today, as they have been since the appearance of what we know as life; and where the spectacle of living creatures faced by the cosmic realities of their world is crystal clear.

1955

James Baldwin

Notes of a Native Son

ONE

On the twenty-ninth of July, in 1943, my father died. On the same day, a few hours later, his last child was born. Over a month before this, while all our energies were concentrated in waiting for these events, there had been, in Detroit, one of the bloodiest race riots of the century. A few hours after my father's funeral, while he lay in state in the undertaker's chapel, a race riot broke out in Harlem. On the morning of the third of August, we drove my father to the graveyard through a wilderness of smashed plate glass.

The day of my father's funeral had also been my nineteenth birthday. As we drove him to the graveyard, the spoils of injustice, anarchy, discontent, and hatred were all around us. It seemed to me that God himself had devised, to mark my father's end, the most sustained and brutally dissonant of codas. And it seemed to me, too, that the violence which rose all about us as my father left the world had been devised as a corrective for the pride of his eldest son. I had declined to believe in that apocalypse which had been central to my father's vision; very well, life seemed to be saying, here is something that will certainly pass for an apocalypse until the real thing comes along. I had inclined to be contemptuous of my father for the conditions of his life, for the conditions of our lives. When his life had ended I began to wonder about that life and also, in a new way, to be apprehensive about my own.

I had not known my father very well. We had got on badly, partly because we shared, in our different fashions, the vice of stubborn pride.

First published in *Harper's Magazine*, 1955; collected in *Notes of a Native Son*, 1955.

When he was dead I realized that I had hardly ever spoken to him. When he had been dead a long time I began to wish I had. It seems to be typical of life in America, where opportunities, real and fancied, are thicker than anywhere else on the globe, that the second generation has no time to talk to the first. No one, including my father, seems to have known exactly how old he was, but his mother had been born during slavery. He was of the first generation of free men. He, along with thousands of other Negroes, came North after 1919 and I was part of that generation which had never seen the landscape of what Negroes sometimes call the Old Country.

He had been born in New Orleans and had been a quite young man there during the time that Louis Armstrong, a boy, was running errands for the dives and honky-tonks of what was always presented to me as one of the most wicked of cities — to this day, whenever I think of New Orleans, I also helplessly think of Sodom and Gomorrah. My father never mentioned Louis Armstrong, except to forbid us to play his records; but there was a picture of him on our wall for a long time. One of my father's strong-willed female relatives had placed it there and forbade my father to take it down. He never did, but he eventually maneuvered her out of the house and when, some years later, she was in trouble and near death, he refused to do anything to help her.

He was, I think, very handsome. I gather this from photographs and from my own memories of him, dressed in his Sunday best and on his way to preach a sermon somewhere, when I was little. Handsome, proud, and ingrown, "like a toenail," somebody said. But he looked to me, as I grew older, like pictures I had seen of African tribal chieftains: he really should have been naked, with warpaint on and barbaric mementos, standing among spears. He could be chilling in the pulpit and indescribably cruel in his personal life and he was certainly the most bitter man I have ever met; yet it must be said that there was something else in him, buried in him, which lent him his tremendous power and, even, a rather crushing charm. It had something to do with his blackness, I think — he was very black — with his blackness and his beauty, and with the fact that he knew that he was black but did not know that he was beautiful. He claimed to be proud of his blackness but it had also been the cause of much humiliation and it had fixed bleak boundaries to his life. He was not a young man when we were growing up and he had already suffered many kinds of ruin; in his outrageously demanding and protective way he loved his children, who were black like him and menaced, like him; and all these things sometimes showed in his face when he tried, never to my knowledge with any success, to establish contact with any of us. When he took one of his children on his knee to play, the child always became fretful and began to cry; when he tried to help one of us with our homework the absolutely unabating tension which emanated from him caused our minds and our tongues to become paralyzed, so that he, scarcely knowing why, flew into a rage and the child, not knowing why, was punished. If it ever entered his head to bring a surprise home for his children, it was, almost unfailingly, the wrong surprise and even the big watermelons he often brought home on his back in the summertime led to the most appalling scenes. I do not remember, in all those years, that one of his children was ever glad to see him come home. From what I was able to gather of his early life, it seemed that this inability to establish contact with other people had always marked him and had been one of the things which had driven him out of New Orleans. There was something in him, therefore, groping and tentative, which was never expressed and which was buried with him. One saw it most clearly when he was facing new people and hoping to impress them. But he never did, not for long. We went from church to smaller and more improbable church, he found himself in less and less demand as a minister, and by the time he died none of his friends had come to see him for a long time. He had lived and died in an intolerable bitterness of spirit and it frightened me, as we drove him to the graveyard through those unquiet, ruined streets, to see how powerful and overflowing this bitterness could be and to realize that this bitterness now was mine.

When he died I had been away from home for a little over a year. In that year I had had time to become aware of the meaning of all my father's bitter warnings, had discovered the secret of his proudly pursed lips and rigid carriage: I had discovered the weight of white people in the world. I saw that this had been for my ancestors and now would be for me an awful thing to live with and that the bitterness which had helped to kill my father could also kill me.

He had been ill a long time — in the mind, as we now realized, reliving instances of his fantastic intransigence in the new light of his affliction and endeavoring to feel a sorrow for him which never, quite, came true. We had not known that he was being eaten up by paranoia, and the discovery that his cruelty, to our bodies and our minds, had been one of the symptoms of his illness was not, then, enough to enable us to forgive him. The younger children felt, quite simply, relief that he would not be coming home anymore. My mother's observation that it was he, after all, who had kept them alive all these years meant nothing because the problems of keeping children alive are not real for children. The older children felt, with my father gone, that they could invite their friends to the house without fear that their friends would be insulted or, as had sometimes happened with me, being told that their friends were in league with the devil and intended to rob our family of everything we owned. (I didn't fail to wonder, and it made me hate him, what on earth we owned that anybody else would want.)

His illness was beyond all hope of healing before anyone realized that he was ill. He had always been so strange and had lived, like a prophet, in such unimaginably close communion with the Lord that his long silences which were punctuated by moans and hallelujahs and snatches of old songs while he sat at the living-room window never seemed odd to us. It was not until he refused to eat because, he said, his family was trying to poison him that my mother was forced to accept as a fact what had, until then, been only an unwilling suspicion. When he was committed, it was discovered that he had tuberculosis and, as it turned out, the disease of his mind allowed the disease of his body to destroy him. For the doctors could not force him to eat, either, and, though he was fed intravenously, it was clear from the beginning that there was no hope for him.

In my mind's eye I could see him, sitting at the window, locked up in his terrors; hating and fearing every living soul including his children who had betrayed him, too, by reaching toward the world which had despised him. There were nine of us. I began to wonder what it could have felt like for such a man to have had nine children whom he could barely feed. He used to make little jokes about our poverty, which never, of course, seemed very funny to us; they could not have seemed very funny to him, either, or else our all too feeble response to them would never have caused such rages. He spent great energy and achieved, to our chagrin, no small amount of success in keeping us away from the people who surrounded us, people who had all-night rent parties to which we listened when we should have been sleeping, people who cursed and drank and flashed razor blades on Lenox Avenue. He could not understand why, if they had so much energy to spare, they could not use it to make their lives better. He treated almost everybody on our block with a most uncharitable asperity and neither they, nor, of course, their children were slow to reciprocate.

The only white people who came to our house were welfare workers and bill collectors. It was almost always my mother who dealt with them, for my father's temper, which was at the mercy of his pride, was never to be trusted. It was clear that he felt their very presence in his home to be a violation: this was conveyed by his carriage, almost ludicrously stiff, and by his voice, harsh and vindictively polite. When I was around nine or ten I wrote a play which was directed by a young, white schoolteacher, a woman, who then took an interest in me, and gave me books to read and, in order to corroborate my theatrical bent, decided to take me to see what she somewhat tactlessly referred to as "real" plays. Theater-going was forbidden in our house, but, with the really cruel intuitiveness of a child, I suspected that the color of this woman's skin would carry the day for me. When, at school, she suggested taking me to the theater, I did not, as I might have done if she had been a Negro, find a way of discouraging her, but agreed that she should pick me up at my house one evening. I then, very cleverly, left all the rest to my mother, who suggested to my father, as I knew she would, that it would not be very nice to let such a kind woman make the trip for nothing. Also, since it was a schoolteacher, I imagine that my mother countered the idea of sin with the idea of "education," which word, even with my father, carried a kind of bitter weight.

Before the teacher came my father took me aside to ask *why* she was coming, what *interest* she could possibly have in our house, in a boy like me. I said I didn't know but I, too, suggested that it had something to do with education. And I understood that my father was waiting for me to say something — I didn't quite know what; perhaps that I wanted his protection against this teacher and her "education." I said none of these things and the teacher came and we went out. It was clear, during the brief interview in our living room, that my father was agreeing very much against his will and that he would have refused permission if he had dared. The fact that he did not dare caused me to despise him: I had no way of knowing that he was facing in that living room a wholly unprecedented and frightening situation.

Later, when my father had been laid off from his job, this woman became very important to us. She was really a very sweet and generous woman and went to a great deal of trouble to be of help to us, particularly during one awful winter. My mother called her by the highest name she knew: she said she was a "christian." My father could scarcely disagree but during the four or five years of our relatively close association he never trusted her and was always trying to surprise in her open, Midwestern face the genuine, cunningly hidden, and hideous motivation. In later years, particularly when it began to be clear that this "education" of mine was going to lead me to perdition, he became more explicit and warned me that my white friends in high school were not really my friends and that I would see, when I was older, how white people would do anything to keep a Negro down. Some of them could be nice, he admitted, but none of them were to be trusted and most of them were not even nice. The best thing was to have as little to do with them as possible. I did not feel this way and I was certain, in my innocence, that I never would.

But the year which preceded my father's death had made a great change in my life. I had been living in New Jersey, working in defense plants, working and living among southerners, white and black. I knew about the south, of course, and about how southerners treated Negroes and how they expected them to behave, but it had never entered my mind that anyone would look at me and expect *me* to behave that way. I learned in New Jersey that to be a Negro meant, precisely, that one was never looked at but was simply at the mercy of the reflexes the color of one's skin caused in other people. I acted in New Jersey as I had always acted, that is as though I thought a great deal of myself — I had to *act* that way — with results that were, simply, unbelievable. I had scarcely arrived before I had earned the enmity, which was extraordinarily ingenious, of all my superiors and nearly all my co-workers. In the beginning, to make matters worse, I simply did not know what was happening. I did not know what I had done, and I shortly began to wonder what *anyone* could possibly do, to bring about such unanimous, active, and unbearably vocal hostility. I knew about jim crow but I had never experienced it. I went to the same self-service restaurant three times and stood with all the Princeton boys before the counter, waiting for a hamburger and coffee; it was always an extraordinarily long time before anything was set before me; but it was not until the fourth visit that I learned that, in fact, nothing had ever been set before me: I had simply picked something up. Negroes were not served there, I was told, and they had been waiting for me to realize that I was always the only Negro present. Once I was told this, I determined to go there all the time. But now they were ready for me and, though some dreadful scenes were subsequently enacted in that restaurant, I never ate there again.

It was the same story all over New Jersey, in bars, bowling alleys, diners, places to live. I was always being forced to leave, silently, or with mutual imprecations. I very shortly became notorious and children giggled behind me when I passed and their elders whispered or shouted — they really believed that I was mad. And it did begin to work on my mind, of course; I began to be afraid to go anywhere and to compensate for this I went places to which I really should not have gone and where, God knows, I had no desire to be. My reputation in town naturally enhanced my reputation at work and my working day became one long series of acrobatics designed to keep me out of trouble. I cannot say that these acrobatics succeeded. It began to seem that the machinery of the organization I worked for was turning over, day and night, with but one aim: to eject me. I was fired once, and contrived, with the aid of a friend from New York, to get back on the payroll; was fired again, and bounced back again. It took a while to fire me for the third time, but the third time took. There were no loopholes anywhere. There was not even any way of getting back inside the gates.

That year in New Jersey lives in my mind as though it were the year during which, having an unsuspected predilection for it, I first contracted some dread, chronic disease, the unfailing symptom of which is a kind of blind fever, a pounding in the skull and fire in the bowels. Once this disease is contracted, one can never be really carefree again, for the fever, without an instant's warning, can recur at any moment. It can wreck more important things than race relations. There is not a Negro alive who does not have this rage in his blood — one has the choice, merely, of living with it consciously or surrendering to it. As for me, this fever has recurred in me, and does, and will until the day I die.

My last night in New Jersey, a white friend from New York took me to the nearest big town, Trenton, to go to the movies and have a few drinks. As it turned out, he also saved me from, at the very least, a violent whipping. Almost every detail of that night stands out very clearly in my memory. I even remember the name of the movie we saw because its title impressed me as being so patly ironical. It was a movie about the German occupation of France, starring Maureen O'Hara and Charles Laughton and called *This Land Is Mine*. I remember the name of the diner we walked into when the movie ended: it was the "American Diner." When we walked in the counterman asked what we wanted and I remember answering with the casual sharpness which had become my habit: "We want a hamburger and a cup of coffee, what do you think we want?" I do not know why, after a year of such rebuffs, I so completely failed to anticipate his answer, which was, of course, "we don't serve Negroes here." This reply failed to discompose me, at least for the moment. I made some sardonic comment about the name of the diner and we walked out into the streets.

This was the time of what was called the "brownout," when the lights in all American cities were very dim. When we reentered the streets something happened to me which had the force of an optical illusion, or a nightmare. The streets were very crowded and I was facing north. People were moving in every direction but it seemed to me, in that instant, that all of the people I could see, and many more than that, were moving toward me, against me, and that everyone was white. I remember how their faces gleamed. And I felt, like a physical sensation, a *click* at the nape of my neck as though some interior string connecting my head to my body had been cut. I began to walk. I heard my friend call after me, but I ignored him. Heaven only knows what was going on in his mind, but he had the good sense not to touch me — I don't know what would have happened if he had — and to keep me in sight. I don't know what was going on in my mind, either; I certainly had no conscious plan. I wanted to do something to crush these white faces, which were crushing me. I walked for perhaps a block or two until I came to an enormous, glittering, and fashionable restaurant in which I knew not even the intercession of the Virgin would cause me to be served. I pushed through the doors and took the first vacant seat I saw, at a table for two, and waited.

I do not know how long I waited and I rather wonder, until today, what I could possibly have looked like. Whatever I looked like, I frightened the waitress who shortly appeared, and the moment she appeared all of my fury flowed toward her. I hated her for her white face, and for her great, astounded, frightened eyes. I felt that if she found a black man so frightening I would make her fright worthwhile.

She did not ask me what I wanted, but repeated, as though she had learned it somewhere, "We don't serve Negroes here." She did not say it with the blunt, derisive hostility to which I had grown so accustomed, but, rather, with a note of apology in her voice, and fear. This made me colder and more murderous than ever. I felt I had to do something with my hands. I wanted her to come close enough for me to get her neck between my hands.

So I pretended not to have understood her, hoping to draw her closer. And she did step a very short step closer, with her pencil poised incongruously over her pad, and repeated the formula: ". . . don't serve Negroes here."

Somehow, with the repetition of that phrase, which was already ringing in my head like a thousand bells of a nightmare, I realized that she would never come any closer and that I would have to strike from a distance. There was nothing on the table but an ordinary watermug half full of water, and I picked this up and hurled it with all my strength at her. She ducked and it missed her and shattered against the mirror behind the bar. And, with that sound, my frozen blood abruptly thawed, I returned from wherever I had been, I *saw*, for the first time, the restaurant, the people with their mouths open, already, as it seemed to me, rising as one man, and I realized what I had done, and where I was, and I was frightened. I rose and began running for the door. A round, potbellied man grabbed me by the nape of the neck just as I reached the doors and began to beat me about the face. I kicked him and got loose and ran into the streets. My friend whispered, *"Run!"* and I ran.

My friend stayed outside the restaurant long enough to misdirect my pursuers and the police, who arrived, he told me, at once. I do not know what I said to him when he came to my room that night. I could not have said much. I felt, in the oddest, most awful way, that I had somehow betrayed him. I lived it over and over and over again, the way one relives an automobile accident after it has happened and one finds oneself alone and safe. I could not get over two facts, both equally difficult for the imagination to grasp, and one was that I could have been murdered. But the other was that I had been ready to commit murder. I saw nothing very clearly but I did see this: that my life, my *real* life, was in danger, and not from anything other people might do but from the hatred I carried in my own heart.

TWO

I had returned home around the second week in June — in great haste because it seemed that my father's death and my mother's confinement were both but a matter of hours. In the case of my mother, it soon became clear that she had simply made a miscalculation. This had always been her tendency and I don't believe that a single one of us arrived in the world, or has since arrived anywhere else, on time. But none of us dawdled so intolerably about the business of being born as did my baby sister. We sometimes amused ourselves, during those endless, stifling weeks, by picturing the baby sitting within in the safe, warm dark, bitterly regretting the necessity of becoming a part of our chaos and stubbornly putting it off as long as possible. I understood her perfectly and congratulated her on showing such good sense so soon. Death, however, sat as purposefully at my father's bedside as life stirred within my mother's womb and it was harder to understand why he so lingered in that long shadow. It seemed that he had bent, and for a long time, too, all of his energies toward dying. Now death was ready for him but my father held back.

All of Harlem, indeed, seemed to be infected by waiting. I had never before known it to be so violently still. Racial tensions throughout this country were exacerbated during the early years of the war, partly because the labor market brought together hundreds of thousands of ill-prepared people and partly because Negro soldiers, regardless of where they were born, received their military training in the south. What happened in defense plants and army camps had repercussions, naturally, in every Negro ghetto. The situation in Harlem had grown bad enough for clergymen, policemen, educators, politicians, and social workers to assert in one breath that there was no "crime wave" and to offer, in the very next breath, suggestions as to how to combat it. These suggestions always seemed to involve playgrounds, despite the fact that racial skirmishes were occurring in the playgrounds, too. Playground or not, crime wave or not, the Harlem police force had been augmented in March, and the unrest grew — perhaps, in fact, partly as a result of the ghetto's instinctive hatred of policemen. Perhaps the most revealing news item, out of the steady parade of reports of muggings, stabbings, shootings, assaults, gang wars, and accusations of police brutality, is the item concerning six Negro girls who set upon a white girl in the subway because, as they all too accurately put it, she was stepping on their toes. Indeed she was, all over the nation.

I had never before been so aware of policemen, on foot, on horseback, on corners, everywhere, always two by two. Nor had I ever been so aware of small knots of people. They were on stoops and on corners and in doorways, and what was striking about them, I think, was that they did not seem to be talking. Never, when I passed these groups, did the usual sound of a curse or a laugh ring out and neither did there seem to be any hum of gossip. There was certainly, on the other hand, occurring between them communication extraordinarily intense. Another thing that was striking was the unexpected diversity of the people who made up these groups. Usually, for example, one would see a group of sharpies standing on the street corner, jiving the passing chicks; or a group of older men, usually, for some reason, in the vicinity of a barber shop, discussing baseball scores, or the numbers, or making rather chilling observations about women they had known. Women, in a general way, tended to be seen less often together — unless they were church women, or very young girls, or prostitutes met together for an unprofessional instant. But that summer I saw the strangest combinations: large, respectable, churchly matrons standing on the stoops or the corners with their hair tied up, together with a girl in sleazy satin whose face bore the marks of gin and the razor, or heavy-set, abrupt, no-nonsense older men, in company with the most disreputable and fanatical "race" men, or these same "race" men with the sharpies, or these sharpies with the churchly women. Seventh Day Adventists and Methodists and Spiritualists seemed to be hobnobbing with Holyrollers and they were all, alike, entangled with the most flagrant disbelievers; something heavy in their stance seemed to indicate that they had all, incredibly, seen a common vision, and on each face there seemed to be the same strange, bitter shadow.

The churchly women and the matter-of-fact, no-nonsense men had children in the Army. The sleazy girls they talked to had lovers there, the sharpies and the "race" men had friends and brothers there. It would have demanded an unquestioning patriotism, happily as uncommon in this country as it is undesirable, for these people not to have been disturbed by the bitter letters they received, by the newspaper stories they read, not to have been enraged by the posters, then to be found all over New York, which described the Japanese as "yellow-bellied Japs." It was only the "race" men, to be sure, who spoke ceaselessly of being revenged — how this vengeance was to be exacted was not clear — for the indignities and dangers suffered by Negro boys in uniform; but everybody felt a directionless, hopeless bitterness, as well as that panic which can scarcely be suppressed when one knows that a human being one loves is beyond one's reach, and in danger. This helplessness and this gnawing uneasiness does something, at length, to even the toughest mind. Perhaps the best way to sum all this up is to say that the people I knew felt, mainly, a peculiar kind of relief when they knew that their boys were being shipped out of the south, to do battle overseas. It was, perhaps, like feeling that the most dangerous part of a dangerous journey had been passed and that now, even if death should come, it would come with honor and without the complicity of their countrymen. Such a death would be, in short, a fact with which one could hope to live.

It was on the twenty-eighth of July, which I believe was a Wednesday, that I visited my father for the first time during his illness and for the last time in his life. The moment I saw him I knew why I had put off this visit so long. I had told my mother that I did not want to see him because I hated him. But this was not true. It was only that I *had* hated him and I wanted to hold on to this hatred. I did not want to look on him as a ruin: it was not a ruin I had hated. I imagine that one of the reasons people cling to their hates so stubbornly is because they sense, once hate is gone, that they will be forced to deal with pain.

We traveled out to him, his older sister and myself, to what seemed to be the very end of a very Long Island. It was hot and dusty and we wrangled, my aunt and I, all the way out, over the fact that I had recently begun to smoke and, as she said, to give myself airs. But I knew that she wrangled with me because she could not bear to face the fact of her brother's dying. Neither could I endure the reality of her despair, her unstated bafflement as to what had happened to her brother's life, and her own. So we wrangled and I smoked and from time to time she fell into a heavy reverie. Covertly, I watched her face, which was the face of an old woman; it had fallen in, the eyes were sunken and lightless; soon she would be dying, too.

In my childhood — it had not been so long ago — I had thought her beautiful. She had been quick-witted and quick-moving and very generous with all the children and each of her visits had been an event. At one time one of my brothers and myself had thought of running away to live with her. Now she could no longer produce out of her handbag some unexpected and yet familiar delight. She made me feel pity and revulsion and fear. It was awful to realize that she no longer caused me to feel affection. The closer we came to the hospital the more querulous she became and at the same time, naturally, grew more dependent on me. Between pity and guilt and fear I began to feel that there was another me trapped in my skull like a jack-in-the-box who might escape my control at any moment and fill the air with screaming.

She began to cry the moment we entered the room and she saw him lying there, all shriveled and still, like a little black monkey. The great, gleaming apparatus which fed him and would have compelled him to be still even if he had been able to move brought to mind, not beneficence, but torture; the tubes entering his arm made me think of pictures I had seen when a child, of Gulliver, tied down by the pygmies on that island. My aunt wept and wept, there was a whistling sound in my father's throat; nothing was said; he could not speak. I wanted to take his hand, to say something. But I do not know what I could have said, even if he could have heard me. He was not really in that room with us, he had at last really embarked on his journey; and though my aunt told me that he said he was going to meet Jesus, I did not hear anything except that whistling in his throat. The doctor came back and we left, into that unbearable train again, and home. In the morning came the telegram saying that he was dead. Then the house was suddenly full of relatives, friends, hysteria, and confusion and I quickly left my mother and the children to the care of those impressive women, who, in Negro communities at least, automatically appear at times of bereavement armed with lotions, proverbs, and patience, and an ability to cook. I went downtown. By the time I returned, later the same day, my mother had been carried to the hospital and the baby had been born.

THREE

For my father's funeral I had nothing black to wear and this posed a nagging problem all day long. It was one of those problems, simple, or impossible of solution, to which the mind insanely clings in order to avoid the mind's real trouble. I spent most of that day at the downtown apartment of a girl I knew, celebrating my birthday with whisky and wondering what to wear that night. When planning a birthday celebration one naturally does not expect that it will be up against competition from a funeral and this girl had anticipated taking me out that night, for a big dinner and a night club afterwards. Sometime during the course of that long day we decided that we would go out anyway, when my father's funeral service was over. I imagine I decided it, since, as the funeral hour approached, it became clearer and clearer to me that I would not know what to do with myself when it was over. The girl, stifling her very lively concern as to the possible effects of the whisky on one of my father's chief mourners, concentrated on being conciliatory and practically helpful. She found a black shirt for me somewhere and ironed it and, dressed in the darkest pants and jacket I owned, and slightly drunk, I made my way to my father's funeral.

The chapel was full, but not packed, and very quiet. There were, mainly, my father's relatives, and his children, and here and there I saw faces I had not seen since childhood, the faces of my father's one-time friends. They were very dark and solemn now, seeming somehow to suggest that they had known all along that something like this would happen. Chief among the mourners was my aunt, who had quarreled with my father all his life; by which I do not mean to suggest that her mourning was insincere or that she had not loved him. I suppose that she was one of the few people in the world who had, and their incessant quarreling proved precisely the strength of the tie that bound them. The only other person in the world, as far as I knew, whose relationship to my father rivaled my aunt's in depth was my mother, who was not there.

It seemed to me, of course, that it was a very long funeral. But it was, if anything, a rather shorter funeral than most, nor, since there were no overwhelming, uncontrollable expressions of grief, could it be called — if I dare to use the word — successful. The minister who preached my father's funeral sermon was one of the few my father had still been seeing as he neared his end. He presented to us in his sermon a man whom none of us had ever seen — a man thoughtful, patient, and forbearing, a Christian inspiration to all who knew him, and a model for his children. And no doubt the children, in their disturbed and guilty state, were almost ready to believe this; he had been remote enough to be anything and, anyway, the shock of the incontrovertible, that it was really our father lying up there in that casket, prepared the mind for anything. His sister moaned and this grief-stricken moaning was taken as corroboration. The other faces held a dark, noncommittal thoughtfulness. This was not the man they had known, but they had scarcely expected to be confronted with *him;* this was, in a sense deeper than questions of fact, the man they had not known, and the man they had not known may have been the real one. The real man, whoever he had been, had suffered and now he was dead: this was all that was sure and all that mattered now. Every man in the chapel hoped that when his hour came he, too, would be eulogized, which is to say forgiven, and that all of his lapses, greeds, errors, and strayings from the truth would be invested with coherence and looked upon with charity. This was perhaps the last thing human beings could give each other and it was what they demanded, after all, of the Lord. Only the Lord saw the midnight tears, only He was present when one of His children, moaning and wringing hands, paced up and down the room. When one slapped one's child in anger the recoil in the heart reverberated through heaven and became part of the pain of the universe. And when the children were hungry and sullen and distrustful and one watched them, daily, growing wilder, and further away, and running headlong into danger, it was the Lord who knew what the charged heart endured as the strap was laid to the backside; the Lord alone who knew what one *would* have said if one had had, like the Lord, the gift of the living word. It was the Lord who knew of the impossibility every parent in that room faced: how to prepare the child for the day when the child would be despised and how to *create* in the child — by what means? — a stronger antidote to this poison than one had found for oneself. The avenues, side streets, bars, billiard halls, hospitals, police stations, and even the playgrounds of Harlem — not to mention the houses of correction, the jails, and the morgue — testified to the potency of the poison while remaining silent as to the efficacy of whatever antidote, irresistibly raising the question of whether or not such an antidote existed; raising, which was worse, the question of whether or not an antidote was desirable; perhaps poison should be fought with poison. With these several schisms in the mind and with more terrors in the heart than could be named, it was better not to judge the man who had gone down under an impossible burden. It was better to remember: *Thou knowest this man's fall; but thou knowest not his wrassling.*

While the preacher talked and I watched the children — years of changing their diapers, scrubbing them, slapping them, taking them to school, and scolding them had had the perhaps inevitable result of making me love them, though I am not sure I knew this then — my mind was busily breaking out with a rash of disconnected impressions. Snatches of popular songs, indecent jokes, bits of books I had read, movie sequences, faces, voices, political issues — I thought I was going mad; all these impressions suspended, as it were, in the solution of the faint nausea produced in me by the heat and liquor. For a moment I had the impression that my alcoholic breath, inefficiently disguised with chewing gum, filled the entire chapel. Then someone began singing one of my father's favorite songs and, abruptly, I was with him, sitting on his knee, in the hot, enormous, crowded church which was the first church we attended. It was the Abyssinian Baptist Church on 138th Street. We had not gone there long. With this image, a host of others came. I had forgotten, in the rage of my growing up, how proud my father had been of me when I was little. Apparently, I had had a voice and my father had liked to show me off before the members of the church. I had forgotten what he had looked like when he was pleased but now I remembered that he had always been grinning with pleasure when my solos ended. I even remembered certain expressions on his face when he teased my mother — had he loved her? I would never know. And when had it all begun to change? For now it seemed that he had not always been cruel. I remembered being taken for a haircut and scraping my knee on the footrest of the barber's chair and I remembered my father's face as he soothed my crying and applied the stinging iodine. Then I remembered our fights, fights which had been of the worst possible kind because my technique had been silence.

I remembered the one time in all our life together when we had really spoken to each other.

It was on a Sunday and it must have been shortly before I left home.

We were walking, just the two of us, in our usual silence, to or from church. I was in high school and had been doing a lot of writing and I was, at about this time, the editor of the high school magazine. But I had also been a Young Minister and had been preaching from the pulpit. Lately, I had been taking fewer engagements and preached as rarely as possible. It was said in the church, quite truthfully, that I was "cooling off."

My father asked me abruptly, "You'd rather write than preach, wouldn't you?"

I was astonished at his question — because it was a real question. I answered, "Yes."

That was all we said. It was awful to remember that that was all we had *ever* said.

The casket now was opened and the mourners were being led up the aisle to look for the last time on the deceased. The assumption was that the family was too overcome with grief to be allowed to make this journey alone and I watched while my aunt was led to the casket and, muffled in black, and shaking, led back to her seat. I disapproved of forcing the children to look on their dead father, considering that the shock of his death, or, more truthfully, the shock of death as a reality, was already a little more than a child could bear, but my judgment in this matter had been overruled and there they were, bewildered and frightened and very small, being led, one by one, to the casket. But there is also something very gallant about children at such moments. It has something to do with their silence and gravity and with the fact that one cannot help them. Their legs, somehow, seem *exposed*, so that it is at once incredible and terribly clear that their legs are all they have to hold them up.

I had not wanted to go to the casket myself and I certainly had not wished to be led there, but there was no way of avoiding either of these forms. One of the deacons led me up and I looked on my father's face. I cannot say that it looked like him at all. His blackness had been equivocated by powder and there was no suggestion in that casket of what his power had or could have been. He was simply an old man dead, and it was hard to believe that he had ever given anyone either joy or pain. Yet, his life filled that room. Further up the avenue his wife was holding his newborn child. Life and death so close together, and love and hatred, and right and wrong, said something to me which I did not want to hear concerning man, concerning the life of man.

After the funeral, while I was downtown desperately celebrating my birthday, a Negro soldier, in the lobby of the Hotel Braddock, got into a fight with a white policeman over a Negro girl. Negro girls, white policemen, in or out of uniform, and Negro males — in or out of uniform — were part of the furniture of the lobby of the Hotel Braddock and this was certainly not the first time such an incident had occurred. It was destined, however, to receive an unprecedented publicity, for the fight between the policeman and the soldier ended with the shooting of the soldier. Rumor, flowing immediately to the streets outside, stated that the soldier had been shot in the back, an instantaneous and revealing invention, and that the soldier had died protecting a Negro woman. The facts were somewhat different — for example, the soldier had not been shot in the back, and was not dead, and the girl seems to have been as dubious a symbol of womanhood as her white counterpart in Georgia usually is, but no one was interested in the facts. They preferred the invention because this invention expressed and corroborated their hates and fears so perfectly. It is just as well to remember that people are always doing this. Perhaps many of those legends, including Christianity, to which the world clings began their conquest of the world with just some such concerted surrender to distortion. The effect, in Harlem, of this particular legend was like the effect of a lit match in a tin of gasoline. The mob gathered before the doors of the Hotel Braddock simply began to swell and to spread in every direction, and Harlem exploded.

The mob did not cross the ghetto lines. It would have been easy, for example, to have gone over Morningside Park on the west side or to have crossed the Grand Central railroad tracks at 125th Street on the east side, to wreak havoc in white neighborhoods. The mob seems to have been mainly interested in something more potent and real than the white face, that is, in white power, and the principal damage done during the riot of the summer of 1943 was to white business establishments in Harlem. It might have been a far bloodier story, of course, if, at the hour the riot began, these establishments had still been open. From the Hotel Braddock the mob fanned out, east and west along 125th Street, and for the entire length of Lenox, Seventh, and Eighth avenues. Along each of these avenues, and along each major side street — 116th, 125th, 135th, and so on — bars, stores, pawnshops, restaurants, even little luncheonettes had been smashed open and entered and looted — looted, it might be added, with more haste than efficiency. The shelves really looked as though a bomb had struck them. Cans of beans and soup and dog food, along with toilet paper, corn flakes, sardines and milk tumbled every which way, and abandoned cash registers and cases of beer leaned crazily out of the splintered windows and were strewn along the avenues. Sheets, blankets, and clothing of every description formed a kind of path, as though people had dropped them while running. I truly had not realized that Harlem *had* so many stores until I saw them all smashed open; the first time the word *wealth* ever entered my mind in relation to Harlem was when I saw it scattered in the streets. But one's first, incongruous impression of plenty was countered immediately by an impression of waste. None of this was doing anybody any good. It would have been better to have left the plate glass as it had been and the goods lying in the stores.

It would have been better, but it would also have been intolerable, for Harlem had needed something to smash. To smash something is the ghetto's chronic need. Most of the time it is the members of the ghetto who smash each other, and themselves. But as long as the ghetto walls arc standing thcrc will always come a moment when these outlets do not work. That summer, for example, it was not enough to get into a fight on Lenox Avenue, or curse out one's cronies in the barber shops. If ever, indeed, the violence which fills Harlem's churches, pool halls, and bars erupts outward in a more direct fashion, Harlem and its citizens are likely to vanish in an apocalyptic flood. That this is not likely to happen is due to a great many reasons, most hidden and powerful among them the Negro's real relation to the white American. This relation prohibits, simply, anything as uncomplicated and satisfactory as pure hatred. In order really to hate white people, one has to blot so much out of the mind — and the heart — that this hatred itself becomes an exhausting and self-destructive pose. But this does not mean, on the other hand, that love comes easily: the white world is too powerful, too complacent, too ready with gratuitous humiliation, and, above all, too ignorant and too innocent for that. One is absolutely forced to make perpetual qualifications and one's own reactions are always canceling each other out. It is this, really, which has driven so many people mad, both white and black. One is always in the position of having to decide between amputation and gangrene. Amputation is swift but time may prove that the amputation was not necessary — or one may delay the amputation too long. Gangrene is slow, but it is impossible to be sure that one is reading one's symptoms right. The idea of going through life as a cripple is more than one can bear, and equally unbearable is the risk of swelling up slowly, in agony, with poison. And the trouble, finally, is that the risks are real even if the choices do not exist.

"But as for me and my house," my father had said, "we will serve the

Lord." I wondered, as we drove him to his resting place, what this line had meant for him. I had heard him preach it many times. I had preached it once myself, proudly giving it an interpretation different from my father's. Now the whole thing came back to me, as though my father and I were on our way to Sunday school and I were memorizing the golden text: *And if it seem evil unto you to serve the Lord, choose you this day whom you will serve; whether the gods which your fathers served that were on the other side of the flood, or the gods of the Amorites, in whose land ye dwell: but as for me and my house, we will serve the Lord.* I suspected in these familiar lines a meaning which had never been there for me before. All of my father's texts and songs, which I had decided were meaningless, were arranged before me at his death like empty bottles, waiting to hold the meaning which life would give them for me. This was his legacy: nothing is ever escaped. That bleakly memorable morning I hated the unbelievable streets and the Negroes and whites who had, equally, made them that way. But I knew that it was folly, as my father would have said, this bitterness was folly. It was necessary to hold on to the things that mattered. The dead man mattered, the new life mattered; blackness and whiteness did not matter; to believe that they did was to acquiesce in one's own destruction. Hatred, which could destroy so much, never failed to destroy the man who hated and this was an immutable law.

It began to seem that one would have to hold in the mind forever two ideas which seemed to be in opposition. The first idea was acceptance, the acceptance, totally without rancor, of life as it is, and men as they are: in the light of this idea, it goes without saying that injustice is a commonplace. But this did not mean that one could be complacent, for the second idea was of equal power: that one must never, in one's own life, accept these injustices as commonplace but must fight them with all one's strength. This fight begins, however, in the heart and it now had been laid to my charge to keep my own heart free of hatred and despair. This intimation made my heart heavy and, now that my father was irrecoverable, I wished that he had been beside me so that I could have searched his face for the answers which only the future would give me now.

1956

Loren Eiseley

The Brown Wasps

THERE IS a corner in the waiting room of one of the great Eastern stations where women never sit. It is always in the shadow and overhung
by rows of lockers. It is, however, always frequented — not so much by
genuine travelers as by the dying. It is here that a certain element of the
abandoned poor seeks a refuge out of the weather, clinging for a few
hours longer to the city that has fathered them. In a precisely similar
manner I have seen, on a sunny day in midwinter, a few old brown
wasps creep slowly over an abandoned wasp nest in a thicket. Numbed
and forgetful and frost-blackened, the hum of the spring hive still re-
sounded faintly in their sodden tissues. Then the temperature would
fall and they would drop away into the white oblivion of the snow. Here
in the station it is in no way different save that the city is busy in its
snows. But the old ones cling to their seats as though these were symbolic and could not be given up. Now and then they sleep, their gray old
heads resting with painful awkwardness on the backs of the benches.

Also they are not at rest. For an hour they may sleep in the gasping
exhaustion of the ill-nourished and aged who have to walk in the night.
Then a policeman comes by on his round and nudges them upright.

"You can't sleep here," he growls.

A strange ritual then begins. An old man is difficult to waken. After a
muttered conversation the policeman presses a coin into his hand and
passes fiercely along the benches prodding and gesturing toward the
door. In his wake, like birds rising and settling behind the passage of a
farmer through a cornfield, the men totter up, move a few paces, and
subside once more upon the benches.

First published in *Gentry*, 1956–57, and collected in **The Night Country*, 1966.

One man, after a slight, apologetic lurch, does not move at all. Tubercularly thin, he sleeps on steadily. The policeman does not look back. To him, too, this has become a ritual. He will not have to notice it again officially for another hour.

Once in a while one of the sleepers will not awake. Like the brown wasps, he will have had his wish to die in the great droning center of the hive rather than in some lonely room. It is not so bad here with the shuffle of footsteps and the knowledge that there are others who share the bad luck of the world. There are also the whistles and the sounds of everyone, everyone in the world, starting on journeys. Amidst so many journeys somebody is bound to come out all right. Somebody.

Maybe it was on a like thought that the brown wasps fell away from the old paper nest in the thicket. You hold till the last, even if it is only to a public seat in a railroad station. You want your place in the hive more than you want a room or a place where the aged can be eased gently out of the way. It is the place that matters, the place at the heart of things. It is life that you want, that bruises your gray old head with the hard chairs; a man has a right to his place.

But sometimes the place is lost in the years behind us. Or sometimes it is a thing of air, a kind of vaporous distortion above a heap of rubble. We cling to a time and a place because without them man is lost, not only man but life. This is why the voices, real or unreal, which speak from the floating trumpets at spiritualist seances are so unnerving. They are voices out of nowhere whose only reality lies in their ability to stir the memory of a living person with some fragment of the past. Before the medium's cabinet both the dead and the living revolve endlessly about an episode, a place, an event that has already been engulfed by time.

This feeling runs deep in life; it brings stray cats running over endless miles, and birds homing from the ends of the earth. It is as though all living creatures, and particularly the more intelligent, can survive only by fixing or transforming a bit of time into space or by securing a bit of space with its objects immortalized and made permanent in time. For example, I once saw, on a flower pot in my own living room, the efforts of a field mouse to build a remembered field. I have lived to see this episode repeated in a thousand guises, and since I have spent a large portion of my life in the shade of a nonexistent tree I think I am entitled to speak for the field mouse.

One day as I cut across the field which at that time extended on one side of our suburban shopping center, I found a giant slug feeding from a runnel of pink ice cream in an abandoned Dixie cup. I could see his eyes telescope and protrude in a kind of dim uncertain ecstasy as his dark body bunched and elongated in the curve of the cup. Then, as I stood there at the edge of the concrete, contemplating the slug, I began to realize it was like standing on a shore where a different type of life creeps up and fumbles tentatively among the rocks and sea wrack. It knows its place and will only creep so far until something changes. Little by little as I stood there I began to see more of this shore that surrounds the place of man. I looked with sudden care and attention at things I had been running over thoughtlessly for years. I even waded out a short way into the grass and the wild-rose thickets to see more. A huge black-belted bee went droning by and there were some indistinct scurryings in the underbrush.

Then I came to a sign which informed me that this field was to be the site of a new Wanamaker suburban store. Thousands of obscure lives were about to perish, the spores of puffballs would go smoking off to new fields, and the bodies of little white-footed mice would be crunched under the inexorable wheels of the bulldozers. Life disappears or modifies its appearances so fast that everything takes on an aspect of illusion — a momentary fizzing and boiling with smoke rings, like pouring dissident chemicals into a retort. Here man was advancing, but in a few years his plaster and bricks would be disappearing once more into the insatiable maw of the clover. Being of an archaeological cast of mind, I thought of this fact with an obscure sense of satisfaction and waded back through the rose thickets to the concrete parking lot. As I did so, a mouse scurried ahead of me, frightened of my steps if not of that ominous Wanamaker sign. I saw him vanish in the general direction of my apartment house, his little body quivering with fear in the great open sun on the blazing concrete. Blinded and confused, he was running straight away from his field. In another week scores would follow him.

I forgot the episode then and went home to the quiet of my living room. It was not until a week later, letting myself into the apartment, that I realized I had a visitor. I am fond of plants and had several ferns standing on the floor in pots to avoid the noon glare by the south window.

As I snapped on the light and glanced carelessly around the room, I saw a little heap of earth on the carpet and a scrabble of pebbles that had been kicked merrily over the edge of one of the flower pots. To my astonishment I discovered a full-fledged burrow delving downward among the fern roots. I waited silently. The creature who had made the burrow did not appear. I remembered the wild field then, and the flight of the mice. No house mouse, no *Mus domesticus,* had kicked up this little heap of earth or sought refuge under a fern root in a flower pot. I thought of the desperate little creature I had seen fleeing from the wildrose thicket. Through intricacies of pipes and attics, he, or one of his fellows, had climbed to this high green solitary room. I could visualize what had occurred. He had an image in his head, a world of seed pods and quiet, of green sheltering leaves in the dim light among the weed stems. It was the only world he knew and it was gone.

Somehow in his flight he had found his way to this room with drawn shades where no one would come till nightfall. And here he had smelled green leaves and run quickly up the flower pot to dabble his paws in common earth. He had even struggled half the afternoon to carry his burrow deeper and had failed. I examined the hole, but no whiskered twitching face appeared. He was gone. I gathered up the earth and refilled the burrow. I did not expect to find traces of him again.

Yet for three nights thereafter I came home to the darkened room and my ferns to find the dirt kicked gaily about the rug and the burrow reopened, though I was never able to catch the field mouse within it. I dropped a little food about the mouth of the burrow, but it was never touched. I looked under beds or sat reading with one ear cocked for rustlings in the ferns. It was all in vain; I never saw him. Probably he ended in a trap in some other tenant's room.

But before he disappeared I had come to look hopefully for his evening burrow. About my ferns there had begun to linger the insubstantial vapor of an autumn field, the distilled essence, as it were, of a mouse brain in exile from its home. It was a small dream, like our dreams, carried a long and weary journey along pipes and through spider webs, past holes over which loomed the shadows of waiting cats, and finally, desperately, into this room where he had played in the shuttered daylight for an hour among the green ferns on the floor. Every day these invisible dreams pass us on the street, or rise from beneath our feet, or look out upon us from beneath a bush.

Some years ago the old elevated railway in Philadelphia was torn down and replaced by a subway system. This ancient El with its barnlike stations containing nut-vending machines and scattered food scraps had, for generations, been the favorite feeding ground of flocks of pigeons, generally one flock to a station along the route of the El. Hundreds of pigeons were dependent upon the system. They flapped in and out of its stanchions and steel work or gathered in watchful little audiences about the feet of anyone who rattled the peanut-vending machines. They even watched people who jingled change in their hands, and prospected for food under the feet of the crowds who gathered between trains. Probably very few among the waiting people who tossed a crumb to an eager pigeon realized that this El was like a food-bearing river, and that the life which haunted its banks was dependent upon the running of the trains with their human freight.

I saw the river stop.

The time came when the underground tubes were ready; the traffic was transferred to a realm unreachable by pigeons. It was like a great river subsiding suddenly into desert sands. For a day, for two days, pigeons continued to circle over the El or stand close to the red vending machines. They were patient birds, and surely this great river which had flowed through the lives of unnumbered generations was merely suffering from some momentary drought.

They listened for the familiar vibrations that had always heralded an approaching train; they flapped hopefully about the head of an occasional workman walking along the steel runways. They passed from one empty station to another, all the while growing hungrier. Finally they flew away.

I thought I had seen the last of them about the El, but there was a revival and it provided a curious instance of the memory of living things for a way of life or a locality that has long been cherished. Some weeks after the El was abandoned workmen began to tear it down. I went to work every morning by one particular station, and the time came when the demolition crews reached this spot. Acetylene torches showered passers-by with sparks, pneumatic drills hammered at the base of the structure, and a blind man who, like the pigeons, had clung with his cup to a stairway leading to the change booth, was forced to give up his place.

It was then, strangely, momentarily, one morning that I witnessed the return of a little band of the familiar pigeons. I even recognized one or two members of the flock that had lived around this particular station before they were dispersed into the streets. They flew bravely in and out among the sparks and the hammers and the shouting workmen. They had returned — and they had returned because the hubbub of the wreckers had convinced them that the river was about to flow once more. For several hours they flapped in and out through the empty windows, nodding their heads and watching the fall of girders with attentive little eyes. By the following morning the station was reduced to some burned-off stanchions in the street. My bird friends had gone. It was plain, however, that they retained a memory for an insubstantial structure now compounded of air and time. Even the blind man clung to it. Someone had provided him with a chair, and he sat at the same corner staring sightlessly at an invisible stairway where, so far as he was concerned, the crowds were still ascending to the trains.

I have said my life has been passed in the shade of a nonexistent tree, so that such sights do not offend me. Prematurely I am one of the brown wasps and I often sit with them in the great droning hive of the station, dreaming sometimes of a certain tree. It was planted sixty years ago by a boy with a bucket and a toy spade in a little Nebraska town. That boy was myself. It was a cottonwood sapling and the boy remembered it because of some words spoken by his father and because everyone died or moved away who was supposed to wait and grow old under its shade. The boy was passed from hand to hand, but the tree for some intangible reason had taken root in his mind. It was under its branches that he sheltered; it was from this tree that his memories, which are my memories, led away into the world.

After sixty years the mood of the brown wasps grows heavier upon one. During a long inward struggle I thought it would do me good to go and look upon that actual tree. I found a rational excuse in which to clothe this madness. I purchased a ticket and at the end of two thousand miles I walked another mile to an address that was still the same. The house had not been altered.

I came close to the white picket fence and reluctantly, with great effort, looked down the long vista of the yard. There was nothing there to see. For sixty years that cottonwood had been growing in my mind. Season by season its seeds had been floating farther on the hot prairie winds. We had planted it lovingly there, my father and I, because he had a great hunger for soil and live things growing, and because none of these things had long been ours to protect. We had planted the little sapling and watered it faithfully, and I remembered that I had run out with my small bucket to drench its roots the day we moved away. And all the years since it had been growing in my mind, a huge tree that somehow stood for my father and the love I bore him. I took a grasp on the picket fence and forced myself to look again.

A boy with the hard bird eye of youth pedaled a tricycle slowly up beside me.

"What'cha lookin' at?" he asked curiously.

"A tree," I said.

"What for?" he said.

"It isn't there," I said, to myself mostly, and began to walk away at a pace just slow enough not to seem to be running.

"What isn't there?" the boy asked. I didn't answer. It was obvious I was attached by a thread to a thing that had never been there, or certainly not for long. Something that had to be held in the air, or sustained in the mind, because it was part of my orientation in the universe and I could not survive without it. There was more than an animal's attachment to a place. There was something else, the attachment of the spirit to a grouping of events in time; it was part of our mortality.

So I had come home at last, driven by a memory in the brain as surely as the field mouse who had delved long ago into my flower pot or the pigeons flying forever amidst the rattle of nut-vending machines. These, the burrow under the greenery in my living room and the red-bellied bowls of peanuts now hovering in midair in the minds of pigeons, were all part of an elusive world that existed nowhere and yet everywhere. I looked once at the real world about me while the persistent boy pedaled at my heels.

It was without meaning, though my feet took a remembered path. In sixty years the house and street had rotted out of my mind. But the tree, the tree that no longer was, that had perished in its first season, bloomed on in my individual mind, unblemished as my father's words. "We'll plant a tree here, son, and we're not going to move any more. And when you're an old, old man you can sit under it and think how we planted it here, you and me, together."

I began to outpace the boy on the tricycle.

"Do you live here, Mister?" he shouted after me suspiciously. I took a firm grasp on airy nothing — to be precise, on the bole of a great tree. "I do," I said. I spoke for myself, one field mouse, and several pigeons. We were all out of touch but somehow permanent. It was the world that had changed.

1957

Eudora Welty

....

A Sweet Devouring

WHEN I USED to ask my mother which we were, rich or poor, she re-fused to tell me. I was then nine years old and of course what I was dy-ing to hear was that we were poor. I was reading a book called *Five Little Peppers* and my heart was set on baking a cake for my mother in a stove with a hole in it. Some version of rich, crusty old Mr. King — up till that time not living on our street — was sure to come down the hill in his wheelchair and rescue me if anything went wrong. But before I could start a cake at all I had to find out if we were poor, and poor *enough;* and my mother wouldn't tell me, she said she was too busy. I couldn't wait too long; I had to go on reading and soon Polly Pepper got into more trouble, some that was a little harder on her and easier on me.

Trouble, the backbone of literature, was still to me the original prop-erty of the fairy tale, and as long as there was plenty of trouble for ev-erybody and the rewards for it were falling in the right spots, reading was all smooth sailing. At that age a child reads with higher appetite and gratification, and with those two stars sailing closer together, than ever again in his growing up. The home shelves had been providing me all along with the usual books, and I read them with love — but snap, I finished them. I read everything just alike — snap. I even came to the *Tales from Maria Edgeworth* and went right ahead, without feeling the bump — then. It *was* noticeable that when her characters suffered she punished them for it, instead of rewarding them as a reader had rather been led to hope. In her stories, the children had to make their choice between being unhappy and good about it and being unhappy and bad

First published in *Mademoiselle,* 1957; collected in *The Eye of the Story,* 1977.

about it, and then she helped them to choose wrong. In *The Purple Jar*, it will be remembered, there was the little girl being taken through the shops by her mother and her downfall coming when she chooses to buy something beautiful instead of something necessary. The purple jar, when the shop sends it out, proves to have been purple only so long as it was filled with purple water, and her mother knew it all the time. They don't deliver the water. That's only the cue for stones to start coming through the hole in the victim's worn-out shoe. She bravely agrees she must keep walking on stones until such time as she is offered another choice between the beautiful and the useful. Her father tells her as far as he is concerned she can stay in the house. If I had been at all easy to disappoint, that story would have disappointed me. Of course, I did feel, what is the good of walking on rocks if they are going to let the water out of the jar too? And it seemed to me that even the illustrator fell down on the characters in that book, not alone Maria Edgeworth, for when a rich, crusty old gentleman gave Simple Susan a guinea for some kind deed she'd done him, there was a picture of the transaction and where was the guinea? I couldn't make out a feather. But I liked *reading* the book all right — except that I finished it.

My mother took me to the Public Library and introduced me: "Let her have any book she wants, except *Elsie Dinsmore*." I looked for the book I couldn't have and it was a row. That was how I learned about the Series Books. The *Five Little Peppers* belonged, so did *The Wizard of Oz*, so did *The Little Colonel*, so did *The Green Fairy Book*. There were many of everything, generations of everybody, instead of one. I wasn't coming to the end of reading, after all — I was saved.

Our library in those days was a big rotunda lined with shelves. A copy of *V. V.'s Eyes* seemed to follow you wherever you went, even after you'd read it. I didn't know what I liked, I just knew what there was a lot of. After *Randy's Spring* there came *Randy's Summer, Randy's Fall* and *Randy's Winter.* True, I didn't care very much myself for her spring, but it didn't occur to me that I might not care for her summer, and then her summer didn't prejudice me against her fall, and I still had hopes as I moved on to her winter. I was disappointed in her whole year, as it turned out, but a thing like that didn't keep me from wanting to read every word of it. The pleasures of reading itself — who doesn't remember? — were like those of a Christmas cake, a sweet devouring. The "Randy Books" failed chiefly in being so soon over. Four seasons doesn't make a series.

All that summer I used to put on a second petticoat (our librarian wouldn't let you past the front door if she could see through you), ride my bicycle up the hill and "through the Capitol" (shortcut) to the library with my two read books in the basket (two was the limit you could take out at one time when you were a child and also as long as you lived), and tiptoe in ("Silence") and exchange them for two more in two minutes. Selection was no object. I coasted the two new books home, jumped out of my petticoat, read (I suppose I ate and bathed and answered questions put to me), then in all hope put my petticoat back on and rode those two books back to the library to get my next two.

The librarian was the lady in town who wanted to be it. She called me by my full name and said, "Does your mother know where you are? You know good and well the fixed rule of this library: *Nobody is going to come running back here with any book on the same day they took it out.* Get both those things out of here and don't come back till tomorrow. And I can practically see through you."

My great-aunt in Virginia, who understood better about needing more to read than you *could* read, sent me a book so big it had to be read on the floor — a bound volume of six or eight issues of *St. Nicholas* from a previous year. In the very first pages a serial began: *The Lucky Stone* by Abbie Farwell Brown. The illustrations were right down my alley: a heroine so poor she was ragged, a witch with an extremely pointed hat, a rich, crusty old gentleman in — better than a wheelchair — a runaway carriage; and I set to. I gobbled up installment after installment through the whole luxurious book, through the last one, and then came the words, turning me to *un*lucky stone: "To be concluded." The book had come to an end and *The Lucky Stone* wasn't finished! The witch had it! I couldn't believe this infidelity from my aunt. I still had my secret childhood feeling that if you hunted long enough in a book's pages, you could find what you were looking for, and long after I knew books better than that, I used to hunt again for the end of *The Lucky Stone.* It never occurred to me that the story had an existence anywhere else outside the pages of that single green-bound book. The last chapter was just something I would have to do without. Polly Pepper could do it. And then suddenly I tried something — I read it again, as much as I had of it. I was in love with books at least partly for what they looked like; I loved the printed page.

In my little circle books were almost never given for Christmas, they cost too much. But the year before, I'd been given a book and got a shock. It was from the same classmate who had told me there was no Santa Claus. She gave me a book, all right — *Poems by Another Little Girl.* It looked like a real book, was printed like a real book — but it was *by her.* Homemade poems? Illusion-dispelling was her favorite game. She was in such a hurry, she had such a pile to get rid of — her mother's electric runabout was stacked to the bud vases with copies — that she hadn't even time to say, "Merry Christmas!" With only the same raucous laugh with which she had told me, "Been filling my own stocking for years!" she shot me her book, received my Japanese pencil box with a moonlight scene on the lid and a sharpened pencil inside, jumped back into the car and was sped away by her mother. I stood right where they had left me, on the curb in my Little Nurse's uniform, and read that book, and I had no better way to prove when I got through than I had when I started that this was not a real book. But of course it wasn't. The printed page is not absolutely everything.

Then this Christmas was coming, and my grandfather in Ohio sent along in his box of presents an envelope with money in it for me to buy myself the book I wanted.

I went to Kress's. Not everybody knew Kress's sold books, but children just before Christmas know everything Kress's ever sold or will sell. My father had showed us the mirror he was giving my mother to hang above her desk, and Kress's is where my brother and I went to reproduce that by buying a mirror together to give her ourselves, and where our little brother then made us take him and he bought her one his size for fifteen cents. Kress's had also its version of the Series Books, called, exactly like another series, "The Camp Fire Girls," beginning with *The Camp Fire Girls in the Woods.*

I believe they were ten cents each and I had a dollar. But they weren't all that easy to buy, because the series stuck, and to buy some of it was like breaking into a loaf of French bread. Then after you got home, each single book was as hard to open as a box stuck in its varnish, and when it gave way it popped like a firecracker. The covers once prized apart would never close; those books once open stayed open and lay on their backs helplessly fluttering their leaves like a turned-over June bug. They were as light as a matchbox. They were printed on yellowed paper with corners that crumbled, if you pinched on them too hard, like old graham crackers, and they smelled like attic trunks, caramelized glue, their own confinement with one another and, over all, the Kress's smell —

bandannas, peanuts and sandalwood from the incense counter. Even without reading them I loved them. It was hard, that year, that Christmas is a day you can't read.

What could have happened to those books? — but I can tell you about the leading character. His name was Mr. Holmes. He was not a Camp Fire Girl: he wanted to catch one. Through every book of the series he gave chase. He pursued Bessie and Zara — those were the Camp Fire Girls — and kept scooping them up in his touring car, while they just as regularly got away from him. Once Bessie escaped from the second floor of a strange inn by climbing down a gutter pipe. Once she escaped by driving away from Mr. Holmes in his own automobile, which she had learned to drive by watching him. What Mr. Holmes wanted with them — either Bessie or Zara would do — didn't give me pause; I was too young to be a Camp Fire Girl; I was just keeping up. I wasn't alarmed by Mr. Holmes — when I cared for a chill, I knew to go to Dr. Fu Manchu, who had his own series in the library. I wasn't fascinated either. There was one thing I wanted from those books, and that was for me to have ten to read at one blow.

Who in the world wrote those books? I knew all the time they were the false "Camp Fire Girls" and the ones in the library were the authorized. But book reviewers sometimes say of a book that if anyone else had written it, it might not have been this good, and I found it out as a child — their warning is justified. This was a proven case, although a case of the true not being as good as the false. In the true series the characters were either totally different or missing (Mr. Holmes was missing), and there was too much time given to teamwork. The Kress's Campers, besides getting into a more reliable kind of trouble than the Carnegie Campers, had adventures that even they themselves weren't aware of: the pages were in wrong. There were transposed pages, repeated pages, and whole sections in upside down. There was no way of telling if there was anything missing. But if you knew your way in the woods at all, you could enjoy yourself tracking it down. I read the library "Camp Fire Girls," since that's what they were there for, but though they could be read by poorer light they were not as good.

And yet, in a way, the false Campers were no better either. I wonder whether I felt some flaw at the heart of things or whether I was just tired of not having any taste; but it seemed to me when I had finished that the last nine of those books weren't as good as the first one. And the same went for all Series Books. As long as they are keeping a series going, I was afraid, nothing can really happen. The whole thing is one grand prevention. For my greed, I might have unwittingly dealt with myself in the same way Maria Edgeworth dealt with the one who put her all into the purple jar — I had received word it was just colored water.

And then I went again to the home shelves and my lucky hand reached and found Mark Twain — twenty-four volumes, not a series, and good all the way through.

Donald Hall

....

A Hundred Thousand
Straightened Nails

WHEN I WAS growing up, I spent every summer helping out on my grandparents' farm. My grandfather was a great storyteller and told me anecdotes to go with every face whose portrait hung in the farmhouse gallery, those long rows of silhouettes, daguerreotypes, tinted photographs and snapshots which my grandmother kept in the parlor and the sitting room. The portraits had names which I recognized on headstones when we visited graveyards. Though I loved the bright flowery borders and the white paint of the farmhouse, and though I loved our haying in the dry heat of the fields, I was always aware that New Hampshire was more dead than alive. Walking in the dense woods, I learned to be careful not to fall into the cellar holes.

If I was morbid, it was not my grandfather's fault. He was interested only in lively stories about the dead, and he lived so completely in the dramatic scenes of his memory that everything was continually present to him. My grandmother was occasionally elegiac, but not enough to influence me. When I was nine I saw my Great-Aunt Nannie, blind and insane, dying for one long summer on a cot in the parlor, yet my own lamentation for the dead and the past had begun even earlier. Many of my grandfather's stories were symptoms, to me and not to him, of the decay of New Hampshire; a story might include a meadow where the farm boys had played baseball, or a wood through which a railroad had once run.

First published in *The American Scholar, 1961; incorporated in String Too Short to Be Saved, 1961.

I found myself, too, taking some of the characters in his stories at a value different from his. So many of them lived a half-life, a life of casual waste. He often talked about Washington Woodward, who was a cousin of ours. I knew Washington well, yet my image of him was a mixture of what I had observed and what my grandfather had told me. The whole farm was composed of things which Washington had made or at least repaired, so there was no end of devices to remind my grandfather of a story about him. Most of them were funny, for Washington was eccentric, yet after I had finished laughing, even perhaps when I lay in bed at night and thought over what had happened in the day, the final effect of the stories was not comic. I turned Washington into a sign of the dying place. I loved him, and I could feel his affection for me. Yet when I thought of the disease that afflicted New Hampshire, I knew that my grandfather's face was the exception to disease. The face of sickness was the mouth and moving beard, the ingenious futility of Washington Woodward.

This was a paradox, for Washington hated corruption and spied it everywhere like a prophet. Yet unlike a prophet he retired from corruption to the hills, meditated it, and never returned to denounce it. He bought a few acres high up New Canada Road, on Ragged Mountain, in 1895. He lived there alone, with few forays into the world, for the more than fifty years until he died.

I have seen pictures of him, in the farmhouse gallery, taken when he was a young man. He was short and muscular of body, handsome and stern, with a full black mustache over a downcurved mouth. I remembered him only as old, for even in my first memories he must have been sixty. The image I retained had him bent nearly double from the waist, with quick bright eyes and his mouth jiggling his beard in an incessant monotone.

When Washington was young, my grandfather told me, he was already the misanthrope who would exile himself. He had been the youngest of eleven children in a family related to my grandmother. His father, everyone admits, was lazy and mean. Their house burned down, and the children were boarded with various relatives. Washington was only six but already embittered and even surly when he came to live with the Kenestons. My grandmother was a baby. He stayed until he was twelve, and he always looked back to those years as a golden age; my grandmother's family was the great exception to the misanthropic rule. To my grandmother, he was an older brother; when she nursed him

during illnesses late in his life, she was remembering someone who had
been kind to her when she was as dependent as he had become.

He would never have left the Keneston house of his own will. When
Washington was twelve, his father drove into the farmyard on his
broken-down wagon and called for him until he came out of the barn
where he had been wandering with little Katie. Washington knew the
sort of man his father was, but he knew that sons obeyed fathers. When
he had reached the wagon his father told him to lift a hundred-pound
sack of grain out onto the ground, and then back into the wagon again.
When he did it without straining, his father said, "You're big enough to
work. Get packed up. You're coming home."

Washington ran away four years later and set up on his own as a
hired hand and an odd-jobber. He was a hard worker and skillful. The
best thing about him was his pride in good work. By the time he was
twenty-five, he had repaired or built everything but a locomotive. Give
him a forge and some scraps of old iron, my grandfather said, and he
could make a locomotive too. I knew him to shoe a horse, install
plumbing, dig a well, make a gun, build a road, lay a dry stone wall, do
the foundation and frame of a house, invent a new kind of trap for bea-
vers, manufacture his own shotgun shells, grind knives and turn a baseball bat on a lathe. The bat was made out of rock maple, and so heavy
that I could barely lift it to my shoulders when he made it for my thirteenth birthday. The trouble was that he was incredibly slow. He was
not interested in your problems, but in the problems of the job itself.
He didn't care if it took him five weeks to shingle an outhouse that
plumbing was going to outmode in a year. This was one outhouse that
would *stay* shingled, although the shingles might protect only the spi-
ders and the mother cat.

His slowness cost him money, but money did not matter to him. He
did not even call it an abomination like drinking, cardplaying, smoking,
swearing, lipstick and dancing; he simply did not think of it. He needed
no more for supper than bread and milk. Did anyone else? If he didn't
care about money, he cared about people sticking to their word; he
cared about honor, whether it concerned his pay or the hour at which
he was to finish a job. Once a deacon of the church asked Washington to
fix the rickety wheels of a carriage. Washington told him it would be
four dollars, and he spent six full days at the forge strengthening the
wheels and adding supports until the axles would have carried five tons
of hay, much less the deacon and his thin wife. But the deacon said,

when the carriage was delivered, that four dollars was too much, and that three dollars was what the job was worth. Washington refused to take anything, and he never sat in his pew again, for if deacons cheated, churches were corrupt. He read his Bible by himself.

During all his years of solitude, he was extraordinarily sociable whenever he saw his family, as if the taciturnity he had assumed with his solitude was unnatural. He stored up, alone in his shack, acres of volubility which the sight of a relative discovered. If I remarked to him that an apple he had given me was a good apple, he might say, "Well, I remember; that apple came from the tree by the woodchuck hole in the northeast corner that leans toward the south; though it don't lean too much; down in that patch there; it's from a splice, that branch is, from a big tree, high as a house, on John Wentworth's land; his orchard behind his cowbarn beside the saphouse; well, the tree, old John Wentworth's been dead twenty years' tree, was always a good one for apples, big and meaty with plenty of juice to them; and one summer about 1919, no, 1920 I guess, I was working up to John's; I was fixing some sap pails had leaks and I shingled the icehouse, the back of it, where you couldn't see from the road but it was about gone; I'd done the front before and I told him the back would need doing; I was there as much as two months, ten weeks I guess; and it come apple time while I was there, and I helped him picking and he come up here and helped me; and I had my few trees up here, not so many as now, not half so many, as I reckon it, and one time I was mending a water pipe that fed the horse trough, it had come loose, and John didn't have no more solder, so I had to come all the way back to the shop; and as I was going I stopped to look at the tree, the big one, and I thought about asking John if I could splice off a limb as part pay; well, I never did get back that day because I saw a deer in the peas when I got here. . . ." And then he would tell how he waited for the deer and shot him, and what he had done with the pelt, and what John Wentworth had said to him when he asked for the limb, and how he had spliced it to his own tree, and on and on until, if the body had been strong enough, Washington would have talked out the whole contents of his mind. Scratch him anywhere and you touched his auto-biography. Any detail was sufficiently relevant if it kept the tongue moving and the silence broken. My grandfather's many memories, on the other hand, were separated into stories with just enough irrelevant material of the past to keep them circumstantial; they had form, and you knew when he had come to a stopping point. Washington was a talking machine capable of producing the recall of every sensation, every motive, of a lifetime; and all the objects of his world could serve him like Proust's *madeleine*.

It was not the past that interested him, but talking. If he had known about contemporary politics, he would have been willing to use it as his pretext for speech; but in the pursuit of independence he had cut himself off from everything but his daily sensations. The talking was the same when he was young and when he was old. When we visited him at his shack, he would invariably trot alongside the car or buggy as we left, jogging a hundred yards farther with the story he couldn't end. My mother remembers from her girlhood, and I from twenty-five years later, how my grandparents would go to bed while he was talking, and how he would drone on for hours in the dark. When he was old and sick, he would talk in his chair in the kitchen while they read in the living room. Sometimes he would laugh a little and pause, as he reached a brief resting space in his unfinishable monologue. My grandmother learned to say, "Is that so?" whenever there was a pause. My grandfather swore that she could do it in her sleep.

Washington always wore the same costume in the years I knew him. The only thing that ever differed about his appearance was his beard, for he shaved in the summer and let his hair grow for warmth in the winter. He wore heavy brown overalls, patched and stitched, and a lighter brown workshirt stitched so extensively that the cloth had nearly vanished under the coarse stitches; over these he wore a light, nondescript workcoat, and in winter a thick, ancient overcoat with safety pins instead of buttons. He often spent his evenings sewing by the light of a candle until his eyes hurt.

Washington had built his shack on the slope of Ragged Mountain on the western, downward side of New Canada Road, two miles up from U. S. 3 by the road, but half a mile as the crow flies. He had a small pasture for cattle, a hen yard, geese wandering loose, a good orchard of various apple trees and other northern fruits, and at various times he kept pigs, goats, ducks and a dog. His shack was small, and it had grown smaller inside every year. Layers of things saved grew inward from the walls until Washington could barely move inside it. A tiny path among the boxes and animal pelts led from the door to a cross path from an iron stove to a Morris chair. Washington slept upright in the chair every night.

If he found a board in a ditch as he walked home from the day's work, and if the board had a bent nail in it, he would hammer the nail out of the board with a rock and take it home. If the board would make kindling or if it was strong enough to build with, he would take it along too. He would straighten the nail with a hammer on the anvil at his lean-to shop and put it in a box with other nails of the same dimensions. He might have to move a dozen other boxes to find the right one, but he would know where it was. It wasn't that he was a miser, because he cared nothing for the money he saved by collecting used nails. And when he died he did not, like the misers reported in the newspapers, leave a hundred thousand dollars in the back of a mirror; he left a hundred thousand straightened nails. He saved the nails because it was a sin to allow good material to go to waste. Everyone knows the story about the box of pieces of string, found in an old attic, labeled "String too short to be saved."

Besides nails, Washington kept a complete line of hardware and parts: clasps, hinges, brackets, braces, hoe handles, axe heads and spare rungs for ladders. He also saved elk, moose, bear, beaver, fox and deer pelts. On the wall beside the door were his rifle and shotgun and boxes of shells and cartridges. He was a good shot and a patient hunter. Until he was old he shot a big buck every year and ate nothing but venison until the bones were bare. Once a year, in the early fall, he had my grandmother bake him a woodchuck in her big oven. Only when his legs were so bad that he did not dare to wait out an animal, for fear that he would not be able to move after being still, did the woodchucks and hedgehogs manage to eat his peas and his apples and in this way avenge their ancestors.

He ate one kind of food exclusively until he finished his supply of it. Often it would be nothing but oatmeal for a week. Again he would buy two dozen loaves of stale bread and eat nothing else until the last moldy crust was gone. I remember him eating his way through a case of corn flakes; and when the woodchucks had eaten his garden, one winter, he ate a case of canned peas. It was no principle with him, but simply the easiest thing to do. When he was old and sick, living a winter in the rocking chair in my grandmother's kitchen beside Christopher, the canary, he bought his own food and kept it separately, in a cardboard box beside him. At this time he had a run on graham crackers. He did not eat on any schedule, and sometimes my grandparents would wake up in the middle of the night to hear him gumming a cracker, his false teeth lost in the darkness of a Mason jar.

When he was younger he must have been nearly self-sufficient. For much of each year he would refuse outside jobs from anyone, unless my grandfather particularly needed a mowing machine fixed or a scythe handle made when the store was out of them. And often he wouldn't take any money from my grandfather, although my grandmother would try to pay him in disguise with shirts and canned vegetables and pies. To pay the taxes on his land he worked a few days a year on the county road gang, repairing the dirt roads that laced the hills and connected the back farms with the main road in the valley. For clothing he had his gifts, and I know that he once made himself a coat out of fur he had trapped. For food he had all the game he shot, and he kept potatoes and apples and carrots and turnips in a lean-to (the food covered with burlap a foot thick to keep it from freezing) beside his shack, and he canned on his small stove dozens of jars of peas, tomatoes, corn and wax beans.

When he took an outside job or made a little money by peddling patent medicines like Quaker Oil or Rawleigh's Salve, he might buy himself a candy bar or five postcards or a pad of paper, or he might give it away. When my mother and her sister were at college, they sometimes had a letter from Washington with a nickel carefully wrapped inside. The patent medicines were before my time, and my grandfather told me about them. Washington would occasionally fill a large basket with his vials and jars, cut himself a walking stick, and set out to peddle on the back roads. He would sleep in barns, barter for his food, and return after a week with a pocketful of change. A room on the second floor of the farmhouse was always full of cases marked in the trade name of a cough syrup or a tonic. Everyone in the family sniffed up drops of Quaker Oil to stop sneezing, or ate a few drops on a lump of sugar for coughing.

Washington worked hard at tending his trees and garden and animals, and when he was through with his chores he invented more work for himself. He spent considerable time and energy at what I could only call his hobby. He moved big rocks. His ingenuity, which was always providing him with the creation of new, usually trivial tools (tools which took him four days to make and which simplified a fifteen-minute job), invented a massive instrument of three tall pine logs and an arrangement of pulleys. It looked like the tripod of a camera, but the camera would have been as big as a Model A. By means of this engine, he was able to move huge rocks; I don't know how he moved the whole contraption after the rock was lifted, though when I was a boy I must have heard detailed descriptions of a hundred rock-moves. (I was another who learned to shut the door between his ears and his brain.) He moved any rock for whose displacement he could find an excuse: small boulders that obstructed his fields; rocks near the house whose appearance offended him; rocks beside the road into which a car might sometime, possibly, crash; rocks, even, in the way of other people's cows in other people's pastures. When he was old and couldn't use the machine any more, it weathered beside the front door of his shack, and when he died someone took it away for the pine.

It was the cows he was thinking of, not the farmers, when he moved rocks in a pasture. However seriously he meant it, he often indicated that, except for his family and one or two others, humanity was morally inferior to animals; at least to the animals which were, like his family, his own creatures. He had developed a gorgeous line of cattle, out of a combination of devotion and shrewd trading. It was when I knew him that he had Phoebe, the last beast that he truly loved. Phoebe was a Holstein, a prodigy among milkers and the only cow in the world who thought she was a collie dog. Treated like a house pet from birth, she acted like one with Washington. She came frisking to him when he called her, romped with him, and all but whined when she couldn't follow him into the shack and curl her great bulk at his feet. Washington fed her apples and peas in the pod while he ate stale bread. She slept on the other side of a plank wall from him, so that he could hear any irregularity in her breathing. He washed her every day. When she was old and lame, Washington invented a rig like his rock-mover to help her stand or lie down. He nursed her when she was sick, and he was caressing her when she died.

My grandfather told me about an earlier pet, Old Duke the ox. Washington taught Old Duke to shake hands and roll over. He made a cart and a sled which Old Duke could pull, and it would take him a whole forenoon to drive the two and a half miles from his shack to the farmhouse. The only time Washington ever showed romantic interest in a woman was when a young girl named Esther Dodge helped out at the farm one harvest. Washington paid court by asking Esther, a pretty red-cheeked country girl as my mother remembers her, to go for a ride behind Old Duke. Esther would only go if the girls, my ten-year-old mother and her younger sister Caroline, could come along, and they giggled all the way.

When Washington was seventy-eight, Anson Buck found him in a coma one morning when he came to deliver a package on his R.F.D. route. Anson carried him into the back seat and drove fourteen miles to the hospital at Franklin, where they operated. When he recovered, he went back to his shack. One day the following December, my grandmother made some mince pies and decided to send one to Wash. She flagged down a young lumberman as he passed by in his blue 1934 Chevrolet and asked him to leave it off on his way up New Canada to work. He was back almost as soon as he left, saying, "He's looney. Old Wash is looney." After Great-Aunt Nannie, no such announcement was liable to surprise my grandmother. She called "Yoo-hoo" to the barn and told my grandfather what had happened. The lumberman drove them to the shack.

They found Washington sitting on the floor of his cabin between his sleeping chair and his cold stove, which my grandfather said hadn't been lit all night. Washington didn't seem to notice that they were there but kept on talking as they had heard him talk before they entered. What he said was incoherent at first, but they could tell that it was about building a road, about white hogs and about two ladies. He allowed himself to be helped over the thick snow into the Model A and driven back to the house.

Washington told his story for many days, over and over, until my grandparents finally understood its sequence. My grandfather told me all about it the next summer. The night before he was found, Wash said, he took a walk to look at a timber lot of my grandfather's north of his shack. (His legs were so bad that he never walked any farther than his well that winter; the timber was three-quarters of a mile away.) When he got there he saw a whole crowd of people working, though it was nearly dark, and they were cutting a big new road. They had bulldozers, which were white, and a big herd of white horses. He walked up to some of the people and tried to talk to them, but they acted as if they couldn't see him, and they were jabbering in a language he couldn't make out, but it wasn't Canuck. He walked away from the crowd and climbed a little rise, and when he looked down on the other side of the rise to a cleared field he saw about a hundred hogs, all pure white. In front of them were the biggest sow and the biggest boar he had ever seen, both pure white, and they were mating. Washington started to walk down the hill and he stubbed his boot on the nose of a horse that was sticking up through the snow. He and the horse fell in the snow, down and down, until the people lifted them up on the huge piece of chicken wire that was underneath the snow. Then two women among the people took him back to his cabin and stayed there all night with him. He watched, all night long, the tips of their hats against the background of starlight from the cracks in the cabin walls. Though he asked them questions, they never answered.

The doctor came and listened to Washington and gave him morphine. When he woke up he seemed fine except that he kept on with his story. My grandfather told him that there was no road going into his timber lot, and Washington was only indignant. After a week he began to ask visitors about the road, and they all told him there wasn't any, and he stopped telling the story. In the spring he paid a boy with a flivver to drive him past the place so that he could see with his own eyes.

He never had delusions again. Perhaps he had left his cabin for water and had fallen in the snow when his legs failed him. Perhaps he had crawled for an hour in pain through all that whiteness back to his shack where he had talked to the boxes all night. By April he was back at his cabin again, and that summer he was eighty years old.

He died in a state nursing home. My grandfather and I went to see him a month before he died, and his cheeks were flushed above the white beard, and his eyes shone while he performed his monologue. He joked with us and showed us the sores on his legs. He displayed me to his nurses and to the silent old men in the room with him. It was a little like all the other times I had met him, yet seeing him ready to die I was all the more impressed by the waste of him — the energy, the ingenuity, the strength to do what he wanted — as he lay frail and bearded in a nightgown provided by the legislature. The waste that he hated, I thought, was through him like blood in his veins. He had saved nails and wasted life. He had lived alone, but if he was a hermit he was neither religious nor philosophical. His fanaticisms, which might have been creative, were as petulant as his break from the church. I felt that he was intelligent, or it would not have mattered, but I had no evidence to support my conviction. His only vision was a delusion of white hogs. He worked hard all his life at being himself, but there were no principles to examine when his life was over. It was as if there had been a moral skeleton which had lacked the flesh of the intellect and the blood of experience. The life that he could recall totally was not worth recalling; it was a box of string too short to be saved.

Standing beside him in the nursing home, I saw ahead for one moment into the residue, five years from then, of Washington Woodward's life: the shack has caved in and his straightened nails have rusted into the dirt of Ragged Mountain; though the rocks stay where he moved them, no one knows how they got there; his animals are dead and their descendants have made bad connections; his apple trees produce small and sour fruits; the best built hayracks rot under rotting sheds; in New Hampshire the frost tumbles the cleverest wall; those who knew him best are dead or dying, and his gestures have assumed the final waste of irrelevance.

1963

Martin Luther King, Jr.

....

Letter from Birmingham Jail

Martin Luther King, Jr.
Birmingham City Jail
April 16, 1963

Bishop C.C.J. Carpenter, *Bishop* Joseph A. Durick,
Rabbi Milton L. Grafman, *Bishop* Paul Hardin,
Bishop Nolan B. Harmon, *The Rev.* George M. Murray,
The Rev. Edward V. Ramage, *The Rev.* Earl Stallings

My dear Fellow Clergymen,
While confined here in the Birmingham City Jail, I came across your recent statement calling our present activities "unwise and untimely." Seldom, if ever, do I pause to answer criticism of my work and ideas. If I sought to answer all of the criticisms that cross my desk, my secretaries would be engaged in little else in the course of the day and I would have no time for constructive work. But since I feel that you are men of gen-

---

There are essentially two versions of this historic response to eight white Alabama clergymen who published a newspaper letter earlier that January calling on King to end his policy of nonviolent resistance and allow the issue of integration to be handled in the courts. According to King, who was in jail for civil rights demonstrations, he began writing the letter "on the margins of the newspaper in which the statement appeared" and continued it "on scraps of writing paper supplied by a friendly Negro trusty," and concluded it "on a pad my attorneys were eventually permitted to leave me." King's open letter was first published in 1963 as a *pamphlet by the American Friends Committee and then in 1964 revised and collected by King for *Why We Can't Wait*. The first version, written spontaneously and under great pressure, better reflects the immediate occasion that inspired one of King's greatest persuasive efforts and was thus chosen for this volume.

uine good will and your criticisms are sincerely set forth, I would like to answer your statement in what I hope will be patient and reasonable terms.

I think I should give the reason for my being in Birmingham, since you have been influenced by the argument of "outsiders coming in." I have the honor of serving as president of the Southern Christian Leadership Conference, an organization operating in every Southern state with headquarters in Atlanta, Georgia. We have some eighty-five affiliate organizations all across the South — one being the Alabama Christian Movement for Human Rights. Whenever necessary and possible we share staff, educational, and financial resources with our affiliates. Several months ago our local affiliate here in Birmingham invited us to be on call to engage in a nonviolent direct action program if such were deemed necessary. We readily consented and when the hour came we lived up to our promises. So I am here, along with several members of my staff, because we were invited here. I am here because I have basic organizational ties here. Beyond this, I am in Birmingham because injustice is here. Just as the eighth century prophets left their little villages and carried their "thus saith the Lord" far beyond the boundaries of their home town, and just as the Apostle Paul left his little village of Tarsus and carried the gospel of Jesus Christ to practically every hamlet and city of the Graeco-Roman world, I too am compelled to carry the gospel of freedom beyond my particular home town. Like Paul, I must constantly respond to the Macedonian call for aid.

Moreover, I am cognizant of the interrelatedness of all communities and states. I cannot sit idly by in Atlanta and not be concerned about what happens in Birmingham. Injustice anywhere is a threat to justice everywhere. We are caught in an inescapable network of mutuality tied in a single garment of destiny. Whatever affects one directly affects all indirectly. Never again can we afford to live with the narrow, provincial "outside agitator" idea. Anyone who lives inside the United States can never be considered an outsider anywhere in this country.

You deplore the demonstrations that are presently taking place in Birmingham. But I am sorry that your statement did not express a similar concern for the conditions that brought the demonstrations into being. I am sure that each of you would want to go beyond the superficial social analyst who looks merely at effects, and does not grapple with underlying causes. I would not hesitate to say that it is unfortunate that so-called demonstrations are taking place in Birmingham at this time, but I would say in more emphatic terms that it is even more unfortunate that the white power structure of this city left the Negro community with no other alternative.

In any nonviolent campaign there are four basic steps: (1) collection of the facts to determine whether injustices are alive; (2) negotiation; (3) self-purification; and (4) direct action. We have gone through all of these steps in Birmingham. There can be no gainsaying of the fact that racial injustice engulfs this community. Birmingham is probably the most thoroughly segregated city in the United States. Its ugly record of police brutality is known in every section of this country. Its unjust treatment of Negroes in the courts is a notorious reality. There have been more unsolved bombings of Negro homes and churches in Birmingham than any city in this nation. These are the hard, brutal, and unbelievable facts. On the basis of these conditions Negro leaders sought to negotiate with the city fathers. But the political leaders consistently refused to engage in good faith negotiation.

Then came the opportunity last September to talk with some of the leaders of the economic community. In these negotiating sessions certain promises were made by the merchants — such as the promise to remove the humiliating racial signs from the stores. On the basis of these promises Rev. Shuttlesworth and the leaders of the Alabama Christian Movement for Human Rights agreed to call a moratorium on any type of demonstrations. As the weeks and months unfolded we realized that we were the victims of a broken promise. The signs remained. As in so many experiences of the past we were confronted with blasted hopes, and the dark shadow of a deep disappointment settled upon us. So we had no alternative except that of preparing for direct action, whereby we would present our very bodies as a means of laying our case before the conscience of the local and national community. We were not unmindful of the difficulties involved. So we decided to go through a process of self-purification. We started having workshops on nonviolence and repeatedly asked ourselves the questions, "Are you able to accept blows without retaliating?" "Are you able to endure the ordeals of jail?"

We decided to set our direct action program around the Easter season, realizing that with the exception of Christmas, this was the largest shopping period of the year. Knowing that a strong economic withdrawal program would be the by-product of direct action, we felt that this was the best time to bring pressure on the merchants for the needed changes. Then it occurred to us that the March election was ahead, and so we speedily decided to postpone action until after election day. When we discovered that Mr. Connor was in the run-off, we decided again to postpone so that the demonstrations could not be used to cloud the issues. At this time we agreed to begin our nonviolent witness the day after the run-off.

This reveals that we did not move irresponsibly into direct action. We too wanted to see Mr. Connor defeated; so we went through postponement after postponement to aid in this community need. After this we felt that direct action could be delayed no longer.

You may well ask, "Why direct action? Why sit-ins, marches, etc.? Isn't negotiation a better path?" You are exactly right in your call for negotiation. Indeed, this is the purpose of direct action. Nonviolent direct action seeks to create such a crisis and establish such creative tension that a community that has constantly refused to negotiate is forced to confront the issue. It seeks so to dramatize the issue that it can no longer be ignored. I just referred to the creation of tension as a part of the work of the nonviolent resister. This may sound rather shocking. But I must confess that I am not afraid of the word tension. I have earnestly worked and preached against violent tension, but there is a type of constructive nonviolent tension that is necessary for growth. Just as Socrates felt that it was necessary to create a tension in the mind so that individuals could rise from the bondage of myths and half-truths to the unfettered realm of creative analysis and objective appraisal, we must see the need of having nonviolent gadflies to create the kind of tension in society that will help men rise from the dark depths of prejudice and racism to the majestic heights of understanding and brotherhood. So the purpose of the direct action is to create a situation so crisis-packed that it will inevitably open the door to negotiation. We, therefore, concur with you in your call for negotiation. Too long has our beloved Southland been bogged down in the tragic attempt to live in monologue rather than dialogue.

One of the basic points in your statement is that our acts are untimely. Some have asked, "Why didn't you give the new administration time to act?" The only answer that I can give to this inquiry is that the new administration must be prodded about as much as the outgoing one before it acts. We will be sadly mistaken if we feel that the election of Mr. Boutwell will bring the millennium to Birmingham. While Mr. Boutwell is much more articulate and gentle than Mr. Connor, they are both segregationists dedicated to the task of maintaining the status quo. The hope I see in Mr. Boutwell is that he will be reasonable enough to see the futility of massive resistance to desegregation. But he will not see this without pressure from the devotees of civil rights. My friends, I must say to you that we have not made a single gain in civil rights without determined legal and nonviolent pressure. History is the long and tragic story of the fact that privileged groups seldom give up their privileges voluntarily. Individuals may see the moral light and voluntarily give up their unjust posture; but as Reinhold Niebuhr has reminded us, groups are more immoral than individuals.

We know through painful experience that freedom is never voluntarily given by the oppressor; it must be demanded by the oppressed. Frankly I have never yet engaged in a direct action movement that was "well timed," according to the timetable of those who have not suffered unduly from the disease of segregation. For years now I have heard the word "Wait!" It rings in the ear of every Negro with a piercing familiarity. This "wait" has almost always meant "never." It has been a tranquilizing thalidomide, relieving the emotional stress for a moment, only to give birth to an ill-formed infant of frustration. We must come to see with the distinguished jurist of yesterday that "justice too long delayed is justice denied." We have waited for more than three hundred and forty years for our constitutional and God-given rights. The nations of Asia and Africa are moving with jet-like speed toward the goal of political independence, and we still creep at horse and buggy pace toward the gaining of a cup of coffee at a lunch counter.

I guess it is easy for those who have never felt the stinging darts of segregation to say wait. But when you have seen vicious mobs lynch your mothers and fathers at will and drown your sisters and brothers at whim; when you have seen hate filled policemen curse, kick, brutalize, and even kill your black brothers and sisters with impunity; when you see the vast majority of your twenty million Negro brothers smothering in an air-tight cage of poverty in the midst of an affluent society; when you suddenly find your tongue twisted and your speech stammering as you seek to explain to your six-year-old daughter why she can't go to the public amusement park that has just been advertised on television, and see tears welling up in her little eyes when she is told that Funtown is closed to colored children, and see the depressing clouds of inferiority begin to form in her little mental sky, and see her begin to distort her little personality by unconsciously developing a bitterness toward white people; when you have to concoct an answer for a five-year-old son asking in agonizing pathos: "Daddy, why do white people treat colored people so mean?"; when you take a cross country drive and find it necessary to sleep night after night in the uncomfortable corners of your automobile because no motel will accept you; when you are humiliated day in and day out by nagging signs reading "white" men and "colored"; when your first name becomes "nigger" and your middle name becomes "boy" (however old you are) and your last name becomes "John," and when your wife and mother are never given the respected title "Mrs."; when you are harried by day and haunted by night by the fact that you are a Negro, living constantly at tip-toe stance never quite knowing what to expect next, and plagued with inner fears and outer resentments; when you are forever fighting a degenerating sense of "nobodiness"; — then you will understand why we find it difficult to wait. There comes a time when the cup of endurance runs over, and men are no longer willing to be plunged into an abyss of injustice where they experience the bleakness of corroding despair. I hope, sirs, you can understand our legitimate and unavoidable impatience.

You express a great deal of anxiety over our willingness to break laws. This is certainly a legitimate concern. Since we so diligently urge people to obey the Supreme Court's decision of 1954 outlawing segregation in the public schools, it is rather strange and paradoxical to find us consciously breaking laws. One may well ask, "How can you advocate breaking some laws and obeying others?" The answer is found in the fact that there are two types of laws. There are *just* laws and there are *unjust* laws. I would be the first to advocate obeying just laws. One has not only a legal but moral responsibility to obey just laws. Conversely, one has a moral responsibility to disobey unjust laws. I would agree with Saint Augustine that "An unjust law is no law at all."

Now what is the difference between the two? How does one determine when a law is just or unjust? A just law is a man-made code that squares with the moral law or the law of God. An unjust law is a code that is out of harmony with the moral law. To put it in the terms of Saint Thomas Aquinas, an unjust law is a human law that is not rooted in eternal and natural law. Any law that uplifts human personality is just. Any law that degrades human personality is unjust. All segregation statutes are unjust because segregation distorts the soul and damages the personality. It gives the segregator a false sense of superiority and the segregated a false sense of inferiority. To use the words of Martin Buber, the great Jewish philosopher, segregation substitutes an "I-it" relationship for the "I-thou" relationship, and ends up relegating persons to the status of things. So segregation is not only politically, economically, and sociologically unsound, but it is morally wrong and sinful. Paul Tillich has said that sin is separation. Isn't segregation an existential expression of man's tragic separation, an expression of his awful es-trangement, his terrible sinfulness? So I can urge men to obey the 1954 decision of the Supreme Court because it is morally right, and I can urge them to disobey segregation ordinances because they are morally wrong.

Let us turn to a more concrete example of just and unjust laws. An unjust law is a code that a majority inflicts on a minority that is not binding on itself. This is *difference* made legal. On the other hand a just law is a code that a majority compels a minority to follow that it is will-ing to follow itself. This is *sameness* made legal.

Let me give another explanation. An unjust law is a code inflicted upon a minority which that minority had no part in enacting or creat-ing because they did not have the unhampered right to vote. Who can say the legislature of Alabama which set up the segregation laws was democratically elected? Throughout the state of Alabama all types of conniving methods are used to prevent Negroes from becoming regis-tered voters and there are some counties without a single Negro regis-tered to vote despite the fact that the Negro constitutes a majority of the population. Can any law set up in such a state be considered democrati-cally structured?

These are just a few examples of unjust and just laws. There are some instances when a law is just on its face but unjust in its application. For instance, I was arrested Friday on a charge of parading without a per-mit. Now there is nothing wrong with an ordinance which requires a permit for a parade, but when the ordinance is used to preserve segre-gation and to deny citizens the First Amendment privilege of peaceful assembly and peaceful protest, then it becomes unjust.

I hope you can see the distinction I am trying to point out. In no sense do I advocate evading or defying the law as the rabid segregation-ist would do. This would lead to anarchy. One who breaks an unjust law must do it *openly, lovingly* (not hatefully as the white mothers did in New Orleans when they were seen on television screaming "nigger, nigger, nigger") and with a willingness to accept the penalty. I submit that an individual who breaks a law that conscience tells him is unjust, and willingly accepts the penalty by staying in jail to arouse the con-science of the community over its injustice, is in reality expressing the very highest respect for law.

Of course there is nothing new about this kind of civil disobedi-ence. It was seen sublimely in the refusal of Shadrach, Meshach, and Abednego to obey the laws of Nebuchadnezzar because a higher moral law was involved. It was practiced superbly by the early Christians who were willing to face hungry lions and the excruciating pain of chopping blocks, before submitting to certain unjust laws of the Roman Empire. To a degree academic freedom is a reality today because Socrates practiced civil disobedience.

We can never forget that everything Hitler did in Germany was "legal" and everything the Hungarian freedom fighters did in Hungary was "illegal." It was "illegal" to aid and comfort a Jew in Hitler's Germany. But I am sure that, if I had lived in Germany during that time, I would have aided and comforted my Jewish brothers even though it was illegal. If I lived in a communist country today where certain principles dear to the Christian faith are suppressed, I believe I would openly advocate disobeying those antireligious laws.

I must make two honest confessions to you, my Christian and Jewish brothers. First I must confess that over the last few years I have been gravely disappointed with the white moderate. I have almost reached the regrettable conclusion that the Negroes' great stumbling block in the stride toward freedom is not the White Citizens' "Counciler" or the Ku Klux Klanner, but the white moderate who is more devoted to "order" than to justice; who prefers a negative peace which is the absence of tension to a positive peace which is the presence of justice; who constantly says "I agree with you in the goal you seek, but I can't agree with your methods of direct action"; who paternalistically feels that he can set the timetable for another man's freedom; who lives by the myth of time and who constantly advises the Negro to wait until a "more convenient season." Shallow understanding from people of good will is more frustrating than absolute misunderstanding from people of ill will. Lukewarm acceptance is much more bewildering than outright rejection.

I had hoped that the white moderate would understand that law and order exist for the purpose of establishing justice, and that when they fail to do this they become the dangerously structured dams that block the flow of social progress. I had hoped that the white moderate would understand that the present tension in the South is merely a necessary phase of the transition from an obnoxious negative peace, where the Negro passively accepted his unjust plight, to a substance-filled positive peace, where all men will respect the dignity and worth of human personality. Actually, we who engage in nonviolent direct action are not the creators of tension. We merely bring to the surface the hidden tension that is already alive. We bring it out in the open where it can be seen and dealt with. Like a boil that can never be cured as long as it is covered up but must be opened with all its pus-flowing ugliness to the natural medicines of air and light, injustice must likewise be exposed, with all of the tension its exposing creates, to the light of human conscience and the air of national opinion before it can be cured.

In your statement you asserted that our actions, even though peaceful, must be condemned because they precipitate violence. But can this assertion be logically made? Isn't this like condemning the robbed man because his possession of money precipitated the evil act of robbery? Isn't this like condemning Socrates because his unswerving commitment to truth and his philosophical delvings precipitated the misguided popular mind to make him drink the hemlock? Isn't this like condemning Jesus because His unique God consciousness and never-ceasing devotion to His will precipitated the evil act of crucifixion? We must come to see, as federal courts have consistently affirmed, that it is immoral to urge an individual to withdraw his efforts to gain his basic constitutional rights because the quest precipitates violence. Society must protect the robbed and punish the robber.

I had also hoped that the white moderate would reject the myth of time. I received a letter this morning from a white brother in Texas which said: "All Christians know that the colored people will receive equal rights eventually, but is it possible that you are in too great of a religious hurry? It has taken Christianity almost 2000 years to accomplish what it has. The teachings of Christ take time to come to earth." All that is said here grows out of a tragic misconception of time. It is the strangely irrational notion that there is something in the very flow of time that will inevitably cure all ills. Actually time is neutral. It can be used either destructively or constructively. I am coming to feel that the people of ill will have used time much more effectively than the people of good will. We will have to repent in this generation not merely for the vitriolic words and actions of the bad people, but for the appalling silence of the good people. We must come to see that human progress never rolls in on wheels of inevitability. It comes through the tireless efforts and persistent work of men willing to be co-workers with God, and without this hard work time itself becomes an ally of the forces of social stagnation.

We must use time creatively, and forever realize that the time is always ripe to do right. Now is the time to make real the promise of democracy, and transform our pending national elegy into a creative psalm of brotherhood. Now is the time to lift our national policy from the quicksand of racial injustice to the solid rock of human dignity.

You spoke of our activity in Birmingham as extreme. At first I was rather disappointed that fellow clergymen would see my nonviolent efforts as those of the extremist. I started thinking about the fact that I stand in the middle of two opposing forces in the Negro community. One is a force of complacency made up of Negroes who, as a result of long years of oppression, have been so completely drained of self-respect and a sense of "somebodiness" that they have adjusted to segregation, and of a few Negroes in the middle class who, because of a degree of academic and economic security, and because at points they profit by segregation, have unconsciously become insensitive to the problems of the masses. The other force is one of bitterness and hatred and comes perilously close to advocating violence. It is expressed in the various black nationalist groups that are springing up over the nation, the largest and best known being Elijah Muhammad's Muslim movement. This movement is nourished by the contemporary frustration over the continued existence of racial discrimination. It is made up of people who have lost faith in America, who have absolutely repudiated Christianity, and who have concluded that the white man is an incurable "devil." I have tried to stand between these two forces saying that we need not follow the "do-nothingism" of the complacent or the hatred and despair of the black nationalist. There is the more excellent way of love and nonviolent protest. I'm grateful to God that, through the Negro church, the dimension of nonviolence entered our struggle. If this philosophy had not emerged I am convinced that by now many streets of the South would be flowing with floods of blood. And I am further convinced that if our white brothers dismiss us as "rabble rousers" and "outside agitators" — those of us who are working through the channels of nonviolent direct action — and refuse to support our nonviolent efforts, millions of Negroes, out of frustration and despair, will seek solace and security in black nationalist ideologies, a development that will lead inevitably to a frightening racial nightmare.

Oppressed people cannot remain oppressed forever. The urge for freedom will eventually come. This is what has happened to the American Negro. Something within has reminded him of his birthright of freedom; something without has reminded him that he can gain it. Consciously and unconsciously, he has been swept in by what the Germans call the *Zeitgeist,* and with his black brothers of Africa, and his brown and yellow brothers of Asia, South America, and the Caribbean, he is moving with a sense of cosmic urgency toward the promised land of racial justice. Recognizing this vital urge that has engulfed the Negro community, one should readily understand public demonstrations. The Negro has many pent-up resentments and latent frustrations. He has to get them out. So let him march sometime; let him have his prayer pilgrimages to the city hall; understand why he must have sit-ins and freedom rides. If his repressed emotions do not come out in these nonviolent ways, they will come out in ominous expressions of violence. This is not a threat; it is a fact of history. So I have not said to my people, "Get rid of your discontent." But I have tried to say that this normal and healthy discontent can be channeled through the creative outlet of nonviolent direct action. Now this approach is being dismissed as extremist. I must admit that I was initially disappointed in being so categorized.

But as I continued to think about the matter I gradually gained a bit of satisfaction from being considered an extremist. Was not Jesus an extremist in love? "Love your enemies, bless them that curse you, pray for them that despitefully use you." Was not Amos an extremist for justice — "Let justice roll down like waters and righteousness like a mighty stream." Was not Paul an extremist for the gospel of Jesus Christ — "I bear in my body the marks of the Lord Jesus." Was not Martin Luther an extremist — "Here I stand; I can do none other so help me God." Was not John Bunyan an extremist — "I will stay in jail to the end of my days before I make a butchery of my conscience." Was not Abraham Lincoln an extremist — "This nation cannot survive half slave and half free." Was not Thomas Jefferson an extremist — "We hold these truths to be self evident that all men are created equal." So the question is not whether we will be extremist but what kind of extremist will we be. Will we be extremists for hate or will we be extremists for love? Will we be extremists for the preservation of injustice — or will we be extremists for the cause of justice? In that dramatic scene on Calvary's hill three men were crucified. We must never forget that all three were crucified for the same crime — the crime of extremism. Two were extremists for immorality, and thus fell below their environment. The other, Jesus Christ, was an extremist for love, truth, and goodness, and thereby rose above His environment. So, after all, maybe the South, the nation, and the world are in dire need of creative extremists.

I had hoped that the white moderate would see this. Maybe I was too optimistic. Maybe I expected too much. I guess I should have realized

that few members of a race that has oppressed another race can understand or appreciate the deep groans and passionate yearnings of those
that have been oppressed, and still fewer have the vision to see that injustice must be rooted out by strong, persistent, and determined action.
I am thankful, however, that some of our white brothers have grasped
the meaning of this social revolution and committed themselves to it.
They are still all too small in quantity, but they are big in quality. Some
like Ralph McGill, Lillian Smith, Harry Golden, and James Dabbs have
written about our struggle in eloquent, prophetic, and understanding
terms. Others have marched with us down nameless streets of the
South. They have languished in filthy, roach-infested jails, suffering the
abuse and brutality of angry policemen who see them as "dirty nigger
lovers." They, unlike so many of their moderate brothers and sisters,
have recognized the urgency of the moment and sensed the need for
powerful "action" antidotes to combat the disease of segregation.

Let me rush on to mention my other disappointment. I have been
so greatly disappointed with the white Church and its leadership. Of
course there are some notable exceptions. I am not unmindful of the
fact that each of you has taken some significant stands on this issue. I
commend you, Rev. Stallings, for your Christian stand on this past
Sunday, in welcoming Negroes to your worship service on a nonsegre-
gated basis. I commend the Catholic leaders of this state for integrating
Springhill College several years ago.

But despite these notable exceptions I must honestly reiterate that I
have been disappointed with the Church. I do not say that as one of
those negative critics who can always find something wrong with the
Church. I say it as a minister of the gospel, who loves the Church; who
was nurtured in its bosom; who has been sustained by its spiritual
blessings and who will remain true to it as long as the cord of life shall
lengthen.

I had the strange feeling when I was suddenly catapulted into the
leadership of the bus protest in Montgomery several years ago that we
would have the support of the white Church. I felt that the white ministers, priests, and rabbis of the South would be some of our strongest al-
lies. Instead, some have been outright opponents, refusing to understand the freedom movement and misrepresenting its leaders; all too
many others have been more cautious than courageous and have remained silent behind the anesthetizing security of stained glass windows.

In spite of my shattered dreams of the past, I came to Birmingham with the hope that the white religious leadership of the community would see the justice of our cause and, with deep moral concern, serve as the channel through which our just grievances could get to the power structure. I had hoped that each of you would understand. But again I have been disappointed.

I have heard numerous religious leaders of the South call upon their worshippers to comply with a desegregation decision because it is the law, but I have longed to hear white ministers say follow this decree because integration is morally right and the Negro is your brother. In the midst of blatant injustices inflicted upon the Negro, I have watched white churches stand on the sideline and merely mouth pious irrelevancies and sanctimonious trivialities. In the midst of a mighty struggle to rid our nation of racial and economic injustice, I have heard so many ministers say, "Those are social issues with which the Gospel has no real concern," and I have watched so many churches commit themselves to a completely otherworldly religion which made a strange distinction between body and soul, the sacred and the secular.

So here we are moving toward the exit of the twentieth century with a religious community largely adjusted to the status quo, standing as a tail light behind other community agencies rather than a headlight leading men to higher levels of justice.

I have travelled the length and breadth of Alabama, Mississippi, and all the other Southern states. On sweltering summer days and crisp autumn mornings I have looked at her beautiful churches with their spires pointing heavenward. I have beheld the impressive outlay of her massive religious education buildings. Over and over again I have found myself asking: "Who worships here? Who is their God? Where were their voices when the lips of Governor Barnett dripped with words of interposition and nullification? Where were they when Governor Wallace gave the clarion call for defiance and hatred? Where were their voices of support when tired, bruised, and weary Negro men and women decided to rise from the dark dungeons of complacency to the bright hills of creative protest?"

Yes, these questions are still in my mind. In deep disappointment, I have wept over the laxity of the Church. But be assured that my tears have been tears of love. There can be no deep disappointment where there is not deep love. Yes, I love the Church; I love her sacred walls. How could I do otherwise? I am in the rather unique position of being the son, the grandson, and the great grandson of preachers. Yes, I see the Church as the body of Christ. But, oh! How we have blemished

and scarred that body through social neglect and fear of being noncon-
formists.

There was a time when the Church was very powerful. It was during
that period when the early Christians rejoiced when they were deemed
worthy to suffer for what they believed. In those days the Church was
not merely a thermometer that recorded the ideas and principles of
popular opinion; it was a thermostat that transformed the mores of society. Wherever the early Christians entered a town the power structure
got disturbed and immediately sought to convict them for being "dis-
turbers of the peace" and "outside agitators." But they went on with the
conviction that they were a "colony of heaven" and had to obey God
rather than man. They were small in number but big in commitment.
They were too God-intoxicated to be "astronomically intimidated."
They brought an end to such ancient evils as infanticide and gladiato-
rial contest.

Things are different now. The contemporary Church is so often a
weak, ineffectual voice with an uncertain sound. It is so often the
archsupporter of the status quo. Far from being disturbed by the presence of the Church, the power structure of the average community is
consoled by the Church's silent and often vocal sanction of things as
they are.

But the judgment of God is upon the Church as never before. If the
Church of today does not recapture the sacrificial spirit of the early
Church, it will lose its authentic ring, forfeit the loyalty of millions, and
be dismissed as an irrelevant social club with no meaning for the twentieth century. I am meeting young people every day whose disappointment with the Church has risen to outright disgust.

Maybe again I have been too optimistic. Is organized religion too in-
extricably bound to the status quo to save our nation and the world?
Maybe I must turn my faith to the inner spiritual Church, the church
within the Church, as the true *ecclesia* and the hope of the world. But
again I am thankful to God that some noble souls from the ranks of organized religion have broken loose from the paralyzing chains of conformity and joined us as active partners in the struggle for freedom.
They have left their secure congregations and walked the streets of Albany, Georgia, with us. They have gone through the highways of the
South on torturous rides for freedom. Yes, they have gone to jail with
us. Some have been kicked out of their churches and lost the support of
their bishops and fellow ministers. But they have gone with the faith
that right defeated is stronger than evil triumphant. These men have

been the leaven in the lump of the race. Their witness has been the spiritual salt that has preserved the true meaning of the Gospel in these troubled times. They have carved a tunnel of hope through the dark mountain of disappointment.

I hope the Church as a whole will meet the challenge of this decisive hour. But even if the Church does not come to the aid of justice, I have no despair about the future. I have no fear about the outcome of our struggle in Birmingham, even if our motives are presently misunderstood. We will reach the goal of freedom in Birmingham and all over the nation, because the goal of America is freedom. Abused and scorned though we may be, our destiny is tied up with the destiny of America. Before the pilgrims landed at Plymouth, we were here. Before the pen of Jefferson etched across the pages of history the majestic words of the Declaration of Independence, we were here. For more than two centuries our foreparents labored in this country without wages; they made cotton "king"; and they built the homes of their masters in the midst of brutal injustice and shameful humiliation — and yet out of a bottomless vitality they continued to thrive and develop. If the inexpressible cruelties of slavery could not stop us, the opposition we now face will surely fail. We will win our freedom because the sacred heritage of our nation and the eternal will of God are embodied in our echoing demands.

I must close now. But before closing I am impelled to mention one other point in your statement that troubled me profoundly. You warmly commended the Birmingham police force for keeping "order" and "preventing violence." I don't believe you would have so warmly commended the police force if you had seen its angry violent dogs literally biting six unarmed, nonviolent Negroes. I don't believe you would so quickly commend the policemen if you would observe their ugly and inhuman treatment of Negroes here in the city jail; if you would watch them push and curse old Negro women and young Negro girls; if you would see them slap and kick old Negro men and young Negro boys; if you will observe them, as they did on two occasions, refuse to give us food because we wanted to sing our grace together. I'm sorry that I can't join you in your praise for the police department.

It is true that they have been rather disciplined in their public handling of the demonstrators. In this sense they have been rather publicly "nonviolent." But for what purpose? To preserve the evil system of segregation. Over the last few years I have consistently preached that nonviolence demands that the means we use must be as pure as the ends we seek. So I have tried to make it clear that it is wrong to use immoral means to attain moral ends. But now I must affirm that it is just as wrong, or even more so, to use moral means to preserve immoral ends. Maybe Mr. Connor and his policemen have been rather publicly nonviolent, as Chief Pritchett was in Albany, Georgia, but they have used the moral means of nonviolence to maintain the immoral end of flagrant racial injustice. T. S. Eliot has said that there is no greater treason than to do the right deed for the wrong reason.

I wish you had commended the Negro sit-inners and demonstrators of Birmingham for their sublime courage, their willingness to suffer, and their amazing discipline in the midst of the most inhuman provocation. One day the South will recognize its real heroes. They will be the James Merediths, courageously and with a majestic sense of purpose, facing jeering and hostile mobs and the agonizing loneliness that characterizes the life of the pioneer. They will be old, oppressed, battered Negro women, symbolized in a seventy-two year old woman of Montgomery, Alabama, who rose up with a sense of dignity and with her people decided not to ride the segregated buses, and responded to one who inquired about her tiredness with ungrammatical profundity: "My feets is tired, but my soul is rested." They will be young high school and college students, young ministers of the gospel and a host of the elders, courageously and nonviolently sitting in at lunch counters and willingly going to jail for conscience sake. One day the South will know that when these disinherited children of God sat down at lunch counters they were in reality standing up for the best in the American dream and the most sacred values in our Judeo-Christian heritage, and thus carrying our whole nation back to great wells of democracy which were dug deep by the founding fathers in the formulation of the Constitution and the Declaration of Independence.

Never before have I written a letter this long (or should I say a book?). I'm afraid that it is much too long to take your precious time. I can assure you that it would have been much shorter if I had been writing from a comfortable desk, but what else is there to do when you are alone for days in the dull monotony of a narrow jail cell other than write long letters, think strange thoughts, and pray long prayers?

If I have said anything in this letter that is an overstatement of the truth and is indicative of an unreasonable impatience, I beg you to forgive me. If I have said anything in this letter that is an understatement of the truth and is indicative of my having a patience that makes me patient with anything less than brotherhood, I beg God to forgive me.

I hope this letter finds you strong in the faith. I also hope that circumstances will soon make it possible for me to meet each of you, not as an integrationist or a civil rights leader, but as a fellow clergyman and a Christian brother. Let us all hope that the dark clouds of racial prejudice will soon pass away and the deep fog of misunderstanding will be lifted from our fear-drenched communities and in some not too distant tomorrow the radiant stars of love and brotherhood will shine over our great nation with all of their scintillating beauty.

Yours for the cause of Peace and Brotherhood
Martin Luther King, Jr.

1964

Tom Wolfe

....

Putting Daddy On

PARKER WANTS me to go down to the Lower East Side and help him
retrieve his son from the hemp-smoking flipniks. He believes all newspaper reporters know their way around in the lower depths. "Come on
down and ride shotgun for me," he says. Parker has a funny way of
speaking, using a lot of ironic metonymy and metaphor. He picked it
up at Yale twenty-five years ago and has nurtured it through many
lunches in the East 50's. On the other hand, he doesn't want to appear
to be too uneasy. "I just want you to size it up for me," he says. "The
whole thing is ridiculous, except that it is just as pathetic as hell. I feel
like I'm on my back with all four feet up in the air." Parker says his son,
Ben, suddenly left Columbia in his junior year, without saying anything, and moved to the Lower East Side. Parker speaks of the Lower
East Side as the caravansary for flipniks. Flipniks is his word for beat-
niks. As Parker pictures it, his son, Ben, now lies around on the floor
in lofts and four-story walkups on the Lower East Side, eaten by lice
and aphids, smoking pot and having visions of the Oneness of the hip
life.

I think Parker is a casualty of the Information Crisis. The world has
had a good seventy-five years of Freud, Darwin, Pavlov, Max Weber,
Sir James Frazer, Dr. Spock, Vance Packard and Rose Franzblau, and everything they have had to say about human motivation has filtered
through Parker and all of Parker's friends in college, at parties, at lunch,
in the magazines and novels they read and the conversations they have
at home with wives who share the same esoterica. As a result, Parker

First published in the *New York Herald Tribune*'s Sunday magazine, *New York*, 1964; collected in **The Kandy-Kolored Tangerine-Flake Streamline Baby*, 1965.

understands everybody's motives, including his own, which he has a tendency to talk about and revile.

He understands, for example, that he is now forty-six years old and close to becoming a vice-president of the agency and that at this particular age and status he now actually feels the *need* to go to the kind of barbershop where one makes an appointment and has the same barber each time and the jowls are anointed with tropical oils. It is as if Parker were looking through a microscope at a convulsive amoeba, himself, Parker. "I can't go into any other kind of barbershop," he says. "It has gotten so I have an *actual, physical* need to have my hair cut in that kind of barbershop." He can go on like this about the clothes he buys, about the clubs he joins, the music he listens to, the way he feels about Negroes, anything.

He understands why pot-smoking is sort of a religion. He understands Oneness, lofts, visions, the Lower East Side. He understands why Ben has given up everything. He understands why his wife, Regina, says he is a —— and has to *do* something. Her flannel mouth is supposed to goad him into action. He understands everything, the whole thing, and he is in a hopeless funk.

So here are Parker and I walking along Avenue B on the Lower East Side. Parker is wearing a brown Chesterfield and a Madison Avenue crash helmet. Madison Avenue crash helmet is another of Parker's terms. It refers to the kind of felt hat that is worn with a crease down the center and no dents in the sides, a sort of homburg without a flanged brim. He calls it a Madison Avenue crash helmet and then wears one. Inevitably, Parker is looking over his own shoulder, following his own progress down Avenue B. Here is Parker with his uptown clothes and his anointed jowls, walking past the old Avenue B Cinema, a great rotting building with lions' heads and shattered lepers' windows. Here is Parker walking past corner stores with posters for Kassel, Kaplan, Aldrich and the others, plastered, torn, one on top of the other, like scales. Here is Parker walking along narrow streets with buildings all overhung with fire escapes on both sides. Here is this ripening, forty-six-year-old agency executive walking along amid the melted storefronts. There are whole streets on the Lower East Side where it looks as if the place had been under intense heat and started melting and then was suddenly frozen in amber. Half the storefronts are empty and there is a gray film inside the windows. Pipes, bins, shafts of wood and paper are all sort of sliding down the walls. The ceilings are always covered with squares of sheet metal with quaint moldings on them to make an all-over design, and they are all buckling. The signs have all flaked down to metal the color of weathered creosote, even the ones that say *Bodega y Carneceria*. Everything is collapsing under New York moss, which is a combination of lint and soot. In a print shop window, under the soot and lint, is a sample of a wedding announcement. Mr. and Mrs. Benjamin Arnschmidt announce the marriage of their daughter, Lillian, to Mr. Aaron Kornilov, on October 20, 1951. This seems to deepen Parker's funk. He is no doubt asking himself what sort of hopeless amber fix Lillian Arnschmidt and Aaron Kornilov are frozen in today.

Parker sticks his head inside a doorway. Then he walks in. Then he turns around and says, "Are you sure?"

"You said 488," I tell him, "this is 488."

"Nifty," Parker says.

Here is Parker in the entryway of a slum tenement. Slum tenements are worse than they sound. The hallway is painted with a paint that looks exactly the color, thickness and lumpiness of real mud. Parker and I walk in, and there are three big cans of garbage by the stairway. Behind them are two doors, one to the basement apartment, one to the first-floor apartment, out of which two or three children have overflowed when the mother rises in the doorway like a moon reflecting a 25-watt light and yells something in Spanish. The children squeeze back, leaving us with the garbage and the interesting mud tableau. At some point they painted the mud color over everything, even over the doorbell-buzzer box. They didn't bother to pull the wiring out. They just cut the wires and painted over the stubs. And there they have it, the color called Landlord's Brown, immune to time, flood, tropic heat, arctic chill, punk rumbles, slops, blood, leprotic bugs, cockroaches the size of mice, mice the size of rats, rats the size of Airedales, and lumpenprole tenants.

On the way up there are so many turns amid the muddy gloom, I can't tell what floor we stop at. But Parker finds the door up there and knocks.

For a while we don't hear anything, but there is a light through the door. Then somebody inside says, "Who is it?"

"Ben!" says Parker. "It's me."

There is another long pause, and then the door opens. There in the doorway, lit up from behind by an ochre light, is a boy with a very thick head of hair and a kind of Rasputin beard. It is a strange combination, the hair and the beard. The hair is golden, a little red, but mostly golden and very thick, thatchy, matted down over his ears and his forehead. But the beard is one of those beards that come out a different color. It is red and stiff like a nylon brush.

"Ah," says Parker, "the whole scene."

Ben says nothing. He just stands there in a pair of white ducks and rubber Zorrie sandals. He has no shirt on. He looks as robust as a rice pudding.

"The whole scene," Parker says again and motions toward Ben's Rasputin beard.

Ben is obviously pained to hear his old man using hip talk. He gives a peeved twist to his mouth. He is rather startling to look at, a little chunk of rice pudding with all this ferocious hair. Parker, the understanding, understands, but he is embarrassed, which is his problem.

"When did all this happen?" says Parker. "The beaver. When did you grow the beaver?"

Ben still just stands there. Then he narrows his eyes and clamps his upper teeth over his lower lip in the Italian tough guy manner, after the fashion of Jack Palance in *Panic in the Streets*.

"Beaver is a very old expression," says Parker. "Before you were born. About 1803. I was using a very old expression, from my childhood. Did you ever hear a song that goes 'Alpha, beta, delta handa poker?' That was a very hip song."

Then he says, "I didn't mean that, Ben. I just want to talk to you a minute."

"All right," says Ben, and he opens the door wider and we walk in.

We walk into a sort of kitchen. There is a stove with all four gas burners turned up, apparently for heat. The apartment is all one room, of the sort that might be termed extremely crummy. The walls actually have big slags of plaster missing and the lathing showing, as in a caricature of an extremely crummy place. The floor is impacted with dirt and looks as if it has been chewed up by something. And off to one side is more of the day's gathering gaffe: two more kids.

They are both up against the wall as if they have been squashed there. One of them is slouched up against the wall in an upright position. He is a chubby boy with receding blond hair and a walrus mustache. The other, a thin, Latin-looking boy with miles of black hair, is right next to him, only he is sitting down on the floor, with his back propped against the wall. They are both looking at us like the tar baby or a couple of those hard-cheese mestizos on the road to Acapulco. There is a sweet smell in the room. The understanding Parker isn't going to start in on that, however. Parker looks a little as if he has just been pole-axed and the sympathetic nervous system is trying to decide whether to twitch or fold up. Here is Parker in the net of the flipniks, in the caravansary.

Nobody is saying a word. Finally Ben nods toward the chubby boy and says, "This is Jaywak." Then he nods toward the boy on the floor and says, "This is Aywak."

Jaywak stares at Parker a little longer with the tar-baby look, and then he fans his lips out very slowly, very archly, into a smile. After what seems about eight or ten seconds, he holds out his hand. Parker shakes his hand, and as soon as he starts to do that, the boy on the floor, Aywak, sticks his hand straight up in the air. He doesn't get up or even look at Parker. He just sticks his hand straight up in the air and waits for Parker. Parker is so flustered he shakes it. Then Parker introduces me. All this time Ben never introduces Parker. He never says this is my father. One's old man does not show up in a brown Chesterfield with ratchety pleas in his poor old voice, such as he wants to talk to you.

"Well, take off your coat," says Ben. But when he says something to Parker, he looks at Jaywak and Aywak.

Parker keeps his coat wrapped around him like a flag and a shield. Parker can't take his eyes off the place. Between the kitchen and the other part of the apartment is a low divider, like a half-wall, with two funny pillars between it and the ceiling. God knows what the room was for originally. In the back part there is another big craggy space on the wall, apparently where a mantelpiece has been ripped off. Some kind of ratty cloth is over the windows. It is not the decor that gets you. It is this kind of special flipnik litter. Practically every Lower East Side pad has it. Little objects are littered all over the floor, a sock, a Zorrie sandal, a T shirt, a leaflet from the Gospel Teachers, some kind of wool stuffing, a rubber door wedge, a toothbrush, cigarette butts, an old pair of blue wool bathing trunks with a white belt, a used Band-aid, all littered around the chewed-up floor. There is almost no furniture, just a mattress in the corner with a very lumpy-looking blanket over it. There is also a table top, with no legs, propped up on some boxes. Parker keeps gawking.

"Very colorful," he says.

"It's not very colorful," Ben says. "It's a place."

Ben's voice tends to groan with pretentious simplicity.

Suddenly Aywak, the tar baby on the floor, speaks up.

"It has a lot of potential," he says. "It really has a lot of potential. Doesn't it? Or doesn't it?"

He looks straight at Parker with his eyes rolled up sadly.

"We're helping Bewak," he says. "We're helping Bewak put down the tiles. Bewak's going to do a lot with this place because it has a lot of potential. We talked it over. We're going to put all these tiles over he-e-e-ere, and then, over he-e-e-ere, on this wall, all these bricks. White bricks. We're going to paint them white. I kind of like the idea, all these white bricks and the tiles. I mean, it's not *much*. I'm not saying it's a *lot*. But the important thing is to know what you've got to do and then do something about it and *improve* on it, you know?"

"Cool it," says Ben.

This is all very bad for Parker. Suddenly Parker turns to Jaywak and says, "He's an interior decorator. What do you do?"

"I'm not an interior decorator," says Aywak, "I've got a trade."

"I'm a social worker," says Jaywak. Jaywak spreads his face out into the smile again.

"Who do you social work for?" says Parker.

"Well, it's sort of like the Big Brothers," says Jaywak. "You know the Big Brothers?"

Jaywak says this very seriously, looking at Parker with a very open look on his face, so that Parker has to nod.

"Yes," Parker says.

"Well, it's like them," says Jaywak, "only . . . only . . ." — his voice becomes very distant and he looks off to where the mantelpiece used to be — "only it's different. We work with older people. I can't tell you how different it is."

"I'm not an interior decorator," says Aywak. "I don't want you to think I'm an interior decorator. We're not going to do miracles in here. This is *not* the greatest building in the world. I mean, that's probably pretty obvious. But I mean, like I was going on about it — but that just happens to be the way I *feel* about it."

"What are you if you're not an interior decorator?" says Jaywak.

"You mean, what do I *do?*" says Aywak.

"I mean, what do you *do*," says Jaywak.

"That's a very important question," says Aywak, "and I think he's right about it."

"'What do you do?'"

"Yes."

"Someone ask Aywak what he does," Jaywak says.

"I have a trade," says Aywak. "I'm a cooper. I make barrels. Barrels and barrels and barrels. You probably think I'm kidding."

So Parker turns on Ben. He speaks severely his only time. "Just what do *you* do?" he says to Ben. "I'd really like to know!"

"What do *you* do?" says Ben. "What are you doing right now?"

"Look," says Parker, "I don't care what you want to look like in front of these —"

Ben reaches into an old tin of tea and pulls out a string of dried figs. This is one of the Lower East Side's arty foods, along with Ukrainian sausages. Ben turns completely away from Parker and says to me, "Do you want a fig?"

I shake my head no, but even that much seems stupid.

"Are you going to listen?" says Parker.

"They're very good for you," says Aywak, "only they're filling. You know what I mean?"

"Yeah," Jaywak says to me, "sometimes you *want* to be hungry. You know? Suppose you want to be hungry, only you aren't hungry. Then you want to *get* hungry, you know? You're just waiting to get hungry again. You think about it. You want it. You want to get hungry again, but the time won't pass."

"A dried fig ruins it," says Aywak.

"Yeah!" says Jaywak.

I have the eerie feeling they're starting in on me.

"Are you going to listen?" Parker is saying to Ben.

"Sure," says Ben. "Let's have a talk. What's new? Is something new?"

Parker seems to be deflating inside his Chesterfield. Here is Parker amid the flipniks, adrift amid the litter while the gas jets burn.

Parker turns to me. "I'm sorry," he says. Then he turns to Ben. "O.K., we're going."

"O.K.," says Ben.

"Only one thing," says Parker. "What do you want me to . . ."

He doesn't finish. He turns around and walks toward the door. Then he wheels around again.

"What do you want me to tell your mother?"

"What do you mean?" Ben says.

"Do you have a message for her?"

"Such as what?"

"Well, she's been praying for you again."

"Are you being funny?"

"No, it's true," says Parker. "She has been praying for you again. I hear her in the bedroom. She has her eyes shut tight, like this, and she is on her knees. She says things like, 'O dear Lord, guide and protect my Ben wherever he may be tonight. Do you remember, O Lord, how my sweet Ben stood before me in the morning so that I might kiss him upon his forehead in the early brightness? Do you remember, O Lord, the golden promise of this child, my Ben?' Well, you know, Bewak, things like that. I don't want to embarrass you."

"That was extremely witty," Ben says.

"What do you want me to tell her?" says Parker.

"Why don't you just go?" Ben says.

"Well, we're all going to be on our knees praying tonight, Bewak," says Parker. "So long, Bewak."

Down in the hallway, in the muddy tableau, Parker begins chuckling.

"I know what I'm going to tell Regina," he says. "I'm going to tell her Ben has become a raving religious fanatic and was down on his knees in a catatonic trance when we got there."

"What is all this about kneeling in prayer?"

"I don't know," Parker says. "I just want everybody who is japping me to get down on their knees, locked in a battle of harmless zeal. I discovered something up there."

"Which was?"

"He's repulsive," says Parker. "The whole thing was repulsive. After a while I didn't see it from the inside. It wasn't me looking at my own son. I saw it from the outside. It repelled me, that was all. It repelled me."

At the corner of Avenue B and 2d Street Parker sticks out his hand and bygod there is a cab. It is amazing. There are no cabs cruising the Lower East Side. Parker looks all around before he gets in the cab. Up the street, up Avenue B, you can see the hulk of the Avenue B Cinema and the edge of the park.

"That is a good augury," he tells me. "If you can walk right out on the street and get a cab — any time, any place, just stick out your hand and a cab stops — if you can do that, that is the sign that you are on top of it in New York."

Parker doesn't say anything more until we're riding up Fourth Avenue, or Park Avenue South, as it now is, up around 23d Street, by the Metropolitan Life Insurance Building.

"You tell me," he says. "What could I say to him? I couldn't say anything to him. I threw out everything I had. I couldn't make anything skip across the pond. None of them. Not one."

1964

Susan Sontag

....

Notes on "Camp"

MANY THINGS in the world have not been named; and many things, even if they have been named, have never been described. One of these is the sensibility — unmistakably modern, a variant of sophistication but hardly identical with it — that goes by the cult name of "Camp."

A sensibility (as distinct from an idea) is one of the hardest things to talk about; but there are special reasons why Camp, in particular, has never been discussed. It is not a natural mode of sensibility, if there be any such. Indeed the essence of Camp is its love of the unnatural: of artifice and exaggeration. And Camp is esoteric — something of a private code, a badge of identity even, among small urban cliques. Apart from a lazy two-page sketch in Christopher Isherwood's novel *The World in the Evening* (1954), it has hardly broken into print. To talk about Camp is therefore to betray it. If the betrayal can be defended, it will be for the edification it provides, or the dignity of the conflict it resolves. For myself, I plead the goal of self-edification, and the goad of a sharp conflict in my own sensibility. I am strongly drawn to Camp, and almost as strongly offended by it. That is why I want to talk about it, and why I can. For no one who wholeheartedly shares in a given sensibility can analyze it; he can only, whatever his intention, exhibit it. To name a sensibility, to draw its contours and to recount its history, requires a deep sympathy modified by revulsion.

Though I am speaking about sensibility only — and about a sensibility that, among other things, converts the serious into the frivolous — these are grave matters. Most people think of sensibility or taste as the

---

First published in *Partisan Review,* 1964; collected in **Against Interpretation,* 1966.

realm of purely subjective preferences, those mysterious attractions, mainly sensual, that have not been brought under the sovereignty of reason. They *allow* that considerations of taste play a part in their reactions to people and to works of art. But this attitude is naïve. And even worse. To patronize the faculty of taste is to patronize oneself. For taste governs every free — as opposed to rote — human response. Nothing is more decisive. There is taste in people, visual taste, taste in emotion — and there is taste in acts, taste in morality. Intelligence, as well, is really a kind of taste: taste in ideas. (One of the facts to be reckoned with is that taste tends to develop very unevenly. It's rare that the same person has good visual taste *and* good taste in people *and* taste in ideas.)

Taste has no system and no proofs. But there is something like a logic of taste: the consistent sensibility which underlies and gives rise to a certain taste. A sensibility is almost, but not quite, ineffable. Any sensibility which can be crammed into the mold of a system, or handled with the rough tools of proof, is no longer a sensibility at all. It has hardened into an idea. . . .

To snare a sensibility in words, especially one that is alive and powerful,* one must be tentative and nimble. The form of jottings, rather than an essay (with its claim to a linear, consecutive argument), seemed more appropriate for getting down something of this particular fugitive sensibility. It's embarrassing to be solemn and treatise-like about Camp. One runs the risk of having, oneself, produced a very inferior piece of Camp.

These notes are for Oscar Wilde.

> "One should either be a work of art, or wear a work of art."
> — *Phrases & Philosophies for the Use of the Young*

1. To start very generally: Camp is a certain mode of aestheticism. It is one way of seeing the world as an aesthetic phenomenon. That way, the way of Camp, is not in terms of beauty, but in terms of the degree of artifice, of stylization.

2. To emphasize style is to slight content, or to introduce an attitude which is neutral with respect to content. It goes without saying

---

* The sensibility of an era is not only its most decisive, but also its most perishable, aspect. One may capture the ideas (intellectual history) and the behavior (social history) of an epoch without ever touching upon the sensibility or taste which informed those ideas, that behavior. Rare are those historical studies — like Huizinga on the late Middle Ages, Febvre on 16th century France — which do tell us something about the sensibility of the period.

that the Camp sensibility is disengaged, depoliticized — or at least apolitical.

3. Not only is there a Camp vision, a Camp way of looking at things. Camp is as well a quality discoverable in objects and the behavior of persons. There are "campy" movies, clothes, furniture, popular songs, novels, people, buildings. . . . This distinction is important. True, the Camp eye has the power to transform experience. But not everything can be seen as Camp. It's not *all* in the eye of the beholder.

4. Random examples of items which are part of the canon of Camp:

Zuleika Dobson
Tiffany lamps
Scopitone films
The Brown Derby restaurant on Sunset Boulevard in LA
The Enquirer, headlines and stories
Aubrey Beardsley drawings
Swan Lake
Bellini's operas
Visconti's direction of *Salome* and *'Tis Pity She's a Whore*
certain turn-of-the-century picture postcards
Schoedsack's *King Kong*
the Cuban pop singer La Lupe
Lynn Ward's novel in woodcuts, *God's Man*
the old Flash Gordon comics
women's clothes of the twenties (feather boas, fringed and beaded
    dresses, etc.)
the novels of Ronald Firbank and Ivy Compton-Burnett
stag movies seen without lust

5. Camp taste has an affinity for certain arts rather than others. Clothes, furniture, all the elements of visual décor, for instance, make up a large part of Camp. For Camp art is often decorative art, emphasizing texture, sensuous surface, and style at the expense of content. Concert music, though, because it is contentless, is rarely Camp. It offers no opportunity, say, for a contrast between silly or extravagant content and rich form. . . . Sometimes whole art forms become saturated with Camp. Classical ballet, opera, movies have seemed so for a long time. In the last two years, popular music (post–rock 'n' roll, what the French call *yé yé*) has been annexed. And movie criticism (like lists of "The 10 Best Bad Movies I Have Seen") is probably the greatest popularizer of Camp taste today, because most people still go to the movies in a high-spirited and unpretentious way.

6. There is a sense in which it is correct to say: "It's too good to be Camp." Or "too important," not marginal enough. (More on this later.) Thus, the personality and many of the works of Jean Cocteau are Camp, but not those of André Gide; the operas of Richard Strauss, but not those of Wagner; concoctions of Tin Pan Alley and Liverpool, but not jazz. Many examples of Camp are things which, from a "serious" point of view, are either bad art or kitsch. Not all, though. Not only is Camp not necessarily bad art, but some art which can be approached as Camp (example: the major films of Louis Feuillade) merits the most serious admiration and study.

> "The more we study Art, the less we care for Nature."
>
> — *The Decay of Lying*

7. All Camp objects, and persons, contain a large element of artifice. Nothing in nature can be campy. . . . Rural Camp is still man-made, and most campy objects are urban. (Yet, they often have a serenity — or a naïveté — which is the equivalent of pastoral. A great deal of Camp suggests Empson's phrase, "urban pastoral.")

8. Camp is a vision of the world in terms of style — but a particular kind of style. It is the love of the exaggerated, the "off," of things-being-what-they-are-not. The best example is in Art Nouveau, the most typical and fully developed Camp style. Art Nouveau objects, typically, convert one thing into something else: the lighting fixtures in the form of flowering plants, the living room which is really a grotto. A remarkable example: the Paris Métro entrances designed by Hector Guimard in the late 1890s in the shape of cast-iron orchid stalks.

9. As a taste in persons, Camp responds particularly to the markedly attenuated and to the strongly exaggerated. The androgyne is certainly one of the great images of Camp sensibility. Examples: the swooning, slim, sinuous figures of pre-Raphaelite painting and poetry; the thin, flowing, sexless bodies in Art Nouveau prints and posters, presented in relief on lamps and ashtrays; the haunting androgynous vacancy behind the perfect beauty of Greta Garbo. Here, Camp taste draws on a mostly unacknowledged truth of taste: the most refined form of sexual attractiveness (as well as the most refined form of sexual pleasure) consists in going against the grain of one's sex. What is most beautiful in virile men is something feminine; what is most beautiful in feminine women is something masculine. . . . Allied to the Camp taste for the androgynous is something that seems quite different but isn't: a rel-

ish for the exaggeration of sexual characteristics and personality mannerisms. For obvious reasons, the best examples that can be cited are
movie stars. The corny flamboyant femaleness of Jayne Mansfield, Gina
Lollobrigida, Jane Russell, Virginia Mayo; the exaggerated he-man-ness
of Steve Reeves, Victor Mature. The great stylists of temperament and
mannerism, like Bette Davis, Barbara Stanwyck, Tallulah Bankhead,
Edwige Feuillère.

10. Camp sees everything in quotation marks. It's not a lamp, but a
"lamp"; not a woman, but a "woman." To perceive Camp in objects and
persons is to understand Being-as-Playing-a-Role. It is the farthest extension, in sensibility, of the metaphor of life as theater.

11. Camp is the triumph of the epicene style. (The convertibility of
"man" and "woman," "person" and "thing.") But all style, that is, artifice, is, ultimately, epicene. Life is not stylish. Neither is nature.

12. The question isn't, "Why travesty, impersonation, theatricality?"
The question is, rather, "When does travesty, impersonation, theatrical-
ity acquire the special flavor of Camp?" Why is the atmosphere of
Shakespeare's comedies (As You Like It, etc.) not epicene, while that of
Der Rosenkavalier is?

13. The dividing line seems to fall in the 18th century; there the origins of Camp taste are to be found (Gothic novels, Chinoiserie, caricature, artificial ruins, and so forth.) But the relation to nature was quite
different then. In the 18th century, people of taste either patronized nature (Strawberry Hill) or attempted to remake it into something artificial (Versailles). They also indefatigably patronized the past. Today's
Camp taste effaces nature, or else contradicts it outright. And the relation of Camp taste to the past is extremely sentimental.

14. A pocket history of Camp might, of course, begin farther back —
with the mannerist artists like Pontormo, Rosso, and Caravaggio, or the
extraordinarily theatrical painting of Georges de La Tour, or Euphuism.
(Lyly, etc.) in literature. Still, the soundest starting point seems to be the
late 17th and early 18th century, because of that period's extraordinary
feeling for artifice, for surface, for symmetry; its taste for the picturesque and the thrilling, its elegant conventions for representing instant feeling and the total presence of character — the epigram and the
rhymed couplet (in words), the flourish (in gesture and in music). The
late 17th and early 18th century is the great period of Camp: Pope,
Congreve, Walpole, etc., but not Swift; les précieux in France; the rococo
churches of Munich; Pergolesi. Somewhat later: much of Mozart. But in
the 19th century, what had been distributed throughout all of high cul-

ture now becomes a special taste; it takes on overtones of the acute, the esoteric, the perverse. Confining the story to England alone, we see Camp continuing wanly through 19th century aestheticism (Burne-Jones, Pater, Ruskin, Tennyson), emerging full-blown with the Art Nouveau movement in the visual and decorative arts, and finding its conscious ideologists in such "wits" as Wilde and Firbank.

15. Of course, to say all these things are Camp is not to argue they are simply that. A full analysis of Art Nouveau, for instance, would scarcely equate it with Camp. But such an analysis cannot ignore what in Art Nouveau allows it to be experienced as Camp. Art Nouveau is full of "content," even of a political-moral sort; it was a revolutionary movement in the arts, spurred on by a utopian vision (somewhere between William Morris and the Bauhaus group) of an organic politics and taste. Yet there is also a feature of the Art Nouveau objects which suggests a disengaged, unserious, "aesthete's" vision. This tells us something important about Art Nouveau — and about what the lens of Camp, which blocks out content, is.

16. Thus, the Camp sensibility is one that is alive to a double sense in which some things can be taken. But this is not the familiar split-level construction of a literal meaning, on the one hand, and a symbolic meaning, on the other. It is the difference, rather, between the thing as meaning something, anything, and the thing as pure artifice.

17. This comes out clearly in the vulgar use of the word Camp as a verb, "to camp," something that people do. To camp is a mode of seduction — one which employs flamboyant mannerisms susceptible of a double interpretation; gestures full of duplicity, with a witty meaning for cognoscenti and another, more impersonal, for outsiders. Equally and by extension, when the word becomes a noun, when a person or a thing is "a camp," a duplicity is involved. Behind the "straight" public sense in which something can be taken, one has found a private zany experience of the thing.

> "To be natural is such a very difficult pose to keep up."
> — *An Ideal Husband*

18. One must distinguish between naïve and deliberate Camp. Pure Camp is always naïve. Camp which knows itself to be Camp ("camping") is usually less satisfying.

19. The pure examples of Camp are unintentional; they are dead serious. The Art Nouveau craftsman who makes a lamp with a snake coiled

around it is not kidding, nor is he trying to be charming. He is saying, in all earnestness: Voilà! the Orient! Genuine Camp — for instance, the numbers devised for the Warner Brothers musicals of the early thirties (*42nd Street; The Gold Diggers of 1933; . . . of 1935; . . . of 1937;* etc.) by Busby Berkeley — does not *mean* to be funny. Camping — say, the plays of Noel Coward — does. It seems unlikely that much of the traditional opera repertoire could be such satisfying Camp if the melodramatic absurdities of most opera plots had not been taken seriously by their composers. One doesn't need to know the artist's private intentions. The work tells all. (Compare a typical 19th century opera with Samuel Barber's *Vanessa,* a piece of manufactured, calculated Camp, and the difference is clear.)

20. Probably, intending to be campy is always harmful. The perfection of *Trouble in Paradise* and *The Maltese Falcon,* among the greatest Camp movies ever made, comes from the effortless smooth way in which tone is maintained. This is not so with such famous would-be Camp films of the fifties as *All About Eve* and *Beat the Devil.* These more recent movies have their fine moments, but the first is so slick and the second so hysterical; they want so badly to be campy that they're continually losing the beat. . . . Perhaps, though, it is not so much a question of the unintended effect versus the conscious intention, as of the delicate relation between parody and self-parody in Camp. The films of Hitchcock are a showcase for this problem. When self-parody lacks ebullience but instead reveals (even sporadically) a contempt for one's themes and one's materials — as in *To Catch a Thief, Rear Window, North by Northwest* — the results are forced and heavy-handed, rarely Camp. Successful Camp — a movie like Carné's *Drôle de Drame;* the film performances of Mae West and Edward Everett Horton; portions of the Goon Show — even when it reveals self-parody, reeks of self-love.

21. So, again, Camp rests on innocence. That means Camp discloses innocence, but also, when it can, corrupts it. Objects, being objects, don't change when they are singled out by the Camp vision. Persons, however, respond to their audiences. Persons begin "camping": Mae West, Bea Lillie, La Lupe, Tallulah Bankhead in *Lifeboat,* Bette Davis in *All About Eve.* (Persons can even be induced to camp without their knowing it. Consider the way Fellini got Anita Ekberg to parody herself in *La Dolce Vita.*)

22. Considered a little less strictly, Camp is either completely naïve or else wholly conscious (when one plays at being campy). An example of the latter: Wilde's epigrams themselves.

"It's absurd to divide people into good and bad. People are either charming or tedious."

— *Lady Windemere's Fan*

23. In naïve, or pure, Camp, the essential element is seriousness, a seriousness that fails. Of course, not all seriousness that fails can be redeemed as Camp. Only that which has the proper mixture of the exaggerated, the fantastic, the passionate, and the naïve.

24. When something is just bad (rather than Camp), it's often because it is too mediocre in its ambition. The artist hasn't attempted to do anything really outlandish. ("It's too much," "It's too fantastic," "It's not to be believed," are standard phrases of Camp enthusiasm.)

25. The hallmark of Camp is the spirit of extravagance. Camp is a woman walking around in a dress made of three million feathers. Camp is the paintings of Carlo Crivelli, with their real jewels and *trompe-l'oeil* insects and cracks in the masonry. Camp is the outrageous aestheticism of Sternberg's six American movies with Dietrich, all six, but especially the last, *The Devil Is a Woman.* . . . In Camp there is often something *démesuré* in the quality of the ambition, not only in the style of the work itself. Gaudí's lurid and beautiful buildings in Barcelona are Camp not only because of their style but because they reveal — most notably in the Cathedral of the Sagrada Familia — the ambition on the part of one man to do what it takes a generation, a whole culture to accomplish.

26. Camp is art that proposes itself seriously, but cannot be taken altogether seriously because it is "too much." *Titus Andronicus* and *Strange Interlude* are almost Camp, or could be played as Camp. The public manner and rhetoric of de Gaulle, often, are pure Camp.

27. A work can come close to Camp, but not make it, because it succeeds. Eisenstein's films are seldom Camp because, despite all exaggeration, they do succeed (dramatically) without surplus. If they were a little more "off," they could be great Camp — particularly *Ivan the Terrible I & II*. The same for Blake's drawings and paintings, weird and mannered as they are. They aren't Camp; though Art Nouveau, influenced by Blake, is.

What is extravagant in an inconsistent or an unpassionate way is not Camp. Neither can anything be Camp that does not seem to spring from an irrepressible, a virtually uncontrolled sensibility. Without passion, one gets pseudo-Camp — what is merely decorative, safe, in a word, chic. On the barren edge of Camp lie a number of attractive things: the sleek fantasies of Dali, the haute couture preciosity of Albicocco's *The Girl with the Golden Eyes*. But the two things — Camp and preciosity — must not be confused.

28. Again, Camp is the attempt to do something extraordinary. But extraordinary in the sense, often, of being special, glamorous. (The curved line, the extravagant gesture.) Not extraordinary merely in the sense of effort. Ripley's Believe-It-Or-Not items are rarely campy. These items, either natural oddities (the two-headed rooster, the eggplant in the shape of a cross) or else the products of immense labor (the man who walked from here to China on his hands, the woman who engraved the New Testament on the head of a pin), lack the visual reward — the glamour, the theatricality — that marks off certain extravagances as Camp.

29. The reason a movie like *On the Beach*, books like *Winesburg, Ohio* and *For Whom the Bell Tolls* are bad to the point of being laughable, but not bad to the point of being enjoyable, is that they are too dogged and pretentious. They lack fantasy. There is Camp in such bad movies as *The Prodigal* and *Samson and Delilah*, the series of Italian color spectacles featuring the super-hero Maciste, numerous Japanese science fiction films *(Rodan, The Mysterians, The H-Man)* because, in their relative unpretentiousness and vulgarity, they are more extreme and irresponsible in their fantasy — and therefore touching and quite enjoyable.

30. Of course, the canon of Camp can change. Time has a great deal to do with it. Time may enhance what seems simply dogged or lacking in fantasy now because we are too close to it, because it resembles too closely our own everyday fantasies, the fantastic nature of which we don't perceive. We are better able to enjoy a fantasy as fantasy when it is not our own.

31. This is why so many of the objects prized by Camp taste are old-fashioned, out-of-date, démodé. It's not a love of the old as such. It's simply that the process of aging or deterioration provides the necessary detachment — or arouses a necessary sympathy. When the theme is important, and contemporary, the failure of a work of art may make us indignant. Time can change that. Time liberates the work of art from moral relevance, delivering it over to the Camp sensibility. . . . Another effect: time contracts the sphere of banality. (Banality is, strictly speaking, always a category of the contemporary.) What was banal can, with the passage of time, become fantastic. Many people who listen with delight to the style of Rudy Vallee revived by the English pop group, The

Temperance Seven, would have been driven up the wall by Rudy Vallee in his heyday.

Thus, things are campy, not when they become old — but when we become less involved in them, and can enjoy, instead of be frustrated by, the failure of the attempt. But the effect of time is unpredictable. Maybe "Method" Acting (James Dean, Rod Steiger, Warren Beatty) will seem as Camp some day as Ruby Keeler's does now — or as Sarah Bernhardt's does, in the films she made at the end of her career. And maybe not.

32. Camp is the glorification of "character." The statement is of no importance — except, of course, to the person (Loie Fuller, Gaudí, Cecil B. De Mille, Crivelli, de Gaulle, etc.) who makes it. What the Camp eye appreciates is the unity, the force of the person. In every move the aging Martha Graham makes she's being Martha Graham, etc., etc. . . . This is clear in the case of the great serious idol of Camp taste, Greta Garbo. Garbo's incompetence (at the least, lack of depth) as an *actress* enhances her beauty. She's always herself.

33. What Camp taste responds to is "instant character" (this is, of course, very 18th century); and, conversely, what it is not stirred by is the sense of the development of character. Character is understood as a state of continual incandescence — a person being one, very intense thing. This attitude toward character is a key element of the theatrical-ization of experience embodied in the Camp sensibility. And it helps account for the fact that opera and ballet are experienced as such rich treasures of Camp, for neither of these forms can easily do justice to the complexity of human nature. Wherever there is development of character, Camp is reduced. Among operas, for example, *La Traviata* (which has some small development of character) is less campy than *Il Trovatore* (which has none).

> "Life is too important a thing ever to talk seriously about it."
> — *Vera, or The Nihilists*

34. Camp taste turns its back on the good-bad axis of ordinary aes-thetic judgment. Camp doesn't reverse things. It doesn't argue that the good is bad, or the bad is good. What it does is to offer for art (and life) a different — a supplementary — set of standards.

35. Ordinarily we value a work of art because of the seriousness and dignity of what it achieves. We value it because it succeeds — in being what it is and, presumably, in fulfilling the intention that lies behind it. We assume a proper, that is to say, straightforward relation between in-

tention and performance. By such standards, we appraise *The Iliad,* Aristophanes' plays, The Art of the Fugue, *Middlemarch,* the paintings of Rembrandt, Chartres, the poetry of Donne, *The Divine Comedy,* Beethoven's quartets, and — among people — Socrates, Jesus, St. Francis, Napoleon, Savonarola. In short, the pantheon of high culture: truth, beauty, and seriousness.

36. But there are other creative sensibilities besides the seriousness (both tragic and comic) of high culture and of the high style of evaluating people. And one cheats oneself, as a human being, if one has respect only for the style of high culture, whatever else one may do or feel on the sly.

For instance, there is the kind of seriousness whose trademark is anguish, cruelty, derangement. Here we do accept a disparity between intention and result. I am speaking, obviously, of a style of personal existence as well as of a style in art; but the examples had best come from art. Think of Bosch, Sade, Rimbaud, Jarry, Kafka, Artaud, think of most of the important works of art of the 20th century, that is, art whose goal is not that of creating harmonies but of overstraining the medium and introducing more and more violent, and unresolvable, subject matter. This sensibility also insists on the principle that an *oeuvre* in the old sense (again, in art, but also in life) is not possible. Only "fragments" are possible. . . . Clearly, different standards apply here than to traditional high culture. Something is good not because it is achieved, but because another kind of truth about the human situation, another experience of what it is to be human — in short, another valid sensibility — is being revealed.

And third among the great creative sensibilities is Camp: the sensibility of failed seriousness, of the theatricalization of experience. Camp refuses both the harmonies of traditional seriousness, and the risks of fully identifying with extreme states of feeling.

37. The first sensibility, that of high culture, is basically moralistic. The second sensibility, that of extreme states of feeling, represented in much contemporary "avant-garde" art, gains power by a tension between moral and aesthetic passion. The third, Camp, is wholly aesthetic.

38. Camp is the consistently aesthetic experience of the world. It incarnates a victory of "style" over "content," "aesthetics" over "morality," of irony over tragedy.

39. Camp and tragedy are antitheses. There is seriousness in Camp (seriousness in the degree of the artist's involvement) and, often, pa-

thos. The excruciating is also one of the tonalities of Camp; it is the quality of excruciation in much of Henry James (for instance, *The Europeans, The Awkward Age, The Wings of the Dove*) that is responsible for the large element of Camp in his writings. But there is never, never tragedy.

40. Style is everything. Genet's ideas, for instance, are very Camp. Genet's statement that "the only criterion of an act is its elegance"* is virtually interchangeable, as a statement, with Wilde's "in matters of great importance, the vital element is not sincerity, but style." But what counts, finally, is the style in which ideas are held. The ideas about morality and politics in, say, *Lady Windemere's Fan* and in *Major Barbara* are Camp, but not just because of the nature of the ideas themselves. It is those ideas, held in a special playful way. The Camp ideas in *Our Lady of the Flowers* are maintained too grimly, and the writing itself is too successfully elevated and serious, for Genet's books to be Camp.

41. The whole point of Camp is to dethrone the serious. Camp is playful, anti-serious. More precisely, Camp involves a new, more complex relation to "the serious." One can be serious about the frivolous, frivolous about the serious.

42. One is drawn to Camp when one realizes that "sincerity" is not enough. Sincerity can be simple philistinism, intellectual narrowness.

43. The traditional means for going beyond straight seriousness — irony, satire — seem feeble today, inadequate to the culturally oversaturated medium in which contemporary sensibility is schooled. Camp introduces a new standard: artifice as an ideal, theatricality.

44. Camp proposes a comic vision of the world. But not a bitter or polemical comedy. If tragedy is an experience of hyperinvolvement, comedy is an experience of underinvolvement, of detachment.

"I adore simple pleasures, they are the last refuge of the complex."
— *A Woman of No Importance*

45. Detachment is the prerogative of an elite; and as the dandy is the 19th century's surrogate for the aristocrat in matters of culture, so Camp is the modern dandyism. Camp is the answer to the problem: how to be a dandy in the age of mass culture.

46. The dandy was overbred. His posture was disdain, or else *ennui.* He sought rare sensations, undefiled by mass appreciation. (Models:

* Sartre's gloss on this in *Saint Genet* is: "Elegance is the quality of conduct which transforms the greatest amount of being into appearing."

Des Esseintes in Huysmans' *À Rebours, Marius the Epicurean*, Valéry's *Monsieur Teste.*) He was dedicated to "good taste."

The connoisseur of Camp has found more ingenious pleasures. Not in Latin poetry and rare wines and velvet jackets, but in the coarsest, commonest pleasures, in the arts of the masses. Mere use does not defile the objects of his pleasure, since he learns to possess them in a rare way. Camp — Dandyism in the age of mass culture — makes no distinction between the unique object and the mass-produced object. Camp taste transcends the nausea of the replica.

47. Wilde himself is a transitional figure. The man who, when he first came to London, sported a velvet beret, lace shirts, velveteen knee-breeches and black silk stockings, could never depart too far in his life from the pleasures of the old-style dandy; this conservatism is reflected in *The Picture of Dorian Gray.* But many of his attitudes suggest something more modern. It was Wilde who formulated an important element of the Camp sensibility — the equivalence of all objects — when he announced his intention of "living up" to his blue-and-white china, or declared that a doorknob could be as admirable as a painting. When he proclaimed the importance of the necktie, the boutonniere, the chair, Wilde was anticipating the democratic *esprit* of Camp.

48. The old-style dandy hated vulgarity. The new-style dandy, the lover of Camp, appreciates vulgarity. Where the dandy would be continually offended or bored, the connoisseur of Camp is continually amused, delighted. The dandy held a perfumed handkerchief to his nostrils and was liable to swoon; the connoisseur of Camp sniffs the stink and prides himself on his strong nerves.

49. It is a feat, of course. A feat goaded on, in the last analysis, by the threat of boredom. The relation between boredom and Camp taste cannot be overestimated. Camp taste is by its nature possible only in affluent societies, in societies or circles capable of experiencing the psychopathology of affluence.

> "What is abnormal in Life stands in normal relations to Art. It is the only thing in Life that stands in normal relations to Art."
> — A Few Maxims for the Instruction of the Over-Educated

50. Aristocracy is a position vis-à-vis culture (as well as vis-à-vis power), and the history of Camp taste is part of the history of snob taste. But since no authentic aristocrats in the old sense exist today to sponsor special tastes, who is the bearer of this taste? Answer: an impro-

vised self-elected class, mainly homosexuals, who constitute themselves as aristocrats of taste.

51. The peculiar relation beween Camp taste and homosexuality has to be explained. While it's not true that Camp taste is homosexual taste, there is no doubt a peculiar affinity and overlap. Not all liberals are Jews, but Jews have shown a peculiar affinity for liberal and reformist causes. So, not all homosexuals have Camp taste. But homosexuals, by and large, constitute the vanguard — and the most articulate audience — of Camp. (The analogy is not frivolously chosen. Jews and homosexuals are the outstanding creative minorities in contemporary urban culture. Creative, that is, in the truest sense: they are creators of sensibilities. The two pioneering forces of modern sensibility are Jewish moral seriousness and homosexual aestheticism and irony.)

52. The reason for the flourishing of the aristocratic posture among homosexuals also seems to parallel the Jewish case. For every sensibility is self-serving to the group that promotes it. Jewish liberalism is a gesture of self-legitimization. So is Camp taste, which definitely has something propagandistic about it. Needless to say, the propaganda operates in exactly the opposite direction. The Jews pinned their hopes for integrating into modern society on promoting the moral sense. Homosexuals have pinned their integration into society on promoting the aesthetic sense. Camp is a solvent of morality. It neutralizes moral indignation, sponsors playfulness.

53. Nevertheless, even though homosexuals have been its vanguard, Camp taste is much more than homosexual taste. Obviously, its metaphor of life as theater is peculiarly suited as a justification and projec tion of a certain aspect of the situation of homosexuals. (The Camp insistence on not being "serious," on playing, also connects with the homosexual's desire to remain youthful.) Yet one feels that if homosexuals hadn't more or less invented Camp, someone else would. For the aristocratic posture with relation to culture cannot die, though it may persist only in increasingly arbitrary and ingenious ways. Camp is (to repeat) the relation to style in a time in which the adoption of style — as such — has become altogether questionable. (In the modern era, each new style, unless frankly anachronistic, has come on the scene as an anti-style.)

> "One must have a heart of stone to read the death of Little Nell without laughing."
>
> — *In conversation*

54. The experiences of Camp are based on the great discovery that the sensibility of high culture has no monopoly upon refinement. Camp asserts that good taste is not simply good taste; that there exists, indeed, a good taste of bad taste. (Genet talks about this in *Our Lady of the Flowers.*) The discovery of the good taste of bad taste can be very liberating. The man who insists on high and serious pleasures is depriving himself of pleasure; he continually restricts what he can enjoy; in the constant exercise of his good taste he will eventually price himself out of the market, so to speak. Here Camp taste supervenes upon good taste as a daring and witty hedonism. It makes the man of good taste cheerful, where before he ran the risk of being chronically frustrated. It is good for the digestion.

55. Camp taste is, above all, a mode of enjoyment, of appreciation — not judgment. Camp is generous. It wants to enjoy. It only seems like malice, cynicism. (Or, if it is cynicism, it's not a ruthless but a sweet cynicism.) Camp taste doesn't propose that it is in bad taste to be serious; it doesn't sneer at someone who succeeds in being seriously dramatic. What it does is to find the success in certain passionate failures.

56. Camp taste is a kind of love, love for human nature. It relishes, rather than judges, the little triumphs and awkward intensities of "character." . . . Camp taste identifies with what it is enjoying. People who share this sensibility are not laughing at the thing they label as "a camp," they're enjoying it. Camp is a *tender* feeling.

(Here, one may compare Camp with much of Pop Art, which — when it is not just Camp — embodies an attitude that is related, but still very different. Pop Art is more flat and more dry, more serious, more detached, ultimately nihilistic.)

57. Camp taste nourishes itself on the love that has gone into certain objects and personal styles. The absence of this love is the reason why such kitsch items as *Peyton Place* (the book) and the Tishman Building aren't Camp.

58. The ultimate Camp statement: it's good *because* it's awful. . . . Of course, one can't always say that. Only under certain conditions, those which I've tried to sketch in these notes.

1966

Vladimir Nabokov

....

Perfect Past

1

THE CRADLE ROCKS above an abyss, and common sense tells us that our existence is but a brief crack of light between two eternities of darkness. Although the two are identical twins, man, as a rule, views the prenatal abyss with more calm than the one he is heading for (at some forty-five hundred heartbeats an hour). I know, however, of a young chronophobiac who experienced something like panic when looking for the first time at homemade movies that had been taken a few weeks before his birth. He saw a world that was practically unchanged — the same house, the same people — and then realized that he did not exist there at all and that nobody mourned his absence. He caught a glimpse of his mother waving from an upstairs window, and that unfamiliar gesture disturbed him, as if it were some mysterious farewell. But what particularly frightened him was the sight of a brand-new baby carriage standing there on the porch, with the smug, encroaching air of a coffin; even that was empty, as if, in the reverse course of events, his very bones had disintegrated.

Such fancies are not foreign to young lives. Or, to put it otherwise, first and last things often tend to have an adolescent note — unless, possibly, they are directed by some venerable and rigid religion. Nature expects a full-grown man to accept the two black voids, fore and aft, as stolidly as he accepts the extraordinary visions in between.

First published in *The New Yorker*, 1950; revised and expanded for *Conclusive Evidence*, 1951; and enlarged again as chapter 1 of *Speak, Memory*, 1966.

Imagination, the supreme delight of the immortal and the immature, should be limited. In order to enjoy life, we should not enjoy it too much.

I rebel against this state of affairs. I feel the urge to take my rebellion outside and picket nature. Over and over again, my mind has made colossal efforts to distinguish the faintest of personal glimmers in the impersonal darkness on both sides of my life. That this darkness is caused merely by the walls of time separating me and my bruised fists from the free world of timelessness is a belief I gladly share with the most gaudily painted savage. I have journeyed back in thought — with thought hopelessly tapering off as I went — to remote regions where I groped for some secret outlet only to discover that the prison of time is spherical and without exits. Short of suicide, I have tried everything. I have doffed my identity in order to pass for a conventional spook and steal into realms that existed before I was conceived. I have mentally endured the degrading company of Victorian lady novelists and retired colonels who remembered having, in former lives, been slave messengers on a Roman road or sages under the willows of Lhasa. I have ransacked my oldest dreams for keys and clues — and let me say at once that I reject completely the vulgar, shabby, fundamentally medieval world of Freud, with its crankish quest for sexual symbols (something like searching for Baconian acrostics in Shakespeare's works) and its bitter little embryos spying, from their natural nooks, upon the love life of their parents.

Initially, I was unaware that time, so boundless at first blush, was a prison. In probing my childhood (which is the next best to probing one's eternity) I see the awakening of consciousness as a series of spaced flashes, with the intervals between them gradually diminishing until bright blocks of perception are formed, affording memory a slippery hold. I had learned numbers and speech more or less simultaneously at a very early date, but the inner knowledge that I was I and that my parents were my parents seems to have been established only later, when it was directly associated with my discovering their age in relation to mine. Judging by the strong sunlight that, when I think of that revelation, immediately invades my memory with lobed sun flecks through overlapping patterns of greenery, the occasion may have been my mother's birthday, in late summer, in the country, and I had asked questions and had assessed the answers I received. All this is as it should be according to the theory of recapitulation; the beginning of reflexive consciousness in the brain of our remotest ancestor must surely have coincided with the dawning of the sense of time.

Thus, when the newly disclosed, fresh and trim formula of my own age, four, was confronted with the parental formulas, thirty-three and twenty-seven, something happened to me. I was given a tremendously invigorating shock. As if subjected to a second baptism, on more divine lines than the Greek Catholic ducking undergone fifty months earlier by a howling, half-drowned half-Victor (my mother, through the half-closed door, behind which an old custom bade parents retreat, managed to correct the bungling archpresbyter, Father Konstantin Vetvenitski), I felt myself plunged abruptly into a radiant and mobile medium that was none other than the pure element of time. One shared it — just as excited bathers share shining seawater — with creatures that were not oneself but that were joined to one by time's common flow, an environment quite different from the spatial world, which not only man but apes and butterflies can perceive. At that instant, I became acutely aware that the twenty-seven-year-old being, in soft white and pink, holding my left hand, was my mother, and that the thirty-three-year-old being, in hard white and gold, holding my right hand, was my father. Between them, as they evenly progressed, I strutted, and trotted, and strutted again, from sun fleck to sun fleck, along the middle of a path, which I easily identify today with an alley of ornamental oaklings in the park of our country estate, Vyra, in the former Province of St. Petersburg, Russia. Indeed, from my present ridge of remote, isolated, almost uninhabited time, I see my diminutive self as celebrating, on that August day 1903, the birth of sentient life. If my left-hand-holder and my right-hand-holder had both been present before in my vague infant world, they had been so under the mask of a tender incognito; but now my father's attire, the resplendent uniform of the Horse Guards, with that smooth golden swell of cuirass burning upon his chest and back, came out like the sun, and for several years afterward I remained keenly interested in the age of my parents and kept myself informed about it, like a nervous passenger asking the time in order to check a new watch.

My father, let it be noted, had served his term of military training long before I was born, so I suppose he had that day put on the trappings of his old regiment as a festive joke. To a joke, then, I owe my first gleam of complete consciousness — which again has recapitulatory implications, since the first creatures on earth to become aware of time were also the first creatures to smile.

2

It was the primordial cave (and not what Freudian mystics might suppose) that lay behind the games I played when I was four. A big cretonne-covered divan, white with black trefoils, in one of the drawing rooms at Vyra rises in my mind, like some massive product of a geological upheaval before the beginning of history. History begins (with the promise of fair Greece) not far from one end of this divan, where a large potted hydrangea shrub, with pale blue blossoms and some greenish ones, half conceals, in a corner of the room, the pedestal of a marble bust of Diana. On the wall against which the divan stands, another phase of history is marked by a gray engraving in an ebony frame — one of those Napoleonic-battle pictures in which the episodic and the allegoric are the real adversaries and where one sees, all grouped together on the same plane of vision, a wounded drummer, a dead horse, trophies, one soldier about to bayonet another, and the invulnerable emperor posing with his generals amid the frozen fray.

With the help of some grown-up person, who would use first both hands and then a powerful leg, the divan would be moved several inches away from the wall, so as to form a narrow passage which I would be further helped to roof snugly with the divan's bolsters and close up at the ends with a couple of its cushions. I then had the fantastic pleasure of creeping through that pitch-dark tunnel, where I lingered a little to listen to the singing in my ears — that lonesome vibration so familiar to small boys in dusty hiding places — and then, in a burst of delicious panic, on rapidly thudding hands and knees I would reach the tunnel's far end, push its cushion away, and be welcomed by a mesh of sunshine on the parquet under the canework of a Viennese chair and two gamesome flies settling by turns. A dreamier and more delicate sensation was provided by another cave game, when upon awakening in the early morning I made a tent of my bedclothes and let my imagination play in a thousand dim ways with shadowy snowslides of linen and with the faint light that seemed to penetrate my penumbral covert from some immense distance, where I fancied that strange, pale animals roamed in a landscape of lakes. The recollection of my crib, with its lateral nets of fluffy cotton cords, brings back, too, the pleasure of handling a certain beautiful, delightfully solid, garnet-dark crystal egg left over from some unremembered Easter; I used to chew a corner of the bedsheet until it was thoroughly soaked and then wrap the egg in it tightly, so as to admire and re-lick the warm, ruddy glitter of the snugly enveloped facets that came seeping through with a miraculous completeness of glow and color. But that was not yet the closest I got to feeding upon beauty.

How small the cosmos (a kangaroo's pouch would hold it), how paltry and puny in comparison to human consciousness, to a single individual recollection, and its expression in words! I may be inordinately fond of my earliest impressions, but then I have reason to be grateful to them. They led the way to a veritable Eden of visual and tactile sensations. One night, during a trip abroad, in the fall of 1903, I recall kneeling on my (flattish) pillow at the window of a sleeping car (probably on the long-extinct Mediterranean Train de Luxe, the one whose six cars had the lower part of their body painted in umber and the panels in cream) and seeing with an inexplicable pang, a handful of fabulous lights that beckoned to me from a distant hillside, and then slipped into a pocket of black velvet: diamonds that I later gave away to my characters to alleviate the burden of my wealth. I had probably managed to undo and push up the tight tooled blind at the head of my berth, and my heels were cold, but I still kept kneeling and peering. Nothing is sweeter or stranger than to ponder those first thrills. They belong to the harmonious world of a perfect childhood and, as such, possess a naturally plastic form in one's memory, which can be set down with hardly any effort; it is only starting with the recollections of one's adolescence that Mnemosyne begins to get choosy and crabbed. I would moreover submit that, in regard to the power of hoarding up impressions, Russian children of my generation passed through a period of genius, as if destiny were loyally trying what it could for them by giving them more than their share, in view of the cataclysm that was to remove completely the world they had known. Genius disappeared when everything had been stored, just as it does with those other, more specialized child prodigies — pretty, curly-headed youngsters waving batons or taming enormous pianos, who eventually turn into second-rate musicians with sad eyes and obscure ailments and something vaguely misshapen about their eunuchoid hindquarters. But even so, the individual mystery remains to tantalize the memoirist. Neither in environment nor in heredity can I find the exact instrument that fashioned me, the anonymous roller that pressed upon my life a certain intricate watermark whose unique design becomes visible when the lamp of art is made to shine through life's foolscap.

3

To fix correctly, in terms of time, some of my childhood recollections, I have to go by comets and eclipses, as historians do when they tackle the fragments of a saga. But in other cases there is no dearth of data. I see myself, for instance, clambering over wet black rocks at the seaside while Miss Norcott, a languid and melancholy governess, who thinks I am following her, strolls away along the curved beach with Sergey, my younger brother. I am wearing a toy bracelet. As I crawl over those rocks, I keep repeating, in a kind of zestful, copious, and deeply gratifying incantation, the English word "childhood," which sounds mysterious and new, and becomes stranger and stranger as it gets mixed up in my small, overstocked, hectic mind, with Robin Hood and Little Red Riding Hood, and the brown hoods of old hunchbacked fairies. There are dimples in the rocks, full of tepid seawater, and my magic muttering accompanies certain spells I am weaving over the tiny sapphire pools.

The place is of course Abbazia, on the Adriatic. The thing around my wrist, looking like a fancy napkin ring, made of semitranslucent, pale-green and pink, celluloidish stuff, is the fruit of a Christmas tree, which Onya, a pretty cousin, my coeval, gave me in St. Petersburg a few months before. I sentimentally treasured it until it developed dark streaks inside which I decided as in a dream were my hair cuttings which somehow had got into the shiny substance together with my tears during a dreadful visit to a hated hairdresser in nearby Fiume. On the same day, at a waterside café, my father happened to notice, just as we were being served, two Japanese officers at a table near us, and we immediately left — not without my hastily snatching, a whole *bombe* of lemon sherbet, which I carried away secreted in my aching mouth. The year was 1904. I was five. Russia was fighting Japan. With hearty relish, the English illustrated weekly Miss Norcott subscribed to reproduced war pictures by Japanese artists that showed how the Russian locomotives — made singularly toylike by the Japanese pictorial style — would drown if our Army tried to lay rails across the treacherous ice of Lake Baikal.

But let me see. I had an even earlier association with that war. One afternoon at the beginning of the same year, in our St. Petersburg house, I was led down from the nursery into my father's study to say how-do-you-do to a friend of the family, General Kuropatkin. His thickset, uniform-encased body creaking slightly, he spread out to amuse me a handful of matches, on the divan where he was sitting, placed ten of them end to end to make a horizontal line, and said, "This is the sea in calm weather." Then he tipped up each pair so as to turn the straight line into a zigzag — and that was "a stormy sea." He scrambled the matches and was about to do, I hoped, a better trick when we were interrupted. His aide-de-camp was shown in and said something to him. With a Russian, flustered grunt, Kuropatkin heavily rose from his seat, the loose matches jumping up on the divan as his weight left it. That day, he had been ordered to assume supreme command of the Russian Army in the Far East.

This incident had a special sequel fifteen years later, when at a certain point of my father's flight from Bolshevik-held St. Petersburg to southern Russia he was accosted while crossing a bridge, by an old man who looked like a gray-bearded peasant in his sheepskin coat. He asked my father for a light. The next moment each recognized the other. I hope old Kuropatkin, in his rustic disguise, managed to evade Soviet imprisonment, but that is not the point. What pleases me is the evolution of the match theme: those magic ones he had shown me had been trifled with and mislaid, and his armies had also vanished, and everything had fallen through, like my toy trains that, in the winter of 1904–05, in Wiesbaden, I tried to run over the frozen puddles in the grounds of the Hotel Oranien. The following of such thematic designs through one's life should be, I think, the true purpose of autobiography.

4

The close of Russia's disastrous campaign in the Far East was accompanied by furious internal disorders. Undaunted by them, my mother, with her three children, returned to St. Petersburg after almost a year of foreign resorts. This was in the beginning of 1905. State matters required the presence of my father in the capital; the Constitutionalist Democratic Party, of which he was one of the founders, was to win a majority of seats in the First Parliament the following year. During one of his short stays with us in the country that summer, he ascertained, with patriotic dismay, that my brother and I could read and write English but not Russian (except KAKAO and MAMA). It was decided that the village schoolmaster should come every afternoon to give us lessons and take us for walks.

With a sharp and merry blast from the whistle that was part of my first sailor suit, my childhood calls me back into that distant past to have me shake hands again with my delightful teacher. Vasiliy Martïnovich Zhernosekov had a fuzzy brown beard, a balding head, and china-blue eyes, one of which bore a fascinating excrescence on the upper lid. The first day he came he brought a boxful of tremendously appetizing blocks with a different letter painted on each side; these cubes he would manipulate as if they were infinitely precious things, which for that matter, they were (besides forming splendid tunnels for toy trains). He revered my father who had recently rebuilt and modernized the village school. In old-fashioned token of free thought, he sported a flowing black tie carelessly knotted in a bowlike arrangement. When addressing me, a small boy, he used the plural of the second person — not in the stiff way servants did, and not as my mother would do in moments of intense tenderness, when my temperature had gone up or I had lost a tiny train-passenger (as if the singular were too thin to bear the load of her love), but with the polite plainness of one man speaking to another whom he does not know well enough to use "thou." A fiery revolutionary, he would gesture vehemently on our country rambles and speak of humanity and freedom and the badness of warfare and the sad (but interesting, I thought) necessity of blowing up tyrants, and sometimes he would produce the then popular pacifist book *Doloy Oruzhie!* (a translation of Bertha von Suttner's *Die Waffen Nieder!*), and treat me, a child of six, to tedious quotations; I tried to refute them: at that tender and bellicose age I spoke up for bloodshed in angry defense of my world of toy pistols and Arthurian knights. Under Lenin's regime, when all non-Communist radicals were ruthlessly persecuted, Zhernosekov was sent to a hard-labor camp but managed to escape abroad, and died in Narva in 1939.

To him, in a way, I owe the ability to continue for another stretch along my private footpath which runs parallel to the road of that troubled decade. When, in July 1906, the Tsar unconstitutionally dissolved the Parliament, a number of its members, my father among them, held a rebellious session in Viborg and issued a manifesto that urged the people to resist the government. For this, more than a year and a half later they were imprisoned. My father spent a restful, if somewhat lonesome, three months in solitary confinement, with his books, his collapsible bathtub, and his copy of J. P. Muller's manual of home gymnastics. To the end of her days, my mother preserved the letters he managed to smuggle through to her — cheerful epistles written in pencil on toilet paper (these I have published in 1965, in the fourth issue of the Russian-language review *Vozdushnïe puti,* edited by Roman Grynberg in New York). We were in the country when he regained his liberty, and it was the village schoolmaster who directed the festivities and arranged the bunting (some of it frankly red) to greet my father on his way home from the railway station, under archivolts of fir needles and crowns of bluebottles, my father's favorite flower. We children had gone down to the village, and it is when I recall that particular day that I see with the utmost clarity the sun-spangled river; the bridge, the dazzling tin of a can left by a fisherman on its wooden railing; the linden-treed hill with its rosy-red church and marble mausoleum where my mother's dead reposed; the dusty road to the village; the strip of short, pastel-green grass, with bald patches of sandy soil, between the road and the lilac bushes behind which walleyed, mossy log cabins stood in a rickety row; the stone building of the new schoolhouse near the wooden old one; and, as we swiftly drove by, the little black dog with very white teeth that dashed out from among the cottages at a terrific pace but in absolute silence, saving his voice for the brief outburst he would enjoy when his muted spurt would at last bring him close to the speeding carriage.

5

The old and the new, the liberal touch and the patriarchal one, fatal poverty and fatalistic wealth got fantastically interwoven in that strange first decade of our century. Several times during a summer it might happen that in the middle of luncheon, in the bright, many-windowed, walnut-paneled dining room on the first floor of our Vyra manor, Aleksey, the butler, with an unhappy expression on his face, would bend over and inform my father in a low voice (especially low if we had company) that a group of villagers wanted to see the *barin* outside. Briskly my father would remove his napkin from his lap and ask my mother to excuse him. One of the windows at the west end of the dining room gave upon a portion of the drive near the main entrance. One could see the top of the honeysuckle bushes opposite the porch. From that direction the courteous buzz of a peasant welcome would reach us as the invisible group greeted my invisible father. The ensuing parley, conducted in ordinary tones, would not be heard, as the windows underneath which it took place were closed to keep out the heat. It presumably had to do with a plea for his mediation in some local feud, or with some special subsidy, or with the permission to harvest some bit of our land or cut down a coveted clump of our trees. If, as usually happened, the request was at once granted, there would be again that buzz, and then, in token of gratitude, the good *barin* would be put through the national ordeal of being rocked and tossed up and securely caught by a score or so of strong arms.

In the dining room, my brother and I would be told to go on with our food. My mother, a tidbit between finger and thumb, would glance under the table to see if her nervous and gruff dachshund was there. *"Un jour ils vont le laisser tomber"* would come from Mlle Golay, a primly pessimistic old lady who had been my mother's governess and still dwelt with us (on awful terms with our own governesses). From my place at table I would suddenly see through one of the west windows a marvelous case of levitation. There, for an instant, the figure of my father in his wind-rippled white summer suit would be displayed, gloriously sprawling in midair, his limbs in a curiously casual attitude, his handsome, imperturbable features turned to the sky. Thrice, to the mighty heave-ho of his invisible tossers, he would fly up in this fashion, and the second time he would go higher than the first and then there he would be, on his last and loftiest flight, reclining, as if for good, against the cobalt blue of the summer noon, like one of those paradisiac personages who comfortably soar, with such a wealth of folds in their garments, on the vaulted ceiling of a church while below, one by one, the wax tapers in mortal hands light up to make a swarm of minute flames in the mist of incense, and the priest chants of eternal repose, and funeral lilies conceal the face of whoever lies there, among the swimming lights, in the open coffin.

1967

N. Scott Momaday

The Way to Rainy Mountain

A SINGLE KNOLL rises out of the plain in Oklahoma, north and west of the Wichita Range. For my people, the Kiowas, it is an old landmark, and they gave it the name Rainy Mountain. The hardest weather in the world is there. Winter brings blizzards, hot tornadic winds arise in the spring, and in summer the prairie is an anvil's edge. The grass turns brittle and brown, and it cracks beneath your feet. There are green belts along the rivers and creeks, linear groves of hickory and pecan, willow and witch hazel. At a distance in July or August the steaming foliage seems almost to writhe in fire. Great green and yellow grasshoppers are everywhere in the tall grass, popping up like corn to sting the flesh, and tortoises crawl about on the red earth, going nowhere in the plenty of time. Loneliness is an aspect of the land. All things in the plain are isolate; there is no confusion of objects in the eye, but *one* hill or *one* tree or *one* man. To look upon that landscape in the early morning, with the sun at your back, is to lose the sense of proportion. Your imagination comes to life, and this, you think, is where Creation was begun.

I returned to Rainy Mountain in July. My grandmother had died in the spring, and I wanted to be at her grave. She had lived to be very old and at last infirm. Her only living daughter was with her when she died, and I was told that in death her face was that of a child.

I like to think of her as a child. When she was born, the Kiowas were living the last great moment of their history. For more than a hundred years they had controlled the open range from the Smoky Hill River to the Red, from the headwaters of the Canadian to the fork of the Arkan-

First published in *The Reporter,* 1967; reprinted as the introduction to *The Way to Rainy Mountain,* 1969.

sas and Cimarron. In alliance with the Comanches, they had ruled the whole of the southern Plains. War was their sacred business, and they were among the finest horsemen the world has ever known. But warfare for the Kiowas was preeminently a matter of disposition rather than of survival, and they never understood the grim, unrelenting advance of the U.S. Cavalry. When at last, divided and ill-provisioned, they were driven onto the Staked Plains in the cold rains of autumn, they fell into panic. In Palo Duro Canyon they abandoned their crucial stores to pillage and had nothing then but their lives. In order to save themselves, they surrendered to the soldiers at Fort Sill and were imprisoned in the old stone corral that now stands as a military museum. My grandmother was spared the humiliation of those high gray walls by eight or ten years, but she must have known from birth the affliction of defeat, the dark brooding of old warriors.

Her name was Aho, and she belonged to the last culture to evolve in North America. Her forebears came down from the high country in western Montana nearly three centuries ago. They were a mountain people, a mysterious tribe of hunters whose language has never been positively classified in any major group. In the late seventeenth century they began a long migration to the south and east. It was a journey toward the dawn, and it led to a golden age. Along the way the Kiowas were befriended by the Crows, who gave them the culture and religion of the Plains. They acquired horses, and their ancient nomadic spirit was suddenly free of the ground. They acquired Tai-me, the sacred Sun Dance doll, from that moment the object and symbol of their worship, and so shared in the divinity of the sun. Not least, they acquired the sense of destiny, therefore courage and pride. When they entered upon the southern Plains they had been transformed. No longer were they slaves to the simple necessity of survival; they were a lordly and dangerous society of fighters and thieves, hunters and priests of the sun. According to their origin myth, they entered the world through a hollow log. From one point of view, their migration was the fruit of an old prophecy, for indeed they emerged from a sunless world.

Although my grandmother lived out her long life in the shadow of Rainy Mountain, the immense landscape of the continental interior lay like memory in her blood. She could tell of the Crows, whom she had never seen, and of the Black Hills, where she had never been. I wanted to see in reality what she had seen more perfectly in the mind's eye, and traveled fifteen hundred miles to begin my pilgrimage.

Yellowstone, it seemed to me, was the top of the world, a region of deep lakes and dark timber, canyons and waterfalls. But, beautiful as it is, one might have the sense of confinement there. The skyline in all directions is close at hand, the high wall of the woods and deep cleavages of shade. There is a perfect freedom in the mountains, but it belongs to the eagle and the elk, the badger and the bear. The Kiowas reckoned their stature by the distance they could see, and they were bent and blind in the wilderness.

Descending eastward, the highland meadows are a stairway to the plain. In July the inland slope of the Rockies is luxuriant with flax and buckwheat, stonecrop and larkspur. The earth unfolds and the limit of the land recedes. Clusters of trees, and animals grazing far in the distance, cause the vision to reach away and wonder to build upon the mind. The sun follows a longer course in the day, and the sky is immense beyond all comparison. The great billowing clouds that sail upon it are shadows that move upon the grain like water, dividing light. Farther down, in the land of the Crows and Blackfeet, the plain is yellow. Sweet clover takes hold of the hills and bends upon itself to cover and seal the soil. There the Kiowas paused on their way; they had come to the place where they must change their lives. The sun is at home on the plains. Precisely there does it have the certain character of a god. When the Kiowas came to the land of the Crows, they could see the dark lees of the hills at dawn across the Bighorn River, the profusion of light on the grain shelves, the oldest deity ranging after the solstices. Not yet would they veer southward to the caldron of the land that lay below; they must wean their blood from the northern winter and hold the mountains a while longer in their view. They bore Tai-me in procession to the east.

A dark mist lay over the Black Hills, and the land was like iron. At the top of a ridge I caught sight of Devil's Tower upthrust against the gray sky as if in the birth of time the core of the earth had broken through its crust and the motion of the world was begun. There are things in nature that engender an awful quiet in the heart of man; Devil's Tower is one of them. Two centuries ago, because they could not do otherwise, the Kiowas made a legend at the base of the rock. My grandmother said:

Eight children were there at play, seven sisters and their brother. Suddenly the boy was struck dumb; he trembled and began to run upon his hands and feet. His fingers became claws, and his body was covered with fur. Directly there was a bear where the boy had been. The sisters were terrified; they ran, and the bear after them. They came to the stump of a great tree, and the tree spoke to them. It bade them climb upon it, and as they did so it began to rise

into the air. The bear came to kill them, but they were just beyond its reach.
It reared against the tree and scored the bark all around with its claws.
The seven sisters were borne into the sky, and they became the stars of the
Big Dipper.

From that moment, and so long as the legend lives, the Kiowas have kinsmen in the night sky. Whatever they were in the mountains, they could be no more. However tenuous their well-being, however much they had suffered and would suffer again, they had found a way out of the wilderness.

My grandmother had a reverence for the sun, a holy regard that now is all but gone out of mankind. There was a wariness in her, and an ancient awe. She was a Christian in her later years, but she had come a long way about, and she never forgot her birthright. As a child she had been to the Sun Dances; she had taken part in those annual rites, and by them she had learned the restoration of her people in the presence of Tai-me. She was about seven when the last Kiowa Sun Dance was held in 1887 on the Washita River above Rainy Mountain Creek. The buffalo were gone. In order to consummate the ancient sacrifice — to impale the head of a buffalo bull upon the medicine tree — a delegation of old men journeyed into Texas, there to beg and barter for an animal from the Goodnight herd. She was ten when the Kiowas came together for the last time as a living Sun Dance culture. They could find no buffalo; they had to hang an old hide from the sacred tree. Before the dance could begin, a company of soldiers rode out from Fort Sill under orders to disperse the tribe. Forbidden without cause the essential act of their faith, having seen the wild herds slaughtered and left to rot upon the ground, the Kiowas backed away forever from the medicine tree. That was July 20, 1890, at the great bend of the Washita. My grandmother was there. Without bitterness, and for as long as she lived, she bore a vision of deicide.

Now that I can have her only in memory, I see my grandmother in the several postures that were peculiar to her: standing at the wood stove on a winter morning and turning meat in a great iron skillet; sitting at the south window, bent above her beadwork, and afterwards, when her vision failed, looking down for a long time into the fold of her hands; going out upon a cane, very slowly as she did when the weight of age came upon her; praying. I remember her most often at prayer. She made long, rambling prayers out of suffering and hope, having seen many things. I was never sure that I had the right to hear, so exclusive were they of all mere custom and company. The last time I saw her she prayed standing by the side of her bed at night, naked to the waist, the light of a kerosene lamp moving upon her dark skin. Her long, black hair, always drawn and braided in the day, lay upon her shoulders and against her breasts like a shawl. I do not speak Kiowa, and I never understood her prayers, but there was something inherently sad in the sound, some merest hesitation upon the syllables of sorrow. She began in a high and descending pitch, exhausting her breath to silence; then again and again — and always the same intensity of effort, of something that is, and is not, like urgency in the human voice. Transported so in the dancing light among the shadows of her room, she seemed beyond the reach of time. But that was illusion; I think I knew then that I should not see her again.

Houses are like sentinels in the plain, old keepers of the weather watch. There, in a very little while, wood takes on the appearance of great age. All colors wear soon away in the wind and rain, and then the wood is burned gray and the grain appears and the nails turn red with rust. The windowpanes are black and opaque; you imagine there is nothing within, and indeed there are many ghosts, bones given up to the land. They stand here and there against the sky, and you approach them for a longer time than you expect. They belong in the distance; it is their domain.

Once there was a lot of sound in my grandmother's house, a lot of coming and going, feasting and talk. The summers there were full of excitement and reunion. The Kiowas are a summer people; they abide the cold and keep to themselves, but when the season turns and the land becomes warm and vital they cannot hold still; an old love of going returns upon them. The aged visitors who came to my grandmother's house when I was a child were made of lean and leather, and they bore themselves upright. They wore great black hats and bright ample shirts that shook in the wind. They rubbed fat upon their hair and wound their braids with strips of colored cloth. Some of them painted their faces and carried the scars of old and cherished enmities. They were an old council of warlords, come to remind and be reminded of who they were. Their wives and daughters served them well. The women might indulge themselves; gossip was at once the mark and compensation of their servitude. They made loud and elaborate talk among themselves, full of jest and gesture, fright and false alarm. They went abroad in fringed and flowered shawls, bright beadwork and German silver. They were at home in the kitchen, and they prepared meals that were banquets.

There were frequent prayer meetings, and great nocturnal feasts. When I was a child I played with my cousins outside, where the lamplight fell upon the ground and the singing of the old people rose up around us and carried away into the darkness. There were a lot of good things to eat, a lot of laughter and surprise. And afterwards, when the quiet returned, I lay down with my grandmother and could hear the frogs away by the river and feel the motion of the air.

Now there is a funeral silence in the rooms, the endless wake of some final word. The walls have closed in upon my grandmother's house. When I returned to it in mourning, I saw for the first time in my life how small it was. It was late at night, and there was a white moon, nearly full. I sat for a long time on the stone steps by the kitchen door. From there I could see out across the land; I could see the long row of trees by the creek, the low light upon the rolling plains, and the stars of the Big Dipper. Once I looked at the moon and caught sight of a strange thing. A cricket had perched upon the handrail, only a few inches away from me. My line of vision was such that the creature filled the moon like a fossil. It had gone there, I thought, to live and die, for there, of all places, was its small definition made whole and eternal. A warm wind rose up and purled like the longing within me.

The next morning I awoke at dawn and went out on the dirt road to Rainy Mountain. It was already hot, and the grasshoppers began to fill the air. Still, it was early in the morning, and the birds sang out of the shadows. The long yellow grass on the mountain shone in the bright light, and a scissortail hied above the land. There, where it ought to be, at the end of a long and legendary way, was my grandmother's grave. Here and there on the dark stones were ancestral names. Looking back once, I saw the mountain and came away.

1968

Elizabeth Hardwick

....

The Apotheosis
of Martin Luther King

Memphis, Atlanta, 1968
THE DECAYING, downtown shopping section of Memphis — still another Main Street — lay, the weekend before Martin Luther King's funeral, under a siege. The deranging curfew and that state of civic existence called "tension" made the town seem to be sinister, again very much like a film set, perhaps for a television drama, of breakdown, catastrophe. Since films and television have staged everything imaginable before it happens, a true event, taking place in the real world, brings to mind the landscape of films. There is no meaning in this beyond description and real life only looks like a fabrication and does not feel so.

The streets are completely empty of traffic and persons and yet the emptiness is the signal of dire and dramatic possibilities. In the silence, the horn of a tug gliding up the dark Mississippi is background. The hotel, downtown, overlooking the city park, is a tomb and perhaps that is usual since it is downtown where nobody wants to go in middle-sized cities. It is a shabby place, poorly staffed by aged persons, not grown old in their duties, but newly hired, untrained, depressed, worn-out old people.

The march was called for the next day, a march originally called by King as a renewal of his efforts in the Memphis garbage strike, efforts interrupted by a riot in the poor, black sections the week before. Now he was murdered and the march was called to honor him. Fear of riots,

First published in *The New York Review of Books,* 1968; collected in **Bartleby in Manhattan and Other Essays,* 1983.

rage, had brought the curfew and the National Guard. Perhaps there was fear, but in civic crises there is always something exciting and even a sort of humidity of smugness seemed to hang over the town. Children kept home from school, bank and ten-cent store closed. If one was not in clear danger, there seemed to be a complacent pleasure in thinking, We have been brought to this by Them.

Beyond and beneath the glassy beige curtains of the hotel room, the courthouse square was spread out like a target, the destination of the next day's march and ceremony. All night long little hammer blows, a ghostly percussion, rang out as the structure for the "event" was being put together. The stage, slowly forming, plank by plank, seemed in the deluding curfew emptiness and silence like a scaffolding being prepared for a beheading. These overwrought and exaggerated images came to me from the actual scene and from a crush of childhood memories. Memphis was a Southern town in which a murder had taken place. The killer might be over yonder in that deep blue thicket, or holed up in the woods on the edge of town, ready to come back at night. Of course this was altogether different. The assassin's work was completed. Here in Memphis it was not the killer, whoever he might be, who was feared, but the killed one and what his death might bring.

Not far from the downtown was the leprous little hovel where, from a squalid toilet window, the assassin had been able to look across and target the new and hopeful Lorraine Motel. Now the motel was being visited by mourners. The black people of Memphis, dressed in their best, filed silently up and down the ramp, glancing shyly into the room which King had occupied. At the ramp before the door of the room where he fell there were flowers, glads and potted azaleas.

All over the Negro section, rickety little stores, emptied in the "consumer rebellion," were boarded up, burned out, or simply empty, with the windows broken. The stores were for the most part of great modesty. Who owned that one? I asked the taxi driver.

"Well, that happened to be Chinee," he said.

Shops are a dwelling and their goods and stuffs, counters and cash registers are a form of interior decoration. Sacked and disordered, these Memphis boxes were amazingly small and only an active sense of possibility could conceive of them as the site of commercial enterprise. It did not seem possible that by stocking a few shelves these squares of rotting timber could merit ownership, license, investment and produce a profitable exchange. They are lean-tos, chicken coops — measly and optimistic. Looters had sought the consolations of television sets and whiskey. The intrepid dramas of refrigerators and living room suites, deftly transported from store to home, were beyond the range of this poor section of the romantic city on the river.

The day of the march came to the gray, empty streets. The march was solemn and impressive, but on the other hand perhaps somewhat disappointing. A compulsive exaggeration dogs most of the expectations of ideological gatherings and thereby turns success to failure. The forty to sixty thousand predicted belittled the eighteen thousand present. The National Guard, alert with gun and bayonet as if for some important marine landing, made the quiet, orderly march appear a bit of a sell.

The numbers of the National Guard, the body count, spoke almost of a sort of psychotic imagining. They were on every street, blocking every intersection, cutting off each highway. There, in their large brown trucks, crawling out from under the olive-brown canvas, were men in full battle dress, in helmets and chin straps which concealed most of their pale, red-flecked and rather alarmed Southern faces. They guarded the alleys and the horizon, the river and the muddy playground, thoroughfare and esplanade, newspaper store and bank. It was as if by some cancerous multiplication the sensible and necessary had been turned into a monstrous glut.

The march, after all, was mostly made up of Memphis blacks. Was this a victory or a defeat? There were also some local white students from Southwestern, a few young ministers, and from New York members of the teachers' union with a free day off and a lunch box. Mrs. King came from Atlanta for the gathering, a tribute to her husband and also a tribute to the poor sanitation workers for whom it had all begun.

The people gathered early and waited long in the streets. They stood in neat lines to indicate the absence of unruly feelings. Part of the ritual of every public show of opinion and solidarity is the presence of a name or, preferably, the body of a Notable ("Notable" for a routine occasion, and "Dignitary" for a more solemn and affecting event such as the funeral to be held in Atlanta the next day). Notables are often from the entertainment world and the rest are usually to be known for political activities. Like a foundation of stone moved from site to site, only on the notables can the petition for funds be based, the protest developed, the idea constructed.

The marchers waited without restlessness for the chartered airplane to arrive and to announce that it could then truly begin. A limousine will be waiting to take the noted ones to the front of the line, or to leave them off at the stage door. The motors are kept running. After an appearance, a speech, a mere presence, out they go by the back doors used by the celebrated, out to the waiting limousine, off to the waiting plane, and then off.

These persons are symbols of a larger consensus that can be transferred to the mass of the unknown faithful. They are priests giving sanction to idea, struggle, defiance. It is believed that only the famous, the busy, the talented have the power to solicit funds from the rich, notice from the press, and envy from the opposition. Also they are a sunshine, warming. They have the appeal of the lucky.

The march of Memphis was quiet; it was designed as a silent memorial, like a personal prayer. Hold your head high, the instructions read. No gum chewing. For protection in case of trouble, no smoking, no umbrellas, no earrings in pierced ears, no fountain pens in jacket pockets. One woman said, "If they make me take off my shades, I'm quitting the march." Among those who had come from some distance a decision had been made in favor of the small gathering in Memphis over the "national" funeral in Atlanta the following day. "I feel this is more important," they would say.

In the march and at the funeral of Martin Luther King, the mood of the earlier Civil Rights days in Alabama and Mississippi returned, a reunion at the grave of squabbling, competitive family members. And no one could doubt that there had been a longing for reunion among the white ministers and students and the liberals from the large cities. The "love" — locked arms, hymns, good feeling — all of that was remembered with feeling.

This love, if not always refused, was now seldom forthcoming in relations with new black militants, who were set against dependency upon the checkbooks and cooperation of the guilty, longing, loving whites. Everything separated the old Civil Rights people from the new black militants; it could be said, and for once truly, that they did not speak the same language. A harsh, obscene style, unforgiving stares, posturings, insulting accusations and refusal to make distinctions among those of the white world — this was humbling and perplexing. Many of the white people had created their very self-identity out of issues and distinctions and they felt cast off, ill at ease, with the new street rhetoric of "self-defense" and "self-determination."

Comradeship, yes, and being in the South again gave one a remembrance of the meaning of the merely legislative, the newly visible. Back at the hotel in the late afternoon the marchers were breaking up. The dining room was suddenly filled with not-too-pleasing young black boys — not black notables with cameras and briefcases, or in the company of intimidating, busy-looking persons from afar — no, just poor boys from Memphis. The aged waitresses padded about on aching feet and finally approached with the questions of function. Menu? Yes. Cream in the coffee? A little.

So, at last business was business, not friendship. The old white waitresses themselves were deeply wrinkled by the stains of plebeianism. Manner, accent marked them as "disadvantaged"; they were diffident, ignorant, and poor and would themselves cast a blight on the cheerful claims of many dining places. They seemed to be the enduring remnants of many an old retired trailer camp couple, the men with tattooed arms and the women in bright colored stretch pants; those who wander the warm roads and whose traveling kitchenettes and motorized toilets are a distress to the genteel and tasteful.

In any case, joy and flush-cheeked nuns were past history, a folk epic, full of poetry, simplicity and piety. The pastoral period of the Civil Rights Movement had gone by.

At the funeral in Atlanta, rising above the crowd, the *nez pointu* of Richard Nixon . . . Lester Maddox, short-toothed little marmoset, peeking from behind the draperies of the Georgia State House . . . Many Christians have died without the scruples of Christian principles being to the point. The *belief* of Martin Luther King — what an unexpected curiosity it was, the strength of it. His natural mode of address was the sermon. "So I say to you, seek God and discover Him and make Him a power in your life. Without Him all our efforts turn to ashes and our sunrises into darkest nights."

At the end of his life, King seemed in some transfigured state, even though politically he had become more radical and there were traces of disillusionment — with what? messianic hope perhaps. He had observed that America was sicker, more intransigent than he had realized when he began his work. The last, ringing, "I have been to the mountaintop!" gave voice to a transcendent experience. It is this visionary strain that makes him a man elusive in the extreme, difficult to understand as a character.

How was it possible for one so young as King to seem to contain, in himself, so much of the American past? At the very least, the impression he gave was of an experience of life coterminous with the years of his father. The depression, the dust bowl, the sharecropper, the old back-country churches, and even the militance of the earlier IWW — he suggested all of this. He did not appear to belong to the time of Billy Graham (God bless you real good) but to a previous and more spiritual evangelism, to a time of solitude and refined simplicity. In *Adam Bede,* Dinah preaches that Jesus came down from Heaven to tell the good news about God to the poor. "Why, you and me, dear friends, are poor. We have been brought up in poor cottages, and have been reared on oatcake and lived coarse. . . . It doesn't cost Him much to give us our little handful of victual and bit of clothing, but how do we know He cares for us any more than we care for the worms . . . so long as we rear our carrots and onions?" There remains this old, pure tradition in King. Rare elements of the godly and the political come together, with an affecting naturalness. His political work was indeed a Mission, as well as a political cause.

In spite of the heat of his sermon oratory, King seems lofty and often removed by the singleness of his concentration — an evangelical aristocrat. There is even a coldness in his public character, an impenetrability and solidity often seen in those who have given their entire lives to ideas and causes. The racism in America acts finally as an exhaustion to all except the strongest of black leaders. It leads to the urban, manic frenzy, the sleeplessness, hurry, and edginess that are a contrast to King's steadiness and endurance.

Small-town Christianity, staged in some sense as it was, made King's funeral supremely moving. Its themes were root American, bathed in memory, in forgotten prayers and hymns and dreams. Mule carts, sharecroppers, dusty poverty, sleepy Sunday morning services, and late Wednesday night prayer meetings *after work.* There in the reserved pews it was something else — candidates, former candidates, and hopeful candidates, illuminated, as it were, on prime viewing time, free of charge, you might say, free of past contributions to the collection plate, free of the envelopes of future pledges.

The rare young man was mourned and, without him, the world was fearful indeed. The other side of the funeral, Act Two ready in the wings, was the looting and anger of a black population inconsolable for its many losses.

"Jesus is a trick on niggers," a character in Flannery O'Connor's *Wise Blood* says. The strength of belief revealed in King and in such associates as the Reverend Abernathy was a chastening irregularity, not a regionalism absorbed. It stands apart from our perfunctory addresses to "this nation under God." In a later statement Abernathy has said that

God, not Lester Maddox or George Wallace, rules over the South. So, Negro justice is God's work and God's will.

The popular Wesleyan hymns have always urged decent, sober behavior, or that is part of the sense of the urgings. As you sing, "I can hear my Savior calling," you are invited to accept the community of the church and also, quite insistently, to behave yourself, stop drinking, gambling and running around. Non-violence of a sort, but personal, thinking of the home and the family, and looking back to an agricultural or small-town life, far from the uprooted, inchoate, *communal* explosions in the ghettos of the cities. The political non-violence of Martin Luther King was an act of brilliant intellectual conviction, very sophisticated and yet perfectly consistent with evangelical religion, but not a necessary condition as we know from the white believers.

One of the cruelties of the South and part of the pathos of Martin Luther King's funeral and the sadness that edges his rhetoric is that the same popular religion is shared by many bellicose white communicants. The religion seems to have sent few peaceful messages to them insofar as their brothers in Christ, the Negroes, are concerned. Experience leads one to suppose there was more respect for King among Jews, atheists, and comfortable Episcopalians, more sympathy and astonishment, than among the white congregations who use, with a different cadence, the same religious tone and the same hymns heard in the Ebenezer Church. Under the robes of the Klan there is an evangelical skin; its dogmatism is touched with the Scriptural, however perverse the reading of the text.

At one of the memorial services in Central Park after the murder, a radical speaker shouted, "You have killed the last good nigger!" This posturing exclamation was not meant to dishonor King, but to speak of his kind as something gone by, its season over. And perhaps so. The inclination of white leaders to characterize everything unpleasant to themselves in black response to American conditions as a desecration of King's memory was a sordid footnote to what they had named the "redemptive moment." But it told in a self-serving way of the peculiarity of the man, of the survival in him of habits of mind from an earlier time.

King's language in the pulpit and in his speeches was effective but not remarkably interesting. His style compares well, however, with the speeches of recent Presidents and even with those of Adlai Stevenson, most of them bland and flat in print. In many ways, King was not Southern and rural in his address, although he had a melting Georgia accent and his discourse was saturated in the Bible. His was a practical, not a frenzied exhortation, inspiring the Southern Negroes to the sacrifices and dangers of protest and yet reassuring them by its clarity and humanity.

His speech was most beautiful in the less oracular cadences, as when he summed up the meaning of the Poor People's March on Washington with, "We have come for our checks!" The language of the younger generation is another thing altogether. It has the brutality of the city and an assertion of threatening power at hand, not to come. It is military, theatrical, and at its most coherent probably a lasting repudiation of empty courtesy and bureaucratic euphemism.

The murder of Martin Luther King was a "national disgrace." That we said again and again and it would be cynical to hint at fraudulent feelings in the scramble for suitable acts of penance. Levittowns would henceforth not abide by local rulings, but would practice open housing; Walter Reuther offered $50,000 to the beleagured sanitation workers of Memphis; the Field Foundation gave a million to the Southern Christian Leadership movement; Congress acted on the open housing bill. Nevertheless, the mundane continued to nudge the eternal. In 125 cities there was burning and looting. Smoke rose over Washington, D.C.

The Reverend Abernathy spoke of a plate of salad shared with Dr. King at the Lorraine Motel, creating a grief-laden scenery of the Last Supper. How odd it was after all, this exalted Black Liberation, played out at the holy table and at Gethsemane, "in the Garden," as the hymns have it. A moment in history, each instance filled with symbolism and the aura of Christian memory. Perhaps what was celebrated in Atlanta was an end, not a beginning — the waning of the slow, sweet dream of Salvation, through Christ, for the Negro masses.

1969

Michael Herr

Illumination Rounds

WE WERE ALL strapped into the seats of the Chinook, fifty of us, and something, someone was hitting it from the outside with an enormous hammer. How do they do that? I thought, we're a thousand feet in the air! But it had to be that, over and over, shaking the helicopter, making it dip and turn in a horrible out-of-control motion that took me in the stomach. I had to laugh, it was so exciting, it was the thing I had wanted, almost what I had wanted except for that wrenching, resonant metal-echo; I could hear it even above the noise of the rotor blades. And they were going to fix that, I knew they would make it stop. They had to, it was going to make me sick.

They were all replacements going in to mop up after the big battles on Hills 875 and 876, the battles that had already taken on the name of one great battle, the battle of Dak To. And I was new, brand new, three days in-country, embarrassed about my boots because they were so new. And across from me, ten feet away, a boy tried to jump out of the straps and then jerked forward and hung there, his rifle barrel caught in the red plastic webbing of the seat back. As the chopper rose again and turned, his weight went back hard against the webbing and a dark spot the size of a baby's hand showed in the center of his fatigue jacket. And it grew — I knew what it was, but not really — it got up to his armpits and then started down his sleeves and up over his shoulders at the same time. It went all across his waist and down his legs, covering the canvas

First published in *The New American Review* #7, 1969, and collected in *Dispatches, 1977. Herr employs a number of military abbreviations; a few useful to know here are EM (enlisted men), lz (landing zone), ARVN (Army of the Republic of Vietnam), and LOH (light observation helicopter).

on his boots until they were dark like everything else he wore, and it was running in slow, heavy drops off of his fingertips. I thought I could hear the drops hitting the metal strip on the chopper floor. Hey! . . . Oh, but this isn't anything at all, it's not real, it's just some *thing* they're going through that isn't real. One of the door gunners was heaped up on the floor like a cloth dummy. His hand had the bloody raw look of a pound of liver fresh from the butcher paper. We touched down on the same lz we had just left a few minutes before, but I didn't know it until one of the guys shook my shoulder, and then I couldn't stand up. All I could feel of my legs was their shaking, and the guy thought I'd been hit and helped me up. The chopper had taken eight hits, there was shattered plastic all over the floor, a dying pilot up front, and the boy was hanging forward in the straps again, he was dead, but not (I knew) really dead.

It took me a month to lose that feeling of being a spectator to something that was part game, part show. That first afternoon, before I'd boarded the Chinook, a black sergeant had tried to keep me from going. He told me I was too new to go near the kind of shit they were throwing around up in those hills. ("You a reporter?" he'd asked, and I'd said, "No, a writer," dumbass and pompous, and he'd laughed and said, "Careful. You can't use no eraser up where you wanna go.") He'd pointed to the bodies of all the dead Americans lined in two long rows near the chopper pad, so many that they could not even cover all of them decently. But they were not real then, and taught me nothing. The Chinook had come in, blowing my helmet off, and I grabbed it up and joined the replacements waiting to board. "Okay, man," the sergeant said. "You gotta go, you gotta go. All's I can say is, I hope you get a clean wound."

The battle for Hill 875 was over, and some survivors were being brought in by Chinook to the landing strip at Dak To. The 173rd Airborne had taken over 400 casualties, nearly 200 killed, all on the previous afternoon and in the fighting that had gone on all through the night. It was very cold and wet up there, and some girls from the Red Cross had been sent up from Pleiku to comfort the survivors. As the troops filed out of the helicopters, the girls waved and smiled at them from behind their serving tables. "Hi, soldier! What's your name?" "Where you from, soldier?" "I'll bet some hot coffee would hit the spot about now."

And the men from the 173rd just kept walking without answering, staring straight ahead, their eyes rimmed with red from fatigue, their faces pinched and aged with all that had happened during the night. One of them dropped out of line and said something to a loud, fat girl who wore a Peanuts sweatshirt under her fatigue blouse and she started to cry. The rest just walked past the girls and the large, olive-drab coffee urns. They had no idea of where they were.

A senior NCO in the Special Forces was telling the story: "We was back at Bragg, in the NCO Club, and this schoolteacher comes in an' she's real good-lookin'. Dusty here grabs her by the shoulders and starts runnin' his tongue all over her face like she's a fuckin' ice-cream cone. An' you know what she says? She says, 'I like you. You're different.'"

At one time they would have lighted your cigarette for you on the terrace of the Continental Hotel. But those days are almost twenty years gone, and anyway, who really misses them? Now there is a crazy American who looks like George Orwell, and he is always sleeping off his drinks in one of the wicker chairs there, slumped against a table, starting up with violence, shouting and then going back to sleep. He makes everyone nervous, especially the waiters; the old ones who had served the French and the Japanese and the first American journalists and OSS types ("those noisy bastards at the Continental," Graham Greene called them) and the really young ones who bussed the tables and pimped in a modest way. The little elevator boy still greets the guests each morning with a quiet "*Ça va?*" but he is seldom answered, and the old baggage man (he also brings us grass) will sit in the lobby and say, "How are you tomorrow?"

"Ode to Billy Joe" plays from speakers mounted on the terrace's corner columns, but the air seems too heavy to carry the sound right, and it hangs in the corners. There is an exhausted, drunk master sergeant from the 1st Infantry Division who has bought a flute from the old man in khaki shorts and pith helmet who sells instruments along Tu Do Street. The old man will lean over the butt-strewn flower boxes that line the terrace and play "Frère Jacques" on a wooden stringed instrument. The sergeant has bought the flute, and he is playing it quietly, pensively, badly.

The tables are crowded with American civilian construction engineers, men getting $30,000 a year from their jobs on government contracts and matching that easily on the black market. Their faces have the look of aerial photos of silicone pits, all hung with loose flesh and visible veins. Their mistresses were among the prettiest, saddest girls in Vietnam. I always wondered what they had looked like before they'd made their arrangements with the engineers. You'd see them at the tables there, smiling their hard, empty smiles into those rangy, brutal, scared faces. No wonder those men all looked alike to the Vietnamese. After a while they all looked alike to me. Out on the Bien Hoa Highway, north of Saigon, there is a monument to the Vietnamese war dead, and it is one of the few graceful things left in the country. It is a modest pagoda set above the road and approached by long flights of gently rising steps. One Sunday, I saw a bunch of these engineers gunning their Harleys up those steps, laughing and shouting in the afternoon sun. The Vietnamese had a special name for them to distinguish them from all other Americans; it translated out to something like "The Terrible Ones," although I'm told that this doesn't even approximate the odium carried in the original.

There was a young sergeant in the Special Forces, stationed at the C Detachment in Can Tho, which served as the SF headquarters for IV Corps. In all, he had spent thirty-six months in Vietnam. This was his third extended tour, and he planned to come back again as soon as he possibly could after this current hitch was finished. During his last tour he had lost a finger and part of a thumb in a firefight, and he had been generally shot up enough times for the three Purple Hearts which mean that you don't have to fight in Vietnam anymore. After all that, I guess they thought of him as a combat liability, but he was such a hard charger that they gave him the EM Club to manage. He ran it well and seemed happy, except that he had gained a lot of weight in the duty, and it set him apart from the rest of the men. He loved to horse around with the Vietnamese in the compound, leaping on them from behind, leaning heavily on them, shoving them around and pulling their ears, sometimes punching them a little hard in the stomach, smiling a stiff small smile that was meant to tell them all that he was just being playful. The Vietnamese would smile too, until he turned to walk away. He loved the Vietnamese, he said, he really *knew* them after three years. As far as he was concerned, there was no place in the world as fine as Vietnam. And back home in North Carolina he had a large, glass-covered display case in which he kept his medals and decorations and citations, the photographs taken during three tours and countless battles, letters from past commanders, a few souvenirs. The case stood in the center of the living room, he said, and every night his wife and three kids would move the kitchen table out in front of it and eat their dinner there.

At 800 feet we knew we were being shot at. Something hit the underside of the chopper but did not penetrate it. They weren't firing tracers, but we saw the brilliant flickering blips of light below, and the pilot circled and came down very fast, working the button that released fire from the flex guns mounted on either side of the Huey. Every fifth round was a tracer, and they sailed out and down, incomparably graceful, closer and closer, until they met the tiny point of light coming from the jungle. The ground fire stopped, and we went on to land at Vinh Long, where the pilot yawned and said, "I think I'll go to bed early tonight and see if I can wake up with any enthusiasm for this war."

A twenty-four-year-old Special Forces captain was telling me about it. "I went out and killed one VC and liberated a prisoner. Next day the major called me in and told me that I'd killed fourteen VC and liberated six prisoners. You want to see the medal?"

There was a little air-conditioned restaurant on the corner of Le Loi and Tu Do, across from the Continental Hotel and the old opera house which now served as the Vietnamese Lower House. Some of us called it the Graham Greene Milk Bar (a scene in *The Quiet American* had taken place there), but its name was Givral. Every morning they baked their own baguettes and croissants, and the coffee wasn't too bad. Sometimes, I'd meet there with a friend of mine for breakfast.

He was a Belgian, a tall, slow-moving man of thirty who'd been born in the Congo. He professed to know and love war, and he affected the mercenary sensibility. He'd been photographing the Vietnam thing for seven or eight years now, and once in a while he'd go over to Laos and run around the jungles there with the government, searching for the dreaded Pathet Lao, which he pronounced "Paddy Lao." Other people's stories of Laos always made it sound like a lotus land where no one wanted to hurt anyone, but he said that whenever he went on ops there he always kept a grenade taped to his belly because he was a Catholic and knew what the Paddy Lao would do to him if he were captured. But he was a little crazy that way, and tended to dramatize his war stories.

He always wore dark glasses, probably even during operations. His pictures sold to the wire services, and I saw a few of them in the American news magazines. He was very kind in a gruff, offhanded sort of way, kindness embarrassed him, and he was so graceless among people, so eager to shock, that he couldn't understand why so many of us liked him. Irony was the effect he worked for in conversation, that and a sense of how exquisite the war could be when all of its machinery was running right. He was explaining the finish of an operation he'd just been on in War Zone C, above Cu Chi.

"There were a lot of dead VC," he said. "Dozens and dozens of them! A lot of them were from that same village that has been giving you so much trouble lately. VC from top to bottom — Michael, in that village the fucking *ducks* are VC. So the American commander had twenty or thirty of the dead flown up in a sling load and dropped into the village. I should say it was a drop of at least two hundred feet, all those dead Viet Congs, right in the middle of the village."

He smiled (I couldn't see his eyes).

"Ah, Psywar!" he said, kissing off the tips of his fingers.

Bob Stokes of *Newsweek* told me this: In the big Marine hospital in Danang they have what is called the "White Lie Ward," where they bring some of the worst cases, the ones who can be saved but who will never be the same again. A young Marine was carried in, still unconscious and full of morphine, and his legs were gone. As he was being carried into the ward, he came out of it briefly and saw a Catholic chaplain standing over him.

"Father," he said, "am I all right?"

The chaplain didn't know what to say. "You'll have to talk about that with the doctors, son."

"Father, are my legs okay?"

"Yes," the chaplain said. "Sure."

By the next afternoon the shock had worn off and the boy knew all about it. He was lying on his cot when the chaplain came by.

"Father," the Marine said, "I'd like to ask you for something."

"What, son?"

"I'd like to have that cross." And he pointed to the tiny silver insignia on the chaplain's lapel.

"Of course," the chaplain said. "But why?"

"Well, it was the first thing I saw when I came to yesterday, and I'd like to have it."

The chaplain removed the cross and handed it to him. The Marine held it tightly in his fist and looked at the chaplain.

"You lied to me, Father," he said. "You cocksucker. You lied to me."

His name was Davies, and he was a gunner with a helicopter group based at Tan Son Nhut airport. On paper, by the regulations, he was billeted in one of the big "hotel" BEQ's in Cholon, but he only kept his things there. He actually lived in a small two-story Vietnamese house deeper inside of Cholon, as far from the papers and the regulations as he could get. Every morning he took an Army bus with wire-grille windows out to the base and flew missions, mostly around War Zone C, along the Cambodian border, and most nights he returned to the house in Cholon where he lived with his "wife" (whom he'd found in one of the bars) and some other Vietnamese who were said to be the girl's family. Her mamma-san and her brother were always there, living on the first floor, and there were others who came and went. He seldom saw the brother, but every few days he would find a pile of labels and brand names torn from cardboard cartons, American products that the brother wanted from the PX.

The first time I saw him he was sitting alone at a table on the Continental terrace, drinking a beer. He had a full, drooping mustache and sharp, sad eyes, and he was wearing a denim workshirt and wheat jeans. He also carried a Leica and a copy of *Ramparts,* and I just assumed at first that he was a correspondent. I didn't know then that you could buy *Ramparts* at the PX, and after I'd borrowed and returned it we began to talk. It was the issue that featured left-wing Catholics like Jesus Christ and Fulton Sheen on the cover. "*Catholique?*" one of the bar girls said later that night. "*Moi aussi,*" and she kept the magazine. That was when we were walking around Cholon in the rain trying to find Hoa, his wife. Mamma-san had told us that she'd gone to the movies with some girlfriends, but Davies knew what she was doing.

"I hate that shit," he said. "It's so uncool."

"Well, don't put up with it."

"Yeah."

Davies' house was down a long, narrow alley that became nothing more than a warren at the end, smelling of camphor smoke and fish, crowded but clean. He would not speak to Mamma-san, and we walked straight up to the second floor. It was one long room that had a sleeping area screened off in an arrangement of filmy curtains. At the top of the stairs there was a large poster of Lenny Bruce, and beneath it, in a shrine effect, was a low table with a Buddha and lighted incense on it.

"Lenny," Davies said.

Most of one wall was covered with a collage that Davies had done with the help of some friends. It included glimpses of burning monks, stacked Viet Cong dead, wounded Marines screaming and weeping, Cardinal Spellman waving from a chopper, Ronald Reagan, his face halved and separated by a stalk of cannabis; pictures of John Lennon peering through wire-rimmed glasses, Mick Jagger, Jimi Hendrix, Dylan, Eldridge Cleaver, Rap Brown; coffins draped with American flags whose stars were replaced by swastikas and dollar signs; odd parts clipped from *Playboy* pictures, newspaper headlines (FARMERS BUTCHER HOGS TO PROTEST PORK PRICE DIP), photo captions (*President Jokes with Newsmen*), beautiful girls holding flowers, showers of peace symbols; Ky standing at attention and saluting, a small mushroom cloud forming where his genitalia should have been; a map of the western United States with the shape of Vietnam reversed and fitted over California and one large, long figure that began at the bottom with shiny leather boots and rouged knees and ascended in a microskirt, bare breasts, graceful shoulders and a long neck, topped by the burned, blackened face of a dead Vietnamese woman.

By the time Davies' friends showed up, we were already stoned. We could hear them below, laughing and rapping with Mama, and then they came up the stairs, three spades and two white guys.

"It sure do smell *peculiar* up here," one of them said.

"Hi, you freaky li'l fuckers."

"This grass is Number Ten," Davies said. "Every time I smoke this grass over here it gives me a bad trip."

"Ain' nuthin' th' matter with that grass," someone said. "It ain't the grass."

"Where's Hoa?"

"Yeah, Davies, where's your ole lady at?"

"She's out hustling Saigon tea, and I'm fucking sick of it." He tried to look really angry, but he only looked unhappy.

One of them handed off a joint and stretched out. "Hairy day today," he said.

"Where'd you fly?"

"Bu Dop."

"Bu Dop!" one of the spades said, and he started to move toward the joint, jiving and working his shoulders, bopping his head. "Bu Dop, budop, bu dop dop *dop!*"

"Funky funky Bu Dop."

"Hey, man, can you OD on grass?"

"I dunno, baby. Maybe we could get jobs at the Aberdeen Proving Grounds smokin' dope for Uncle Sugar."

"Wow, I'm stoned. Hey, Davies, you stoned?"

"Yeah," Davies said.

It started to rain again, so hard that you couldn't hear drops, only the full force of the water pouring down on the metal roof. We smoked a little more, and then the others started to leave. Davies looked like he was sleeping with his eyes open.

"That goddamn pig," he said. "Fuckin' whore. Man, I'm paying out all this bread for the house and those people downstairs. I don't even know who they are, for Christ's sake. I'm really . . . I'm getting sick of it."

"You're pretty short now," someone said. "Why don't you cut out?"

"You mean just split?"

"Why not?"

Davies was quiet for a long time.

"Yeah," he finally said. "This is bad. This is really bad. I think I'm going to get out of here."

A bird colonel, commanding a brigade of the 4th Infantry Division: "I'll bet you always wondered why we call 'em Dinks up in this part of the country. I thought of it myself. I'll tell you, I never *did* like hearing them called Charlie. See, I had an uncle named Charlie, and I liked him too. No, Charlie was just too damn good for the little bastards. So I just thought, What are they *really* like? and I came up with rinky-dink. Suits 'em just perfect, Rinky-Dink. 'Cept that was too long, so we cut it down some. And that's why we call 'em Dinks."

One morning before dawn, Ed Fouhy, a former Saigon bureau chief for CBS, went out to 8th Aerial Port at Tan Son Nhut to catch the early military flight to Danang. They boarded as the sun came up, and Fouhy strapped in next to a kid in rumpled fatigues, one of those soldiers you see whose weariness has gone far beyond physical exhaustion, into that state where no amount of sleep will ever give him the kind of rest he needs. Every torpid movement they make tells you that they are tired, that they'll stay tired until their tours are up and the big bird flies them back to the World. Their eyes are dim with it, their faces almost puffy, and when they smile you have to accept it as a token.

There was a standard question you could use to open a conversation with troops, and Fouhy tried it. "How long you been in-country?" he asked.

The kid half lifted his head; that question could *not* be serious. The weight was really on him, and the words came slowly.

"All fuckin' day," he said.

"You guys ought do a story on me suntahm," the kid said. He was a helicopter gunner, six-three with an enormous head that sat in bad proportion to the rest of his body and a line of picket teeth that were always on show in a wet, uneven smile. Every few seconds he would have to wipe his mouth with the back of his hand, and when he talked to you his face was always an inch from yours, so that I had to take my glasses off to keep them dry. He was from Kilgore, Texas, and he was on his seventeenth consecutive month in-country.

"Why should we do a story about you?"

"'Cause I'm so fuckin' good," he said, "'n' that ain' no shit, neither. Got me one hunnert 'n' fifty-se'en gooks kilt. 'N' fifty caribou." He grinned and stanched the saliva for a second. "Them're all certified," he added.

The chopper touched down at Ba Xoi and we got off, not unhappy about leaving him. "Lis'n," he said, laughing, "you git up onna ridgeline, see y' keep yer head down. Y'heah?"

"Say, how'd you get to be a co-respondent an' come ovah to this raggedy-ass motherfucker?"

He was a really big spade, rough-looking even when he smiled, and he wore a gold nose-bead fastened through his left nostril. I told him that the nose-bead blew my mind, and he said that was all right, it blew everybody's mind. We were sitting by the chopper pad of an lz above Kontum. He was trying to get to Dak To, I was heading for Pleiku, and we both wanted to get out of there before nightfall. We took turns running out to the pad to check the choppers that kept coming in and taking off, neither of us was having any luck, and after we'd talked for an hour he laid a joint on me and we smoked.

"I been here mor'n eight months now," he said. "I bet I been in mor'n twenny firefights. An' I ain' hardly fired back once."

"How come?"

"Shee-it, I go firin' back, I might kill one a th' Brothers, you dig it?"

I nodded, no Viet Cong ever called *me* honky, and he told me that in his company alone there were more than a dozen Black Panthers and that he was one of them. I didn't say anything, and then he said that he wasn't just a Panther; he was an agent for the Panthers, sent over here to recruit. I asked him what kind of luck he'd been having, and he said fine, real fine. There was a fierce wind blowing across the lz, and the joint didn't last very long.

"Hey, baby," he said, "that was just some shit I tol' you. Shit, I ain' no Panther. I was just fuckin' with you, see what you'd say."

"But the Panthers have guys over here. I've met some."

"Tha' could be," he said, and he laughed.

A Huey came in, and he jogged out to see where it was headed. It was going to Dak To, and he came back to get his gear. "Later, baby," he said. "An' luck." He jumped into the chopper, and as it rose from the strip he leaned out and laughed, bringing his arm up and bending it back toward him, palm out and the fist clenched tightly in the Sign.

One day I went out with the ARVN on an operation in the rice paddies above Vinh Long, forty terrified Vietnamese troops and five Americans, all packed into three Hueys that dropped us up to our hips in paddy muck. I had never been in a rice paddy before. We spread out and moved toward the marshy swale that led to the jungle. We were still twenty feet from the first cover, a low paddy wall, when we took fire from the treeline. It was probably the working half of a crossfire that had somehow gone wrong. It caught one of the ARVN in the head, and he dropped back into the water and disappeared. We made it to the wall with two casualties. There was no way of stopping their fire, no room to send in a flanking party, so gunships were called and we crouched behind the wall and waited. There was a lot of fire coming from the trees, but we were all right as long as we kept down. And I was thinking, Oh man, so this is a rice paddy, yes, wow! when I suddenly heard an electric guitar shooting right up in my ear and a mean, rapturous black voice singing, coaxing, "Now c'mon baby, stop actin' so crazy," and when I got it all together I turned to see a grinning black corporal hunched over a cassette recorder. "Might's well," he said. "We ain' goin' *no*where till them gunships come."

That's the story of the first time I ever heard Jimi Hendrix, but in a war where a lot of people talked about Aretha's "Satisfaction" the way other people speak of Brahms' Fourth, it was more than a story; it was

Credentials. "Say, that Jimi Hendrix is my main man," someone would say. "He has *definitely* got his shit together!" Hendrix had once been in the 101st Airborne, and the Airborne in Vietnam was full of wiggy-brilliant spades like him, really mean and really good, guys who always took care of you when things got bad. That music meant a lot to them. I never once heard it played over the Armed Forces Radio Network.

I met this kid from Miles City, Montana, who read the *Stars and Stripes* every day, checking the casualty lists to see if by some chance anybody from his town had been killed. He didn't even know if there was anyone else from Miles City in Vietnam, but he checked anyway because he knew for sure that if there *was* someone else and they got killed, he would be all right. "I mean, can you just see *two* guys from a raggedy-ass town like Miles City getting killed in Vietnam?" he said.

The sergeant had lain out near the clearing for almost two hours with a wounded medic. He had called over and over for a medevac, but none had come. Finally, a chopper from another outfit, a LOH, appeared, and he was able to reach it by radio. The pilot told him that he'd have to wait for one of his own ships, they weren't coming down, and the sergeant told the pilot that if he did not land for them he was going to open fire from the ground and fucking well *bring* him down. So they were picked up that way, but there were repercussions.

The commander's code name was Mal Hombre, and he reached the sergeant later that afternoon from a place with the call signal Violent Meals.

"God *damn* it, Sergeant," he said through the static, "I thought you were a professional soldier."

"I waited as long as I could, Sir. Any longer, I was gonna lose my man."

"This outfit is perfectly capable of taking care of its own dirty laundry. Is that clear, Sergeant?"

"Colonel, since when is a wounded trooper 'dirty laundry'?"

"At ease, Sergeant," Mal Hombre said, and radio contact was broken.

There was a spec 4 in the Special Forces at Can Tho, a shy Indian boy from Chinle, Arizona, with large, wet eyes the color of ripe olives and a quiet way of speaking, a really nice way of putting things, kind to everyone without ever being stupid or soft about it. On the night that the compound and the airstrip were hit, he came and asked me if there was a chaplain anywhere around. He wasn't very religious, he said, but he was worried about tonight. He'd just volunteered for a "suicide squad," two jeeps that were going to drive across the airstrip with mortars and a recoilless rifle. It looked bad, I had to admit it; there were so few of us in the compound that they'd had to put me on the reaction force. It might be bad. He just had a feeling about it, he'd seen what always happened to guys whenever they got that feeling, at least he *thought* it was that feeling, a bad one, the worst he'd ever had.

I told him that the only chaplains I could think of would be in the town, and we both knew that the town was cut off.

"Oh," he said. "Look, then. If I get it tonight . . ."

"It'll be okay."

"Listen, though. If it happens . . . I think it's going to . . . will you make sure the colonel tells my folks I was looking for a chaplain anyway?"

I promised, and the jeeps loaded and drove off. I heard later that there had been a brief firefight, but that no one had been hurt. They didn't have to use the recoilless. They all drove back into the compound two hours later. The next morning at breakfast he sat at another table, saying a lot of loud, brutal things about the gooks, and he wouldn't look at me. But at noon he came over and squeezed my arm and smiled, his eyes fixed somewhere just to the right of my own.

For two days now, ever since the Tet Offensive had begun, they had been coming by the hundreds to the province hospital at Can Tho. They were usually either very young or very old or women, and their wounds were often horrible. The more lightly wounded were being treated quickly in the hospital yard, and the more serious cases were simply placed in one of the corridors to die. There were just too many of them to treat, the doctors had worked without a break, and now, on the second afternoon, the Viet Cong began shelling the hospital.

One of the Vietnamese nurses handed me a cold can of beer and asked me to take it down the hall where one of the Army surgeons was operating. The door of the room was ajar, and I walked right in. I probably should have looked first. A little girl was lying on the table, looking with wide dry eyes at the wall. Her left leg was gone, and a sharp piece of bone about six inches long extended from the exposed stump. The leg itself was on the floor, half wrapped in a piece of paper. The doctor was a major, and he'd been working alone. He could not have looked worse if he'd lain all night in a trough of blood. His hands were so slippery that I had to hold the can to his mouth for him and tip it up as his head went back. I couldn't look at the girl.

"Is it all right?" he said quietly.

"It's okay now. I expect I'll be sick as hell later on."

He placed his hand on the girl's forehead and said, "Hello, little darling." He thanked me for bringing the beer. He probably thought that he was smiling, but nothing changed anywhere in his face. He'd been working this way for nearly twenty hours.

The Intel report lay closed on the green field table, and someone had scrawled "What does it all mean?" across the cover sheet. There wasn't much doubt about who had done that; the S-2 was a known ironist. There were so many like him, really young captains and majors who had the wit to cut back their despair, a wedge to set against the bitterness. What got to them sooner or later was an inability to reconcile their love of service with their contempt for the war, and a lot of them finally had to resign their commissions, leave the profession.

We were sitting in the tent waiting for the rain to stop, the major, five grunts and myself. The rains were constant now, ending what had been a dry monsoon season, and you could look through the tent flap and think about the Marines up there patrolling the hills. Someone came in to report that one of the patrols had discovered a small arms cache.

"An arms cache!" the major said. "What happened was, one of the grunts was out there running around, and he tripped and fell down. That's about the only way we ever find any of this shit."

He was twenty-nine, young in rank, and this was his second tour. The time before, he had been a captain commanding a regular Marine company. He knew all about grunts and patrols, arms caches and the value of most Intelligence.

It was cold, even in the tent, and the enlisted Marines seemed uncomfortable about lying around with a stranger, a correspondent there. The major was a cool head, they knew that; there wasn't going to be any kind of hassle until the rain stopped. They talked quietly among themselves at the far end of the tent, away from the light of the lantern. Reports kept coming in: reports from the Vietnamese, from recon, from Division, situation reports, casualty reports, three casualty reports in twenty minutes. The major looked them all over.

"Did you know that a dead Marine costs eighteen thousand dollars?" he said. The grunts all turned around and looked at us. They knew how the major had meant that because they knew the major. They were just seeing about me.

The rain stopped, and they left. Outside, the air was still cool, but heavy, too, as though a terrible heat was coming on. The major and I stood by the tent and watched while an F-4 flew nose-down, released its load against the base of a hill, leveled and flew upward again.

"I've been having this dream," the major said. "I've had it two times now. I'm in a big examination room back at Quantico. They're handing out questionnaires for an aptitude test. I take one and look at it, and the first question says, 'How many kinds of animals can you kill with your hands?'"

We could see rain falling in a sheet about a kilometer away. Judging by the wind, the major gave it three minutes before it reached us.

"After the first tour, I'd have the goddamndest nightmares. You know, the works. Bloody stuff, bad fights, guys dying, *me* dying . . . I thought they were the worst," he said. "But I sort of miss them now."

1970

Maya Angelou

I Know Why the Caged Bird Sings

"What you looking at me for?
I didn't come to stay . . ."

I HADN'T so much forgot as I couldn't bring myself to remember. Other things were more important.

"What you looking at me for?
I didn't come to stay . . ."

Whether I could remember the rest of the poem or not was immaterial. The truth of the statement was like a wadded-up handkerchief, sopping wet in my fists, and the sooner they accepted it the quicker I could let my hands open and the air would cool my palms.

"What you looking at me for . . . ?"

The children's section of the Colored Methodist Episcopal Church of Stamps, Arkansas, was wiggling and giggling over my well-known forgetfulness.

The dress I wore was lavender taffeta, and each time I breathed it rustled, and now that I was sucking in air to breathe out shame it sounded like crepe paper on the back of hearses.

As I'd watched Momma put ruffles on the hem and cute little tucks around the waist, I knew that once I put it on I'd look like a movie star. (It was silk and that made up for the awful color.) I was going to look like one of the sweet little white girls who were everybody's dream of what was right with the world. Hanging softly over the black Singer

Published under this title in *Harper's Magazine* in February 1970, the essay was adapted from the opening sections of Angelou's 1969 book, *I Know Why the Caged Bird Sings*.

sewing machine, it looked like magic, and when people saw me wearing it they were going to run up to me and say, "Marguerite [sometimes it was 'dear Marguerite'], forgive us, please, we didn't know who you were," and I would answer generously, "No, you couldn't have known. Of course I forgive you."

Just thinking about it made me go around with angel's dust sprinkled over my face for days. But Easter's early morning sun had shown the dress to be a plain ugly cut-down from a white woman's once-was-purple throwaway. It was old-lady-long too, but it didn't hide my skinny legs, which had been greased with Blue Seal Vaseline and powdered with the Arkansas red clay. The age-faded color made my skin look dirty like mud, and everyone in church was looking at my skinny legs.

Wouldn't they be surprised when one day I woke out of my black ugly dream, and my real hair, which was long and blond, would take the place of the kinky mass that Momma wouldn't let me straighten? My light-blue eyes were going to hypnotize them, after all the things they said about "my daddy must of been a Chinaman" (I thought they meant made out of china, like a cup) because my eyes were so small and squinty. Then they would understand why I had never picked up a Southern accent, or spoken the common slang, and why I had to be forced to eat pigs' tails and snouts. Because I was really white and because a cruel fairy stepmother, who was understandably jealous of my beauty, had turned me into a too-big Negro girl, with nappy black hair, broad feet, and a space between her teeth that would hold a number-two pencil.

"What you looking . . ." The minister's wife leaned toward me, her long yellow face full of sorry. She whispered, "I just come to tell you, it's Easter Day." I repeated, jamming the words together, "Ijustcometo-tellyouit'sEasterDay," as low as possible. The giggles hung in the air like melting clouds that were waiting to rain on me. I held up two fingers, close to my chest, which meant that I had to go to the toilet, and tiptoed toward the rear of the church. Dimly, somewhere over my head, I heard ladies saying, "Lord bless the child" and, "Praise God." My head was up and my eyes were open, but I didn't see anything. Halfway down the aisle, the church exploded with, "Were you there when they crucified my Lord?" and I tripped over a foot stuck out from the children's pew. I stumbled and started to say something, or maybe to scream, but a green persimmon, or it could have been a lemon, caught me between the legs and squeezed. I tasted the sour on my tongue and felt it in the back of my mouth. Then before I reached the door, the sting was burning down my legs and into my Sunday socks. I tried to hold, to squeeze it back, to keep it from speeding, but when I reached the church porch I knew I'd have to let it go, or it would probably run right back up to my head and my poor head would burst like a dropped watermelon, and all the brains and spit and tongue and eyes would roll all over the place. So I ran down into the yard and let it go. I ran, peeing and crying, not toward the toilet out back but to our house. I'd get a whipping for it, to be sure, and the nasty children would have something new to tease me about. I laughed anyway, partially for the sweet release; still, the greater joy came not from being liberated from the silly church but from the knowledge that I wouldn't die from a busted head.

If growing up is painful for the Southern Black girl, being aware of her displacement is the rust on the razor that threatens the throat. It is an unnecessary insult.

1

My brother Bailey and I had come to the musty little town of Stamps when I was three and he four. We had arrived wearing tags on our wrists which instructed — "To Whom It May Concern" — that we were Marguerite and Bailey Johnson, Jr., from Long Beach, California, en route to Stamps, Arkansas, c/o Mrs. Annie Henderson.

Our parents had decided to put an end to their calamitous marriage, and Father shipped us home to his mother. A porter had been charged with our welfare — he got off the train the next day in Arizona — and our tickets were pinned to my brother's inside coat pocket.

I don't remember much of the trip, but after we reached the segregated Southern part of the journey, things must have looked up. Negro passengers, who always traveled with loaded lunch boxes, felt sorry for "the poor little motherless darlings" and plied us with cold fried chicken and potato salad. Years later I discovered that the United States had been crossed thousands of times by frightened Black children traveling alone to their newly affluent parents in Northern cities, or back to grandmothers in Southern towns when the urban North reneged on its economic promises.

The town reacted to us as its inhabitants had reacted to all things new before our coming. It regarded us awhile without curiosity but with caution, and after we were seen to be harmless (and children) it closed in around us, as a real mother embraces a stranger's child. Warmly, but not too familiarly.

We lived with our grandmother and uncle in the rear of the Store (it was always spoken of with a capital *s*), which she had owned some twenty-five years. Early in the century, Momma (we soon stopped calling her Grandmother) sold lunches to the sawmen in the lumberyard (east Stamps) and the seedmen at the cotton gin (west Stamps). Her crisp meat pies and cool lemonade, when joined to her miraculous ability to be in two places at the same time, assured her business success. From having a mobile lunch counter, she set up a stand between the two points of fiscal interest and supplied the workers' needs for a few years. Then she had the Store built in the heart of the Negro area. Over the years it became the lay center of activities in town. On Saturdays, barbers sat their customers in the shade on the porch of the Store, and troubadours on their ceaseless crawlings through the South leaned across its benches and sang their sad songs of The Brazos while they played juice harps and cigar-box guitars.

The formal name of the Store was the Wm. Johnson General Merchandise Store. Customers could find food staples, a good variety of colored thread, mash for hogs, corn for chickens, coal oil for lamps, light bulbs for the wealthy, shoestrings, hair dressing, balloons, and flower seeds. Anything not visible had only to be ordered. Until we became familiar enough to belong to the Store and it to us, we were locked up in a Fun House of Things where the attendant had gone home for life.

Each year I watched the field across from the Store turn caterpillar green, then gradually frosty white. I knew exactly how long it would be before the big wagons would pull into the front yard and load on the cotton pickers at daybreak to carry them to the remains of slavery's plantations.

During the picking season my grandmother would get out of bed at four o'clock (she never used an alarm clock) and creak down to her knees and chant in a sleep-filled voice, "Our Father, thank you for letting me see this New Day. Thank you that you didn't allow the bed I lay on last to be my cooling board, nor my blanket my winding sheet. Guide my feet this day along the straight and narrow, and help me to put a bridle on my tongue. Bless this house, and everybody in it. Thank you, in the name of your Son, Jesus Christ, Amen." Before she had quite arisen, she called our names and issued orders, and pushed her large feet into home slippers and across the bare lye-washed wooden floor to light the coal-oil lamp.

The lamplight in the Store gave a soft make-believe feeling to our world which made me want to whisper and walk about on tiptoe. The odors of onions and oranges and kerosene had been mixing all night and wouldn't be disturbed until the wooded slat was removed from the door and the early morning air forced its way in with the bodies of people who had walked miles to reach the pickup place.

"Sister, I'll have two cans of sardines."

"I'm gonna work so fast today I'm gonna make you look like you standing still."

"Lemme have a hunk uh cheese and some sody crackers."

"Just gimme a coupla them fat peanut paddies." That would be from a picker who was taking his lunch. The greasy brown-paper sack was stuck behind the bib of his overalls. He'd use the candy as a snack before the noon sun called the workers to rest.

In those tender mornings the Store was full of laughing, joking, boasting, and bragging. One man was going to pick two hundred pounds of cotton, and another three hundred. Even the children were promising to bring home fo' bits and six bits. The champion picker of the day before was the hero of the dawn. If he prophesied that the cotton in today's field was going to be sparse and stick to the bolls like glue, every listener would grunt a hearty agreement. The sound of the empty cotton sacks dragging over the floor and the murmurs of waking people were sliced by the cash register as we rang up the five-cent sales.

If the morning sounds and smells were touched with the supernatural, the late afternoon had all the features of the normal Arkansas life. In the dying sunlight the people dragged, rather than their empty cotton sacks. Brought back to the Store, the pickers would step out of the backs of trucks and fold down, dirt-disappointed, to the ground. No matter how much they had picked, it wasn't enough. Their wages wouldn't even get them out of debt to my grandmother, not to mention the staggering bill that waited on them at the white commissary downtown.

The sounds of the new morning had been replaced with grumbles about cheating houses, weighted scales, snakes, skimpy cotton, and dusty rows. In later years I was to confront the stereotyped picture of gay song-singing cotton pickers with such inordinate rage that I was told even by fellow Blacks that my paranoia was embarrassing. But I had seen the fingers cut by the mean little cotton bolls, and I had witnessed the backs and shoulders and arms and legs resisting any further demands.

Some of the workers would leave their sacks at the Store to be picked up the following morning, but a few had to take them home for repairs.

I winced to picture them sewing the coarse material under a coal-oil lamp with fingers stiffening from the day's work. In too few hours they would have to walk back to Sister Henderson's Store, get vittles, and load, again, onto the trucks. Then they would face another day of trying to earn enough for the whole year with the heavy knowledge that they were going to end the season as they started it. Without the money or credit necessary to sustain a family for three months. In cotton-picking time the late afternoons revealed the harshness of Black Southern life, which in the early morning had been softened by nature's blessing of grogginess, forgetfulness, and the soft lamplight.

2

When Bailey was six and I a year younger, we used to rattle off the times tables with the speed I was later to see Chinese children in San Francisco employ on their abacuses. Our summer-gray potbellied stove bloomed rosy red during winter, and became a severe disciplinarian threat if we were so foolish as to indulge in making mistakes.

Uncle Willie used to sit, like a giant black Z (he had been crippled as a child), and hear us testify to the Lafayette County Training School's abilities. His face pulled down on the left side, as if a pulley had been attached to his lower teeth, and his left hand was only a mite bigger than Bailey's, but on the second mistake or on the third hesitation his big overgrown right hand would catch one of us behind the collar, and in the same moment would thrust the culprit toward the dull red heater, which throbbed like a devil's toothache. We were never burned, although once I might have been when I was so terrified I tried to jump onto the stove to remove the possibility of its remaining a threat. Like most children, I thought if I could face the worst danger voluntarily, and *triumph*, I would forever have power over it. But in my case of sacrificial effort I was thwarted. Uncle Willie held tight to my dress and I only got close enough to smell the clean dry scent of hot iron. We learned the times tables without understanding their grand principle, simply because we had the capacity and no alternative.

The tragedy of lameness seems so unfair to children that they are embarrassed in its presence. And they, most recently off nature's mold, sense that they have only narrowly missed being another of her jokes. In relief at the narrow escape, they vent their emotions in impatience and criticism of the unlucky cripple.

Momma related times without end, and without any show of emotion, how Uncle Willie had been dropped when he was three years old by a woman who was minding him. She seemed to hold no rancor against the baby-sitter, nor for her just God who allowed the accident. She felt it necessary to explain over and over again to those who knew the story by heart that he wasn't "born that way."

In our society, where two-legged, two-armed strong Black men were able at best to eke out only the necessities of life, Uncle Willie, with his starched shirts, shined shoes, and shelves full of food, was the whipping boy and butt of jokes of the underemployed and underpaid. Fate not only disabled him but laid a double-tiered barrier in his path. He was also proud and sensitive. Therefore he couldn't pretend that he wasn't crippled, nor could he deceive himself that people were not repelled by his defect.

Only once in all the years of trying not to watch him, I saw him pretend to himself and others that he wasn't lame. Coming home from school one day, I saw a dark car in our front yard. I rushed in to find a strange man and woman (Uncle Willie said later they were schoolteachers from Little Rock) drinking Dr. Peppers in the cool of the Store. I sensed a wrongness around me, like an alarm clock that had gone off without being set.

I knew it couldn't be the strangers. Not frequently, but often enough, travelers pulled off the main road to buy tobacco or soft drinks in the only Negro store in Stamps. When I looked at Uncle Willie, I knew what was pulling my mind's coattails. He was standing erect behind the counter, not leaning forward or resting on the small shelf that had been built for him. Erect. His eyes seemed to hold me with a mixture of threat and appeal.

I dutifully greeted the strangers and roamed my eyes around for his walking stick. It was nowhere to be seen. He said, "Uh . . . this this . . . this . . . uh, my niece. She's . . . uh . . . just come from school." Then to the couple — "You know . . . how, uh, children are . . . th-th-these days . . . they play all d-d-day at school and c-c-can't wait to get home and pl-play some more."

The people smiled, very friendly.

He added, "Go on out and pl-play, Sister."

The lady laughed in a soft Arkansas voice and said, "Well, you know, Mr. Johnson, they say, You're only a child once. Have you children of your own?"

Uncle Willie looked at me with an impatience I hadn't seen in his face even when he took thirty minutes to loop the laces over his high-topped shoes. "I . . . I thought I told you to go . . . go outside and play."

Before I left I saw him lean back on the shelves of Garret Snuff, Prince Albert, and Spark Plug chewing tobacco.

"No ma'am . . . no ch-children and no wife." He tried a laugh. "I have an old m-m-mother and my brother's t-two children to l-look after."

The couple left after a few minutes, and from the back of the house I watched the red car scare chickens, raise dust, and disappear toward Magnolia.

Uncle Willie was making his way down the long shadowed aisle between the shelves and the counter — hand over hand, like a man climbing out of a dream. I stayed quiet and watched him lurch from one side, bumping to the other, until he reached the coal-oil tank. He put his hand behind that dark recess and took his cane in the strong fist and shifted his weight on the wooden support. He thought he had pulled it off.

I'll never know why it was important to him that the couple (he said later that he'd never seen them before) would take a picture of a whole Mr. Johnson back to Little Rock. He must have tired of being crippled, as prisoners tire of penitentiary bars and the guilty tire of blame. The high-topped shoes and the cane, his uncontrollable muscles and thick tongue, and the looks he suffered of either contempt or pity had simply worn him out, and for one afternoon, one part of an afternoon, he wanted no part of them.

I understood and felt closer to him at the moment than ever before or since.

During these years in Stamps, I met and fell in love with William Shakespeare. He was my first white love. Although I enjoyed and respected Kipling, Poe, Butler, Thackeray, and Henley, I saved my young and loyal passion for Paul Lawrence Dunbar, Langston Hughes, James Weldon Johnson, and W.E.B. Du Bois's "Litany at Atlanta." But it was Shakespeare who said, "When in disgrace with fortune and men's eyes." It was a state with which I felt myself most familiar. I pacified myself about his whiteness by saying that after all he had been dead so long it couldn't matter to anyone anymore.

Bailey and I decided to memorize a scene from *The Merchant of Venice,* but we realized that Momma would question us about the author and that we'd have to tell her that Shakespeare was white, and it wouldn't matter to her whether he was dead or not. So we chose "The Creation" by James Weldon Johnson instead.

3

Until I was thirteen and left Arkansas for good, the Store was my favorite place to be. Alone and empty in the mornings, it looked like an unopened present from a stranger. Opening the front doors was pulling the ribbon off the unexpected gift. The light would come in softly (we faced north), easing itself over the shelves of mackerel, salmon, tobacco, thread. It fell flat on the big vat of lard and by noontime during the summer the grease had softened to a thick soup. Whenever I walked into the Store in the afternoon, I sensed that it was tired. I alone could hear the slow pulse of its job half done. But just before bedtime, after numerous people had walked in and out, had argued over their bills, or joked about their neighbors, or just dropped in "to give Sister Henderson a 'Hi y'all,'" the promise of magic mornings returned to the Store and spread itself over the family in washed life waves.

Momma opened boxes of crispy crackers and we sat around the meat block at the rear of the Store. I sliced onions, and Bailey opened two or even three cans of sardines and allowed their juice of oil and fishing boats to ooze down and around the sides. That was supper. In the evening, when we were alone like that, Uncle Willie didn't stutter or shake or give any indication that he had an "affliction." It seemed that the peace of a day's ending was an assurance that the covenant God made with children, Negroes, and the crippled was still in effect.

Throwing scoops of corn to the chickens and mixing sour dry mash with leftover food and oily dishwater for the hogs were among our evening chores. Bailey and I sloshed down twilight trails to the pigpens, and standing on the first fence rungs we poured down the unappealing concoctions to our grateful hogs. They mashed their tender pink snouts down into the slop, and rooted and grunted their satisfaction. We always grunted a reply only half in jest. We were also grateful that we had concluded the dirtiest of chores and had only gotten the evil-smelling swill on our shoes, stockings, feet, and hands.

Late one day, as we were attending to the pigs, I heard a horse in the front yard (it really should have been called a driveway, except that there was nothing to drive into it), and ran to find out who had come riding up on a Thursday evening. The used-to-be sheriff sat rakishly astraddle his horse. His nonchalance was meant to convey his authority and power over even dumb animals. How much more capable he would be with Negroes, it went without saying.

His twang jogged in the brittle air. From the side of the Store, Bailey and I heard him say to Momma, "Annie, tell Willie he better lay low to-night. A crazy nigger messed with a white lady today. Some of the boys'll be coming over here later." Even after the slow drag of years, I remember the sense of fear which filled my mouth with hot, dry air, and made my body light.

The "boys"? Those cement faces and eyes of hate that burned the clothes off you if they happened to see you lounging on the main street downtown on Saturday. Boys? It seemed that youth had never happened to them. Boys? No, rather men who were covered with graves' dust and age without beauty or learning. The ugliness and rottenness of old abominations.

If on Judgment Day I were summoned by St. Peter to give testimony to the used-to-be sheriff's act of kindness, I would be unable to say anything in his behalf. His confidence that my uncle and every other Black man who heard of the Klan's coming ride would scurry under their houses to hide in chicken droppings was too humiliating to hear. Without waiting for Momma's thanks, he rode out of the yard, sure that things were as they should be and that he was a gentle squire, saving those deserving serfs from the laws of the land, which he condoned.

Immediately, while his horse's hoofs were still loudly thudding the ground, Momma blew out the coal-oil lamps. She had a quiet, hard talk with Uncle Willie and called Bailey and me into the Store.

We were told to take the potatoes and onions out of their bins and knock out the dividing walls that kept them apart. Then with a tedious and fearful slowness Uncle Willie gave me his rubber-tipped cane and bent down to get into the now-enlarged empty bin. It took forever before he lay down flat, and then we covered him with potatoes and onions, layer upon layer, like a casserole. Grandmother knelt praying in the darkened Store.

It was fortunate that the "boys" didn't ride into our yard that evening and insist that Momma open the Store. They would have surely found Uncle Willie and just as surely lynched him. He moaned the whole night through as if he had, in fact, been guilty of some heinous crime. The heavy sounds pushed their way up out of the blanket of vegetables and I pictured his mouth pulling down on the right side and his saliva flowing into the eyes of new potatoes and waiting there like dewdrops for the warmth of morning.

4

Bailey was the greatest person in my world. And the fact that he was my brother, my only brother, and I had no sisters to share him with, was such good fortune that it made me want to live a Christian life just to show God that I was grateful. Where I was big, elbowy, and grating, he was small, graceful, and smooth. When I was described by our playmates as being shit color, he was lauded for his velvet-black skin. His hair fell down in black curls, and my head was covered with black steel wool. And yet he loved me.

When our elders said unkind things about my features (my family was handsome to a point of pain for me), Bailey would wink at me from across the room, and I knew that it was a matter of time before he would take revenge. He would allow the old ladies to finish wondering how on earth I came about, then he would ask, in a voice like cooling bacon grease, "Oh Mizeriz Coleman, how is your son? I saw him the other day, and he looked sick enough to die."

Aghast, the ladies would ask, "Die? From what? He ain't sick."

And in a voice oilier than the one before, he'd answer with a straight face, "From the Uglies."

I would hold my laugh, bite my tongue, grit my teeth, and very seriously erase even the touch of a smile from my face. Later, behind the house by the black-walnut tree, we'd laugh and laugh and howl. Bailey could count on very few punishments for his consistently outrageous behavior, for he was the pride of the Henderson/Johnson family.

His movements, as he was later to describe those of an acquaintance, were activated with oiled precision. He was also able to find more hours in the day than I thought existed. He finished chores, homework, read more books than I, and played the group games on the side of the hill with the best of them. He could even pray out loud in church, and was apt at stealing pickles from the barrel that sat under the fruit counter and Uncle Willie's nose.

After our early chores were done, while Uncle Willie or Momma minded the Store, we were free to play the children's games, as long as we stayed within yelling distance. Playing hide-and-seek, his voice was easily identified, singing, "Last night, night before, twenty-four robbers at my door. Who all is hid? Ask me to let them in, hit 'em in the head with a rolling pin. Who all is hid?" In follow-the-leader, naturally he was the one who created the most daring and interesting things to do. And when he was on the tail of the pop-the-whip, he would twirl off the end like a top, spinning, falling, laughing, finally stopping just before my heart beat its last, and then he was back in the game, still laughing.

Of all the needs (there are none imaginary) a lonely child has, the one that must be satisfied, if there is going to be hope and a hope of wholeness, is the unshaking need for an unshakable God. My pretty Black brother was my Kingdom Come.

In Stamps the segregation was so complete that most Black children didn't really, absolutely know what whites looked like. Other than that they were different, to be dreaded, and in that dread was included the hostility of the powerless against the powerful, the poor against the rich, the worker against the worked-for, and the ragged against the well-dressed. I remember never believing that whites were really real.

Many women who worked in their kitchens traded at our Store, and when they carried their finished laundry back to town they often set the big baskets down on our front porch to pull a singular piece from the starched collection and show either how graceful was their ironing hand or how rich and opulent was the property of their employers.

I looked at the items that weren't on display. I knew, for instance, that white men wore shorts, as Uncle Willie did, and that they had an opening for taking out their "things" and peeing, and that white women's breasts weren't built into their dresses, as people said, because I saw their brassieres in the baskets. But I couldn't force myself to think of them as people. People were Mrs. LaGrone, Mrs. Hendricks, Momma, Reverend Sneed, Lillie B, and Louise and Rex. Whitefolks couldn't be people because their feet were too small, their skin too white and see-throughy, and they didn't walk on the balls of their feet the way people did — they walked on their heels like horses.

People were those who lived on my side of town. I didn't like them all, or, in fact, any of them very much, but they were people. These others, the strange pale creatures that lived in their alien unlife, weren't considered folks. They were whitefolks.

5

Some families of powhitetrash lived on Momma's farmland behind the school. Sometimes a gaggle of them came to the Store, filling the whole room, chasing out the air, and even changing the well-known scents. The children crawled over the shelves and into the potato and onion bins, twanging all the time in their sharp voices like cigar-box guitars. They took liberties in my Store that I would never dare. Since Momma told us that the less you say to whitefolks (or even powhitetrash) the better, Bailey and I would stand, solemn, quiet, in the displaced air. But if one of the playful apparitions got close to us, I pinched it. Partly out of angry frustration and partly because I didn't believe in its flesh reality.

They called my uncle by his first name and ordered him around the Store. He, to my crying shame, obeyed them in his limping dip-straight-dip fashion. My grandmother, too, followed their orders, except that she didn't seem to be servile because she anticipated their needs.

"Here's sugar, Miz Potter, and here's baking powder. You didn't buy soda last month, you'll probably be needing some."

Momma always directed her statements to the adults, but sometimes, oh painful sometimes, the grimy, snotty-nosed girls would answer her. "Naw, Annie . . ." — to Momma? Who owned the land they lived on? Who forgot more than they would ever learn? If there was any justice in the world, God should strike them dumb at once! — "Just give us some extry sody crackers, and some more mackerel."

At least they never looked in her face, or I never caught them doing so. Nobody with a smidgen of training, not even the worst roustabout, would look right in a grown person's face. It meant the person was trying to take the words out before they were formed. The dirty little children didn't do that, but they threw their orders around the Store like lashes from a cat-o'-nine-tails.

When I was around ten years old, those scruffy children caused me the most painful and confusing experience I had ever had with my grandmother. One summer morning, after I had swept the dirt yard of leaves, spearmint-gum wrappers, and Vienna-sausage labels, I raked the yellow-red dirt, and made half-moons carefully, so that the design stood out clearly and masklike. I put the rake behind the Store and came through the back of the house to find Grandmother on the front porch in her big, wide white apron. The apron was so stiff by virtue of the starch that it could have stood alone. Momma was admiring the yard, so I joined her. It truly looked like a flat redhead that had been raked with a big-toothed comb. Momma didn't say anything but I knew she liked it. She looked around, hoping one of the community pillars would see the design before the day's business wiped it out. Then she looked upward toward the school. My head had swung with hers, so at just about the same time we saw a troop of the powhitetrash kids marching over the hill and down by the side of the school.

I looked to Momma for direction. She did an excellent job of sagging from her waist down, but from the waist up she seemed to be pulling for the top of the oak tree across the road. Then she began to moan a hymn. Maybe not to moan, but the tune was so slow and the meter so strange that she could have been moaning. She didn't look at me again. When the children reached halfway down the hill, halfway to the Store, she said without turning, "Sister, go on inside."

I wanted to beg her, "Momma, don't wait for them. Come on inside with me. If they come in the Store, you go to the bedroom and let me wait on them. They only frighten me if you're around. Alone I know how to handle them," but of course I couldn't say anything, so I went in and stood behind the screen door.

Before the girls got to the porch I heard their laughter crackling and popping like pine logs in a cooking stove. I suppose my lifelong paranoia was born in those cold, molasses-slow minutes. They came finally to stand on the ground in front of Momma. At first they pretended seriousness. Then one of them wrapped her right arm in the crook of her left, pushed out her mouth, and started to hum. I realized that she was aping my grandmother. Another said, "Naw, Helen, you ain't standing like her. This here's it." Then she lifted her chest, folded her arms, and mocked that strange carriage that was Annie Henderson. Another laughed. "Naw, you can't do it. Your mouth ain't pooched out enough. It's like this."

I thought about the rifle behind the door, but I knew I'd never be able to hold it straight, and the .410, our sawed-off shotgun, which stayed loaded and was fired every New Year's night, was locked in the trunk and Uncle Willie had the key on his chain. Through the fly-specked screen door, I could see that the arms of Momma's apron jiggled from the vibrations of her humming. But her knees seemed to have locked as if they would never bend again.

She sang on. No louder than before, but no softer either. No slower or faster.

The dirt of the girls' cotton dresses continued on their legs, feet, arms, and faces to make them all of a piece. Their greasy uncolored hair hung down, uncombed, with a grim finality. I knelt to see them better, to remember them for all time. The tears that had slipped down my

dress left unsurprising dark spots, and made the front yard blurry and
even more unreal. The world had taken a deep breath and was having
doubts about continuing to revolve.

The girls had tired of mocking Momma and turned to other means
of agitation. One crossed her eyes, stuck her thumbs in both sides of her
mouth, and said, "Look here, Annie." Grandmother hummed on and
the apron strings trembled. I wanted to throw a handful of black pepper
in their faces, to throw lye on them, to scream that they were dirty,
scummy peckerwoods, but I knew I was as clearly imprisoned behind
the scene as the actors outside were confined to their roles.

One of the smaller girls did a kind of puppet dance while her fellow
clowns laughed at her. But the tall one, who was almost a woman, said
something very quietly, which I couldn't hear. They all moved backward
from the porch, still watching Momma. For an awful second I thought
they were going to throw a rock at Momma, who seemed (except for the
apron strings) to have turned into stone herself. But the big girl turned
her back, bent down, and put her hands flat on the ground — she didn't
pick up anything. She simply shifted her weight and did a handstand.

Her dirty bare feet and long legs went straight for the sky. Her dress
fell down around her shoulders, and she had on no drawers. The slick
pubic hair made a brown triangle where her legs came together. She
hung in the vacuum of that lifeless morning for only a few seconds,
then wavered and tumbled. The other girls clapped her on the back and
slapped their hands.

Momma changed her song to "Bread of Heaven, bread of Heaven,
feed me till I want no more."

I found that I was praying too. How long could Momma hold out?
What new indignity would they think of to subject her to? Would I be
able to stay out of it? What would Momma really like me to do?

Then they were moving out of the yard, on their way to town. They
bobbed their heads and shook their slack behinds and turned, one at a
time:

"'Bye, Annie."

"'Bye, Annie."

"'Bye, Annie."

Momma never turned her head or unfolded her arms, but she
stopped singing and said, "'Bye, Miz Helen, 'bye, Miz Ruth, 'bye, Miz
Eloise."

I burst. A firecracker July-the-Fourth burst. How could Momma call
them Miz? The mean nasty things. Why couldn't she have come inside

the sweet, cold Store when we saw them breasting the hill? What did she prove? And then if they were dirty, mean, and impudent, why did Momma have to call them Miz?

She stood another whole song through and then opened the screen door to look down on me crying in rage. She looked until I looked up. Her face was a brown moon that shone on me. She was beautiful. Something had happened out there, which I couldn't completely understand, but I could see that she was happy. Then she bent down and touched me as mothers of the church "lay hands on the sick and afflicted" and I quieted.

"Go wash your face, Sister." And she went behind the candy counter and hummed, "Glory, glory, hallelujah, when I lay my burden down." I threw the well water on my face and used the weekday handkerchief to blow my nose. Whatever the contest had been out front, I knew Momma had won.

I took the rake back to the front yard. The smudged footprints were easy to erase. I worked for a long time on my new design and laid the rake behind the wash pot. When I came back in the Store, I took Momma's hand and we both walked outside to look at the pattern.

It was a large heart with lots of hearts growing smaller inside, and piercing from the outside rim to the smallest heart was an arrow. Momma said, "Sister, that's right pretty." Then she turned back to the Store and resumed, "Glory, glory hallelujah, when I lay my burden down."

1971

Lewis Thomas

The Lives of a Cell

WE ARE TOLD that the trouble with Modern Man is that he has been trying to detach himself from nature. He sits in the topmost tiers of polymer, glass, and steel, dangling his pulsing legs, surveying at a distance the writhing life of the planet. In this scenario, Man comes on as a stupendous lethal force, and the earth is pictured as something delicate, like rising bubbles at the surface of a country pond, or flights of fragile birds.

But it is illusion to think that there is anything fragile about the life of the earth; surely this is the toughest membrane imaginable in the universe, opaque to probability, impermeable to death. We are the delicate part, transient and vulnerable as cilia. Nor is it a new thing for man to invent an existence that he imagines to be above the rest of life; this has been his most consistent intellectual exertion down the millennia. As illusion, it has never worked out to his satisfaction in the past, any more than it does today. Man is embedded in nature.

The biologic science of recent years has been making this a more urgent fact of life. The new, hard problem will be to cope with the dawning, intensifying realization of just how interlocked we are. The old, clung-to notions most of us have held about our special lordship are being deeply undermined.

Item. A good case can be made for our nonexistence as entities. We are not made up, as we had always supposed, of successively enriched packets of our own parts. We are shared, rented, occupied. At the interior of our cells, driving them, providing the oxidative energy that

First published in *The New England Journal of Medicine* in 1971; collected in *The Lives of a Cell*, 1974.

sends us out for the improvement of each shining day, are the mitochondria, and in a strict sense they are not ours. They turn out to be little separate creatures, the colonial posterity of migrant prokaryocytes, probably primitive bacteria that swam into ancestral precursors of our eukaryotic cells and stayed there. Ever since, they have maintained themselves and their ways, replicating in their own fashion, privately, with their own DNA and RNA quite different from ours. They are as much symbionts as the rhizobial bacteria in the roots of beans. Without them, we would not move a muscle, drum a finger, think a thought.

Mitochondria are stable and responsible lodgers, and I choose to trust them. But what of the other little animals, similarly established in my cells, sorting and balancing me, clustering me together? My centrioles, basal bodies, and probably a good many other more obscure tiny beings at work inside my cells, each with its own special genome, are as foreign, and as essential, as aphids in anthills. My cells are no longer the pure line entities I was raised with; they are ecosystems more complex than Jamaica Bay.

I like to think that they work in my interest, that each breath they draw for me, but perhaps it is they who walk through the local park in the early morning, sensing my senses, listening to my music, thinking my thoughts.

I am consoled, somewhat, by the thought that the green plants are in the same fix. They could not be plants, or green, without their chloroplasts, which run the photosynthetic enterprise and generate oxygen for the rest of us. As it turns out, chloroplasts are also separate creatures with their own genomes, speaking their own language.

We carry stores of DNA in our nuclei that may have come in, at one time or another, from the fusion of ancestral cells and the linking of ancestral organisms in symbiosis. Our genomes are catalogues of instructions from all kinds of sources in nature, filed for all kinds of contingencies. As for me, I am grateful for differentiation and speciation, but I cannot feel as separate an entity as I did a few years ago, before I was told these things, nor, I should think, can anyone else.

Item. The uniformity of the earth's life, more astonishing than its diversity, is accountable by the high probability that we derived, originally, from some single cell, fertilized in a bolt of lightning as the earth cooled. It is from the progeny of this parent cell that we take our looks; we still share genes around, and the resemblance of the enzymes of grasses to those of whales is a family resemblance.

The viruses, instead of being single-minded agents of disease and death, now begin to look more like mobile genes. Evolution is still an infinitely long and tedious biologic game, with only the winners staying at the table, but the rules are beginning to look more flexible. We live in a dancing matrix of viruses; they dart, rather like bees, from organism to organism, from plant to insect to mammal to me and back again, and into the sea, tugging along pieces of this genome, strings of genes from that, transplanting grafts of DNA, passing around heredity as though at a great party. They may be a mechanism for keeping new, mutant kinds of DNA in the widest circulation among us. If this is true, the odd virus disease, on which we must focus so much of our attention in medicine, may be looked on as an accident, something dropped.

Item. I have been trying to think of the earth as a kind of organism, but it is no go. I cannot think of it this way. It is too big, too complex, with too many working parts lacking visible connections. The other night, driving through a hilly, wooded part of southern New England, I wondered about this. If not like an organism, what is it like, what is it *most* like? Then, satisfactorily for that moment, it came to me: it is *most* like a single cell.

John McPhee

···

The Search for Marvin Gardens

Go. I roll the dice — a six and a two. Through the air I move my token, the flatiron, to Vermont Avenue, where dog packs range.

The dogs are moving (some are limping) through ruins, rubble, fire damage, open garbage. Doorways are gone. Lath is visible in the crumbling walls of the buildings. The street sparkles with shattered glass. I have never seen, anywhere, so many broken windows. A sign — "Slow, Children at Play" — has been bent backward by an automobile. At the lighthouse, the dogs turn up Pacific and disappear. George Meade, Army engineer, built the lighthouse — brick upon brick, six hundred thousand bricks, to reach up high enough to throw a beam twenty miles over the sea. Meade, seven years later, saved the Union at Gettysburg.

·

I buy Vermont Avenue for $100. My opponent is a tall, shadowy figure, across from me, but I know him well, and I know his game like a favorite tune. If he can, he will always go for the quick kill. And when it is foolish to go for the quick kill he will be foolish. On the whole, though, he is a master assessor of percentages. It is a mistake to underestimate him. His eleven carries his top hat to St. Charles Place, which he buys for $140.

·

The sidewalks of St. Charles Place have been cracked to shards by through-growing weeds. There are no buildings. Mansions, hotels once

---

First published in *The New Yorker*, 1972; collected in **Pieces of the Frame*, 1975.

stood here. A few street lamps now drop cones of light on broken glass and vacant space behind a chain-link fence that some great machine has in places bent to the ground. Five plane trees — in full summer leaf, flecking the light — are all that live on St. Charles Place.

.

Block upon block, gradually, we are cancelling each other out — in the blues, the lavenders, the oranges, the greens. My opponent follows a plan of his own devising. I use the Hornblower & Weeks opening and the Zuricher defense. The first game draws tight, will soon finish. In 1971, a group of people in Racine, Wisconsin, played for seven hundred and sixty-eight hours. A game begun a month later in Danville, California, lasted eight hundred and twenty hours. These are official records, and they stun us. We have been playing for eight minutes. It amazes us that Monopoly is thought of as a long game. It is possible to play to a complete, absolute, and final conclusion in less than fifteen minutes, all within the rules as written. My opponent and I have done so thousands of times. No wonder we are sitting across from each other now in this best-of-seven series for the international singles championship of the world.

.

On Illinois Avenue, three men lean out from second-story windows. A girl is coming down the street. She wears dungarees and a bright-red shirt, has ample breasts and a Hadendoan Afro, a black halo, two feet in diameter. Ice rattles in the glasses in the hands of the men.

"Hey, sister!"

"Come on up!"

She looks up, looks from one to another to the other, looks them flat in the eye.

"What for?" she says, and she walks on.

.

I buy Illinois for $240. It solidifies my chances, for I already own Kentucky and Indiana. My opponent pales. If he had landed first on Illinois, the game would have been over then and there, for he has houses built on Boardwalk and Park Place, we share the railroads equally, and we have cancelled each other everywhere else. We never trade.

.

In 1852, R. B. Osborne, an immigrant Englishman, civil engineer, sur-
veyed the route of a railroad line that would run from Camden to
Absecon Island, in New Jersey, traversing the state from the Delaware
River to the barrier beaches of the sea. He then sketched in the plan of a
"bathing village" that would surround the eastern terminus of the line.
His pen flew glibly, framing and naming spacious avenues parallel to
the shore — Mediterranean, Baltic, Oriental, Ventnor — and narrower
transsecting avenues: North Carolina, Pennsylvania, Vermont, Connecticut, States, Virginia, Tennessee, New York, Kentucky, Indiana, Illi-
nois. The place as a whole had no name, so when he had completed
the plan Osborne wrote in large letters over the ocean, "Atlantic City."
No one ever challenged the name, or the names of Osborne's streets.
Monopoly was invented in the early nineteen-thirties by Charles B.
Darrow, but Darrow was only transliterating what Osborne had created. The railroads, crucial to any player, were the making of Atlantic
City. After the rails were down, houses and hotels burgeoned from
Mediterranean and Baltic to New York and Kentucky. Properties —
building lots — sold for as little as six dollars apiece and as much as a
thousand dollars. The original investors in the railroads and the real estate called themselves the Camden & Atlantic Land Company. Rever-
ently, I repeat their names: Dwight Bell, William Coffin, John DaCosta,
Daniel Deal, William Fleming, Andrew Hay, Joseph Porter, Jonathan
Pitney, Samuel Richards — founders, fathers, forerunners, archetypical
masters of the quick kill.

•

My opponent and I are now in a deep situation of classical Monopoly. The torsion is almost perfect — Boardwalk and Park Place versus
the brilliant reds. His cash position is weak, though, and if I escape him
now he may fade. I land on Luxury Tax, contiguous to but in sanctuary
from his power. I have four houses on Indiana. He lands there. He
concedes.

•

Indiana Avenue was the address of the Brighton Hotel, gone now.
The Brighton was exclusive — a word that no longer has retail value in
the city. If you arrived by automobile and tried to register at the Brighton, you were sent away. Brighton-class people came in private railroad
cars. Brighton-class people had other private railroad cars for their
horses — dawn rides on the firm sand at water's edge, skirts flying. Col-

onel Anthony J. Drexel Biddle — the sort of name that would constrict throats in Philadelphia — lived, much of the year, in the Brighton.

•

Colonel Sanders' fried chicken is on Kentucky Avenue. So is Clifton's Club Harlem, with the Sepia Revue and the Sepia Follies, featuring the Honey Bees, the Fashions, and the Lords.

•

My opponent and I, many years ago, played 2,428 games of Monopoly in a single season. He was then a recent graduate of the Harvard Law School, and he was working for a downtown firm, looking up law. Two people we knew — one from Chase Manhattan, the other from Morgan, Stanley — tried to get into the game, but after a few rounds we found that they were not in the conversation and we sent them home. Monopoly should always be *mano a mano* anyway. My opponent won 1,199 games, and so did I. Thirty were ties. He was called into the Army, and we stopped just there. Now, in Game 2 of the series, I go immediately to jail, and again to jail while my opponent seines property. He is dumbfoundingly lucky. He wins in twelve minutes.

•

Visiting hours are daily, eleven to two; Sunday, eleven to one; evenings, six to nine. "NO MINORS, NO FOOD, Immediate Family Only Allowed in Jail." All this above a blue steel door in a blue cement wall in the windowless interior of the basement of the city hall. The desk sergeant sits opposite the door to the jail. In a cigar box in front of him are pills in every color, a banquet of fruit salad an inch and a half deep — leapers, co-pilots, footballs, truck drivers, peanuts, blue angels, yellow jackets, redbirds, rainbows. Near the desk are two soldiers, waiting to go through the blue door. They are about eighteen years old. One of them is trying hard to light a cigarette. His wrists are in steel cuffs. A military policeman waits, too. He is a year or so older than the soldiers, taller, studious in appearance, gentle, fat. On a bench against a wall sits a good-looking girl in slacks. The blue door rattles, swings heavily open. A turnkey stands in the doorway. "Don't you guys kill yourselves back there now," says the sergeant to the soldiers.

"One kid, he overdosed himself about ten and a half hours ago," says the M.P.

The M.P., the soldiers, the turnkey, and the girl on the bench are white. The sergeant is black. "If you take off the handcuffs, take off the belts," says the sergeant to the M.P. "I don't want them hanging themselves back there." The door shuts and its tumblers move. When it opens again, five minutes later, a young white man in sandals and dungarees and a blue polo shirt emerges. His hair is in a ponytail. He has no beard. He grins at the good-looking girl. She rises, joins him. The sergeant hands him a manila envelope. From it he removes his belt and a small notebook. He borrows a pencil, makes an entry in the notebook. He is out of jail, free. What did he do? He offended Atlantic City in some way. He spent a night in the jail. In the nineteen-thirties, men visiting Atlantic City went to jail, directly to jail, did not pass Go, for appearing in topless bathing suits on the beach. A city statute requiring all men to wear full-length bathing suits was not seriously challenged until 1937, and the first year in which a man could legally go bare-chested on the beach was 1940.

·

Game 3. After seventeen minutes, I am ready to begin construction on overpriced and sluggish Pacific, North Carolina, and Pennsylvania. Nothing else being open, opponent concedes.

·

The physical profile of streets perpendicular to the shore is something like a playground slide. It begins in the high skyline of Boardwalk hotels, plummets into warrens of "side-avenue" motels, crosses Pacific, slopes through church missions, convalescent homes, burlesque houses, rooming houses, and liquor stores, crosses Atlantic, and runs level through the bombed-out ghetto as far — Baltic, Mediterranean — as the eye can see. North Carolina Avenue, for example, is flanked at its beach end by the Chalfonte and the Haddon Hall (908 rooms, air-conditioned), where, according to one biographer, John Philip Sousa (1854–1932) first played when he was twenty-two, insisting, even then, that everyone call him by his entire name. Behind these big hotels, motels — Barbizon, Catalina — crouch. Between Pacific and Atlantic is an occasional house from 1910 — wooden porch, wooden mullions, old yellow paint — and two churches, a package store, a strip show, a dealer in fruits and vegetables. Then, beyond Atlantic Avenue, North Carolina moves on into the vast ghetto, the bulk of the city, and it looks like Metz in 1919, Cologne in 1944. Nothing has actually exploded. It is not bomb damage. It is deep and complex decay. Roofs are off. Bricks are scattered in the street. People sit on porches, six deep, at nine on a Monday morning. When they go off to wait in unemployment lines, they wait sometimes two hours. Between Mediterranean and Baltic runs a chain-link fence, enclosing rubble. A patrol car sits idling by the curb. In the back seat is a German shepherd. A sign on the fence says, "Beware of Bad Dogs."

Mediterranean and Baltic are the principal avenues of the ghetto. Dogs are everywhere. A pack of seven passes me. Block after block, there are three-story brick row houses. Whole segments of them are abandoned, a thousand broken windows. Some parts are intact, occupied. A mattress lies in the street, soaking in a pool of water. Wet stuffing is coming out of the mattress. A postman is having a rye and a beer in the Plantation Bar at nine-fifteen in the morning. I ask him idly if he knows where Marvin Gardens is. He does not. "HOOKED AND NEED HELP? CONTACT N.A.R.C.O." "REVIVAL NOW GOING ON, CONDUCTED BY REVEREND H. HENDERSON OF TEXAS." These are signboards on Mediterranean and Baltic. The second one is upside down and leans against a boarded-up window of the Faith Temple Church of God in Christ. There is an old peeling poster on a warehouse wall showing a figure in an electric chair. "The Black Panther Manifesto" is the title of the poster, and its message is, or was, that "the fascists have already decided in advance to murder Chairman Bobby Seale in the electric chair." I pass an old woman who carries a bucket. She wears blue sneakers, worn through. Her feet spill out. She wears red socks, rolled at the knees. A white handkerchief, spread over her head, is knotted at the corners. Does she know where Marvin Gardens is? "I sure don't know," she says, setting down the bucket. "I sure don't know. I've heard of it somewhere, but I just can't say where." I walk on, through a block of shattered glass. The glass crunches underfoot like coarse sand. I remember when I first came here — a long train ride from Trenton, long ago, games of poker in the train — to play basketball against Atlantic City. We were half black, they were all black. We scored forty points, they scored eighty, or something like it. What I remember most is that they had glass backboards — glittering, pendent, expensive glass backboards, a rarity then in high schools, even in colleges, the only ones we played on all year.

I turn on Pennsylvania, and start back toward the sea. The windows of the Hotel Astoria, on Pennsylvania near Baltic, are boarded up. A sheet of unpainted plywood is the door, and in it is a triangular peephole that now frames an eye. The plywood door opens. A man answers my question. Rooms there are six, seven, and ten dollars a week. I thank him for the information and move on, emerging from the ghetto at the Catholic Daughters of America Women's Guest House, between Atlantic and Pacific. Between Pacific and the Boardwalk are the blinking vacancy signs of the Aristocrat and Colton Manor motels. Pennsylvania terminates at the Sheraton-Seaside — thirty-two dollars a day, ocean corner. I take a walk on the Boardwalk and into the Holiday Inn (twenty-three stories). A guest is registering. "You reserved for Wednesday, and this is Monday," the clerk tells him. "But that's all right. We have *plenty* of rooms." The clerk is very young, female, and has soft brown hair that hangs below her waist. Her superior kicks her.

He is a middle-aged man with red spiderwebs in his face. He is jacketed and tied. He takes her aside. "Don't say 'plenty,'" he says. "Say 'You are fortunate, sir. We have rooms available.'"

The face of the young woman turns sour. "We have all the rooms you need," she says to the customer, and, to her superior, "How's that?"

·

Game 4. My opponent's luck has become abrasive. He has Boardwalk and Park Place, and has sealed the board.

·

Darrow was a plumber. He was, specifically, a radiator repairman who lived in Germantown, Pennsylvania. His first Monopoly board was a sheet of linoleum. On it he placed houses and hotels that he had carved from blocks of wood. The game he thus invented was brilliantly conceived, for it was an uncannily exact reflection of the business milieu at large. In its depth, range, and subtlety, in its luck-skill ratio, in its sense of infrastructure and socio-economic parameters, in its philosophical characteristics, it reached to the profundity of the financial community. It was as scientific as the stock market. It suggested the manner and means through which an underdeveloped world had been developed. It was chess at Wall Street level. "Advance token to the nearest Railroad and pay owner twice the rental to which he is otherwise entitled. If Railroad is unowned, you may buy it from the Bank. Get out of Jail, free. Advance token to nearest Utility. If unowned, you may buy it from Bank. If owned, throw dice and pay owner a total ten times the amount thrown. You are assessed for street repairs: $40 per house, $115

per hotel. Pay poor tax of $15. Go to Jail. Go directly to Jail. Do not pass
Go. Do not collect $200."

•

The turnkey opens the blue door. The turnkey is known to the inmates as Sidney K. Above his desk are ten closed-circuit-TV screens —
assorted viewpoints of the jail. There are three cellblocks — men,
women, juvenile boys. Six days is the average stay. Showers twice a week.
The steel doors and the equipment that operates them were made in
San Antonio. The prisoners sleep on bunks of butcher block. There are
no mattresses. There are three prisoners to a cell. In winter, it is cold in
here. Prisoners burn newspapers to keep warm. Cell corners are black
with smudge. The jail is three years old. The men's block echoes with
chatter. The man in the cell nearest Sidney K. is pacing. His shirt is covered with broad stains of blood. The block for juvenile boys is, by contrast, utterly silent — empty corridor, empty cells. There is only one
prisoner. He is small and black and appears to be thirteen. He says he is
sixteen and that he has been alone in here for three days.
  "Why are you here? What did you do?"
  "I hit a jitney driver."

•

The series stands at three all. We have split the fifth and sixth games.
We are scrambling for property. Around the board we fairly fly. We
move so fast because we do our own banking and search our own
deeds. My opponent grows tense.

•

Ventnor Avenue, a street of delicatessens and doctors' offices, is leafy
with plane trees and hydrangeas, the city flower. Water Works is on the
mainland. The water comes over in submarine pipes. Electric Company
gets power from across the state, on the Delaware River, in Deepwater.
States Avenue, now a wasteland like St. Charles, once had gardens running down the middle of the street, a horse-drawn trolley, private
homes. States Avenue was as exclusive as the Brighton. Only an apartment house, a small motel, and the All Wars Memorial Building — mo-
nadnocks spaced widely apart — stand along States Avenue now. Pawnshops, convalescent homes, and the Paradise Soul Saving Station are on
Virginia Avenue. The soul-saving station is pink, orange, and yellow. In
the windows flanking the door of the Virginia Money Loan Office are

Nikons, Polaroids, Yashicas, Sony TVs, Underwood typewriters, Singer sewing machines, and pictures of Christ. On the far side of town, beside a single track and locked up most of the time, is the new railroad station, a small hut made of glazed firebrick, all that is left of the lines that built the city. An authentic phrenologist works on New York Avenue close to Frank's Extra Dry Bar and a church where the sermon today is "Death in the Pot." The church is of pink brick, has blue and amber windows and two red doors. St. James Place, narrow and twisting, is lined with boarding houses that have wooden porches on each of three stories, suggesting a New Orleans made of salt-bleached pine. In a vacant lot on Tennessee is a white Ford station wagon stripped to the chassis. The windows are smashed. A plastic Clorox bottle sits on the driver's seat. The wind has pressed newspaper against the chain-link fence around the lot. Atlantic Avenue, the city's principal thoroughfare, could be seventeen American Main Streets placed end to end — discount vitamins and Vienna Corset shops, movie theatres, shoe stores, and funeral homes. The Boardwalk is made of yellow pine and Douglas fir, soaked in pentachlorophenol. Downbeach, it reaches far beyond the city. Signs everywhere — on windows, lampposts, trash baskets — proclaim "Bienvenue Canadiens!" The salt air is full of Canadian French. In the Claridge Hotel, on Park Place, I ask a clerk if she knows where Marvin Gardens is. She says, "Is it a floral shop?" I ask a cabdriver, parked outside. He says, "Never heard of it." Park Place is one block long, Pacific to Boardwalk. On the roof of the Claridge is the Solarium, the highest point in town — panoramic view of the ocean, the bay, the salt-water ghetto. I look down at the rooftops of the side-avenue motels and into swimming pools. There are hundreds of people around the rooftop pools, sunbathing, reading — many more people than are on the beach. Walls, windows, and a block of sky are all that is visible from these pools — no sand, no sea. The pools are craters, and with the people around them they are countersunk into the motels.

•

The seventh, and final, game is ten minutes old and I have hotels on Oriental, Vermont, and Connecticut. I have Tennessee and St. James. I have North Carolina and Pacific. I have Boardwalk, Atlantic, Ventnor, Illinois, Indiana. My fingers are forming a "V." I have mortgaged most of these properties in order to pay for others, and I have mortgaged the others to pay for the hotels. I have seven dollars. I will pay off the mortgages and build my reserves with income from the three hotels. My cash position may be low, but I feel like a rocket in an underground silo. Meanwhile, if I could just go to jail for a time I could pause there, wait there, until my opponent, in his inescapable rounds, pays the rates of my hotels. Jail, at times, is the strategic place to be. I roll boxcars from the Reading and move the flatiron to Community Chest. "Go to Jail. Go directly to Jail."

•

The prisoners, of course, have no pens and no pencils. They take paper napkins, roll them tight as crayons, char the ends with matches, and write on the walls. The things they write are not entirely idiomatic; for example, "In God We Trust." All is in carbon. Time is required in the writing. "Only humanity could know of such pain." "God So Loved the World." "There is no greater pain than life itself." In the women's block now, there are six blacks, giggling, and a white asleep in red shoes. She is drunk. The others are pushers, prostitutes, an auto thief, a burglar caught with pistol in purse. A sixteen-year-old accused of murder was in here last week. These words are written on the wall of a now empty cell: "Laying here I see two bunks about six inches thick, not counting the one I'm laying on, which is hard as brick. No cushion for my back. No pillow for my head. Just a couple scratchy blankets which is best to use it's said. I wake up in the morning so shivery and cold, waiting and waiting till I am told the food is coming. It's on its way. It's not worth waiting for, but I eat it anyway. I know one thing when they set me free I'm gonna be good if it kills me."

•

How many years must a game be played to produce an Anthony J. Drexel Biddle and chestnut geldings on the beach? About half a century was the original answer, from the first railroad to Biddle at his peak. Biddle, at his peak, hit an Atlantic City streetcar conductor with his fist, laid him out with one punch. This increased Biddle's legend. He did not go to jail. While John Philip Sousa led his band along the Boardwalk playing "The Stars and Stripes Forever" and Jack Dempsey ran up and down in training for his fight with Gene Tunney, the city crossed the high curve of its parabola. Al Capone held conventions here — upstairs with his sleeves rolled, apportioning among his lieutenant governors the states of the Eastern seaboard. The natural history of an American resort proceeds from Indians to French Canadians via Biddles and Capones. French Canadians, whatever they may be at home, are Visigoths here. Bienvenue Visigoths!

．

My opponent plods along incredibly well. He has got his fourth railroad, and patiently, unbelievably, he has picked up my potential winners until he has blocked me everywhere but Marvin Gardens. He has avoided, in the fifty-dollar zoning, my increasingly petty hotels. His cash flow swells. His railroads are costing me two hundred dollars a minute. He is building hotels on States, Virginia, and St. Charles. He has temporarily reversed the current. With the yellow monopolies and my blue monopolies, I could probably defeat his lavenders and his railroads. I have Atlantic and Ventnor. I need Marvin Gardens. My only hope is Marvin Gardens.

．

There is a plaque at Boardwalk and Park Place, and on it in relief is the leonine profile of a man who looks like an officer in a metropolitan bank — "Charles B. Darrow, 1889–1967, inventor of the game of Monopoly." "Darrow," I address him, aloud. "Where is Marvin Gardens?" There is, of course, no answer. Bronze, impassive, Darrow looks south down the Boardwalk. "Mr. Darrow, please, where is Marvin Gardens?" Nothing. Not a sign. He just looks south down the Boardwalk.

．

My opponent accepts the trophy with his natural ease, and I make, from notes, remarks that are even less graceful than his.

．

Marvin Gardens is the one color-block Monopoly property that is not in Atlantic City. It is a suburb within a suburb, secluded. It is a planned compound of seventy-two handsome houses set on curvilinear private streets under yews and cedars, poplars and willows. The compound was built around 1920, in Margate, New Jersey, and consists of solid buildings of stucco, brick, and wood, with slate roofs, tile roofs, multi-mullioned porches, Giraldic towers, and Spanish grilles. Marvin Gardens, the ultimate outwash of Monopoly, is a citadel and sanctuary of the middle class. "We're heavily patrolled by police here. We don't take no chances. Me? I'm living here nine years. I paid seventeen thousand dollars and I've been offered thirty. Number one, I don't want to move. Number two, I don't need the money. I have four bedrooms, two and a half baths, front den, back den. No basement. The Atlantic is down there. Six feet down and you float. A lot of people have a hard time finding this place. People that lived in Atlantic City all their life don't know how to find it. They don't know where the hell they're going. They just know it's south, down the Boardwalk."

William H. Gass

....

The Doomed in Their Sinking

CRANE WENT sudden as a springboard. The Gulf gave nothing back. My mother, I remember, took her time. She held the house around her as she held her bathrobe, safely doorpinned down its floorlength, the metal threads glinting like those gay gold loops which close the coat of a grenadier, though there were gaps of course . . . unseemly as sometimes a door is on a chain . . . so that to urinate she had to hoist the whole thing like a skirt, collecting the cloth in fat pleats with her fingers, wads which soon out-oozed her fists and sprang slowly away . . . one conse-quence . . . so that she felt she had to hover above the hole, the seat (clouds don't care about *their* aim), unsteadily . . . necessarily . . . more and more so as the nighttime days drew on, so that the robe grew damp the way the sweater on a long drink grows, soggy from edge to center, until I found I cared with what success she peed when what she swal-lowed was herself and what streamed out of her in consequence seemed me.

Though Hart shed his bathrobe frugally before he jumped, my mother, also saving, would have worn hers like the medal on a hussar straight through living room and loony bin, every nursing home and needle house we put her in, if those points hadn't had to come out (they confiscate your pins, belts, buckles, jewelry, teeth, and they'd take the air, too, if it had an edge, because the crazy can garrote themselves with a length of breath, their thoughts are open razors, their eyes go off like guns), though there was naturally no danger in these baubles to herself, for my mother was living the long death, her whole life passing before

First published in *The New York Review of Books,* 1972; revised and collected in **The World Within the Word,* 1978.

her as she went, the way those who drown themselves are said to have theirs pass . . . and consequence, yes . . . her own ocean like a message in a bottle so that she sank slowly somewhere as a stone sill sinks beneath the shoes of pilgrims and tourists, not like Plath with pills, or Crane or Woolf with water, Plath again by gas, or Berryman from a bridge, but, I now believe, in the best way possible, because the long death is much more painful and punishing than even disembowelment or bleach, and it inflicts your dying on those you are blaming for it better than burning or blowing up — during an exquisitely extended stretch — since the same substance which both poisons you, preserves, you both have and eat, enjoy and suffer your revenges together, as well as the illusion that you can always change your mind.

Yet my mother wasn't what we call a suicide even though she died as though she'd cut her throat when the vessels burst there finally, and my father, who clenched his teeth till neither knees nor elbows would unfist, dying of his own murderous wishes like the scorpion who's supposed to sting itself to death — no — he wasn't one either: both had a terribly tenacious grip on life . . . so that some suicides will survive anything, and many who court death have no desire to wed her . . . it mixes us up . . .

Should a suicide be regarded as the last stage of a series of small acts against the self, since the murderer who arsenics his wife little by little is still a murderer though she takes a decade dying; or does this confuse kinds of hostility in a serious way, because harsh words aren't the same as blows or their bruises, desire isn't adultery whatever Jesus preached, not even a degree of it? Cigarettes shorten our life, but the alcoholic's fuddle mimics death (the loss of control, the departure of the soul) in a way the smoker's never does. What can we make of that? We shall manage something.

My mother managed. She was what we call a dedicated passive . . . liquidly acquiescent . . . supinely on the go. Still, she went in her own way — the way, for instance, her robe was fastened.

Socrates acquiesced in his own execution, others demand theirs. The Kamikaze pilot intends his death, but does not desire it. Malcolm Lowry, who choked on his vomit, evidently desired his, but did not intend it. Soldiers charging the guns at Verdun neither wished for death nor were bent on it, though death was what they expected. My mother accepted.

I used to think my father was the actively aggressive one because

while he sat, temporized, bided and brooded and considered and consolidated, he growled, swore, and made horrible faces.

During the decline of Christian morals, few groups have risen so rapidly in the overall estimation of society. It was dangerous for Donne to
suggest that suicide was sometimes not a sin. It was still daring for
Hume to reason that it was sometimes not a crime. Later one had to
point out that it was sometimes not simply a sickness of the soul. Now
it seems necessary to argue that it is sometimes not a virtue.

To paraphrase Freud, what does a suicide want? Not what he gets,
surely.

Some simply think of death as the absence of their present state, a
state which pursues them like a malignant disease and which cannot be
otherwise escaped. Others consider it quite positively, as though to die
were to get on in the world. Seventh Heaven, after all, is a most desirable
address. Still others spend their life like money, purchasing this or that,
but their aim is to buy, not to go broke. Are we to say to them (all and
every kind) what we often say to children? no, Freddie, you don't want a
pet boa, you wouldn't like the way it swallows mice.

It doesn't follow at all that because it is easy enough to kill yourself, it
is easy enough to get, in that case, what you want. Can you really be said
to want what you cannot possibly understand? or what you are in abys-
mal confusion about? or what is provenly contrary to your interests? or
is plainly impossible? Is "I'd rather be dead" anything like: "I want to be
a chewed-up marshmallow"; or: "I want 6 and 3 to make 10"; or: "I
want to be a Fiji princess"; or: "I want a foot-long dong"; or: "I want
that seventh scotch-on-the-rocks"; or "I would love to make it with
Lena Horne"?

It's been said that suicide is a crime of status. Poverty limits it, as it
virtuously inhibits so many other vices. It occurs, we are also told, when
its victim is not properly folded into the general batter of society, and
when external constraints upon one's behavior are weak. (The super-
ego, however, can come down on conscience like a hammer.) So suicide
is a disease of singularity and selfhood, because as we are elevated in the
social system, and authorities "over" us are removed, as we wobble out
on our own, the question of whether it is better to be or not to be arises
with real relevance for the first time, since the burden of being is felt
most fully by the self-determining self.

In a sense, society has already rejected the prospective suicide, hurled
him overboard as Jonah was. His beliefs, all that was beloved, have for-

saken him. He is a jinx. Once in the water, is it his fault he drowns? Hamlet, of course, has too many motives. Death and adultery have parted him from his family — murder and adultery from his king — imbecility from his love. He's in the firmly impalpable grip of guilt. Above all, he is too fine a spirit for this wormy world. Don't we often think so?

The logic of misery hides its premises to forget its fallacies: Hamlet's a prison; Hamlet's a Dane; Denmark's a prison; then is the world one.

On the other hand, if I were to commit suicide, I am sure it would be from a surfeit of family and society, in a desperate effort to escape its selfish swallowing hug; yet to feel that way may already signify the absence of the necessary melodic relation. To be ruled by Reason, rather than by Father, Nature, King, or God, is an antisocial resolve. The autonomous self listens only to its own voice, unaffected by the grate of force, the lure of bribes, or the temptations of love.

Anyway, men have been killing themselves, we may suppose, as long as life has afforded them the opportunity, but to be sick of life is not the same as having a painful illness or suffering a shame so denobling life is no longer endurable. The presence everywhere of decay, disease, coarseness, brutality, and death — the flow of value into a blank abyss — this death-in-life that made living like the aftertaste of drunken vomit — was the black center of the plague of melancholy which afflicted the Elizabethans.

Hamlet's question, indeed, throws everything in doubt. The doubt becomes a commonplace, and a century later Pope defends the self-slaughter of an unfortunate lady in an elegant poem which takes for granted what continually shocked the Elizabethans — the democracy of death.

> Poets themselves must fall, like those they sung;
> Deaf the prais'd ear, and mute the tuneful tongue.
> Ev'n he, whose soul now melts in mournful lays,
> Shall shortly want the gen'rous tear he pays;
> Then from his closing eyes thy form shall part,
> And the last pang shall tear thee from his heart,
> Life's idle business at one gasp be o'er,
> The Muse forgot, and thou belov'd no more!

Definitions of suicide, like definitions of adultery, are invariably normative, and frequently do little more than reflect the shallowest social attitudes, embody the most parochial perspectives. Above all, these attitudes are for the most part deeply irrational. Failures may be executed, for example, while the corpses of successes are assaulted. Studies of suicide, including those of Alvarez and Choron,* are soon elaborately confused about desire, intention, deed, and consequence, ownership and responsibility (whether we belong to ourselves, society, or God); neglect the difference between act and action, refuse to decide whether to include deaths of soul (Rimbaud?) as well as deaths of body, since holy living may indeed be holy dying, so that physical and metaphysical murders become hopelessly intertwined; and they are content to record, with a tourist's widened eyes, the sweet, sour, wise, or benighted opinions of nearly everyone.

If we are to call suicide every self-taken way out of the world, then even the Platonic pursuit of knowledge, involving as it does the separation of reason from passion and appetite, is suicidal . . . as are, of course, the search for ecstatic states, and longings for mystical union. It is the habit of such examinations to mess up these matters as if they were so many paints whose purpose was purely to give pleasure to the fingers.

Nowadays the significance of a suicide for the suicide and the significance of that suicide for society are seldom the same. If, according to the social workers' comforting cliché, they are often a cry for help, they're just as frequently a solemn vow of silence. Nevertheless, it is easy to imagine circumstances under which some of our conventional kinds of suicide would be impossible — impossible because we would simply refuse to recognize them. The liver fails. The veins collapse. Sleep seizes the wheel. No suicides there. Suppose that starving yourself were a "going-home-to-God" (no suicide there), while slashing your wrists were a "cowardly-copping-out." In order to speak your piece properly you might have to shoot, hang, or poison yourself. Sprott records the case of "one that hang'd himself, upon his Knees, with a Bible on a Stool open before him, and a Paper to signifie that he had repented."† The liberated woman must do something manly, shotgun herself at the very least, avoid sleeping pills like the devil — that soothing syrup of the oppressed sex. If you don't want the manner of your dying to be a message to mankind, if your aim is just to get the hell out, then you will have

---

* A. Alvarez, *The Savage God* (New York: Random House, 1972), and Jacques Choron, *Suicide* (New York: Scribner's, 1972).

† S. E. Sprott, *The English Debate on Suicide from Donne to Hume* (La Salle, Illinois: Open Court, 1961).

to be as clever at disarming symbols as Mallarmé. Alas, the way we think and write about suicides would provide many with still another motive, an additional despair, were they alive again and mercilessly aware.

Breeding is not out of place even here. Petronius, the critics say, had class. Cato has consistently had a good press. And we write cheery loving thank-you notes; we put our affairs in order; we do not leap on top of people, run in front of cars owned by innocent strangers, bleed in public, allow the least hint of indecision, ambiguity, or failure to spoil our aim, and avoid every form of vulgar display. The ledge-huggers want to be coaxed, for instance. That's a suicide for shopgirls. On the other hand, if you are, like Mishima, too stylish, your actions risk being thought incomprehensible. My favorites are rather theatrical, though. Choron tells us how Arria, the wife of a Roman senator who'd been caught plotting, in order to stimulate her husband to his duty, plunged a sword into her breast and then handed it to him with the words: *Paete, non dolet* (It does not hurt). Others seek the third rail and interrupt the service; swallow combs, crosses, safety pins, fountain pens, needles, nails; they blow up the planes they are riding in, smother themselves in plastic Baggies, or simply find a wall and dash out their brains. Sprott says that by 1600

> Suicidal types had become traditional: the epicure, the disappointed lover, the great spirit, the melancholiac, the jealous man, the frightened child, the debauched apprentice, the unfortunate merchant, the bloody murderer despairing of God's pardon, the desperate zealot, the "tender Conscience't Despairer" . . . (Sprott, p. 36)

Though methods, motives, meanings differ ("Whose head is hanging from the swollen strap?" asked Crane), most can be expected to mess up their deaths exactly as they've messed up their lives. Poor folks. Poor ways.

Never mind. If you pay with your life you get a ticket to the tent: martyrs, daredevils, the accident-prone, those who cheat "justice" as Hannibal did, or are condemned by it as Seneca was; those who would die rather than surrender, even *en masse*, as the Jews died at Massada; those too poor, too rich, too proud, too ineffably wicked; all addicts, Cleopatras, all desolate Didos, mystics, faddists, young sorrowful Werthers; the fundamentally frigid, who cannot allow life to give them any pleasure; the incurably ill, the mad, the metaphysically gloomy; widows who go up with the rest of the property, and all those who from disgust or rage protest this life with emblematic ignitions and ritual sacrifice . . . it's like cataloguing books according to the color of their covers . . . the mourners, the divided selves (not just Cartesians, severed into bum and bicycle as Beckett's men are, but those who are cut up into competing personalities as vicious as sisters in some *Cinderella*); then the downright stupid, the inept and careless, the sublimely heroic, the totally disgraced . . . the color may be significant (the blue cover of *Ulysses* is), but it is scarcely a mode of classification which carves reality at the joints . . . those whom guilt feeds on as if they were already carrion; the Virginia Woolfs, too, who enter their own imagery, and the ones for whom death is a deer park, a convent, a place in outer space; also the impotent, ugly, acned, lonely; the inadvertently pregnant, and otherwise those who embrace their assassins, or who have felt only the hold of their own hand, thus to come and go finally in the same way . . . from little death to large . . . everyone's welcome.

Lost in lists, in the surveyor's sweepings, borne along on conjecture like gutter water, the same act can signify anything you like, depending on the system — even the mood or the line of the eye — which gives it meaning: I cock my head one way and it appears to me that my mother was murdered; I cock it another and she seems a specially vindictive suicide; while if I face firmly forward as one in military ranks she seems to have been overcome by a rather complex illness, a chronic and progressively worsening disease. Simply examining "suicides" is like trying to establish a science of — let's say — *sallescape,* which we can imagine contains the whys and wherefores of room-leaving. The word confers a fictitious unity upon a rabble of factors, and the ironic thing about suicide itself, intrinsically considered (and what my little litanies have been designed to demonstrate), is that it is a wholly empty act. It is — more than Rigaut, the Dada hero, was — an empty suitcase.

And if the suicide believes his final gesture, like the last line of an obscure poem, will unite, clarify, and give meaning to all that has gone before; or if actual poems have held offhand hints —

> The news from Spain got worse. The President of my Form
> at South Kent turned up at Clare, one of the last let out of Madrid.
> He designed the Chapel the School later built
> & killed himself, I never heard why
> or just how, it was something to do with a bridge.
>
> (Berryman: "Transit")

or seemed like chilling scenarios —

We have come so far, it is over.

Each dead child coiled, a white serpent,
One at each little

Pitcher of milk, now empty.

(Plath: "Edge")

so that the line between literature and life appears underdrawn (before she killed herself, Sylvia Plath put out two mugs of milk for her children); or if he has fallen for a romantic comparison like Camus's "An act like this is prepared within the silence of the heart, as is a great work of art," then at least he will suffer no further disappointment dead, because, of course, acts aren't language, and there's no poetry at all in suicide, only in some accounts of it . . . significance, value *in this sense*, belongs solely to sentences. Actions, and other similar events, have meaning only secondarily, as we impute it to them, and so may mean many things to many people. Words are acts only secondarily. They principally exist in the systems which establish and define them (as numbers do in mathematics), so while feasting may mean one thing to a Jew and quite another to a Samoan, the word *"Traum,"* uttered anywhere by anybody, remains irrevocably German.

Death will not fill up an empty life and in a line of verse it occupies only five letters of space.

Choron's readable little handbook, with its capsule summaries of speculation, its few tables of statistics, brief histories of opinions, merely provokes its questions, instead of asking them, and touches so lightly on all its subjects, they never feel it. Totally porous, the data are simply slowed down a trifle in seeping through. It resembles Choron's earlier *Death and Modern Man* in being a kind of easy introductory text.

Alvarez, observing the immense diversity of his material, wisely offers no solutions. Yet because he does not rigorously differentiate sorts, define terms, regulate interpretations, exclude kinds, but is content to report, reflect, admonish, and look on, his "study" turns out to be gossipy and anecdotal, though sometimes splendidly so, as his account of the suicide of Sylvia Plath is, because Alvarez is sensitive and sympathetic, knows how to handle a text, and writes with conscience and skill about a subject which is close enough to his own personal concerns (he is himself a "failed" suicide) that one could reasonably expect it to shake both skill and conscience as though they were rags in a gale.

It must have seemed like a good idea to sandwich his historical and literary studies of suicide between two kinds of direct acquaintance with it, all the more so when Alvarez's dissatisfaction with most theoretical investigations lies in their natural lack of contact with inner feeling, although much the same might be said of the physical laws for falling bodies, especially when the falling body is your own. The result of this division has not been entirely happy, however. Natural reticence, moral restraint, and simple lack of knowledge make his accounts of suicide from the inside-side seriously deficient in essential data, and therefore reduce them to sensitively told and frequently moving *stories*, although with less excuse Choron manages to make even the expounding of a theory sound like gossip (in effect: "Do you know what Plato said? Well — you won't believe this — but *he* said . . .").

Throughout *The Savage God*, too, again because it has no ruling principle, details fly out like sparks from every point that's struck, to fade without a purpose. The conditions surrounding Chatterton's suicide, for example, are certainly interesting, and Alvarez recites them nicely enough, but which ones really count, and which ones don't, and how do they count if they do, and if they do by how much? Vivid details, picturesque circumstances . . . my mother's copterlike bathroom posture, her gap-pinned robe, miscolored toes . . . well, their relevance isn't clear. Perhaps they have mainly a vaudeville function — to enliven without enlightening. Throughout, my mention of my mother merely mimics the problem.

The value of *The Savage God*, and it is high, lies mainly in the humanity of the mind which composed it, in the literary excellence of its composition, and the suggestiveness of many of its passages — the moment-by-moment thoughtfulness of its author as a reader.

The world of the suicidal is, in a certain sense (for all its familiar elements: pain, grief, confusion, failure, loss . . .), a private and impenetrable one, hence the frustration of those who are trying to help, and whose offers to do so, as raps on the glass disturb fish, often simply insult the suicide immersed in his situation. It is a consciousness trapped, enclosed by a bell jar, in the image which encloses Plath's novel, and Alvarez's book should do a great deal to correct the sentimentalist's happy thought that art is a kind of therapy for the sick, trapped, homeless, and world-weary, and that through it, deep personal problems get worked benignly out.

Poetry is cathartic only for the unserious, for in front of the rush of expressive need stands the barrier of form, and when the hurdler's scissored legs and outstretched arms carry him over the bars, the limp in his life, the headache in his heart, the emptiness he's full of, are as absent as his street-shoes, which will pinch and scrape his feet in all the old leathery ways once the race is over and he has to walk through the front door of his future like a brushman with some feckless patter and a chintzy plastic prize.

Rilke sometimes took this therapeutic attitude toward the writing of *Malte Laurids Brigge*, but if writing kept him sane, as he thought, it was one of the chief sources of his misery as well. If life is hard, art is harder. Plath's last poems, considered in this way, are announcements and warnings; they are promises; and their very excellence was a threat to the existence of their author, a woman whom success had always vanquished, and who was certainly defeated without it. Not only does the effort of creation often cultivate our problems at their roots, as Alvarez notes, the rich eloquence of their eventual formulation may give to some "solutions" an allure that is abnormal, one that art confers, not life. And if we have tried often enough, warned, performed and promised, must we not sometime keep that promise, if only to ensure that our sufferings have not been mockeries and showoffs, and succeed at failure one final time?

Malcolm Lowry, that eminent drunk, perhaps put Plath's particular case best when he wrote:

> When the doomed are most eloquent in their sinking,
> It seems that then we are least strong to save.

Writing. Not writing. Twin terrors. Putting one's mother into words . . . It may have been easier to put her in her grave.

1975

Maxine Hong Kingston

···

No Name Woman

"You MUST NOT tell anyone," my mother said, "what I am about to tell you. In China your father had a sister who killed herself. She jumped into the family well. We say that your father has all brothers because it is as if she had never been born.

"In 1924 just a few days after our village celebrated seventeen hurry-up weddings — to make sure that every young man who went 'out on the road' would responsibly come home — your father and his brothers and your grandfather and his brothers and your aunt's new husband sailed for America, the Gold Mountain. It was your grandfather's last trip. Those lucky enough to get contracts waved goodbye from the decks. They fed and guarded the stowaways and helped them off in Cuba, New York, Bali, Hawaii. 'We'll meet in California next year,' they said. All of them sent money home.

"I remember looking at your aunt one day when she and I were dressing; I had not noticed before that she had such a protruding melon of a stomach. But I did not think, 'She's pregnant,' until she began to look like other pregnant women, her shirt pulling and the white tops of her black pants showing. She could not have been pregnant, you see, because her husband had been gone for years. No one said anything. We did not discuss it. In early summer she was ready to have the child, long after the time when it could have been possible.

"The village had also been counting. On the night the baby was to be born the villagers raided our house. Some were crying. Like a great saw, teeth strung with lights, files of people walked zigzag across our land, tearing the rice. Their lanterns doubled in the disturbed black water,

First published in *Viva*, 1975; collected in *The Woman Warrior*, 1976.

which drained away through the broken bunds. As the villagers closed in, we could see that some of them, probably men and women we knew well, wore white masks. The people with long hair hung it over their faces. Women with short hair made it stand up on end. Some had tied white bands around their foreheads, arms, and legs.

"At first they threw mud and rocks at the house. Then they threw eggs and began slaughtering our stock. We could hear the animals scream their deaths — the roosters, the pigs, a last great roar from the ox. Familiar wild heads flared in our night windows; the villagers encircled us. Some of the faces stopped to peer at us, their eyes rushing like searchlights. The hands flattened against the panes, framed heads, and left red prints.

"The villagers broke in the front and the back doors at the same time, even though we had not locked the doors against them. Their knives dripped with the blood of our animals. They smeared blood on the doors and walls. One woman swung a chicken, whose throat she had slit, splattering blood in red arcs about her. We stood together in the middle of our house, in the family hall with the pictures and tables of the ancestors around us, and looked straight ahead.

"At that time the house had only two wings. When the men came back, we would build two more to enclose our courtyard and a third one to begin a second courtyard. The villagers pushed through both wings, even your grandparents' rooms, to find your aunt's, which was also mine until the men returned. From this room a new wing for one of the younger families would grow. They ripped up her clothes and shoes and broke her combs, grinding them underfoot. They tore her work from the loom. They scattered the cooking fire and rolled the new weaving in it. We could hear them in the kitchen breaking our bowls and banging the pots. They overturned the great waist-high earthenware jugs; duck eggs, pickled fruits, vegetables burst out and mixed in acrid torrents. The old woman from the next field swept a broom through the air and loosed the spirits-of-the-broom over our heads. 'Pig.' 'Ghost.' 'Pig,' they sobbed and scolded while they ruined our house.

"When they left, they took sugar and oranges to bless themselves. They cut pieces from the dead animals. Some of them took bowls that were not broken and clothes that were not torn. Afterward we swept up the rice and sewed it back up into sacks. But the smells from the spilled preserves lasted. Your aunt gave birth in the pigsty that night. The next morning when I went for the water, I found her and the baby plugging up the family well.

"Don't let your father know that I told you. He denies her. Now that you have started to menstruate, what happened to her could happen to you. Don't humiliate us. You wouldn't like to be forgotten as if you had never been born. The villagers are watchful."

Whenever she had to warn us about life, my mother told stories that ran like this one, a story to grow up on. She tested our strength to establish realities. Those in the emigrant generations who could not reassert brute survival died young and far from home. Those of us in the first American generations have had to figure out how the invisible world the emigrants built around our childhoods fits in solid America.

The emigrants confused the gods by diverting their curses, misleading them with crooked streets and false names. They must try to confuse their offspring as well, who, I suppose, threaten them in similar ways — always trying to get things straight, always trying to name the unspeakable. The Chinese I know hide their names; sojourners take new names when their lives change and guard their real names with silence.

Chinese-Americans, when you try to understand what things in you are Chinese, how do you separate what is peculiar to childhood, to poverty, insanities, one family, your mother who marked your growing with stories, from what is Chinese? What is Chinese tradition and what is the movies?

If I want to learn what clothes my aunt wore, whether flashy or ordinary, I would have to begin, "Remember Father's drowned-in-the-well sister?" I cannot ask that. My mother has told me once and for all the useful parts. She will add nothing unless powered by Necessity, a riverbank that guides her life. She plants vegetable gardens rather than lawns; she carries the odd-shaped tomatoes home from the fields and eats food left for the gods.

Whenever we did frivolous things, we used up energy; we flew high kites. We children came up off the ground over the melting cones our parents brought home from work and the American movie on New Year's Day — *Oh, You Beautiful Doll* with Betty Grable one year, and *She Wore a Yellow Ribbon* with John Wayne another year. After the one carnival ride each, we paid in guilt; our tired father counted his change on the dark walk home.

Adultery is extravagance. Could people who hatch their own chicks and eat the embryos and the heads for delicacies and boil the feet in vinegar for party food, leaving only the gravel, eating even the gizzard lining — could such people engender a prodigal aunt? To be a woman, to have a daughter in starvation time was a waste enough. My aunt could not have been the lone romantic who gave up everything for sex. Women in the old China did not choose. Some man had commanded her to lie with him and be his secret evil. I wonder whether he masked himself when he joined the raid on her family.

Perhaps she had encountered him in the fields or on the mountain where the daughters-in-law collected fuel. Or perhaps he first noticed her in the marketplace. He was not a stranger because the village housed no strangers. She had to have dealings with him other than sex. Perhaps he worked an adjoining field, or he sold her the cloth for the dress she sewed and wore. His demand must have surprised, then terrified her. She obeyed him; she always did as she was told.

When the family found a young man in the next village to be her husband, she had stood tractably beside the best rooster, his proxy, and promised before they met that she would be his forever. She was lucky that he was her age and she would be the first wife, an advantage secure now. The night she first saw him, he had sex with her. Then he left for America. She had almost forgotten what he looked like. When she tried to envision him, she only saw the black and white face in the group photograph the men had had taken before leaving.

The other man was not, after all, much different from her husband. They both gave orders: she followed. "If you tell your family, I'll beat you. I'll kill you. Be here again next week." No one talked sex, ever. And she might have separated the rapes from the rest of living if only she did not have to buy her oil from him or gather wood in the same forest. I want her fear to have lasted just as long as rape lasted so that the fear could have been contained. No drawn-out fear. But women at sex hazarded birth and hence lifetimes. The fear did not stop but permeated everywhere. She told the man, "I think I'm pregnant." He organized the raid against her.

On nights when my mother and father talked about their life back home, sometimes they mentioned an "outcast table" whose business they still seemed to be settling, their voices tight. In a commensal tradition, where food is precious, the powerful older people made wrongdoers eat alone. Instead of letting them start separate new lives like the Japanese, who could become samurais and geishas, the Chinese family, faces averted but eyes glowering sideways, hung on to the offenders and fed them leftovers. My aunt must have lived in the same house as my parents and eaten at an outcast table. My mother spoke about the raid as if she had seen it, when she and my aunt, a daughter-in-law to a different household, should not have been living together at all. Daughters-in-law lived with their husbands' parents, not their own; a synonym for marriage in Chinese is "taking a daughter-in-law." Her husband's parents could have sold her, mortgaged her, stoned her. But they had sent her back to her own mother and father, a mysterious act hinting at disgraces not told me. Perhaps they had thrown her out to deflect the avengers.

She was the only daughter; her four brothers went with her father, husband, and uncles "out on the road" and for some years became western men. When the goods were divided among the family, three of the brothers took land, and the youngest, my father, chose an education. After my grandparents gave their daughter away to her husband's family, they had dispensed all the adventure and all the property. They expected her alone to keep the traditional ways, which her brothers, now among the barbarians, could fumble without detection. The heavy, deep-rooted women were to maintain the past against the flood, safe for returning. But the rare urge west had fixed upon our family, and so my aunt crossed boundaries not delineated in space.

The work of preservation demands that the feelings playing about in one's guts not be turned into action. Just watch their passing like cherry blossoms. But perhaps my aunt, my forerunner, caught in a slow life, let dreams grow and fade and after some months or years went toward what persisted. Fear at the enormities of the forbidden kept her desires delicate, wire and bone. She looked at a man because she liked the way the hair was tucked behind his ears, or she liked the question-mark line of a long torso curving at the shoulder and straight at the hip. For warm eyes or a soft voice or a slow walk — that's all — a few hairs, a line, a brightness, a sound, a pace, she gave up family. She offered us up for a charm that vanished with tiredness, a pigtail that didn't toss when the wind died. Why, the wrong lighting could erase the dearest thing about him.

It could very well have been, however, that my aunt did not take subtle enjoyment of her friend, but, a wild woman, kept rollicking company. Imagining her free with sex doesn't fit, though. I don't know any women like that, or men either. Unless I see her life branching into mine, she gives me no ancestral help.

To sustain her being in love, she often worked at herself in the mirror, guessing at the colors and shapes that would interest him, changing them frequently in order to hit on the right combination. She wanted him to look back.

On a farm near the sea, a woman who tended her appearance reaped a reputation for eccentricity. All the married women blunt-cut their hair in flaps about their ears or pulled it back in tight buns. No nonsense. Neither style blew easily into heart-catching tangles. And at their weddings they displayed themselves in their long hair for the last time. "It brushed the backs of my knees," my mother tells me. "It was braided, and even so, it brushed the backs of my knees."

At the mirror my aunt combed individuality into her bob. A bun could have been contrived to escape into black streamers blowing in the wind or in quiet wisps about her face, but only the older women in our picture album wear buns. She brushed her hair back from her forehead, tucking the flaps behind her ears. She looped a piece of thread, knotted into a circle between her index fingers and thumbs, and ran the double strand across her forehead. When she closed her fingers as if she were making a pair of shadow geese bite, the string twisted together catching the little hairs. Then she pulled the thread away from her skin, ripping the hairs out neatly, her eyes watering from the needles of pain. Opening her fingers, she cleaned the thread, then rolled it along her hairline and the tops of her eyebrows. My mother did the same to me and my sisters and herself. I used to believe that the expression "caught by the short hairs" meant a captive held with a depilatory string. It especially hurt at the temples, but my mother said we were lucky we didn't have to have our feet bound when we were seven. Sisters used to sit on their beds and cry together, she said, as their mothers or their slaves removed the bandages for a few minutes each night and let the blood gush back into their veins. I hope that the man my aunt loved appreciated a smooth brow, that he wasn't just a tits-and-ass man.

Once my aunt found a freckle on her chin, at a spot that the almanac said predestined her for unhappiness. She dug it out with a hot needle and washed the wound with peroxide.

More attention to her looks than these pullings of hairs and pickings at spots would have caused gossip among the villagers. They owned work clothes and good clothes, and they wore good clothes for feasting the new seasons. But since a woman combing her hair hexes beginnings, my aunt rarely found an occasion to look her best. Women looked like great sea snails — the corded wood, babies, and laundry they carried were the whorls on their backs. The Chinese did not admire a bent back; goddesses and warriors stood straight. Still there must have been a marvelous freeing of beauty when a worker laid down her burden and stretched and arched.

Such commonplace loveliness, however, was not enough for my aunt. She dreamed of a lover for the fifteen days of New Year's, the time for families to exchange visits, money, and food. She plied her secret comb. And sure enough she cursed the year, the family, the village, and herself.

Even as her hair lured her imminent lover, many other men looked at her. Uncles, cousins, nephews, brothers would have looked, too, had they been home between journeys. Perhaps they had already been restraining their curiosity, and they left, fearful that their glances, like a field of nesting birds, might be startled and caught. Poverty hurt, and that was their first reason for leaving. But another, final reason for leaving the crowded house was the never-said.

She may have been unusually beloved, the precious only daughter, spoiled and mirror gazing because of the affection the family lavished on her. When her husband left, they welcomed the chance to take her back from the in-laws; she could live like the little daughter for just a while longer. There are stories that my grandfather was different from other people, "crazy ever since the little Jap bayoneted him in the head." He used to put his naked penis on the dinner table, laughing. And one day he brought home a baby girl, wrapped up inside his brown western-style greatcoat. He had traded one of his sons, probably my father, the youngest, for her. My grandmother made him trade back. When he finally got a daughter of his own, he doted on her. They must have all loved her, except perhaps my father, the only brother who never went back to China, having once been traded for a girl.

Brothers and sisters, newly men and women, had to efface their sexual color and present plain miens. Disturbing hair and eyes, a smile like no other, threatened the ideal of five generations living under one roof. To focus blurs, people shouted face to face and yelled from room to room. The immigrants I know have loud voices, unmodulated to American tones even after years away from the village where they called their friendships out across the fields. I have not been able to stop my mother's screams in public libraries or over telephones. Walking erect (knees straight, toes pointed forward, not pigeon-toed, which is Chinese-feminine) and speaking in an inaudible voice, I have tried to turn myself American-feminine. Chinese communication was loud, public. Only sick people had to whisper. But at the dinner table, where the family members came nearest one another, no one could talk, not the outcasts nor any eaters. Every word that falls from the mouth is a coin lost. Silently they gave and accepted food with both hands. A preoccupied child who took his bowl with one hand got a sideways glare. A complete moment of total attention is due everyone alike. Children and lovers have no singularity here, but my aunt used a secret voice, a separate attentiveness.

She kept the man's name to herself throughout her labor and dying; she did not accuse him that he be punished with her. To save her inseminator's name she gave silent birth.

He may have been somebody in her own household, but intercourse with a man outside the family would have been no less abhorrent. All the village were kinsmen, and the titles shouted in loud country voices never let kinship be forgotten. Any man within visiting distance would have been neutralized as a lover — "brother," "younger brother," "older brother" — one hundred and fifteen relationship titles. Parents researched birth charts probably not so much to assure good fortune as to circumvent incest in a population that has but one hundred surnames. Everybody has eight million relatives. How useless then sexual mannerisms, how dangerous.

As if it came from an atavism deeper than fear, I used to add "brother" silently to boys' names. It hexed the boys, who would or would not ask me to dance, and made them less scary and as familiar and deserving of benevolence as girls.

But, of course, I hexed myself also — no dates. I should have stood up, both arms waving, and shouted out across libraries, "Hey, you! Love me back." I had no idea, though, how to make attraction selective, how to control its direction and magnitude. If I made myself American-pretty so that the five or six Chinese boys in the class fell in love with me, everyone else — the Caucasian, Negro, and Japanese boys — would too. Sisterliness, dignified and honorable, made much more sense.

Attraction eludes control so stubbornly that whole societies designed to organize relationships among people cannot keep order, not even when they bind people to one another from childhood and raise them together. Among the very poor and the wealthy, brothers married their adopted sisters, like doves. Our family allowed some romance, paying adult brides' prices and providing dowries so that their sons and daughters could marry strangers. Marriage promises to turn strangers into friendly relatives — a nation of siblings.

In the village structure, spirits shimmered among the live creatures, balanced and held in equilibrium by time and land. But one human being flaring up into violence could open up a black hole, a maelstrom that pulled in the sky. The frightened villagers, who depended on one another to maintain the real, went to my aunt to show her a personal, physical representation of the break she had made in the "roundness." Misallying couples snapped off the future, which was to be embodied in true offspring. The villagers punished her for acting as if she could have a private life, secret and apart from them.

If my aunt had betrayed the family at a time of large grain yields and peace, when many boys were born, and wings were being built on many houses, perhaps she might have escaped such severe punishment. But the men — hungry, greedy, tired of planting in dry soil — had been forced to leave the village in order to send food-money home. There were ghost plagues, bandit plagues, wars with the Japanese, floods. My Chinese brother and sister had died of an unknown sickness. Adultery, perhaps only a mistake during good times, became a crime when the village needed food.

The round moon cakes and round doorways, the round tables of graduated sizes that fit one roundness inside another, round windows and rice bowls — these talismans had lost their power to warn this family of the law: a family must be whole, faithfully keeping the descent line by having sons to feed the old and the dead, who in turn look after the family. The villagers came to show my aunt and her lover-in-hiding a broken house. The villagers were speeding up the circling of events because she was too shortsighted to see that her infidelity had already harmed the village, that waves of consequences would return unpredictably, sometimes in disguise, as now, to hurt her. This roundness had to be made coin-sized so that she would see its circumference: punish her at the birth of her baby. Awaken her to the inexorable. People who refused fatalism because they could invent small resources insisted on culpability. Deny accidents and wrest fault from the stars.

After the villagers left, their lanterns now scattering in various directions toward home, the family broke their silence and cursed her. "Aiaa, we're going to die. Death is coming. Death is coming. Look what you've done. You've killed us. Ghost! Dead ghost! Ghost! You've never been born." She ran out into the fields, far enough from the house so that she could no longer hear their voices, and pressed herself against the earth, her own land no more. When she felt the birth coming, she thought that she had been hurt. Her body seized together. "They've hurt me too much," she thought. "This is gall, and it will kill me." With forehead and knees against the earth, her body convulsed and then relaxed. She turned on her back, lay on the ground. The black well of sky and stars went out and out and out forever; her body and her complexity seemed to disappear. She was one of the stars, a bright dot in blackness, without home, without a companion, in eternal cold and silence. An agoraphobia rose in her, speeding higher and higher, bigger and bigger; she would not be able to contain it; there would be no end to fear.

Flayed, unprotected against space, she felt pain return, focusing her body. This pain chilled her — a cold, steady kind of surface pain. Inside, spasmodically, the other pain, the pain of the child, heated her. For hours she lay on the ground, alternately body and space. Sometimes a vision of normal comfort obliterated reality: she saw the family in the evening gambling at the dinner table, the young people massaging their elders' backs. She saw them congratulating one another, high joy on the mornings the rice shoots came up. When these pictures burst, the stars drew yet further apart. Black space opened.

She got to her feet to fight better and remembered that old-fashioned women gave birth in their pigsties to fool the jealous, pain-dealing gods, who do not snatch piglets. Before the next spasms could stop her, she ran to the pigsty, each step a rushing out into emptiness. She climbed over the fence and knelt in the dirt. It was good to have a fence enclosing her, a tribal person alone.

Laboring, this woman who had carried her child as a foreign growth that sickened her every day, expelled it at last. She reached down to touch the hot, wet, moving mass, surely smaller than anything human, and could feel that it was human after all — fingers, toes, nails, nose. She pulled it up on to her belly, and it lay curled there, butt in the air, feet precisely tucked one under the other. She opened her loose shirt and buttoned the child inside. After resting, it squirmed and thrashed and she pushed it up to her breast. It turned its head this way and that until it found her nipple. There, it made little snuffling noises. She clenched her teeth at its preciousness, lovely as a young calf, a piglet, a little dog.

She may have gone to the pigsty as a last act of responsibility: she would protect this child as she had protected its father. It would look after her soul, leaving supplies on her grave. But how would this tiny child without family find her grave when there would be no marker for her anywhere, neither in the earth nor the family hall? No one would give her a family hall name. She had taken the child with her into the wastes. At its birth the two of them had felt the same raw pain of separation, a wound that only the family pressing tight could close. A child with no descent line would not soften her life but only trail after her, ghostlike, begging her to give it purpose. At dawn the villagers on their way to the fields would stand around the fence and look.

Full of milk, the little ghost slept. When it awoke, she hardened her breasts against the milk that crying loosens. Toward morning she picked up the baby and walked to the well.

Carrying the baby to the well shows loving. Otherwise abandon it. Turn its face into the mud. Mothers who love their children take them along. It was probably a girl; there is some hope of forgiveness for boys.

"Don't tell anyone you had an aunt. Your father does not want to hear her name. She has never been born." I have believed that sex was unspeakable and words so strong and fathers so frail that "aunt" would do my father mysterious harm. I have thought that my family, having settled among immigrants who had also been their neighbors in the ancestral land, needed to clean their name, and a wrong word would incite the kinspeople even here. But there is more to this silence: they want me to participate in her punishment. And I have.

In the twenty years since I heard this story I have not asked for details nor said my aunt's name; I do not know it. People who can comfort the dead can also chase after them to hurt them further — a reverse ancestor worship. The real punishment was not the raid swiftly inflicted by the villagers, but the family's deliberately forgetting her. Her betrayal so maddened them, they saw to it that she would suffer forever, even after death. Always hungry, always needing, she would have to beg food from other ghosts, snatch and steal it from those whose living descendants give them gifts. She would have to fight the ghosts massed at crossroads for the buns a few thoughtful citizens leave to decoy her away from village and home so that the ancestral spirits could feast unharassed. At peace, they could act like gods, not ghosts, their descent lines providing them with paper suits and dresses, spirit money, paper houses, paper automobiles, chicken, meat, and rice into eternity — essences delivered up in smoke and flames, steam and incense rising from each rice bowl. In an attempt to make the Chinese care for people outside the family, Chairman Mao encourages us now to give our paper replicas to the spirits of outstanding soldiers and workers, no matter whose ancestors they may be. My aunt remains forever hungry. Goods are not distributed evenly among the dead.

My aunt haunts me — her ghost drawn to me because now, after fifty years of neglect, I alone devote pages of paper to her, though not origamied into houses and clothes. I do not think she always means me well. I am telling on her, and she was a spite suicide, drowning herself in the drinking water. The Chinese are always very frightened of the drowned one, whose weeping ghost, wet hair hanging and skin bloated, waits silently by the water to pull down a substitute.

Alice Walker

Looking for Zora

On January 16, 1959, Zora Neale Hurston, suffering from the effects of a stroke and writing painfully in longhand, composed a letter to the "editorial department" of Harper & Brothers inquiring if they would be interested in seeing "the book I am laboring upon at present — a life of Herod the Great." One year and twelve days later, Zora Neale Hurston died without funds to provide for her burial, a resident of the St. Lucie County, Florida, Welfare Home. She lies today in an unmarked grave in a segregated cemetery in Fort Pierce, Florida, a resting place generally symbolic of the black writer's fate in America.

Zora Neale Hurston is one of the most significant unread authors in America, the author of two minor classics and four other major books.

— Robert Hemenway, "Zora Hurston and the Eatonville Anthropology,"
in *The Harlem Renaissance Remembered*

On August 15, 1973, I wake up just as the plane is lowering over Sanford, Florida, which means I am also looking down on Eatonville, Zora Neale Hurston's birthplace. I recognize it from Zora's description in *Mules and Men:* "the city of five lakes, three croquet courts, three hundred brown skins, three hundred good swimmers, plenty guavas, two schools, and no jailhouse." Of course I cannot see the guavas, but the five lakes are still there, and it is the lakes I count as the plane prepares to land in Orlando.

From the air, Florida looks completely flat, and as we near the ground this impression does not change. This is the first time I have seen the interior of the state, which Zora wrote about so well, but there

First published in *Ms.*, 1975; collected in *In Search of Our Mothers' Gardens, 1983.

are the acres of orange groves, the sand, mangrove trees, and scrub pine that I know from her books. Getting off the plane I walk through the humid air of midday into the tacky but air-conditioned airport. I search for Charlotte Hunt, my companion on the Zora Hurston expedition. She lives in Winter Park, Florida, very near Eatonville, and is writing her graduate dissertation on Zora. I see her waving — a large, pleasant-faced white woman in dark glasses. We have written to each other for several weeks, swapping our latest finds (mostly hers) on Zora, and trying to make sense out of the mass of information obtained (often erroneous or simply confusing) from Zora herself — through her stories and autobiography — and from people who wrote about her.

Eatonville has lived for such a long time in my imagination that I can hardly believe it will be found existing in its own right. But after twenty minutes on the expressway, Charlotte turns off and I see a small settlement of houses and stores set with no particular pattern in the sandy soil off the road. We stop in front of a neat gray building that has two fascinating signs: EATONVILLE POST OFFICE and EATONVILLE CITY HALL.

Inside the Eatonville City Hall half of the building, a slender, dark-brown-skin woman sits looking through letters on a desk. When she hears we are searching for anyone who might have known Zora Neale Hurston, she leans back in thought. Because I don't wish to inspire foot-dragging in people who might know something about Zora they're not sure they should tell, I have decided on a simple, but I feel profoundly *useful*, lie.

"I am Miss Hurston's niece," I prompt the young woman, who brings her head down with a smile.

"I think Mrs. Moseley is about the only one still living who might remember her," she says.

"Do you mean *Mathilda* Moseley, the woman who tells those 'woman-is-smarter-than-man' lies in Zora's book?"

"Yes," says the young woman. "Mrs. Moseley is real old now, of course. But this time of day, she should be at home."

I stand at the counter looking down on her, the first Eatonville resident I have spoken to. Because of Zora's books, I feel I know something about her; at least I know what the town she grew up in was like years before she was born.

"Tell me something," I say. "Do the schools teach Zora's books here?"

"No," she says, "they don't. I don't think most people know anything about Zora Neale Hurston, or know about any of the great things she did. She was a fine lady. I've read all of her books myself, but I don't think many other folks in Eatonville have."

"Many of the church people around here, as I understand it," says Charlotte in a murmured aside, "thought Zora was pretty loose. I don't think they appreciated her writing about them."

"Well," I say to the young woman, "thank you for your help." She clarifies her directions to Mrs. Moseley's house and smiles as Charlotte and I turn to go.

> The letter to Harper's does not expose a publisher's rejection of an unknown masterpiece, but it does reveal how the bright promise of the Harlem Renaissance deteriorated for many of the writers who shared in its exuberance. It also indicates the personal tragedy of Zora Neale Hurston: Barnard graduate, author of four novels, two books of folklore, one volume of autobiography, the most important collector of Afro-American folklore in America, reduced by poverty and circumstance to seek a publisher by unsolicited mail.
>
> — Robert Hemenway

> Zora Hurston was born in 1901, 1902, or 1903 — depending on how old she felt herself to be at the time someone asked.
>
> — Librarian, Beinecke Library, Yale University

The Moseley house is small and white and snug, its tiny yard nearly swallowed up by oleanders and hibiscus bushes. Charlotte and I knock on the door. I call out. But there is no answer. This strikes us as peculiar. We have had time to figure out an age for Mrs. Moseley — not dates or a number, just old. I am thinking of a quivery, bedridden invalid when we hear the car. We look behind us to see an old black and white Buick — paint peeling and grillwork rusty — pulling into the drive. A neat old lady in a purple dress and with white hair is straining at the wheel. She is frowning because Charlotte's car is in the way.

Mrs. Moseley looks at us suspiciously. "Yes, I knew Zora Neale," she says, unsmilingly and with a rather cold stare at Charlotte (who, I imagine, feels very *white* at that moment), "but that was a long time ago, and I don't want to talk about it."

"Yes, ma'am," I murmur, bringing all my sympathy to bear on the situation.

"Not only that," Mrs. Moseley continues. "I've been sick. Been in the hospital for an operation. Ruptured artery. The doctors didn't believe I was going to live, but you see me alive, don't you?"

"Looking well, too," I comment.

Mrs. Moseley is out of her car. A thin, sprightly woman with nice gold-studded false teeth, uppers and lowers. I like her because she stands there *straight* beside her car, with a hand on her hip and her straw pocketbook on her arm. She wears white T-strap shoes with heels that show off her well-shaped legs.

"I'm eighty-two years old, you know," she says. "And I just can't remember things the way I used to. Anyhow, Zora Neale left here to go to school and she never really came back to live. She'd come here for material for her books, but that was all. She spent most of her time down in South Florida."

"You know, Mrs. Moseley, I saw your name in one of Zora's books."

"You did?" She looks at me with only slightly more interest. "I read some of her books a long time ago, but then people got to borrowing and borrowing and they borrowed them all away."

"I could send you a copy of everything that's been reprinted," I offer. "Would you like me to do that?"

"No," says Mrs. Moseley promptly. "I don't read much any more. Besides, all of that was *so* long ago. . . ."

Charlotte and I settle back against the car in the sun. Mrs. Moseley tells us at length and with exact recall every step in her recent operation, ending with: "What those doctors didn't know — when they were expecting me to die (and they didn't even think I'd live long enough for them to have to take out my stitches!) — is that Jesus is the best doctor, and if *He* says for you to get well, that's all that counts."

With this philosophy, Charlotte and I murmur quick assent: being Southerners and church bred, we have heard that belief before. But what we learn from Mrs. Moseley is that she does not remember much beyond the year 1938. She shows us a picture of her father and mother and says that her father was Joe Clarke's brother. Joe Clarke, as every Zora Hurston reader knows, was the first mayor of Eatonville; his fictional counterpart is Jody Starks of *Their Eyes Were Watching God*. We also get directions to where Joe Clarke's store *was* — where Club Eaton is now. Club Eaton, a long orange-beige nightspot we had seen on the main road, is apparently famous for the good times in it regularly had by all. It is, perhaps, the modern equivalent of the store porch, where all the men of Zora's childhood came to tell "lies," that is, black folk tales, that were "made and used on the spot," to take a line from Zora. As for Zora's exact birthplace, Mrs. Moseley has no idea.

After I have commented on the healthy growth of her hibiscus bushes, she becomes more talkative. She mentions how much she *loved* to dance, when she was a young woman, and talks about how good her husband was. When he was alive, she says, she was completely happy because he allowed her to be completely free. "I was so free I had to pinch myself sometimes to tell if I was a married woman."

Relaxed now, she tells us about going to school with Zora. "Zora and I went to the same school. It's called Hungerford High now. It *was* only to the eighth grade. But our teachers were so good that by the time you left you knew college subjects. When I went to Morris Brown in Atlanta, the teachers there were just teaching me the same things I had already learned right in Eatonville. I wrote Mama and told her I was going to come home and help her with her babies. I wasn't learning anything new."

"Tell me something, Mrs. Moseley," I ask. "Why do you suppose Zora was against integration? I read somewhere that she was against school desegregation because she felt it was an insult to black teachers."

"Oh, one of them [white people] came around asking me about integration. One day I was doing my shopping. I heard 'em over there talking about it in the store, about the schools. And I got on out of the way because I knew if they asked me, they wouldn't like what I was going to tell 'em. But they came up and asked me anyhow. 'What do you think about this integration?' one of them said. I acted like I thought I had heard wrong. 'You're asking *me* what *I* think about integration?' I said. 'Well, as you can see, I'm just an old colored woman' — I was seventy-five or seventy-six then — 'and this is the first time anybody ever asked me about integration. And nobody asked my grandmother what she thought, either, but her daddy was one of you all.'" Mrs. Moseley seems satisfied with this memory of her rejoinder. She looks at Charlotte. "I have the blood of three races in my veins," she says belligerently, "white, black, and Indian, and nobody asked me *anything* before."

"Do you think living in Eatonville made integration less appealing to you?"

"Well, I can tell you this: I have lived in Eatonville all my life, and I've been in the governing of this town. I've been everything but mayor and I've been *assistant* mayor. Eatonville was and is an all-black town. We have our own police department, post office, and town hall. Our own school and good teachers. Do I need integration?

"They took over Goldsboro, because the black people who lived there never incorporated, like we did. And now I don't even know if any black folks live there. They built big houses up there around the lakes. But we didn't let that happen in Eatonville, and we don't sell land to just any-body. And you see, we're still here."

When we leave, Mrs. Moseley is standing by her car, waving. I think of the letter Roy Wilkins wrote to a black newspaper blasting Zora Neale for her lack of enthusiasm about the integration of schools. I wonder if he knew the experience of Eatonville she was coming from. Not many black people in America have come from a self-contained, all-black community where loyalty and unity are taken for granted. A place where black pride is nothing new.

There is, however, one thing Mrs. Moseley said that bothered me.

"Tell me, Mrs. Moseley," I had asked, "why is it that thirteen years af-ter Zora's death, no marker has been put on her grave?"

And Mrs. Moseley answered: "The reason she doesn't have a stone is because she wasn't buried here. She was buried down in South Florida somewhere. I don't think anybody really knew where she was."

> Only to reach a wider audience, need she ever write books — because she is a perfect book of entertainment in herself. In her youth she was always getting scholarships and things from wealthy white people, some of whom simply paid her just to sit around and represent the Negro race for them, she did it in such a racy fashion. She was full of sidesplitting anecdotes, humorous tales, and tragicomic stories, re-membered out of her life in the South as a daughter of a traveling minister of God. She could make you laugh one minute and cry the next. To many of her white friends, no doubt, she was a perfect "darkie," in the nice meaning they give the term — that is, a naïve, childlike, sweet, humorous, and highly colored Negro.
>
> But Miss Hurston was clever, too — a student who didn't let college give her a broad "a" and who had great scorn for all pretensions, aca-demic or otherwise. That is why she was such a fine folklore collector, able to go among the people and never act as if she had been to school at all. Almost nobody else could stop the average Harlemite on Lenox Avenue and measure his head with a strange-looking, anthropological device and not get bawled out for the attempt, except Zora, who used to stop anyone whose head looked interesting, and measure it.
>
> — Langston Hughes, *The Big Sea*

> What does it matter what white folks must have thought about her?
>
> — Student, black women writers' class, Wellesley College

Mrs. Sarah Peek Patterson is a handsome, red-haired woman in her late forties, wearing orange slacks and gold earrings. She is the director of Lee-Peek Mortuary in Fort Pierce, the establishment that handled

Zora's burial. Unlike most black funeral homes in Southern towns that sit like palaces among the general poverty, Lee-Peek has a run-down, *small* look. Perhaps this is because it is painted purple and white, as are its Cadillac chariots. These colors do not age well. The rooms are cluttered and grimy, and the bathroom is a tiny, stale-smelling prison, with a bottle of black hair dye (apparently used to touch up the hair of the corpses) dripping into the face bowl. Two pine burial boxes are resting in the bathtub.

Mrs. Patterson herself is pleasant and helpful.

"As I told you over the phone, Mrs. Patterson," I begin, shaking her hand and looking into her penny-brown eyes, "I am Zora Neale Hurston's niece, and I would like to have a marker put on her grave. You said, when I called you last week, that you could tell me where the grave is."

By this time I am, of course, completely into being Zora's niece, and the lie comes with perfect naturalness to my lips. Besides, as far as I'm concerned, she *is* my aunt — and that of all black people as well.

"She was buried in 1960," exclaims Mrs. Patterson. "That was when my father was running this funeral home. He's sick now or I'd let you talk to him. But I know where she's buried. She's in the old cemetery, the Garden of the Heavenly Rest, on Seventeenth Street. Just when you go in the gate there's a circle, and she's buried right in the middle of it. Hers is the only grave in that circle — because people don't bury in that cemetery any more."

She turns to a stocky, black-skinned woman in her thirties, wearing a green polo shirt and white jeans cut off at the knee. "This lady will show you where it is," she says.

"I can't tell you how much I appreciate this," I say to Mrs. Patterson, as I rise to go. "And could you tell me something else? You see, I never met my aunt. When she died, I was still a junior in high school. But could you tell me what she died of, and what kind of funeral she had?"

"I don't know exactly what she died of," Mrs. Patterson says. "I know she didn't have any money. Folks took up a collection to bury her. . . . I believe she died of malnutrition."

"*Malnutrition?*"

Outside, in the blistering sun, I lean my head against Charlotte's even more blistering car top. The sting of the hot metal only intensifies my anger. "*Malnutrition,*" I manage to mutter. "Hell, our condition hasn't changed *any* since Phillis Wheatley's time. *She* died of malnutrition!"

"Really?" says Charlotte. "I didn't know that."

One cannot overemphasize the extent of her commitment. It was so
great that her marriage in the spring of 1927 to Herbert Sheen was
short-lived. Although divorce did not come officially until 1931, the
two separated amicably after only a few months, Hurston to continue
her collecting, Sheen to attend Medical School. Hurston never married again.

— Robert Hemenway

"What is your name?" I ask the woman who has climbed into the
back seat.

"Rosalee," she says. She has a rough, pleasant voice, as if she is a
singer who also smokes a lot. She is homely, and has an air of ready indifference.

"Another woman came by here wanting to see the grave," she says,
lighting up a cigarette. "She was a little short, dumpty white lady from
one of these Florida schools. Orlando or Daytona. But let me tell you
something before we gets started. All I know is where the cemetery is. I
don't know one thing about that grave. You better go back in and ask
her to draw you a map."

A few moments later, with Mrs. Patterson's diagram of where the
grave is, we head for the cemetery.

We drive past blocks of small, pastel-colored houses and turn right
onto Seventeenth Street. At the very end, we reach a tall curving gate,
with the words "Garden of the Heavenly Rest" fading into the stone. I
expected, from Mrs. Patterson's small drawing, to find a small circle —
which would have placed Zora's grave five or ten paces from the road.
But the "circle" is over an acre large and looks more like an abandoned
field. Tall weeds choke the dirt road and scrape against the sides of the
car. It doesn't help either that I step out into an active ant hill.

"I don't know about y'all," I say, "but I don't even believe this." I am
used to the haphazard cemetery-keeping that is traditional in most
Southern black communities, but this neglect is staggering. As far as I
can see there is nothing but bushes and weeds, some as tall as my waist.
One grave is near the road, and Charlotte elects to investigate it. It is
fairly clean, and belongs to someone who died in 1963.

Rosalee and I plunge into the weeds; I pull my long dress up to my
hips. The weeds scratch my knees, and the insects have a feast. Looking
back, I see Charlotte standing resolutely near the road.

"Aren't you coming?" I call.

"No," she calls back. "I'm from these parts and I know what's out there." She means snakes.

"Shit," I say, my whole life and the people I love flashing melodramatically before my eyes. Rosalee is a few yards to my right.

"How're you going to find anything out here?" she asks. And I stand still a few seconds, looking at the weeds. Some of them are quite pretty, with tiny yellow flowers. They are thick and healthy, but dead weeds under them have formed a thick gray carpet on the ground. A snake could be lying six inches from my big toe and I wouldn't see it. We move slowly, very slowly, our eyes alert, our legs trembly. It is hard to tell where the center of the circle is since the circle is not really round, but more like half of something round. There are things crackling and hissing in the grass. Sandspurs are sticking to the inside of my skirt. Sand and ants cover my feet. I look toward the road and notice that there are, indeed, *two* large curving stones, making an entrance and exit to the cemetery. I take my bearings from them and try to navigate to exact center. But the center of anything can be very large, and a grave is not a pinpoint. Finding the grave seems positively hopeless. There is only one thing to do:

"Zora!" I yell, as loud as I can (causing Rosalee to jump). "Are you out here?"

"If she is, I sho hope she don't answer you. If she do, I'm gone."

"Zora!" I call again. "I'm here. Are you?"

"If she is," grumbles Rosalee, "I hope she'll keep it to herself."

"Zora!" Then I start fussing with her. "I hope you don't think I'm going to stand out here all day, with these snakes watching me and these ants having a field day. In fact, I'm going to call you just one or two more times." On a clump of dried grass, near a small bushy tree, my eye falls on one of the largest bugs I have ever seen. It is on its back, and is as large as three of my fingers. I walk toward it, and yell "Zo-ra!" and my foot sinks into a hole. I look down. I am standing in a sunken rectangle that is about six feet long and about three or four feet wide. I look up to see where the two gates are.

"Well," I say, "this is the center, or approximately anyhow. It's also the only sunken spot we've found. Doesn't this look like a grave to you?"

"For the sake of not going no farther through these bushes," Rosalee growls, "yes, it do."

"Wait a minute," I say, "I have to look around some more to be sure this is the only spot that resembles a grave. But you don't have to come."

Rosalee smiles — a grin, really — beautiful and tough.

"Naw," she says, "I feels sorry for you. If one of these snakes got ahold of you out here by yourself I'd feel *real* bad." She laughs. "I done come this far, I'll go on with you."

"Thank you, Rosalee," I say. "Zora thanks you too."

"Just as long as she don't try to tell me in person," she says, and together we walk down the field.

> The gusto and flavor of Zora Neal[e] Hurston's storytelling, for example, long before the yarns were published in "Mules and Men" and other books, became a local legend which might . . . have spread further under different conditions. A tiny shift in the center of gravity could have made them best-sellers.
>
> — Arna Bontemps, *Personals*

> Bitter over the rejection of her folklore's value, especially in the black community, frustrated by what she felt was her failure to convert the Afro-American world view into the forms of prose fiction, Hurston finally gave up.
>
> — Robert Hemenway

When Charlotte and I drive up to the Merritt Monument Company, I immediately see the headstone I want.

"How much is this one?" I ask the young woman in charge, pointing to a tall black stone. It looks as majestic as Zora herself must have been when she was learning voodoo from those root doctors down in New Orleans.

"Oh, *that* one," she says, "that's our finest. That's Ebony Mist."

"Well, how much is it?"

"I don't know. But wait," she says, looking around in relief, "here comes somebody who'll know."

A small, sunburned man with squinty green eyes comes up. He must be the engraver, I think, because his eyes are contracted into slits, as if he has been keeping stone dust out of them for years.

"That's Ebony Mist," be says. "That's our best."

"How much is it?" I ask, beginning to realize I probably *can't* afford it.

He gives me a price that would feed a dozen Sahelian drought victims for three years. I realize I must honor the dead, but between the dead great and the living starving, there is no choice.

"I have a lot of letters to be engraved," I say, standing by the plain gray marker I have chosen. It is pale and ordinary, not at all like Zora, and makes me momentarily angry that I am not rich.

We go into his office and I hand him a sheet of paper that has:

> ZORA NEALE HURSTON
> "A GENIUS OF THE SOUTH"
> NOVELIST   FOLKLORIST
> ANTHROPOLOGIST
> 1901   1960

"A genius of the South" is from one of Jean Toomer's poems.

"Where is this grave?" the monument man asks. "If it's in a new cemetery, the stone has to be flat."

"Well, it's not a new cemetery and Zora — my aunt — doesn't need anything flat, because with the weeds out there, you'd never be able to see it. You'll have to go out there with me."

He grunts.

"And take a long pole and 'sound' the spot," I add. "Because there's no way of telling it's a grave, except that it's sunken."

"Well," he says, after taking my money and writing up a receipt, in the full awareness that he's the only monument dealer for miles, "you take this flag" (he hands me a four-foot-long pole with a red-metal marker on top) "and take it out to the cemetery and put it where you think the grave is. It'll take us about three weeks to get the stone out there."

I wonder if he knows he is sending me to another confrontation with the snakes. He probably does. Charlotte has told me she will cut my leg and suck out the blood if I am bit.

"At least send me a photograph when it's done, won't you?"

He says he will.

Hurston's return to her folklore-collecting in December of 1927 was made possible by Mrs. R. Osgood Mason, an elderly white patron of the arts, who at various times also helped Langston Hughes, Alain Locke, Richmond Barthe, and Miguel Covarrubias. Hurston apparently came to her attention through the intercession of Locke, who frequently served as a kind of liaison between the young black talent and Mrs. Mason. The entire relationship between this woman and the Harlem Renaissance deserves extended study, for it represents much of the ambiguity involved in white patronage of black artists. All her artists were instructed to call her "Godmother"; there was a decided emphasis on the "primitive" aspects of black culture, apparently a holdover from Mrs. Mason's interest in the Plains Indians. In

Hurston's case there were special restrictions imposed by her patron: although she was to be paid a handsome salary for her folklore collecting, she was to limit her correspondence and publish nothing of her research without prior approval.

— Robert Hemenway

You have to read the chapters Zora *left out* of her autobiography.

— Student, Special Collections Room, Beinecke Library, Yale University

Dr. Benton, a friend of Zora's and a practicing M.D. in Fort Pierce, is one of those old, good-looking men whom I always have trouble not liking. (It no longer bothers me that I may be constantly searching for father figures; by this time, I have found several and dearly enjoyed knowing them all.) He is shrewd, with steady brown eyes under hair that is almost white. He is probably in his seventies, but doesn't look it. He carries himself with dignity, and has cause to be proud of the new clinic where he now practices medicine. His nurse looks at us with suspicion, but Dr. Benton's eyes have the penetration of a scalpel cutting through skin. I guess right away that if he knows anything at all about Zora Hurston, he will not believe I am her niece. "Eatonville?" Dr. Benton says, leaning forward in his chair, looking first at me, then at Charlotte. "Yes, I know Eatonville; I grew up not far from there. I knew the whole bunch of Zora's family." (He looks at the shape of my cheekbones, the size of my eyes, and the nappiness of my hair.) "I knew her daddy. The old man. He was a hard-working, Christian man. Did the best he could for his family. He was the mayor of Eatonville for a while, you know.

"My father was the mayor of Goldsboro. You probably never heard of it. It never incorporated like Eatonville did, and has just about disappeared. But Eatonville is still all black."

He pauses and looks at me. "And you're Zora's niece," he says wonderingly.

"Well," I say with shy dignity, yet with some tinge, I hope, of a nineteenth-century blush, "I'm illegitimate. That's why I never knew Aunt Zora."

I love him for the way he comes to my rescue. "You're *not* illegitimate!" he cries, his eyes resting on me fondly. "All of us are God's children! Don't you even *think* such a thing!"

And I hate myself for lying to him. Still, I ask myself, would I have gotten this far toward getting the headstone and finding out about Zora Hurston's last days without telling my lie? Actually, I probably would have. But I don't like taking chances that could get me stranded in central Florida.

"Zora didn't get along with her family. I don't know why. Did you read her autobiography, *Dust Tracks on a Road?*"

"Yes, I did," I say. "It pained me to see Zora pretending to be naïve and grateful about the old white 'Godmother' who helped finance her research, but I loved the part where she ran off from home after falling out with her brother's wife."

Dr. Benton nods. "When she got sick, I tried to get her to go back to her family, but she refused. There wasn't any real hatred; they just never had gotten along and Zora wouldn't go to them. She didn't want to go to the county home, either, but she had to, because she couldn't do a thing for herself."

"I was surprised to learn she died of malnutrition."

Dr. Benton seems startled. "Zora *didn't* die of malnutrition," he says indignantly. "Where did you get that story from? She had a stroke and she died in the welfare home." He seems peculiarly upset, distressed, but sits back reflectively in his chair. "She was an incredible woman," he muses. "Sometimes when I closed my office, I'd go by her house and just talk to her for an hour or two. She was a well-read, well-traveled woman and always had her own ideas about what was going on. . . ."

"I never knew her, you know. Only some of Carl Van Vechten's photographs and some newspaper photographs . . . What did she look like?"

"When I knew her, in the fifties, she was a big woman, *erect*. Not quite as light as I am [Dr. Benton is dark beige], and about five foot seven inches, and she weighed about two hundred pounds. Probably more. She . . ."

"What! Zora was *fat!* She wasn't, in Van Vechten's pictures!"

"Zora loved to eat," Dr. Benton says complacently. "She could sit down with a mound of ice cream and just eat and talk till it was all gone."

While Dr. Benton is talking, I recall that the Van Vechten pictures were taken when Zora was still a young woman. In them she appears tall, tan, and healthy. In later newspaper photographs — when she was in her forties — I remembered that she seemed heavier and several shades lighter. I reasoned that the earlier photographs were taken while she was busy collecting folklore materials in the hot Florida sun.

"She had high blood pressure. Her health wasn't good . . . She used to live in one of my houses — on School Court Street. It's a block house. . . . I don't recall the number. But my wife and I used to invite her over to the house for dinner. *She always ate well,*" he says emphatically.

"That's comforting to know," I say, wondering where Zora ate when she wasn't with the Bentons.

"Sometimes she would run out of groceries — after she got sick — and she'd call me. 'Come over here and see 'bout me,' she'd say. And I'd take her shopping and buy her groceries.

"She was always studying. Her mind — before the stroke — just worked all the time. She was always going somewhere, too. She once went to Honduras to study something. And when she died, she was working on that book about Herod the Great. She was so intelligent! And really had perfect expressions. Her English was beautiful." (I suspect this is a clever way to let me know Zora herself didn't speak in the "black English" her characters used.)

"I used to read all of her books," Dr. Benton continues, "but it was a long time ago. I remember one about . . . it was called, I think, 'The Children of God' [*Their Eyes Were Watching God*], and I remember Janie and Teapot [Teacake) and the mad dog riding on the cow in that hurricane and bit old Teapot on the cheek. . . ."

I am delighted that he remembers even this much of the story, even if the names are wrong, but seeing his affection for Zora I feel I must ask him about her burial. "Did she *really* have a pauper's funeral?"

"She *didn't* have a pauper's funeral!" he says with great heat. "Everybody around here *loved* Zora."

"We just came back from ordering a headstone," I say quietly, because he *is* an old man and the color is coming and going on his face, "but to tell the truth, I can't be positive what I found is the grave. All I know is the spot I found was the only grave-size hole in the area."

"I remember it wasn't near the road," says Dr. Benton, more calmly. "Some other lady came by here and we went out looking for the grave and I took a long iron stick and poked all over that part of the cemetery but we didn't find anything. She took some pictures of the general area. Do the weeds still come up to your knees?"

"And beyond," I murmur. This time there isn't any doubt. Dr. Benton feels ashamed.

As he walks us to our car, he continues to talk about Zora. "She couldn't really write much near the end. She had the stroke and it left her weak; her mind was affected. She couldn't think about anything for long.

"She came here from Daytona, I think. She owned a houseboat over there. When she came here, she sold it. She lived on that money, then she worked as a maid — for an article on maids she was writing — and she worked for the *Chronicle* writing the horoscope column.

"I think black people here in Florida got mad at her because she was for some politician they were against. She said this politician *built* schools for blacks while the one they wanted just talked about it. And although Zora wasn't egotistical, what she thought, she thought; and generally what she thought, she said."

When we leave Dr. Benton's office, I realize I have missed my plane back home to Jackson, Mississippi. That being so, Charlotte and I decide to find the house Zora lived in before she was taken to the county welfare home to die. From among her many notes, Charlotte locates a letter of Zora's she has copied that carries the address: 1734 School Court Street. We ask several people for directions. Finally, two old gentlemen in a dusty gray Plymouth offer to lead us there. School Court Street is not paved, and the road is full of mud puddles. It is dismal and squalid, redeemed only by the brightness of the late afternoon sun. Now I can understand what a "block" house is. It is a house shaped like a block, for one thing, surrounded by others just like it. Some houses are blue and some are green or yellow. Zora's is light green. They are tiny — about fifty by fifty feet, squatty with flat roofs. The house Zora lived in looks worse than the others, but that is its only distinction. It also has three ragged and dirty children sitting on the steps.

"Is this where y'all live?" I ask, aiming my camera.

"No, ma'am" they say in unison, looking at me earnestly. "We live over yonder. This Miss So-and-So's house; but she in the horspital."

We chatter inconsequentially while I take more pictures. A car drives up with a young black couple in it. They scowl fiercely at Charlotte and don't look at me with friendliness, either. They get out and stand in their doorway across the street. I go up to them to explain. "Did you know Zora Hurston used to live right across from you?" I ask.

"Who?" They stare at me blankly, then become curiously attentive, as if they think I made the name up. They are both Afroed and he is somberly dashikied.

I suddenly feel frail and exhausted. "It's too long a story," I say, "but tell me something: is there anybody on this street who's lived here for more than thirteen years?"

"That old man down there," the young man says, pointing. Sure enough, there is a man sitting on his steps three houses down. He has graying hair and is very neat, but there is a weakness about him. He reminds me of Mrs. Turner's husband in *Their Eyes Were Watching God*. He's rather "vanishing" looking, as if his features have been sanded down. In the old days, before black was beautiful, he was probably considered attractive, because he has wavy hair and light-brown skin; but now, well, light skin has ceased to be its own reward.

After the preliminaries, there is only one thing I want to know: "Tell me something," I begin, looking down at Zora's house. "Did Zora like flowers?"

He looks at me queerly. "As a matter of fact," he says, looking regretfully at the bare, rough yard that surrounds her former house, "she was crazy about them. And she was a great gardener. She loved azaleas, and that running and blooming vine [morning-glories], and she really loved that night-smelling flower [gardenia]. She kept a vegetable garden year-round, too. She raised collards and tomatoes and things like that.

"Everyone in this community thought well of Miss Hurston. When she died, people all up and down this street took up a collection for her burial. We put her away nice."

"Why didn't somebody put up a headstone?"

"Well, you know, one was never requested. Her and her family didn't get along. They didn't even come to the funeral."

"And did she live down there by herself?"

"Yes, until they took her away. She lived with — just her and her companion, Sport."

My ears perk up. "Who?"

"Sport, you know, her dog. He was her only companion. He was a big brown and white dog."

When I walk back to the car, Charlotte is talking to the young couple on their porch. They are relaxed and smiling.

"I told them about the famous lady who used to live across the street from them," says Charlotte as we drive off. "Of course they had no idea Zora ever lived, let alone that she lived across the street. I think I'll send some of her books to them."

"That's real kind of you," I say.

> I am not tragically colored. There is no great sorrow dammed up in my soul, nor lurking behind my eyes. I do not mind at all. I do not belong to the sobbing school of Negrohood who hold that nature some-

how has given them a lowdown dirty deal and whose feelings are all hurt about it. . . . No, I do not weep at the world — I am too busy sharpening my oyster knife.

— Zora Neale Hurston, "How It Feels to Be Colored Me,"
World Tomorrow, 1928

There are times — and finding Zora Hurston's grave was one of them — when normal responses of grief, horror, and so on do not make sense because they bear no real relation to the depth of the emotion one feels. It was impossible for me to cry when I saw the field full of weeds where Zora is. Partly this is because I have come to know Zora through her books and she was not a teary sort of person herself; but partly, too, it is because there is a point at which even grief feels absurd. And at this point, laughter gushes up to retrieve sanity.

It is only later, when the pain is not so direct a threat to one's own existence, that what was learned in that moment of comical lunacy is understood. Such moments rob us of both youth and vanity. But perhaps they are also times when greater disciplines are born.

1977

Adrienne Rich

....

Women and Honor:
Some Notes on Lying

These notes are concerned with relationships between and among women. When "personal relationship" is referred to, I mean a relationship between two women. It will be clear in what follows when I am talking about women's relationships with men.

The old, male idea of honor. A man's "word" sufficed — to other men — without guarantee.

"Our Land Free, Our Men Honest, Our Women Fruitful" — a popular colonial toast in America.

Male honor also having something to do with killing: *I could not love thee, Dear, so much / Lov'd I not Honour more,* ("To Lucasta, On Going to the Wars"). Male honor as something needing to be avenged: hence, the duel.

Women's honor, something altogether else: virginity, chastity, fidelity to a husband. Honesty in women has not been considered important. We have been depicted as generically whimsical, deceitful, subtle, vacillating. And we have been rewarded for lying.

Men have been expected to tell the truth about facts, not about feelings. They have not been expected to talk about feelings at all.

First published as a pamphlet by Motheroot Press in 1977 and collected in *On Lies, Secrets, and Silence,* 1979. Rich first read the notes at a women writers' workshop in Oneonta, New York, in 1975.

Yet even about facts they have continually lied.

We assume that politicians are without honor. We read their statements trying to crack the code. The scandals of their politics: not that men in high places lie, only that they do so with such indifference, so endlessly, still expecting to be believed. We are accustomed to the contempt inherent in the political lie.

•

To discover that one has been lied to in a personal relationship, however, leads one to feel a little crazy.

•

Lying is done with words, and also with silence.

The woman who tells lies in her personal relationships may or may not plan or invent her lying. She may not even think of what she is doing in a calculated way.

A subject is raised which the liar wishes buried. She has to go downstairs, her parking meter will have run out. Or, there is a telephone call she ought to have made an hour ago.

She is asked, point-blank, a question which may lead into painful talk: "How do you feel about what is happening between us?" Instead of trying to describe her feelings in their ambiguity and confusion, she asks, "How do *you* feel?" The other, because she is trying to establish a ground of openness and trust, begins describing her own feelings. Thus the liar learns more than she tells.

And she may also tell herself a lie: that she is concerned with the other's feelings, not with her own.

But the liar is concerned with her own feelings.

The liar lives in fear of losing control. She cannot even desire a relationship without manipulation, since to be vulnerable to another person means for her the loss of control.

The liar has many friends, and leads an existence of great loneliness.

•

The liar often suffers from amnesia. Amnesia is the silence of the unconscious.

To lie habitually, as a way of life, is to lose contact with the unconscious. It is like taking sleeping pills, which confer sleep but blot out dreaming. The unconscious wants truth. It ceases to speak to those who want something else more than truth.

In speaking of lies, we come inevitably to the subject of truth. There is nothing simple or easy about this idea. There is no "the truth," "a truth" — truth is not one thing, or even a system. It is an increasing complexity. The pattern of the carpet is a surface. When we look closely, or when we become weavers, we learn of the tiny multiple threads unseen in the overall pattern, the knots on the underside of the carpet.

This is why the effort to speak honestly is so important. Lies are usually attempts to make everything simpler — for the liar — than it really is, or ought to be.

In lying to others we end up lying to ourselves. We deny the importance of an event, or a person, and thus deprive ourselves of a part of our lives. Or we use one piece of the past or present to screen out another. Thus we lose faith even with our own lives.

The unconscious wants truth, as the body does. The complexity and fecundity of dreams come from the complexity and fecundity of the unconscious struggling to fulfill that desire. The complexity and fecundity of poetry come from the same struggle.

•

An honorable human relationship — that is, one in which two people have the right to use the word "love" — is a process, delicate, violent, often terrifying to both persons involved, a process of refining the truths they can tell each other.

It is important to do this because it breaks down human self-delusion and isolation.

It is important to do this because in so doing we do justice to our own complexity.

It is important to do this because we can count on so few people to go that hard way with us.

•

I come back to the questions of women's honor. Truthfulness has not been considered important for women, as long as we have remained physically faithful to a man, or chaste.

We have been expected to lie with our bodies: to bleach, redden, unkink or curl our hair, pluck eyebrows, shave armpits, wear padding in various places or lace ourselves, take little steps, glaze finger and toe nails, wear clothes that emphasized our helplessness.

We have been required to tell different lies at different times, depending on what the men of the time needed to hear. The Victorian wife or the white southern lady, who were expected to have no sensuality, to "lie still"; the twentieth-century "free" woman who is expected to fake orgasms.

We have had the truth of our bodies withheld from us or distorted; we have been kept in ignorance of our most intimate places. Our instincts have been punished: clitoridectomies for "lustful" nuns or for "difficult" wives. It has been difficult, too, to know the lies of our complicity from the lies we believed.

The lie of the "happy marriage," of domesticity — we have been complicit, have acted out the fiction of a well-lived life, until the day we testify in court of rapes, beatings, psychic cruelties, public and private humiliations.

Patriarchal lying has manipulated women both through falsehood and through silence. Facts we needed have been withheld from us. False witness has been borne against us.

And so we must take seriously the question of truthfulness between women, truthfulness among women. As we cease to lie with our bodies, as we cease to take on faith what men have said about us, is a truly womanly idea of honor in the making?

•

Women have been forced to lie, for survival, to men. How to unlearn this among other women?

"Women have always lied to each other."
"Women have always whispered the truth to each other."
Both of these axioms are true.

"Women have always been divided against each other."
"Women have always been in secret collusion."
Both of these axioms are true.

In the struggle for survival we tell lies. To bosses, to prison guards, the police, men who have power over us, who legally own us and our children, lovers who need us as proof of their manhood.

There is a danger run by all powerless people: that we forget we are lying, or that lying becomes a weapon we carry over into relationships with people who do not have power over us.

•

I want to reiterate that when we talk about women and honor, or women and lying, we speak within the context of male lying, the lies of the powerful, the lie as false source of power.

Women have to think whether we want, in our relationships with each other, the kind of power that can be obtained through lying.

Women have been driven mad, "gaslighted," for centuries by the refutation of our experience and our instincts in a culture which validates only male experience. The truth of our bodies and our minds has been mystified to us. We therefore have a primary obligation to each other: not to undermine each other's sense of reality for the sake of expediency; not to gaslight each other.

Women have often felt insane when cleaving to the truth of our experience. Our future depends on the sanity of each of us, and we have a profound stake, beyond the personal, in the project of describing our reality as candidly and fully as we can to each other.

•

There are phrases which help us not to admit we are lying: "my privacy," "nobody's business but my own." The choices that underlie these phrases may indeed be justified; but we ought to think about the full meaning and consequences of such language.

Women's love for women has been represented almost entirely through silence and lies. The institution of heterosexuality has forced the lesbian to dissemble, or be labeled a pervert, a criminal, a sick or dangerous woman, etc., etc. The lesbian, then, has often been forced to lie, like the prostitute or the married woman.

Does a life "in the closet" — lying, perhaps of necessity, about ourselves to bosses, landlords, clients, colleagues, family, because the law and public opinion are founded on a lie — does this, can it, spread into private life, so that lying (described as *discretion*) becomes an easy way to avoid conflict or complication? can it become a strategy so ingrained that it is used even with close friends and lovers?

Heterosexuality as an institution has also drowned in silence the erotic feelings between women. I myself lived half a lifetime in the lie of that denial. That silence makes us all, to some degree, into liars.

When a woman tells the truth she is creating the possibility for more truth around her.

•

The liar leads an existence of unutterable loneliness.

The liar is afraid.

But we are all afraid: without fear we become manic, hubristic, self-destructive. What is this particular fear that possesses the liar?

She is afraid that her own truths are not good enough.

She is afraid, not so much of prison guards or bosses, but of something unnamed within her.

The liar fears the void.

The void is not something created by patriarchy, or racism, or capitalism. It will not fade away with any of them. It is part of every woman.

"The dark core," Virginia Woolf named it, writing of her mother. The dark core. It is beyond personality; beyond who loves us or hates us.

We begin out of the void, out of darkness and emptiness. It is part of the cycle understood by the old pagan religions, that materialism denies. Out of death, rebirth; out of nothing, something.

The void is the creatrix, the matrix. It is not mere hollowness and anarchy. But in women it has been identified with lovelessness, barrenness, sterility. We have been urged to fill our "emptiness" with children. We are not supposed to go down into the darkness of the core.

Yet, if we can risk it, the something born of that nothing is the beginning of our truth.

The liar in her terror wants to fill up the void, with anything. Her lies are a denial of her fear; a way of maintaining control.

·

Why do we feel slightly crazy when we realize we have been lied to in a relationship?

We take so much of the universe on trust. You tell me: "In 1950 I lived on the north side of Beacon Street in Somerville." You tell me: "She and I were lovers, but for months now we have only been good friends." You tell me: "It is seventy degrees outside and the sun is shining." Because I love you, because there is not even a question of lying between us, I take these accounts of the universe on trust: your address twenty-five years ago, your relationship with someone I know only by sight, this morning's weather. I fling unconscious tendrils of belief, like slender green threads, across statements such as these, statements made so unequivocally, which have no tone or shadow of tentativeness. I build them into the mosaic of my world. I allow my universe to change in minute, significant ways, on the basis of things you have said to me, of my trust in you.

I also have faith that you are telling me things it is important I should know; that you do not conceal facts from me in an effort to spare me, or yourself, pain.

Or, at the very least, that you will say, "There are things I am not telling you."

When we discover that someone we trusted can be trusted no longer, it forces us to reexamine the universe, to question the whole instinct and concept of trust. For a while, we are thrust back onto some bleak, jutting ledge, in a dark pierced by sheets of fire, swept by sheets of rain, in a world before kinship, or naming, or tenderness exist; we are brought close to formlessness.

·

The liar may resist confrontation, denying that she lied. Or she may use other language: forgetfulness, privacy, the protection of someone else. Or, she may bravely declare herself a coward. This allows her to go on lying, since that is what cowards do. She does not say, *I was afraid*, since this would open the question of other ways of handling her fear. It would open the question of what is actually feared.

She may say, *I didn't want to cause pain.* What she really did not want is to have to deal with the other's pain. The lie is a short-cut through another's personality.

•

Truthfulness, honor, is not something which springs ablaze of itself; it has to be created between people.

This is true in political situations. The quality and depth of the politics evolving from a group depends in very large part on their understanding of honor.

Much of what is narrowly termed "politics" seems to rest on a longing for certainty even at the cost of honesty, for an analysis which, once given, need not be reexamined. Such is the deadendedness — for women — of Marxism in our time.

Truthfulness anywhere means a heightened complexity. But it is a movement into evolution. Women are only beginning to uncover our own truths; many of us would be grateful for some rest in that struggle, would be glad just to lie down with the sherds we have painfully unearthed, and be satisfied with those. Often I feel this like an exhaustion in my own body.

The politics worth having, the relationships worth having, demand that we delve still deeper.

•

The possibilities that exist between two people, or among a group of people, are a kind of alchemy. They are the most interesting thing in life. The liar is someone who keeps losing sight of these possibilities.

When relationships are determined by manipulation, by the need for control, they may possess a dreary, bickering kind of drama, but they cease to be interesting. They are repetitious; the shock of human possibilities has ceased to reverberate through them.

When someone tells me a piece of the truth which has been withheld from me, and which I needed in order to see my life more clearly, it may bring acute pain, but it can also flood me with a cold, sea-sharp wash of relief. Often such truths come by accident, or from strangers.

It isn't that to have an honorable relationship with you, I have to understand everything, or tell you everything at once, or that I can know, beforehand, everything I need to tell you.

It means that most of the time I am eager, longing for the possibility of telling you. That these possibilities may seem frightening, but not destructive, to me. That I feel strong enough to hear your tentative and groping words. That we both know we are trying, all the time, to extend the possibilities of truth between us.

The possibility of life between us.

1979

Joan Didion

··

The White Album

1

WE TELL OURSELVES stories in order to live. The princess is caged in the consulate. The man with the candy will lead the children into the sea. The naked woman on the ledge outside the window on the sixteenth floor is a victim of accidie, or the naked woman is an exhibitionist, and it would be "interesting" to know which. We tell ourselves that it makes some difference whether the naked woman is about to commit a mortal sin or is about to register a political protest or is about to be, the Aristophanic view, snatched back to the human condition by the fireman in priest's clothing just visible in the window behind her, the one smiling at the telephoto lens. We look for the sermon in the suicide, for the social or moral lesson in the murder of five. We interpret what we see, select the most workable of the multiple choices. We live entirely, especially if we are writers, by the imposition of a narrative line upon disparate images, by the "ideas" with which we have learned to freeze the shifting phantasmagoria which is our actual experience.

Or at least we do for a while. I am talking here about a time when I began to doubt the premises of all the stories I had ever told myself, a common condition but one I found troubling. I suppose this period began around 1966 and continued until 1971. During those five years I appeared, on the face of it, a competent enough member of some community or another, a signer of contracts and Air Travel cards, a citizen: I

Parts 3, 6, and 9 of the essay were first published in Didion's "Points West" column in *The Saturday Evening Post* in 1968 and 1969. "The White Album: A Chronicle of Survival" was published in *New West* in 1979. It is the title essay of Didion's collection **The White Album*, 1979.

wrote a couple of times a month for one magazine or another, published two books, worked on several motion pictures; participated in the paranoia of the time, in the raising of a small child, and in the entertainment of large numbers of people passing through my house; made gingham curtains for spare bedrooms, remembered to ask agents if any reduction of points would be *pari passu* with the financing studio, put lentils to soak on Saturday night for lentil soup on Sunday, made quarterly F.I.C.A. payments and renewed my driver's license on time, missing on the written examination only the question about the financial responsibility of California drivers. It was a time of my life when I was frequently "named." I was named godmother to children. I was named lecturer and panelist, colloquist and conferee. I was even named, in 1968, a *Los Angeles Times* "Woman of the Year," along with Mrs. Ronald Reagan, the Olympic swimmer Debbie Meyer, and ten other California women who seemed to keep in touch and do good works. I did no good works but I tried to keep in touch. I was responsible. I recognized my name when I saw it. Once in a while I even answered letters addressed to me, not exactly upon receipt but eventually, particularly if the letters had come from strangers. "During my absence from the country these past eighteen months," such replies would begin.

This was an adequate enough performance, as improvisations go. The only problem was that my entire education, everything I had ever been told or had told myself, insisted that the production was never meant to be improvised: I was supposed to have a script, and had mislaid it. I was supposed to hear cues, and no longer did. I was meant to know the plot, but all I knew was what I saw: flash pictures in variable sequence, images with no "meaning" beyond their temporary arrangement, not a movie but a cutting-room experience. In what would probably be the middle of my life I wanted still to believe in the narrative and in the narrative's intelligibility, but to know that one could change the sense with every cut was to begin to perceive the experience as rather more electrical than ethical.

During this period I spent what were for me the usual proportions of time in Los Angeles and New York and Sacramento. I spent what seemed to many people I knew an eccentric amount of time in Honolulu, the particular aspect of which lent me the illusion that I could any minute order from room service a revisionist theory of my own history, garnished with a vanda orchid. I watched Robert Kennedy's funeral on a verandah at the Royal Hawaiian Hotel in Honolulu, and also the first reports from My Lai. I reread all of George Orwell on the Royal Hawaiian Beach, and I also read, in the papers that came one day late from the mainland, the story of Betty Lansdown Fouquet, a 26-year-old woman with faded blond hair who put her five-year-old daughter out to die on the center divider of Interstate 5 some miles south of the last Bakersfield exit. The child, whose fingers had to be pried loose from the Cyclone fence when she was rescued twelve hours later by the California Highway Patrol, reported that she had run after the car carrying her mother and stepfather and brother and sister for "a long time." Certain of these images did not fit into any narrative I knew.

Another flash cut:

"In June of this year patient experienced an attack of vertigo, nausea, and a feeling that she was going to pass out. A thorough medical evaluation elicited no positive findings and she was placed on Elavil, Mg 20, tid. . . . The Rorschach record is interpreted as describing a personality in process of deterioration with abundant signs of failing defenses and increasing inability of the ego to mediate the world of reality and to cope with normal stress. . . . Emotionally, patient has alienated herself almost entirely from the world of other human beings. Her fantasy life appears to have been virtually completely preempted by primitive, regressive libidinal preoccupations many of which are distorted and bizarre. . . . In a technical sense basic affective controls appear to be intact but it is equally clear that they are insecurely and tenuously maintained for the present by a variety of defense mechanisms including intellectualization, obsessive-compulsive devices, projection, reaction-formation, and somatization, all of which now seem inadequate to their task of controlling or containing an underlying psychotic process and are therefore in process of failure. The content of patient's responses is highly unconventional and frequently bizarre, filled with sexual and anatomical preoccupations, and basic reality contact is obviously and seriously impaired at times. In quality and level of sophistication patient's responses are characteristic of those of individuals of high average or superior intelligence but she is now functioning intellectually in impaired fashion at barely average level. Patient's thematic productions on the Thematic Apperception Test emphasize her fundamentally pessimistic, fatalistic, and depressive view of the world around her. It is as though she feels deeply that all human effort is foredoomed to failure, a conviction which seems to push her further into a dependent, passive withdrawal. In her view she lives in a world of people moved by strange, conflicted, poorly comprehended, and, above all, devious motivations which commit them inevitably to conflict and failure . . ."

The patient to whom this psychiatric report refers is me. The tests mentioned — the Rorschach, the Thematic Apperception Test, the Sentence Completion Test and the Minnesota Multiphasic Personality Index — were administered privately, in the outpatient psychiatric clinic at St. John's Hospital in Santa Monica, in the summer of 1968, shortly after I suffered the "attack of vertigo and nausea" mentioned in the first sentence and shortly before I was named a Los Angeles Times "Woman of the Year." By way of comment I offer only that an attack of vertigo and nausea does not now seem to me an inappropriate response to the summer of 1968.

2

In the years I am talking about I was living in a large house in a part of Hollywood that had once been expensive and was now described by one of my acquaintances as a "senseless-killing neighborhood." This house on Franklin Avenue was rented, and paint peeled inside and out, and pipes broke and window sashes crumbled and the tennis court had not been rolled since 1933, but the rooms were many and high-ceilinged and, during the five years that I lived there, even the rather sinistral inertia of the neighborhood tended to suggest that I should live in the house indefinitely.

In fact I could not, because the owners were waiting only for a zoning change to tear the house down and build a high-rise apartment building, and for that matter it was precisely this anticipation of imminent but not exactly immediate destruction that lent the neighborhood its particular character. The house across the street had been built for one of the Talmadge sisters, had been the Japanese consulate in 1941, and was now, although boarded up, occupied by a number of unrelated adults who seemed to constitute some kind of therapy group. The house next door was owned by Synanon. I recall looking at a house around the corner with a rental sign on it: this house had once been the Canadian consulate, had 28 large rooms and two refrigerated fur closets, and could be rented, in the spirit of the neighborhood, only on a month-to-month basis, unfurnished. Since the inclination to rent an unfurnished 28-room house for a month or two is a distinctly special one, the neighborhood was peopled mainly by rock-and-roll bands, therapy groups, very old women wheeled down the street by practical nurses in soiled uniforms, and by my husband, my daughter and me.

Q. And what else happened, if anything. . . .
A. He said that he thought that I could be a star, like, you know, a young Burt Lancaster, you know, that kind of stuff.
Q. Did he mention any particular name?
A. Yes, sir.
Q. What name did he mention?
A. He mentioned a lot of names. He said Burt Lancaster. He said Clint Eastwood. He said Fess Parker. He mentioned a lot of names. . . .
Q. Did you talk after you ate?
A. While we were eating, after we ate. Mr. Novarro told our fortunes with some cards and he read our palms.
Q. Did he tell you you were going to have a lot of good luck or bad luck or what happened?
A. He wasn't a good palm reader.

These are excerpts from the testimony of Paul Robert Ferguson and Thomas Scott Ferguson, brothers, ages 22 and 17 respectively, during their trial for the murder of Ramon Novarro, age 69, at his house in Laurel Canyon, not too far from my house in Hollywood, on the night of October 30, 1968. I followed this trial quite closely, clipping reports from the newspapers and later borrowing a transcript from one of the defense attorneys. The younger of the brothers, "Tommy Scott" Ferguson, whose girl friend testified that she had stopped being in love with him "about two weeks after Grand Jury," said that he had been unaware of Mr. Novarro's career as a silent film actor until he was shown, at some point during the night of the murder, a photograph of his host as Ben-Hur. The older brother, Paul Ferguson, who began working carnivals when he was 12 and described himself at 22 as having had "a fast life and a good one," gave the jury, upon request, his definition of a hustler: "A hustler is someone who can talk — not just to men, to women, too. Who can cook. Can keep company. Wash a car. Lots of things make up a hustler. There are a lot of lonely people in this town, man." During the course of the trial each of the brothers accused the other of the murder. Both were convicted. I read the transcript several times, trying to bring the picture into some focus which did not suggest that I lived, as my psychiatric report had put it, "in a world of people moved by strange, conflicted, poorly comprehended and, above all, devious motivations"; I never met the Ferguson brothers.

I did meet one of the principals in another Los Angeles County murder trial during those years: Linda Kasabian, star witness for the prosecution in what was commonly known as the Manson Trial. I once asked Linda what she thought about the apparently chance sequence of events which had brought her first to the Spahn Movie Ranch and then to the Sybil Brand Institute for Women on charges, later dropped, of murdering Sharon Tate Polanski, Abigail Folger, Jay Sebring, Voytek Frykowski, Steven Parent, and Rosemary and Leno LaBianca. "Everything was to teach me something," Linda said. Linda did not believe that chance was without pattern. Linda operated on what I later recognized as dice theory, and so, during the years I am talking about, did I.

It will perhaps suggest the mood of those years if I tell you that during them I could not visit my mother-in-law without averting my eyes from a framed verse, a "house blessing," which hung in a hallway of her house in West Hartford, Connecticut.

> God bless the corners of this house,
> And be the lintel blest —
> And bless the hearth and bless the board
> And bless each place of rest —
> And bless the crystal windowpane that lets the starlight in
> And bless each door that opens wide, to stranger as to kin.

This verse had on me the effect of a physical chill, so insistently did it seem the kind of "ironic" detail the reporters would seize upon, the morning the bodies were found. In my neighborhood in California we did not bless the door that opened wide to stranger as to kin. Paul and Tommy Scott Ferguson were the strangers at Ramon Novarro's door, up on Laurel Canyon. Charles Manson was the stranger at Rosemary and Leno LaBianca's door, over in Los Feliz. Some strangers at the door knocked, and invented a reason to come inside: a call, say, to the Triple A, about a car not in evidence. Others just opened the door and walked in, and I would come across them in the entrance hall. I recall asking one such stranger what he wanted. We looked at each other for what seemed a long time, and then he saw my husband on the stair landing. "Chicken Delight," he said finally, but we had ordered no Chicken Delight, nor was he carrying any. I took the license number of his panel truck. It seems to me now that during those years I was always writing down the license numbers of panel trucks, panel trucks circling the block, panel trucks parked across the street, panel trucks idling at the intersection. I put these license numbers in a dressing-table drawer where they could be found by the police when the time came.

That the time would come I never doubted, at least not in the inaccessible places of the mind where I seemed more and more to be living. So many encounters in those years were devoid of any logic save that of the dreamwork. In the big house on Franklin Avenue many people seemed to come and go without relation to what I did. I knew where the sheets and towels were kept but I did not always know who was sleeping in every bed. I had the keys but not the key. I remember taking a 25-mg. Compazine one Easter Sunday and making a large and elaborate lunch for a number of people, many of whom were still around on Monday. I remember walking barefoot all day on the worn hardwood floors of that house and I remember "Do You Wanna Dance" on the record player, "Do You Wanna Dance" and "Visions of Johanna" and a song called "Midnight Confessions." I remember a babysitter telling me that she saw death in my aura. I remember chatting with her about reasons why this might be so, paying her, opening all the French windows and going to sleep in the living room.

It was hard to surprise me in those years. It was hard to even get my attention. I was absorbed in my intellectualization, my obsessive-compulsive devices, my projection, my reaction-formation, my somatization, and in the transcript of the Ferguson trial. A musician I had met a few years before called from a Ramada Inn in Tuscaloosa to tell me how to save myself through Scientology. I had met him once in my life, had talked to him for maybe half an hour about brown rice and the charts, and now he was telling me from Alabama about E-meters, and how I might become a Clear. I received a telephone call from a stranger in Montreal who seemed to want to enlist me in a narcotics operation. "Is it cool to talk on this telephone?" he asked several times. "Big Brother isn't listening?"

I said that I doubted it, although increasingly I did not.

"Because what we're talking about, basically, is applying the Zen philosophy to money and business, dig? And if I say we are going to finance the underground, and if I mention major money, you know what I'm talking about because you know what's going down, right?"

Maybe he was not talking about narcotics. Maybe he was talking about turning a profit on M-1 rifles: I had stopped looking for the logic in such calls. Someone with whom I had gone to school in Sacramento and had last seen in 1952 turned up at my house in Hollywood in 1968 in the guise of a private detective from West Covina, one of very few licensed women private detectives in the State of California. "They call us Dickless Tracys," she said, idly but definitely fanning out the day's mail on the hall table. "I have a lot of very close friends in law enforcement," she said then. "You might want to meet them." We exchanged promises to keep in touch but never met again: a not atypical encounter of the period. The Sixties were over before it occurred to me that this visit might have been less than entirely social.

3

It was six, seven o'clock of an early spring evening in 1968 and I was sitting on the cold vinyl floor of a sound studio on Sunset Boulevard, watching a band called The Doors record a rhythm track. On the whole my attention was only minimally engaged by the preoccupations of rock-and-roll bands (I had already heard about acid as a transitional stage and also about the Maharishi and even about Universal Love, and after a while it all sounded like marmalade skies to me), but The Doors were different, The Doors interested me. The Doors seemed unconvinced that love was brotherhood and the Kama Sutra. The Doors' music insisted that love was sex and sex was death and therein lay salvation. The Doors were the Norman Mailers of the Top Forty, missionaries of apocalyptic sex. *Break on through*, their lyrics urged, and *Light my fire*, and:

> Come on baby, gonna take a little ride
> Goin' down by the ocean side
> Gonna get real close
> Get real tight
> Baby gonna drown tonight —
> Goin' down, down, down.

On this evening in 1968 they were gathered together in uneasy symbiosis to make their third album, and the studio was too cold and the lights were too bright and there were masses of wires and banks of the ominous blinking electronic circuitry with which musicians live so easily. There were three of the four Doors. There was a bass player borrowed from a band called Clear Light. There were the producer and the engineer and the road manager and a couple of girls and a Siberian husky named Nikki with one gray eye and one gold. There were paper bags half filled with hard-boiled eggs and chicken livers and cheeseburgers and empty bottles of apple juice and California rosé. There was everything and everybody The Doors needed to cut the rest of this third album except one thing, the fourth Door, the lead singer, Jim Morrison, a 24-year-old graduate of U.C.L.A. who wore black vinyl pants and no underwear and tended to suggest some range of the possible just beyond a suicide pact. It was Morrison who had described The Doors as "erotic politicians." It was Morrison who had defined the group's interests as "anything about revolt, disorder, chaos, about activity that appears to have no meaning." It was Morrison who got arrested in Miami in December of 1967 for giving an "indecent" performance. It was Morrison who wrote most of The Doors' lyrics, the peculiar character of which was to reflect either an ambiguous paranoia or a quite unambiguous insistence upon the love-death as the ultimate high. And it was Morrison who was missing. It was Ray Manzarek and Robby Krieger and John Densmore who made The Doors sound the way they sounded, and maybe it was Manzarek and Krieger and Densmore who made seventeen out of twenty interviewees on *American Bandstand* prefer The Doors over all other bands, but it was Morrison who got up there in his black vinyl pants with no underwear and projected the idea, and it was Morrison they were waiting for now.

"Hey listen," the engineer said. "I was listening to an FM station on the way over here, they played three Doors songs, first they played 'Back Door Man' and then 'Love Me Two Times' and 'Light My Fire.'"

"I heard it," Densmore muttered. "I heard it."

"So what's wrong with somebody playing three of your songs?"

"This cat dedicates it to his family."

"Yeah? To his family?"

"To his family. Really crass."

Ray Manzarek was hunched over a Gibson keyboard. "You think *Morrison's* going to come back?" he asked to no one in particular.

No one answered.

"So we can do some *vocals?*" Manzarek said.

The producer was working with the tape of the rhythm track they had just recorded. "I hope so," he said without looking up.

"Yeah," Manzarek said. "So do I."

My leg had gone to sleep, but I did not stand up; unspecific tensions seemed to be rendering everyone in the room catatonic. The producer played back the rhythm track. The engineer said that he wanted to do his deep-breathing exercises. Manzarek ate a hard-boiled egg. "Tennyson made a mantra out of his own name," he said to the engineer. "I don't know if he said 'Tennyson Tennyson Tennyson' or 'Alfred Alfred Alfred' or 'Alfred Lord Tennyson,' but anyway, he did it. Maybe he just said 'Lord Lord Lord.'"

"Groovy," the Clear Light bass player said. He was an amiable enthu-
siast, not at all a Door in spirit.

"I wonder what Blake said," Manzarek mused. "Too bad *Morrison's*
not here. *Morrison* would know."

It was a long while later. Morrison arrived. He had on his black vinyl
pants and he sat down on a leather couch in front of the four big blank
speakers and he closed his eyes. The curious aspect of Morrison's arrival
was this: no one acknowledged it. Robby Krieger continued working
out a guitar passage. John Densmore tuned his drums. Manzarek sat at
the control console and twirled a corkscrew and let a girl rub his shoulders. The girl did not look at Morrison, although he was in her direct line of sight. An hour or so passed, and still no one had spoken to
Morrison. Then Morrison spoke to Manzarek. He spoke almost in a
whisper, as if he were wresting the words from behind some disabling
aphasia.

"It's an hour to West Covina," he said. "I was thinking maybe we
should spend the night out there after we play."

Manzarek put down the corkscrew. "Why?" he said.

"Instead of coming back."

Manzarek shrugged. "We were planning to come back."

"Well, I was thinking, we could rehearse out there."

Manzarek said nothing.

"We could get in a rehearsal, there's a Holiday Inn next door."

"We could do that," Manzarek said. "Or we could rehearse Sunday, in
town."

"I guess so." Morrison paused. "Will the place be ready to rehearse
Sunday?"

Manzarek looked at him for a while. "No," he said then.

I counted the control knobs on the electronic console. There were
seventy-six. I was unsure in whose favor the dialogue had been resolved,
or if it had been resolved at all. Robby Krieger picked at his guitar, and
said that he needed a fuzz box. The producer suggested that he borrow
one from the Buffalo Springfield, who were recording in the next studio. Krieger shrugged. Morrison sat down again on the leather couch
and leaned back. He lit a match. He studied the flame awhile and then
very slowly, very deliberately, lowered it to the fly of his black vinyl
pants. Manzarek watched him. The girl who was rubbing Manzarek's
shoulders did not look at anyone. There was a sense that no one was go-

ing to leave the room, ever. It would be some weeks before The Doors finished recording this album. I did not see it through.

4

Someone once brought Janis Joplin to a party at the house on Franklin Avenue: she had just done a concert and she wanted brandy-and-Benedictine in a water tumbler. Music people never wanted ordinary drinks. They wanted sake, or champagne cocktails, or tequila neat. Spending time with music people was confusing, and required a more fluid and ultimately a more passive approach than I ever acquired. In the first place time was never of the essence: we would have dinner at nine unless we had it at eleven-thirty, or we could order in later. We would go down to U.S.C. to see the Living Theater if the limo came at the very moment when no one had just made a drink or a cigarette or an arrangement to meet Ultra Violet at the Montecito. In any case David Hockney was coming by. In any case Ultra Violet was not at the Montecito. In any case we would go down to U.S.C. and see the Living Theater tonight or we would see the Living Theater another night, in New York, or Prague. First we wanted sushi for twenty, steamed clams, vegetable vindaloo and many rum drinks with gardenias for our hair. First we wanted a table for twelve, fourteen at the most, although there might be six more, or eight more, or eleven more: there would never be one or two more, because music people did not travel in groups of "one" or "two." John and Michelle Phillips, on their way to the hospital for the birth of their daughter Chynna, had the limo detour into Hollywood in order to pick up a friend, Anne Marshall. This incident, which I often embroider in my mind to include an imaginary second detour, to the Luau for gardenias, exactly describes the music business to me.

5

Around five o'clock on the morning of October 28, 1967, in the desolate district between San Francisco Bay and the Oakland estuary that the Oakland police call Beat 101A, a 25-year-old black militant named Huey P. Newton was stopped and questioned by a white police officer named John Frey, Jr. An hour later Huey Newton was under arrest at Kaiser Hospital in Oakland, where he had gone for emergency treatment of a gunshot wound in his stomach, and a few weeks later he was indicted by the Alameda County Grand Jury on charges of murdering John Frey, wounding another officer, and kidnapping a bystander.

In the spring of 1968, when Huey Newton was awaiting trial, I went to see him in the Alameda County Jail. I suppose I went because I was interested in the alchemy of issues, for an issue is what Huey Newton had by then become. To understand how that had happened you must first consider Huey Newton, who he was. He came from an Oakland family, and for a while he went to Merritt College. In October of 1966 he and a friend named Bobby Seale organized what they called the Black Panther Party. They borrowed the name from the emblem used by the Freedom Party in Lowndes County, Alabama, and, from the beginning, they defined themselves as a revolutionary political group. The Oakland police knew the Panthers, and had a list of the twenty or so Panther cars. I am telling you neither that Huey Newton killed John Frey nor that Huey Newton did not kill John Frey, for in the context of revolutionary politics Huey Newton's guilt or innocence was irrelevant. I am telling you only how Huey Newton happened to be in the Alameda County Jail, and why rallies were held in his name, demonstrations organized whenever he appeared in court. LET'S SPRING HUEY, the buttons read (fifty cents each), and here and there on the courthouse steps, among the Panthers with their berets and sunglasses, the chants would go up:

> Get your M-
> 31.
> 'Cause baby we gonna
> Have some fun.
> BOOM BOOM. BOOM BOOM.

"Fight on, brother," a woman would add in the spirit of a good-natured amen. "Bang-bang."

> Bullshit bullshit
> Can't stand the game
> White man's playing.
> One way out, one way out.
> BOOM BOOM. BOOM BOOM.

In the corridor downstairs in the Alameda County Courthouse there was a crush of lawyers and CBC correspondents and cameramen and people who wanted to "visit Huey."

"Eldridge doesn't mind if I go up," one of the latter said to one of the lawyers.

"If Eldridge doesn't mind, it's all right with me," the lawyer said. "If you've got press credentials."

"I've got kind of dubious credentials."

"I can't take you up then. *Eldridge* has got dubious credentials. One's bad enough. I've got a good working relationship up there, I don't want to blow it." The lawyer turned to a cameraman. "You guys rolling yet?"

On that particular day I was allowed to go up, and a *Los Angeles Times* man, and a radio newscaster. We all signed the police register and sat around a scarred pine table and waited for Huey Newton. "The only thing that's going to free Huey Newton," Rap Brown had said recently at a Panther rally in Oakland Auditorium, "is gunpowder." "Huey Newton laid down his life for us," Stokely Carmichael had said the same night. But of course Huey Newton had not yet laid down his life at all, was just here in the Alameda County Jail waiting to be tried, and I wondered if the direction these rallies were taking ever made him uneasy, ever made him suspect that in many ways he was more useful to the revolution behind bars than on the street. He seemed, when he finally came in, an extremely likable young man, engaging, direct, and I did not get the sense that he had intended to become a political martyr. He smiled at us all and waited for his lawyer, Charles Garry, to set up a tape recorder, and he chatted softly with Eldridge Cleaver, who was then the Black Panthers' Minister of Information. (Huey Newton was still the Minister of Defense.) Eldridge Cleaver wore a black sweater and one gold earring and spoke in an almost inaudible drawl and was allowed to see Huey Newton because he had those "dubious credentials," a press card from *Ramparts*. Actually his interest was in getting "statements" from Huey Newton, "messages" to take outside; in receiving a kind of prophecy to be interpreted as needed.

"We need a statement, Huey, about the ten-point program," Eldridge Cleaver said, "so I'll ask you a question, see, and you answer it . . ."

"How's Bobby," Huey Newton asked.

"He's got a hearing on his misdemeanors, see . . ."

"I thought he had a felony."

"Well, that's another thing, the felony, he's also got a couple of misdemeanors . . ."

Once Charles Garry had set up the tape recorder Huey Newton stopped chatting and started lecturing, almost without pause. He talked, running the words together because he had said them so many times before, about "the American capitalistic-materialistic system" and "so-called free enterprise" and "the fight for the liberation of black people throughout the world." Every now and then Eldridge Cleaver would signal Huey Newton and say something like, "There are a lot of people interested in the Executive Mandate Number Three you've issued to the Black Panther Party, Huey. Care to comment?"

And Huey Newton would comment. "Yes. Mandate Number Three is this demand from the Black Panther Party speaking for the black community. Within the Mandate we admonish the racist police force . . ." I kept wishing that he would talk about himself, hoping to break through the wall of rhetoric, but he seemed to be one of those autodidacts for whom all things specific and personal present themselves as mine fields to be avoided even at the cost of coherence, for whom safety lies in generalization. The newspaperman, the radio man, they tried:

Q. Tell us something about yourself, Huey, I mean your life before the Panthers.
A. Before the Black Panther Party my life was very similar to that of most black people in this country.
Q. Well, your family, some incidents you remember, the influences that shaped you —
A. Living in America shaped me.
Q. Well, yes, but more specifically —
A. It reminds me of a quote from James Baldwin: "To be black and conscious in America is to be in a constant state of rage."

"To be black and conscious in America is to be in a constant state of rage," Eldridge Cleaver wrote in large letters on a pad of paper, and then he added: *"Huey P. Newton quoting James Baldwin."* I could see it emblazoned above the speakers' platform at a rally, imprinted on the letterhead of an ad hoc committee still unborn. As a matter of fact almost everything Huey Newton said had the ring of being a "quotation," a "pronouncement" to be employed when the need arose. I had heard Huey P. Newton On Racism ("The Black Panther Party is against racism"), Huey P. Newton On Cultural Nationalism ("The Black Panther Party believes that the only culture worth holding onto is revolutionary culture"), Huey P. Newton On White Radicalism, On Police Occupation of the Ghetto, On The European Versus The African. "The European started to be sick when he denied his sexual nature," Huey Newton said, and Charles Garry interrupted then, bringing it back to first principles.

"Isn't it true, though, Huey," he said, "that racism got its start for *economic* reasons?"

This weird interlocution seemed to take on a life of its own. The small room was hot and the fluorescent light hurt my eyes and I still did not know to what extent Huey Newton understood the nature of the role in which he was cast. As it happened I had always appreciated the logic of the Panther position, based as it was on the proposition that political power began at the end of the barrel of a gun (exactly what gun had even been specified, in an early memorandum from Huey P. Newton: *"Army .45; carbine; 12-gauge Magnum shotgun with 18″ barrel, preferably the brand of High Standard; M-16; .357 Magnum pistols; P-38"*), and I could appreciate as well the particular beauty in Huey Newton as "issue." In the politics of revolution everyone was expendable, but I doubted that Huey Newton's political sophistication extended to seeing himself that way: the value of a Scottsboro case is easier to see if you are not yourself the Scottsboro boy. "Is there anything else you want to ask Huey?" Charles Garry asked. There did not seem to be. The lawyer adjusted his tape recorder. "I've had a request, Huey," he said, "from a high-school student, a reporter on his school paper, and he wanted a statement from you, and he's going to call me tonight. Care to give me a message for him?"

Huey Newton regarded the microphone. There was a moment in which he seemed not to remember the name of the play, and then he brightened. "I would like to point out," he said, his voice gaining volume as the memory disks clicked, *high school, student, youth, message to youth,* "that America is becoming a very young nation . . ."

I heard a moaning and a groaning, and I went over and it was — this Negro fellow was there. He had been shot in the stomach and at the time he didn't appear in any acute distress and so I said I'd see, and I asked him if he was a Kaiser, if he belonged to Kaiser, and he said, "Yes, yes. Get a doctor. Can't you see I'm bleeding? I've been shot. Now get someone out here." And I asked him if he had his Kaiser card and he got upset at this and he said, "Come on, get a doctor out here, I've been shot." I said, "I see this, but you're not in any acute distress." . . . So I told him we'd have to check to make sure he was a member. . . . And this kind of upset him more and he called me a few nasty names and said, "Now get a doctor out here right now, I've been shot and I'm bleeding." And he took his coat off and his shirt and he threw it on the desk there and he said, "Can't you see all this blood?" And I said, "I see it." And it wasn't that much, and so I said, "Well, you'll have to sign our admission sheet before you can be seen by a doctor." And he said, "I'm not signing anything." And I said, "You cannot be seen by a doctor unless you sign the admission sheet," and he said, "I don't have to sign anything" and a few more choice words . . .

This is an excerpt from the testimony before the Alameda County Grand Jury of Corrine Leonard, the nurse in charge of the Kaiser Foundation Hospital emergency room in Oakland at 5:30 A.M. on October 28, 1967. The "Negro fellow" was of course Huey Newton, wounded that morning during the gunfire which killed John Frey. For a long time I kept a copy of this testimony pinned to my office wall, on the theory that it illustrated a collision of cultures, a classic instance of an historical outsider confronting the established order at its most petty and impenetrable level. This theory was shattered when I learned that Huey Newton was in fact an enrolled member of the Kaiser Foundation Health Plan, i.e., in Nurse Leonard's words, "a Kaiser."

6

One morning in 1968 I went to see Eldridge Cleaver in the San Francisco apartment he then shared with his wife, Kathleen. To be admitted to this apartment it was necessary to ring first and then stand in the middle of Oak Street, at a place which could be observed clearly from the Cleavers' apartment. After this scrutiny the visitor was, or was not, buzzed in. I was, and I climbed the stairs to find Kathleen Cleaver in the kitchen frying sausage and Eldridge Cleaver in the living room listening to a John Coltrane record and a number of other people all over the apartment, people everywhere, people standing in doorways and people moving around in one another's peripheral vision and people making and taking telephone calls. "When can you move on that?" I would hear in the background, and "You can't bribe me with a dinner, man, those *Guardian* dinners are all Old Left, like a wake." Most of these other people were members of the Black Panther Party, but one of them, in the living room, was Eldridge Cleaver's parole officer. It seems to me that I stayed about an hour. It seems to me that the three of us — Eldridge Cleaver, his parole officer and I — mainly discussed the commercial prospects of *Soul on Ice*, which, it happened, was being published that day. We discussed the advance ($5,000). We discussed the size of the first printing (10,000 copies). We discussed the advertising budget and we discussed the bookstores in which copies were or were not available. It was a not unusual discussion between writers, with the difference that one of the writers had his parole officer there and the other had stood out on Oak Street and been visually frisked before coming inside.

7

TO PACK AND WEAR:

2 skirts
2 jerseys or leotards
1 pullover sweater
2 pair shoes
stockings
bra
nightgown, robe, slippers
cigarettes
bourbon
bag with:
    shampoo
    toothbrush and paste
    Basis soap
    razor, deodorant
    aspirin, prescriptions, Tampax
    face cream, powder, baby oil

TO CARRY:

mohair throw
typewriter
2 legal pads and pens
files
house key

This is a list which was taped inside my closet door in Hollywood during those years when I was reporting more or less steadily. The list enabled me to pack, without thinking, for any piece I was likely to do. Notice the deliberate anonymity of costume: in a skirt, a leotard, *and stockings,* I could pass on either side of the culture. Notice the mohair throw for trunk-line flights (i.e., no blankets) and for the motel room in which the air conditioning could not be turned off. Notice the bourbon for the same motel room. Notice the typewriter for the airport, coming home: the idea was to turn in the Hertz car, check in, find an empty bench, and start typing the day's notes.

It should be clear that this was a list made by someone who prized control, yearned after momentum, someone determined to play her role as if she had the script, heard her cues, knew the narrative. There is on this list one significant omission, one article I needed and never had: a watch. I needed a watch not during the day, when I could turn on the car radio or ask someone, but at night, in the motel. Quite often I would ask the desk for the time every half hour or so, until finally, embarrassed to ask again, I would call Los Angeles and ask my husband. In other words I had skirts, jerseys, leotards, pullover sweater, shoes, stockings, bra, nightgown, robe, slippers, cigarettes, bourbon, shampoo, toothbrush and paste, Basis soap, razor, deodorant, aspirin, prescriptions, Tampax, face cream, powder, baby oil, mohair throw, typewriter, legal pads, pens, files and a house key, but I didn't know what time it was. This may be a parable, either of my life as a reporter during this period or of the period itself.

8

Driving a Budget Rent-A-Car between Sacramento and San Francisco one rainy morning in November of 1968 I kept the radio on very loud. On this occasion I kept the radio on very loud not to find out what time it was but in an effort to erase six words from my mind, six words which had no significance for me but which seemed that year to signal the onset of anxiety or fright. The words, a line from Ezra Pound's "In a Station of the Metro," were these: *Petals on a wet black bough.* The radio played "Wichita Lineman" and "I Heard It Through the Grapevine." *Petals on a wet black bough.* Somewhere between the Yolo Causeway and Vallejo it occurred to me that during the course of any given week I met too many people who spoke favorably about bombing power stations. Somewhere between the Yolo Causeway and Vallejo it also occurred to me that the fright on this particular morning was going to present itself as an inability to drive this Budget Rent-A-Car across the Carquinas Bridge. *The Wichita Lineman was still on the job.* I closed my eyes and drove across the Carquinas Bridge, because I had appointments, because I was working, because I had promised to watch the revolution being made at San Francisco State College and because there was no place in Vallejo to turn in a Budget Rent-A-Car and because nothing on my mind was in the script as I remembered it.

9

At San Francisco State College on that particular morning the wind was blowing the cold rain in squalls across the muddied lawns and against the lighted windows of empty classrooms. In the days before there had been fires set and classes invaded and finally a confrontation with the San Francisco Police Tactical Unit, and in the weeks to come the campus would become what many people on it were pleased to call "a battlefield." The police and the Mace and the noon arrests would become the routine of life on the campus, and every night the combatants would review their day on television: the waves of students advancing, the commotion at the edge of the frame, the riot sticks flashing, the instant of jerky camera that served to suggest at what risk the film was obtained; then a cut to the weather map. In the beginning there had been the necessary "issue," the suspension of a 22-year-old instructor who happened as well to be Minister of Education for the Black Panther Party, but that issue, like most, had soon ceased to be the point in the minds of even the most dense participants. Disorder was its own point.

I had never before been on a campus in disorder, had missed even Berkeley and Columbia, and I suppose I went to San Francisco State expecting something other than what I found there. In some not at all trivial sense, the set was wrong. The very architecture of California state colleges tends to deny radical notions, to reflect instead a modest and hopeful vision of progressive welfare bureaucracy, and as I walked across the campus that day and on later days the entire San Francisco State dilemma — the gradual politicization, the "issues" here and there, the obligatory "Fifteen Demands," the continual arousal of the police and the outraged citizenry — seemed increasingly off-key, an instance of the *enfants terribles* and the Board of Trustees unconsciously collaborating on a wishful fantasy (Revolution on Campus) and playing it out in time for the six o'clock news. "Adjet-prop committee meeting in the Redwood Room," read a scrawled note on the cafeteria door one morning; only someone who needed very badly to be alarmed could respond with force to a guerrilla band that not only announced its meetings on the enemy's bulletin board but seemed innocent of the spelling, and so the meaning, of the words it used. "Hitler Hayakawa," some of the faculty had begun calling S. I. Hayakawa, the semanticist who had become the college's third president in a year and had incurred considerable displeasure by trying to keep the campus open. "*Eichmann*," Kay Boyle had screamed at him at a rally. In just such broad strokes was the picture being painted in the fall of 1968 on the pastel campus at San Francisco State.

The place simply never seemed serious. The headlines were dark that first day, the college had been closed "indefinitely," both Ronald Reagan and Jesse Unruh were threatening reprisals; still, the climate inside the Administration Building was that of a musical comedy about college life. "No *chance* we'll be open tomorrow," secretaries informed callers. "Go skiing, have a good time." Striking black militants dropped in to chat with the deans; striking white radicals exchanged gossip in the corridors. "No interviews, no press," announced a student strike leader who happened into a dean's office where I was sitting; in the next moment he was piqued because no one had told him that a Huntley-Brinkley camera crew was on campus. "We can still plug into that," the dean said soothingly. Everyone seemed joined in a rather festive camaraderie, a shared jargon, a shared sense of moment: the future was no longer arduous and indefinite but immediate and programmatic, aglow with the prospect of problems to be "addressed," plans to be "implemented." It was agreed all around that the confrontations could be "a very healthy development," that maybe it took a shutdown "to get something done." The mood, like the architecture, was 1948 functional, a model of pragmatic optimism.

Perhaps Evelyn Waugh could have gotten it down exactly right: Waugh was good at scenes of industrious self-delusion, scenes of people absorbed in odd games. Here at San Francisco State only the black militants could be construed as serious: they were at any rate picking the games, dictating the rules, and taking what they could from what seemed for everyone else just an amiable evasion of routine, of institutional anxiety, of the tedium of the academic calendar. Meanwhile the administrators could talk about programs. Meanwhile the white radicals could see themselves, on an investment of virtually nothing, as urban guerrillas. It was working out well for everyone, this game at San Francisco State, and its peculiar virtues had never been so clear to me as they became one afternoon when I sat in on a meeting of fifty or sixty SDS members. They had called a press conference for later that day, and now they were discussing "just what the format of the press conference should be."

"This has to be on our terms," someone warned. "Because they'll ask very leading questions, they'll ask *questions.*"

"Make them submit any questions in writing," someone else suggested. "The Black Student Union does that very successfully, then they just don't answer anything they don't want to answer."

"That's it, don't fall into their trap."

"Something we should stress at this press conference is *who owns the media.*"

"You don't think it's common knowledge that the papers represent corporate interests?" a realist among them interjected doubtfully.

"I don't think it's *understood.*"

Two hours and several dozen hand votes later, the group had selected four members to tell the press who owned the media, had decided to appear *en masse* at an opposition press conference, and had debated various slogans for the next day's demonstration. "Let's see, first we have 'Hearst Tells It Like It Ain't', then 'Stop Press Distortion' — that's the one there was some political controversy about. . . ."

And, before they broke up, they had listened to a student who had driven up for the day from the College of San Mateo, a junior college down the peninsula from San Francisco. "I came up here today with some Third World students to tell you that we're with you, and we hope you'll be with *us* when we try to pull off a strike next week, because we're really into it, we carry our motorcycle helmets all the time, can't think, can't go to class."

He had paused. He was a nice-looking boy, and fired with his task. I considered the tender melancholy of life in San Mateo, which is one of the richest counties per capita in the United States of America, and I considered whether or not the Wichita Lineman and the petals on the wet black bough represented the aimlessness of the bourgeoisie, and I considered the illusion of aim to be gained by holding a press conference, the only problem with press conferences being that the press asked questions. "I'm here to tell you that at College of San Mateo we're living like *revolutionaries,*" the boy said then.

10

We put "Lay Lady Lay" on the record player, and "Suzanne." We went down to Melrose Avenue to see the Flying Burritos. There was a jasmine vine grown over the verandah of the big house on Franklin Avenue, and in the evenings the smell of jasmine came in through all the open doors and windows. I made bouillabaisse for people who did not eat meat. I imagined that my own life was simple and sweet, and sometimes it was, but there were odd things going around town. There were rumors. There were stories. Everything was unmentionable but nothing was unimaginable. This mystical flirtation with the idea of "sin" — this sense that it was possible to go "too far," and that many people were doing it — was very much with us in Los Angeles in 1968 and 1969. A demented and seductive vortical tension was building in the community. The jitters were setting in. I recall a time when the dogs barked every night and the moon was always full. On August 9, 1969, I was sitting in the shallow end of my sister-in-law's swimming pool in Beverly Hills when she received a telephone call from a friend who had just heard about the murders at Sharon Tate Polanski's house on Cielo Drive. The phone rang many times during the next hour. These early reports were garbled and contradictory. One caller would say hoods, the next would say chains. There were twenty dead, no, twelve, ten, eighteen. Black masses were imagined, and bad trips blamed. I remember all of the day's misinformation very clearly, and I also remember this, and wish I did not: *I remember that no one was surprised.*

11

When I first met Linda Kasabian in the summer of 1970 she was wearing her hair parted neatly in the middle, no makeup, Elizabeth Arden "Blue Grass" perfume, and the unpressed blue uniform issued to inmates at the Sybil Brand Institute for Women in Los Angeles. She was at Sybil Brand in protective custody, waiting out the time until she could testify about the murders of Sharon Tate Polanski, Abigail Folger, Jay Sebring, Voytek Frykowski, Steven Parent, and Rosemary and Leno LaBianca, and, with her lawyer, Gary Fleischman, I spent a number of evenings talking to her there. Of these evenings I remember mainly my dread at entering the prison, at leaving for even an hour the infinite possibilities I suddenly perceived in the summer twilight. I remember driving downtown on the Hollywood Freeway in Gary Fleischman's Cadillac convertible with the top down. I remember watching a rabbit graze on the grass by the gate as Gary Fleischman signed the prison register. Each of the half-dozen doors that locked behind us as we entered Sybil Brand was a little death, and I would emerge after the interview like Persephone from the underworld, euphoric, elated. Once home I would have two drinks and make myself a hamburger and eat it ravenously.

"Dig it," Gary Fleischman was always saying. One night when we were driving back to Hollywood from Sybil Brand in the Cadillac convertible with the top down he demanded that I tell him the population of India. I said that I did not know the population of India. "Take a guess," he prompted. I made a guess, absurdly low, and he was disgusted. He had asked the same question of his niece ("a college girl"), of Linda, and now of me, and none of us had known. It seemed to confirm some idea he had of women, their essential ineducability, their similarity under the skin. Gary Fleischman was someone of a type I met only rarely, a comic realist in a porkpie hat, a business traveler on the far frontiers of the period, a man who knew his way around the courthouse and Sybil Brand and remained cheerful, even jaunty, in the face of the awesome and impenetrable mystery at the center of what he called "the case." In fact we never talked about "the case," and referred to its central events only as "Cielo Drive" and "LaBianca." We talked instead about Linda's childhood pastimes and disappointments, her high-school romances and her concern for her children. This particular juxtaposition of the spoken and the unspeakable was eerie and unsettling, and made my notebook a litany of little ironies so obvious as to be of interest only to dedicated absurdists. An example: Linda dreamed of opening a combination restaurant-boutique and pet shop.

12

Certain organic disorders of the central nervous system are characterized by periodic remissions, the apparent complete recovery of the afflicted nerves. What happens appears to be this: as the lining of a nerve becomes inflamed and hardens into scar tissue, thereby blocking the passage of neural impulses, the nervous system gradually changes its circuitry, finds other, unaffected nerves to carry the same messages. During the years when I found it necessary to revise the circuitry of my mind I discovered that I was no longer interested in whether the woman on the ledge outside the window on the sixteenth floor jumped or did not jump, or in why. I was interested only in the picture of her in my mind: her hair incandescent in the floodlights, her bare toes curled inward on the stone ledge.

In this light all narrative was sentimental. In this light all connections were equally meaningful, and equally senseless. Try these: on the morning of John Kennedy's death in 1963 I was buying, at Ransohoff's in San Francisco, a short silk dress in which to be married. A few years later this dress of mine was ruined when, at a dinner party in Bel-Air, Roman Polanski accidentally spilled a glass of red wine on it. Sharon Tate was also a guest at this party, although she and Roman Polanski were not yet married. On July 27, 1970, I went to the Magnin-Hi Shop on the third floor of I. Magnin in Beverly Hills and picked out, at Linda Kasabian's request, the dress in which she began her testimony about the murders at Sharon Tate Polanski's house on Cielo Drive. "Size 9 Petite," her instructions read. "Mini but not extremely mini. In velvet if possible. Emerald green or gold. Or: A Mexican peasant-style dress, smocked or embroidered." She needed a dress that morning because the district attorney, Vincent Bugliosi, had expressed doubts about the dress she had planned to wear, a long white homespun shift. "Long is for evening," he had advised Linda. Long was for evening and white was for brides. At her own wedding in 1965 Linda Kasabian had worn a white brocade suit. Time passed, times changed. Everything was to teach us something. At 11:20 on that July morning in 1970 I delivered the dress in which she would testify to Gary Fleischman, who was waiting in front of his office on Rodeo Drive in Beverly Hills. He was wearing his porkpie hat and he was standing with Linda's second husband, Bob Kasabian, and their friend Charlie Melton, both of whom were wearing long white robes. Long was for Bob and Charlie, the dress in the I. Magnin box was for Linda. The three of them took the I. Magnin box and got into Gary Fleischman's Cadillac convertible with the top down and drove off in the sunlight toward the freeway downtown, waving back at me. I believe this to be an authentically senseless chain of correspondences, but in the jingle-jangle morning of that summer it made as much sense as anything else did.

13

I recall a conversation I had in 1970 with the manager of a motel in which I was staying near Pendleton, Oregon. I had been doing a piece for *Life* about the storage of VX and GB nerve gas at an Army arsenal in Umatilla County, and now I was done, and trying to check out of the motel. During the course of checking out I was asked this question by the manager, who was a Mormon: *If you can't believe you're going to heaven in your own body and on a first-name basis with all the members of your family, then what's the point of dying?* At that time I believed that my basic affective controls were no longer intact, but now I present this to you as a more cogent question than it might at first appear, a kind of koan of the period.

14

Once I had a rib broken, and during the few months that it was painful to turn in bed or raise my arms in a swimming pool I had, for the first time, a sharp apprehension of what it would be like to be old. Later I forgot. At some point during the years I am talking about here, after a series of periodic visual disturbances, three electroencephalograms, two complete sets of skull and neck X-rays, one five-hour glucose tolerance test, two electromyelograms, a battery of chemical tests and consultations with two ophthalmologists, one internist and three neurologists, I was told that the disorder was not really in my eyes, but in my central nervous system. I might or might not experience symptoms of neural damage all my life. These symptoms, which might or might not appear, might or might not involve my eyes. They might or might not involve my arms or legs, they might or might not be disabling. Their effects might be lessened by cortisone injections, or they might not. It could not be predicted. The condition had a name, the kind of name usually associated with telethons, but the name meant nothing and the neurologist did not like to use it. The name was multiple sclerosis, but the name had no meaning. This was, the neurologist said, an exclusionary diagnosis, and meant nothing.

I had, at this time, a sharp apprehension not of what it was like to be old but of what it was like to open the door to the stranger and find that the stranger did indeed have the knife. In a few lines of dialogue in a neurologist's office in Beverly Hills, the improbable had become the probable, the norm: things which happened only to other people could in fact happen to me. I could be struck by lightning, could dare to eat a peach and be poisoned by the cyanide in the stone. The startling fact was this: my body was offering a precise physiological equivalent to what had been going on in my mind. "Lead a simple life," the neurologist advised. "Not that it makes any difference we know about." In other words it was another story without a narrative.

15

Many people I know in Los Angeles believe that the Sixties ended abruptly on August 9, 1969, ended at the exact moment when word of the murders on Cielo Drive traveled like brushfire through the community, and in a sense this is true. The tension broke that day. The paranoia was fulfilled. In another sense the Sixties did not truly end for me until January of 1971, when I left the house on Franklin Avenue and moved to a house on the sea. This particular house on the sea had itself been very much a part of the Sixties, and for some months after we took possession I would come across souvenirs of that period in its history — a piece of Scientology literature beneath a drawer lining, a copy of *Stranger in a Strange Land* stuck deep on a closet shelf — but after a while we did some construction, and between the power saws and the sea wind the place got exorcised.

I have known, since then, very little about the movements of the people who seemed to me emblematic of those years. I know of course that Eldridge Cleaver went to Algeria and came home an entrepreneur. I know that Jim Morrison died in Paris. I know that Linda Kasabian fled in search of the pastoral to New Hampshire, where I once visited her; she also visited me in New York, and we took our children on the Staten Island Ferry to see the Statue of Liberty. I also know that in 1975 Paul Ferguson, while serving a life sentence for the murder of Ramon Novarro, won first prize in a PEN fiction contest and announced plans to "continue my writing." Writing had helped him, he said, to "reflect on experience and see what it means." Quite often I reflect on the big house in Hollywood, on "Midnight Confessions" and on Ramon Novarro and on the fact that Roman Polanski and I are godparents to the same child, but writing has not yet helped me to see what it means.

1968–1978

1980

Richard Rodriguez

....

Aria: A Memoir
of a Bilingual Childhood

I REMEMBER, to start with, that day in Sacramento, in a California now nearly thirty years past, when I first entered a classroom — able to understand about fifty stray English words. The third of four children, I had been preceded by my older brother and sister to a neighborhood Roman Catholic school. But neither of them had revealed very much about their classroom experiences. They left each morning and returned each afternoon, always together, speaking Spanish as they climbed the five steps to the porch. And their mysterious books, wrapped in brown shopping-bag paper, remained on the table next to the door, closed firmly behind them.

An accident of geography sent me to a school where all my classmates were white and many were the children of doctors and lawyers and business executives. On that first day of school, my classmates must certainly have been uneasy to find themselves apart from their families, in the first institution of their lives. But I was astonished. I was fated to be the "problem student" in class.

The nun said, in a friendly but oddly impersonal voice: "Boys and girls, this is Richard Rodriguez." (I heard her sound it out — *Rich-heard Road-ree-guess*.) It was the first time I had heard anyone say my name in English. "Richard," the nun repeated more slowly, writing my name down in her book. Quickly I turned to see my mother's face dissolve in a watery blur behind the pebbled-glass door.

*

First published in *The American Scholar,* 1980; collected in *Hunger of Memory: The Education of Richard Rodriguez,* 1981.

Now, many years later, I hear of something called "bilingual education" — a scheme proposed in the late 1960s by Hispanic-American social activists, later endorsed by a congressional vote. It is a program that seeks to permit non-English-speaking children (many from lower-class homes) to use their "family language" as the language of school. Such, at least, is the aim its supporters announce. I hear them, and am forced to say no: It is not possible for a child, any child, ever to use his family's language in school. Not to understand this is to misunderstand the public uses of schooling and to trivialize the nature of intimate life.

Memory teaches me what I know of these matters. The boy reminds the adult. I was a bilingual child, but of a certain kind: "socially disadvantaged," the son of working-class parents, both Mexican immigrants.

In the early years of my boyhood, my parents coped very well in America. My father had steady work. My mother managed at home. They were nobody's victims. When we moved to a house many blocks from the Mexican-American section of town, they were not intimidated by those two or three neighbors who initially tried to make us unwelcome. ("Keep your brats away from my sidewalk!") But despite all they achieved, or perhaps because they had so much to achieve, they lacked any deep feeling of ease, of belonging in public. They regarded the people at work or in crowds as being very distant from us. Those were the others, *los gringos*. That term was interchangeable in their speech with another, even more telling: *los americanos*.

I grew up in a house where the only regular guests were my relations. On a certain day, enormous families of relatives would visit us, and there would be so many people that the noise and the bodies would spill out to the backyard and onto the front porch. Then for weeks no one would come. (If the doorbell rang, it was usually a salesman.) Our house stood apart — gaudy yellow in a row of white bungalows. We were the people with the noisy dog, the people who raised chickens. We were the foreigners on the block. A few neighbors would smile and wave at us. We waved back. But until I was seven years old, I did not know the name of the old couple living next door or the names of the kids living across the street.

In public, my father and mother spoke a hesitant, accented, and not always grammatical English. And then they would have to strain, their bodies tense, to catch the sense of what was rapidly said by *los gringos*. At home, they returned to Spanish. The language of their Mexican past sounded in counterpoint to the English spoken in public. The words would come quickly, with ease. Conveyed through those sounds was the pleasing, soothing, consoling reminder that one was at home.

During those years when I was first learning to speak, my mother and father addressed me only in Spanish; in Spanish I learned to reply. By contrast, English (*inglés*) was the language I came to associate with gringos, rarely heard in the house. I learned my first words of English overhearing my parents speaking to strangers. At six years of age, I knew just enough words for my mother to trust me on errands to stores one block away — but no more.

I was then a listening child, careful to hear the very different sounds of Spanish and English. Wide-eyed with hearing, I'd listen to sounds more than to words. First, there were English (gringo) sounds. So many words still were unknown to me that when the butcher or the lady at the drugstore said something, exotic polysyllabic sounds would bloom in the midst of their sentences. Often the speech of people in public seemed to me very loud, booming with confidence. The man behind the counter would literally ask, "What can I do for you?" But by being so firm and clear, the sound of his voice said that he was a gringo; he belonged in public society. There were also the high, nasal notes of middle-class American speech — which I rarely am conscious of hearing today because I hear them so often, but could not stop hearing when I was a boy. Crowds at Safeway or at bus stops were noisy with the birdlike sounds of *los gringos*. I'd move away from them all — all the chirping chatter above me.

My own sounds I was unable to hear, but I knew that I spoke English poorly. My words could not extend to form complete thoughts. And the words I did speak I didn't know well enough to make distinct sounds. (Listeners would usually lower their heads to hear better what I was trying to say.) But it was one thing for *me* to speak English with difficulty; it was more troubling to hear my parents speaking in public: their high-whining vowels and guttural consonants; their sentences that got stuck with "eh" and "ah" sounds; the confused syntax; the hesitant rhythm of sounds so different from the way gringos spoke. I'd notice, moreover, that my parents' voices were softer than those of gringos we would meet.

I am tempted to say now that none of this mattered. (In adulthood I am embarrassed by childhood fears.) And, in a way, it didn't matter very much that my parents could not speak English with ease. Their linguistic difficulties had no serious consequences. My mother and father made themselves understood at the county hospital clinic and at government offices. And yet, in another way, it mattered very much. It was unsettling to hear my parents struggle with English. Hearing them, I'd grow nervous, and my clutching trust in their protection and power would be weakened.

There were many times like the night at a brightly lit gasoline station (a blaring white memory) when I stood uneasily hearing my father talk to a teenage attendant. I do not recall what they were saying, but I cannot forget the sounds my father made as he spoke. At one point his words slid together to form one long word — sounds as confused as the threads of blue and green oil in the puddle next to my shoes. His voice rushed through what he had left to say. Toward the end, he reached falsetto notes, appealing to his listener's understanding. I looked away at the lights of passing automobiles. I tried not to hear any more. But I heard only too well the attendant's reply, his calm, easy tones. Shortly afterward, headed for home, I shivered when my father put his hand on my shoulder. The very first chance that I got, I evaded his grasp and ran on ahead into the dark, skipping with feigned boyish exuberance.

But then there was Spanish: *español,* the language rarely heard away from the house; *español,* the language which seemed to me therefore a private language, my family's language. To hear its sounds was to feel myself specially recognized as one of the family, apart from *los otros.* A simple remark, an inconsequential comment could convey that assurance. My parents would say something to me and I would feel embraced by the sounds of their words. Those sounds said: *I am speaking with ease in Spanish. I am addressing you in words I never use with* los gringos. *I recognize you as someone special, close, like no one outside. You belong with us. In the family. Ricardo.*

At the age of six, well past the time when most middle-class children no longer notice the difference between sounds uttered at home and words spoken in public, I had a different experience. I lived in a world compounded of sounds. I was a child longer than most. I lived in a magical world, surrounded by sounds both pleasing and fearful. I shared with my family a language enchantingly private — different from that used in the city around us.

Just opening or closing the screen door behind me was an important experience. I'd rarely leave home all alone or without feeling reluctance. Walking down the sidewalk, under the canopy of tall trees, I'd warily notice the (suddenly) silent neighborhood kids who stood warily watching me. Nervously, I'd arrive at the grocery store to hear there the sounds of the gringo, reminding me that in this so-big world I was a foreigner. But if leaving home was never routine, neither was coming back. Walking toward our house, climbing the steps from the sidewalk, in summer when the front door was open, I'd hear voices beyond the screen door talking in Spanish. For a second or two I'd stay, linger there listening. Smiling, I'd hear my mother call out, saying in Spanish, "Is that you, Richard?" Those were her words, but all the while her sounds would assure me: *You are home now. Come closer inside. With us.* "Sí," I'd reply.

Once more inside the house, I would resume my place in the family. The sounds would grow harder to hear. Once more at home, I would grow less conscious of them. It required, however, no more than the blurt of the doorbell to alert me all over again to listen to sounds. The house would turn instantly quiet while my mother went to the door. I'd hear her hard English sounds. I'd wait to hear her voice turn to soft-sounding Spanish, which assured me, as surely as did the clicking tongue of the lock on the door, that the stranger was gone.

Plainly it is not healthy to hear such sounds so often. It is not healthy to distinguish public from private sounds so easily. I remained cloistered by sounds, timid and shy in public, too dependent on the voices at home. And yet I was a very happy child when I was at home. I remember many nights when my father would come back from work, and I'd hear him call out to my mother in Spanish, sounding relieved. In Spanish, his voice would sound the light and free notes that he never could manage in English. Some nights I'd jump up just hearing his voice. My brother and I would come running into the room where he was with our mother. Our laughing (so deep was the pleasure!) became screaming. Like others who feel the pain of public alienation, we transformed the knowledge of our public separateness into a consoling reminder of our intimacy. Excited, our voices joined in a celebration of sounds. *We are speaking now the way we never speak out in public — we are together,* the sounds told me. Some nights no one seemed willing to loosen the hold that sounds had on us. At dinner we invented new words that sounded Spanish, but made sense only to us. We pieced together new words by taking, say, an English verb and giving it Spanish endings. My mother's instructions at bedtime would be lacquered with mock-urgent tones. Or a word like *sí*, sounded in several notes, would convey added measures of feeling. Tongues lingered around the edges of words, especially fat vowels. And we happily sounded that military drum roll, the

twirling roar of the Spanish *r*. Family language, my family's sounds: the
voices of my parents and sisters and brother. Their voices insisting: *You
belong here. We are family members. Related. Special to one another. Listen!* Voices singing and sighing, rising and straining, then surging,
teeming with pleasure which burst syllables into fragments of laughter.
At times it seemed there was steady quiet only when, from another
room, the rustling whispers of my parents faded and I edged closer to
sleep.

Supporters of bilingual education imply today that students like me
miss a great deal by not being taught in their family's language. What
they seem not to recognize is that, as a socially disadvantaged child, I regarded Spanish as a private language. It was a ghetto language that
deepened and strengthened my feeling of public separateness. What I
needed to learn in school was that I had the right, and the obligation, to
speak the public language. The odd truth is that my first-grade classmates could have become bilingual, in the conventional sense of the
word, more easily than I. Had they been taught early (as upper middle-
class children often are taught) a "second language" like Spanish or
French, they could have regarded it simply as another public language.
In my case, such bilingualism could not have been so quickly achieved.
What I did not believe was that I could speak a single public language.

Without question, it would have pleased me to have heard my teachers address me in Spanish when I entered the classroom. I would have
felt much less afraid. I would have imagined that my instructors were
somehow "related" to me; I would indeed have heard their Spanish as
my family's language. I would have trusted them and responded with
ease. But I would have delayed — postponed for how long? — having to
learn the language of public society. I would have evaded — and for
how long? — learning the great lesson of school: that I had a public
identity.

Fortunately, my teachers were unsentimental about their responsibility. What they understood was that I needed to speak public English. So
their voices would search me out, asking me questions. Each time I
heard them I'd look up in surprise to see a nun's face frowning at me.
I'd mumble, not really meaning to answer. The nun would persist.
"Richard, stand up. Don't look at the floor. Speak up. Speak to the entire class, not just to me!" But I couldn't believe English could be my
language to use. (In part, I did not want to believe it.) I continued to

mumble. I resisted the teacher's demands. (Did I somehow suspect that once I learned this public language my family life would be changed?) Silent, waiting for the bell to sound, I remained dazed, diffident, afraid.

Because I wrongly imagined that English was intrinsically a public language and Spanish was intrinsically private, I easily noted the difference between classroom language and the language of home. At school, words were directed to a general audience of listeners. ("Boys and girls . . .") Words were meaningfully ordered. And the point was not self-expression alone, but to make oneself understood by many others. The teacher quizzed: "Boys and girls, why do we use that word in this sentence? Could we think of a better word to use there? Would the sentence change its meaning if the words were differently arranged? Isn't there a better way of saying much the same thing?" (I couldn't say. I wouldn't try to say.)

Three months passed. Five. A half year. Unsmiling, ever watchful, my teachers noted my silence. They began to connect my behavior with the slow progress my brother and sisters were making. Until, one Saturday morning, three nuns arrived at the house to talk to our parents. Stiffly they sat on the blue living-room sofa. From the doorway of another room, spying on the visitors, I noted the incongruity, the clash of two worlds, the faces and voices of school intruding upon the familiar setting of home. I overheard one voice gently wondering, "Do your children speak only Spanish at home, Mrs. Rodriguez?" While another voice added, "That Richard especially seems so timid and shy."

That Rich-heard!

With great tact, the visitors continued, "Is it possible for you and your husband to encourage your children to practice their English when they are home?" Of course my parents complied. What would they not do for their children's well-being? And how could they question the Church's authority which those women represented? In an instant they agreed to give up the language (the sounds) which had revealed and accentuated our family's closeness. The moment after the visitors left, the change was observed. "*Ahora,* speak to us only *en inglés,*" my father and mother told us.

At first, it seemed a kind of game. After dinner each night, the family gathered together to practice "our" English. It was still then *inglés,* a language foreign to us, so we felt drawn to it as strangers. Laughing, we would try to define words we could not pronounce. We played with strange English sounds, often over-anglicizing our pronunciations. And we filled the smiling gaps of our sentences with familiar Spanish sounds. But that was cheating, somebody shouted, and everyone laughed.

In school, meanwhile, like my brother and sisters, I was required to attend a daily tutoring session. I needed a full year of this special work. I also needed my teachers to keep my attention from straying in class by calling out, *"Rich-heard!"* — their English voices slowly loosening the ties to my other name, with its three notes, *Ri-car-do*. Most of all, I needed to hear my mother and father speak to me in a moment of seriousness in "broken" — suddenly heartbreaking — English. This scene was inevitable. One Saturday morning I entered the kitchen where my parents were talking, but I did not realize that they were talking in Spanish until, the moment they saw me, their voices changed and they began speaking English. The gringo sounds they uttered startled me. Pushed me away. In that moment of trivial misunderstanding and profound insight, I felt my throat twisted by unsounded grief. I simply turned and left the room. But I had no place to escape to where I could grieve in Spanish. My brother and sisters were speaking English in another part of the house.

Again and again in the days following, as I grew increasingly angry, I was obliged to hear my mother and father encouraging me: "Speak to us *en inglés*." Only then did I determine to learn classroom English. Thus, sometime afterward it happened: one day in school, I raised my hand to volunteer an answer to a question. I spoke out in a loud voice and I did not think it remarkable when the entire class understood. That day I moved very far from being the disadvantaged child I had been only days earlier. Taken hold at last was the belief, the calming assurance, that I *belonged* in public.

Shortly after, I stopped hearing the high, troubling sounds of *los gringos*. A more and more confident speaker of English, I didn't listen to how strangers sounded when they talked to me. With so many English-speaking people around me, I no longer heard American accents. Conversations quickened. Listening to persons whose voices sounded eccentrically pitched, I might note their sounds for a few seconds, but then I'd concentrate on what they were saying. Now when I heard someone's tone of voice — angry or questioning or sarcastic or happy or sad — I didn't distinguish it from the words it expressed. Sound and word were thus tightly wedded. At the end of each day I was often bemused, and always relieved, to realize how "soundless," though crowded with words, my day in public had been. An eight-year-old boy, I finally came to accept what had been technically true since my birth: I was an American citizen.

But diminished by then was the special feeling of closeness at home. Gone was the desperate, urgent, intense feeling of being at home among those with whom I felt intimate. Our family remained a loving family, but one greatly changed. We were no longer so close, no longer bound tightly together by the knowledge of our separateness from *los gringos*. Neither my older brother nor my sisters rushed home after school any more. Nor did I. When I arrived home, often there would be neighborhood kids in the house. Or the house would be empty of sounds.

Following the dramatic Americanization of their children, even my parents grew more publicly confident — especially my mother. First she learned the names of all the people on the block. Then she decided we needed to have a telephone in our house. My father, for his part, continued to use the word gringo, but it was no longer charged with bitterness or distrust. Stripped of any emotional content, the word simply became a name for those Americans not of Hispanic descent. Hearing him, sometimes, I wasn't sure if he was pronouncing the Spanish word *gringo*, or saying gringo in English.

There was a new silence at home. As we children learned more and more English, we shared fewer and fewer words with our parents. Sentences needed to be spoken slowly when one of us addressed our mother or father. Often the parent wouldn't understand. The child would need to repeat himself. Still the parent misunderstood. The young voice, frustrated, would end up saying, "Never mind" — the subject was closed. Dinners would be noisy with the clinking of knives and forks against dishes. My mother would smile softly between her remarks; my father, at the other end of the table, would chew and chew his food while he stared over the heads of his children.

My mother! My father! After English became my primary language, I no longer knew what words to use in addressing my parents. The old Spanish words (those tender accents of sound) I had earlier used — *mamá* and *papá* — I couldn't use any more. They would have been all-too-painful reminders of how much had changed in my life. On the other hand, the words I heard neighborhood kids call their parents seemed equally unsatisfactory. "Mother" and "father," "ma," "papa," "pa," "dad," "pop" (how I hated the all-American sound of that last word) — all these I felt were unsuitable terms of address for *my* parents. As a result, I never used them at home. Whenever I'd speak to my parents, I would try to get their attention by looking at them. In public conversations, I'd refer to them as my "parents" or my "mother" and "father."

My mother and father, for their part, responded differently, as their children spoke to them less. My mother grew restless, seemed troubled and anxious at the scarceness of words exchanged in the house. She would question me about my day when I came home from school. She smiled at my small talk. She pried at the edges of my sentences to get me to say something more. ("What . . .?") She'd join conversations she overheard, but her intrusions often stopped her children's talking. By contrast, my father seemed to grow reconciled to the new quiet. Though his English somewhat improved, he tended more and more to retire into silence. At dinner he spoke very little. One night his children and even his wife helplessly giggled at his garbled English pronunciation of the Catholic "Grace Before Meals." Thereafter he made his wife recite the prayer at the start of each meal, even on formal occasions when there were guests in the house.

Hers became the public voice of the family. On official business it was she, not my father, who would usually talk to strangers on the phone or in stores. We children grew so accustomed to his silence that years later we would routinely refer to his "shyness." (My mother often tried to explain: both of his parents died when he was eight. He was raised by an uncle who treated him as little more than a menial servant. He was never encouraged to speak. He grew up alone — a man of few words.) But I realized my father was not shy whenever I'd watch him speaking Spanish with relatives. Using Spanish, he was quickly effusive. Especially when talking with other men, his voice would spark, flicker, flare alive with varied sounds. In Spanish he expressed ideas and feelings he rarely revealed when speaking English. With firm Spanish sounds he conveyed a confidence and authority that English would never allow him.

The silence at home, however, was not simply the result of fewer words passing between parents and children. More profound for me was the silence created by my inattention to sounds. At about the time I no longer bothered to listen with care to the sounds of English in public, I grew careless about listening to the sounds made by the family when they spoke. Most of the time I would hear someone speaking at home and didn't distinguish his sounds from the words people uttered in public. I didn't even pay much attention to my parents' accented and ungrammatical speech — at least not at home. Only when I was with them in public would I become alert to their accents. But even then their sounds caused me less and less concern. For I was growing increasingly confident of my own public identity.

I would have been happier about my public success had I not recalled, sometimes, what it had been like earlier, when my family conveyed its intimacy through a set of conveniently private sounds. Sometimes in public, hearing a stranger, I'd hark back to my lost past. A Mexican farm worker approached me one day downtown. He wanted directions to some place. "*Hijito* . . . ," he said. And his voice stirred old longings. Another time I was standing beside my mother in the visiting room of a Carmelite convent, before the dense screen which rendered the nuns shadowy figures. I heard several of them speaking Spanish in their busy, singsong, overlapping voices, assuring my mother that, yes, yes, we were remembered, all our family was remembered, in their prayers. Those voices echoed faraway family sounds. Another day a dark-faced old woman touched my shoulder lightly to steady herself as she boarded a bus. She murmured something to me I couldn't quite comprehend. Her Spanish voice came near, like the face of a never-before-seen relative in the instant before I was kissed. That voice, like so many of the Spanish voices I'd hear in public, recalled the golden age of my childhood.

Bilingual educators say today that children lose a degree of "individuality" by becoming assimilated into public society. (Bilingual schooling is a program popularized in the seventies, that decade when middle-class "ethnics" began to resist the process of assimilation — the "American melting pot.") But the bilingualists oversimplify when they scorn the value and necessity of assimilation. They do not seem to realize that a person is individualized in two ways. So they do not realize that, while one suffers a diminished sense of *private* individuality by being assimilated into public society, such assimilation makes possible the achievement of *public* individuality.

Simplistically again, the bilingualists insist that a student should be reminded of his difference from others in mass society, of his "heritage." But they equate mere separateness with individuality. The fact is that only in private — with intimates — is separateness from the crowd a prerequisite for individuality; an intimate "tells" me that I am unique, unlike all others, apart from the crowd. In public, by contrast, full individuality is achieved, paradoxically, by those who are able to consider themselves members of the crowd. Thus it happened for me. Only when I was able to think of myself as an American, no longer an alien in gringo society, could I seek the rights and opportunities necessary for full public individuality. The social and political advantages I enjoy as a man began on the day I came to believe that my name is indeed *Rich-heard Road-ree-guess*. It is true that my public society today is often impersonal; in fact, my public society is usually mass society. But despite the anonymity of the crowd, and despite the fact that the individuality I achieve in public is often tenuous — because it depends on my being one in a crowd — I celebrate the day I acquired my new name. Those middle-class ethnics who scorn assimilation seem to me filled with decadent self-pity, obsessed by the burden of public life. Dangerously, they romanticize public separateness and trivialize the dilemma of those who are truly socially disadvantaged.

If I rehearse here the changes in my private life after my Americanization, it is finally to emphasize a public gain. The loss implies the gain. The house I returned to each afternoon was quiet. Intimate sounds no longer greeted me at the door. Inside there were other noises. The telephone rang. Neighborhood kids ran past the door of the bedroom where I was reading my schoolbooks — covered with brown shopping-bag paper. Once I learned the public language, it would never again be easy for me to hear intimate family voices. More and more of my day was spent hearing words, not sounds. But that may only be a way of saying that on the day I raised my hand in class and spoke loudly to an entire roomful of faces, my childhood started to end.

I grew up the victim of a disconcerting confusion. As I became fluent in English, I could no longer speak Spanish with confidence. I continued to understand spoken Spanish, and in high school I learned how to read and write Spanish. But for many years I could not pronounce it. A powerful guilt blocked my spoken words; an essential glue was missing whenever I would try to connect words to form sentences. I would be unable to break a barrier of sound, to speak freely. I would speak, or try to speak, Spanish, and I would manage to utter halting, hiccuping sounds which betrayed my unease. (Even today I speak Spanish very slowly, at best.)

When relatives and Spanish-speaking friends of my parents came to the house, my brother and sisters would usually manage to say a few words before being excused. I never managed so gracefully. Each time I'd hear myself addressed in Spanish, I couldn't respond with any success. I'd know the words I wanted to say, but I couldn't say them. I would try to speak, but everything I said seemed to me horribly anglicized. My mouth wouldn't form the sounds right. My jaw would tremble. After a phrase or two, I'd stutter, cough up a warm, silvery sound, and stop.

My listeners were surprised to hear me. They'd lower their heads to grasp better what I was trying to say. They would repeat their questions in gentle, affectionate voices. But then I would answer in English. No, no, they would say, we want you to speak to us in Spanish (*"en español"*). But I couldn't do it. Then they would call me *Pocho.* Sometimes playfully, teasing, using the tender diminutive — *mi pochito.* Sometimes not so playfully but mockingly, *pocho.* (A Spanish dictionary defines that word as an adjective meaning "colorless" or "bland." But I heard it as a noun, naming the Mexican-American who, in becoming an American, forgets his native society.) *"¡Pocho!"* my mother's best friend muttered, shaking her head. And my mother laughed, somewhere behind me. She said that her children didn't want to practice "our Spanish" after they started going to school. My mother's smiling voice made me suspect that the lady who faced me was not really angry at me. But searching her face, I couldn't find the hint of a smile.

Embarrassed, my parents would often need to explain their children's inability to speak fluent Spanish during those years. My mother encountered the wrath of her brother, her only brother, when he came up from Mexico one summer with his family and saw his nieces and nephews for the very first time. After listening to me, he looked away and said what a disgrace it was that my siblings and I couldn't speak Spanish, *"su propria idioma."* He made that remark to my mother, but I noticed that he stared at my father.

One other visitor from those years I clearly remember: a long-time friend of my father from San Francisco who came to stay with us for several days in late August. He took great interest in me after he realized that I couldn't answer his questions in Spanish. He would grab me, as I started to leave the kitchen. He would ask me something. Usually he wouldn't bother to wait for my mumbled response. Knowingly, he'd murmur, *"¿Ay pocho, pocho, donde vas?"* And he would press his thumbs into the upper part of my arms, making me squirm with pain. Dumbly I'd stand there, waiting for his wife to notice us and call him off with a benign smile. I'd giggle, hoping to deflate the tension between us, pretending that I hadn't seen the glittering scorn in his glance.

I recount such incidents only because they suggest the fierce power that Spanish had over many people I met at home, how strongly Spanish was associated with closeness. Most of those people who called me a *pocho* could have spoken English to me, but many wouldn't. They seemed to think that Spanish was the only language we could use among ourselves, that Spanish alone permitted our association. (Such persons are always vulnerable to the ghetto merchant and the politician who have learned the value of speaking their clients' "family language" so as to gain immediate trust.) For my part, I felt that by learning English I had somehow committed a sin of betrayal. But betrayal against whom? Not exactly against the visitors to the house. Rather, I felt I had betrayed my immediate family. I knew that my parents had encouraged me to learn English. I knew that I had turned to English with angry reluctance. But once I spoke English with ease, I came to feel guilty. I sensed that I had broken the spell of intimacy which had once held the family so close together. It was this original sin against my family that I recalled whenever anyone addressed me in Spanish and I responded, confounded.

Yet even during those years of guilt, I was coming to grasp certain consoling truths about language and intimacy — truths that I learned gradually. Once, I remember playing with a friend in the backyard when my grandmother appeared at the window. Her face was stern with suspicion when she saw the boy (the *gringo* boy) I was with. She called out to me in Spanish, sounding the whistle of her ancient breath. My companion looked up and watched her intently as she lowered the window and moved (still visible) behind the light curtain, watching us both. He wanted to know what she had said. I started to tell him, to translate her Spanish words into English. The problem was, however, that though I knew how to translate exactly what she had told me, I realized that any translation would distort the deepest meaning of her message: it had been directed only to me. This message of intimacy could never be translated because it did not lie in the actual words she had used but passed through them. So any translation would have seemed wrong; the words would have been stripped of an essential meaning. Finally I decided not to tell my friend anything — just that I didn't hear all she had said.

This insight was unfolded in time. As I made more and more friends outside my house, I began to recognize intimate messages spoken in English in a close friend's confidential tone or secretive whisper. Even more remarkable were those instances when, apparently for no special reason, I'd become conscious of the fact that my companion was speaking *only to me*. I'd marvel then, just hearing his voice. It was a stunning event to be able to break through the barrier of public silence, to be able to hear the voice of the other, to realize that it was directed just to me. After such moments of intimacy outside the house, I began to trust what I heard intimately conveyed through my family's English. Voices at home at last punctured sad confusion. I'd hear myself addressed as an intimate — in English. Such moments were never as raucous with sound as in past times, when we had used our "private" Spanish. (Our English-sounding house was never to be as noisy as our Spanish-sounding house had been.) Intimate moments were usually moments of soft sound. My mother would be ironing in the dining room while I did my homework nearby. She would look over at me, smile, and her voice sounded to tell me that I was her son. *Richard.*

Intimacy thus continued at home; intimacy was not stilled by English. Though there were fewer occasions for it — a change in my life that I would never forget — there were also times when I sensed the deep truth about language and intimacy: *Intimacy is not created by a particular language; it is created by intimates.* Thus the great change in my life was not linguistic but social. If, after becoming a successful student, I no longer heard intimate voices as often as I had earlier, it was not because I spoke English instead of Spanish. It was because I spoke public language for most of my day. I moved easily at last, a citizen in a crowded city of words.

As a man I spend most of my day in public, in a world largely devoid of speech sounds. So I am quickly attracted by the glamorous quality of certain alien voices. I still am gripped with excitement when someone passes me on the street, speaking in Spanish. I have not moved beyond the range of the nostalgic pull of those sounds. And there is something very compelling about the sounds of lower-class blacks. Of all the accented versions of English that I hear in public, I hear theirs most intently. The Japanese tourist stops me downtown to ask me a question and I inch my way past his accent to concentrate on what he is saying. The eastern European immigrant in the neighborhood delicatessen speaks to me and, again, I do not pay much attention to his sounds, nor to the Texas accent of one of my neighbors or the Chicago accent of the woman who lives in the apartment below me. But when the ghetto black teenagers get on the city bus, I hear them. Their sounds in my society are the sounds of the outsider. Their voices annoy me for being so loud — so self-sufficient and unconcerned by my presence, but for the same reason they are glamorous: a romantic gesture against public acceptance. And as I listen to their shouted laughter, I realize my own quietness. I feel envious of them — envious of their brazen intimacy.

I warn myself away from such envy, however. Overhearing those teenagers, I think of the black political activists who lately have argued in favor of using black English in public schools — an argument that varies only slightly from that of foreign-language bilingualists. I have heard "radical" linguists make the point that black English is a complex and intricate version of English. And I do not doubt it. But neither do I think that black English should be a language of public instruction. What makes it inappropriate in classrooms is not something in the language itself but, rather, what lower-class speakers make of it. Just as Spanish would have been a dangerous language for me to have used at the start of my education, so black English would be a dangerous language to use in the schooling of teenagers for whom it reinforces feelings of public separateness.

This seems to me an obvious point to make, and yet it must be said. In recent years there have been many attempts to make the language of the alien a public language. "Bilingual education, two ways to understand . . ." television and radio commercials glibly announce. Proponents of bilingual education are careful to say that above all they want every student to acquire a good education. Their argument goes something like this: Children permitted to use their family language will not be so alienated and will be better able to match the progress of English-speaking students in the crucial first months of schooling. Increasingly confident of their ability, such children will be more inclined to apply themselves to their studies in the future. But then the bilingualists also claim another very different goal. They say that children who use their family language in school will retain a sense of their ethnic heritage and their family ties. Thus the supporters of bilingual education want it both ways. They propose bilingual schooling as a way of helping students acquire the classroom skills crucial for public success. But they likewise insist that bilingual instruction will give students a sense of their identity apart from the English-speaking public.

Behind this scheme gleams a bright promise for the alien child: one can become a public person while still remaining a private person. Who would not want to believe such an appealing idea? Who can be surprised that the scheme has the support of so many middle-class ethnic Americans? If the barrio or ghetto child can retain his separateness even while being publicly educated, then it is almost possible to believe that no private cost need be paid for public success. This is the consolation offered by any of the number of current bilingual programs. Consider, for example, the bilingual voter's ballot. In some American cities one can cast a ballot printed in several languages. Such a document implies that it is possible for one to exercise that most public of rights — the right to vote — while still keeping oneself apart, unassimilated in public life.

It is not enough to say that such schemes are foolish and certainly doomed. Middle-class supporters of public bilingualism toy with the confusion of those Americans who cannot speak standard English as well as they do. Moreover, bilingual enthusiasts sin against intimacy. A Hispanic-American tells me, "I will never give up my family language," and he clutches a group of words as though they were the source of his family ties. He credits to language what he should credit to family members. This is a convenient mistake, for as long as he holds on to certain familiar words, he can ignore how much else has actually changed in his life.

It has happened before. In earlier decades, persons ambitious for social mobility, and newly successful, similarly seized upon certain "family words." Workingmen attempting to gain political power, for example, took to calling one another "brother." The word as they used it, however, could never resemble the word (the sound) "brother" exchanged by two people in intimate greeting. The context of its public delivery made it at best a metaphor; with repetition it was only a vague echo of the intimate sound. Context forced the change. Context could not be overruled. Context will always protect the realm of the intimate from public misuse. Today middle-class white Americans continue to prove the importance of context as they try to ignore it. They seize upon idioms of the black ghetto, but their attempt to appropriate such expressions invariably changes the meaning. As it becomes a public expression, the ghetto idiom loses its sound, its message of public separateness and strident intimacy. With public repetition it becomes a series of words, increasingly lifeless.

The mystery of intimate utterance remains. The communication of intimacy passes through the word and enlivens its sound, but it cannot be held by the word. It cannot be retained or ever quoted because it is too fluid. It depends not on words but on persons.

My grandmother! She stood among my other relations mocking me when I no longer spoke Spanish. *Pocho*, she said. But then it made no difference. She'd laugh, and our relationship continued because language was never its source. She was a woman in her eighties during the first decade of my life — a mysterious woman to me, my only living grandparent, a woman of Mexico in a long black dress that reached down to her shoes. She was the one relative of mine who spoke no word of English. She had no interest in gringo society and remained completely aloof from the public. She was protected by her daughters, protected even by me when we went to Safeway together and I needed to act as her translator. An eccentric woman. Hard. Soft.

When my family visited my aunt's house in San Francisco, my grandmother would search for me among my many cousins. When she found me, she'd chase them away. Pinching her granddaughters, she would warn them away from me. Then she'd take me to her room, where she had prepared for my coming. There would be a chair next to the bed, a dusty jellied candy nearby, and a copy of *Life en Español* for me to examine. "There," she'd say. And I'd sit content, a boy of eight. *Pocho,* her favorite. I'd sift through the pictures of earthquake-destroyed Latin-American cities and blond-wigged Mexican movie stars. And all the while I'd listen to the sound of my grandmother's voice. She'd pace around the room, telling me stories of her life. Her past. They were stories so familiar that I couldn't remember when I'd heard them for the first time. I'd look up sometimes to listen. Other times she'd look over at me, but she never expected a response. Sometimes I'd smile or nod. (I understood exactly what she was saying.) But it never seemed to matter to her one way or the other. It was enough that I was there. The words she spoke were almost irrelevant to that fact. We were content. And the great mystery remained: intimate utterance.

I learn nothing about language and intimacy listening to those social activists who propose using one's family language in public life. I learn much more simply by listening to songs on a radio, or hearing a great voice at the opera, or overhearing the woman downstairs at an open window singing to herself. Singers celebrate the human voice. Their lyrics are words, but, animated by voice, those words are subsumed into sounds. (This suggests a central truth about language: all words are capable of becoming sounds as we fill them with the "music" of our life.) With excitement I hear the words yielding their enormous power to sound, even though their meaning is never totally obliterated. In most songs, the drama or tension results from the way that the singer moves between words (sense) and notes (song). At one moment the song simply "says" something; at another moment the voice stretches out the words and moves to the realm of pure sound. Most songs are about love: lost love, celebrations of loving, pleas. By simply being occasions when sounds soar through words, however, songs put me in mind of the most intimate moments of life.

Finally, among all types of music, I find songs created by lyric poets most compelling. On no other public occasion is sound so important for me. Written poems on a page seem at first glance a mere collection of words. And yet, without musical accompaniment, the poet leads me to hear the sounds of the words that I read. As song, a poem moves between the levels of sound and sense, never limited to one realm or the other. As a public artifact, the poem can never offer truly intimate sound, but it helps me to recall the intimate times of my life. As I read in my room, I grow deeply conscious of being alone, sounding my voice in search of another. The poem serves, then, as a memory device; it forces remembrance. And it refreshes; it reminds me of the possibility of escaping public words, the possibility that awaits me in intimate meetings.

The child reminds the adult: to seek intimate sounds is to seek the company of intimates. I do not expect to hear those sounds in public. I would dishonor those I have loved, and those I love now, to claim anything else. I would dishonor our intimacy by holding on to a particular language and calling it my family language. Intimacy cannot be trapped within words; it passes through words. It passes. Intimates leave the room. Doors close. Faces move away from the window. Time passes, and voices recede into the dark. Death finally quiets the voice. There is no way to deny it, no way to stand in the crowd claiming to utter one's family language.

The last time I saw my grandmother I was nine years old. I can tell you some of the things she said to me as I stood by her bed, but I cannot quote the message of intimacy she conveyed with her voice. She laughed, holding my hand. Her voice illumined disjointed memories as it passed them again. She remembered her husband — his green eyes, his magic name of Narcissio, his early death. She remembered the farm in Mexico, the eucalyptus trees nearby (their scent, she remembered, like incense). She remembered the family cow, the bell around its neck heard miles away. A dog. She remembered working as a seamstress, how she'd leave her daughters and son for long hours to go into Guadalajara to work. And how my mother would come running toward her in the sun — in her bright yellow dress — on her return. "MMMMAAAAMMMMÁÁÁÁÁ," the old lady mimicked her daughter (my mother) to her daughter's son. She laughed. There was the snap of a cough. An aunt came into the room and told me it was time I should leave. "You can see her tomorrow," she promised. So I kissed my grand-mother's cracked face. And the last thing I saw was her thin, oddly youthful thigh, as my aunt rearranged the sheet on the bed.

At the funeral parlor a few days after, I remember kneeling with my relatives during the rosary. Among their voices I traced, then lost, the sounds of individual aunts in the surge of the common prayer. And I heard at that moment what since I have heard very often — the sound the women in my family make when they are praying in sadness. When I went up to look at my grandmother, I saw her through the haze of a veil draped over the open lid of the casket. Her face looked calm — but distant and unyielding to love. It was not the face I remembered seeing most often. It was the face she made in public when the clerk at Safeway asked her some question and I would need to respond. It was her public face that the mortician had designed with his dubious art.

Gretel Ehrlich

The Solace of Open Spaces

IT'S MAY and I've just awakened from a nap, curled against sagebrush the way my dog taught me to sleep — sheltered from wind. A front is pulling the huge sky over me, and from the dark a hailstone has hit me on the head. I'm trailing a band of two thousand sheep across a stretch of Wyoming badlands, a fifty-mile trip that takes five days because sheep shade up in hot sun and won't budge until it's cool. Bunched together now, and excited into a run by the storm, they drift across dry land, tumbling into draws like water and surge out again onto the rugged, choppy plateaus that are the building blocks of this state.

The name Wyoming comes from an Indian word meaning "at the great plains," but the plains are really valleys, great arid valleys, sixteen hundred square miles, with the horizon bending up on all sides into mountain ranges. This gives the vastness a sheltering look.

Winter lasts six months here. Prevailing winds spill snowdrifts to the east, and new storms from the northwest replenish them. This white bulk is sometimes dizzying, even nauseating, to look at. At twenty, thirty, and forty degrees below zero, not only does your car not work, but neither do your mind and body. The landscape hardens into a dungeon of space. During the winter, while I was riding to find a new calf, my jeans froze to the saddle, and in the silence that such cold creates I felt like the first person on earth, or the last.

Today the sun is out — only a few clouds billowing. In the east, where the sheep have started off without me, the benchland tilts up in a series of eroded red-earthed mesas, planed flat on top by a million years of

First published in *The Atlantic Monthly*, 1981; collected in **The Solace of Open Spaces*, 1985.

water; behind them, a bold line of muscular scarps rears up ten thousand feet to become the Big Horn Mountains. A tidal pattern is engraved into the ground, as if left by the sea that once covered this state. Canyons curve down like galaxies to meet the oncoming rush of flat land.

To live and work in this kind of open country, with its hundred-mile views, is to lose the distinction between background and foreground. When I asked an older ranch hand to describe Wyoming's openness, he said, "It's all a bunch of nothing — wind and rattlesnakes — and so much of it you can't tell where you're going or where you've been and it don't make much difference." John, a sheepman I know, is tall and handsome and has an explosive temperament. He has a perfect intuition about people and sheep. They call him "Highpockets," because he's so long-legged; his graceful stride matches the distances he has to cover. He says, "Open space hasn't affected me at all. It's all the people moving in on it." The huge ranch he was born on takes up much of one county and spreads into another state; to put 100,000 miles on his pickup in three years and never leave home is not unusual. A friend of mine has an aunt who ranched on Powder River and didn't go off her place for eleven years. When her husband died, she quickly moved to town, bought a car, and drove around the States to see what she'd been missing.

Most people tell me they've simply driven through Wyoming, as if there were nothing to stop for. Or else they've skied in Jackson Hole, a place Wyomingites acknowledge uncomfortably because its green beauty and chic affluence are mismatched with the rest of the state. Most of Wyoming has a "lean-to" look. Instead of big, roomy barns and Victorian houses, there are dugouts, low sheds, log cabins, sheep camps, and fence lines that look like driftwood blown haphazardly into place. People here still feel pride because they live in such a harsh place, part of the glamorous cowboy past, and they are determined not to be the victims of a mining-dominated future.

Most characteristic of the state's landscape is what a developer euphemistically describes as "indigenous growth right up to your front door" — a reference to waterless stands of salt sage, snakes, jack rabbits, deerflies, red dust, a brief respite of wildflowers, dry washes, and no trees. In the Great Plains the vistas look like music, like Kyries of grass, but Wyoming seems to be the doing of a mad architect — tumbled and twisted, ribboned with faded, deathbed colors, thrust up and pulled down as if the place had been startled out of a deep sleep and thrown into a pure light.

I came here four years ago. I had not planned to stay, but I couldn't make myself leave. John, the sheepman, put me to work immediately. It was spring, and shearing time. For fourteen days of fourteen hours each, we moved thousands of sheep through sorting corrals to be sheared, branded, and deloused. I suspect that my original motive for coming here was to "lose myself" in new and unpopulated territory. Instead of producing the numbness I thought I wanted, life on the sheep ranch woke me up. The vitality of the people I was working with flushed out what had become a hallucinatory rawness inside me. I threw away my clothes and bought new ones; I cut my hair. The arid country was a clean slate. Its absolute indifference steadied me.

Sagebrush covers 58,000 square miles of Wyoming. The biggest city has a population of fifty thousand, and there are only five settlements that could be called cities in the whole state. The rest are towns, scattered across the expanse with as much as sixty miles between them, their populations two thousand, fifty, or ten. They are fugitive-looking, perched on a barren, windblown bench, or tagged onto a river or a railroad, or laid out straight in a farming valley with implement stores and a block-long Mormon church. In the eastern part of the state, which slides down into the Great Plains, the new mining settlements are boomtowns, trailer cities, metal knots on flat land.

Despite the desolate look, there's a coziness to living in this state. There are so few people (only 470,000) that ranchers who buy and sell cattle know one another statewide; the kids who choose to go to college usually go to the state's one university, in Laramie; hired hands work their way around Wyoming in a lifetime of hirings and firings. And despite the physical separation, people stay in touch, often driving two or three hours to another ranch for dinner.

Seventy-five years ago, when travel was by buckboard or horseback, cowboys who were temporarily out of work rode the grub line — drifting from ranch to ranch, mending fences or milking cows, and receiving in exchange a bed and meals. Gossip and messages traveled this slow circuit with them, creating an intimacy between ranchers who were three and four weeks' ride apart. One old-time couple I know, whose turn-of-the-century homestead was used by an outlaw gang as a relay station for stolen horses, recall that if you were traveling, desperado or not, any lighted ranch house was a welcome sign. Even now, for someone who lives in a remote spot, arriving at a ranch or coming to town for supplies is cause for celebration. To emerge from isolation can be disorienting. Everything looks bright, new, vivid. After I had been herding sheep for only three days, the sound of the camp tender's pickup flustered me. Longing for human company, I felt a foolish grin take over my face; yet I had to resist an urgent temptation to run and hide.

Things happen suddenly in Wyoming, the change of seasons and weather; for people, the violent swings in and out of isolation. But good-naturedness is concomitant with severity. Friendliness is a tradition. Strangers passing on the road wave hello. A common sight is two pickups stopped side by side far out on a range, on a dirt track winding through the sage. The drivers will share a cigarette, uncap their thermos bottles, and pass a battered cup, steaming with coffee, between windows. These meetings summon up the details of several generations, because, in Wyoming, private histories are largely public knowledge.

Because ranch work is a physical and, these days, economic strain, being "at home on the range" is a matter of vigor, self-reliance, and common sense. A person's life is not a series of dramatic events for which he or she is applauded or exiled but a slow accumulation of days, seasons, years, fleshed out by the generational weight of one's family and anchored by a land-bound sense of place.

In most parts of Wyoming, the human population is visibly outnumbered by the animal. Not far from my town of fifty, I rode into a narrow valley and startled a herd of two hundred elk. Eagles look like small people as they eat car-killed deer by the road. Antelope, moving in small, graceful bands, travel at sixty miles an hour, their mouths open as if drinking in the space.

The solitude in which westerners live makes them quiet. They telegraph thoughts and feelings by the way they tilt their heads and listen; pulling their Stetsons into a steep dive over their eyes, or pigeon-toeing one boot over the other, they lean against a fence with a fat wedge of Copenhagen beneath their lower lips and take in the whole scene. These detached looks of quiet amusement are sometimes cynical, but they can also come from a dry-eyed humility as lucid as the air is clear.

Conversation goes on in what sounds like a private code; a few phrases imply a complex of meanings. Asking directions, you get a curious list of details. While trailing sheep I was told to "ride up to that kinda upturned rock, follow the pink wash, turn left at the dump, and then you'll see the water hole." One friend told his wife on roundup to "turn at the salt lick and the dead cow," which turned out to be a scattering of bones and no salt lick at all.

Sentence structure is shortened to the skin and bones of a thought. Descriptive words are dropped, even verbs; a cowboy looking over a corral full of horses will say to a wrangler, "Which one needs rode?" People hold back their thoughts in what seems to be a dumbfounded silence, then erupt with an excoriating perceptive remark. Language, so compressed, becomes metaphorical. A rancher ended a relationship with one remark: "You're a bad check," meaning bouncing in and out was intolerable, and even coming back would be no good.

What's behind this laconic style is shyness. There is no vocabulary for the subject of feelings. It's not a hangdog shyness, or anything coy — always there's a robust spirit in evidence behind the restraint, as if the earth-dredging wind that pulls across Wyoming had carried its people's voices away but everything else in them had shouldered confidently into the breeze.

I've spent hours riding to sheep camp at dawn in a pickup when nothing was said; eaten meals in the cookhouse when the only words spoken were a mumbled "Thank you, ma'am" at the end of dinner. The silence is profound. Instead of talking, we seem to share one eye. Keenly observed, the world is transformed. The landscape is engorged with detail, every movement on it chillingly sharp. The air between people is charged. Days unfold, bathed in their own music. Nights become hallucinatory; dreams, prescient.

Spring weather is capricious and mean. It snows, then blisters with heat. There have been tornadoes. They lay their elephant trunks out in the sage until they find houses, then slurp everything up and leave. I've noticed that melting snowbanks hiss and rot, viperous, then drip into calm pools where ducklings hatch and livestock, being trailed to summer range, drink. With the ice cover gone, rivers churn a milkshake brown, taking culverts and small bridges with them. Water in such an arid place (the average annual rainfall where I live is less than eight inches) is like blood. It festoons drab land with green veins; a line of cottonwoods following a stream; a strip of alfalfa; and, on ditch banks, wild asparagus growing.

I've moved to a small cattle ranch owned by friends. It's at the foot of the Big Horn Mountains. A few weeks ago, I helped them deliver a calf who was stuck halfway out of his mother's body. By the time he was freed, we could see a heartbeat, but he was straining against a swollen tongue for air. Mary and I held him upside down by his back feet, while Stan, on his hands and knees in the blood, gave the calf mouth-to-mouth resuscitation. I have a vague memory of being pneumonia-choked as a child, my mother giving me her air, which may account for my romance with this windswept state.

If anything is endemic to Wyoming, it is wind. This big room of space is swept out daily, leaving a bone yard of fossils, agates, and carcasses in every stage of decay. Though it was water that initially shaped the state, wind is the meticulous gardener, raising dust and pruning the sage.

I try to imagine a world in which I could ride my horse across uncharted land. There is no wilderness left; wildness, yes, but true wilderness has been gone on this continent since the time of Lewis and Clark's overland journey.

Two hundred years ago, the Crow, Shoshone, Arapaho, Cheyenne, and Sioux roamed the intermountain West, orchestrating their movements according to hunger, season, and warfare. Once they acquired horses, they traversed the spines of all the big Wyoming ranges — the Absarokas, the Wind Rivers, the Tetons, the Big Horns — and wintered on the unprotected plains that fan out from them. Space was life. The world was their home.

What was life-giving to Native Americans was often nightmarish to sodbusters who had arrived encumbered with families and ethnic pasts to be transplanted in nearly uninhabitable land. The great distances, the shortage of water and trees, and the loneliness created unexpected hardships for them. In her book *O Pioneers!,* Willa Cather gives a settler's version of the bleak landscape:

> The little town behind them had vanished as if it had never been, had fallen behind the swell of the prairie, and the stern frozen country received them into its bosom. The homesteads were few and far apart; here and there a windmill gaunt against the sky, a sod house crouching in a hollow.

The emptiness of the West was for others a geography of possibility. Men and women who amassed great chunks of land and struggled to preserve unfenced empires were, despite their self-serving motives, unwitting geographers. They understood the lay of the land. But by the 1850s the Oregon and Mormon trails sported bumper-to-bumper traffic. Wealthy landowners, many of them aristocratic absentee landlords, known as remittance men because they were paid to come West and get out of their families' hair, overstocked the range with more than a million head of cattle. By 1885 the feed and water were desperately short, and the winter of 1886 laid out the gaunt bodies of dead animals so closely together that when the thaw came, one rancher from Kaycee claimed to have walked on cowhide all the way to Crazy Woman Creek, twenty miles away.

Territorial Wyoming was a boy's world. The land was generous with everything but water. At first there was room enough, food enough, for everyone. And, as with all beginnings, an expansive mood set in. The young cowboys, drifters, shopkeepers, schoolteachers, were heroic, lawless, generous, rowdy, and tenacious. The individualism and optimism generated during those times have endured.

John Tisdale rode north with the trail herds from Texas. He was a college-educated man with enough money to buy a small outfit near the Powder River. While driving home from the town of Buffalo with a buckboard full of Christmas toys for his family and a winter's supply of food, he was shot in the back by an agent of the cattle barons who resented the encroachment of small-time stockmen like him. The wealthy cattlemen tried to control all the public grazing land by restricting membership in the Wyoming Stock Growers Association, as if it were a country club. They ostracized from roundups and brandings cowboys and ranchers who were not members, then denounced them as rustlers. Tisdale's death, the second such cold-blooded murder, kicked off the Johnson County cattle war, which was no simple good-guy-bad-guy shoot-out but a complicated class struggle between landed gentry and less affluent settlers — a shocking reminder that the West was not an egalitarian sanctuary after all.

Fencing ultimately enforced boundaries, but barbed wire abrogated space. It was stretched across the beautiful valleys, into the mountains, over desert badlands, through buffalo grass. The "anything is possible" fever — the lure of any new place — was constricted. The integrity of the land as a geographical body, and the freedom to ride anywhere on it, were lost.

I punched cows with a young man named Martin, who is the great-grandson of John Tisdale. His inheritance is not the open land that Tisdale knew and prematurely lost but a rage against restraint.

Wyoming tips down as you head northeast; the highest ground — the Laramie Plains — is on the Colorado border. Up where I live, the Big Horn River leaks into difficult, arid terrain. In the basin where it's dammed, sandhill cranes gather and, with delicate legwork, slice through the stilled water. I was driving by with a rancher one morning when he commented that cranes are "old-fashioned." When I asked why, he said, "Because they mate for life." Then he looked at me with a twinkle in his eyes, as if to say he really did believe in such things but also understood why we break our own rules.

In all this open space, values crystalize quickly. People are strong on scruples but tenderhearted about quirky behavior. A friend and I found one ranch hand, who's "not quite right in the head," sitting in front of the badly decayed carcass of a cow, shaking his finger and saying, "Now, I don't want you to do this ever again!" When I asked what was wrong with him, I was told, "He's goofier than hell, just like the rest of us." Perhaps because the West is historically new, conventional morality is still felt to be less important than rock-bottom truths. Though there's always a lot of teasing and sparring, people are blunt with one another, sometimes even cruel, believing honesty is stronger medicine than sympathy, which may console but often conceals.

The formality that goes hand in hand with the rowdiness is known as the Western Code. It's a list of practical do's and don'ts, faithfully observed. A friend, Cliff, who runs a trapline in the winter, cut off half his foot while chopping a hole in the ice. Alone, he dragged himself to his pickup and headed for town, stopping to open the ranch gate as he left, and getting out to close it again, thus losing, in his observance of rules, precious time and blood. Later, he commented, "How would it look, them having to come to the hospital to tell me their cows had gotten out?"

Accustomed to emergencies, my friends doctor each other from the vet's bag with relish. When one old-timer suffered a heart attack in hunting camp, his partner quickly stirred up a brew of red horse liniment and hot water and made the half-conscious victim drink it, then tied him onto a horse and led him twenty miles to town. He regained consciousness and lived.

The roominess of the state has affected political attitudes as well. Ranchers keep up with world politics and the convulsions of the economy but are basically isolationists. Being used to running their own small empires of land and livestock, they're suspicious of big government. It's a "don't fence me in" holdover from a century ago. They still want the elbow room their grandfathers had, so they're strongly conservative, but with a populist twist.

Summer is the season when we get our "cowboy tans" — on the lower parts of our faces and on three fourths of our arms. Excessive heat, in the nineties and higher, sends us outside with the mosquitoes. In winter we're tucked inside our houses, and the white wasteland outside appears to be expanding, but in summer all the greenery abridges space. Summer is a go-ahead season. Every living thing is off the block and in the race: battalions of bugs in flight and biting; bats swinging around my log cabin as if the bases were loaded and someone had hit a home run. Some of summer's high-speed growth is ominous: larkspur, death camas, and green greasewood can kill sheep — an ironic idea, dying in this desert from eating what is too verdant. With sixteen hours of daylight, farmers and ranchers irrigate feverishly. There are first, second, and third cuttings of hay, some crews averaging only four hours of sleep a night for weeks. And, like the cowboys who in summer ride the night rodeo circuit, nighthawks make daredevil dives at dusk with an eerie whirring sound like a plane going down on the shimmering horizon.

In the town where I live, they've had to board up the dance-hall windows because there have been so many fights. There's so little to do except work that people wind up in a state of idle agitation that becomes fatalistic, as if there were nothing to be done about all this untapped energy. So the dark side to the grandeur of these spaces is the small-mindedness that seals people in. Men become hermits; women go mad. Cabin fever explodes into suicides, or into grudges and lifelong family feuds. Two sisters in my area inherited a ranch but found they couldn't get along. They fenced the place in half. When one's cows got out and mixed with the other's, the women went at each other with shovels. They ended up in the same hospital room but never spoke a word to each other for the rest of their lives.

After the brief lushness of summer, the sun moves south. The range grass is brown. Livestock is trailed back down from the mountains. Water holes begin to frost over at night. Last fall Martin asked me to accompany him on a pack trip. With five horses, we followed a river into the mountains behind the tiny Wyoming town of Meeteetse. Groves of aspen, red and orange, gave off a light that made us look toasted. Our hunting camp was so high that clouds skidded across our foreheads, then slowed to sail out across the warm valleys. Except for a bull moose who wandered into our camp and mistook our black gelding for a rival, we shot at nothing.

One of our evening entertainments was to watch the night sky. My dog, a dingo bred to herd sheep, also came on the trip. He is so used to the silence and empty skies that when an airplane flies over he always looks up and eyes the distant intruder quizzically. The sky, lately, seems to be much more crowded than it used to be. Satellites make their silent passes in the dark with great regularity. We counted eighteen in one hour's viewing. How odd to think that while they circumnavigated the planet, Martin and I had moved only six miles into our local wilderness and had seen no other human for the two weeks we stayed there.

At night, by moonlight, the land is whittled to slivers — a ridge, a river, a strip of grassland stretching to the mountains, then the huge sky. One morning a full moon was setting in the west just as the sun was rising. I felt precariously balanced between the two as I loped across a meadow. For a moment, I could believe that the stars, which were still visible, work like cooper's bands, holding together everything above Wyoming.

Space has a spiritual equivalent and can heal what is divided and burdensome in us. My grandchildren will probably use space shuttles for a honeymoon trip or to recover from heart attacks, but closer to home we might also learn how to carry space inside ourselves in the effortless way we carry our skins. Space represents sanity, not a life purified, dull, or "spaced out" but one that might accommodate intelligently any idea or situation.

From the clayey soil of northern Wyoming is mined bentonite, which is used as a filler in candy, gum, and lipstick. We Americans are great on fillers, as if what we have, what we are, is not enough. We have a cultural tendency toward denial, but, being affluent, we strangle ourselves with what we can buy. We have only to look at the houses we build to see how we build *against* space, the way we drink against pain and loneliness. We fill up space as if it were a pie shell, with things whose opacity further obstructs our ability to see what is already there.

1982

Annie Dillard

Total Eclipse

I

IT HAD BEEN LIKE DYING, that sliding down the mountain pass. It had been like the death of someone, irrational, that sliding down the mountain pass and into the region of dread. It was like slipping into fever, or falling down that hole in sleep from which you wake yourself whimpering. We had crossed the mountains that day, and now we were in a strange place — a hotel in central Washington, in a town near Yakima. The eclipse we had traveled here to see would occur early the next morning.

I lay in bed. My husband, Gary, was reading beside me. I lay in bed and looked at the painting on the hotel room wall. It was a print of a detailed and lifelike painting of a smiling clown's head, made out of vegetables. It was a painting of the sort which you do not intend to look at, and which, alas, you never forget. Some tasteless fate presses it upon you; it becomes part of the complex interior junk you carry with you wherever you go. Two years have passed since the total eclipse of which I write. During those years I have forgotten, I assume, a great many things I wanted to remember — but I have not forgotten that clown painting or its lunatic setting in the old hotel.

The clown was bald. Actually, he wore a clown's tight rubber wig, painted white; this stretched over the top of his skull, which was a cabbage. His hair was bunches of baby carrots. Inset in his white clown makeup, and in his cabbage skull, were his small and laughing human

First published in *Antaeus*, 1982; collected in * *Teaching a Stone to Talk*, 1982.

eyes. The clown's glance was like the glance of Rembrandt in some of the self-portraits: lively, knowing, deep, and loving. The crinkled shadows around his eyes were string beans. His eyebrows were parsley. Each of his ears was a broad bean. His thin, joyful lips were red chili peppers; between his lips were wet rows of human teeth and a suggestion of a real tongue. The clown print was framed in gilt and glassed.

To put ourselves in the path of the total eclipse, that day we had driven five hours inland from the Washington coast, where we lived. When we tried to cross the Cascades range, an avalanche had blocked the pass.

A slope's worth of snow blocked the road; traffic backed up. Had the avalanche buried any cars that morning? We could not learn. This highway was the only winter road over the mountains. We waited as highway crews bulldozed a passage through the avalanche. With two-by-fours and walls of plyboard, they erected a one-way, roofed tunnel through the avalanche. We drove through the avalanche tunnel, crossed the pass, and descended several thousand feet into central Washington and the broad Yakima valley, about which we knew only that it was orchard country. As we lost altitude, the snows disappeared; our ears popped; the trees changed, and in the trees were strange birds. I watched the landscape innocently, like a fool, like a diver in the rapture of the deep who plays on the bottom while his air runs out.

The hotel lobby was a dark, derelict room, narrow as a corridor, and seemingly without air. We waited on a couch while the manager vanished upstairs to do something unknown to our room. Beside us on an overstuffed chair, absolutely motionless, was a platinum-blond woman in her forties wearing a black silk dress and a strand of pearls. Her long legs were crossed; she supported her head on her fist. At the dim far end of the room, their backs toward us, sat six bald old men in their shirtsleeves, around a loud television. Two of them seemed asleep. They were drunks. "Number six!" cried the man on television, "Number six!"

On the broad lobby desk, lighted and bubbling, was a ten-gallon aquarium containing one large fish; the fish tilted up and down in its water. Against the long opposite wall sang a live canary in its cage. Beneath the cage, among spilled millet seeds on the carpet, were a decorated child's sand bucket and matching sand shovel.

Now the alarm was set for six. I lay awake remembering an article I had read downstairs in the lobby, in an engineering magazine. The article was about gold mining.

In South Africa, in India, and in South Dakota, the gold mines extend so deeply into the earth's crust that they are hot. The rock walls burn the miners' hands. The companies have to air-condition the mines; if the air conditioners break, the miners die. The elevators in the mine shafts run very slowly, down, and up, so the miners' ears will not pop in their skulls. When the miners return to the surface, their faces are deathly pale.

Early the next morning we checked out. It was February 26, 1979, a Monday morning. We would drive out of town, find a hilltop, watch the eclipse, and then drive back over the mountains and home to the coast. How familiar things are here; how adept we are; how smoothly and professionally we check out! I had forgotten the clown's smiling head and the hotel lobby as if they had never existed. Gary put the car in gear and off we went, as off we have gone to a hundred other adventures.

It was before dawn when we found a highway out of town and drove into the unfamiliar countryside. By the growing light we could see a band of cirrostratus clouds in the sky. Later the rising sun would clear these clouds before the eclipse began. We drove at random until we came to a range of unfenced hills. We pulled off the highway, bundled up, and climbed one of these hills.

II

The hill was five hundred feet high. Long winter-killed grass covered it, as high as our knees. We climbed and rested, sweating in the cold; we passed clumps of bundled people on the hillside who were setting up telescopes and fiddling with cameras. The top of the hill stuck up in the middle of the sky. We tightened our scarves and looked around.

East of us rose another hill like ours. Between the hills, far below, was the highway which threaded south into the valley. This was the Yakima valley; I had never seen it before. It is justly famous for its beauty, like every planted valley. It extended south into the horizon, a distant dream of a valley, a Shangri-la. All its hundreds of low, golden slopes bore orchards. Among the orchards were towns, and roads, and plowed and fallow fields. Through the valley wandered a thin, shining river; from the river extended fine, frozen irrigation ditches. Distance blurred and blued the sight, so that the whole valley looked like a thickness or sediment at the bottom of the sky. Directly behind us was more sky, and empty lowlands blued by distance, and Mount Adams. Mount Adams was an enormous, snow-covered volcanic cone rising flat, like so much scenery.

Now the sun was up. We could not see it; but the sky behind the band of clouds was yellow, and, far down the valley, some hillside orchards had lighted up. More people were parking near the highway and climbing the hills. It was the West. All of us rugged individualists were wearing knit caps and blue nylon parkas. People were climbing the nearby hills and setting up shop in clumps among the dead grasses. It looked as though we had all gathered on hilltops to pray for the world on its last day. It looked as though we had all crawled out of spaceships and were preparing to assault the valley below. It looked as though we were scattered on hilltops at dawn to sacrifice virgins, make rain, set stone stelae in a ring. There was no place out of the wind. The straw grasses banged our legs.

Up in the sky where we stood the air was lusterless yellow. To the west the sky was blue. Now the sun cleared the clouds. We cast rough shadows on the blowing grass; freezing, we waved our arms. Near the sun, the sky was bright and colorless. There was nothing to see.

It began with no ado. It was odd that such a well-advertised public event should have no starting gun, no overture, no introductory speaker. I should have known right then that I was out of my depth. Without pause or preamble, silent as orbits, a piece of the sun went away. We looked at it through welders' goggles. A piece of the sun was missing; in its place we saw empty sky.

I had seen a partial eclipse in 1970. A partial eclipse is very interesting. It bears almost no relation to a total eclipse. Seeing a partial eclipse bears the same relation to seeing a total eclipse as kissing a man does to marrying him, or as flying in an airplane does to falling out of an airplane. Although the one experience precedes the other, it in no way prepares you for it. During a partial eclipse the sky does not darken — not even when 94 percent of the sun is hidden. Nor does the sun, seen colorless through protective devices, seem terribly strange. We have all seen a sliver of light in the sky; we have all seen the crescent moon by day. However, during a partial eclipse the air does indeed get cold, precisely as if someone were standing between you and the fire. And blackbirds do fly back to their roosts. I had seen a partial eclipse before, and here was another.

What you see in an eclipse is entirely different from what you know.

It is especially different for those of us whose grasp of astronomy is so frail that, given a flashlight, a grapefruit, two oranges, and fifteen years, we still could not figure out which way to set the clocks for Daylight Saving Time. Usually it is a bit of a trick to keep your knowledge from blinding you. But during an eclipse it is easy. What you see is much more convincing than any wild-eyed theory you may know.

You may read that the moon has something to do with eclipses. I have never seen the moon yet. You do not see the moon. So near the sun, it is as completely invisible as the stars are by day. What you see before your eyes is the sun going through phases. It gets narrower and narrower, as the waning moon does, and, like the ordinary moon, it travels alone in the simple sky. The sky is of course background. It does not appear to eat the sun; it is far behind the sun. The sun simply shaves away; gradually, you see less sun and more sky.

The sky's blue was deepening, but there was no darkness. The sun was a wide crescent, like a segment of tangerine. The wind freshened and blew steadily over the hill. The eastern hill across the highway grew dusky and sharp. The towns and orchards in the valley to the south were dissolving into the blue light. Only the thin river held a trickle of sun.

Now the sky to the west deepened to indigo, a color never seen. A dark sky usually loses color. This was a saturated, deep indigo, up in the air. Stuck up into that unworldly sky was the cone of Mount Adams, and the alpenglow was upon it. The alpenglow is that red light of sunset which holds out on snowy mountaintops long after the valleys and tablelands are dimmed. "Look at Mount Adams," I said, and that was the last sane moment I remember.

I turned back to the sun. It was going. The sun was going, and the world was wrong. The grasses were wrong; they were platinum. Their every detail of stem, head, and blade shone lightless and artificially distinct as an art photographer's platinum print. This color has never been seen on earth. The hues were metallic; their finish was matte. The hillside was a nineteenth-century tinted photograph from which the tints had faded. All the people you see in the photograph, distinct and detailed as their faces look, are now dead. The sky was navy blue. My hands were silver. All the distant hills' grasses were finespun metal which the wind laid down. I was watching a faded color print of a movie filmed in the Middle Ages; I was standing in it, by some mistake. I was standing in a movie of hillside grasses filmed in the Middle Ages. I missed my own century, the people I knew, and the real light of day.

I looked at Gary. He was in the film. Everything was lost. He was a platinum print, a dead artist's version of life. I saw on his skull the darkness of night mixed with the colors of day. My mind was going out; my eyes were receding the way galaxies recede to the rim of space. Gary was light-years away, gesturing inside a circle of darkness, down the wrong end of a telescope. He smiled as if he saw me; the stringy crinkles around his eyes moved. The sight of him, familiar and wrong, was something I was remembering from centuries hence, from the other side of death: yes, *that* is the way he used to look, when we were living. When it was our generation's turn to be alive. I could not hear him; the wind was too loud. Behind him the sun was going. We had all started down a chute of time. At first it was pleasant; now there was no stopping it. Gary was chuting away across space, moving and talking and catching my eye, chuting down the long corridor of separation. The skin on his face moved like thin bronze plating that would peel.

The grass at our feet was wild barley. It was the wild einkorn wheat which grew on the hilly flanks of the Zagros Mountains, above the Euphrates valley, above the valley of the river we called *River*. We harvested the grass with stone sickles, I remember. We found the grasses on the hillsides; we built our shelter beside them and cut them down. That is how he used to look then, that one, moving and living and catching my eye, with the sky so dark behind him, and the wind blowing. God save our life.

From all the hills came screams. A piece of sky beside the crescent sun was detaching. It was a loosened circle of evening sky, suddenly lighted from the back. It was an abrupt black body out of nowhere; it was a flat disk; it was almost over the sun. That is when there were screams. At once this disk of sky slid over the sun like a lid. The sky snapped over the sun like a lens cover. The hatch in the brain slammed. Abruptly it was dark night, on the land and in the sky. In the night sky was a tiny ring of light. The hole where the sun belongs is very small. A thin ring of light marked its place. There was no sound. The eyes dried, the arteries drained, the lungs hushed. There was no world. We were the world's dead people rotating and orbiting around and around, embedded in the planet's crust, while the earth rolled down. Our minds were light-years distant, forgetful of almost everything. Only an extraordinary act of will could recall to us our former, living selves and our contexts in matter and time. We had, it seems, loved the planet and loved our lives, but could no longer remember the way of them. We got the light wrong. In the sky was something that should not be there. In the black sky was a ring of light. It was a thin ring, an old, thin silver wedding band, an old, worn ring. It was an old wedding band in the sky, or a morsel of bone. There were stars. It was all over.

III

It is now that the temptation is strongest to leave these regions. We have seen enough; let's go. Why burn our hands any more than we have to? But two years have passed; the price of gold has risen. I return to the same buried alluvial beds and pick through the strata again.

I saw, early in the morning, the sun diminish against a backdrop of sky. I saw a circular piece of that sky appear, suddenly detached, blackened, and backlighted; from nowhere it came and overlapped the sun. It did not look like the moon. It was enormous and black. If I had not read that it was the moon, I could have seen the sight a hundred times and never thought of the moon once. (If, however, I had not read that it was the moon — if, like most of the world's people throughout time, I had simply glanced up and seen this thing — then I doubtless would not have speculated much, but would have, like Emperor Louis of Bavaria in 840, simply died of fright on the spot.) It did not look like a dragon, although it looked more like a dragon than the moon. It looked like a lens cover, or the lid of a pot. It materialized out of thin air — black, and flat, and sliding, outlined in flame.

Seeing this black body was like seeing a mushroom cloud. The heart screeched. The meaning of the sight overwhelmed its fascination. It obliterated meaning itself. If you were to glance out one day and see a row of mushroom clouds rising on the horizon, you would know at once that what you were seeing, remarkable as it was, was intrinsically not worth remarking. No use running to tell anyone. Significant as it was, it did not matter a whit. For what is significance? It is significance for people. No people, no significance. This is all I have to tell you.

In the deeps are the violence and terror of which psychology has warned us. But if you ride these monsters deeper down, if you drop with them farther over the world's rim, you find what our sciences cannot locate or name, the substrate, the ocean or matrix or ether which buoys the rest, which gives goodness its power for good, and evil its power for evil, the unified field: our complex and inexplicable caring for each other, and for our life together here. This is given. It is not learned.

The world which lay under darkness and stillness following the closing of the lid was not the world we know. The event was over. Its devastation lay round about us. The clamoring mind and heart stilled, almost indifferent, certainly disembodied, frail, and exhausted. The hills were hushed, obliterated. Up in the sky, like a crater from some distant cataclysm, was a hollow ring.

You have seen photographs of the sun taken during a total eclipse. The corona fills the print. All of those photographs were taken through telescopes. The lenses of telescopes and cameras can no more cover the breadth and scale of the visual array than language can cover the breadth and simultaneity of internal experience. Lenses enlarge the sight, omit its context, and make of it a pretty and sensible picture, like something on a Christmas card. I assure you, if you send any shepherds a Christmas card on which is printed a three-by-three photograph of the angel of the Lord, the glory of the Lord, and a multitude of the heavenly host, they will not be sore afraid. More fearsome things can come in envelopes. More moving photographs than those of the sun's corona can appear in magazines. But I pray you will never see anything more awful in the sky.

You see the wide world swaddled in darkness; you see a vast breadth of hilly land, and an enormous, distant, blackened valley; you see towns' lights, a river's path, and blurred portions of your hat and scarf; you see your husband's face looking like an early black-and-white film; and you see a sprawl of black sky and blue sky together, with unfamiliar stars in it, some barely visible bands of cloud, and over there, a small white ring. The ring is as small as one goose in a flock of migrating geese — if you happen to notice a flock of migrating geese. It is one 360th part of the visible sky. The sun we see is less than half the diameter of a dime held at arm's length.

The Crab Nebula, in the constellation Taurus, looks, through binoculars, like a smoke ring. It is a star in the process of exploding. Light from its explosion first reached the earth in 1054; it was a supernova then, and so bright it shone in the daytime. Now it is not so bright, but it is still exploding. It expands at the rate of seventy million miles a day. It is interesting to look through binoculars at something expanding seventy million miles a day. It does not budge. Its apparent size does not increase. Photographs of the Crab Nebula taken fifteen years ago seem identical to photographs of it taken yesterday. Some lichens are similar. Botanists have measured some ordinary lichens twice, at fifty-year intervals, without detecting any growth at all. And yet their cells divide; they live.

The small ring of light was like these things — like a ridiculous lichen up in the sky, like a perfectly still explosion 4,200 light-years away: it was interesting, and lovely, and in witless motion, and it had nothing to do with anything.

It had nothing to do with anything. The sun was too small, and too cold, and too far away, to keep the world alive. The white ring was not enough. It was feeble and worthless. It was as useless as a memory; it was as off kilter and hollow and wretched as a memory.

When you try your hardest to recall someone's face, or the look of a place, you see in your mind's eye some vague and terrible sight such as this. It is dark; it is insubstantial; it is all wrong.

The white ring and the saturated darkness made the earth and the sky look as they must look in the memories of the careless dead. What I saw, what I seemed to be standing in, was all the wrecked light that the memories of the dead could shed upon the living world. We had all died in our boots on the hilltops of Yakima, and were alone in eternity. Empty space stoppered our eyes and mouths; we cared for nothing. We remembered our living days wrong. With great effort we had remembered some sort of circular light in the sky — but only the outline. Oh, and then the orchard trees withered, the ground froze, the glaciers slid down the valleys and overlapped the towns. If there had ever been people on earth, nobody knew it. The dead had forgotten those they had loved. The dead were parted one from the other and could no longer remember the faces and lands they had loved in the light. They seemed to stand on darkened hilltops, looking down.

IV

We teach our children one thing only, as we were taught: to wake up. We teach our children to look alive there, to join by words and activities the life of human culture on the planet's crust. As adults we are almost all adept at waking up. We have so mastered the transition we have forgotten we ever learned it. Yet it is a transition we make a hundred times a day, as, like so many will-less dolphins, we plunge and surface, lapse and emerge. We live half our waking lives and all of our sleeping lives in some private, useless, and insensible waters we never mention or recall. Useless, I say. Valueless, I might add — until someone hauls their wealth up to the surface and into the wide-awake city, in a form that people can use.

I do not know how we got to the restaurant. Like Roethke, "I take my waking slow." Gradually I seemed more or less alive, and already forgetful. It was now almost nine in the morning. It was the day of a solar eclipse in central Washington, and a fine adventure for everyone. The sky was clear; there was a fresh breeze out of the north.

The restaurant was a roadside place with tables and booths. The other eclipse-watchers were there. From our booth we could see their cars' California license plates, their University of Washington parking stickers. Inside the restaurant we were all eating eggs or waffles; people were fairly shouting and exchanging enthusiasms, like fans after a World Series game. Did you see . . . ? Did you see . . . ? Then somebody said something which knocked me for a loop.

A college student, a boy in a blue parka who carried a Hasselblad, said to us, "Did you see that little white ring? It looked like a Life Saver. It looked like a Life Saver up in the sky."

And so it did. The boy spoke well. He was a walking alarm clock. I myself had at that time no access to such a word. He could write a sentence, and I could not. I grabbed that Life Saver and rode it to the surface. And I had to laugh. I had been dumbstruck on the Euphrates River, I had been dead and gone and grieving, all over the sight of something which, if you could claw your way up to that level, you would grant looked very much like a Life Saver. It was good to be back among people so clever; it was good to have all the world's words at the mind's disposal, so the mind could begin its task. All those things for which we have no words are lost. The mind — the culture — has two little tools, grammar and lexicon: a decorated sand bucket and a matching shovel. With these we bluster about the continents and do all the world's work. With these we try to save our very lives.

There are a few more things to tell from this level, the level of the restaurant. One is the old joke about breakfast. "It can never be satisfied, the mind, never." Wallace Stevens wrote that, and in the long run he was right. The mind wants to live forever, or to learn a very good reason why not. The mind wants the world to return its love, or its awareness; the mind wants to know all the world, and all eternity, and God. The mind's sidekick, however, will settle for two eggs over easy.

The dear, stupid body is as easily satisfied as a spaniel. And, incredibly, the simple spaniel can lure the brawling mind to its dish. It is everlastingly funny that the proud, metaphysically ambitious, clamoring mind will hush if you give it an egg.

Further: while the mind reels in deep space, while the mind grieves or fears or exults, the workaday senses, in ignorance or idiocy, like so many computer terminals printing out market prices while the world blows up, still transcribe their little data and transmit them to the warehouse in the skull. Later, under the tranquilizing influence of fried eggs, the mind can sort through this data. The restaurant was a halfway house, a decompression chamber. There I remembered a few things more.

The deepest, and most terrifying, was this: I have said that I heard screams. (I have since read that screaming, with hysteria, is a common reaction even to expected total eclipses.) People on all the hillsides, including, I think, myself, screamed when the black body of the moon detached from the sky and rolled over the sun. But something else was happening at that same instant, and it was this, I believe, which made us scream.

The second before the sun went out we saw a wall of dark shadow come speeding at us. We no sooner saw it than it was upon us, like thunder. It roared up the valley. It slammed our hill and knocked us out. It was the monstrous swift shadow cone of the moon. I have since read that this wave of shadow moves 1,800 miles an hour. Language can give no sense of this sort of speed — 1,800 miles an hour. It was 195 miles wide. No end was in sight — you saw only the edge. It rolled at you across the land at 1,800 miles an hour, hauling darkness like plague behind it. Seeing it, and knowing it was coming straight for you, was like feeling a slug of anesthetic shoot up your arm. If you think very fast, you may have time to think, "Soon it will hit my brain." You can feel the deadness race up your arm; you can feel the appalling, inhuman speed of your own blood. We saw the wall of shadow coming, and screamed before it hit.

This was the universe about which we have read so much and never

before felt: the universe as a clockwork of loose spheres flung at stupe-
fying, unauthorized speeds. How could anything moving so fast not
crash, not veer from its orbit amok like a car out of control on a turn?

Less than two minutes later, when the sun emerged, the trailing edge
of the shadow cone sped away. It coursed down our hill and raced eastward over the plain, faster than the eye could believe; it swept over the
plain and dropped over the planet's rim in a twinkling. It had clobbered
us, and now it roared away. We blinked in the light. It was as though an
enormous, loping god in the sky had reached down and slapped the
earth's face.

Something else, something more ordinary, came back to me along
about the third cup of coffee. During the moments of totality, it was so
dark that drivers on the highway below turned on their cars' headlights.
We could see the highway's route as a strand of lights. It was bumper-
to-bumper down there. It was eight-fifteen in the morning, Monday
morning, and people were driving into Yakima to work. That it was as
dark as night, and eerie as hell, an hour after dawn, apparently meant
that in order to *see* to drive to work, people had to use their headlights.
Four or five cars pulled off the road. The rest, in a line at least five miles
long, drove to town. The highway ran between hills; the people could
not have seen any of the eclipsed sun at all. Yakima will have another total eclipse in 2,086. Perhaps, in 2086, businesses will give their employ-
ees an hour off.

From the restaurant we drove back to the coast. The highway crossing
the Cascades range was open. We drove over the mountain like old
pros. We joined our places on the planet's thin crust; it held. For the
time being, we were home free.

Early that morning at six, when we had checked out, the six bald men
were sitting on folding chairs in the dim hotel lobby. The television was
on. Most of them were awake. You might drown in your own spittle,
God knows, at any time; you might wake up dead in a small hotel, a
cabbage head watching TV while snows pile up in the passes, watching
TV while the chili peppers smile and the moon passes over the sun and
nothing changes and nothing is learned because you have lost your
bucket and shovel and no longer care. What if you regain the surface
and open your sack and find, instead of treasure, a beast which jumps at
you? Or you may not come back at all. The winches may jam, the scaf-

folding buckle, the air conditioning collapse. You may glance up one day and see by your headlamp the canary keeled over in its cage. You may reach into a cranny for pearls and touch a moray eel. You yank on your rope; it is too late.

Apparently people share a sense of these hazards, for when the total eclipse ended, an odd thing happened.

When the sun appeared as a blinding bead on the ring's side, the eclipse was over. The black lens cover appeared again, backlighted, and slid away. At once the yellow light made the sky blue again; the black lid dissolved and vanished. The real world began there. I remember now: we all hurried away. We were born and bored at a stroke. We rushed down the hill. We found our car; we saw the other people streaming down the hillsides; we joined the highway traffic and drove away.

We never looked back. It was a general vamoose, and an odd one, for when we left the hill, the sun was still partially eclipsed — a sight rare enough, and one which, in itself, we would probably have driven five hours to see. But enough is enough. One turns at last even from glory itself with a sigh of relief. From the depths of mystery, and even from the heights of splendor, we bounce back and hurry for the latitudes of home.

Cynthia Ozick

....

A Drugstore in Winter

THIS IS ABOUT READING; a drugstore in winter; the gold leaf on the dome of the Boston State House; also loss, panic, and dread.

First, the gold leaf. (This part is a little like a turn-of-the-century pulp tale, though only a little. The ending is a surprise, but there is no plot.) Thirty years ago I burrowed in the Boston Public Library one whole afternoon, to find out — not out of curiosity — how the State House got its gold roof. The answer, like the answer to most Bostonian questions, was Paul Revere. So I put Paul Revere's gold dome into an "article," and took it (though I was just as scared by recklessness then as I am now) to the *Boston Globe*, on Washington Street. The Features Editor had a bare severe head, a closed parenthesis mouth, and silver Dickensian spectacles. He made me wait, standing, at the side of his desk while he read; there was no bone in me that did not rattle. Then he opened a drawer and handed me fifteen dollars. Ah, joy of Homer, joy of Milton! Grub Street bliss!

The very next Sunday, Paul Revere's gold dome saw print. Appetite for more led me to a top-floor chamber in Filene's department store: Window Dressing. But no one was in the least bit dressed — it was a dumbstruck nudist colony up there, a mob of naked frozen enigmatic manikins, tall enameled skinny ladies with bald breasts and skulls, and legs and wrists and necks that horribly unscrewed. Paul Revere's dome paled beside this gold mine! A sight — mute numb Walpurgisnact — easily worth another fifteen dollars. I had a master's degree (thesis topic: "Parable in the Later Novels of Henry James") and a job as an ad-

First published in *The New York Times Book Review*, 1982; collected in *Art & Ardor*, 1984.

vertising copywriter (9 A.M. to 6 P.M. six days a week, forty dollars per week; if you were male and had no degree at all, sixty dollars). Filene's Sale Days — Crib Bolsters! Lulla-Buys! Jonnie-Mops! Maternity Skirts with Expanding Invisible Trick Waist! And a company show; gold watches to mark the retirement of elderly Irish salesladies; for me the chance to write song lyrics (to the tune of "On Top of Old Smoky") honoring our Store. But "Mute Numb Walpurgisnacht in Secret Downtown Chamber" never reached the *Globe*. Melancholy and meaning business, the Advertising Director forbade it. Grub Street was bad form, and I had to promise never again to sink to another article. Thus ended my life in journalism.

Next: reading, and certain drugstore winter dusks. These come together. It is an aeon before Filene's, years and years before the Later Novels of Henry James. I am scrunched on my knees at a round glass table near a plate glass door on which is inscribed, in gold leaf Paul Revere never put there, letters that must be read backward: YƆAMЯAHԀ WƎIV ʞЯAԀ . There is an evening smell of late coffee from the fountain, and all the librarians are lined up in a row on the tall stools, sipping and chattering. They have just stepped in from the cold of the Traveling Library, and so have I. The Traveling Library is a big green truck that stops, once every two weeks, on the corner of Continental Avenue, just a little way in from Westchester Avenue, not far from a house that keeps a pig. Other houses fly pigeons from their roofs, other yards have chickens, and down on Mayflower there is even a goat. This is Pelham Bay, the Bronx, in the middle of the Depression, all cattails and weeds, such a lovely place and tender hour! Even though my mother takes me on the subway far, far downtown to buy my winter coat in the frenzy of Klein's on Fourteenth Street, and even though I can recognize the heavy power of a quarter, I don't know it's the Depression. On the trolley on the way to Westchester Square I see the children who live in the boxcar strangely set down in an empty lot some distance from Spy Oak (where a Revolutionary traitor was hanged — served him right for siding with redcoats); the lucky boxcar children dangle their stick-legs from their train-house maw and wave; how I envy them! I envy the orphans of the Gould Foundation, who have their own private swings and seesaws. Sometimes I imagine I am an orphan, and my father is an impostor pretending to be my father.

My father writes in his prescription book: *#59330 Dr. O'Flaherty Pow .60/ #59331 Dr. Mulligan Gtt .65/ #59332 Dr. Thron Tab .90*. Ninety cents! A terrifically expensive medicine; someone is really sick. When I deliver a prescription around the corner or down the block, I am offered a nickel tip. I always refuse, out of conscience; I am, after all, the Park View Pharmacy's own daughter, and it wouldn't be seemly. My father grinds and mixes powders, weighs them out in tiny snowy heaps on an apothecary scale, folds them into delicate translucent papers or meticulously drops them into gelatin capsules.

In the big front window of the Park View Pharmacy there is a startling display — goldfish bowls, balanced one on the other in amazing pyramids. A German lady enters, one of my father's cronies — his cronies are both women and men. My quiet father's eyes are water-color blue, he wears his small skeptical quiet smile and receives the neighborhood's life-secrets. My father is discreet and inscrutable. The German lady pokes a punchboard with a pin, pushes up a bit of rolled paper, and cries out — she has just won a goldfish bowl, with two swimming goldfish in it! Mr. Jaffe, the salesman from McKesson & Robbins, arrives, trailing two mists: winter steaminess and the animal fog of his cigar, which melts into the coffee smell, the tarpaper smell, the eerie honeyed tangled drugstore smell. Mr. Jaffe and my mother and father are intimates by now, but because it is the 1930s, so long ago, and the old manners still survive, they address one another gravely as Mr. Jaffe, Mrs. Ozick, Mr. Ozick. My mother calls my father Mr. O, even at home, as in a Victorian novel. In the street my father tips his hat to ladies. In the winter his hat is a regular fedora; in the summer it is a straw boater with a black ribbon and a jot of blue feather.

What am I doing at this round glass table, both listening and not listening to my mother and father tell Mr. Jaffe about their struggle with "Tessie," the lion-eyed landlady who has just raised, threefold, in the middle of that Depression I have never heard of, the Park View Pharmacy's devouring rent? My mother, not yet forty, wears bandages on her ankles, covering oozing varicose veins; back and forth she strides, dashes, runs, climbing cellar stairs or ladders; she unpacks cartons, she toils behind drug counters and fountain counters. Like my father, she is on her feet until one in the morning, the Park View's closing hour. My mother and father are in trouble, and I don't know it. I am too happy. I feel the secret center of eternity, nothing will ever alter, no one will ever die. Through the window, past the lit goldfish, the gray oval sky deepens over our neighborhood wood, where all the dirt paths lead down to seagull-specked water. I am familiar with every frog-haunted monument: Pelham Bay Park is thronged with WPA art — statuary, fountains, immense rococo staircases cascading down a hillside, Bacchus-faced stelae

— stone Roman glories afterward mysteriously razed by an avenging Robert Moses. One year — how distant it seems now, as if even the climate is past returning — the bay froze so hard that whole families, mine among them, crossed back and forth to City Island, strangers saluting and calling out in the ecstasy of the bright trudge over such a sudden wilderness of ice.

In the Park View Pharmacy, in the winter dusk, the heart in my body is revolving like the goldfish fleet-finned in their clear bowls. The librarians are still warming up over their coffee. They do not recognize me, though only half an hour ago I was scrabbling in the mud around the two heavy boxes from the Traveling Library — oafish crates tossed with a thump to the ground. One box contains magazines — *Boy's Life, The American Girl, Popular Mechanix.* But the other, the other! The other transforms me. It is tumbled with storybooks, with clandestine intimations and transfigurations. In school I am a luckless goosegirl, friendless and forlorn. In P.S. 71 I carry, weighty as a cloak, the ineradicable knowledge of my scandal — I am cross-eyed, dumb, an imbecile at arithmetic; in P.S. 71 I am publicly shamed in Assembly because I am caught not singing Christmas carols; in P.S. 71 I am repeatedly accused of deicide. But in the Park View Pharmacy, in the winter dusk, branches blackening in the park across the road, I am driving in rapture through the Violet Fairy Book and the Yellow Fairy Book, insubstantial chariots snatched from the box in the mud. I have never been *inside* the Traveling Library; only grownups are allowed. The boxes are for the children. No more than two books may be borrowed, so I have picked the fattest ones, to last. All the same, the Violet and the Yellow are melting away. Their pages dwindle. I sit at the round glass table, dreaming, dreaming. Mr. Jaffe is murmuring advice. He tells a joke about Wrong-Way Corrigan. The librarians are buttoning up their coats. A princess, captive of an ogre, receives a letter from her swain and hides it in her bosom. I can visualize her bosom exactly — she clutches it against her chest. It is a tall and shapely vase, with a hand-painted flower on it, like the vase on the secondhand piano at home.

I am incognito. No one knows who I truly am. The teachers in P.S. 71 don't know. Rabbi Meskin, my *cheder* teacher, doesn't know. Tessie the lion-eyed landlady doesn't know. Even Hymie the fountain clerk can't know — though he understands other things better than anyone: how to tighten roller skates with a skatekey, for instance, and how to ride a horse. On Friday afternoons, when the new issue is out, Hymie and my brother fight hard over who gets to see *Life* magazine first. My brother is older than I am, and doesn't like me; he builds radios in his bedroom, he is already W2LOM, and operates his transmitter (*da-di-da-dit, da-da-di-da*) so penetratingly on Sunday mornings that Mrs. Eva Brady, across the way, complains. Mrs. Eva Brady has a subscription to *The Writer;* I fill a closet with her old copies. How to Find a Plot. Narrative and Character, the Writer's Tools. Because my brother has his ham license, I say, "I have a license too." "What kind of license?" my brother asks, falling into the trap. "Poetic license," I reply; my brother hates me, but anyhow his birthday presents are transporting: one year *Alice in Wonderland, Pinocchio* the next, then *Tom Sawyer.* I go after Mark Twain, and find *Joan of Arc* and my first satire, *Christian Science.* My mother surprises me with *Pollyanna,* the admiration of her Lower East Side childhood, along with *The Lady of the Lake.* Mrs. Eva Brady's daughter Jeannie has outgrown her Nancy Drews and Judy Boltons, so on rainy afternoons I cross the street and borrow them, trying not to march away with too many — the child of immigrants, I worry that the Bradys, true and virtuous Americans, will judge me greedy or careless. I wrap the Nancy Drews in paper covers to protect them. Old Mrs. Brady, Jeannie's grandmother, invites me back for more. I am so timid I can hardly speak a word, but I love her dark parlor; I love its black bookcases. Old Mrs. Brady sees me off, embracing books under an umbrella; perhaps she divines who I truly am. My brother doesn't care. My father doesn't notice. I think my mother knows. My mother reads the *Saturday Evening Post* and the *Woman's Home Companion;* sometimes the *Ladies' Home Journal,* but never *Good Housekeeping.* I read all my mother's magazines. My father reads *Drug Topics* and *Der Tog,* the Yiddish daily. In Louie Davidowitz's house (waiting our turn for the rabbi's lesson, he teaches me chess in *cheder*) there is a piece of furniture I am in awe of: a shining circular table that is also a revolving bookshelf holding a complete set of Charles Dickens. I borrow *Oliver Twist.* My cousins turn up with *Gulliver's Travels, Just So Stories, Don Quixote,* Oscar Wilde's *Fairy Tales,* uncannily different from the usual kind. Blindfolded, I reach into a Thanksgiving grab-bag and pull out *Mrs. Leicester's School,* Mary Lamb's desolate stories of rejected children. Books spill out of rumor, exchange, miracle. In the Park View Pharmacy's lending library I discover, among the nurse romances, a browning, brittle miracle: *Jane Eyre.* Uncle Morris comes to visit (*his* drugstore is on the other side of the Bronx) and leaves behind, just like that, a three-volume Shakespeare. Peggy and Betty Provan, Scottish sisters around the corner, lend me their *Swiss Family Robinson.* Norma Foti, a whole year older, transmits a rumor about Louisa May Alcott; afterward I read *Little Women* a thousand times. Ten thousand! I am no longer incognito, not even to myself. I am Jo in her "vortex"; not Jo exactly, but some Jo-of-the-future. I am under an enchantment: who I truly am must be deferred, waited for and waited for. My father, silently filling capsules, is grieving over his mother in Moscow. I write letters in Yiddish to my Moscow grandmother, whom I will never know. I will know my Russian aunts, uncles, cousins. In Moscow there is suffering, deprivation, poverty. My mother, threadbare, goes without a new winter coat so that packages can be sent to Moscow. Her fiery justice-eyes are semaphores I cannot decipher.

Someday, when I am free of P.S. 71, I will write stories; meanwhile, in winter dusk, in the Park View, in the secret bliss of the Violet Fairy Book, I both see and do not see how these grains of life will stay forever, papa and mama will live forever, Hymie will always turn my skatekey.

Hymie, after Italy, after the Battle of the Bulge, comes back from the war with a present: *From Here to Eternity*. Then he dies, young. Mama reads *Pride and Prejudice* and every single word of Willa Cather. Papa reads, in Yiddish, all of Sholem Aleichem and Peretz. He reads Malamud's *The Assistant* when I ask him to.

Papa and mama, in Staten Island, are under the ground. Some other family sits transfixed in the sun parlor where I read *Jane Eyre* and *Little Women* and, long afterward, *Middlemarch*. The Park View Pharmacy is dismantled, turned into a Hallmark card shop. It doesn't matter! I close my eyes, or else only stare, and everything is in its place again, and everyone.

A writer is dreamed and transfigured into being by spells, wishes, goldfish, silhouettes of trees, boxes of fairy tales dropped in the mud, uncles' and cousins' books, tablets and capsules and powders, papa's Moscow ache, his drugstore jacket with his special fountain pen in the pocket, his beautiful Hebrew paragraphs, his Talmudist's rationalism, his Russian-Gymnasium Latin and German, mama's furnace-heart, her masses of memoirs, her paintings of autumn walks down to the sunny water, her braveries, her reveries, her old, old school hurts.

A writer is buffeted into being by school hurts — Orwell, Forster, Mann! — but after a while other ambushes begin: sorrows, deaths, disappointments, subtle diseases, delays, guilts, the spite of the private haters of the poetry side of life, the snubs of the glamorous, the bitterness of those for whom resentment is a daily gruel, and so on and so on; and then one day you find yourself leaning here, writing at that selfsame round glass table salvaged from the Park View Pharmacy — writing this, an impossibility, a summary of how you came to be where you are now, and where, God knows, is that? Your hair is whitening, you are a well of tears, what you meant to do (beauty and justice) you have not done, papa and mama are under the earth, you live in panic and dread, the future shrinks and darkens, stories are only vapor, your inmost craving is for nothing but an old scarred pen, and what, God knows, is that?

1987

William Manchester

Okinawa: The Bloodiest Battle of All

ON OKINAWA TODAY, Flag Day will be observed with an extraordinary ceremony: two groups of elderly men, one Japanese, the other American, will gather for a solemn rite. They could scarcely have less in common. Their motives are mirror images; each group honors the memory of men who tried to slay the men honored by those opposite them. But theirs is a common grief. After forty-two years the ache is still there. They are really united by death, the one great victor in modern war.

They have come to Okinawa to dedicate a lovely monument in remembrance of the Americans, Japanese and Okinawans killed there in the last and bloodiest battle of the Pacific war. More than 200,000 perished in the 82-day struggle — twice the number of Japanese lost at Hiroshima and more American blood than had been shed at Gettysburg. My own regiment — I was a sergeant in the 29th Marines — lost more than 80 percent of the men who had landed on April 1, 1945. Before the battle was over, both the Japanese and American commanding generals lay in shallow graves.

Okinawa lies 330 miles southwest of the southernmost Japanese island of Kyushu; before the war, it was Japanese soil. Had there been no atom bombs — and at that time the most powerful Americans, in Washington and at the Pentagon, doubted that the device would work — the invasion of the Nipponese homeland would have been staged from Okinawa, beginning with a landing on Kyushu to take place November 1. The six Marine divisions, storming ashore abreast, would lead

First published in *The New York Times Magazine*, 1987; selected by Annie Dillard for *The Best American Essays 1988*.

the way. President Truman asked General Douglas MacArthur, whose estimates of casualties on the eve of battles had proved uncannily accurate, about Kyushu. The general predicted a million Americans would die in that first phase.

Given the assumption that nuclear weapons would contribute nothing to victory, the battle of Okinawa had to be fought. No one doubted the need to bring Japan to its knees. But some Americans came to hate the things we had to do, even when convinced that doing them was absolutely necessary; they had never understood the bestial, monstrous and vile means required to reach the objective — an unconditional Japanese surrender. As for me, I could not reconcile the romanticized view of war that runs like a red streak through our literature — and the glowing aura of selfless patriotism that had led us to put our lives at forfeit — with the wet, green hell from which I had barely escaped. Today, I understand. I was there, and was twice wounded. This is the story of what I knew and when I knew it.

To our astonishment, the Marine landing on April 1 was uncontested. The enemy had set a trap. Japanese strategy called first for kamikazes to destroy our fleet, cutting us off from supply ships; then Japanese troops would methodically annihilate the men stranded ashore using the trench-warfare tactics of World War I — cutting the Americans down as they charged heavily fortified positions. One hundred and ten thousand Japanese troops were waiting on the southern tip of the island. Intricate entrenchments, connected by tunnels, formed the enemy's defense line, which ran across the waist of Okinawa from the Pacific Ocean to the East China Sea.

By May 8, after more than five weeks of fighting, it became clear that the anchor of this line was a knoll of coral and volcanic ash, which the Marines christened Sugar Loaf Hill. My role in mastering it — the crest changed hands more than eleven times — was the central experience of my youth, and of all the military bric-a-brac that I put away after the war, I cherish most the Commendation from General Lemuel C. Shepherd, Jr., U.S.M.C., our splendid division commander, citing me for "gallantry in action and extraordinary achievement," adding, "Your courage was a constant source of inspiration . . . and your conduct throughout was in keeping with the highest tradition of the United States Naval Service."

The struggle for Sugar Loaf lasted ten days; we fought under the worst possible conditions — a driving rain that never seemed to slacken, day or night. (I remember wondering, in an idiotic moment — no man in combat is really sane — whether the battle could be called off, or at least postponed, because of bad weather.)

Newsweek called Sugar Loaf "the most critical local battle of the war." *Time* described a company of Marines — 270 men — assaulting the hill. They failed; fewer than 30 returned. Fletcher Pratt, the military historian, wrote that the battle was unmatched in the Pacific war for "closeness and desperation." Casualties were almost unbelievable. In the 22d and 29th Marine regiments, two out of every three men fell. The struggle for the dominance of Sugar Loaf was probably the costliest engagement in the history of the Marine Corps. But by early evening on May 18, as night thickened over the embattled armies, the 29th Marines had taken Sugar Loaf, this time for keeps.

On Okinawa today, the ceremony will be dignified, solemn, seemly. It will also be anachronistic. If the Japanese dead of 1945 were resurrected to witness it, they would be appalled by the acceptance of defeat, the humiliation of their emperor — the very idea of burying Japanese near the barbarians from across the sea and then mourning them together. Americans, meanwhile, risen from their graves, would ponder the evolution of their own society, and might wonder, What ever happened to patriotism?

When I was a child, a bracket was screwed to the sill of a front attic window; its sole purpose was to hold the family flag. At first light, on all legal holidays — including Election Day, July 4, Memorial Day and, of course, Flag Day — I would scamper up to show it. The holidays remain, but mostly they mean long weekends.

In the late 1920s, during my childhood, the whole town of Attleboro, Massachusetts, would turn out to cheer the procession on Memorial Day. The policemen always came first, wearing their number-one uniforms and keeping perfect step. Behind them was a two-man vanguard — the mayor and, at his side, my father, hero of the 5th Marines and Belleau Wood, wearing his immaculate dress blues and looking like a poster of a Marine, with one magnificent flaw: the right sleeve of his uniform was empty. He had lost the arm in the Argonne. I now think that, as I watched him pass by, my own military future was already determined.

The main body of the parade was led by five or six survivors of the Civil War, too old to march but sitting upright in open Pierce-Arrows and Packards, wearing their blue uniforms and broad-brimmed hats. Then, in perfect step, came a contingent of men in their fifties, with their blanket rolls sloping diagonally from shoulder to hip — the Spanish-American War veterans. After these — and anticipated by a great roar from the crowd — came the doughboys of World War I, some still in their late twenties. They were acclaimed in part because theirs had been the most recent conflict, but also because they had fought in the war that — we then thought — had ended all wars.

Americans still march in Memorial Day parades, but attendance is light. One war has led to another and another and yet another, and the cruel fact is that few men, however they die, are remembered beyond the lifetimes of their closest relatives and friends. In the early 1940s, one of the forces that kept us on the line, under heavy enemy fire, was the conviction that this battle was of immense historical import, and that those of us who survived it would be forever cherished in the hearts of Americans. It was rather diminishing to return in 1945 and discover that your own parents couldn't even pronounce the names of the islands you had conquered.

But what of those who *do* remain faithful to patriotic holidays? What are they commemorating? Very rarely are they honoring what actually happened, because only a handful know, and it's not their favorite topic of conversation. In World War II, 16 million Americans entered the armed forces. Of these, fewer than a million saw action. Logistically, it took nineteen men to back up one man in combat. All who wore uniforms are called veterans, but more than 90 percent of them are as uninformed about the killing zones as those on the home front.

If all Americans understood the nature of battle, they might be vulnerable to truth. But the myths of warfare are embedded deep in our ancestral memories. By the time children have reached the age of awareness, they regard uniforms, decorations and Sousa marches as exalted, and those who argue otherwise are regarded as unpatriotic.

General MacArthur, quoting Plato, said: "Only the dead have seen the end of war." One hopes he was wrong, for war, as it had existed for over four thousand years, is now obsolete. As late as the spring of 1945, it was possible for one man, with a rifle, to make a difference, however infinitesimal, in the struggle to defeat an enemy who had attacked us and threatened our West Coast. The bomb dropped on Hiroshima made the man ludicrous, even pitiful. Soldiering has been relegated to Sartre's theater of the absurd. The image of the man as protector and defender of the home has been destroyed (and I suggest that that seed of thought eventually led women to re-examine their own role in society).

Until nuclear weapons arrived, the glorifying of militarism was the nation's hidden asset. Without it, we would almost certainly have been defeated by the Japanese, probably by 1943. In 1941 American youth was isolationist and pacifist. Then war planes from Imperial Japan destroyed our fleet at Pearl Harbor on December 7, and on December 8 recruiting stations were packed. Some of us later found fighting rather different from what had been advertised. Yet in combat these men risked their lives — and often lost them — in hope of winning medals. There is an old soldier's saying: "A man won't sell you his life, but he'll give it to you for a piece of colored ribbon."

Most of the men who hit the beaches came to scorn eloquence. They preferred the 130-year-old "Word of Cambronne." As dusk darkened the Waterloo battlefield, with the French in full retreat, the British sent word to General Pierre Cambronne, commander of the Old Guard. His position, they pointed out, was hopeless, and they suggested he capitulate. Every French textbook reports his reply as "The Old Guard dies but never surrenders." What he actually said was *"Merde."*

If you mention this incident to members of the U.S. 101st Airborne Division, they will immediately understand. "Nuts" was not Brigadier General Anthony C. McAuliffe's answer to the Nazi demand that he hoist a white flag over Bastogne. Instead, he quoted Cambronne.

The character of combat has always been determined by the weapons available to men when their battles were fought. In the beginning they were limited to hand weapons — clubs, rocks, swords, lances. At the Battle of Camlann in 539, England's Arthur — a great warrior, not a king — led a charge that slew 930 Saxons, including their leader.

It is important to grasp the fact that those 930 men were not killed by snipers, grenades or shells. The dead were bludgeoned or stabbed to death, and we have a pretty good idea how this was done. One of the facts withheld from civilians during World War II was that Kabar fighting knives, with seven-inch blades honed to such precision that you could shave with them, were issued to Marines and that we were taught to use them. You never cut downward. You drove the point of your blade into a man's lower belly and ripped upward. In the process, you yourself became soaked in the other man's gore. After that charge at Camlann, Arthur must have been half drowned in blood.

The Battle of Agincourt, fought nearly one thousand years later, represented a slight technical advance: crossbows and long bows had appeared. All the same, Arthur would have recognized the battle. Like all engagements of the time, this one was short. Killing by hand is hard work, and hot work. It is so exhausting that even men in peak condition collapse once the issue of triumph or defeat is settled. And Henry V's spear carriers and archers were drawn from social classes that had been undernourished for as long as anyone could remember. The duration of medieval battles could have been measured in hours, even minutes.

The Battle of Waterloo, fought exactly four hundred years later, is another matter. By 1815, the Industrial Revolution had begun cranking out appliances of death, primitive by today's standards, but revolutionary for infantrymen of that time. And Napoleon had formed mass armies, pressing every available man into service. It was a long step toward total war, and its impact was immense. Infantrymen on both sides fought with single-missile weapons — muskets or rifles — and were supported by (and were the target of) artillery firing cannonballs.

The fighting at Waterloo continued for three days; for a given regiment, however, it usually lasted one full day, much longer than medieval warfare. A half century later, Gettysburg lasted three days and cost 43,497 men. Then came the marathon slaughters of 1914–1918, lasting as long as ten months (Verdun) and producing hundreds of thousands of corpses lying, as F. Scott Fitzgerald wrote afterward, "like a million bloody rugs." Winston Churchill, who had been a dashing young cavalry officer when Victoria was queen, said of the new combat: "War, which was cruel and magnificent, has become cruel and squalid."

It may be said that the history of war is one of men packed together, getting closer and closer to the ground and then deeper and deeper into it. In the densest combat of World War I, battalion frontage — the length of the line into which the 1,000-odd men were squeezed — had been 800 yards. On Okinawa, on the Japanese fortified line, it was less than 600 yards — about 18 inches per man. We were there and deadlocked for more than a week in the relentless rain. During those weeks we lost nearly 4,000 men.

And now it is time to set down what this modern battlefield was like.

All greenery had vanished; as far as one could see, heavy shellfire had denuded the scene of shrubbery. What was left resembled a cratered moonscape. But the craters were vanishing, because the rain had transformed the earth into a thin porridge — too thin even to dig foxholes.

At night you lay on a poncho as a precaution against drowning during the barrages. All night, every night, shells erupted close enough to shake the mud beneath you at the rate of five or six a minute. You could hear the cries of the dying but could do nothing. Japanese infiltration was always imminent, so the order was to stay put. Any man who stood up was cut in half by machine guns manned by fellow Marines.

By day, the mud was hip deep; no vehicles could reach us. As you moved up the slope of the hill, artillery and mortar shells were bursting all around you, and, if you were fortunate enough to reach the top, you encountered the Japanese defenders, almost face to face, a few feet away. To me, they looked like badly wrapped brown paper parcels someone had soaked in a tub. Their eyes seemed glazed. So, I suppose, did ours.

Japanese bayonets were fixed; ours weren't. We used the knives, or, in my case, a .45 revolver and M1 carbine. The mud beneath our feet was deeply veined with blood. It was slippery. Blood is very slippery. So you skidded around, in deep shock, fighting as best you could until one side outnumbered the other. The outnumbered side would withdraw for reinforcements and then counterattack.

During those ten days I ate half a candy bar. I couldn't keep anything down. Everyone had dysentery, and this brings up an aspect of war even Robert Graves, Siegfried Sassoon, Edmund Blunden and Ernest Hemingway avoided. If you put more than a quarter million men in a line for three weeks, with no facilities for the disposal of human waste, you are going to confront a disgusting problem. We were fighting and sleeping in one vast cesspool. Mingled with that stench was another — the corrupt and corrupting odor of rotting human flesh.

My luck ran out on June 5, more than two weeks after we had taken Sugar Loaf Hill and killed the seven thousand Japanese soldiers defending it. I had suffered a slight gunshot wound above the right knee on June 2, and had rejoined my regiment to make an amphibious landing on Oroku Peninsula behind enemy lines. The next morning several of us were standing in a stone enclosure outside some Okinawan tombs when a six-inch rocket mortar shell landed among us.

The best man in my section was blown to pieces, and the slime of his viscera enveloped me. His body had cushioned the blow, saving my life; I still carry a piece of his shinbone in my chest. But I collapsed, and was left for dead. Hours later corpsmen found me still breathing, though blind and deaf, with my back and chest a junkyard of iron fragments — including, besides the piece of shinbone, four pieces of shrapnel too close to the heart to be removed. (They were not dangerous, a Navy surgeon assured me, but they still set off the metal detector at the Buffalo airport.)

Between June and November I underwent four major operations and was discharged as 100 percent disabled. But the young have strong recuperative powers. The blindness was caused by shock, and my vision returned. I grew new eardrums. In three years I was physically fit. The invisible wounds remain.

Most of those who were closest to me in the early 1940s had left New England campuses to join the Marines, knowing it was the most dangerous branch of the service. I remember them as bright, physically strong and inspired by an idealism and love of country they would have been too embarrassed to acknowledge. All of us despised the pompousness and pretentiousness of senior officers. It helped that, almost without exception, we admired and respected our commander in chief. But despite our enormous pride in being Marines, we saw through the scam that had lured so many of us to recruiting stations.

Once we polled a rifle company, asking each man why he had joined the Marines. A majority cited *To the Shores of Tripoli*, a marshmallow of a movie starring John Payne, Randolph Scott and Maureen O'Hara. Throughout the film the uniform of the day was dress blues; requests for liberty were always granted. The implication was that combat would be a lark, and when you returned, spangled with decorations, a Navy nurse like Maureen O'Hara would be waiting in your sack. It was peacetime again when John Wayne appeared on the silver screen as Sergeant Stryker in *Sands of Iwo Jima*, but that film underscores the point; I went to see it with another ex-Marine, and we were asked to leave the theater because we couldn't stop laughing.

After my evacuation from Okinawa, I had the enormous pleasure of seeing Wayne humiliated in person at Aiea Heights Naval Hospital in Hawaii. Only the most gravely wounded, the litter cases, were sent there. The hospital was packed, the halls lined with beds. Between Iwo Jima and Okinawa, the Marine Corps was being bled white.

Each evening, Navy corpsmen would carry litters down to the hospital theater so the men could watch a movie. One night they had a surprise for us. Before the film the curtains parted and out stepped John Wayne, wearing a cowboy outfit — ten-gallon hat, bandanna, checkered shirt, two pistols, chaps, boots and spurs. He grinned his awshucks grin, passed a hand over his face and said, "Hi ya, guys!" He was greeted by a stony silence. Then somebody booed. Suddenly everyone was booing. This man was a symbol of the fake machismo we had come to hate, and we weren't going to listen to him. He tried and tried to make himself heard, but we drowned him out, and eventually he quit and left. If you liked *Sands of Iwo Jima,* I suggest you be careful. Don't tell it to the Marines.

And so we weren't macho. Yet we never doubted the justice of our cause. If we had failed — if we had lost Guadalcanal, and the Navy's pilots had lost the Battle of Midway — the Japanese would have invaded Australia and Hawaii, and California would have been in grave danger. In 1942 the possibility of an Axis victory was very real. It is possible for me to loathe war — and with reason — yet still honor the brave men, many of them boys, really, who fought with me and died beside me. I have been haunted by their loss these forty-two years, and I shall mourn them until my own death releases me. It does not seem too much to ask that they be remembered on one day each year. After all, they sacrificed their futures that you might have yours.

Yet I will not be on Okinawa for the dedication today. I would enjoy being with Marines; the ceremony will be moving, and we would be solemn, remembering our youth and the beloved friends who died there.

Few, if any, of the Japanese survivors agreed to attend the ceremony. However, Edward L. Fox, chairman of the Okinawa Memorial Shrine Committee, capped almost six years' campaigning for a monument when he heard about a former Japanese naval officer, Yoshio Yazaki — a meteorologist who had belonged to a four-thousand-man force led by Rear Admiral Minoru Ota — and persuaded him to attend.

On March 31, 1945, Yazaki-san had been recalled to Tokyo, and thus missed the battle of Okinawa. Ten weeks later — exactly forty-two years ago today — Admiral Ota and his men committed seppuku, killing themselves rather than face surrender. Ever since then Yazaki has been tormented by the thought that his comrades have joined their ancestors and he is here, not there.

Finding Yazaki was a great stroke of luck for Fox, for whom an Okinawa memorial had become an obsession. His own division commander tried to discourage him. The Japanese could hardly be expected to back a memorial on the site of their last great military defeat. But Yazaki made a solution possible.

If Yazaki can attend, why can't I? I played a role in the early stages of

Buzz Fox's campaign and helped write the tribute to the Marines that is engraved on the monument. But when I learned that Japanese were also participating, I quietly withdrew. There are too many graves between us, too much gore, too many memories of too many atrocities.

In 1978, revisiting Guadalcanal, I encountered a Japanese business-man who had volunteered to become a kamikaze pilot in 1945 and was turned down at the last minute. Mutual friends suggested that we meet. I had expected no difficulty; neither, I think, did he. But when we confronted each other, we froze.

I trembled, suppressing the sudden, startling surge of primitive rage within. And I could see, from his expression, that this was difficult for him, too. Nations may make peace. It is harder for fighting men. On simultaneous impulse we both turned and walked away.

I set this down in neither pride nor shame. The fact is that some wounds never heal. Yazaki, unlike Fox, is dreading the ceremony. He does not expect to be shriven of his guilt. He knows he must be there but can't say why. Men are irrational, he explains, and adds that he feels very sad.

So do I, Yazaki-san, so do I.

1988

Edward Hoagland

....

Heaven and Nature

A FRIEND OF MINE, a peaceable soul who has been riding the New York subways for thirty years, finds himself stepping back from the tracks once in a while and closing his eyes as the train rolls in. This, he says, is not only to suppress an urge to throw himself in front of it but because every couple of weeks an impulse rises in him to push a stranger onto the tracks, any stranger, thus ending his own life too. He blames this partly on apartment living, "pigeonholes without being able to fly."

It is profoundly startling not to trust oneself after decades of doing so. I don't dare keep ammunition in my country house for a small rifle I bought secondhand two decades ago. The gun had sat in a cupboard in the back room with the original box of .22 bullets under the muzzle all that time, seldom fired except at a few apples hanging in a tree every fall to remind me of my army training near the era of the Korean War, when I'd been considered quite a marksman. When I bought the gun I didn't trust either my professional competence as a writer or my competence as a father as much as I came to, but certainly believed I could keep myself alive. I bought it for protection, and the idea that someday I might be afraid of shooting myself with the gun would have seemed inconceivable — laughable.

One's fifties can be giddy years, as anybody fifty knows. Chest pains, back pains, cancer scares, menopausal or prostate complications are not the least of it, and the fidelities of a lifetime, both personal and professional, may be called into question. Was it a mistake to have stuck so

First published in *Harper's Magazine*, 1988; collected in *Heart's Desire: The Best of Edward Hoagland*, 1988; selected by Geoffrey Wolff for *The Best American Essays 1989*.

long with one's marriage, and to have stayed with a lackluster well-paying job? (Or *not* to have stayed and stuck?) People not only lose faith in their talents and their dreams or values; some simply tire of them. Grow tired, too, of the smell of fried-chicken grease, once such a delight, and the cold glutinosity of ice cream, the boredom of beer, the stop-go of travel, the hiccups of laughter, and of two rush hours a day, then the languor of weekends, of athletes as well as accountants, and even the frantic birdsong of spring — red-eyed vireos that have been clocked singing twenty-two thousand times in a day. Life is a matter of cultivating the six senses, and an equilibrium with nature and what I think of as its subdivision, human nature, trusting no one completely but almost everyone at least a little; but this is easier said than done.

More than thirty thousand Americans took their own lives last year, men mostly, with the highest rate being among those older than sixty-five. When I asked a friend why three times as many men kill themselves as members of her own sex, she replied with sudden anger, "I'm not going to go into the self-indulgence of men." They won't bend to failure, she said, and want to make themselves memorable. Suicide is an exasperating act as often as it is pitiable. "Committing" suicide is in bad odor in our culture even among those who don't believe that to cash in your chips ahead of time and hand back to God his gifts to you is a blasphemous sin. We the living, in any case, are likely to feel accused by this person who "voted with his feet." It appears to cast a subversive judgment upon the social polity as a whole that what was supposed to work in life — religion, family, friendship, commerce, and industry — did not, and furthermore it frightens the horses in the street, as Shaw's friend Mrs. Patrick Campbell once defined wrongful behavior.

Many suicides inflict outrageous trauma, burning permanent injuries in the minds of their children, though they may have joked beforehand only of "taking a dive." And sometimes the gesture has a peevish or cowardly aspect, or seems to have been senselessly shortsighted as far as an outside observer can tell. There are desperate suicides and crafty suicides, people who do it to cause others trouble and people who do it to save others trouble, deranged exhibitionists who yell from a building ledge and close-mouthed, secretive souls who swim out into the ocean's anonymity. Suicide may in fact be an attempt to escape death, shortcut the dreadful deteriorating processes, abort one's natural trajectory, elude "the ruffian on the stairs," in A. E. Housman's phrase for a cruelly painful, anarchic death — make it neat and not messy. The deed can be grandiose or self-abnegating, vindictive or drably mousy, rationally plotted or plainly insane. People sidle toward death, intent upon out-witting their own bodies' defenses, or they may dramatize the chance to make one last, unambiguous, irrevocable decision, like a captain scuttling his ship — death before dishonor — leaping toward oblivion through a curtain of pain, like a frog going down the throat of a snake. One man I knew hosted a quietly affectionate evening with several un-knowing friends on the night before he swallowed too many pills. An-other waved an apologetic goodbye to a bystander on a bridge. Seldom shy ordinarily, and rarely considerate, he turned shy and apologetic in the last moment of life. Never physically inclined, he made a great vault toward the ice on the Mississippi.

In the army, we wore dog tags with a notch at one end by which these numbered pieces of metal could be jammed between our teeth, if we lay dead and nameless on a battlefield, for later sorting. As "servicemen" our job would be to kill people who were pointed out to us as enemies, or make "the supreme sacrifice" for a higher good than enjoying the rest of our lives. Life was very much a possession, in other words — not only God's, but the soldier's own to dispose of. Working in an army hospital, I frequently did handle dead bodies, but this never made me feel I would refuse to kill another man whose uniform was pointed out to me as being inimical, or value my life more tremulously and vigilantly. The notion of dying for my country never appealed to me as much as dying free-lance for my ideas (in the unlikely event that I *could* do that), but I was ready. People were taught during the 1940s and 1950s that one should be ready to die for one's beliefs. Heroes were revered because they had deliberately chosen to give up their lives. Life would not be worth living under the tyranny of an invader and Nathan Hale appar-ently hadn't paused to wonder whether God might not have other uses for him besides being hung. Nor did the pilot Colin Kelly hesitate be-fore plunging his plane into a Japanese battleship, becoming America's first well-publicized hero in World War II.

I've sometimes wondered why people who know that they are termi-nally ill, or who are headed for suicide, so very seldom have paused to take a bad guy along with them. It is lawless to consider an act of assas-sination, yet hardly more so, really, than suicide is regarded in some quarters (or death itself, in others). Government bureaucracies, includ-ing our own, in their majesty and as the executors of laws, regularly weigh the pros and cons of murdering foreign antagonists. Of course the answer is that most individuals are fortunately more timid as well as humbler in their judgment than government officialdom, but beyond that, when dying or suicidal, they no longer care enough to devote their final energies to doing good works of any kind — Hitler himself in their gunsights they would have passed up. Some suicides become so crushed and despairing that they can't recognize the consequences of anything they do, and it's not primarily vindictiveness that wreaks such havoc upon their survivors but their derangement from ordinary life.

Courting the idea is different from the real impulse. "When he begged for help, we took him and locked him up," another friend of mine says, speaking of her husband. "Not till then. Wishing to be out of the situation you are in — feeling helpless and unable to cope — is not the same as wishing to be dead. If I actually wished to be dead, even my children's welfare would have no meaning."

You might think the ready option of divorce available lately would have cut suicide rates, offering an escape to battered wives, lovelorn husbands, and other people in despair. But it doesn't work that way. When the number of choices people have increases, an entire range of possibilities opens up. Suicide among teenagers has almost quadrupled since 1950, although the standard of comfort that their families enjoy is up. Black Americans, less affluent than white Americans, have had less of a rise in suicides, and the rate among them remains about half of that for whites.

Still, if a fiftyish fellow with fine teeth and a foolproof pension plan, a cottage at the beach and the Fourth of July weekend coming up, kills himself, it seems truculent. We would look at him bafflingly if he told us he no longer likes the Sturm und Drang of banging fireworks.

Then stay at your hideaway! we'd argue with him.

"Big mouths eat little mouths. Nature isn't 'timeless.' Whole lives are squeezed into three months or three days."

What about your marriage?

"She's become more mannish than me. I loved women. I don't believe in marriage between men."

Remarry, then!

"I've gone impotent, and besides, when I see somebody young and pretty I guess I feel like dandling her on my knee."

Marriage is friendship. You can find someone your own age.

"I'm tired of it."

But how about your company? — a widows-and-orphans stock that's on the cutting edge of the silicon frontier? That's interesting.

"I know what wins. It's less and less appetizing."

You're not scared of death anymore?

"It interests me less than it did."

What are you so sick of? The rest of us keep going.

"I'm tired of weathermen and sportscasters on the screen. Of being patient and also of impatience. I'm tired of the president, whoever the president happens to be, and sleeping badly, with forty-eight half-hours in the day — of breaking two eggs every morning and putting sugar on something. I'm tired of the drone of my own voice, but also of us jabbering like parrots at each other — of all our stumpy ways of doing everything."

You're bored with yourself?

That's an understatement. I'm maybe the least interesting person I know."

But to kill yourself?

"You know, it's a tradition, too," he remarks quietly, not making so bold as to suggest that the tradition is an honorable one, though his tone of voice might be imagined to imply this. "I guess I've always been a latent maverick."

Except in circumstances which are themselves a matter of life and death, I'm reluctant to agree with the idea that suicide is not the result of mental illness. No matter how reasonably the person appears to have examined his options, it goes against the grain of nature for him to destroy himself. And any illness that threatens his life changes a person. Suicidal thinking, if serious, can be a kind of death scare, comparable to suffering a heart attack or undergoing a cancer operation. One survives such a phase both warier and chastened. When — two years ago — I emerged from a bad dip into suicidal speculation, I felt utterly exhausted and yet quite fearless of ordinary dangers, vastly afraid of myself but much less scared of extraneous eventualities. The fact of death may not be tragic; many people die with a bit of a smile that captures their mouths at the last instant, and most people who are revived after a deadly accident are reluctant to be brought to life, resisting resuscitation, and carrying back confusing, beamish, or ecstatic memories. But the same impetuosity that made him throw himself out of the window might have enabled the person to love life all the more if he'd been calibrated somewhat differently at the time of the emergency. Death's edge is so abrupt and near that many people who expect a short and momentary dive may be astounded to find that it is bottomless and change their minds and start to scream when they are only halfway down.

Although my fright at my mind's anarchy superseded my fear of death in the conventional guise of automobile or airplane crashes, heart seizures, and so on, nightmares are more primitive and in my dreams I continued to be scared of a death not sought after — dying from driving too fast and losing control of the car, breaking through thin ice while skating and drowning in the cold, or falling off a cliff. When I am tense and sleeping raggedly, my worst nightmare isn't drawn from anxious prep school memories or my stint in the army or the bad spells of my marriages or any other of adulthood's vicissitudes. Nothing else from the past half century has the staying power in my mind of the elevated-train rides that my father and I used to take down Third Avenue to the Battery in New York City on Sunday afternoon when I was three or four or five so I could see the fish at the aquarium. We were probably pretty good companions in those years, but the wooden platforms forty feet up shook terribly as trains from both directions pulled in and out. To me they seemed worse than rickety — ready to topple. And the roar was fearful, and the railings left large gaps for a child to fall through, after the steep climb up the slat-sided, windy, shaking stairway from street level. It's a rare dream, but several times a year I still find myself on such a perch, without his company or anybody else's, on a boyish or a grown-up's mission, when the elevated platform begins to rattle desperately, seesaw, heel over, and finally come apart, disintegrate, while I cling to struts and trusses.

My father, as he lay dying at home of bowel cancer, used to enjoy watching Tarzan reruns on the children's hour of television. Like a strong green vine, they swung him far away from his deathbed to a world of skinny-dipping and friendly animals and scenic beauty linked to the lost realities of his adolescence in Kansas City. Earlier, when he had still been able to walk without much pain, he'd paced the house for several hours at night, contemplating suicide, I expect, along with other anguishing thoughts, regrets, remembrances, and yearnings, while the rest of us slept. But he decided to lie down and die the slower way. I don't know how much of that decision was for the sake of his wife and children, how much was because he didn't want to be a "quitter," as he sometimes put it, and how much was due to his believing that life belongs to God (which I'm not even sure he did). He was not a churchgoer after his thirties. He had belonged to J. P. Morgan's church, St. George's, on Stuyvesant Square — Morgan was a hero of his — but when things went a little wrong for him at the Wall Street law firm he worked for and he changed jobs and moved out to the suburbs, he became a skeptic on religious matters, and gradually, in the absence of faith of that previous kind, he adhered to a determined allegiance to the social order. Wendell Willkie or Dwight D. Eisenhower instead of J. P. Morgan became the sort of hero he admired, and suicide would have seemed an act of insurrection against the laws and conventions of the society, internationalist-Republican, that he believed in.

I was never particularly afraid that I might plan a suicide, swallowing a bunch of pills and keeping them down — only of what I think of as being Anna Karenina's kind of death. This most plausible self-killing in all of literature is frightening because it was unwilled, regretted at midpoint, and came as a complete surprise to Anna herself. After rushing impulsively, in great misery, to the Moscow railway station to catch a train, she ended up underneath another one, dismayed, astonished, and trying to climb out from under the wheels even as they crushed her. Many people who briefly verge on suicide undergo a mental somersault for a terrifying interval during which they're upside down, their perspective topsy-turvy, skidding, churning; and this is why I got rid of the bullets for my .22.

Nobody expects to trust his body overmuch after the age of fifty. Incipient cataracts or arthritis, outlandish snores, tooth-grinding, ankles that threaten to turn, are part of the game. But not to trust one's *mind?* That's a surprise. The single attribute that older people were sure to have (we thought as boys) was a stodgy dependability, a steady temperance or caution. Adults might be vain, unimaginative, pompous, and callous, but they did have their affairs tightly in hand. It was not till my thirties that I began to know friends who were in their fifties on equal terms, and I remember being amused, piqued, irritated, and slightly bewildered to learn that some of them still felt as marginal or rebellious or in a quandary about what to do with themselves for the next dozen years as my contemporaries were likely to. That close to retirement, some of them harbored a deep-seated contempt for the organizations they had been working for, ready to walk away from almost everybody they had known and the efforts and expertise of whole decades with very little sentiment. Nor did twenty years of marriage necessarily mean more than two or three — they might be just as ready to walk away from that also, and didn't really register it as twenty years at all. Rather, life could be about to begin all over again. "Bummish" was how one man described himself, with a raffish smile — "Lucky to have a roof over my head" — though he'd just put a child through Yale. He was quitting his job and claimed with exasperation that his wife still cried for her mother in her sleep, as if they'd never been married.

The great English traveler Richard Burton quoted an Arab proverb that speaks for many middle-aged men of the old-fashioned variety: "Conceal thy Tenets, thy Treasure, and thy Traveling." These are serious matters, in other words. People didn't conceal their tenets in order to betray them, but to fight for them more opportunely. And except for kings and princelings, concealing whatever treasure one had went almost without saying. As for travel, a man's travels were also a matter of gravity. Travel was knowledge, ambiguity, dalliances or misalliances, divided loyalty, forbidden thinking; and besides, someday he might need to make a run for it and go to ground someplace where he had made some secret friends. Friends of mine whose husbands or whose wives have died have been quite startled afterward to discover caches of money or traveler's checks concealed around the house, or a bundle of cash in a safe deposit box.

Burton, like any other desert adage-spinner and most individuals over fifty, would have agreed to an addition so obvious that it wasn't included to begin with: "Conceal thy Illnesses." I can remember how urgently my father worried that word would get out, after a preliminary operation for his cancer. He didn't want to be written off, counted out of the running at the corporation he worked for and in other enclaves of competition. Men often compete with one another until the day they die; comradeship consists of rubbing shoulders jocularly with a competitor. As breadwinners, they must be considered fit and sound by friend as well as foe, and so there's lots of truth to the most common answer I heard when asking why three times as many men as women kill themselves: "They keep their troubles to themselves"; "They don't know how to ask for help." Men greet each other with a sock on the arm, women with a hug, and the hug wears better in the long run.

I'm not entirely like that, and I discovered that when I confided something of my perturbation to a woman friend she was likely to keep telephoning me or mailing cheery postcards, whereas a man would usually listen with concern, communicate his sympathy, and maybe intimate that he had pondered the same drastic course of action himself a few years back and would end up respecting my decision either way. Open-mindedness seems an important attribute to a good many men, who pride themselves on being objective, hearing all sides of an issue, on knowing that truth and honesty do not always coincide with social dicta, and who may even cherish a subterranean outlaw streak that, like being ready to violently defend one's family, reputation, and country, is by tradition male.

Men, being so much freer than women in society, used to feel they had less of a stake in the maintenance of certain churchly conventions and enjoyed speaking irreverently about various social truisms, including even the principle that people ought to die on schedule, not cutting in ahead on their assigned place in line. Contemporary women, after their triumphant irreverence during the 1960s and 1970s, cannot be generalized about so easily, however. They turn as skeptical and saturnine as any man. In fact, women attempt suicide more frequently, but favor pills or other methods, whereas two-thirds of the men who kill themselves have used a gun. In 1985, 85 percent of suicides by means of firearms were done by men. An overdose of medication hasn't the same finality. It may be reversible if the person is discovered quickly, or be subject to benign miscalculation to start with. Even if it works, perhaps it can be fudged by a kindly doctor in the record-keeping. Like an enigmatic drowning or a single-car accident that baffles the suspicions of the insurance company, a suicide by drugs can be a way to avoid making a loud statement, and merely illustrate the final modesty of a person who didn't wish to ask for too much of the world's attention.

Unconsummated attempts at suicide can strike the rest of us as self-pitying and self aggrandizing, or plaintive plea-bargaining — "childish," we say, though actually the suicide of children is ghastly beyond any stunt of self-mutilation an adult may indulge in because of the helplessness that echoes through the act. It would be hard to define chaos better than as a world where children decide that they don't want to live.

Love is the solution to all dilemmas, we sometimes hear, and in those moments when the spirit bathes itself in beneficence and manages to transcend the static of personalities rubbing fur off of each other, indeed it is. Without love nothing matters, Paul told the Corinthians, a mystery which, if true, has no ready Darwinian explanation. Love without a significant sexual component and for people who are unrelated to us serves little practical purpose. It doesn't help us feed our families, win struggles, thrive and prosper. It distracts us from the ordinary business of sizing people up and making a living, and is not even conducive to intellectual observation, because instead of seeing them, we see right through them to the bewildered child and dreaming adolescent who inhabited their bodies earlier, the now-tired idealist who fell in love and out of love, got hired and quit, hired and fired, bought cars and wore them out, liked black-eyed Susans, blueberry muffins, and roosters crowing — liked roosters crowing better than skyscrapers but now likes skyscrapers better than roosters crowing. As swift as thought, we select the details that we need to see in order to be able to love them.

Yet at other times we'll dispense with these same poignancies and choose only their grunginess to look at, their pinched mouths and shifty eyes, their thirst for gin at noon and indifference to their kids, their greed for the best tidbit on the buffet table and penchant for poking their penises up the excretory end of other human beings. I tend to gaze quite closely at the faces of priests I meet on the street to see if a lifetime of love has marked them noticeably. Real serenity or asceticism I no longer expect, and I take for granted the beefy calm that frequently goes with Catholic celibacy, but I am watching for the marks of love and often see mere resignation or tenacity.

Many men are romantics, likely to plunge, go for broke, take action in a spirit of exigency rather than waiting for the problem to resolve itself. Then, on the contrary, still as romantics, they may drift into despairing passivity, stare at the TV all day long, and binge with a bottle. Women too may turn frenetic for a while and then throw up their hands; but though they may not seem as grandiosely fanciful and romantic at the outset, they are more often believers — at least I think they tend to believe in God or in humanity, the future, and so on. We have above us the inviting eternity of "the heavens," if we choose to look at it, lying on our backs in the summer grass under starlight, some of which had left its source before mankind became man. But because we live in our heads more than in nature nowadays, even the summer sky is a mine field for people whose memories are mined. With the sky no longer humbling, the sunshine only a sort of convenience, and no godhead located anywhere outside our own heads, every problem may seem insolubly interlocked. When the telephone has become impossible to answer at home, sometimes it finally becomes impossible to stride down the gangplank of a cruise ship in Mombasa too, although no telephones will ring for you there.

But if escapist travel is ruled out in certain emergencies, surely you can *pray?* Pray, yes; but to whom? That requires a bit of preparation. Rarely do people obtain much relief from praying if they haven't stood in line awhile to get a visa. It's an appealing idea that you can just *go,* and in a previous era perhaps you could have, like on an old-fashioned shooting safari. But it's not so simple now. What do you believe in? Whom are you praying to? What are you praying for? There's no crèche on the courthouse lawn; you're not supposed to adhere exactly even to what your parents had believed. Like psychotherapy, praying takes time, even if you know which direction to face when you kneel.

Love is powerfully helpful when the roof falls in — loving other people with a high and hopeful heart and as a kind of prayer. Yet that feat too requires new and sudden insights or long practice. The beatitude of loving strangers as well as friends — loving them on sight with a leap of empathy and intuition — is a form of inspiration, edging, of course, in some cases toward madness, as other states of beatitude can do. But there's no question that a genuine love for the living will stymie suicidal depressions not chemical in origin. Love is an elixir, changing the life of the lover like no other. And many of us have experienced this — a temporary lightening of our leery, prickly disapproval of much of the rest of the world when at a wedding or a funeral of shared emotion, or when we have fallen in love.

Yet the zest for life of those unusual men and women who make a great zealous success of living is due more often in good part to the craftiness and pertinacity with which they manage to overlook the misery of others. You can watch them watch life beat the stuffing out of the faces of their friends and acquaintances, yet they themselves seem to outwit the dense delays of social custom, the tedious tick-tock of bureaucratic obfuscation, accepting loss and age and change and disappointment without suffering punctures in their stomach lining. Breathlessness or strange dull pains from their nether organs don't nonplus them. They fret and doubt in moderation, and love a lobster roast, squeeze lemon juice on living clams on the half shell to prove that the clams are alive, laugh as robins tussle a worm out of the ground or a kitten flees a dog. Like the problem drinkers, pork eaters, and chain smokers who nevertheless finish out their allotted years, succumbing to a stroke at a nice round biblical age when the best vitamin-eating vegetarian has long since died, their faces become veritable walnuts of fine character, with the same smile lines as the rarer individual whose grin has been affectionate all of his life.

We spend our lives getting to know ourselves, yet wonders never cease. During my adolescent years my states of mind, though undulant, seemed seamless; even when I was unhappy no cracks or fissures made me wonder if I was a danger to myself. My confidence was such that I treaded the slippery lips of waterfalls, fought forest fires, drove ancient cars cross-country night and day, and scratched the necks of menagerie leopards in the course of various adventures which enhanced the joy of being alive. The chemistry of the mind, because unfathomable, is more frightening. In the city, I live on the waterfront and occasionally will notice an agitated-looking figure picking his way along the pilings and string-pieces of the timbered piers nearby, staring at the sliding whorls on the surface of the Hudson as if teetering over an abyss. Our building, across the street, seems imposing from the water and over the years has acted as a magnet for a number of suicides — people who have dreaded the clammy chill, the onerous smothering essential to their first plan. One woman climbed out after jumping in and took the elevator to the roof (my neighbors remember how wringing wet she was) and leapt off, banging window ledges on the way down, and hit with the whap of a sack of potatoes, as others have.

Yet what is more remarkable than that a tiny minority of souls reach a point where they entrust their bodies to the force of gravity is that so few of the rest of us splurge an hour of a summer day gazing at the trees and sky. How many summers do we *have?* One sees prosperous families in the city who keep plants in their apartment windows that have grown so high they block the sunlight and appear to be doing the living for the tenants who are bolted inside. But beauty is nobody's sure salvation: not the beauty of a swimming hole if you get a cramp, and not the beauty of a woman if she doesn't care for you. The swimming hole looks inviting under the blue sky, with its amber bottom, green sedges sticking up in the shallows, and curls of gentle current over a water-logged basswood tree two feet beneath the surface near the brook that feeds it. Come back at dusk, however, and the pond turns black — as dark as death, or on the contrary, a restful dark, a dark to savor. Take it as you will.

People with sunny natures do seem to live longer than people who are nervous wrecks; yet mankind didn't evolve out of the animal kingdom by being unduly sunny-minded. Life was fearful and phantasmagoric, supernatural and preternatural, as well as encompassing the kind of clockwork regularity of our well-governed day. It had numerous superstitious (from the Latin, "standing over") elements, such as we are likely to catch a whiff of only when we're peering at a dead body. And it was not just our optimism but our pessimistic premonitions, our dark moments as a species, our irrational, frightful speculations, our strange mutations upon the simple theme of love, and our sleepless, obsessive inventiveness — our dread as well as our faith — that made us human beings. Staking one's life on the more general good came to include risking suicide also. Brilliant, fecund people sometimes kill themselves.

"Joy to the world . . . Let heaven and nature sing, and heaven and na-

ture sing . . . Repeat the sounding joy . . ." The famous Christmas carol invokes not only glee but unity: heaven with nature, not always a Christian combination. It's a rapturous hymn, and no one should refuse to surrender to such a pitch of revelation when it comes. But the flip side of rapture can be a riptide of panic, of hysterical gloom. Our faces are not molded as if joy were a preponderant experience. (Nor is a caribou's or a thrush's.) Our faces in repose look stoic or battered, and people of the sunniest temperament sometimes die utterly unstrung, doubting everything they have ever believed in or have done.

Let heaven and nature sing! the hymn proclaims. But *is* there such harmony? Are God and Mother Nature really the same? Are they even compatible? And will we risk burning our wings if we mount high enough to try to see? I've noticed that woods soil in Italy smells the same as woods soil in New England when you pick up a handful of it and enjoy its aromas — but is God there the same? It can be precarious to wonder. I don't rule out suicide as being unthinkable for people who have tried to live full lives, and don't regard it as negating the work and faith and satisfaction and fun and even ecstasy they may have known before. In killing himself a person acknowledges his failures during a time span when perhaps heaven and earth had caught him like a pair of scissors — but not his life span. Man is different from animals in that he speculates, a high-risk activity.

Stephen Jay Gould

The Creation Myths of Cooperstown

You MAY EITHER look upon the bright side and say that hope springs eternal or, taking the cynic's part, you may mark P. T. Barnum as an astute psychologist for his proclamation that suckers are born every minute. The end result is the same: you can, Honest Abe notwithstanding, fool most of the people all of the time. How else to explain the long and continuing compendium of hoaxes — from the medieval shroud of Turin to Edwardian Piltdown Man to an ultramodern array of flying saucers and astral powers — eagerly embraced for their consonance with our hopes or their resonance with our fears?

Some hoaxes make a sufficient mark upon history that their products acquire the very status initially claimed by fakery — legitimacy (although as an object of human or folkloric, rather than natural, history. I once held the bones of Piltdown Man and felt that I was handling an important item of Western culture).

The Cardiff Giant, the best American entry for the title of paleontological hoax turned into cultural history, now lies on display in a shed behind a barn at the Farmer's Museum in Cooperstown, New York. This gypsum man, more than ten feet tall, was "discovered" by workmen digging a well on a farm near Cardiff, New York, in October 1869. Eagerly embraced by a gullible public, and ardently displayed by its creators at fifty cents a pop, the Cardiff Giant caused quite a brouhaha around Syracuse, and then nationally, for the few months of its active life between exhumation and exposure.

The Cardiff Giant was the brainchild of George Hull, a cigar manu-

First published in *Natural History*, 1989; selected by Justin Kaplan for *The Best American Essays 1990*; collected in *Bully for Brontosaurus*, 1991.

facturer (and general rogue) from Binghamton, New York. He quarried a large block of gypsum from Fort Dodge, Iowa, and shipped it to Chicago, where two marble cutters fashioned the rough likeness of a naked man. Hull made some crude and minimal attempts to give his statue an aged appearance. He chipped off the carved hair and beard because experts told him that such items would not petrify. He drove darning needles into a wooden block and hammered the statue, hoping to simulate skin pores. Finally, he dumped a gallon of sulfuric acid all over his creation to simulate extended erosion. Hull then shipped his giant in a large box back to Cardiff.

Hull, as an accomplished rogue, sensed that his story could not hold for long and, in that venerable and alliterative motto, got out while the getting was good. He sold a three-quarter interest in the Cardiff Giant to a consortium of highly respectable businessmen, including two former mayors of Syracuse. These men raised the statue from its original pit on November 5 and carted it off to Syracuse for display.

The hoax held on for a few more weeks, and Cardiff Giant fever swept the land. Debate raged in newspapers and broadsheets between those who viewed the giant as a petrified fossil and those who regarded it as a statue wrought by an unknown and wondrous prehistoric race. But Hull had left too many tracks — at the gypsum quarries in Fort Dodge, at the carver's studio in Chicago, along the roadways to Cardiff (several people remembered seeing an awfully large box passing on a cart just days before the supposed discovery). By December, Hull was ready to recant, but held his tongue a while longer. Three months later, the two Chicago sculptors came forward, and the Cardiff Giant's brief rendezvous with fame and fortune ended.

The common analogy of the Cardiff Giant with Piltdown Man works only to a point (both were frauds passed off as human fossils) and fails in one crucial respect. Piltdown was cleverly wrought and fooled professionals for forty years, while the Cardiff Giant was preposterous from the start. How could a man turn to solid gypsum while preserving all his soft anatomy, from cheeks to toes to penis? Geologists and paleontologists never accepted Hull's statue. O. C. Marsh, later to achieve great fame as a discoverer of dinosaurs, echoed a professional consensus in his unambiguous pronouncement: "It is of very recent origin and a decided humbug."

Why, then, was the Cardiff Giant so popular, inspiring a wave of interest and discussion as high as any tide in the affairs of men during its short time in the sun? If the fraud had been well executed, we might attribute this great concern to the dexterity of the hoaxers (just as we grant grudging attention to a few of the most accomplished art fakers for their skills as copyists). But since the Cardiff Giant was so crudely done, we can only attribute its fame to the deep issue, the raw nerve, touched by the subject of its fakery — human origins. Link an absurd concoction to a noble and mysterious subject and you may prevail, at least for a while. My opening reference to P. T. Barnum was not meant sarcastically; he was one of the great practical psychologists of the nineteenth century — and his motto applies with special force to the Cardiff Giant: "No humbug is great without truth at bottom." (Barnum made a copy of the Cardiff Giant and exhibited it in New York City. His mastery of hype and publicity assured that his model far outdrew the "real" fake when the original went on display at a rival establishment in the same city.)

For some reason (to be explored but not resolved in this essay), we are powerfully drawn to the subject of beginnings. We yearn to know about origins, and we readily construct myths when we do not have data (or we suppress data in favor of legend when a truth strikes us as too commonplace). The hankering after an origin myth has always been especially strong for the closest subject of all — the human race. But we extend the same psychic need to our accomplishments and institutions — and we have origin myths and stories for the beginning of hunting, of language, of art, of kindness, of war, of boxing, bowties, and brassieres. Most of us know that the Great Seal of the United States pictures an eagle holding a ribbon reading *e pluribus unum*. Fewer would recognize the motto on the other side (check it out on the back of a dollar bill): *annuit coeptis* — "he smiles on our beginnings."

Cooperstown may house the Cardiff Giant, but the fame of this small village in central New York does not rest upon its celebrated namesake, author James Fenimore, or its lovely Lake Otsego or the Farmer's Museum. Cooperstown is "on the map" by virtue of a different origin myth — one more parochial but no less powerful for many Americans than the tales of human beginnings that gave life to the Cardiff Giant. Cooperstown is the sacred founding place in the official myth about the origin of baseball.

Origin myths, since they are so powerful, can engender enormous practical problems. Abner Doubleday, as we shall soon see, most emphatically did not invent baseball at Cooperstown in 1839 as the official tale proclaims; in fact, no one invented baseball at any moment or in any spot. Nonetheless, this creation myth made Cooperstown the official home of baseball, and the Hall of Fame, with its associated museum and library, set its roots in this small village, inconveniently located near nothing in the way of airports or accommodations. We all revel in bucolic imagery on the field of dreams, but what a hassle when tens of thousands line the roads, restaurants, and port-a-potties during the annual Hall of Fame weekend, when new members are enshrined and two major league teams arrive to play an exhibition game at Abner Doubleday Field, a sweet little ten-thousand-seater in the middle of town. Put your compass point at Cooperstown, make your radius at Albany — and you'd better reserve a year in advance if you want any accommodation within the enormous resulting circle.

After a lifetime of curiosity, I finally got the opportunity to witness this annual version of forty students in a telephone booth or twenty circus clowns in a Volkswagen. Since Yaz (former Boston star Carl Yastrzemski to the uninitiated) was slated to receive baseball's Nobel in 1989, and his old team was playing in the Hall of Fame game, and since I'm a transplanted Bostonian (although still a New Yorker and not-so-secret Yankee fan at heart), Tom Heitz, chief of the wonderful baseball library at the Hall of Fame, kindly invited me to join the sardines in this most lovely of all cans.

The silliest and most tendentious of baseball writing tries to wrest profundity from the spectacle of grown men hitting a ball with a stick by suggesting linkages between the sport and deep issues of morality, parenthood, history, lost innocence, gentleness, and so on, seemingly ad infinitum. (The effort reeks of silliness because baseball is profound all by itself and needs no excuses; people who don't know this are not fans and are therefore unreachable anyway.) When people ask me how baseball imitates life, I can only respond with what the more genteel newspapers used to call a "barnyard epithet," but now, with growing bravery, usually render as "bullbleep." Nonetheless, baseball is a major item of our culture, and it does have a long and interesting history. Any item or institution with these two properties must generate a set of myths and stories (perhaps even some truths) about its beginnings. And the subject of beginnings is the bread and butter of this column on evolution in the broadest sense. I shall make no woolly analogies between baseball and life; this is an essay on the origins of baseball, with some musings on why beginnings of all sorts hold such fascination for us. (I thank Tom Heitz not only for the invitation to Cooperstown at its yearly acme

but also for drawing the contrast between creation and evolution stories of baseball, and for supplying much useful information from his
unparalleled storehouse.)

Stories about beginnings come in only two basic modes. An entity
either has an explicit point of origin, a specific time and place of creation, or else it evolves and has no definable moment of entry into the
world. Baseball provides an interesting example of this contrast because
we know the answer and can judge received wisdom by the two chief
criteria, often opposed, of external fact and internal hope. Baseball
evolved from a plethora of previous stick-and-ball games. It has no true
Cooperstown and no Doubleday. Yet we seem to prefer the alternative
model of origin by a moment of creation — for then we can have heroes
and sacred places. By contrasting the myth of Cooperstown with the
fact of evolution, we can learn something about our cultural practices
and their frequent disrespect for truth.

The official story about the beginning of baseball is a creation myth,
and a review of the reasons and circumstances of its fabrication may
give us insight into the cultural appeal of stories in this mode. A. G.
Spalding, baseball's first great pitcher during his early career, later
founded the sporting goods company that still bears his name and became one of the great commercial moguls of America's gilded age. As
publisher of the annual *Spalding's Official Base Ball Guide,* he held max-
imal power in shaping both public and institutional opinion on all facets of baseball and its history. As the sport grew in popularity, and the
pattern of two stable major leagues coalesced early in our century,
Spalding and others felt the need for clarification (or merely for codification) of opinion on the hitherto unrecorded origins of an activity
that truly merited its common designation as America's "national pastime."

In 1907, Spalding set up a blue ribbon committee to investigate and
resolve the origins of baseball. The committee, chaired by A. G. Mills
and including several prominent businessmen and two senators who
had also served as presidents of the National League, took much testimony but found no smoking gun for a beginning. Then, in July 1907,
Spalding himself transmitted to the committee a letter from an Abner
Graves, then a mining engineer in Denver, who reported that Abner
Doubleday had, in 1839, interrupted a marbles game behind the tailor's
shop in Cooperstown, New York, to draw a diagram of a baseball field,
explain the rules of the game, and designate the activity by its modern
name of "base ball" (then spelled as two words).

Such "evidence" scarcely inspired universal confidence, but the commission came up with nothing better — and the Doubleday myth, as we shall soon see, was eminently functional. Therefore, in 1908, the Mills Commission reported its two chief findings: first, "that base ball had its origins in the United States"; and second, "that the first scheme for playing it, according to the best evidence available to date, was devised by Abner Doubleday, at Cooperstown, New York, in 1839." This "best evidence" consisted only of "a circumstantial statement by a reputable gentleman" — namely Graves's testimony as reported by Spalding himself.

When cited evidence is so laughably insufficient, one must seek motivations other than concern for truth value. The key to underlying reasons stands in the first conclusion of Mills's committee: hoopla and patriotism (cardboard version) decreed that a national pastime must have an indigenous origin. The idea that baseball had evolved from a wide variety of English stick-and-ball games — although true — did not suit the mythology of a phenomenon that had become so quintessentially American. In fact, Spalding had long been arguing, in an amiable fashion, with Henry Chadwick, another pioneer and entrepreneur of baseball's early years. Chadwick, born in England, had insisted for years that baseball had developed from the British stick-and-ball game called rounders; Spalding had vociferously advocated a purely American origin, citing the Colonial game of "one old cat" as a distant precursor, but holding that baseball itself represented something so new and advanced that a pinpoint of origin — a creation myth — must be sought.

Chadwick considered the matter of no particular importance, arguing (with eminent justice) that an English origin did not "detract one iota from the merit of its now being unquestionably a thoroughly American field sport, and a game too, which is fully adapted to the American character." (I must say that I have grown quite fond of Mr. Chadwick, who certainly understood evolutionary change and its chief principle that historical origin need not match contemporary function.) Chadwick also viewed the committee's whitewash as a victory for his side. He labeled the Mills report as "a masterful piece of special pleading which lets my dear old friend Albert [Spalding] escape a bad defeat. The whole matter was a joke between Albert and myself."

We may accept the psychic need for an indigenous creation myth, but why Abner Doubleday, a man with no recorded tie to the game and who, in the words of Donald Honig, probably "didn't know a baseball from a kumquat"? I had wondered about this for years, but only ran into the answer serendipitously during a visit to Fort Sumter in the harbor of Charleston, South Carolina. There, an exhibit on the first skirmish of the Civil War points out that Abner Doubleday, as captain of the Union artillery, had personally sighted and given orders for firing the first responsive volley following the initial Confederate attack on the fort. Doubleday later commanded divisions at Antietam and Fredericksburg, became at least a minor hero at Gettysburg, and retired as a brevet major general. In fact, A. G. Mills, head of the commission, had served as part of an honor guard when Doubleday's body lay in state in New York City, following his death in 1893.

If you have to have an American hero, could anyone be better than the man who fired the first shot (in defense) of the Civil War? Needless to say, this point was not lost on the members of Mills's committee. Spalding, never one to mince words, wrote to the committee when submitting Graves's dubious testimony: "It certainly appeals to an American pride to have had the great national game of base ball created and named by a Major General in the United States Army." Mills then concluded in his report: "Perhaps in the years to come, in view of the hundreds of thousands of people who are devoted to base ball, and the millions who will be, Abner Doubleday's fame will rest evenly, if not quite as much, upon the fact that he was its inventor . . . as upon his brilliant and distinguished career as an officer in the Federal Army."

And so, spurred by a patently false creation myth, the Hall of Fame stands in the most incongruous and inappropriate locale of a charming little town in central New York. Incongruous and inappropriate, but somehow wonderful. Who needs another museum in the cultural maelstroms (and summer doldrums) of New York, Boston, or Washington? Why not a major museum in a beautiful and bucolic setting? And what could be more fitting than the spatial conjunction of two great American origin myths — the Cardiff Giant and the Doubleday Fable? Thus, I too am quite content to treat the myth gently, while honesty requires fessing up. The exhibit on Doubleday in the Hall of Fame Museum sets just the right tone in its caption: "In the hearts of those who love baseball, he is remembered as the lad in the pasture where the game was invented. Only cynics would need to know more." Only in the hearts; not in the minds.

Baseball evolved. Since the evidence is so clear (as epitomized below), we must ask why these facts have been so little appreciated for so long, and why a creation myth like the Doubleday story ever gained a foothold. Two major reasons have conspired: first, the positive block of our attraction to creation stories; second, the negative impediment of unfamiliar sources outside the usual purview of historians. English stick-and-ball games of the nineteenth century can be roughly classified into two categories along social lines. The upper and educated classes played cricket, and the history of this sport is copiously documented because the literati write about their own interests, and because the activities of men in power are well recorded (and constitute virtually all of history, in the schoolboy version). But the ordinary pastimes of rural and urban working people can be well nigh invisible in conventional sources of explicit commentary. Working people played a different kind of stick-and-ball game, existing in various forms and designated by many names, including "rounders" in western England, "feeder" in London, and "base ball" in southern England. For a large number of reasons, forming the essential difference between cricket and baseball, cricket matches can last up to several days (a batsman, for example, need not run after he hits the ball and need not expose himself to the possibility of being put out every time he makes contact). The leisure time of working people does not come in such generous gobs, and the lower-class stick-and-ball games could not run more than a few hours.

Several years ago, at the Victoria and Albert Museum in London, I learned an important lesson from an excellent exhibit on the late-nineteenth-century history of the British music hall. This is my favorite period (Darwin's century, after all), and I consider myself tolerably well informed on cultural trends of the time. I can sing any line from any of the Gilbert and Sullivan operas (a largely middle-class entertainment), and I know the general drift of high cultural interests in literature and music. But here was a whole world of entertainment for millions, a world with its heroes, its stars, its top forty songs, its gaudy theaters — and I knew nothing, absolutely nothing, about it. I felt chagrined, but my ignorance had an explanation beyond personal insensitivity (and the exhibit had been mounted explicitly to counteract the selective invisibility of certain important trends in history). The music hall was the chief entertainment of Victorian working classes, and the history of working people is often invisible in conventional written sources. It must be rescued and reconstituted from different sorts of data; in this case, from posters, playbills, theater accounts, persistence of some songs in the oral tradition (most were never published as sheet music), recollections of old-timers who knew the person who knew the person . . .

The early history of baseball — the stick-and-ball game of working people — presents the same problem of conventional invisibility — and the same promise of rescue by exploration of unusual sources. Work continues and intensifies as the history of sport becomes more and more academically respectable, but the broad outlines (and much fascinating detail) are not well established. As the upper classes played a codified and well-documented cricket, working people played a largely unrecorded and much more diversified set of stick-and-ball games ancestral to baseball. Many sources, including primers and boys' manuals, depict games recognizable as precursors to baseball well into the early eighteenth century. Occasional references even spill over into high culture. In *Northanger Abbey*, written at the close of the eighteenth century, Jane Austen remarks: "It was not very wonderful that Catherine . . . should prefer cricket, base ball, riding on horseback, and running about the country, at the age of fourteen, to books." As this quotation illustrates, the name of the game is no more Doubleday's than the form of play.

These ancestral styles of baseball came to America with early settlers and were clearly well established by Colonial times. But they were driven ever further underground by Puritan proscriptions of sport for adults. They survived largely as children's games and suffered the double invisibility of location among the poor and the young. But two major reasons brought these games into wider repute and led to a codification of standard forms quite close to modern baseball between the 1820s and the 1850s. First, a set of social reasons, from the decline of Puritanism to increased concern about health and hygiene in crowded cities, made sport an acceptable activity for adults. Second, middle-class and professional people began to take up these early forms of baseball, and with this upward social drift came teams, leagues, written rules, uniforms, stadiums, guidebooks: in short, all the paraphernalia of conventional history.

I am not arguing that these early games could be called baseball with a few trivial differences (evolution means substantial change, after all), but only that they stand in a complex lineage, better called a nexus, from which modern baseball emerged, eventually in a codified and canonical form. In those days before instant communication, every region had its own version, just as every set of outdoor steps in New York City generated a different form of stoopball in my youth, without threatening the basic identity of the game. These games, most commonly called town ball, differed from modern baseball in substantial ways. In the Massachusetts Game, a codification of the late 1850s drawn up by ballplayers in New England towns, four bases and three strikes identify the genus, but many specifics are strange by modern standards. The bases were made of wooden stakes projecting four feet from the ground. The batter (called the striker) stood between first and fourth base. Sides changed after a single out. One hundred runs (called tallies), not higher score after a specified number of innings, spelled victory. The field contained no foul lines, and balls hit in any direction were in play. Most importantly, runners were not tagged out but were retired by "plugging," that is, being hit with a thrown ball while running between bases. Consequently, since baseball has never been a game for masochists, balls were soft — little more than rags stuffed into leather covers — and could not be hit far. (Tom Heitz has put together a team of Cooperstown worthies to re-create town ball for interested parties and prospective opponents. Since few other groups are well schooled in this lost art, Tom's team hasn't been defeated in ages, if ever. "We are the New York Yankees of town ball," he told me. His team is called, quite appropriately in general but especially for this essay, the Cardiff Giants.)

Evolution is continual change, but not insensibly gradual transition; in any continuum, some points are always more interesting than others. The conventional nomination for most salient point in this particular continuum goes to Alexander Joy Cartwright, leader of a New York team that started to play in lower Manhattan, eventually rented some changing rooms and a field in Hoboken (just a quick ferry ride across the Hudson), and finally drew up a set of rules in 1845, later known as the New York Game. Cartwright's version of town ball is much closer to modern baseball, and many clubs followed his rules — for standardization became ever more vital as the popularity of early baseball grew and opportunity for play between regions increased. In particular, Cartwright introduced two key innovations that shaped the disparate forms of town ball into a semblance of modern baseball. First, he eliminated plugging and introduced tagging in the modern sense; the ball could now be made harder, and hitting for distance became an option. Second, he introduced foul lines, again in the modern sense, as his batter stood at a home plate and had to hit the ball within lines defined from home through first and third bases. The game could now become a spectator sport because areas close to the field but out of action could, for the first time, be set aside for onlookers.

The New York Game may be the highlight of a continuum, but it provides no origin myth for baseball. Cartwright's rules were followed in various forms of town ball. His New York Game still included many curiosities by modern standards (twenty-one runs, called aces, won the game, and balls caught on one bounce were outs). Moreover, our modern version is an amalgam of the New York Game plus other town ball traditions, not Cartwright's baby grown up by itself. Several features of the Massachusetts Game entered the modern version in preference to Cartwright's rules. Balls had to be caught on the fly in Boston, and pitchers threw overhand, not underhand as in the New York Game (and in professional baseball until the 1880s).

Scientists often lament that so few people understand Darwin and the principles of biological evolution. But the problem goes deeper. Too few people are comfortable with evolutionary modes of explanation in any form. I do not know why we tend to think so fuzzily in this area, but one reason must reside in our social and psychic attraction to creation myths in preference to evolutionary stories — for creation myths, as noted before, identify heroes and sacred places, while evolutionary stories provide no palpable, particular thing as a symbol for reverence, worship, or patriotism. Still, we must remember — and an intellectual's most persistent and nagging responsibility lies in making this simple point over and over again, however noxious and bothersome we render ourselves thereby — that truth and desire, fact and comfort, have no necessary, or even preferred, correlation (so rejoice when they do coincide).

To state the most obvious example in our current political turmoil. Human growth is a continuum, and no creation myth can define an instant for the origin of an individual life. Attempts by anti-abortionists to designate the moment of fertilization as the beginning of personhood make no sense in scientific terms (and also violate a long history of social definitions that traditionally focused on the quickening, or detected movement, of the fetus in the womb). I will admit — indeed, I emphasized as a key argument of this essay — that not all points on a continuum are equal. Fertilization is a more interesting moment than most, but it no more provides a clean definition of origin than the most interesting moment of baseball's continuum — Cartwright's codification of the New York Game — defines the beginning of our national pastime. Baseball evolved and people grow; both are continua without definable points of origin. Probe too far back and you reach absurdity, for you will see Nolan Ryan on the hill when the first ape hit a bird with a stone; or you will define both masturbation and menstruation as murder — and who will then cast the first stone? Look for something in the middle, and you find nothing but continuity — always a meaningful "before," and always a more modern "after." (Please note that I am not stating an opinion on the vexatious question of abortion — an ethical issue that can only be decided in ethical terms. I only point out that one side has rooted its case in an argument from science that is not only entirely irrelevant to the proper realm of resolution but also happens to be flat-out false in trying to devise a creation myth within a continuum.)

And besides, why do we prefer creation myths to evolutionary stories? I find all the usual reasons hollow. Yes, heroes and shrines are all very well, but is there not grandeur in the sweep of continuity? Shall we revel in a story for all humanity that may include the sacred ball courts of the Aztecs, and perhaps, for all we know, a group of *Homo erectus* hitting rocks or skulls with a stick or a femur? Or shall we halt beside the mythical Abner Doubleday, standing behind the tailor's shop in Cooperstown, and say "behold the man" — thereby violating truth and, perhaps even worse, extinguishing both thought and wonder?

1990

Gerald Early

....

Life with Daughters: Watching the Miss America Pageant

> The theater is an expression of our dream life — of our unconscious aspirations.
>
> — David Mamet, "A Tradition of the Theater as Art," *Writing in Restaurants*

> Aunt Hester went out one night, — where or for what I do not know, — and happened to be absent when my master desired her presence.
>
> — Frederick Douglass, *Narrative of the Life of Frederick Douglass*

> Adults, older girls, shops, magazines, newspapers, window signs — all the world had agreed that a blue-eyed, yellow-haired, pink-skinned doll was what every girl child treasured.
>
> — Toni Morrison, *The Bluest Eye*

IT IS NOW fast become a tradition — if one can use that word to describe a habit about which I still feel a certain amount of shamefacedness — for our household to watch the Miss America contest on television every year. The source of my embarrassment is that this program remains, despite its attempts in recent years to modernize its frightfully antique quality of "women on parade," a kind of maddeningly barbarous example of the persistent, hard, crass urge to sell: from the plugs for the sponsor that are made a part of the script (that being an antique of fifties and sixties television; the show does not remember its history so much as it seems bent on repeating it) to the constant references to the success of some of the previous contestants and the reminders that

First published in *The Kenyon Review*, 1990; selected by Joyce Carol Oates for *The Best American Essays 1991.*

this is some sort of scholarship competition, the program has all the cheap earnestness of a social uplift project being played as a musical revue in Las Vegas. Paradoxically, it wishes to convince the public that it is a common entertainment while simultaneously wishing to convey that it is more than mere entertainment. The Miss America pageant is the worst sort of "Americanism," the soft smile of sex and the hard sell of toothpaste and hair dye ads wrapped in the dreamy ideological gauze of "making it through one's own effort." In a perverse way, I like the show; it is the only live television left other than sports, news broadcasts, performing arts awards programs, and speeches by the president. I miss live TV. It was the closest thing to theater for the masses. And the Miss America contest is, as it has been for some time, the most perfectly rendered theater in our culture, for it so perfectly captures what we yearn for: a low-class ritual, a polished restatement of vulgarity, that wants to open the door to high-class respectability by way of plain middle-class anxiety and ambition. Am I doing all right? the contestants seem to ask in a kind of reassuring, if numbed, way. The contest brings together all the American classes in a show-biz spectacle of classlessness and tastelessness.

My wife has been interested in the Miss America contest since childhood, and so I ascribe her uninterrupted engagement with America's cultural passage into fall (Miss America, like college and pro football, signifies for us as a nation the end of summer; the contest was invented, back in 1921, by Atlantic City merchants to prolong the summer season past Labor Day) as something mystically and uniquely female. She, as a black woman, had a long-standing quarrel with the contest until Vanessa Williams was chosen the first black Miss America in September 1983. Somehow she felt vindicated by Williams for all those years as a black girl in Dallas, watching white women win the crown and thumb their noses at her, at her blackness, at her straightened hair, her thick lips, her wide nose. She played with white Barbie dolls as a little girl and had, I suppose, a "natural," or at least an understandable and predictable, interest in seeing the National White Barbie Doll chosen every year because for such a long time, of course, the Miss America contest, with few exceptions, was a totemic preoccupation with and representation of a particularly stilted form of patriarchal white supremacy. In short, it was a national white doll contest. And well we know that every black girl growing up in the fifties and early sixties had her peculiar love-hate affair with white dolls, with mythicized white femininity. I am reminded of this historical instance: everyone knows that in the Brown versus Topeka Board of Education case (the case that resulted in the Supreme Court decision to integrate public schools) part of the sociological evidence used by the plaintiffs to show the psychological damage suffered by blacks because of Jim Crow was an account by Kenneth Clarke of how, when offered a choice between a black doll and a white doll, little black girls invariably chose the white doll because they thought it "prettier."

On the front page of the January 6, 1962, *Pittsburgh Courier*, a black weekly, is a picture of a hospitalized black girl named Connie Smith holding a white doll sent to her by Attorney General Robert Kennedy. Something had occurred between 1954, when the Supreme Court made its decision, and 1962 which made it impossible for Kennedy to send the girl a black doll, and this impossibility was to signal, ironically, that the terms of segregation and the terms of racial integration, the very icon of them, were to be exactly the same. Kennedy could not send the girl a black doll, as it would have implied, in the age of integration, that he was, in effect, sending her a Jim Crow toy, a toy that would emphasize the girl's race. In the early sixties such a gesture would have been considered condescending. To give the black girl a white doll in the early sixties was to mainstream the black girl into the culture, to say that she was worthy of the same kind of doll that a white girl would have. But how can it be that conservatism and liberalism, segregation and integration, could produce, fantastically, the same results, the identical iconography: a black girl hugging a white doll because everyone thinks it is best for her to have it? How can it be that at one time the white doll is the sign of the black girl's rejection and inferiority and fewer than ten years later it is the sign of her acceptance and redemption? Those who are knowledgeable about certain aspects of the black mind or the collective black consciousness realize, of course, that the issues of segregation and integration, of conservatism and liberalism, of acceptance and rejection, of redemption and inferiority, are all restatements of the same immovable and relentless reality of the meaning of American blackness; that this is all a matter of the harrowing and compelling intensity that is called, quaintly, race pride. And in this context, the issue of white dolls, this fetishization of young white feminine beauty, and the complexity of black girlhood becomes an unresolved theme stated in a strident key. Blacks have preached for a long time about how to heal their daughters of whiteness: in the November 1908 issue of *The Colored American Magazine*, E. A. Johnson wrote an article entitled, "Negro

Dolls for Negro Babies," in which he said, "I am convinced that one of the best ways to teach Negro children to respect their own color would be to see to it that the children be given colored dolls to play with. . . . To give a Negro child a white doll means to create in it a prejudice against its own color, which will cling to it through life." Lots of black people believed this and, for all I know, probably still do, as race pride, or the lack thereof, burns and crackles like a current through most African-American public and private discourse. Besides, it is no easy matter to wish white dolls away.

A few years ago I was thumbing through an album of old family photographs and saw one of me and my oldest sister taken when I was four and she was nine. It struck me, transfixed me really, as it was a color photo and most of the old family pictures taken when I was a boy were black-and-white because my mother could not afford to have color pictures developed. We, my sister and I, are sitting on an old stuffed blue chair and she is holding a white doll in her hand, displaying it for the picture. I remember the occasion very well, as my sister was to be confirmed in our small, all-black Episcopal church that day, and she was, naturally, proud of the moment and wanted to share it with her favorite toy. That, I remembered, was why these were color pictures. It was a special day for the family, a day my mother wanted to celebrate by taking special pictures. My mother is a very dark woman who has a great deal of race pride and often speaks about my sisters' having black dolls. I was surprised, in looking at the picture recently, that they ever owned a white one, that indeed a white one had been a favorite.

My wife grew up — enjoyed the primary years of black girlhood, so to speak — during the years 1954 through 1962; she was about five or six years younger than my oldest sister. She lived in a southern state, or a state that was a reasonable facsimile of a southern state. She remembers that signs for colored and white bathrooms and water fountains persisted well into the mid-sixties in Texas. She remembers also Phyllis George, the Miss America from Denton, Texas, who went on to become a television personality for several years. She has always been very interested in George's career, and she has always disliked her. "She sounds just like a white girl from Texas," my wife likes to say, always reminding me that while both blacks and whites in Texas have accents, they do not sound alike. George won the contest in 1971, my wife's freshman year at the University of Pennsylvania and around the time she began to wear an Afro, a popular hairstyle for young black women in the days of "our

terrible blackness" or "our black terribleness." It was a year fraught with
complex passages into black womanhood for her. To think that a white
woman from Texas should win the Miss America title that year! For my
wife, the years of watching the Miss America contest were nothing
more, in some sense continue to be nothing more, than an expression
of anger made all the worse by the very unconscious or semiconscious
nature of it. But if the anger has been persistent, so has her enormous
capacity to "take it"; for in all these years it has never occurred to her to
refuse to watch because, like the black girl being offered the white doll,
like all black folk being offered white gifts, she has absolutely no idea
how that is done, and she is not naïve enough to think that a simple refusal would be an act of empowerment. Empowerment comes only
through making demands of our bogeymen, not by trying to convince
ourselves we are not tormented. Yet, paradoxically, among blacks there
is the bitter hope that a simplistic race pride will save us, a creed that
masks its complex contradictions beneath lapping waves of bourgeois
optimism and bourgeois anguish; for race pride clings to the opposing
notions that the great hope (but secret fear) of an African-American future is, first, that blacks will always remain black and, second, that the
great fear (but secret hope) of an African-American future is that blacks
will not always remain black but evolve into something else. Race pride,
which at its most insistent argues that blackness is everything, becomes,
in its attempt to be the psychological quest for sanity, a form of dementia that exists as a response to that form of white dementia that says
blackness is nothing. Existing as it does as a reactive force battling
against a white preemptive presumption, race pride begins to take on
the vices of an unthinking dogma and the virtues of a disciplined religious faith, all in the same instance. With so much at stake, race pride
becomes both the act of making a virtue of a necessity and making a
necessity of a virtue and, finally, making a profound and touching absurdity of both virtue and necessity. In some ways my wife learned her
lessons well in her youth: she never buys our daughters white dolls.

My daughters, Linnet, age ten, and Rosalind, age seven, have become
staunch fans of beauty contests in the last three years. In that time they
have watched, in their entirety, several Miss America pageants, one Miss
Black America contest, and one Miss USA. At first, I ascribed this to the
same impulse that made my wife interested in such events when she
was little: something secretly female, just as an interest in professional
sports might be ascribed to something peculiarly male. Probably it is a

sort of resentment that black girls harbor toward these contests. But that could not really be the case with my daughters. After all, they have seen several black entrants in these contests and have even seen black winners. They also have black dolls.

Back in the fall of 1983 when Vanessa Williams became Miss America, we, as a family, had our picture taken with her when she visited St. Louis. We went, my wife and I, to celebrate the grand moment when white American popular culture decided to embrace black women as something other than sexual subversives or fat, kindly maids cleaning up and caring for white families. We had our own, well, royalty, and royal origins mean a great deal to people who have been denied their myths and their right to human blood. White women reformers may be ready to scrap the Miss America contest. (And the contest has certainly responded to the criticism it has been subjected to in recent years by muting some of the fleshier aspects of the program while, in its attempts to be even more the anxiety-ridden middle-class dream-wish, emphasizing more and more the magic of education and scholarly attainments.) It is now the contest that signifies the quest for profession alism among bourgeois women, and the first achievement of the professional career is to win something in a competition. But if there is a movement afoot to bring down the curtain finally on Miss America, my wife wants no part of it: "Whites always want to reform and end things when black people start getting on the gravy train they've been enjoying for years. What harm does the Miss America contest do?" None, I suppose, especially since black women have been winning lately.

Linnet and Rosalind were too young when we met Vanessa Williams to recall anything about the pictures, but they are amazed to see themselves in a bright, color Polaroid picture with a famous person, being part of an event which does not strike a chord in their consciousness because they cannot remember being alive when it happened. I often wonder if they attach any significance to the pictures at all. They think Vanessa is very pretty, prettier than their mother, but they attach no significance to being pretty — that is to say, no real value; they would not admire someone simply because he or she was good-looking. They think Williams is beautiful, but they do not wish that she was their mother. And this issue of being beautiful is not to be taken lightly in the life of a black girl. About two years ago Linnet started coming home from school wishing aloud that her hair was long and blond so that she could fling it about, the way she saw many of her white classmates doing. As she attends a school that is more than 90 percent white, it seemed inevitable to my wife that one of our daughters would become sensitive about her appearance. At this time Linnet's hair was not straightened and she wore it in braids. Oddly, despite the fact that she wanted a different hairstyle that would permit her hair to "blow in the wind," so to speak, she vehemently opposed having it straightened, although my wife has straightened hair, after having worn an Afro for several years. I am not sure why Linnet did not want her hair straightened; perhaps, after seeing her teenage cousin have her hair straightened on several occasions, the process of hair straightening seemed distasteful or disheartening or frightening. Actually, I do not think Linnet wanted to change her hair to be beautiful; she wanted to be like everyone else. But perhaps this is simply wishful thinking here or playing with words because Linnet must have felt her difference as being a kind of ugliness. Yet she is not a girl who is subject to illusion. Once, about a year earlier, when she had had a particularly rough day in school, I told her, in a father's patronizing way with a daughter, that I thought she was the most beautiful girl in the world. She looked at me strangely when I said that and then replied matter-of-factly: "I don't think I'm beautiful at all. I think I'm just ordinary. There is nothing wrong with that, is there, Daddy? Just to be ordinary?" "Are you unhappy to be ordinary?" I asked. She thought for a moment, then said quietly and finally, "No. Are you?"

Hair straightening, therefore, was not an option and would not have been even if Linnet had wanted it, because my wife was opposed to having Linnet's hair straightened at her age. At first, Linnet began going to school with her hair unbraided. Unfortunately, this turned out to be a disastrous hairdo, as her hair shrank during the course of a day to a tangled mess. Finally, my wife decided to have both Linnet and Rosalind get short Afro haircuts. Ostensibly, this was to ease the problem of taking swim lessons during the summer. In reality, it was to end Linnet's wishes for a white hairstyle by, in effect, foreclosing any possibility that she could remotely capture such a look. Rosalind's hair was cut so that Linnet would not feel that she was being singled out. (Alas, the trials of being both the second and the younger child!) At first, the haircuts caused many problems in school. Some of the children — both black and white — made fun of them. Brillo heads, they were called, and fungus and Afro heads. One group of black girls at school refused to play with Linnet. "You look so ugly with that short hair," they would say.

"Why don't you wear your hair straight like your mom. Your mom's hair is so pretty." Then, for the first time, the girls were called niggers by a white child on their school bus, although I think neither the child nor my daughters completely understood the gravity of that obscenity. People in supermarkets would refer to them as boys unless they were wearing dresses. Both girls went through a period when they suffered most acutely from that particular American disease, that particularly African-American disease, the conjunction of oppression and exhibitionistic desire: self-consciousness. They thought about their hair all the time. My wife called the parents of the children who teased them. The teasing stopped for the most part, although a few of the black girls remained so persistent that the white school counselor suggested that Linnet's and Rosalind's hair be straightened. "I'm white," he said, "and maybe I shouldn't get into this, but they might feel more comfortable if they wore a different hairstyle." My wife angrily rejected that bit of advice. She had them wear dresses more often to make them look unmistakably like girls, although she refused out of hand my suggestion of having their ears pierced. She is convinced that pierced ears are just a form of mutilation, primitive tattooing or scarring passing itself off as something fashionable. Eventually, the girls became used to their hair. Now, after more than a year, they hardly think about it, and even if Linnet wears a sweat suit or jeans, no one thinks she is a boy because she is budding breasts. Poor Rosalind still suffers on occasion in supermarkets because she shows no outward signs of sexual maturity. Once, while watching Linnet look at her mother's very long and silken straight hair, the hair that the other black girls at school admire, always calling it pretty, I asked her if she would like to have hers straightened.

"Not now," she said. "Maybe when I'm older. It'll be something different."

"Do you think you will like it?" I asked.

"Maybe," she said.

And in that "maybe," so calmly and evenly uttered, rests the complex contradictions, the uneasy tentative negotiations of that which cannot be compromised yet can never be realized in this flawed world as an ideal; there is, in that "maybe," the epistemology of race pride for black American women so paradoxically symbolized by their straightened hair. In the February 1939 issue of *The Atlantic Monthly*, a black woman named Kimbal Goffman (possibly a pseudonym) wrote an essay entitled "Black Pride" in which she accused blacks of being ashamed of their heritage and, even more damningly in some of her barbs obviously aimed at black women, of their looks:

> . . . why are so many manufacturers becoming rich through the manufacture of bleaching preparations? Why are hair-straightening combs found in nearly every Negro home? Why is the following remark made so often to a newborn baby, when grandma or auntie visits it for the first time? "Tell Mother she must pinch your nose every morning. If she doesn't, you're gonna have a sure 'nough darky nose."

According to Goffman, blacks do not exploit what society has given them; they are simply ashamed to have what they have, tainted as it is with being associated with a degraded people, and long to be white or to have possessions that would accrue a kind of white status. In the essay, blacks in general receive their share of criticism but only black women are criticized in a gender-specific way that their neurotic sense of inferiority concerning physical appearance is a particularly dangerous form of reactionism as it stigmatizes each new generation. According to Goffman, it is black women, because they are mothers, who perpetuate their sense of inferiority by passing it on to their children. In this largely Du Boisian argument, Goffman advises, "Originality is the backbone of all progress." And, in this sense, originality means understanding blackness as something uncontrolled or uninfluenced by what whites say it is. This is the idealism of race pride that demands both purity and parity. Exactly one year later, in the February 1940 issue of *The Brown American,* a black magazine published in Philadelphia, Lillian Franklin McCall wrote an article about the history of black women beauty shop owners and entrepreneurs entitled "Appointment at Seven." The opening paragraph is filled with dollar signs:

> The business of straightening milady's insistent curls tinkles cash registers in the country to the tune of two million and a half dollars a year. And that covers merely the semi-monthly session with the hairdresser for the estimated four million of Eve's sepia adult daughters by national census. Today there is a growing trend to top off the regular, "Shampoo and wave," with a facial; and, perhaps, a manicure. New oil treatments and rinses prove a lure, too, so milady finds her beauty budget stepped up from approximately $39 yearly for an average $1.25 or $1.50 "hair-do," to $52.00 per year if she adds a facial to the beauty rite, and $10 more, for the manicure.

In a Booker T. Washington tone, McCall goes on to describe how the establishment of a black beauty culture serves as a source of empowerment for black women:

Brown business it is, in all its magnitude for Miss Brown America receives her treatments from the hands of Negro beauticians and her hair preparations and skin dreams come, usually from Negro laboratories.

She then tells the reader that leading companies in this field were founded by black women: Madam C. J. Walker, Mrs. Annie Turbo Malone, Madame Sara Spencer Washington. And one is struck by the absences that this essay evokes, not only in comparison to Goffman's piece but also to Elsie Johnson McDougald's major manifesto on black women, "The Task of Negro Womanhood," that appeared in Alain Locke's seminal 1925 anthology of African-American thought, *The New Negro*. In McDougald's piece, which outlines all the economic status and achievements of black women at the time, there is absolutely no mention of black beauty culture, no mention of Madame C. J. Walker, although her newspaper ads were among the biggest in black newspapers nationwide during the twenties. (And why did McDougald not mention black women's beauty workers and businesspeople culture along with the nurses, domestics, clerks, and teachers she discusses at length? It can scarcely be because she, as a trained and experienced writer on black sociological matters, did not think of it.)[1] It is not simply money or black woman's industry or endeavor that makes the black woman present or a presence; it is beauty culture generally which finally brings her into being, and specifically, her presence is generated by her hair. What for one black woman writer, Goffman, is an absence and thus a sign of degradation, is for another a presence and a sign of economic possibilities inherent in feminine aesthetics.

What did I see as a boy when I passed the large black beauty shop on Broad and South streets in Philadelphia where the name of its owner, Adele Reese, commanded such respect or provoked such jealousy? What did I see there but a long row of black women dressed immaculately in white tunics, washing and styling the hair of other black women. That was a sign of what culture, of what set of politics? The sheen of those straightened heads, the entire enterprise of the making of black feminine beauty: was it an enactment of a degradation inspirited by a bitter inferiority or was it a womanly laying on of hands where black women were, in their way, helping themselves to live through and transcend their degradation? As a boy, I used to watch and wonder as my mother straightened my sisters' hair every Saturday night for church on Sunday morning. Under a low flame on the stove, the hot comb would glow dully; from an open jar of Apex bergamot hair oil or

Dixie Peach, my mother would extract blobs and place them on the back of one hand, deftly applying the oil to strands of my sisters' hair with the other. And the strange talk about a "light press" or a "heavy press" or a "close press" to get the edges and the ends; the concern about the hair "going back" if caught in the rain. Going back where, I wondered. To Africa? To the bush? And the constant worry and vigil about burning, getting too close to the scalp. I can remember hearing my sisters' hair sizzle and crackle as the comb passed through with a kind of pungent smell of actually burning hair. And I, like an intentional moth, with lonely narrow arcs, hovered near this flame of femininity with a fascinated impertinence. Had I witnessed the debilitating nullity of absence or was it the affirmation of an inescapable presence? Had I witnessed a mutilation or a rite of devotion? Black women's hair is; I decided even as a boy, unintelligible. And now I wonder, is the acceptance of the reigns of black women as Miss America a sign that black beauty has become part of the mainstream culture? Is the black woman now truly a presence?

We, I and my wife and our daughters, sat together and watched the latest Miss America contest. We did what we usually do. We ate popcorn. We laughed at all the talent numbers, particularly the ones when the contestants were opera singers or dancers. We laughed when the girls tried to answer grand social questions — such as "How can we inspire children to achieve and stay in school?" or "How can we address the problem of mainstreaming physically disadvantaged people?" — in thirty seconds. In fact, as Rosalind told me after the show, the main reason my daughters watch the Miss America pageant is that "it's funny." My daughters laugh because they cannot understand why the women are doing what they are doing, why they are trying so hard to please, to be pleasing. This must certainly be a refreshing bit of sanity, as the only proper response for such a contest is simply to dismiss it as hilarious; this grandiose version of an elocution, charm school, dance and music recital, which is not a revelation of talent but a reaffirmation of bourgeois cultural conditioning. And this bit of sanity on my daughters' part may prove hopeful for our future, for our American future, for our African-American future, if black girls are, unlike my wife when she was young, no longer angry. When it was announced that Miss Missouri, Debbye Turner, the third black to be Miss America, was the winner, my children were indifferent. It hardly mattered to them who won, and a black woman's victory meant no more than if any other contestant had prevailed. "She's pretty," Linnet said. She won two dollars in a bet with my wife, who did not think it possible that another black Miss America would be chosen. "Vanessa screwed up for the whole race," she told me once. "It's the race burden, the sins of the one become the original sins of us all." Linnet said simply, "She'll win because she is the best." Meritocracy is still a valid concept with the young.

For me, it was almost to be expected that Miss Turner would win. First, she received more precontest publicity than any other contestant in recent years, with the possible exception of the black woman who was chosen Miss Mississippi a few years ago. Second, after the reign of Vanessa Williams, one would think that the Miss America powers that be very much wanted to have another black win and have a successful reign so that the contest itself could both prove its good faith (to blacks) and forestall criticism from white feminists and liberals (who are always put in a difficult position when the object of their disapproval is a black woman). As with the selection of Williams, the contest gained a veneer of postmodernist social and political relevance not only by selecting a black again but by having an Asian, a kidney donor, and a hearing-impaired woman among the top ten finalists. This all smacks of affirmative action or the let's-play-fair-with-the-underrepresented doctrine, which, as Miss Virginia pointed out after the contest, smacks of politics. But the point she missed, of course, is the point that all people who oppose affirmative action miss. The selection process for the Miss America contest has always been political. Back in the days when only white college women, whose main interest in most instances was a degree in MRS, could win, the contest was indeed just as political as it is now, a clear ideological bow to both patriarchal ideals and racism. It is simply a matter of which politics you prefer, and while no politics are perfect, some are clearly better than others. But in America, it must be added, the doctrine of fair play should not even be graced with such a sophisticated term as "political." It is more our small-town, bourgeois Christian, muscular myth of ethical rectitude, the tremendous need Americans feel to be decent. So Miss Turner is intended to be both the supersession of Vanessa Williams — a religious vet student whose ambitions are properly, well, post-modernist Victorianism, preach do-goodism, evoke the name of God whenever you speak of your ambitions, and live with smug humility — and the redemption of the image of black women in American popular culture, since the Miss America contest is one of the few vehicles of display and competition for women in popular culture.

And if my daughters have come to one profound penetration of this cultural rite, it is that the contest ought to be laughed at in some ways, as most of the manifestations of popular culture ought to be for being the shoddy illusions that they are. For one always ought to laugh at someone or a group of someones who are trying to convince you that nothing is something — and that is not really the same as someone trying to convince you that you can have something for nothing, because in the popular culture business, the price for nothing is the same as the price for something; this "nothing is something" is, in fact, in most cases what the merchandising of popular culture is all about. (But as Mother reminded me as a boy: nothing is nothing and something is something. Accept no substitutes!) For my children, the contest can be laughed at because it is so completely meaningless to them; they know it is an illusion despite its veneer as a competition. And it is that magical word, competition, which is used over and over again all night long by the host and hostesses of the Miss America show (a contest, like most others these days, from the SATs to professional sports, that is made up of a series of competitions within the framework of larger competitions in such a pyramid that the entire structure of the outside world, for the bourgeois mind, is a frightful maze, a strangulating skein of competitions), that is the touchstone of reality, the momentous signifier that the sponsors of the pageant hope will give this extravaganza new significance and new life. For everything that we feel is important now is a matter of competition, beating out someone else for a prize, for some cheap prestige, a moment of notice before descending to cipherhood again; competition ranging from high culture (literary prizes, which seem to be awarded every day in the week, and classical music competitions for every instrument in a symphony orchestra, because of course for high culture one can never have enough art) to mid-culture (the entire phenomenon of American education, from academic honors to entrance requirements for prestigious schools, because of course for the middle class one can never have enough education or enough professionalism) to low culture (playing the lottery and various forms of gambling, because of course for the lower class one can never hope enough for money). And the more stringent and compulsively expressed the competition is (and the Miss America contest has reached a new height of hysteria in both the stridency and compulsion of the competition), the more legitimate and noteworthy it is.

Everyone in our culture wants to win a prize. Perhaps that is the grand lesson we have taken with us from kindergarten in the age of the perversions of Dewey-style education: everyone gets a ribbon, and praise becomes a meaningless narcotic to soothe egoistic distemper. And in our bourgeois coming-of-age, we simply crave more and more ribbons and praise, the attainment of which becomes all the more delightful and satisfying if they are gotten at someone else's expense. Competition, therefore, becomes in the end a kind of laissez-faire psychotherapy that structures and orders our impossible rages of ambition, our rages to be noticed. But competition does not produce better people (a myth we have swallowed whole); it does not even produce better candidates; it simply produces more desperately grasping competitors. The "quality" of the average Miss America contestant is not significantly better now than it was twenty-five years ago, although the desires of today's contestants may meet with our approval (who could possibly disapprove of a black woman who wishes to be a vet in this day of careerism as the expression of independence and political empowerment), but then the women of twenty-five years ago wanted what their audiences approved of as well. That is not necessarily an advance or progress; that is simply a recognition that we are all bound by the mood and temper of our time. So, in this vast competition, this fierce theatrical warfare where all the women are supposed to love their neighbor while they wish to beat her brains out, this warfare so pointedly exposed before the nation, what we have chosen is not the Royal American Daughter (although the contest's preoccupation with the terminology of aristocracy mirrors the public's need for such a person as the American princess) but rather the Cosmopolitan Girl. As the magazine ad states:[2]

> Can a girl be too Busy? I'm taking seventeen units at Princeton, pushing on with my career during vacations and school breaks, study singing and dancing when I can, try never to lose track of my five closest chums, steal the time for Michael Jackson and Thomas Hardy, work for an anti-drug program for kids and, oh yes, I hang out with three horses, three cats, two birds and my dog Jack. My favorite magazine says "too busy" just means you don't want to miss anything . . . I love that magazine. I guess you can say I'm That Cosmopolitan Girl.

When one reads about these women in the Miss America contest, that is precisely what they sound like: the Cosmopolitan Girl who knows how to have serious fun, and she has virtually nothing with which to claim our attention except a moralistic bourgeois diligence. To use a twenties term: she sounds "swell." She is an amalgam of both lead characters portrayed by Patty Duke on her old TV show: the studious, serious kid and the "typical" wacky but good-hearted suburban teenager, or, to borrow Ann Douglas's concept, she is the Teen Angel: the bourgeois girl who can do everything, is completely self-absorbed with her leisure, and has a heart of gold. Once again, with the Miss America contest we have America's vehement preoccupation with innocence, with its inability to deal with the darkness of youth, the darkness of its own uselessly expressed ambition, the dark complexity of its own simplistic morality of sunshine and success, the darkness, righteous rage, and bitter depth of its own daughters. Once again, when the new Miss America, victorious and smiling, walks down the runway, we know that runway, that victory march, to be the American catwalk of supreme bourgeois self-consciousness and supreme illusion. We are still being told that nothing is something.

Nonetheless, the fact that Miss Turner won struck both my wife and me as important, as something important for the race. We laughed during the contest, but we did not laugh when she was chosen. We wanted her to win very much; it is impossible to escape that need to see the race uplifted, to thumb your nose at whites in a competition. It is impossible for blacks not to want to see their black daughters elevated to the platforms where white women are. Perhaps this tainted desire, an echoing "Ballad of the Brown Girl" that resounds in the unconscious psyche of all black people, is the unity of feeling which is the only race pride blacks have ever had since they became Americans; for race pride for the African American, finally, is something that can only be understood as existing on the edge of tragedy and history and is, finally, that which binds both together to make the African American the darkly and richly complicated person he or she is. In the end, both black women magazine writers quoted earlier were right: race pride is transcending your degradation while learning to live in it and with it. To paraphrase an idea of Dorothy Sayers, race pride must teach blacks that they are not to be saved *from* degradation but saved *in* it.

A few days after the contest I watched both my daughters playing Barbies, as they call it. They squat on the floor on their knees, moving their dolls around through an imaginary town and in imaginary houses. I decided to join them and squatted down too, asking them the rules of their game, which they patiently explained as though they did not mind having me, the strange adult, invade their children's world. I told them it was hard for me to squat and asked if I could simply sit down, but they said that one always plays Barbies while squatting. It was a rule that had to be obeyed. As they went along, explaining relationships among their myriad dolls and the several landscapes, as complicated a genealogy as anything Faulkner ever dreamed up, a theater as vast as the entire girlhood of the world, they told me that one particular black Ken doll and one particular black Barbie doll were married and that the dolls had a child. Then Rosalind held up a white doll that someone, probably a grandparent, had given them (my wife is fairly strict on the point of our daughters' not having white dolls, but I guess a few have slipped through), explaining that this doll was the daughter of the black Ken and Barbie.

"But," I said, "how could two black dolls have a white daughter?"

"Oh," said Rosalind, looking at me as if I were an object deserving of only her indulgent pity, "we're not racial. That's old-fashioned. Don't you think so, Daddy? Aren't you tired of all that racial stuff?"

Bowing to that wisdom which, it is said, is the only kind that will lead us to Christ and to ourselves, I decided to get up and leave them to their play. My knees had begun to hurt and I realized, painfully, that I was much too old, much too at peace with stiffness and inflexibility, for children's games.

Notes

1. Richard Wright tells a story in his 1956 account of the Bandung conference, entitled *The Color Curtain,* that emphasizes the absence of the black woman. He relates how a white woman journalist knocks on his hotel room door during the course of the conference and confides the strange behavior of her roommate — a black woman journalist from Boston. Her roommate walks around in the middle of the night and the white woman often covertly spies her in "a dark corner of the room . . . bent over a tiny blue light, a very low and a very blue flame. . . . It seemed like she was combing her hair, but I wasn't sure. Her right arm was moving and now and then she would look over her shoulder toward my bed." The white woman thinks that the black woman is practicing voodoo. But Wright soon explains that the black woman is simply straightening her hair.

> "But why would she straighten her hair? Her hair seems all right" [the white woman journalist asks].
> "Her hair is all right. But it's not straight. It's kinky. But she does not want you, a white woman, to see her when she straightens her hair. She would feel embarrassed —"
> "Why?"
> "Because you were born with straight hair, and she wants to look as much like you as possible. . . ."
> The woman stared at me, then clapped her hands to her eyes and exclaimed: "Oh!"
> I leaned back and thought: here in Asia, where everybody was dark, the poor

American Negro woman was worried about the hair she was born with. Here, where practically nobody was white, her hair would have been acceptable; no one would have found her "inferior" because her hair was kinky; on the contrary, the Indonesians would perhaps have found her different and charming.

The conversation continues with an account of the black woman's secretive skin lightening treatments. What is revealing in this dialogue which takes on both political and psychoanalytic proportions is the utter absence of the black woman's voice, her presence. She is simply the dark, neurotic ghost that flits in the other room while the black male and the white female, both in the same room, one with dispassionate curtness and the other with sentimentalized guilt, consider the illness that is enacted before them as a kind of bad theater. Once again, the psychopathology of the black American is symbolized by the black woman's straightened hair, by her beauty culture.

2. Jacques Barzun, "Culture High and Dry," *The Culture We Deserve* (Middletown, Conn.: Wesleyan University Press, 1989).

1993

John Updike

··

The Disposable Rocket

INHABITING A MALE BODY is much like having a bank account; as long as it's healthy, you don't think much about it. Compared to the female body, it is a low-maintenance proposition: a shower now and then, trim the fingernails every ten days, a haircut once a month. Oh yes, shaving — scraping or buzzing away at your face every morning. Byron, in *Don Juan*, thought the repeated nuisance of shaving balanced out the periodic agony, for females, of childbirth. Women are, his lines tell us,

> Condemn'd to child-bed, as men for their sins
> Have shaving too entail'd upon their chins, —
>
> A daily plague, which in the aggregate
> May average on the whole with parturition.

From the standpoint of reproduction, the male body is a delivery system, as the female is a mazy device for retention. Once the delivery is made, men feel a faint but distinct falling-off of interest. Yet against the enduring female heroics of birth and nurture should be set the male's superhuman frenzy to deliver his goods: he vaults walls, skips sleep, risks wallet, health, and his political future all to ram home his seed into the gut of the chosen woman. The sense of the chase lives in him as the key to life. His body is, like a delivery rocket that falls away in space, a disposable means. Men put their bodies at risk to experience the release from gravity.

When my tenancy of a male body was fairly new — of six or so years'

First published in *Michigan Quarterly Review*, 1993; collected in *More Matter*, 1999; selected by Tracy Kidder for * *The Best American Essays 1994*.

duration — I used to jump and fall just for the joy of it. Falling — backwards, downstairs — became a specialty of mine, an attention-getting stunt I was practicing into my thirties, at suburban parties. Falling is, after all, a kind of flying, though of briefer duration than would be ideal. My impulse to hurl myself from high windows and the edges of cliffs belongs to my body, not my mind, which resists the siren call of the chasm with all its might; the interior struggle knocks the wind from my lungs and tightens my scrotum and gives any trip to Europe, with its Alps, castle parapets, and gargoyled cathedral lookouts, a flavor of nightmare. Falling, strangely, no longer figures in my dreams, as it often did when I was a boy and my subconscious was more honest with me. An airplane, that necessary evil, turns the earth into a map so quickly the brain turns aloof and calm; still, I marvel that there is no end of young men willing to become jet pilots.

Any accounting of male-female differences must include the male's superior recklessness, a drive not, I think, toward death, as the darker feminist cosmogonies would have it, but to test the limits, to see what the traffic will bear — a kind of mechanic's curiosity. The number of men who do lasting damage to their young bodies is striking; war and car accidents aside, secondary-school sports, with the approval of parents and the encouragement of brutish coaches, take a fearful toll of skulls and knees. We were made for combat, back in the post-simian, East African days, and the bumping, the whacking, the breathlessness, the pain-smothering adrenaline rush, form a cumbersome and unfashionable bliss, but bliss nevertheless. Take your body to the edge, and see if it flies.

The male sense of space must differ from that of the female, who has such interesting, active, and significant inner space. The space that interests men is outer. The fly ball high against the sky, the long pass spiraling overhead, the jet fighter like a scarcely visible pinpoint nozzle laying down its vapor trail at forty thousand feet, the gazelle haunch flickering just beyond arrow-reach, the uncountable stars sprinkled on their great black wheel, the horizon, the mountaintop, the quasar — these bring portents with them, and awaken a sense of relation with the invisible, with the empty. The ideal male body is taut with lines of potential force, a diagram extending outward; the ideal female body curves around centers of repose. Of course, no one is ideal, and the sexes are somewhat androgynous subdivisions of a species: Diana the huntress is a more trendy body-type nowadays than languid, overweight Venus, and polymorphous Dionysus poses for more underwear ads than Mars. Relatively, though, men's bodies, however elegant, are designed for covering territory, for moving on.

An erection, too, defies gravity, flirts with it precariously. It extends the diagram of outward direction into downright detachability — objective in the case of the sperm, subjective in the case of the testicles and penis. Men's bodies, at this juncture, feel only partly theirs; a demon of sorts has been attached to their lower torsos, whose performance is erratic and whose errands seem, at times, ridiculous. It is like having a (much) smaller brother toward whom you feel both fond and impatient; if he is you, it is you in curiously simplified and ignoble form. This sense, of the male body being two of them, is acknowledged in verbal love play and erotic writing, where the penis is playfully given its own name, an individuation not even the rarest rapture grants a vagina. Here, where maleness gathers to a quintessence of itself, there can be no insincerity, there can be no hiding; for sheer nakedness, there is nothing like a hopeful phallus; its aggressive shape is indivisible from its tender-skinned vulnerability. The act of intercourse, from the point of view of a consenting female, has an element of mothering, of enwrapment, of merciful concealment, even. The male body, for this interval, is tucked out of harm's way.

To inhabit a male body, then, is to feel somewhat detached from it. It is not an enemy, but not entirely a friend. Our essence seems to lie not in cells and muscles but in the traces our thoughts and actions inscribe on the air. The male body skims the surface of nature's deep, wherein the blood and pain and mysterious cravings of women perpetuate the species. Participating less in nature's processes than the female body, the male body gives the impression — false — of being exempt from time. Its powers of strength and reach descend in early adolescence, along with acne and sweaty feet, and depart, in imperceptible increments, after thirty or so. It surprises me to discover, when I remove my shoes and socks, the same paper-white hairless ankles that struck me as pathetic when I observed them on my father. I felt betrayed when, in some tumble of touch football twenty years ago, I heard my tibia snap; and when, between two reading engagements in Cleveland, my appendix tried to burst; and when, the other day, not for the first time, there arose to my nostrils out of my own body the musty attic smell my grandfather's body had.

A man's body does not betray its tenant as rapidly as a woman's. Never as fine and lovely, it has less distance to fall; what rugged beauty it has is wrinkle-proof. It keeps its capability of procreation indecently long. Unless intense athletic demands are made on it, the thing serves well enough to sixty, which is my age now. From here on, it's chancy. There are no breasts or ovaries to admit cancer to the male body, but the prostate, that awkwardly located little source of seminal fluid, shows the strain of sexual function with fits of hysterical cell replication, and all that beer and potato chips add up in the coronary arteries. A writer, whose physical equipment can be minimal, as long as it gets him to the desk, the lectern, and New York City once in a while, cannot but be grateful to his body, especially to his eyes, those tender and intricate sites where the brain extrudes from the skull, and to his hands, which hold the pen or tap the keyboard. His body has been, not himself exactly, but a close pal, pot-bellied and balding like most of his other pals now. A man and his body are like a boy and the buddy who has a driver's license and the use of his father's car for the evening; he goes along, gratefully, for the ride.

Joyce Carol Oates

....

They All Just Went Away

I MUST HAVE been a lonely child. Until the age of twelve or thirteen, my most intense, happiest hours were spent tramping desolate fields, woods, and creek banks near my family's farmhouse in Millersport, New York. No one knew where I went. My father, working most of the day at Harrison's, a division of General Motors in Lockport, and at other times preoccupied, would not have asked; if my mother asked, I might have answered in a way that would deflect curiosity. I was an articulate, verbal child. Yet I could not have explained what drew me to the abandoned houses, barns, silos, corncribs. A hike of miles through fields of spiky grass, across outcroppings of shale as steeply angled as stairs, was a lark if the reward was an empty house.

Some of these houses had been inhabited as "homes" fairly recently — they had not yet reverted to the wild. Others, abandoned during the Depression, had long since begun to rot and collapse, engulfed by vegetation (trumpet vine, wisteria, rose of Sharon, willow) that elsewhere, on our property for instance, was kept neatly trimmed. I was drawn to both kinds of houses, though the more recently inhabited were more forbidding and therefore more inviting.

To push open a door into such silence: the absolute emptiness of a house whose occupants have departed. Often, the crack of broken glass underfoot. A startled buzzing of flies, hornets. The slithering, ticklish sensation of a garter snake crawling across floorboards.

Left behind, as if in haste, were remnants of a lost household. A broken toy on the floor, a baby's bottle. A rain-soaked sofa, looking as if it

First published in *The New Yorker*, 1995; selected by Geoffrey C. Ward for *The Best American Essays 1996*.

has been gutted with a hunter's skilled knife. Strips of wallpaper like shredded skin. Smashed crockery, piles of tin cans; soda, beer, whiskey bottles. An icebox, its door yawning open. Once, on a counter, a dirt-stiffened rag that, unfolded like precious cloth, revealed itself to be a woman's cheaply glamorous "see-through" blouse, threaded with glitter-strips of gold.

This was a long time ago, yet it is more vivid to me than anything now.

This was when I was too young to think the house is the mother's body, you have been expelled and are forbidden now to reenter.

Always, I was prepared to see a face at a high, empty window. A woman's hand uplifted in greeting, or in warning. *Hello! Come in! Stay away! Run! Who are you?* A movement in the corner of my eye: the blurred motion of a person passing through a doorway, or glimpsed through a window. There might be a single shriek of laughter from a barn — piercing as a bird's cry. Murmurous, teasing voices confused with wind rippling through tall, coarse, gone-to-seed grass. Voices that, when you pause to listen, fade immediately and are gone.

The sky in such places of abandonment was always of the hue and brightness of tin, as if the melancholy rural poverty of tin roofs reflected upward.

A house: a structural arrangement of space, geometrically laid out to provide what are called rooms, these divided from one another by verticals and horizontals called walls, ceilings, floors. The house contains the home but is not identical with it. The house anticipates the home and will very likely survive it, reverting again simply to house when home (that is, life) departs. For only where there is life can there be home.

I have never found the visual equivalent of these abandoned farmhouses of upstate New York, of northern Erie County, in the area of the long, meandering Tonawanda Creek and the Barge Canal. You think most immediately of the canvases of Edward Hopper: those dreamily stylized visions of a lost America, houses never depicted as homes, and human beings, if you look closer, never depicted as other than mannequins. For Hopper is not a realist but a surrealist. His dreams are of the ordinary, as if, even in imagination, the artist were trapped in an unyielding daylight consciousness. There seems almost a kind of rage, a revenge against such restraints, in Hopper's studied, endlessly repeated *simplicity.* By contrast, Charles Burchfield, with his numerous oils and watercolors — frequently of upstate New York landscapes, houses, and farms — rendered the real as visionary and luminous, suffused with a Blakean rapture and a kind of radical simplicity, too. Then there are the shimmering New England barns, fields, and skies of our contemporary Wolf Kahn — images evoked by memory, almost on the verge of dissolution. But the "real" — what assaults the eye before the eye begins its work of selection — is never on the verge of dissolution, still less of appropriation. The real is raw, jarring, unexpected, sometimes trashy, sometimes luminous. Above all, the real is arbitrary. For to be a realist (in art or in life) is to acknowledge that all things might be other than they are. That there is no design, no intention, no aesthetic or moral or teleological imprimatur but, rather, the equivalent of Darwin's great vision of a blind, purposeless, ceaseless evolutionary process that yields no "products" — only temporary strategies against extinction.

Yet, being human, we think, To what purpose these broken-off things, if not to be gathered up, at last, in a single ecstatic vision?

There is a strange and profound and unknowable reality to these abandoned houses where jealously guarded, even prized possessions have become mere trash: windowpanes long ago smashed, and the spaces where they had been festooned with cobwebs, and cobwebs brushing against your face, catching in your hair like caresses. The peculiar, dank smell of wood rot and mildew, in one of the houses I most recall that had partly burned down, the smell of smoke and scorch, in early summer pervading even the lyric smell of honeysuckle — these haunting smells, never, at the time of experiencing, given specific sources, names.

Where a house has been abandoned — unworthy of being sold to new tenants, very likely seized by the county for default on taxes and the property held in escrow — you can be sure there has been a sad story. There have been devastated lives. Lives to be spoken of pityingly. How they went wrong. Why did she marry him, why did she stay with him? Just desperate people. Ignorant. Poor white trash. Runs in the family. A wrong turn.

Shall I say for the record that ours was a happy, close-knit, and unextraordinary family for our time, place, and economic status? Yet what was vividly real in the solid-built old farmhouse that contained my home (my family consisted of my father, mother, younger brother, grandfather, and grandmother, who owned the property — a slow-failing farm whose principal crop had become Bartlett pears by the time I was a girl) was of far less significance to me than what was real elsewhere. A gone-to-seed landscape had an authority that seemed to me incontestable: the powerful authority of silence in houses from which the human voice had vanished. For the abandoned house contained the future of any house — the lilac tree pushing through the rotted veranda, hornets' nests beneath eaves, windows smashed by vandals, human excrement left to dry on a parlor floor once scrubbed on hands and knees.

The abandoned, the devastated, was the profound experience, whereas involvement in family life — the fever, the bliss, the abrasions, the infinite distractions of human love — was so clearly temporary. Like a television screen upon which antic images (at this time, in the fifties, minimally varying gradations of gray) appear fleetingly and are gone.

I have seemed to suggest that the abandoned houses were all distant from our house, but in fact the one that had been partly gutted by fire — which I will call the Weidel house — was perhaps a half mile away. If you drove, turning right off Transit Road, which was our road, onto the old Creek Road, it would have been a distance of a mile or more, but if you crossed through our back potato field and through the marshy woods which no one seemed to own, it was a quick walk.

The Weidels' dog, Slossie, a mixed breed with a stumpy, energetic tail and a sweet disposition, sand-colored, rheumy-eyed, as hungry for affection as for the scraps we sometimes fed her, trotted over frequently to play with my brother and me. Though, strictly speaking, Slossie was not wanted at our house. None of the Weidels were wanted.

The "Weidel house," it would be called for years. The "Weidel property." As if the very land — which the family had not owned in any case, but only rented, partly with county-welfare support — were somehow imprinted with that name, a man's identity. Or infamy.

For tales were told of the father who drank, beat and terrorized his family, "did things to" his daughters, and finally set the house on fire and fled and was arrested, disappearing forever from the proper, decent life of our community. There was no romance in Mr. Weidel, whom my father knew only slightly and despised as a drinker, and as a wife- and child-beater. Mr. Weidel was a railway worker in Lockport, or perhaps an ex–railway worker, for he seemed to work only sporadically, though he always wore a railwayman's cap. He and his elder sons were hunters, owning a shotgun among them and one or two deer rifles. His face was broad, fair, vein-swollen, with a look of flushed, alcoholic reproach. He was tall and heavyset, with graying black whiskers that sprouted like quills. His eyes had a way of swerving in their sockets, seeking you out when you could not slip away quickly enough. *H'lo there, little Joyce! Joycie! Joycie Oates, h'lo!* He wore rubber boots that flapped, unbuckled, about his feet.

Mrs. Weidel was a faded-pretty, apologetic woman with a body that seemed to have become bloated, as with a perpetual pregnancy. Her bosom had sunk to her waist. Her legs were encased, sausagelike, in flesh-colored support hose. *How can that woman live with him? That pig.* There was disdain, disgust, in this frequent refrain. *Why doesn't she leave him? Did you see that black eye? Did you hear them the other night? Take the girls away, at least.* It was thought that she could, for Mrs. Weidel was the only one in the family who seemed to work at all regularly. She was hired for seasonal canning in a tomato factory in lower Lockport and may have done housecleaning in the city.

A shifting household of relatives and rumored "boarders" lived in the Weidel house. There were six Weidel children, four sons and two daughters. Ruth was a year older than I, and Dorothy two years younger. There was an older brother of Mr. Weidel's, who walked with a cane and was said to be an ex-convict, from Attica. The eldest Weidel son, Roy, owned a motorcycle, and friends of his often visited, fellow bikers. There were loud parties, frequent disputes, and tales of Mr. Weidel's chasing his wife with a butcher knife, a claw hammer, the shotgun, threatening to "blow her head off." Mrs. Weidel and the younger children fled outdoors in terror and hid in the hayloft. Sheriff's deputies drove out to the house, but no charges were ever pressed against Mr. Weidel. Until the fire, which was so public that it couldn't be denied.

There was the summer day — I was eleven years old — that Mr. Weidel shot Slossie. We heard the poor creature yelping and whimpering for what seemed like hours. When my father came home from work, he went to speak to Mr. Weidel, though my mother begged him not to. By this time, the dog had dragged herself beneath the Weidels' house to die. Mr. Weidel was furious at the intrusion, drunk, defensive — Slossie was his goddam dog, he said, she'd been getting in the way, she was "old." But my father convinced him to put the poor dog out of her misery. So Mr. Weidel made one of his sons drag Slossie out from beneath the house, and he straddled her and shot her a second time, and a third, at close range. My father, who'd never hunted, who'd never owned a gun, backed off, a hand over his eyes.

Afterward, my father would say of that day that walking away from that drunken son of a bitch with a rifle in his hands was about the hardest thing he'd ever done. He'd expected a shot between his shoulders.

The fire was the following year, around Thanksgiving.

After the Weidels were gone from Millersport and the house stood empty, I discovered Slossie's grave. I'm sure it was Slossie's grave. It was beyond the dog hutch, in the weedy back yard, a sunken patch of earth measuring about three feet by four with one of Mrs. Weidel's big whitewashed rocks at the head.

Morning glories grew in clusters on the posts of the front porch. Mrs. Weidel had planted hollyhocks, sunflowers, and trumpet vine in the yard. Tough, weedlike flowers that would survive for years.

It had been said of Ruth and her sister Dorothy that they were "slow." Yet Ruth was never slow to fly into a rage when she was teased by neighborhood boys or by her older brothers. She waved her fists and stammered obscenities, words that stung like hail. Her face darkened with blood, and her full, thick lips quivered with a strange sort of pleasure. How you loved to see Ruth Weidel fly into one of her rages; it was like holding a lighted match to flammable material.

The Weidel house was like any other rundown woodframe house, said by my grandfather to have been "thrown up" in the 1920s. It had no cellar, only a concrete-block foundation — an emptiness that gradually filled with debris. It had an upstairs with several small bedrooms. There was no attic. No insulation. Steep, almost vertical stairs. The previous tenant had started to construct a front porch of raw planks, never completed or painted. (Though Mrs. Weidel added "touches" to the porch — chairs, a woven-rush rug, geraniums in flowerpots.) The roof of the house was made of sheets of tin, scarred and scabbed like skin, and the front was covered in simulated-brick asphalt siding pieced together from lumberyard scraps. All year round, a number of the windows were covered in transparent duct tape and never opened. From a distance, the house was the fading dun color of a deer's winter coat.

Our house had an attic and a cellar and a deep well and a solid cement foundation. My father did all the carpentry on our house, most of the shingling, the painting, the masonry. I would not know until I was an adult that he'd come from what's called a "broken home" himself — what an image, luridly visual, of a house literally broken, split in two, its secrets spilled out onto the ground for all to see, like entrails.

My mother, unlike Mrs. Weidel, had time to houseclean. It was a continuous task, a mother's responsibility. My mother planted vegetables, strawberries, beds of flowers. Petunias and pansies and zinnias. Crimson peonies that flowered for my birthday, in mid-June.

I remember the night of the fire vividly, as if it had been a festive affair to which I'd been invited.

There was the sound of a siren on the Creek Road. There were shouts, and an astonishing burst of flame in the night, in the direction of the Weidel house. The air was moist, and reflected and magnified the fire, surrounding it like a nimbus. My grandparents would claim there had never been such excitement in Millersport, and perhaps that was true. My father dressed hurriedly and went to help the firefighters, and my mother and the rest of us watched from upstairs windows. The fire began at about 1 A.M., and it would be past 4 A.M. before my seven-year-old brother and I got back to bed.

Yet what was so exciting an event was, in fact, an ending, with nothing to follow. Immediately afterward, the Weidels disappeared from Millersport and from our lives. It was said that Mr. Weidel fled "as a fugitive" but was captured and arrested the next day, in Buffalo. The family was broken up, scattered, the younger children placed in foster homes. That quickly, the Weidels were gone.

For a long time, the smell of wood smoke, scorch, pervaded the air of Millersport, the fresh, damp smell of earth sullied by its presence. Neighbors complained that the Weidel house should be razed at the county's expense, bulldozed over, and the property sold. But nothing was done for years. Who knows why? When I went away to college, the old falling-down house was still there.

How swiftly, in a single season, a human habitation can turn wild. The bumpy cinder driveway over which the eldest Weidel son had ridden his motorcycle was soon stippled with tall weeds.

What had happened to Roy Weidel? It was said he'd joined the navy. No, he had a police record and could not have joined the navy. He'd disappeared. Asked by the police to give a sworn statement about the night of his father's "arson," he'd panicked and fled.

Signs were posted — NO TRESPASSING, THIS PROPERTY CONDEMNED BY ERIE CO. — and they, too, over a period of months, became shabby and faded. My parents warned me never to wander onto the Weidel property. There was a well with a loose-fitting cover, among other dangers. As if *I* would fall into a well! I smiled to think how little my parents knew me. How little anyone knew me.

Have I said that my father never struck his children, as Mr. Weidel struck his? And did worse things to them, to the girls sometimes, it was whispered. Yes, and Mrs. Weidel, who seemed so soft and apologetic and sad, she too had beaten the younger children when she'd been drinking. County social workers came around to question neighbors, and spread the story of what they learned along the way.

In fact, I may have been disciplined, spanked, a few times. Like most children, I don't remember. I remember Mr. Weidel spanking his children until they screamed (though I wasn't a witness, was I?), but I don't remember being spanked by my parents, and in any case, if I was, it was no more than I deserved.

I'd seen Mr. Weidel urinating once at the roadside. The loose-flying skein of the kerosene he'd flung around the house before setting the fire must have resembled the stream of his urine, transparent and glittering. But they laughed, saying Mr. Weidel had been too drunk, or too careless, to have done an adequate job of sprinkling kerosene through the downstairs of the house. Wasn't it like him, such a slovenly job. Only part of the house had burned, a wall of the kitchen and an adjoining woodshed.

Had Mr. Weidel wanted to burn his family alive in their beds? Mrs. Weidel testified no, they'd all been awake, they'd run out into the yard before the fire began. They'd never been in any danger, she swore. But Mr. Weidel was indicted on several counts of attempted murder, along with other charges.

For so many years the Weidel house remained standing. There was something defiant about it, like someone who has been mortally wounded but will not die. In the weedy front yard, Mrs. Weidel's display of whitewashed rocks and plaster-of-Paris gnomes and the clay pedestal with the shiny blue glass ball disappeared from view within a year or so. Brambles grew everywhere. I forced myself to taste a small bitter red berry but spat it out, it made my mouth pucker so.

What did it mean that Erie County had "condemned" the Weidel property? The downstairs windows were carelessly boarded over, and both the front and rear doors were unlocked, collapsing on their hinges. Broken glass underfoot and a sickish stench of burn, mildew, decay. Yet there were "touches" — on what remained of a kitchen wall, a Holstein calendar from a local feed store, a child's crayon drawing. Upstairs, children's clothes, socks and old shoes heaped on the floor. I recognized with a thrill of repugnance an old red sweater of Ruth's, angora-fuzzy. There were broken Christmas tree ornaments, a naked pink plastic doll.

Toppled bedsprings, filthy mattresses streaked with yellow and rust-colored stains. The mattresses looked as if they'd been gutted, their stuffing strewn about. The most terrible punishment, I thought, would be to be forced to lie down on such a mattress.

I thought of Mrs. Weidel, her swollen, blackened eyes, her bruised face. Shouts and sirens in the night, the sheriff's patrol car. But no charges filed. The social worker told my mother how Mrs. Weidel had screamed at the county people, insisting her husband hadn't done anything wrong and shouldn't go to jail. The names she'd called them! Unrepeatable.

She was the wife of that man, they'd had babies together. The law had no right to interfere. The law had nothing to do with them.

As a woman and as a writer, I have long wondered at the wellsprings of female masochism. Or what, in despair of a more subtle, less reductive phrase, we can call the congeries of predilections toward self-hurt, self-erasure, self-repudiation in women. These predilections are presumably "learned" — "acquired" — but perhaps also imprinted in our genes, of biological necessity, neurophysiological fate, predilections that predate culture. Indeed, may shape culture. Do not say, "Yes, but these are isolated, peripheral examples. These are marginal Americans, uneducated. They tell us nothing about ourselves." They tell us everything about ourselves, and even the telling, the exposure, is a kind of cutting, an inscription in the flesh.

Yet what could possibly be the evolutionary advantage of self-hurt in the female? Abnegation in the face of another's cruelty? Acquiescence to another's will? This loathsome secret that women do not care to speak of, or even acknowledge.

Two or three years later, in high school, twelve miles away in a consolidated district school to which, as a sophomore, I went by school bus, Ruth Weidel appeared. She was living now with relatives in Lockport. She looked, at sixteen, like a woman in her twenties; big-breasted, with full, strong thighs and burnished-brown hair inexpertly bleached. Ruth's homeroom was "special education," but she took some classes with the rest of us. If she recognized me, in our home economics class, she was careful to give no sign.

There was a tacit understanding that "something had happened" to Ruth Weidel, and her teachers treated her guardedly. Ruth was special, the way a handicapped person is special. She was withdrawn, quiet; if still prone to violent outbursts of rage, she might have been on medication to control it. Her eyes, like her father's, seemed always about to swerve in their sockets. Her face was round, fleshy, like a pudding, her nose oily-pored. Yet she wore lipstick, she was "glamorous" — almost. In gym class, Ruth's large breasts straining against her T-shirt and the shining rippled muscles and fatty flesh of her thighs were amazing to us; we were so much thinner and less female, so much younger.

I believed that I should protect Ruth Weidel, so I told none of the other students about her family. Even to Ruth, for a long time I pretended not to know who she was. I can't explain how Ruth could have possibly believed me, yet this seems to have been so. Quite purposefully, I befriended Ruth. I thought her face would lose its sallow hardness if she could be made to smile, and so it became a kind of challenge to me to induce Ruth Weidel to smile. She was lonely and miserable at school, and flattered by my attention. For so few "normal" girls sought out "specialed" girls. At first she may have been suspicious, but by degrees she became trusting. I thought of Slossie: trust shows in the eyes.

I sat with Ruth at lunch in the school cafeteria and eventually I asked her about the house on the old Creek Road, and she lied bluntly, to my face, insisting that an uncle of hers had owned that house. She'd only visited a few times. She and her family. I asked, "How did the fire start?" and Ruth said, slowly, each word sucked like a pebble in the mouth, "Lightning. Lightning hit it. One night in a storm." I asked, "Are you living with your mother now, Ruth?" and Ruth shrugged, and made a face, and said, "She's OK. I see her sometimes." I asked about Dorothy. I asked where Mrs. Weidel was. I said that my mother had always liked her mother, and missed her when she went away. But Ruth seemed not to hear. Her gaze had drifted. I said, "Why did you all move away?" Ruth did not reply, though I could hear her breathing hard. "Why did you abandon your house? It could have been fixed. It's still there. Your mom's hollyhocks are still there. You should come out and see it sometime. You could visit me." Ruth shrugged, and laughed. She gave me a sidelong glance, almost flirtatiously. It was startling to see how good-looking she could be, how sullen-sexy; to know how men would stare at her who would never so much as glance at a girl like me. Ruth said slowly, as if she'd come to a final, adamant conclusion to a problem that had long vexed her, "They all just went away."

Another time, after lunch with Ruth, I left a plastic change purse with a few coins in it on the ledge in one of the girls' lavatories, where Ruth was washing her hands. I don't recall whether I left it on purpose or not.

But when I returned, after waiting for Ruth to leave the lavatory, the change purse was gone.

Once or twice, I invited Ruth Weidel to come home with me on the school bus some afternoon, to Millersport, to have supper with my family and stay the night. I must not have truly believed she might accept, for my mother would have been horrified and would have forced me to rescind the invitation. Ruth had hesitated, as if she wanted to say yes, wanted very badly to say yes, but finally she said, "No. I guess I better not."

Saul Bellow

Graven Images

HARRY S. TRUMAN liked to say that as president of this country he was its most powerful citizen — but sometimes he added, smiling, the photographers were even more powerful. They could tell the commander in chief where to go, make him move his chair, cross his legs, hold up a letter, order him to smile or to look stern. He acknowledged their power and, as a political matter, deferred to their judgment. What the people thought of their chief executive would to some extent be decided by the photographers and the picture editors. Photographers may claim to be a priesthood interpreting the laws of light, and light is a universal mystery that the picture takers measure with their light meters. "In nature's book of infinite mystery, a little I can read," says the Egyptian soothsayer in *Antony and Cleopatra*. Pictures taken in the light must be developed in the shallow mystery of darkrooms. But photographers have nothing in common with soothsayers. Their interests, apart from the technical one, are social and political. To some extent, it is they who decide how you are to be publicly seen. Your "visual record" is in their hands.

Broadly speaking, your *amour propre* is the territory invaded by the picture takers. You may wish or not wish to be in public life. Some people have not the slightest desire to be in the papers or on TV. Others feel that papers and TV screens confer immortality. TV crews on a city street immediately attract big crowds. The arrival of television cameras offers people the opportunity each and every one of them has dreamt of

First published in *News from the Republic of Letters*, 1997; selected by Cynthia Ozick for *The Best American Essays 1998*.

— a shot at eternity. Not by deeds, not by prayers, but solely by their faces, grinning and mugging.

But this aspect of modern image-making or idolatry is not, for me, the most interesting one. What I discover when I search my soul is that I have formed a picture of myself as I wish to be seen, and that while photographers are setting up their lights and cameras I am summoning up and fortifying that picture. My intent is to triumph over the photographers' vision of me — their judgment as to what my place in photographic reality is to be. They have *technics* — Science — on their side. On my side there is vanity and deceit — there is, as I have already said, *amour propre;* there is, moreover, a nagging sense that my powers of candor are weakening and sagging, and that my face betrays how heavily it is mortgaged to death. *Amour propre,* with all its hypocritical tricks, is the product of your bourgeois outlook. Your aim is to gain general acceptance for your false self, to make propaganda, concealing your real motives — motives of personal advantage. You persuade people to view you as you need to be viewed if you are to put it over on them. We all are, insofar as we live for our *amour propre,* loyal to nothing except our secret, crippled objectives — the objectives of every "civilized" man.

Et cetera.

Yes, we're all too familiar with *amour propre,* thanks to the great romantic writers of the nineteenth century. But give clever people something to understand and you can count on them to understand it. So in facing the photographers it's not the exposure of my *amour propre* that concerns me. What I feel in making innumerable last-minute ego arrangements is that the real me will decide to withhold itself. I know that the best picture instruments of Germany or "state-of-the-art" Japan are constructed for ends very different from mine. What need is there to bring these powerful lenses up to the very tip of my nose? They will meaninglessly enlarge the pores of my skin. You will supply them with shots that remind viewers of the leg of a mosquito photographed through a microscope. The truth about you is that you have lost more hair than you thought and that your scalp is shining through — the truth is that you have huge paisley-shaped bruises under your eyes and that your bridgework when you smile is far from "photogenic." You are not simply shown — you are exposed. This exposure cannot be prevented. One can only submit to the merciless cruelty of "pure objectivity," which is so hard on your illusions.

Then, too, from a contemporary point of view, the daily and weekly papers — to say nothing of television — do not feel that they are honoring the truth if they do not tear away the tatters of vanity that cover our imperfections. No one is safe from exposure except the owners, the main stockholders, and the leading advertisers of the great national papers. Things weren't always like this. The "gentlemen" described by Aristotle are immune to shame — they are made that way; nothing shameful can touch these aristocrats. But Adam and Eve, when they had eaten the apple of self-consciousness, sewed fig leaves together to cover their nakedness.

It is the (not always conscious) premise of the photographer that his is the art of penetrating your private defenses. We, his subjects, can learn not to care. But we are not by any means an Aristotelian class, trained in the virtues. We are democrats and lead our petty lives in the shadow of shame. And for this as for all our weaknesses and vices there arise, in all civilized countries, entire classes of people, categories of specialists who specialize in *discovery* and exposure.

Their slogan is: Let the Record Show. And what the record shows is, of course, change and decay, instability, weakness and infirmity, darkness as endless and winding as the Malabar Caves as E. M. Forster years ago described them in *A Passage to India*.

A photograph that made me look worse than the Ruins of Athens was published by *Time* together with a line from William Blake: "The lineaments of gratified desire." Nowhere in the novel *Time* was reviewing had I so much as hinted that my face, with its lineaments, was anything like the faces Blake had in mind (faces of prostitutes, as his text explicitly tells us). But there was my dreary, sullen, tired, and aging mug. I was brought low by Blake's blazing words. But it is the prerogative of the mass media to bring you down when they think that you have gotten ahead of yourself — when they suspect you of flying too high. It doesn't damage us to be exposed, to appear in distorted shapes on film or slick paper or newsprint. I often remember how at the age of ninety-nine Freud's grandmother complained that in the paper "they made me look a hundred years old."

But picture editors and journalists often seem to feel that they are the public representatives of truth, and even that they are conferring some sort of immortality on you by singling you out. But you had better be prepared for rough treatment. Often your "privacy" is to them a cover for the lies and manipulations of *amour propre*.

Who would have thought that minor vanities might lead to such vexations. Your secrets will die in the glare of publicity. When the police strip Dimitri Karamazov to his foul underpants, he says to them, "Gentlemen, you have sullied my soul."

But the world has undergone a revolutionary transformation. Such simple, romantic standards of personal dignity and of the respect due to privacy are to be found today only in remote corners of backward countries. Maybe in the Pyrenees or in the forgotten backlands of Corsica — places where I shouldn't care to live. Everywhere else, the forces of insight are on the lookout. The function of their insights is to make your secrets public, for the public has a right to know, and it is the duty of journalists to deliver the secrets of people "in the news" to their readers. For every story has a story behind it — which is to say that your face, in its own way a story, the story that you present, has another, sometimes very different story underlying it, and it is through the skill of the photographer that these layers of story are revealed.

Painters and sculptors, whose publics are smaller, also approach our heads and faces with insight. They class themselves as artists and are more intellectually sophisticated — better educated than photographers. They have generally absorbed a certain amount of twentieth-century psychology, and their portraits may be filled or formed by their ideas and they may have a diagnostic intent. Do you want to know whether X, our subject, is a violent narcissist? Or whether his is a real, a human face, not a false ideological mask or disguise.

The photograph — to narrow it down — reduces us to two dimensions and it makes us small enough to be represented on a piece of paper or a frame of film. We have been trained by the camera to see the external world. We look *at* and not *into*, as one philosopher has put it. We do not allow ourselves to be *drawn* into what we see. We have been trained to go by the externals. The camera shows us only those, and it is we who do the rest. What we do this *with* is the imagination. What photographs have to show us is the external appearance of objects or beings in the real world, and this is only a portion of their reality. It is after all a convention.

I have known — and still know — many excellent photographers whose work I respect. There are demonic, sadistic camera technicians, too. All trades are like that. But neither the kindly nor the wicked ones can show us the realities we so hope — or long — to see.

Finally, there is the ancient Jewish rule forbidding graven images. My maternal grandfather refused to have his picture taken. But when he was dying my mother brought in a photographer and hid him behind the bushes.

This faded picture is one of my Old World legacies. I also inherited the brass family samovar and my mother's silver change purse. In this purse I now carry Betapace, Hytrin, and Coumadin tablets.

My grandfather's picture was taken in the late 1890s. He is sitting, dying in an apple orchard, his beard is spread over his upper body. His elbow rests on the top of his walking stick and his hand supports his head. His big eyes tell you that he is absorbed in *olam ha-bo* — the world to come, the next life. My mother used to say, "He would have been very angry with me. To make pictures was sinful [an *averah*], but I took the *averah* on myself."

When we were very young, my parents told us that until we came of age they would be responsible for our transgressions. But that is an altogether different matter. What I am saying here is that nowadays not even the nobs have their portraits painted, and the masses preserve the faces of ancestors in daguerreotypes and Kodaks. The critical mind sees an insignificant photographer hidden in the bushes, inserting a plate and pulling the cloth over his head. Perhaps the old man knew perfectly well that his picture was being taken. My mother was then old enough to bear the burden of this sin. She committed it because she loved him and was afraid of forgetting what he had looked like.

In any case, I have been not only photographed but cast in bronze and also painted. Since I am too impatient to sit still, painters and sculptors have worked from photographs. The Chicago Public Library exhibits the busts of bookish local boys. The artist who did my head was obliged to measure it while I was watching the Chicago Bulls on television. It was an important game and I didn't intend to miss it.

Considering the bronze head on display in the Harold Washington Library, I think that Pablo Picasso would have done it better. He might perhaps have given me a third eye and two noses. I'd have loved two noses.

But for a one-nose job, the bust in the Chicago library isn't at all bad.

Biographical Notes

The great-grandson of John Adams and grandson of John Quincy Adams, the prominent Bostonian **Henry Adams** (1838–1918) did not follow their illustrious paths to the U.S. presidency. Instead, he devoted himself to writing, producing several multivolume histories of the nation, an enormous quantity of political journalism, and two novels. He is best known today for two nonfiction works (both privately printed) that grew out of his scientific theory of history, *Mont-Saint-Michel and Chartres* (1904) and *The Education of Henry Adams* (1907), a third-person autobiography that imagines Americans in the year 2000 while pursuing one of the earliest investigations into ideas of chaos and complexity. Having moved to Washington in 1877 with his wife (who committed suicide in 1885, an incident not mentioned in the autobiography), Adams quickly became an "insider," forming acquaintances with practically every president until his death at age eighty. See *Henry Adams: Novels, Mont-Saint-Michel, The Education* (ed. Ernest and Jayne N. Samuels, 1983).

One of the few women ever to receive the Nobel Peace Prize, **Jane Addams** (1860–1935) was born into a prominent family in Cedarville, Illinois. She opened the internationally renowned Hull-House in 1889 on Chicago's West Side, where she became head resident and one of the nation's leading social reformers, spearheading movements for civil rights, the first juvenile court laws, and labor legislation while supporting a host of feminist and pacifist causes. In 1896, as she recalls in her memoir *Twenty Years at Hull-House* (1910), she traveled to Russia to seek Leo Tolstoy's spiritual counsel. Found working as usual in the hayfields with the peasants, the count at once embarrassed her by pulling out one of the big sleeves of her fashionable traveling gown, saying it contained enough fabric to make a smock for a little girl. Tolerating this and other discrediting jibes during the encounter, Addams returned to her demanding schedule at Hull-House, concluding that strict adherence to Tolstoy's philosophy would be counterproductive and "utterly preposterous." Her thirteen books include *Democracy and Social Ethics* (1902), *A New Conscience and an Ancient Evil* (1912), *The Long Road of Woman's Memory* (1916), and *The Second Twenty Years at Hull-House* (1930).

Born in Knoxville, Tennessee, **James Agee** (1909–1955) would retain the spiritual and moral values he learned at St. Andrew's, his Tennessee Episcopal school, through Phillips Exeter Academy and then Harvard, where he edited *The Advocate*. Shortly after he joined *Fortune* magazine, he published a prize-winning volume of poetry, *Permit Me Voyage* (1934), and the following year journeyed with the photographer Walker Evans to Hale County, Alabama, on assignment to cover southern sharecropping. They immersed themselves in the daily lives of three families, and afterward Agee submitted perhaps the most richly textured, lyrical, experimental prose report of laborers that the editors of *Fortune* had ever seen. Though the "article" was killed, Agee continued to develop his new forms of writing and observation into a documentary classic, *Let Us Now Praise Famous Men* (1941). Agee also loved film: he served as a regular movie reviewer for *Time* and *The Nation* and is credited with such well-known screenplays as *The African Queen* (1952) and *Night of the Hunter* (1955). *A Death in the Family*, a novel about his father's death (when Agee was six), appeared in 1957, two years after its forty-six-year-old author died suddenly of a massive heart attack.

Maya Angelou (born Marguerite Annie Johnson in 1928) has achieved success as a poet, dramatist, dancer, singer, memoirist, composer, actress, and journalist, winning prestigious awards in nearly all of these endeavors. She was never more in the public eye, however, than when she read her poem "On the Pulse of Morning" at President Clinton's inauguration in 1993. Born in St. Louis, Angelou spent much of her childhood in Stamps, Arkansas, a troubled period she records in *I Know Why the Caged Bird Sings* (1970), a National Book Award nominee, which James Baldwin praised as the "beginning of a new era in the minds and hearts of all black men and women." After high school in San Francisco, she joined a cast of *Porgy and Bess* in 1954 for a twenty-two-nation tour and then performed in several Off-Broadway plays, having moved to Brooklyn. There, encouraged by Baldwin, she began writing about her childhood. Angelou's other memoirs are *Gather Together in My Name* (1974), *Singin' and Swingin' and Gettin' Merry Like Christmas* (1976), *The Heart of a Woman* (1981), and *All God's Children Need Traveling Shoes* (1985). *The Complete Collected Poems of Maya Angelou* appeared in 1994 and an essay collection, *Even the Stars Look Lonesome*, in 1997. Angelou received a Tony Award nomination in 1977 for best supporting actress in *Roots*.

For **James Baldwin** (1924–1987), writing an essay was (to borrow from William James) the "moral equivalent of war." But unlike war, the writer realizes that "a slogan is only a slogan" and must "insist on complexity which people in the battle don't want to think about." Contention and complexity inform all of Baldwin's writing, as he passionately and fearlessly tried to purge from American consciousness what he considered two closely linked, deep-rooted evils: white racism and ingrained puritanism. Born in Harlem, he grew up resisting the inflexible fundamentalism of his stepfather, a fire-and-brimstone lay preacher, memorably portrayed, along with Baldwin's own temporary religious conversion, in his first novel, *Go Tell It on the Mountain* (1953). Baldwin began writing in 1942, soon after high school, and with Richard Wright's help (another "influence" Baldwin would break with), found publishers and fellowships to advance his career. Increasingly distressed over racism and homophobia, he followed Wright to Paris in 1948 and traveled throughout Europe. He settled there permanently, though he visited the United States frequently, especially during the height of the civil rights movement. Besides six other novels, Baldwin published several collections of essays that rank among the century's most important: *Notes of a Native Son* (1955), *Nobody Knows My Name* (1961), and *The Fire Next Time* (1963). A comprehensive collection, *The Price of the Ticket: Collected Nonfiction, 1948–1985* (1985), appeared two years before Baldwin died of stomach cancer in France.

Throughout his fiction, **Saul Bellow** — winner of the Nobel Prize for literature in 1976 — has chronicled the anxieties of displacement and dislocation that have characterized so much of twentieth-century civilization. Bellow was born (1915) in the small town of Lachine in the province of Quebec, the child of religious Jewish immigrants from St. Petersburg, Russia, who moved to Chicago when Bellow was nine. He attended the University of Chicago but completed his degree in the social sciences at Northwestern in 1937. He gave up graduate work in anthropology at the University of Wisconsin because "every time I worked on my thesis, it turned out to be a story." While with the "Great Books" project at the *Encyclopaedia Britannica* in Chicago, Bellow published his first novel, *Dangling Man*, in 1944. He has since won three National Book Awards and a Pulitzer Prize for such novels as *The Adventures of Augie March* (1953), *Seize the Day* (1956), *Henderson the Rain King* (1958), *Herzog* (1964), *Mr. Sammler's Planet* (1970), *Humboldt's Gift* (1975), *More Die of Heartbreak* (1987), and *Ravelstein* (2000). Bellow has held numerous university positions, serving as a member of the Committee on Social Thought at the University of Chicago from 1962 until 1993, when he became a professor of English at Boston University. The author of several short story volumes, Bellow collected some of his favorite essays in 1994 in *It All Adds Up: From the Dim Past to the Uncertain Future.*

Born into a middle-class family in Bloomfield, New Jersey, **Randolph Bourne** (1886–1918) never experienced a normal, comfortable life. The victim of what he called a "terribly messy birth" (his face twisted and ear disfigured by a doctor's forceps), at age four he contracted spinal tuberculosis, which left him dwarfed and hunchbacked. But these disabilities never dampened his enthusiasm for life, love, music, youth, radicalism, and friendship — all of which became important topics of his essays. Family misfortunes forced him to take a variety of jobs for six years until he could attend Columbia, where he studied with the philosopher and educator John Dewey, embroiled himself in one controversy after another, and began writing a series of personal essays for *The Atlantic Monthly*, collected in 1913 as *Youth and Life*. Bourne spent his final years covering progressive education and fiercely opposing America's participation in the First World War, developing the motto "War is the health of the State." He died at thirty-two, one of the twenty million victims worldwide of the 1918 influenza epidemic. See *History of a Literary Radical* (ed. Van Wyck Brooks, 1920; 1956); a generous selection of essays can be found in *Randolph Bourne: The Radical Will* (ed. Olaf Hansen, 1977).

Rachel Carson (1907–1964) abandoned her childhood idea of becoming a poet when she fell in love with the biological sciences at the Pennsylvania College for Women. A rare combination of scientific observation and poetic sensibility resulted in some of the century's most impressive nature writing. Carson completed an M.A. in zoology at Johns Hopkins in 1932 and while working as an aquatic biologist for the U.S. Bureau of Fisheries wrote a lyrical introduction to an official brochure that her supervisor rejected but suggested she send to *The Atlantic Monthly,* which published it in 1937 ("From those four *Atlantic* pages," she wrote, "everything else followed"). The essay established the basis for her first book, *Under the Sea-Wind* (1941), which was succeeded by the National Book Award winner *The Sea Around Us* (1952). *The Edge of the Sea* (1954) completed the best-selling "sea trilogy." Carson, who considered herself more of a writer than a reformer, would have preferred to be remembered for these elegantly composed and superbly textured books, but instead she is popularly known for her fourth bestseller, *Silent Spring* (1962), a devastating attack on pesticides that helped launch the modern environmental movement and that Justice William O. Douglas called "the most important chronicle of this century for the human race." Two years later, Carson died at her Maryland home of breast cancer at age fifty-six.

John Jay Chapman (1862–1933), called by Gore Vidal "America's greatest essayist after Emerson," was born in New York City, the son of a New York Stock Exchange president. Named after his illustrious ancestor John Jay, the first chief justice of the United States, Chapman graduated from Harvard in 1884, where he acquired a heavy dose of Emersonian individualism and formed friendships with such Cambridge intellectuals as William James. He joined Theodore Roosevelt in his city reform movement and for more than a decade experienced the turbulence of hardnosed urban politics. Chapman could be irascible and offensive: at a party he cruelly beat a young man with a stick for paying too much attention to his future wife and afterward in a fit of guilt plunged his left hand into a fire for so long that it had to be amputated. He practiced law until 1898, when he published *Emerson and Other Essays* and decided on a literary career. His twenty-five volumes of plays, poems, translations, and nonfiction include a biography of the abolitionist William Lloyd Garrison (1913; 1921), *Memories and Milestones* (1915), *Greek Genius and Other Essays* (1915), and *Letters and Religion* (1924). He also wrote movingly of his son, the first American pilot to die in World War I. See *The Selected Writings of John Jay Chapman* (ed. Jacques Barzun, 1957) and *Unbought Spirit: A John Jay Chapman Reader* (ed. Richard Stone, 1998).

As a teenager, **Joan Didion** typed out Hemingway's short stories "to learn," as she put it, "how the sentences worked." Born (1934) in Sacramento, California, Didion honed her writing skills while majoring in English at Berkeley, graduating in 1956, shortly after she won *Vogue* magazine's Prix de Paris with an essay on local architecture. She wrote features and film criticism for *Vogue* but after the publication of her first novel, *River Run* (1963), and her marriage to the writer John Gregory Dunne (together they've written several successful screenplays), Didion returned to California, where the two contributed columns to *The Saturday Evening Post.* Her pieces formed the basis of her collection *Slouching Towards Bethlehem* (1968), a landmark in the history of the twentieth-century American essay. The volume was an attempt "to come to terms with disorder" (notably the chaos of the 1960s), an exploration Didion continued in *The White Album* (1979), a collection nominated for both the American Book Award and the National Book Critics Circle Award. Didion's novels include *Play It as It Lays* (1970), *A Book of Common Prayer* (1977), and *Democracy* (1984). A regular contributor to *The New York Review of Books*, in which she writes on politics and culture, Didion has published several other books of nonfiction: *Salvador* (1983), *Miami* (1987), and *After Henry: Sentimental Journeys* (1992).

A writer who cares deeply about the art and craft of the essay, **Annie Dillard** pointedly noted in *Teaching a Stone to Talk* (1982) that "this is not a collection of occasional pieces, such as a writer brings out to supplement his real work; instead this is my real work, such as it is." Born (1945) in Pittsburgh, where through childhood reading she formed an intense and detailed love of the natural world, Dillard received her B.A. and M.A. at rural Hollins College, in Roanoke, Virginia. There she kept the journal of natural and spiritual observations that would crystallize into the Pulitzer Prize–winning *Pilgrim at Tinker Creek* (1974). In 1979 she began teaching at Wesleyan University in Connecticut. She is the author of several poetry collections; a novel, *The Living* (1992); a metaphysical reflection, *Holy the Firm* (1977); a book of criticism, *Living by Fiction* (1982); a travel narrative, *Encounters with Chinese Writers* (1985); a memoir, *An American Childhood* (1987); a book about her chosen profession, *The Writing Life* (1989); and a collection of essays on theological themes, *For the Time Being* (1999). A good introduction to her work is *The Annie Dillard Reader* (1994). She served as the guest editor of *The Best American Essays 1988*.

The first African American to earn a doctoral degree from Harvard, **W(illiam) E(dward) B(urghardt) Du Bois** (1868–1963) wrote *The Souls of Black Folk* (1903) to "show the strange meaning of being black here in the dawning of the Twentieth Century." With *Souls* Du Bois wanted simultaneously to articulate a black consciousness and to expand the limits of the essay. He considered the book "a series of fourteen essays written under various circumstances and for different purposes during a period of seven years . . . There are bits of history and biography, some description of scenes and persons, something of controversy and criticism, some statistics and a bit of storytelling." The last refers to "Of the Coming of John," an essay-parable that Du Bois called "a tale twice told but seldom written." His many volumes of history, essays, and fiction include *The Gift of Black Folk: The Negroes in the Making of America* (1924) and *Black Reconstruction in America* (1935). Du Bois, who was born and raised in Great Barrington, Massachusetts, died a citizen of Ghana at the age of ninety-five, a day before Martin Luther King, Jr., delivered his famous "I Have a Dream" speech. For additional essays and nonfiction, see *W.E.B. Du Bois: Writings* (ed. Nathan I. Huggins, 1986) and *The Souls of Black Folk* (ed. David W. Blight and Robert Gooding-Williams, 1997).

An essayist, scholar, and wide-ranging cultural critic, **Gerald Early** was born (1952) in Philadelphia, where he graduated from the University of Pennsylvania in 1974.

Early received his Ph.D. from Cornell in 1982 and took a teaching position at Washington University in St. Louis, where he is the Merle S. Kling Professor of Modern Letters and director of Afro-American studies. His personal essays and writings on jazz, sports, and culture earned him both a Whiting Foundation Writer's Award and a General Electric Foundation Award for Younger Writers in 1988. His books include *Tuxedo Junction: Essays on American Culture* (1989), *The Culture of Bruising: Essays on Literature, Prizefighting, and Modern American Culture* (1994), which won the National Book Critics Circle Award in criticism, *Daughters: On Family and Fatherhood* (1994), and *One Nation Under a Groove: Motown and American Culture* (1995). Early has contributed essays, reviews, and poetry to a large number of periodicals, such as *The Nation, Harper's Magazine, The Antioch Review, Callaloo, Kenyon Review, Civilization,* and *Hungry Mind Review.* Among the anthologies he has edited on literature, race, and sports are *Lure and Loathing: Essays on Race, Identity, and the Ambivalence of Assimilation* (1993), *The Muhammad Ali Reader* (1998), and a two-volume collection of African American essays, *Speech and Power* (1992).

Educated at Bennington College, the UCLA film school, and the New School for Social Research in New York City, **Gretel Ehrlich** began her career as a filmmaker and published her first volume of poetry in 1970. Born (1946) and raised in California, Ehrlich traveled to Wyoming in 1976 to film a documentary on sheepherders, an experience that proved creatively and professionally pivotal. Falling in love with the land, she moved to Wyoming, where she learned sheep ranching and began composing the journal notes that would form the basis of her award-winning collection of essays *The Solace of Open Spaces* (1985). "The truest art I would strive for in any work," she writes in the book's preface, "would be to give the page the same qualities as earth: weather would land on it harshly; light would elucidate the most difficult truths; wind would sweep away obtuse padding." Besides several volumes of poetry, a collection of short stories (with Edward Hoagland), and a novel about a World War II Wyoming detention camp for Japanese Americans, *Heart Mountain* (1988), her nonfiction books include the essay collection *Islands, the Universe, Home* (1991), *Questions of Heaven: The Chinese Journeys of an American Buddhist* (1997), and her autobiographical account of being almost killed by lightning, *A Match to the Heart* (1994).

A leading scientist and head of the anthropology department of the University of Pennsylvania from 1947 to 1962, **Loren Eiseley** (1907–1977) was born in Lincoln, Nebraska, into a family of original homesteaders. Eiseley survived the scars of a lonely, reclusive, anxious childhood and, after several troubled years of "bumming about" the West, graduated from the University of Nebraska in 1933, receiving his Ph.D. four years later from the University of Pennsylvania. While writing poetry, Eiseley also contributed many scholarly articles to professional publications. As he reached a wider public in *Harper's Magazine, The American Scholar,* and *Scientific American,* he experimented with nonfiction forms, developing the "concealed essay," a creative approach that allowed him to combine his scientific and literary goals and that led to his first book, *The Immense Journey* (1957). Along with several volumes of poetry and studies of natural history, Eiseley's books include the following collections of essays: *The Firmament of Time* (1960), *The Unexpected Universe* (1969), *The Night Country* (1971), and *The Star Thrower* (1978). His haunting autobiography, *All the Strange Hours: The Excavation of a Life* (1975), appeared two years before his death from cancer.

T(homas) S(tearns) Eliot (1888–1965) was born in St. Louis, where his grandfather founded Washington University. He studied literature and philosophy at Harvard, completing his doctoral dissertation but not his degree, having by then moved to England with the intention of pursuing a literary career. The decision caused much family distress, which Eliot then compounded by marrying impulsively in 1915. In desperate need of income, he took a full-time bank position and supplemented his salary with evening lectures and literary reviews. Suffering from constant fatigue and acute depression, he managed, despite a series of nervous collapses, both to succeed at the bank and to establish himself as a leading poet and literary critic, publishing between 1917 and 1920 three volumes of poetry (which included "The Love Song of J. Alfred Prufrock") and a collection of criticism, *The Sacred Wood*. It contained "Tradition and the Individual Talent" — called "quite possibly the most widely anthologized literary essay of the twentieth century" — written around the time he began contemplating the long poem that would become *The Waste Land* (1922). Eliot became a British subject in 1927, an editor at Faber & Faber in 1935, and the recipient of the Nobel Prize for literature in 1948. Although his poetic output was relatively small, he published more than twenty-five books of literary, social, and cultural criticism; they include *Selected Essays* (1932), *The Use of Poetry and the Use of Criticism* (1933), *After Strange Gods* (1934), *Notes Toward a Definition of Culture* (1948), and *The Three Voices of Poetry* (1953). See *Selected Prose* (ed. Frank Kermode, 1975).

A cultural hero of the heady era he labeled "the Jazz Age," **F(rancis) Scott (Key) Fitzgerald** (1896–1940) was born in St. Paul, Minnesota, to prominent, affluent parents — his father supplying the "breeding" and his mother the "money." In 1917 Fitzgerald conveniently left Princeton University, where he performed poorly, to accept an infantry commission. At Fort Leavenworth (Dwight David Eisenhower captained his platoon) he began *This Side of Paradise* (1920), an autobiographical college novel that earned him instant fame and money, enabling him to elevate his infatuation with Zelda Sayre into one of American literature's most publicized and tumultuous marriages. Though his reputation rests largely on *The Great Gatsby* (1925), Fitzgerald wrote nearly two hundred short stories, many essays, and — as his health and finances deteriorated — collaborated on numerous screenplays, including a stint on *Gone with the Wind*. Fitzgerald died suddenly of a heart attack in Hollywood at the age of forty-four. See *The Crack-Up* (edited by Fitzgerald's friend Edmund Wilson, 1945).

Named after the Confederate general, **Robert (Lee) Frost** (1874–1963) was born in San Francisco, where his Harvard-educated father edited a newspaper and unsuccessfully dabbled in politics. When his father died in 1885, the family reclaimed its New England roots, moving, with the help of Frost's grandfather, to Lawrence, Massachusetts, where Frost performed brilliantly in high school, sharing honors with his future wife. Higher education at Dartmouth and then Harvard (reading William James was his "greatest inspiration") was short-lived, though Frost would later acquire so many honorary degrees he had patchwork quilts designed out of all his academic hoods. Success came slowly: after years of farming and teaching, Frost moved at the age of thirty-eight with his wife and four children to England, desperately hoping to launch a literary career. The plan worked. Frost published his first two volumes of poetry, *A Boy's Will* (1913) and *North of Boston* (1914), to such acclaim that he quickly found an American publisher and returned to the States as a leading poet courted by universities and the lecture circuit. Although Frost's family life remained deeply troubled by infant deaths, insanity, depression, and suicide, his literary reputation flourished steadily and culminated in a popularity no other serious American poet has ever experienced. Known primarily for his poetry, Frost nevertheless wrote many pithy, memorable essays. See *Robert Frost: Collected Poems, Prose, and Plays* (ed. Richard Poirier and Mark S. Richardson, 1995) and *The Collected Prose of Robert Frost* (ed. Mark S. Richardson, 1993).

Born (1924) in Fargo, North Dakota, **William H(oward) Gass** grew up in Warren, Ohio, and graduated from Kenyon College in 1947, after serving two years as an ensign in the U.S. Navy. He received a Ph.D. in philosophy from Cornell in 1954, specializing in the theory of metaphor, and then taught philosophy at Purdue from 1954 to 1969, when he moved to Washington University in St. Louis, where in 1979 he became David May Distinguished University Professor in the Humanities. Interested primarily in language and aesthetics, Gass began writing difficult fiction; he said of his first book, the novel *Omensetter's Luck* (1966), that he wrote it "to *not* have readers, while still deserving them." His essays make similar demands on readers and have been collected in *Fiction and the Figures of Life* (1970), *The World Within the Word* (1978), and the National Book Critics Circle Award winners *Habitations of the Word* (1985) and *Finding a Form* (1996). The influence of Gertrude Stein (and her notion of "pure composition") can be seen in his philosophical meditation *On Being Blue* (1976). Gass has also published several volumes of fiction, including the well-known *In the Heart of the Heart of the Country* (1968) and a long-awaited novel, *The Tunnel* (1995).

Stephen Jay Gould is the best-known American scientist on the topic of evolution. Born (1941) in New York City, Gould studied geology at Antioch College in Ohio and received a Ph.D. from Columbia in 1967, the same year he began his lifelong association with Harvard, where he is a professor of zoology and geology as well as curator of invertebrate paleontology at the university's Museum of Comparative Zoology. In 1974 he contributed the first of his nearly three hundred essays to *Natural History* magazine; the immensely popular monthly series ("This View of Life") takes its title from the conclusion of Darwin's *Origin of Species:* "There is grandeur in this view of life." His essays have been collected in nine books, including *Ever Since Darwin* (1977), *The Panda's Thumb* (1980), *The Flamingo's Smile* (1985), *Bully for Brontosaurus* (1991), *Eight Little Piggies* (1993), and *Leonardo's Mountain of Clams and the Diet of Worms* (1998). His books on specific subjects include *The Mismeasure of Man* (1981), a study of the origins of IQ testing that won both the American Book Award and the National Book Critics Circle Award; *Wonderful Life: The Burgess Shale and the Nature of History* (1989); and *Questioning the Millennium* (1997). The recipient of many professional awards and book prizes, Gould also writes frequently on one of his favorite subjects, baseball.

A winner of numerous poetry awards, **Donald Hall** was born (1928) in New Haven, Connecticut, and educated at Exeter, Harvard, Oxford, and the University of Michigan, from which in 1975, after many years of teaching, he resigned to purchase his grandparents' New Hampshire farm and devote himself full time to writing. Hall's first book of poetry appeared in 1952, the year he became the first American to receive Oxford's prestigious Newdigate Prize. Other volumes of poetry include *Exiles and Marriages* (1955), *Kicking the Leaves* (1978), *The One Day* (1988), winner of the National Book Critics Circle Award, *Old and New Poems* (1990), *The Old Life* (1996), and *Without* (1998), a volume commemorating the death of his wife, the poet Jane Kenyon. Hall served as the poet laureate of New Hampshire and has had a successful career as an essayist, a genre he not only practices but has promoted in influential college textbooks. Besides several books of criticism, his major collections of personal essays and nonfiction are *String Too Short to Be Saved* (1961), *Fathers Playing Catch with Sons* (1985), *Seasons at Eagle Pond* (1987), *Here at Eagle Pond* (1990), *Life Work* (1993), and *Principal Products of Portugal* (1995). Hall has also edited numerous literary anthologies, compiled *The Oxford Book of American Literary Anecdotes*, written lyrically of baseball, and published nearly a dozen juvenile books, including the award-winning *Ox-Cart Man* (1979).

Elizabeth Hardwick was born (1916) in Lexington, Kentucky, growing up there and graduating from the University of Kentucky in 1938, where she took an M.A. a year later. After further graduate study at Columbia, Hardwick published her first novel, *The Ghostly Lover* (1945), and soon began contributing social and literary criticism to *Partisan Review*. In 1949 she married the poet Robert Lowell (they divorced in 1972) and continued to publish the essays and fiction that earned her a reputation as one of America's preeminent writers: "One is interested in anything that Elizabeth Hardwick writes," a *New York Times* reviewer claimed. "That is a given." Besides two other novels, *The Simple Truth* (1955) and *Sleepless Nights* (1979), Hardwick has edited *The Selected Letters of William James* (1960; 1993) and published several books of essays: *A View of My Own* (1962), *Seduction and Betrayal* (1974), *Bartleby in Manhattan and Other Essays* (1984), and *Sight Readings* (1998). A founder and advisory editor of *The New York Review of Books*, she helped launch *The Best American Essays* series in 1986, serving as its first guest editor.

His mother hoped he would become a cellist, but **Ernest Hemingway** (1899–1961) constructed instead a public persona that suggested anything but an artistic sensibility. For a biographical note like this one, he once listed his hobbies as "skiing, fishing, shooting, and drinking." Skipping college (he would later study at "Gertrude Stein University" in Paris), Hemingway found work in 1917 as a reporter with the *Kansas City Star*, where he began crafting what would become the most imitated prose style of the twentieth century. War and violence fascinated him, and throughout his career he maneuvered himself to various fronts, whether in World

War I Italy, the Spanish Civil War, or the Normandy invasion on D-day. Bullfighting remained his favorite spectator sport, becoming the subject of his best non-fiction work, *Death in the Afternoon* (1932). His other nonfiction includes *The Green Hills of Africa* (1935) and the episodic memoir *A Moveable Feast* (1964), which appeared a year after his suicide. A generous selection of his numerous dispatches, articles, and essays can be found in *By-Line: Ernest Hemingway* (ed. William White, 1967).

Michael Herr was born (1940) in Syracuse, New York, and attended Syracuse University before starting a freelance career in magazine journalism. He wrote travel articles for *Holiday* and film criticism for *The New Leader*, receiving the biggest assignment of his life when *Esquire* sent him in 1967 to Vietnam. As Geoffrey Wolff put it, Herr "had ears like no one else's ears over there, and he brought an entire language back alive." Herr's pieces appeared in *Esquire, Rolling Stone*, and *New American Review*, but he did not get all of them into book form until 1977, when *Dispatches* appeared to great critical acclaim. As a writer and consultant for two movies about Vietnam, Francis Ford Coppola's *Apocalypse Now* and Stanley Kubrick's *Full Metal Jacket*, Herr helped to imprint the war on the national consciousness. Herr, who moved to London, has also written *The Big Room* (1987), a collection of celebrity sketches with a Las Vegas theme, one of which he expanded into *Walter Winchell* (1990), a novel in the form of a screenplay.

Called by John Updike "the best essayist of my generation," **Edward Hoagland** was born (1932) in New York City and educated at Harvard, winning a Houghton Mifflin Literary Fellowship for his first novel, *Cat Man*, in 1954, the same year he graduated. In addition to serving two years with the U.S. Army, he has traversed the country as a hobo and worked for the circus. Besides four other books of fiction, Hoagland has published two travel books, *African Calliope* (1979) and *Notes from the Century Before: A Journal from British Columbia* (1982), and many essay collections, including *The Courage of Turtles* (1971), *Walking the Dead Diamond River* (1973), *Red Wolves and Black Bears* (1976), *The Tugman's Passage* (1982), *Balancing Acts* (1992), and *Tigers & Ice* (1999). *Heart's Desire* (1988) is a collection of what he considers his best essays from twenty years of writing. "'Heaven and Nature,'" Hoagland comments, "was written in Italy, as my quarter-century marriage was breaking up. Like 'Behold Now Behemoth' (about a spell of blindness) and 'The Threshold and the Jolt of Pain' (about stuttering), it served — among a hundred or so less personal essays — the double purpose of being a sort of life raft for me as well as simply communication." Hoagland, who teaches at Bennington College, served as guest editor of *The Best American Essays 1999*.

The prolific and remarkably versatile **(James) Langston Hughes** (1902–1967) was the first African American writer to achieve an international literary reputation. Born in Joplin, Oklahoma, Hughes showed precocity as a poet, writing one of his best-known works, "The Negro Speaks of Rivers," while still in high school. At his father's urging, Hughes enrolled at Columbia University to study engineering, but he left after a year, joining the merchant marine in 1923 in a move that would prefigure a career of nearly continuous world travel, much of it recorded in his two autobiographies, *The Big Sea* (1940) and *I Wonder as I Wander* (1956). An architect of the Harlem Renaissance and one of its most productive members, Hughes graduated from Lincoln University in Pennsylvania in 1929, having already published two books of highly innovative poetry that borrowed jazz and blues rhythms. In addition to ten volumes of poetry, several biographies, nine plays, nearly a dozen children's books, and nine books of fiction, plus volumes of criticism, translations, anthologies, and history, Hughes published hundreds of fictional character sketches that feature the exploits of a humorous, opinionated Harlem factory worker, Jesse B. Semple (or "Simple"), and an educated friend who does the narrating. Though the conversations are usually comic, the topics cover nearly all the serious issues of the day. Hughes began the series in the *Chicago Defender* in 1943 and collected them in such books as *Simple Speaks His Mind* (1950) and *Simple Takes a Wife* (1952). See *The Best of Simple* (1961).

Zora Neale Hurston (1891–1960) was born in Eatonville, Florida, the nation's first incorporated Negro community. Her mother died when Hurston was thirteen, and she spent her teenage years bouncing back and forth between relatives, supporting herself with odd jobs and not completing high school until her late twenties. After a few years at Howard University, she moved to New York City in 1925 and quickly became a major figure of the Harlem Renaissance. She won a scholarship to Barnard College (becoming the first black woman to be admitted there), where her writing caught the attention of the noted anthropologist Franz Boas, who encouraged her to begin a study of African American folklore. Her research led to two books, *Mules and Men* (1935) and *Tell My Horse* (1938). While living in Jamaica, she wrote the novel *Their Eyes Were Watching God* (1937). Despite an award-winning autobiography, *Dust Tracks on a Road* (1942), and another successful novel, *Seraph on the Suwanee* (1948), Hurston's career went into serious decline in the 1950s, and she died virtually unknown in a county welfare home in her native Florida. For more on Hurston's life, see Alice Walker's essay in this volume, "Looking for Zora." See also *I Love Myself When I Am Laughing . . .* (ed. Alice Walker, 1979).

The older brother of the novelist Henry James, **William James** (1842–1910) was born in New York City and while still in the cradle received Ralph Waldo Emerson's personal "blessing." Educated in science at Harvard, he relished experimentation and completed his studies at Harvard Medical School in 1869, his interest in neurophysiology most likely stimulated by his own physical and mental troubles, which included disabling eye and back problems, nervous symptoms, persistent insomnia, and episodes of suicidal depression. He began teaching at Harvard in 1872, offering innovative courses (to such students as W.E.B. Du Bois and Gertrude Stein) in both psychology and philosophy. His massive textbook, *The Principles of Psychology* (1890), instantly became the bible of the new science he had helped establish. James published numerous professional articles and also advanced the philosophical movement known as pragmatism, yet he reached a wider audience with such books as *The Will to Believe and Other Essays in Popular Philosophy* (1897) and *The Varieties of Religious Experience* (1902) and with persuasive inspirational essays and lectures that exhorted individuals to overcome demoralizing and destructive states of mind by discovering authentic sources of personal energy and moral values. See *William James: Writings 1902–1910* (ed. Bruce Kuklick, 1987).

Although he never intended to be a literary figure, **Martin Luther King, Jr.** (1929–1968), now ranks among the most widely read and quoted Americans. A masterly rhetorician and an eloquent writer, King displayed in childhood a remarkable talent for the spoken word that impressed teachers and won oratorical contests. Born in Atlanta, where his father was pastor of the Ebenezer Baptist Church, King graduated from Morehouse College with a degree in sociology at nineteen. He proceeded to study divinity at Pennsylvania's Crozer Theological Seminary, where he read Gandhi and Thoreau on civil disobedience, and at Boston University, hoping to take a Ph.D. and devote himself to a life of teaching and scholarship. In Boston he met Coretta Scott, a music student, and in 1954, a year after their marriage, feeling the need for more practical experience, King became a pastor in Montgomery, Alabama, where Rosa Parks would soon be arrested for denying her bus seat to a white passenger. King's boycott of the city's transportation system propelled him to national prominence, and from that moment his career would be dedicated to "militant nonviolent resistance" through marches, demonstrations, sit-ins, and protests. King furthered his philosophy in sermons, speeches, and writings. His first book, *Stride Toward Freedom*, appeared in 1958; in the five turbulent years before his assassination in 1968, he also published two volumes of sermons, *The Strength to Love* (1963) and *The Trumpet of Conscience* (1967), along with *Why We Can't Wait* (1964) and *Where Do We Go from Here: Chaos or Community?* (1967).

Maxine Hong Kingston has played a leading role in establishing the personal memoir as a literary form of the late twentieth century. Born (1940) a first-generation American in Stockton, California, Kingston graduated from the University of California, Berkeley, in 1962 and began teaching high school in California and then Hawaii, where she eventually became a college professor in Honolulu. In 1990 she returned to Berkeley as Chancellor's Distinguished Professor. In her work, Kingston fuses autobiography, history, and myth — blurring distinctions between fact and fiction — while drawing narrative inspiration from the "storytalkers" of her Chinese American childhood. Her first book, *The Woman Warrior: Memoirs of a Girlhood among Ghosts* (1976), won the National Book Critics Circle Award and was named by *Time* one of the top ten nonfiction books of the 1970s. She followed it with *China Men* (1980), which won the American Book Award. The recipient of numerous literary prizes, Kingston is also the author of an elegant collection of brief essays, *Hawai'i One Summer* (1987), and a magically transcendent novel, *Tripmaster Monkey: His Fake Book* (1988).

Born (1922) in Attleboro, Massachusetts, the eminent historian and biographer **William Manchester** served throughout the Pacific with the U.S. Marine Corps in World War II, reaching the rank of sergeant and — wounded twice at Okinawa — receiving the Purple Heart, the Navy Cross, and the Silver Star. After the war he completed his studies at the University of Massachusetts, where he developed an enthusiasm for H. L. Mencken, a devotion he took with him to the University of

Missouri, where he wrote a master's thesis on Mencken. It was read by Mencken himself, who found a place for Manchester at the *Baltimore Sun* and authorized what became his first book, *Disturber of the Peace: The Life of H. L. Mencken* (1951). Manchester stayed with the *Sun* as a reporter and wide-ranging foreign correspondent for seven years, leaving in 1954 (a year after the publication of the first of his four novels, *The City of Anger*) and establishing a longtime association with Wesleyan University. Manchester's many biographies and histories include two studies of powerful families (the Rockefellers and the Krupps); three books on John F. Kennedy; *The Glory and the Dream: A Narrative History of America, 1932–1972* (1974); *American Caesar: Douglas MacArthur, 1880–1964* (1978); and a three-volume life of Winston Churchill. He is also the author of *Controversy and Other Essays in Journalism* (1976) and *Goodbye, Darkness: A Memoir of the Pacific War* (1980).

When she was six, **Mary (Therese) McCarthy** (1912–1989) lost both her parents to the worldwide 1918 influenza epidemic. The effect of this loss on McCarthy and her brothers (one, the actor Kevin McCarthy) is vividly told in her autobiography, *Memories of a Catholic Girlhood* (1957). McCarthy lived in Minneapolis for five years, generously supported by her paternal grandparents, who placed the children in the care of nearby relatives. In 1923 she returned to her native Seattle to stay with her maternal grandparents, whom she found more intellectually stimulating. With acting ambitions, McCarthy enrolled at Vassar College in 1929 and impulsively married an actor friend one week after graduation. In 1937 she began reviewing drama for the new *Partisan Review* and a year later married the second of her four husbands, Edmund Wilson, who encouraged her to write fiction. Although her sharp, satiric novels, such as *The Company She Keeps* (1942), *The Groves of Academe* (1952), and the best-selling *The Group* (1963) established her as one of the nation's prominent literary figures, McCarthy wrote an abundance of nonfiction, covering nearly every important issue of the time. Besides travel, criticism, and two more memoirs, she wrote three books on Vietnam (collected as *The Seventeenth Degree,* 1974) and one on Watergate. Her major collection of essays is *On the Contrary* (1961).

For years, **John McPhee** taught a writing course at Princeton called The Literature of Fact. The title conveys the two sides of McPhee's remarkable talent: his conscientious dedication to detail and exactitude and his ability to orchestrate raw information into works of literature. McPhee, who was born (1931) in Princeton and graduated from Princeton University in 1953, usually avoids personal disclosure and writes almost exclusively books about subjects: art, history, geology, sports, science and technology, popular games, crafts, nuclear weapons, shipbuilding, environmentalism — the list can go on to cover practically every section of a giant bookstore. After graduate work at Magdalene College, Cambridge, McPhee worked in television before moving to an editorial position at *Time,* which he left in 1964 to join the staff of *The New Yorker,* where — after having been rejected more than a hundred times — he contributed a profile of a Princeton basketball star, Bill Bradley, that led to his first book, *A Sense of Where You Are* (1965). In 1977 McPhee published his best-selling (and perhaps best-known) book, about the development of the Alaska frontier, *Coming into the Country.* His essays and shorter pieces can be found in _A Roomful of Hovings and Other Profiles_ (1969), _Pieces of the Frame_ (1975), _Giving Good Weight_ (1979), _Table of Contents_ (1985), and _Irons in the Fire_ (1997). See also _The John McPhee Reader_ (ed. William Howarth, 1977) and _The Second John McPhee Reader_ (ed. David Remnick and Patricia Strachan, 1996).

At the age of nine, **H(enry) L(ouis) Mencken** (1880–1956) discovered Mark Twain's recently published _Huckleberry Finn_ and later recalled the moment as "the most stupendous in my whole life." Born in Baltimore to German American parents, Mencken carried on Twain's satirical and independent literary spirit, becoming perhaps the most intellectually feared writer of the first half of the twentieth century — a rash of suicides in the twenties was attributed to reading too much Mencken. Like Twain, he had a sharp eye for pretension; any sort of American quackery or piety could be a target of his excoriating wit. In the summer of 1925, he traveled to the "Bible belt" (he coined the term) to cover the Scopes "monkey trial," which provoked some of his most memorable essays. Mencken, who had become editor in chief of the _Baltimore Sun_ in 1906, collected much of his best writing in the six volumes of his _Prejudices_ series, published between 1919 and 1927. His many other books include _In Defense of Women_ (1918), a masterly study of _The American Language_ (1919), and three volumes of autobiography. Shortly after he suffered a career-ending stroke, Mencken compiled a comprehensive selection of his work in _A Mencken Chrestomathy_ (1949).

"None but an Indian, I think," writes **N(avarre) Scott Momaday,** "knows so much what it is like to have existence in two worlds and security in neither." Born (1934) into a Kiowa family in Lawton, Oklahoma, Momaday grew up on various reservations in northern New Mexico. Before graduating with a degree in political science from the University of New Mexico in 1958, he attended the University of Virginia and met William Faulkner, who exerted a strong influence on his writing. Momaday received a Ph.D. from Stanford in 1963, studying with the critic Yvor Winters and teaching there from 1973 to 1982, when he became a professor at the University of Arizona in Tucson. In 1967 he published _The Journey of Tai-me,_ an exploration of Kiowa folktales, which he enlarged into his best-known book, _The Way to Rainy Mountain_ (1969). Momaday received a Pulitzer Prize for his 1968 novel, _House Made of Dawn._ His other work includes two volumes of poetry, _Angle of Geese and Other Poems_ (1974) and _The Gourd Dancer_ (1976); _The Names: A Memoir_ (1976); an autobiographical novel, _The Ancient Child_ (1989); two collections, _In the Presence of the Sun: Stories and Poems, 1961–1991_ and _The Man Made of Words: Essays, Stories, Passages_ (1997); and an interweaving of poetry and painting (he is an established artist), _In the Bear's House_ (1999).

Born in Dunbar, Scotland, the naturalist and environmental activist **John Muir** (1838–1914) immigrated in 1849 to the United States with his family, who kept moving west, eventually settling in Wisconsin. A phenomenal hiker and mountaineer, Muir turned his wilderness observations into numerous essays for such popular magazines as _The Century, The Atlantic Monthly,_ and _Overland._ Although many of Muir's best-known essays were written in the 1870s and 1880s (and thus not considered for this volume), he waited until 1894 to publish his first book, *The Mountains of California*. Muir played an instrumental role in establishing Yosemite National Park and served in the forefront of the American conservation movement, his essays — especially those collected in *Our National Parks* (1901) and *The Yosemite* (1912) — influencing the policies of Theodore Roosevelt. Muir died in Los Angeles a year after the publication of his autobiography, *The Story of My Boyhood and Youth* (1913). Two recent collections are *Steep Trails* (introduction by Edward Hoagland, 1994) and *John Muir: Nature Writings* (ed. William Cronon, 1997).

"I am," claimed **Vladimir Nabokov** (1899–1977) in a 1963 interview, "an American writer, born in Russia and educated in England, where I studied French literature, before spending fifteen years in Germany. I came to America in 1940 and decided to become an American citizen and made America my home." Born into the Russian nobility, Nabokov escaped to England in 1919 at the end of the civil war that followed the Russian Revolution. By the time he escaped from the Nazis, just before the final collapse of France in May 1940, Nabokov had achieved a full career as a Russian novelist and poet among the large community of his fellow exiles in Western Europe. In the United States, he began a new career as a writer in English, a language that, like French, he had known since childhood (his father had been an admirer of William James). While in Paris, he wrote his first novel in English, *The Real Life of Sebastian Knight* (1941). After he had taught for some years at Wellesley and Cornell, the success of his most famous novel, *Lolita* (1955), allowed him to settle in Switzerland and devote all his time to writing. In the 1940s Nabokov had begun publishing in magazines the separate autobiographical essays that first became *Conclusive Evidence* (1951) and then the substantially enlarged *Speak, Memory: An Autobiography Revisited* (1966). Nabokov hoped to cover his American years in a sequel to be called *Speak On, Memory*, but never did.

"As I am not drawn to art that makes me feel good, comfortable, or at ease," writes **Joyce Carol Oates**, "so I am not drawn to essays that 'smile,' except in the context of larger, more complex ambitions." Born (1938) in Lockport, New York, Oates graduated from Syracuse University in 1960 (having won *Mademoiselle*'s college fiction award a year earlier) and received a master's degree from the University of Wisconsin in 1961. She published the first of more than two dozen novels, *With Shuddering Fall*, in 1964, and with the novel *them* (1969) became the youngest writer ever to receive the National Book Award for fiction. Oates taught in the English department of the University of Windsor, in Ontario, from 1967 to 1978, when she moved to Princeton University, where she is Roger S. Berlind Distinguished Professor. Besides her novels (some of them written under the pseudonym Rosamond Smith) and many volumes of short stories (for which she won an O. Henry Special Award for Continuing Achievement), Oates has published numerous volumes of poetry and plays (many of which have been produced). Her nonfiction includes such literary criticism as *The Edge of Impossibility: Tragic Forms in Literature* (1972) and *New Heaven, New Earth: The Visionary Experience in Literature* (1974) and several essay collections: *Contraries: Essays* (1981), *The Profane Art: Essays and Reviews* (1983), and *(Woman) Writer: Occasions and Opportunities* (1988). She served as guest editor of *The Best American Essays 1991*.

"An essay," claims **Cynthia Ozick,** "is a thing of the imagination . . . A genuine essay has no educational, polemical, or sociopolitical use; it is the movement of a free mind at play." Essays, like the award-winning short stories and novels she is known for, are imaginative and aesthetic experiments — in other words, literature — not position papers. Born (1928) in the Pelham Bay section of the Bronx, Ozick grew up in the atmosphere of a family-operated drugstore. After receiving her B.A. at New York University in 1949 and a year later an M.A. at Ohio State, Ozick called it quits with academic life and set out to take lessons from her master, Henry James, in the demanding art of fiction. Her first novel, *Trust,* appeared in 1966 and was followed by several volumes of short fiction and three more novels, *The Cannibal Galaxy* (1983), *The Messiah of Stockholm* (1987), and *The Puttermesser Papers* (1997). Her personal and literary essays appear in four collections: *Art & Ardor* (1983), *Metaphor & Memory* (1989), *Fame & Folly* (1996), and *Quarrel & Quandary* (2000). She is also the author of two essay collections on writing, *What Henry James Knew* (1993) and *Portrait of the Artist as a Bad Character* (1996). Ozick was guest editor of *The Best American Essays 1998.*

S(idney) J(oseph) Perelman (1904–1979) found no subject sacred, as he proved early by submitting to a high school contest his essay "Why I Am an Atheist." At Brown, the Brooklyn-born writer contributed humor and cartoons to various college publications and met the novelist Nathanael West, whose sister he married in 1929, two years before he became permanently attached to *The New Yorker.* Perelman published numerous collections of his highly distinctive humor, which, in its satirical energy, verbal frolicking, and complex irrationality, often sounds as though James Joyce had collaborated with Mark Twain to write surrealistic accounts of everyday life. *Strictly from Hunger* (1937), Perelman's first major collection in this vein, was followed by such popular volumes as *Look Who's Talking!* (1940), *Crazy Like a Fox* (1944), *Acres and Pains* (1947), and his best-selling satire of travel books, *Westward Ha!; or, Around the World in Eighty Clichés* (1948). Perelman wrote scripts for the Marx Brothers and won an Oscar for his screenplay of the Jules Verne classic *Around the World in Eighty Days* (1956). Along with several other collections of humor, Perelman published three personal compilations: *The Best of S. J. Perelman* (1947), *Perelman's Home Companion* (1955), and *The Most of S. J. Perelman* (1958).

"All the conscious and recollected years of my life," wrote **Katherine Anne Porter** (1890–1980) in 1940, "have been lived to this day under the heavy threat of world catastrophe, and most of the energies of my mind and spirit have been spent in the effort to grasp the meaning of those threats, to trace them to their sources and to understand the logic of this majestic and terrible failure of the life of man in the Western world." The remaining forty years she witnessed of the century would do little to soften this vision. Born in a log cabin in the frontier town of Indian Creek, Texas, Porter received a fragmentary education and as a young woman found work on various newspapers; she would later become the first female faculty member at Washington and Lee University. Her first books of fiction, *Flowering Judas* (1930), *Noon Wine* (1937), *Pale Horse, Pale Rider* (1938), and *The Leaning Tower and Other*

Stories (1944), made a deep and lasting critical impression, but she did not achieve major public recognition until her long-awaited novel *Ship of Fools* appeared in 1962. Her *Collected Stories* (1965) won both the Pulitzer Prize and the National Book Award. Porter's nonfiction includes a collection of essays, *The Days Before* (1952), *The Collected Essays* (1970), and *The Never-Ending Wrong* (1977), a personal memoir of the Sacco and Vanzetti trial.

Adrienne Rich was still a student at Radcliffe when W. H. Auden selected her first book, *A Change of World* (1951), for the Yale Younger Poets series. Born (1929) in Baltimore, where her father practiced medicine, Rich married soon after graduation in 1951 and had three children, but in the turmoil of the 1960s she reinvented herself, resisting the role of "dutiful daughter" and academic wife who wrote formal verse and discovering a new poetic voice as a political radical and feminist, identities that begin to take shape in her fourth book of poetry, *Snapshots of a Daughter-in-Law* (1963). Rich's *Diving into the Wreck* — her best-known volume — won the National Book Award in 1974, four years after her husband committed suicide (the marriage had dissolved) and shortly before she came out as a lesbian. Active in the antiwar, feminist, and gay and lesbian movements, Rich has taught at numerous universities. In 1992, the year after the publication of her prize-winning *An Atlas of the Difficult World*, she received the Robert Frost Silver Medal for lifetime achievement in poetry. Although known mainly as a poet, she has published several nonfiction books and essay collections: *Of Woman Born: Motherhood as Experience and Institution* (1976), *On Lies, Secrets, and Silence* (1979), *Blood, Bread, and Poetry* (1986), and *What Is Found There: Notebooks on Poetry and Politics* (1993).

Born (1944) in San Francisco into a family of working-class Mexican American immigrants, **Richard Rodriguez** could not speak English when he entered the parochial school system in Sacramento, California, where he grew up. After graduating from Stanford (1967) and receiving his M.A. from Columbia (1969), Rodriguez did further graduate work in Renaissance studies at the Warburg Institute in London and the University of California at Berkeley. In 1976, about to launch his academic career, Rodriguez experienced a personal crisis over affirmative action programs and decided to leave graduate school, unable to accept in good conscience the university positions he was being offered because of his "minority" status. He had already published several essays against affirmative action, believing that it favored middle-class students while ignoring the educational needs of the most disadvantaged and arguing that social class and economic need should be the primary factors. His decision (along with subsequent opinions on bilingual education and assimilation) cost Rodriguez a good deal of academic support but led directly to his award-winning memoir, *Hunger of Memory: The Education of Richard Rodriguez* (1982). A reporter and essayist with *The NewsHour* with Jim Lehrer, Rodriguez has published in many magazines and newspapers and is a contributing editor at *Harper's Magazine, U.S. News & World Report*, and the *Los Angeles Times*. He is also the author of a collection of essays, *Days of Obligation: An Argument with My Mexican Father* (1992).

One of the nation's widest-ranging and most versatile intellectuals, **Susan Sontag** was born (1933) in New York City and grew up in California and Arizona. After graduating from the University of Chicago in 1951, she received an M.A. in both English (1954) and philosophy (1955) at Harvard before pursuing further studies in philosophy at Oxford. An independent scholar in the tradition of Edmund Wilson, she began writing for *Partisan Review, Commentary, Harper's Magazine, The Nation,* and *The New York Review of Books,* where she formulated her aesthetic principles and introduced American readers to such modern European thinkers as Roland Barthes and Elias Canetti. The breadth of her cultural concerns can be seen in her three essay collections: *Against Interpretation* (1966), *Styles of Radical Will* (1969), and *Under the Sign of Saturn* (1980). Other nonfiction books include *Trip to Hanoi* (1969), *On Photography* (1977), which won a National Book Critics Circle Award, *Illness as Metaphor* (1978), and *AIDS and Its Metaphors* (1989). The recipient of many prizes and fellowships, Sontag has written and directed four feature-length films and directed plays in the United States and Europe. Her fiction includes short story collections and four novels: *The Benefactor* (1963), *Death Kit* (1967), *The Volcano Lover* (1992), and *In America* (2000). See *A Susan Sontag Reader* (introduction by Elizabeth Hardwick, 1982). She served as guest editor of *The Best American Essays 1992.*

Although now indelibly associated with Paris, **Gertrude Stein** (1874–1946) was born in Allegheny, Pennsylvania, and grew up in Oakland, California ("There is no *there* there"). Financially independent following the deaths of her parents, she studied experimental psychology with William James at Radcliffe, attended medical school at Johns Hopkins, but moved in 1903 to Paris, where her apartment became an international center for such modern painters and writers as Pablo Picasso (who painted her portrait) and Ernest Hemingway. Sensing that the new century was breaking radically from the preceding one, Stein hastened the rupture with several works of fiction so daringly experimental they could only be privately printed. Her reputation grew with *Tender Buttons* (1914) and with her literary theorizing in *Composition as Explanation* (1926), *Narration* (1935), and *What Are Master-pieces* (1940). In 1933, she achieved best-selling fame with her own modernist masterpiece, *The Autobiography of Alice B. Toklas,* written from the perspective of the woman she had lived with since 1909.

When Joyce Carol Oates reviewed **Lewis Thomas**'s first collection in 1974, she praised its "effortless, beautifully-toned style," saying that it "anticipates the kind of writing that will appear more and more frequently, as scientists take on the language of poetry in order to communicate human truths too mysterious for old-fashioned common sense." Born into a medical family in Flushing, New York, Thomas (1913–1993) was educated at Princeton and completed Harvard Medical School in 1937. After active duty with the Navy's Medical Corps throughout World War II (making lieutenant commander), Thomas took teaching and research posts at various medical schools before becoming a professor of pathology at New York University (1954–1969) and Yale University (1969–1973). In 1973 he accepted the presidency of New York's Memorial Sloan-Kettering Cancer Center, where he retained a lifelong association. Thomas had written some two hundred scientific articles before he began contributing in 1971 to *The New England Journal of Medicine* the short essays that formed the basis of the National Book Award–winning *The Lives of a Cell* (1974). It was followed by another award-winning collection, *The Medusa and the Snail* (1979). More of Thomas's essays can be found in his memoir, *The Youngest Science* (1983), *Late Night Thoughts on Listening to Mahler's Ninth Symphony* (1983), *Et Cetera, Et Cetera: Notes of a Word-Watcher* (1990), and *The Fragile Species* (1992).

The career of **James Thurber** (1894–1961) perfectly illustrates the truism that funny people do not necessarily lead funny lives. The victim of a childhood accident that cost him his left eye and in later years led to virtual blindness, Thurber (born in Columbus, Ohio) sporadically attended Ohio State University, where he worked on the newspaper and humor magazine. In 1927, after innumerable rejection slips, he broke into the recently established *New Yorker* and quickly became a staff member, sharing an office with the essayist E. B. White and collaborating with him on *Is Sex Necessary?* (1929). Thurber worked at the magazine, contributing stories, humor, and cartoons, until 1935, when the success of *My Life and Hard Times* permitted him to freelance. Despite a futile series of eye operations, a "five-year nervous crack-up," surgery for a ruptured appendix, and thyroid complications, Thurber continued to produce the inimitable humor that T. S. Eliot found, at bottom, "serious and somber." His best-selling memoir of his *New Yorker* experiences, *The Years with Ross* (1959), cost him a number of old friendships that his death from a brain tumor two years later prevented him from ever mending. For vintage Thurber, see *The Thurber Carnival* (1945); a convenient collection is *James Thurber: Writings and Drawings* (selected by Garrison Keillor, 1996).

Born Samuel Langhorne Clemens in Florida, Missouri, **Mark Twain** (1835–1910) was among the first to use the word "literary" in a pejorative fashion. Throughout his fiction — *The Adventures of Huckleberry Finn* appeared in 1885 — and abundant nonfiction he resisted literary conventions as strenuously as he resisted in his own life the comforts of conventional wisdom. His most important books of nonfiction include *Innocents Abroad* (1869), *Roughing It* (1872), *A Tramp Abroad* (1880), *Life on the Mississippi* (1883), which details his career as a riverboat pilot, *How to Tell a Story and Other Essays* (1897), and *My Debut as a Literary Person* (1903). In his later years he turned increasingly to the essay as a polemical form that would let him express directly his deep hatred of orthodoxy, hypocrisy, prejudice, and "corn-pone opinions." Many of Twain's later essays were published posthumously. See *The Complete Essays* (ed. Charles Neider, 1963), *Collected Tales, Sketches, Speeches, and Essays* (ed. Lewis Budd, 2 vols., 1992), and *Tales, Speeches, Essays, and Sketches* (ed. Tom Quick, 1994).

The author of more than fifty books, **John Updike** was born (1932) and grew up in the small town of Shillington, Pennsylvania, which in his "subjective geography is still the center of the world." After graduating from Harvard in 1954 and studying at the Ruskin School of Drawing and Fine Art in Oxford, Updike worked for *The New Yorker*'s "Talk of the Town" department for two years, establishing what would become a lifetime association with the magazine. In 1957 he moved to Massachusetts, where he has successfully practiced his "solitary trade" as a freelance writer, winning two Pulitzer Prizes, the National Book Award, and the National Book Critics Circle Award for his fiction. His many novels include the sequence *Rabbit, Run* (1960), *Rabbit Redux* (1971), *Rabbit Is Rich* (1981), and *Rabbit at Rest* (1990) as well as *The Centaur* (1963), *Couples* (1968), *Roger's Version* (1986), *In the Beauty of the Lilies* (1996), and *Gertrude and Claudius* (2000). In addition to his numerous volumes of short stories and poetry (his *Collected Poems* appeared in 1993), Updike has established an important presence in American nonfiction. His reviews, criticism, and essays have been collected in *Assorted Prose* (1965), *Picked-Up Pieces* (1975), *Hugging the Shore* (1983), *Just Looking: Essays on Art* (1989), *Odd Jobs* (1991), and *More Matter* (1999). He has also written a memoir, *Self-Consciousness* (1989).

With *The Color Purple* (1982), **Alice Walker** became the first African American woman to win the Pulitzer Prize for fiction. The child of sharecroppers, Walker was born (1944) in Eatonton, Georgia (at one point she lived in a shack near Flannery O'Connor's farm), where she learned to appreciate the everyday artistry and self-expression of poor black southern people, especially the women, whose quilting and gardening Walker celebrates in her first and best-known essay collection, *In Search of Our Mothers' Gardens: The Legacy of Southern Black Women* (1974). An injury when she was eight — she lost an eye when one of her brothers accidentally shot her with a BB gun — turned her inwardly to writing and led to the deep concern with personal identity and self-esteem that can be seen in her work. After two years at Spelman College, Walker graduated from Sarah Lawrence (1965) just in time to work for voter registration in Mississippi, where in 1967 she broke a state law by marrying a white civil rights lawyer (they were divorced in 1977). Strongly influenced by Zora Neale Hurston, whose reputation she helped revive, Walker has published, besides such novels as *The Temple of My Familiar* (1989) and *By the Light of My Father's Smile* (1998), several volumes of poetry, children's literature, short stories, and a good deal of nonfiction, including *Living By the Word* (1988), *The Same River Twice* (1996), and *Anything We Love Can Be Saved* (1997).

Eudora Welty was born (1909) in Jackson, Mississippi, where she has lived for practically her whole life, leaving only to attend the University of Wisconsin (graduating in 1929) and to study advertising at Columbia University Graduate School of Business in New York City. During the Depression, she traveled through Mississippi for the Works Progress Administration, taking the photographs printed years later in *One Time, One Place: Mississippi in the Depression* (1971). In 1941 she published her first collection of stories, *A Curtain of Green* (1941), followed the next year by her first novel, *The Robber Bridegroom*. Her other fiction includes *The Wide Net* (1943), *Delta Wedding* (1946), *The Ponder Heart* (1954), *Losing Battles* (1970), and the Pulitzer Prize–winning *The Optimist's Daughter* (1972). Though known primarily for her fiction, Welty has achieved a solid reputation as a critic and essayist. Her two studies, *Place in Fiction* (1958) and *Three Papers on Fiction* (1962), are frequently cited in criticism of the modern short story. Her more personal writing can be found in *The Eye of the Story* (1978) and her memoir, *One Writer's Beginnings* (1984).

One of America's most celebrated essayists and one universally read in college writing courses, **E(lwyn) B(rooks) White** (1899–1985) wrote continually as a boy growing up in Mount Vernon, New York, winning several prizes and seeing himself in print before he turned fifteen. At Cornell, he edited the daily college paper, pursued a degree in English, and took to heart the concise writing precepts ("Omit needless words!") of Professor Will Strunk, whose little textbook White would one day amplify into *The Elements of Style* (1959), perhaps the most influential writers' manual ever published. After graduation, "Andy" White worked briefly as a reporter in Seattle, then drove a Ford Model T back east, where he spent some unhappy time as a copywriter until the fledgling *New Yorker* hired him in 1926 on the strength of the humor pieces he had been submitting. In 1929 he married an older colleague, the fiction editor Katherine Sergeant Angell, and shortly afterward they bought a saltwater farm in Brooklin, Maine, where they summered and where White would occasionally take a "sabbatical" to escape the city and write. He did so between 1937 and 1943, when he tried unsuccessfully to write a long autobiographical poem but instead discovered his true muse in a series of essays for *Harper's Magazine* that he collected in *One Man's Meat* (1942, enlarged 1944). More essays appeared in *The Wild Flag* (1946), *The Second Tree from the Corner* (1954), and *The Points of My Compass* (1962). White also wrote such successful children's books as *Stuart Little* (1945) and *Charlotte's Web* (1952). See *Essays of E. B. White* (selected and introduced by White, 1977).

Edmund Wilson (1895–1972) was born in Red Bank, New Jersey, into a prosperous though profoundly troubled family. After studies at Princeton (where he met F. Scott Fitzgerald — "the first educated Catholic I had ever known"), Wilson served with a hospital unit in France and moved to New York City in 1919, devoting himself to writing. Between 1929 and 1932, as "the whole structure of American society seemed to be going to pieces," Wilson finished a novel, *I Thought of Daisy;* a groundbreaking study of modern literature, *Axel's Castle;* and a collection of social reportage, *The American Jitters.* Immersed in Marxism and modern history, he visited the Soviet Union in 1935 in preparation for *To the Finland Station* (1940). Wilson began a long association with *The New Yorker* in 1943, just as his third marriage (to Mary McCarthy) was reaching an end. In 1946 he remarried and published a best-selling (and banned) story collection, *Memoirs of Hecate County.* Wilson fearlessly encroached on areas reserved for academic "experts": early Christianity in *The Dead Sea Scrolls* (1955), native American civilization in *Apologies to the Iroquois* (1960), and the American Civil War in *Patriotic Gore* (1962). In 1965 he even began a much-publicized dispute with Vladimir Nabokov over Russian translation. The five posthumously published volumes of his private journals form a tantalizing chronicle of American literary culture over half a century. A convenient collection is *The Portable Edmund Wilson* (ed. Lewis M. Dabney, 1983).

A founder of the "new journalism," **Tom Wolfe** was born (1931) in Richmond, Virginia, graduated from Washington and Lee University, and received a Ph.D. in American Studies at Yale in 1957. Now known for his extravagant prose style, Wolfe first established himself as a reporter with the *Springfield* (Mass.) *Union* and the

Washington Post, winning Washington Newspaper Guild Awards for both humor and foreign news. In 1962 he began working for the *New York Herald Tribune* and contributed features to its Sunday magazine, *New York,* while also freelancing for *Esquire.* On assignment to cover a California custom-car show, Wolfe tried to move beyond the conventional article and ended up producing a piece that not only captured the attention of the literary world but also exquisitely caught the spirit of the go-go sixties. Wolfe's breakthrough story became the title piece of his first book, *The Kandy-Kolored Tangerine-Flake Streamline Baby* (1965). Since then, Wolfe has chronicled the American scene in such nonfiction books as *The Electric Kool-Aid Acid Test* (1968), *The Painted Word* (1975), *The Right Stuff* (1979), which won the American Book Award and the National Book Critics Circle Award, and in two novels, *The Bonfire of the Vanities* (1987) and *A Man in Full* (1998). Wolfe's essays can also be found in *The Pump House Gang* (1968) and *Mauve Gloves & Madmen, Clutter & Vine* (1976).

Born into an impoverished sharecropper family near Natchez, Mississippi, **Richard Wright** (1908–1960) followed the "great migration" to Chicago after he graduated from high school in 1925. He took a series of menial jobs while experimenting with fiction, grew active in radical politics, and joined the Communist Party in 1933. Wright became the Harlem editor of the *Daily Worker* when he moved to New York City in 1937, the year he wrote "The Ethics of Living Jim Crow," the essay that later became part of his first book, *Uncle Tom's Children: Four Novellas* (1938), and laid the groundwork for his best-selling memoir, *Black Boy* (1945). As he struggled with autobiography, Wright discovered "the secret, black, hidden core of race relations in the United States" — "nobody is ever expected to speak honestly about this problem." A Guggenheim fellowship allowed him to complete *Native Son* in 1940, his most successful novel and the first book by an African American to be selected for the Book-of-the-Month Club. Wright left the Communist Party in 1944 and three years later moved permanently with his family to Paris, where Jean-Paul Sartre introduced him to the existentialist philosophy that would shape his later fiction. His nonfiction books include *Black Power* (1954), *The Color Curtain* (1956), *Pagan Spain* (1957), and an essay collection, *White Man Listen!* (1957).

Appendix

Notable Twentieth-Century American Literary Nonfiction

I have listed here only selected collections of personal and critical essays, memoirs, and highly respected works of literary nonfiction. The emphasis is, of course, on the essay and on essayists whose work has appeared or been regularly noted in the annual volumes. Many important, indeed monumental, nonfiction titles — in biography, science, history, politics, professional journalism, philosophy, and so on — are not included because of space limitations and because they would not have been appropriate candidates for this book. — R. A.

EDWARD ABBEY, *Desert Solitaire; Slumgullion Stew*

ANWAR ACCAWI, *The Boy from the Tower of the Moon*

ANDRÉ ACIMAN, *Out of Egypt*

DIANE ACKERMAN, *A Natural History of the Senses*

JOEL AGEE, *Twelve Years*

MARCIA ALDRICH, *Girl Rearing*

PAULA GUNN ALLEN, *Off the Reservation*

HILTON ALS, *The Women*

SHERWOOD ANDERSON, *A Story Teller's Story; Tar: A Midwest Childhood*

ROGER ANGELL, *The Summer Game*

HANNAH ARENDT, *Between Past and Future*

MICHAEL ARLEN, *Passage to Ararat*

BARBARA ASCHER, *Playing After Dark*

MARY AUSTIN, *The Land of Little Rain*

NICHOLSON BAKER, *The Size of Thoughts*

RUSSELL BAKER, *Growing Up*

WILL BAKER, *Mountain Blood*

AMIRI BARAKA, *Blues People*

BILL BARICH, *Laughing in the Hills*

HELEN BAROLINI, *Chiaroscuro*

JACQUES BARZUN, *A Word or Two Before You Go*

RICK BASS, *Wild to the Heart*

JO ANN BEARD, *The Boys of My Youth*

ROBERT BENCHLEY, *20,000 Leagues Under the Sea, or, David Cooperfield; My Ten Years in a Quandary and How They Grew*

JOHN BERENDT, *Midnight in the Garden of Good and Evil*

JEREMY BERNSTEIN, *Science Observed*

WENDELL BERRY, *Recollected Essays*

SVEN BIRKERTS, *The Gutenberg Elegies*

ALFRED KAZIN, *A Walker in the City; Starting Out in the Thirties*

GARRISON KEILLOR, *Lake Wobegon Days*

HELEN KELLER, *The Story of My Life*

TRACY KIDDER, *House; Old Friends*

JAMES KILGO, *Deep Enough for Ivorybills*

JAMAICA KINCAID, *A Small Place; My Brother*

WILLIAM KITTREDGE, *Owning It All*

PERRI KLASS, *Not Entirely a Benign Procedure*

VERLYN KLINKENBORG, *Making Hay; The Last Fine Time*

CAROLINE KNAPP, *Drinking: A Love Story*

ALEX KOTLOWITZ, *There Are No Children Here*

JONATHAN KOZOL, *Death at an Early Age*

JON KRAKAUER, *Into Thin Air*

JANE KRAMER, *The Last Cowboy*

LEONARD KRIEGEL, *Flying Solo; Falling into Life*

JOSEPH WOOD KRUTCH, *The Best of Two Worlds; If You Don't Mind My Saying So*

MAXINE KUMIN, *To Make a Prairie*

NATALIE KUSZ, *Road Song*

LEWIS H. LAPHAM, *Waiting for the Barbarians*

URSULA K. LEGUIN, *Dancing at the Edge of the World*

ALDO LEOPOLD, *A Sand County Almanac*

A. J. LIEBLING, *The Sweet Science*

ALAN LIGHTMAN, *Time Travel and Papa Joe's Pipe; Time for the Stars*

WALTER LIPPMANN, *A Preface to Politics; Public Opinion*

JACK LONDON, *The People of the Abyss; The Road; Revolution; John Barleycorn*

PHILLIP LOPATE, *Against Joie de Vivre; Portrait of My Body*

BARRY LOPEZ, *Of Wolves and Men; Arctic Dreams; Crossing Open Ground*

BRET LOTT, *Fathers, Sons, and Brothers*

NATHAN MCCALL, *Makes Me Wanna Holler*

JAMES MCCONKEY, *Court of Memory*

FRANK MCCOURT, *Angela's Ashes*

DWIGHT MACDONALD, *Against the American Grain*

MICHAEL PATRICK MACDONALD, *All Souls*

NORMAN MACLEAN, *Young Men and Fire*

JAMES A. MCPHERSON, *Crabcakes*

NORMAN MAILER, *The White Negro; Advertisements for Myself; The Armies of the Night; Of a Fire on the Moon*

NANCY MAIRS, *Plaintext*

MALCOLM X (WITH ALEX HALEY), *The Autobiography of Malcolm X*

THOMAS MALLON, *Rockets and Rodeos*

DAVID MAMET, *Some Freaks*

HILARY MASTERS, *In Montaigne's Tower*

PETER MATTHIESSEN, *The Tree Where Man Was Born; The Snow Leopard*

WILLIAM MAXWELL, *Ancestors*

VED MEHTA, *Daddyji; Mamaji; The Stolen Light*

THOMAS MERTON, *The Seven Storey Mountain*

HENRY MILLER, *The Air-Conditioned Nightmare; Remember to Remember*

KATE MILLETT, *Flying*

JOSEPH MITCHELL, *McSorley's Wonderful Saloon*

PAUL MONETTE, *On Becoming a Man*

PAUL ELMER MORE, *Shelburne Essays*

SAMUEL ELIOT MORISON, *By Land and by Sea*

CHRISTOPHER MORLEY, *Plum Pudding; Streamlines; Letters of Askance*

WILLIE MORRIS, *North Toward Home; Good Old Boy*

WRIGHT MORRIS, *Will's Boy*

LAUREN SLATER, *Welcome to My Country*

LOGAN PEARSALL SMITH, *All Trivia*

GARY SOTO, *Living up the Street*

TERRY SOUTHERN, *Red Dirt Marijuana and Other Tastes*

BRENT STAPLES, *Parallel Time*

SHELBY STEELE, *The Content of Our Character*

WALLACE STEGNER, *Wolf Willow; The Sound of Mountain Water*

JOHN STEINBECK, *Travels with Charley*

GLORIA STEINEM, *Outrageous Acts and Everyday Rebellions*

M. G. STEPHENS, *Green Dreams*

ROBERT STEPTO, *Blue As the Lake*

WILLIAM STYRON, *Darkness Visible*

GAY TALESE, *Fame and Obscurity; Unto the Sons*

PAUL THEROUX, *The Great Railway Bazaar; The Old Patagonian Express*

PIRI THOMAS, *Down These Mean Streets*

HUNTER S. THOMPSON, *Fear and Loathing in Las Vegas*

SALLIE TISDALE, *Stepping Westward*

SUSAN ALLEN TOTH, *Blooming*

JAMES TREFIL, *Meditations at 10,000 Feet*

CALVIN TRILLIN, *U.S. Journal; Killings; Remembering Denny*

DIANA TRILLING, *Claremont Essays*

LIONEL TRILLING, *The Liberal Imagination; The Opposing Self; A Gathering of Fugitives*

GEORGE W. S. TROW, *Within the Context of No Context*

WILLIAM TROY, *Selected Essays*

MICHAEL VENTURA, *Shadow Dancing in the USA*

GORE VIDAL, *The Second American Revolution; United States: Essays 1952–1992*

DAN WAKEFIELD, *New York in the Fifties*

JEFFREY WALLEN, *Closed Encounters*

GEOFFREY C. WARD, *American Originals*

WILLIAM W. WARNER, *Beautiful Swimmers*

ROBERT PENN WARREN, *Selected Essays*

ROBERT WARSHOW, *The Immediate Experience*

BOOKER T. WASHINGTON, *Up from Slavery*

GERALD WEISSMANN, *The Woods Hole Cantata*

GLENWAY WESCOTT, *Fear and Trembling*

CORNEL WEST, *Race Matters*

PAUL WEST, *Words for a Deaf Daughter*

EDITH WHARTON, *A Backward Glance*

WILLIAM ALLEN WHITE, *Autobiography*

JOHN EDGAR WIDEMAN, *Brothers and Keepers; Fatheralong*

LEON WIESELTIER, *Kaddish*

GEORGE F. WILL, *The Pursuit of Happiness and Other Sobering Thoughts*

TERRY TEMPEST WILLIAMS, *Pieces of White Shell; Refuge*

WILLIAM CARLOS WILLIAMS, *In the American Grain; Autobiography*

ELLEN WILLIS, *Beginning to See the Light*

GARRY WILLS, *Inventing America; Lincoln at Gettysburg*

YVOR WINTERS, *In Defense of Reason*

LARRY WOIWODE, *What I Think I Did*

GEOFFREY WOLFF, *The Duke of Deception; A Day at the Beach*

TOBIAS WOLFF, *This Boy's Life*

ALEXANDER WOOLLCOTT, *Shouts and Murmers; Going to Pieces*

PAUL ZWEIG, *Departures*